THE
STARCRAFT
ARCHIVE

THE
StarCraft®
ARCHIVE

JEFF GRUBB · GABRIEL MESTA

TRACY HICKMAN · MICKY NEILSON

POCKET BOOKS

NEW YORK   LONDON   TORONTO   SYDNEY

POCKET BOOKS,
A Division of Simon & Schuster, Inc.
1230 Avenue of the Americas
New York, NY 10020

Liberty's Crusade copyright © 2001 by Blizzard Entertainment
Shadow of the Xel'Naga copyright © 2001 by Blizzard Entertainment
Speed of Darkness copyright © 2002 by Blizzard Entertainment
Uprising copyright © 2000 by Blizzard Entertainment

First Pocket Books trade paperback edition November 2007

POCKET and colophon are registered trademarks of Simon & Schuster, Inc.

For information about special discounts for bulk purchases,
please contact Simon & Schuster Special Sales at 1-800-456-6798
or business@simonandschuster.com.

Cover art by Glenn Rane

Interior designed by Mary Austin Speaker

Manufactured in the United States of America

10 9 8 7 6 5 4 3

Library of Congress Cataloging-in-Publication Data is available.

ISBN-13: 978-1-4165-4929-1
ISBN-10:   1-4165-4929-3

These titles were previously published individually by Pocket Books.

CONTENTS

INTRODUCTION

When Chris Metzen asked me to write the introduction for the *StarCraft Archive*, I was pretty excited. This is my first book introduction! That may not be so exciting to you the reader, but I was there the day *StarCraft* was born as an idea. Having watched it grow into the amazing universe that it is now, I am thrilled to share my thoughts about what it is like to be in the right place at the right time, surrounded by the right people.

Eleven years have passed since we first began work on *StarCraft*. Back then, Blizzard had just released two successful RTS (Real Time Strategy) games: *Warcraft: Orcs and Humans* and *Warcraft II: Tides of Darkness*, and it was time to figure out what to do next. Everyone outside of Blizzard wanted and expected us to make *Warcraft III*. From a business standpoint, I couldn't blame them. However, we had been working on Warcraft games for two years straight (which was a long time back then), and our art team was expressing a strong desire to work on something different. We still wanted to make another RTS, but this time we decided it would be set in a sci-fi universe. At one point, we considered working with Lucas Arts to base our game in the Star Wars universe (*StarWarsCraft?*). If we had gone that route, things would be pretty different. For one, I'm thinking no one would have asked me to write an introduction to a collection of stories about the universe.

Each of the Warcraft games took under a year to develop. We knew *StarCraft* would take longer, because we had to design the world, all the units and the gameplay. Furthermore, we wanted to break all sorts of design rules we had followed religiously in the past. In the Warcraft games, the units from the Horde and the Alliance were functionally identical. The two races were basically carbon copies of each other. When we did have variations, we found it very difficult to maintain balance between the two sides. In *StarCraft*, we wanted to create three totally distinct races that would be balanced against each other in a rock/paper/scissors fashion. This was a huge departure for us, and to some measure it was inspired by the game *Magic: The Gathering*, which was very popular around the office at the time. *M:TG* proved to us that it was possible to design a well-balanced game with powerful strategies and effective counters for each strategy. This was a pretty risky decision for us, but the resulting diversity of gameplay is a big reason that gamers continue to play *StarCraft* at a tournament level even today.

We showed an early version of *StarCraft* to the public at the Electronic Entertainment Expo in 1996 after only a few months of work. We had taken the *Warcraft II* game engine, slapped in new artwork and sound effects, and wound up with a game that was rather underwhelming to those who saw it. After the show, gaming magazines referred to our upcoming game as "Orcs in Space." Ouch. This cold reception prompted us to do some soul-searching about the direction we wanted to take the game as well as our ambitions for it. It also brought about the first of two complete rewrites of the game engine.

When I look back on the development of *StarCraft*, we had an amazingly dedicated, passionate team. We all knew that we were creating something that was going to be huge. And anyone who was there also knows how hard we worked. For the last eight months of development, we put every ounce of our time and energy into finishing *StarCraft*. We tried as hard as possible to release the game in time for Christmas of 1997, but the game just wasn't ready. Players became so impatient waiting for the game to come out that a number of them formed a group called Operation CWAL (Can't Wait Any Longer). They posted fictional stories on our Battle.net forums claiming that the game had already been completed but was being held up in an evil plot by Blizzard management. The stories were written in good fun, but the pressure on us to finish the game was real.

When we finally released the game, I actually went to the office the next day, and I was surprised to find others there, just playing the game! You'd think that these guys would have been tired of testing *StarCraft* over and over endlessly for months, but there they were choosing to come in on their own time to create maps and play *StarCraft* on Battle.net. I remember saying "What are you guys doing here? Go home!" but I was thinking "How cool is that?!"

This book you are holding would not exist without the passion of countless people. Certainly Jeff Grubb, Gabriel Mesta, Tracy Hickman, and Blizzard's own Micky Neilson have put their hearts and souls into these stories you are about to read. But the guy I'd like to single out for you is Chris Metzen. Blizzard games are great because of a solid team effort, with different people advocating for different elements in each game. Chris is the guy who showed us how a good story could immerse the player in a game in a way that made the whole game better. Chris is currently our VP of Creative Development, but he started out at Blizzard as an artist back in 1993, when we didn't really see much value in backstory. Storytelling simply wasn't a high priority at Blizzard. We looked at games like *Sonic the Hedgehog*. That was a great game and it didn't even try to have a story (I don't know, did it?). Doesn't matter, it didn't need one. Chris was our champion of the story. As time went on, we all began to recognize that our games required story, history, and lore. It wasn't enough anymore for a faceless voice to provide us with a meaningless mission. We needed a reason to save the universe. Chris rose to the challenge, and he made what we at Blizzard now call Creative Development integral to our game-development process.

This book is a compilation of great stories that will take you on a journey deep into the *StarCraft* universe. I am very proud of these stories: they are a testament that *StarCraft* has become so much more than just a great game. It is home to a fascinating universe of characters with a rich history, and I for one can't wait to return to this universe and experience more. I love *StarCraft*. It remains to this day my favorite Blizzard game. I hope you will enjoy reading these stories as much as I have. Oh, and there is more coming . . .

Mike Morhaime
President
Blizzard Entertainment

THE
StarCraft
ARCHIVE

LIBERTY'S CRUSADE

JEFF GRUBB

ABOUT THE AUTHOR

JEFF GRUBB is the author of *Starcraft: Liberty's Crusade* as well as numerous books for the Forgotten Realms, Dragonlance, and Magic: The Gathering settings, including *Cormyr, a Novel, Lord Toede,* and *The Brothers' War.* His hobby is building worlds, while his job is explaining them to other people. He is currently writing short fiction on Beowulf, cats, and dragons celebrating Christmas (not all at the same time), and creating universes for computer games. He lives in Seattle with his wife, author Kate Novak, and two cats. He keeps an online journal at grubbstreet.blogspot.com.

Dedicated to the fans of StarCraft, in particular my co-workers who have spent countless man-hours perfecting the zergling swarm assault.

ACKNOWLEDGMENTS

This novel is set in the heart of the *StarCraft* universe, which would not exist without the hard work of the talented designers, artists, and programmers at Blizzard Entertainment.

ANTEBELLUM

THE MAN IN THE TATTERED COAT STANDS IN A ROOM of shadows, bathed in light. No, that is wrong: the figure is not illuminated by the light, but rather is light incarnate, light folded and curved in on itself in a holographic replica of its originator. The man speaks to the dimly lit room, unknowing and uncaring if there is anyone present beyond the limits of his own radiance. Phantom smoke, equally luminous, snakes up from the cigarette in his left hand.

He is a shard of the past, a bit of what had gone before, frozen in light, playing to an unseen audience.

"You know me," says the shining figure, pausing to take a drag on his coffin nail. "You've seen my face on the Universe News Network, and you've read the reports under my byline. Some of those were even written by me. Some others, well, let's say I have talented editors." The light-starred figure gives a tired, almost-amused shrug.

The recording presents him as a small mannequin, but he looks as if in real life he would be of normal height and proportions, if a little lanky. His shoulders slope slightly from exhaustion or age. His dirty-blond hair is spattered with lighter striations of gray and is swept back in a ponytail to hide an obvious bald spot. His face is worn, a bit craggier than would be permitted for a traditional newscast, but still recognizable. It remains a famous face, a comfortable face, a well-known face across human space, even in these later war-torn days.

But it is his eyes that demand attention. They are deep-set, and even in the recording seem to reach out. It is the eyes that create the illusion that the shining figure can truly see his audience, and see them to the core of their beings. That has always been his talent, connecting with his audience even when he was light-years away.

The figure takes another pull on his cancer stick, and his head is bathed in a holy nimbus of smoke. "You may have heard the official reports of the fall of the Confederacy of Man and of the glorious rise of the empire called the Terran Dominion. And you may have listened to the stories of the coming of the aliens, the hordes of Zerg and the inhuman, ethereal Protoss. Of the battles of the Sara system and the fall of Tarsonis itself. You've heard the reports. As I said before, some of those reports had my name on them. Parts of them are even true."

In the darkness beyond the light someone shifts uneasily, unseen. The holographic projector lets out only stray bits of light, rogue photons, but the audience remains for the moment a mystery. Somewhere behind the darkness-shrouded audience there is the sound of dripping water.

"You read my words, then, and believed them. I'm here to tell you, in those broadcasts, that most of them were grade-A cow patties, massaged by the powers that be into more suitable and palatable forms. Lies were told, both small and large, lies that have led us in part to our present sorry situation. A situation that is not going to improve unless we start talking about what really happened. What happened on Chau Sara and Mar Sara and Antiga Prime and Tarsonis itself. What happened to me and some friends of mine, and some enemies as well."

The figure pauses, drawing itself up to its full height. It

looks around, its sightless eyes sweeping the darkened room. It looks into the core of its audience's soul.

"I'm Michael Daniel Liberty. I'm a reporter. Call this my most important, perhaps final, report. Call this my manifesto. Call it what you will. I'm just here to tell you what really happened. I'm here to set the record straight. I'm here to tell you the truth."

CHAPTER 1

THE PRESS GANG

Before the war, things were different. Hell, back then, we were just making our daily living, doing our jobs, drawing our paychecks, and stabbing our fellow men and women in the back. We had no idea how bad things would get. We were fat and happy like maggots on a dead animal. There was enough sporadic violence—rebellions and revolutions and balky colonial governments—to keep the military going, but not enough to really threaten the lifestyles we had grown accustomed to. We were, in retrospect, fat and sassy.

And if a real war broke out, well, it was the military's worry. The marines' worry. Not ours.

—The Liberty Manifesto

THE CITY SPRAWLED BENEATH MIKE'S FEET LIKE AN overturned bucket of jade cockroaches. From the dizzying height of Handy Anderson's office, he could almost see the horizon between the taller buildings. The city reached that far, forming a jagged, spiked tear along the edge of the world.

The city of Tarsonis, on the planet Tarsonis. The most important city on the most important planet of the Confederacy of Man. The city so great they named it twice. The city so large its suburbs had greater populations than some planets. A shining beacon of civilization, keeper of the memories of an Earth now lost to history, myth, and earlier generations.

A sleeping dragon. And Michael Liberty could not resist twisting its tail.

"Come back from the edge there, Mickey," said Anderson. The editor-in-chief was firmly ensconced at his desk, a desk as far away from the panoramic view as possible.

Michael Liberty liked to think there was a note of concern in his boss's voice.

"Don't worry," said Mike. "I'm not thinking of jumping." He suppressed a smile.

Mike and the rest of the newsroom knew that the editor-in-chief was acrophobic but could not bear to surrender his stratospheric office view. So on the rare occasions when Liberty was summoned into his boss's office, he always stood near the window. Most of the time he and the other drudges and news hacks worked way down on the fourth floor or in the broadcast booths in the building's basement.

"Jumping I'm not worried about," said Anderson. "Jumping I can handle. Jumping would solve a lot of my problems and give me a lead for tomorrow's edition. I'm more worried about some sniper taking you out from another building."

Liberty turned toward his boss. "Bloodstains that hard to get out of the carpet?"

"Part of it," said Anderson, smiling. "It's also a bitch to replace the glass."

Liberty look one last look at the traffic crawling far below and returned to the overstuffed chairs facing the desk. Anderson tried to be nonchalant, but Mike noted that the editor let out a long, slow breath as Mike moved away from the window.

Michael Liberty settled himself into one of Anderson's

chairs. The chairs were designed to look like normal furniture, but they were stuffed so that they sank an extra inch or two when someone sat down. This made the balding editor-in-chief with his comically oversized eyebrows look more imposing. Mike knew the trick, was not impressed, and set his feet up on the desk.

"So what's the beef?" the reporter asked.

"Have a cigar, Mickey?" Anderson motioned with an open palm toward a teak humidor.

Mike hated being called Mickey. He touched his empty shirt pocket, where he normally stashed a pack of cigarettes. "I'm on the wagon. Trying to cut down."

"They're from beyond the Jaandaran embargo," said Anderson temptingly. "Rolled on the thighs of cinnamon-shaded maidens."

Mike held up both hands and smiled broadly. Everyone knew that Anderson was too cheap to get anything beyond the standard *el ropos* manufactured in some bootleg basement. But the smile was intended to reassure.

"What's the beef?" Mike repeated.

"You've really done it this time," said Anderson, sighing. "Your series on the construction kickbacks on the new Municipal Hall."

"Good stuff. The series should rattle a few cages."

"They've already been rattled," replied Anderson, his chin sinking down to touch his chest. This was known as the bearer-of-bad-news position. It was something that Anderson had learned at some management course but that made him look like a mating ledge-pigeon.

Crap, thought Mike. *He's going to spike the series.*

As if reading his thoughts, Anderson said, "Don't worry, we're going to run the rest of the series. It's solid reporting, well-documented, and best of all, it's true. But you have to know you've made a few people very uncomfortable."

Mike mentally ran through the series. It had been one of his better ones, a classic involving a petty offender who was caught in the wrong place (a public park) at the wrong time (way after midnight) with the wrong thing (mildly radioactive construction waste from the Municipal Hall project). Said offender was more than willing to pass on the name of the man who sent him on this late-night escapade. That individual was in turn willing to tell Mike about some other interesting matters involving the new hall, and so forth, until Mike had, instead of a single story, a whole series about a huge network of graft and corruption that the Universe Network News audience ate up with their collective spoons.

Mike mentally ran through the ward heelers, low-level thugs, and members of the Tarsonis City Council that he had skewered in print, discarding each in turn as a suspect. Any of those august individuals might want to take a shot at him, but such a threat wasn't enough to make Handy Anderson nervous.

The editor-in-chief saw Mike's blank expression and added, "You've made a few powerful, venerable people very uncomfortable."

Mike's left eyebrow rose. Anderson was talking about one of the ruling Families, the power behind the Confederacy for most of its existence, since those early days when the first colony ships (hell, prison ships) landed and/or crashed on various planets in the sector. Somewhere in his reporting, he had nailed somebody with pull, or perhaps somebody close enough to one of the Families to make the old venerables nervous.

Mike resolved to go back over his notes and see what kind of linkages he could make. Perhaps a distaff cousin to one of the Old Families, or a black sheep, or maybe even a direct kickback. God knew that the Old Families ran things from behind the scenes since the year naught. If he could nail one of them . . .

Mike wondered if he was visibly salivating at the prospect.

In the meantime Handy Anderson had risen from his seat and strolled around the side of his desk, perching on the corner nearest Mike. (Another move directly out of the man-agement lectures, Mike realized. Hell, Anderson had assigned him to cover those lectures once.) "Mike, I want you to know you're on dangerous ground here."

Oh God, he called me Mike, thought Liberty. *Next he'll be look-ing plaintively out the window as if lost in thought, wrestling with a momentous decision.*

He said, "I'm used to dangerous ground, boss."

"I know, I know. I just worry about those around you. Your sources. Your friends. Your co-workers . . ."

"Not to mention my superiors."

". . . all of whom would be heartbroken if something hor-rible happened to you."

"Particularly if they were standing nearby when it hap-pened," added the reporter.

Anderson shrugged and stared plaintively out the full-length window. Mike realized that whatever Anderson was afraid of, it was worse than his fear of heights. And this was a man who, if office rumor was correct (and it was), kept a locked room in the subbasement that contained dirt on most of the celebrities and important citizens of the city.

The pause dragged beyond a moment into a minute. Finally Mike broke. He gave a polite cough and said, "So you have an idea how to handle this 'dangerous ground'?"

Handy Anderson nodded slowly. "I want to print the series. It's good work."

"But you don't want me anywhere in the immediate vicin-ity when the next part of that story hits the street."

"I'm thinking of your own safety, Mickey, it's . . ."

"Dangerous ground," finished Mike. "I heard. Here be dragons. Perhaps it would be time for an extended vacation? Maybe a cabin in the mountains?"

"I was thinking more of a special assignment."

Of course, thought Mike. *That way I won't have the chance to figure out whose tail I've inadvertently twisted. And give those involved time to cover their tracks.*

"Another part of the Universe News Network empire?" Mike said with a broad smile, at the same time wondering what godforsaken colony world he would be doing agricultural reports from.

"More of a roving reporter," teased Anderson.

"How roving?" Mike's smile suddenly became flinty and brittle. "Will I need shots for off-planet?"

"Better than getting shot for being on-planet. Sorry, bad joke. The answer is yes, I'm thinking definitely off-planet."

"Come on, spill. Which hellhole do you want to hide me in?"

"I was thinking of the Confederate Marines. As a military reporter, of course."

"What!"

"It would be a temporary posting, of course," continued the editor.

"Are you out of your *mind*?"

"Sort of 'our fighting men in space,' battling against the various forces of rebellion that threaten our great Confederacy. There are rumors that Arcturus Mengsk is rallying more support in the Fringe Worlds. Could turn really hot at any moment."

"The marines?" sputtered Mike. "The Confederate Marines are the biggest collection of criminals in the known universe, outside of the Tarsonis City Council."

"Mike, please. Everyone has *some* criminal blood in them. Hell, all the planets of the Confederacy were settled by exiled convicts."

"Yeah, but most people like to think we grew out of that. The marines still make that one of their basic recruiting requirements. Hell, do you know how many of them have been brain-panned?"

"Neurally Resocialized," corrected Anderson. "No more than fifty percent per unit these days, I understand. Less in some places. And the resocialization is more often done with noninvasive procedures. You probably won't notice."

"Yeah, and they pump them so full of stimpacks they'd kill their own grandpas on the right command."

"Exactly the sort of common misconception that your work can counter," said Anderson, both eyebrows raised in practiced sincerity.

"Look, most of the politicos I've met are naturally nuts. The marines are nuts and *then* they started messing with their heads. No. The marines are not an option."

"It'd make for some good stories. You'd probably get some good contacts."

"No."

"Reporters with experience with the military get perks," said the editor-in-chief. "You get a green tag on your file, and that carries weight with the more venerable families of Tarsonis. In some cases even forgiveness."

"Sorry. Not interested."

"I'll give you your own column."

A pause. Finally Mike said, "How big a column?"

"Full column-page print, or five minutes stand-up for the broadcast. Under your byline, of course."

"Regular?"

"You file, I'll fill."

Another pause. "A raise with that?"

Anderson named a figure, and Mike nodded.

"That's impressive," he said.

"Not chump change," agreed the editor-in-chief.

"I'm a little old to be planet-hopping."

"There's no real danger. And if something does flare up, there's combat pay. Automatic."

"Fifty percent brain-panned?" Mike asked.

"If that."

Another pause. Then Mike said, "Well, it sounds like a challenge."

"And you're just the man for a challenge."

"And it can't be worse than covering the Tarsonis City Council," Mike mused, feeling himself sliding down the slippery slope to acceptance.

"My thoughts exactly," his editor agreed.

"And if it would help the network . . ." Yep, Mike thought, he was on the edge, poised to pitch over into the void.

"You would be a shining light to us all," said Anderson. "A well-paid, shining light. Wave the flag a little, get some personal stories, ride around in a battlecruiser, play some cards. Don't worry about us back here at the office."

"Cush posting?"

"Cushiest. I've got some pull, you know. Was an old green-tag myself. Three months' work, tops. A lifetime of rewards."

There was a final pause, a chasm as deep as the concrete canyon that yawned beyond the window.

"All right," said Mike, "I'll do it."

"Wonderful!" Anderson reached for the humidor, then caught himself and instead offered Mike his hand. "You won't regret it."

"Why do I feel that I already do?" Michael Liberty asked in a small voice as the editor's meaty, sweaty hand ensnared his own.

CHAPTER 2

THE CUSH POSTING

Service in the military, for those of you unfortunate enough never to have experienced it firsthand, consists of long periods of boredom broken by mind-shredding threats to one's life and sanity. From what I can gather from the old tapes, it's always been like that. The best soldiers are those who can wake suddenly, react instantly, and aim precisely.

Unfortunately, none of those traits are shared by the military intelligence that controls those soldiers.

—THE LIBERTY MANIFESTO

"MR. LIBERTY?" SAID THE PERKY MURDERESS AT THE hatchway. "The captain would like a word with you."

Michael Liberty, UNN reporter assigned to the elite Alpha Squadron of the Confederate Marines, propped open one eye and found her, all smiles, standing next to his bunk. An all-night card game had just adjourned, and he was sure the young marine lieutenant had waited until he had lain down before barging into his quarters.

The reporter let out a deep sigh and said, "Does Colonel Duke expect me immediately?"

"No, sir," said the murderess, shaking her head for effect. "He said you should come at your leisure."

"Right," said Mike, swinging his legs over the edge of his bunk and shaking the temptation of sleep from his brain. For Colonel Duke, "at your leisure" usually meant "within the next ten minutes, dammit." Mike reached for his cigarettes, and only when his hand had dipped into the empty shirt pocket did he remember he had given them up.

"Filthy habit anyway," he muttered to himself. To the marine lieutenant he said, "Need a shower. Coffee would be good, too."

Lieutenant Emily Jameson Swallow, Liberty's personal assistant, liaison, minder, and spy for her military superiors, waited only long enough to determine that Mike was serious about getting up, then beetled off to the galley. Mike yawned, figured he must have had all of five minutes' sleep, stripped, and padded off to the sonic cleanser.

The sonic cleanser was a military model, of course. This meant it was similar in construction to those high-pressure jets that blasted the meat off the bones at slaughterhouses. In the past three months Mike had gotten used to it.

In the past three months Michael Liberty had gotten used to a lot of things.

Handy Anderson had been true to his word. The posting was posh, or at least as posh as a military assignment could be. The *Norad II* was a capital ship, one of the Behemoth-class, all neosteel and laser turrets, as befitted the most legendary of Confederate military units, the Alpha Squadron.

Alpha Squadron's primary mission was hunting rebels, particularly the Sons of Korhal, a revolutionary group under the bloodthirsty terrorist Arcturus Mengsk. Unfortunately, the Sons were never where they were supposed to be, and the *Norad II* and her prized crew spent a lot of time showing the flag (a blue diagonal cross filled with white stars against a red background, the memory of a legend of Old Earth) and keeping the local colonial governments in line.

As a result, Mike's biggest challenge so far had been dealing with boredom and finding enough to write about to justify his column. The flag-waving propaganda came easy for the first few stories, but when there was a deficit of real action or achievement, Mike had to reach. A piece on Colonel Edmund Duke, of course. Some human-interest stuff on the well-oiled crew. A bit about the travails of the neurally resocialized that Anderson scotched (out of common decency, Handy explained). Local color on the various planets. Just enough to remind everyone (Handy Anderson in particular) that he was still alive and expected regular payments to his account.

And then there was a long two-parter about the wonders of the Behemoth-class battlecruisers, a story that was decimated by military censors to a mere few paragraphs. Military secrets, it was explained.

Like the Sons of Korhal don't know what we have already, thought Mike as he slipped into his shorts and looked for a less-rumpled shirt and pants. Hanging in his locker was a new traveling coat, a going-away present from the guys in the newsroom. It was a long duster that made him look like a denizen of the Old West, but the crew apparently felt that if Mike was going out to the interplanetary sticks, he might as well look the part.

He slipped into some nondescript pants. Almost on cue, Swallow reappeared with a pot of java and a mug. She poured as Mike buttoned up his shirt.

The brew was military-style "A"—freshly made and scalding, suitable for pouring down on peasants attacking the family castle. The coffee was another thing he had gotten used to.

Of course, he had also gotten used to three squares, sufficient time to write his columns, and a flexible amount of privacy. As well as an ever-changing group of poker partners, all of whom were young, had no place to spend their paychecks, and could not bluff if their lives depended on it.

He had even gotten used to Lieutenant Swallow, though her habitual positive attitude bothered him at first. He had expected some sort of minder, of course, some military attaché who would hang over his shoulder as he wrote and make sure he didn't do anything stupid like drop his pen into the warp coils. But Lieutenant Emily Swallow was like something out of a training film. A particularly cheery training film, the type you show Mom and Dad before shipping their sons and daughters off to extended duty five star systems away. Hell, Lieutenant Emily Swallow looked like she *wrote* that type of training film.

Small, petite, and always smiling, she seemed to take every request from Mike seriously, even if they both knew that there was a snowball's chance that it would be approved. She had no vices, except for the occasional cigarette, accepted with a smile and a guilty shrug. Further, when he hit her up for her own story, she demurred. Most of the crew were stoked up, talking about their lives back home, but Lieutenant Swallow instead just stopped smiling and ran her hand back along the side of her face, as if brushing away long hair that was no longer there.

That was when Mike noticed the small divots behind her ear, the marks of the noninvasive neural resocialization that Anderson had mentioned. Yeah, she had been brain-panned, and good. No one could be that perky without an electrochemical lobotomy.

Mike didn't bring up the subject again, but instead bribed one of the computer techs for some time with the personnel files (this cost him his two emergency packs of smokes, but by that time he was through the worst of the cravings, and the coffin nails were better used in trade than consumption). He found out that before she had involuntarily joined the marines, young Emily Swallow had the interesting hobby of attracting young men in bars, taking them to her home, tying them up, and flaying the skin and meat from their bones with a fillet knife.

Most men would be disconcerted by this news, but Michael Liberty found it reassuring. The murderess of ten young men on Halcyon was much more understandable than the smiling, gung-ho woman who looked like someone from a recruiting poster. Now, following her through the corridors of the *Norad II* to the bridge, Mike wondered how Lieutenant Swallow felt about her medical incarceration and involuntary transformation. He decided that she just didn't dwell on it, and given her original nature, Mike decided not to press the issue.

For a huge ship, the *Norad II* had narrow passageways, built almost as an afterthought after all the landing bays, wardrooms, weapons systems, galleys, computers, and other necessities had been piled in. In the hallways oncoming traffic had to press against walls to pass. Mike noticed large arrows painted on the floor, which Lieutenant Swallow noted were for times when the ship was on alert and soldiers were in full battle armor. Mike realized that the gangways would have been made even narrower had they not been expected to accommodate men in powered combat suits.

They passed several large bays where technicians were already pulling out wiring and cables. The scuttlebutt was that the *Norad II* was due for an overhaul, including an upgrade with the Yamato cannon. Given the number of laser batteries, Wraith-class space fighters, and even the rumored nuclear arms carried on board, the huge spine-mounted cannon would be icing on the cake.

In fact, this was what Mike expected Colonel Duke to tell him—that the *Norad II* was going into dry dock for repairs, and he, Michael Liberty, would be on the next shuttle back to Tarsonis. That would make dealing with the old fossil almost worthwhile.

He revised his opinion when they stepped onto the bridge, and Duke scowled at him. Mind you, Duke never looked particularly pleased to see a member of the press, but this was the deepest and most hostile scowl that Mike had seen yet.

"Mr. Liberty, reporting as requested, sir," said Lieutenant Swallow with a salute as sharp as that in any recruiting video.

The colonel, decked out in his command brown uniform, said nothing but pointed a stubby finger toward his ready room. Lieutenant Swallow led him there, then abandoned him for whatever tasks she did when she wasn't keeping tabs on him. Probably, Mike mused, something involving skinning puppies.

Mike's initial concern grew deeper when he recognized the humanoid shape now hanging from a wall-mounted frame in the ready room. It was a powered combat suit, not one of the standard-issue CMC-300s but a command suit, fitted with its own portable comm system. Colonel Duke's suit, now shined and greased and ready for the great man to step into it.

Mike was less sure now that they were going in for that Yamato refit. Most of the marines kept their armor handy, and drills were as common as meals. Liberty managed to avoid that duty, as he was considered a "soft target" and wasn't cleared for the heavier suits. It was, however, amusing to see the rookies staggering around the narrow passages in full combat armor.

But for the colonel's suit to be here, newly polished and ready, boded very ill indeed.

The suit itself was massive, hunched forward on the hanger under its own weight. In that way, it seemed to Michael Liberty, the empty suit fit its owner well. Colonel Duke reminded Mike of the great apes of Old Earth, the ones that climbed buildings and swatted down primitive aircraft. Gorillas. Duke was an old silverback, the pointy-headed leader of his tribe, and just the way he leaned forward inspired fear in his subordinates.

Mike knew that Duke was from one of the Old Families, the original leaders of the Koprulu Sector colonies. But he must have done something wrong along the way: Edmund Duke was obviously long overdue for his general's stars. Mike wondered what nasty incident stood in the way of his promotion, and surmised that it was loud, messy, and deeply buried in the Confederate military files. He wondered what type of pull it would take to get that information out, and if Handy Anderson had it in his not-so-secret vault.

The door slid open and Colonel Duke strode in like a Goliath-style armored walker scattering infantry units before it. His scowl was even deeper than earlier. He held down a hand to indicate that Mike shouldn't rise (Mike had had no intention of doing so), circled his wide desk, and sat down. He rested his elbows on the polished obsidian desktop and templed his fingers in front of him.

"I trust, Liberty, you have had an enjoyable time with us?" he asked. He had the old, faint drawl that marked the elder Families of the Confederacy.

Mike, who had not expected small talk, managed to stammer out a general affirmative.

"I am afraid it will not last," said the colonel. "Our original orders were to be relieved by the *Theodore G. Bilbo*, and to put in for a retrofit within two weeks. Events have now overtaken us."

Mike said nothing. He had been in enough briefings over the years, even on a civilian level, to know not to interrupt until he had something worth interrupting for.

"We are rerouting our course to the Sara system. I'm afraid it's in the boonies, on the butt end of nowhere. The Confederacy has two colony worlds there, Mar Sara and Chau Sara. This is an extended patrol over and above our initial mission parameters."

Mike just nodded. The colonel was creeping up on the subject, acting like a dog with a chicken bone in its throat— something he had a hard time swallowing and a worse time coughing back up. Mike waited.

"I must remind you that as a member of the press assigned to the Alpha Squadron, you are limited under the Confederate military code in regard to what your duties are and how you perform them."

"Yes, sir," said Mike, sternly enough to give the impression that he gave a rat's ass about the Confederate military code.

"And that this extends to your current assignment as well as to future references to events that occur during your posting here." Duke nodded his pointed head, clearly demanding a response.

"Yes, sir." Mike separated the words clearly to underscore his comprehension.

Another pause, during which Mike could feel the throbbing of the ship around him. Yes, the *Norad II* was vibrating at a different pitch now, a bit higher, more intense, a bit more frantic. Men and women were preparing the ship for subwarp. And perhaps for combat?

Mike suddenly wondered about the wisdom of skipping those combat suit drills.

Colonel Edmund Duke, the dog with the chicken bone in his throat, said, "You know our histories."

It was more of a statement than a question. Mike blinked, suddenly unsure how to respond. He settled for "Sir?"

"How we came to the sector and settled it. Took it for our own," prompted the colonel.

"Aboard the sleeper ships, the supercarriers," Mike said, pulling up the lessons of childhood. "The *Nagglfar*, the *Argo*, the *Sarengo*, and the *Reagan*. The crews of prisoners and outcasts of Old Earth, crashing onto a scattering of habitable worlds."

"And they found three such worlds, right off the bat. And a double-handful nearby that were terrestrial or close enough for army work. But they found no life."

"Begging the colonel's pardon, but there was extensive native life on all three original planets. Plus, most of the colonies and Fringe Worlds have their own ecosystems. Terraforming often, but not always, eradicates native life-forms."

The colonel waved off the comment. "But nothing smarter than your standard watchdog. Some big insects they domesticated on Umoja, and a lot of stuff that was burned when the world was settled and put under the plow. But nothing *smart*."

Mike nodded. "Intelligent life has always been one of the mysteries of the universe. We have found world after world, but nothing to indicate that there is something else out there as smart as we are."

"Until now," said the colonel. "And you will be the first network reporter on the scene."

Mike warmed a bit to the subject. "There have been numerous mysterious formations on many planets that indicate there might have been sentient life at one time. In addition, there are space-haulers' tales of mysterious lights and foo-fighters."

"These aren't lights in the sky or old ruins. This is living proof of ET activity. That we are not alone out here."

Duke let that sink in, and a smirk tugged at the side of his mouth. It did not improve his appearance in the least. Somewhere within the ship a switch closed, and the monstrous engines began to hum.

Mike stroked his chin and asked, "What do we know so far? Has there been an envoy, a representative? Or was this a chance discovery? Did we find a colony, or was there a direct embassy?"

The colonel let out a gruff chortle. "Mr. Liberty, let me make myself quite clear. We have made contact with another alien civilization. This contact consisted of them vaporizing the colony of Chau Sara. They burned it to the ground, and then burned the ground beneath it. We're going there now, but we don't know if the hostiles are still present.

"And you will be the first network reporter on the scene," repeated the colonel. "Congratulations, son."

Mike didn't feel very good about this particular honor.

CHAPTER 3

THE SARA SYSTEM

The first contact with another sentient race, and they blow up a planet. Helluva calling card.

Now, blowing up a planet is nothing new. Christ, we humans did it ourselves not too long ago.

There was a revolt on the planet Korhal IV. The inhabitants didn't care much for the graft and corruption that was part and parcel of the Confederacy. They tried to rebel. At first the Confederacy tried a soft approach: they took out the rebellion's leaders with assassins, ghost-troopers with personal cloaking devices. Unsurprisingly, this approach just made the people of Korhal angrier and more rebellious. So the Confederacy took a harder line.

We nuked Korhal IV from orbit.

Apocalypse-class missiles. About a thousand of them. Some green-tagged idiot on Tarsonis pressed a button, and 35 million people became nothing more than vapor and their homes nothing more than a memory.

Naturally, there were official justifications thereafter about the evil, menacing nature of Korhal, and how they were planning to do it to us if they got even the slightest chance. It was unfortunate that the proof of this accusation was located on a planet covered by blackened glass.

I think that's what really scared the military about the vaporization of Chau Sara: that there was something else out there that was just as crazy as we were.

And they were better at it than we were.

—The Liberty Manifesto

MIKE TOOK ADVANTAGE OF THE TIME THE SHIP WAS in subwarp to pore through the open computer archives on the Sara system. It was a fairly typical fringe system, the ragged leading edge of the Confederacy's ever-increasing sphere of power.

The system had been found by a prospector before the Guild Wars, glommed onto by the Confederacy when it eclipsed that budding rival in space, and was (according to the ship's archives) the home of a growing pair of colony worlds. The only thing that made the Sara system different from about a dozen other similar worlds was that there were two worlds in its habitable band instead of just one.

Chau Sara was the smaller and more outlying of the worlds, and had the larger colony. It had been settled, in Confederate tradition, as a penal colony, and a lot of its (now former) inhabitants had still been serving hard time. Mar Sara had a more eclectic mix of former prospectors and soldiers, along with a couple of religious types that didn't agree with the Tarsonian limits of tolerance for other faiths. Both planets had rich potential for mineral exploitation, but of course the Confederacy had dibs on those resources. The locals would have to either work under Confederate contracts or flee to new Fringe Worlds.

Mike checked the current UNN reports. There was a small bit about a disruption of signals from the Sara system, but most of the broadcast was given over to the latest Sons of Korhal outrage (poison gas in a public plaza on Haji), and a multitrain monorail pileup on Moira.

Mike composed a brief blurb, summarizing his discussion with Colonel Duke and noting that he was under full military restrictions in future reporting. That meant that his report would be checked over before it left the ship and then again before it was broadcast. Handy Anderson would be simultaneously griping about military censorship and dancing around his office in joy for the scoop.

If I'm lucky, thought Mike, *he'll dance too close to that damned window of his.*

Mike prepared a second report, this one scrambled under cipher software and burned onto a minidisk. This one wasn't going anywhere, but if something happened to them, and their bodies were found, someone would know what was going on. It was a grim insurance policy.

He had just finished the second report when a large shadow blocked the light.

Mike looked up into the face of Lieutenant Swallow, now a foot taller and several hundred pounds heavier. She was decked out in a combat suit, her natural strength boosted by servos and mechanisms. An empty belt clip at her side would soon be filled with an 8-millimeter C-14 gauss rifle, an Impaler, for when she went into action.

Her visor was open, and she beamed an excited smile at him. She looked like a girl expecting her first prom dance.

"Sir? We'll be coming out of subwarp soon. The colonel wants you on the bridge, at the soonest possible moment." Then she was gone.

Meaning right damned now, thought Mike, and followed Swallow out of his quarters.

The passageways were no wider now, but with the bulky suits now in preponderance they had become one-way, with movement guided by huge arrows on the floor. At several crossings Swallow held up to let other crewmen pass in front of them, and Mike had the sudden feeling of being the only kindergartner in a sixth-grade class.

"I've got to get me one of those suits," he commented.

"I was unaware you were trained in the CMC powered combat suit, sir," said Swallow.

"I've read the manuals."

"That knowledge would be barely sufficient for your own protection in a crisis situation, sir. However, should something happen, it is my personal responsibility to make sure you get to safety."

"I'm filled with confidence." Mike smiled at Swallow's back, just in case she had a camera trained on him.

The ship gave a transdimensional shudder, and the engines shifted back from subwarp. They were in Sara's space.

The bridge was now bathed in red light, accented by the green monitors that lined the lower deck. Colonel Duke was decked out in his own battle armor. He looked like a gorilla at the court of King Arthur. A gorilla with a pointy head, wearing plate mail. He was surrounded by a small cluster of viewscreens, each with a different talking head feeding data to him.

"Mr. Liberty, reporting as requested, sir," said Swallow, managing another sharp salute, even in the heavy armor.

"Colonel," said Mike.

Duke did not look away from the main screen. He said simply, "We're nearing Chau Sara."

At first Mike thought the main screen was malfunctioning. They were approaching Chau Sara from the night side. The large disk of the outer Saran world was a messy, rainbow smear of light, like that found on oily water.

Then Mike realized that this *was* the surface of Chau Sara he was looking at. It glowed with rippling bands of colors, moored at a handful of locations by bright spikes of orange.

"What . . ." Mike blinked. "What did this?"

"First contact, Liberty," said the colonel. "First contact of the most extreme kind. How are the scans?"

One of the technicians reported, "I get no life readings. Most of the surface area has been liquefied and sterilized. This zone looks to be between twenty and fifty feet deep."

"The settlements?" Mike asked.

The technician continued. "The orange spikes appear to

be magma breaches through the planetary mantle. They are located at the locations of the known settlements." A pause. "Plus at least a dozen other locations."

Mike looked at the swirling, deadly rainbow on the screen. The sun was cresting the horizon ahead of them, and the world looked no better in the sunlight. Only a few dark clouds, thin as crow feathers, dragged across the sunlight side.

"In addition, eighty percent of the atmosphere has been blown off in the attack," continued the technician.

"Any orbital presence?" asked Duke, an armor-plated monolith in their midst.

"Working," said the tech. Finally came the response, "Negative. Nothing of ours. Nothing of unknown origin either. There may be some fragments on a larger scan."

"Widen the scan," said Duke. "I want to know if there's anything out here. Ours or theirs."

"Working . . . Definite fragments. Likely ours. Would need a salvage team to confirm."

"Why did they do this?" Mike asked, but no one answered him. Techs in lighter-weight combat suits tapped displays with gauntleted hands, and the numerous heads on the screens all talked at once to Colonel Duke.

Finally Mike came up with a question he thought they could answer. "What did this? Nukes?"

The word seemed to break Duke from his steady stream of information. He looked at the reporter. "Atomic delivery systems leave blackened glass and burning forests. Even Korhal had some surviving pockets of clear terrain, for a while at least. Chau Sara has been burned down to the liquid core in places. This is much more deadly than even Apocalypse bombs.

"This"—Duke pointed at the screen—"is the work of an alien race, the Protoss. From what I'm being told, they warped in from nowhere, closer to the planet than we would ever attempt. Huge ships, and a lot of them. Caught a few transports and scavenger ships and blew them out of the sky. Then they unleashed whatever-it-was on the planet and sterilized it like a three-minute egg. Then they left again. Mar Sara's on the other side of the sun right now, and they're in a panic that they might be next."

"Protoss." Mike shook his head slightly, digesting the data. Something was wrong there. He looked at the tech's display, showing the deep radar holes punching down to the planet's magma.

"You have enough for your report, Mr. Liberty," Duke said. "We will remain on station in the event of other hostiles for the foreseeable future. You may mention in any report you file that we will be joined by the *Jackson V* and the *Huey Long* within days."

The tech reached for his ear, then said, "Sir, we have anomalous readings."

"Location?" snapped the colonel, turning away from Liberty.

"Zed-Two, Quadrant Five, one AU out. Numerous anomalies."

"Bearing?"

"Working." A pause, and then a defeated shrug crept into the tech's words. "Heading for Mar Sara, sir."

Duke nodded. "Prepare to intercept anomalous readings. Launch fighters when in range."

Mike spoke before he thought, "Are you crazy?"

Duke turned back to the reporter. "That was a rhetorical question, I hope, son."

"We're one ship."

"We're the only ship between them and Mar Sara. We will intercept."

Mike almost said, "Easy for you, you're in a hard-shelled battlesuit," but caught himself. Whatever could go through a planetary crust wouldn't be stopped by a few layers of combat armor.

Instead Mike took a deep breath and just gripped the railing, as if he were hoping that this might ease the eventual blow.

"Approaching visual," said the tech. "Putting on screen."

The main screen flickered to reveal a scattering of fireflies against the night sky. They looked almost pretty against the darkness. Then Mike realized that there were hundreds of them, and that these were only the main ships. Smaller gnats danced around them.

"Are we within launching range for the Wraiths?" the colonel asked.

"Mark at two minutes," replied the tech.

"Launch as soon as possible."

Mike took a deep breath and wished that he had joined in the combat suit drills after all.

Even at long range, the Protoss ships had form and definition. The largest were huge cylindrical creations, similar in appearance to luminous zeppelins. They were surrounded by hungry moths, and Mike realized these had to be their fighters, their equivalents of the A-17 Wraiths that were now in the hangars, just waiting for them to close to within striking range. Other golden ships danced between the larger carriers, glimmering like small stars.

Then, as Mike watched, one of the great carriers seemed to dissolve. There was a flash of light, a soft glowing, and then it was gone. Another moment, and another flash, and another disappearance.

"Sir," said the technician. "Anomalous reading disappearing."

"Cloaking technology?" asked the colonel.

Despite himself, Mike said, "At this scale?"

"Working." A huge pause, as deep as a canyon. "Negative. It appears that they are surrounding themselves with some form of subwarp field. They are retreating."

As Mike watched, more of the ships began to flash and vanish. The great carriers and their brood of smaller ships, the lesser golden vessels, all vanished like fey spirits with the coming of dawn.

Fey spirits that can burn a planet down to its molten core, Mike reminded himself.

The colonel allowed himself a smile. "Good. They're afraid of us. Have all stations stand down, but remain alert for a trick."

Mike shook his head. "This makes no sense. They have the power to toast a planet. Why are they afraid of us?"

"Obvious," said the colonel. "They're spent. They don't have enough force to engage us."

"We're only one ship." Mike shook his head angrily. "There were dozens out there."

"They fear possible reinforcements."

"No, no. Something's going on here. It doesn't make human sense."

"We're not dealing with humans here," said Duke, scowling. "Look at their firepower."

"Exactly. These Protoss have superior numbers and firepower, and *we're* facing them down? Why *are* they here?"

"Mr. Liberty, that will be enough questions for the day." The scowl deepened, but Mike ignored the warning.

"No, something's not jake in all this. Look at the damage reports." Mike pointed at one of the tech's monitors. "They cooked an entire planet, but some places deeper than others. Every major human city, yes, but look." Mike pointed at the wall of data. "There are strike zones on the other side of the planet, far away from any recorded human settlement. I know. I was just checking the archives."

"I said that will be *enough,* mister. We have more to worry about with the Protoss than just how effective they are in choosing their targets."

Mike's face lit up as a connection was made deep in his brain. "And where did we get the name 'Protoss,' Colonel? Is that ours, or theirs?"

"Mister Liberty!" Color was creeping up the sides of Duke's face.

"And if it's their name for themselves, how come *we* know it? Didn't we have to know it in advance? Or did they send a warning before they attacked?" The reporter was raising his voice now, the way he would for a dissembling candidate in a precinct by-election.

"Lieutenant Swallow!" Duke bit off the command.

"Yes, sir?" Another perfect salute.

"Escort Mr. Liberty off the bridge! Now!"

Mike gripped the railing firmly with both hands. A ligatured arm wrapped in metal snaked around his waist. Mike was shouting now, "Dammit, Duke, you know more than you're telling. This stinks to high heaven!"

"I said now, Lieutenant!" Duke snarled.

"This way, sir," said Swallow, breaking Mike's hold and pulling the reporter off his feet. With her prize, she retreated for the lift.

Still shouting questions, Michael Liberty left the bridge. The last thing he heard before the doors slid shut was Colonel Duke ordering the opening of a comm line with the colonial magistrate of Mar Sara.

CHAPTER 4

DOWN ON MAR SARA

There's a period in any war between the first blow and the second. It's a quiet moment, an almost-tranquil time, when the realization of what has happened is just sinking in and everyone feels they know what happens next. Some prepare to flee. Some prepare to hit back. But no one moves. Not yet.

It's a perfect moment, the time when the ball is at the highest point of the throw. The action has been taken, and for one frozen moment everything is moving, but everything is at rest.

Then there are those jackasses who can't leave such things alone. And the ball starts downward again, the second blow is thrown, and we plunge into the maelstrom.

—THE LIBERTY MANIFESTO

MICHAEL LIBERTY WAS NOT ALLOWED OUT OF HIS quarters for the remainder of the action over Mar Sara. Lieutenant Swallow or one of her neurally resocialized comrades stood guard outside his quarters for the next two days. After that it was an escort to the dropship and a shuttle to beautiful Mar Sara itself.

Now, a day after that, he was in the press pool, fleecing the local reporters for most of their life savings while waiting for something that resembled a straight answer from the powers that be.

It was not forthcoming. The official debriefings were pre-shaped pellets of nonnews that stressed the suddenness of the attack on Chau Sara, hailed Duke and the *Norad II* crew as heroes for standing up to the enemy, and claimed that only the ever-watchful vigilance of the Confederacy could protect Mar Sara. The Protoss (still no idea where the name came from) were portrayed as cowards who folded at the first sign of a real fight. The delicate if impressive nature of their lightning-charged ships confirmed that notion: they fled because they were afraid to be hit.

That was the story, anyway, and the marines were sticking with it. In fact, if anyone in the press pool wandered too far from the official version, their reports suddenly started getting lost in transmission. That kept most of the locals in line. They were all issued passes with bar codes that were supposed to be presented upon demand. And, Mike knew, to keep tabs on their whereabouts.

All of the other newshounds knew Liberty's story from aboard the *Norad II*, but no one had yet tried to use any of the information in their own reports.

In the outside world, a planetary lockdown was in force. Officially a civilian protection measure (to quote the official press release), it was effectively a military overthrow of the local government. The locals were being herded into concentration points for supposedly easier evacuation. No mention was made of where the evacuating ships would come from, or even if there was a timetable for abandoning the planet. In the meantime, there were marine patrols on every corner, and those citizens who remained in the city were looking very, very nervous.

In the absence of anything reportable, the newshounds hung out at the large café in front of the Grand Hotel, played cards, waited for the next official newslike release, and speculated madly. Mike, bedecked in his duster, lounged with them, looking more like a native than any of the others.

"Man, I don't think there are any aliens at all," said Rourke between hands of poker. Rourke was a big redhead with a craggy scar across his forehead. "I think the Sons of Korhal finally found enough tech to avenge the nuking of their homeworld."

"Bite your tongue," said Maggs, a crusty old bird from one of the local dailies. "Even joking about the Korholes is enough to get you shot."

"So you have a theory, man?" countered Rourke.

"They're human, but not our type of human," said the old reporter. "They're from Old Earth. I figure that while we were gone they got so wrapped up in genetic purity and such that they are nothing but clones now, and that they've come after us to clear out the rest of the race."

Rourke nodded. "I heard that one. And Thaddeus from the *Post* thinks they're robots, and they have some programming that prevents them from defending themselves. That's why they booked out when the *Norad* took them on."

"You're all wrong," said Murray, a stringer from one of the religious networks. "They're angels, and Judgment Day has arrived."

Both Rourke and Maggs made derisive noises, then Rourke said, "What about you, Liberty? What do you think they are?"

"All I know is what I saw," Mike said. "And what I saw was that whatever they are, they liquefied the surface of the planet next door, and they could be here faster than the Confederacy could react. And we're here at ground zero, playing cards."

A pall hung over the table for a moment, and even Murray the holy stringer was quiet. Finally Rourke let out a long breath and said, "You Tarsonis boys sure know how to squelch a good party. You in or out for the next deal?"

Mike suddenly sat up, staring intently out into the road.

Despite themselves, Murray and Rourke swiveled in their chairs but could see only the usual handful of marines in the street, some in combat armor, some in regulation uniform.

"Quick, Rourke. Give me your press credentials," Mike said.

The big redhead instinctively grabbed the tags around his neck as though they were a life preserver. "No way, man."

"Okay, then let me trade my credentials for yours." Mike held out his own marine-issued ID.

"How come?" Rourke asked, already pulling the chain off over his head.

"You're local press," Mike said. "They'll let you out of the cordon into the hinterland."

"Yeah, but anything I put down goes through the censors anyway," the big man protested, handing over the tags. "Nothing gets out of here."

"Yeah, but I'm going to go crazy hanging out here. Pack of cigs, too."

"I thought you were quitting, man," Rourke said.

"Come on, man."

As soon as Mike had Rourke's cigarettes jammed in his shirt pocket he was up and out of the café, his own press tags still bouncing on the table.

"They breed them crazy on Tarsonis, man," Rourke observed.

"You going to talk or deal?" Maggs asked.

"Lieutenant Swallow!" Mike shouted. He strung Rourke's tags around his neck as he ran, his boots kicking up plumes of dust in the street.

The lieutenant turned and smiled at him. "Mr. Liberty. It is good to see you again." Her smile was warm, though Mike could not tell if the warmth was heartfelt or the result of her reprogramming.

She wasn't in her combat armor anymore, but rather in regulation khakis. That meant she wasn't on MP duty and it was unlikely she would be actively monitored. Still, she had a small slugthrower on one hip and a nasty-looking combat knife on the other.

Mike reached up and pulled the cigarette pack from his pocket. Swallow smiled guiltily and pulled one out.

"I thought you were quitting," she said.

Mike shrugged. "I thought you were, too."

Mike suddenly realized that he didn't have any matches, but Swallow produced a small lighter. A tiny laser ignited the tip's end.

The lieutenant took a long drag and said, "I am sorry about that thing back on the ship. Duty."

Mike shrugged again. "My job is sometimes asking tough questions. Duty. The bruises have healed. You busy?"

"Not at the moment. Is there a problem, sir?"

"I need a lift and a driver for out into the hinterland." Mike made it sound like a simple request. Like bumming a cigarette.

Swallow's face clouded for a moment. "They're letting you out of the cordon? Nothing personal, sir, but I thought the colonel was going to personally kick your backside to Tarsonis after that incident on the bridge."

"Time wounds all heels," said Mike, pulling up Rourke's tags. "They're lengthening my chain a bit. Just a bit of background stuff—talking to the potential refugees."

"Evacuees, sir," corrected Swallow.

"My point exactly. Have to get a line on the brave people of Mar Sara in the face of the threat from space. You interested in shuttling me around?"

"Well, I'm off duty, sir . . ." Swallow hesitated, and Mike touched the cigarette pack again. "I can't see the harm. You sure the colonel is down with this?"

Mike beamed a winning, wise smile. "If he isn't, then we get turned back at the first checkpoint, and I'll introduce you to my card-playing buddies at the café."

Lieutenant Swallow wangled transport, an open-topped, wide-bodied jeep. Rourke's tags got them through the check-

point, a bored MP swiping the card through the reader and getting a green light for the "local reporter." The authorities didn't
seem to be horribly worried about people getting out into the
hinterlands, particularly those with a military escort. They
seemed to be more concerned about people getting back in.

Mar Sara had always been only borderline habitable, in
comparison to the formerly rich jungles of its sister in farther
orbit. Its sky was a dusty orange, and most of its soil varied
between hard-baked mud and stringy scrub. Irrigation had
made parts of this desert bloom, but as they passed outside
the city Mike could see fields already blighted by lack of water.
Watering cranes stood like lonely scarecrows over the brown-
tinged crops.

Such crops needed constant attention, Mike noted in
his recorder, and the displacement of the population was as
deadly for them as an assault from space. The abandonment
of the agricultural areas was a sure sign that the Confederates
expected the Protoss to return.

They came across their first concentration point for refugees (sorry, evacuees) about midafternoon. It was a fabric
city erected in one of the fields, a single Goliath walker over-
seeing the entire complex. Another bored MP didn't even
bother to listen to Mike's full story before swiping Rourke's
card through the reader and, being informed that Mike was
a local, let him in.

Swallow parked the jeep at the feet of the Goliath.

"Let me talk to the ref . . . evacuees alone," Mike said.

"Sir, I am still responsible for your safety," Swallow
responded.

"So watch from a safe distance. People aren't going to open
up too well when one of the Confederacy's own is standing
there in full kit."

Swallow's face clouded, and Mike added, "Of course, anything I get will go through your people before it gets transmitted." That seemed to reassure her enough to keep her near
the jeep while Mike went out to soak up the local color.

The evacuee station was only a few days old, but its facilities were already stressed. It appeared to have been built and supplied for maybe a hundred families, and it currently housed five hundred. Already the overflow of the population was being bundled into square-bodied buses for transportation to other, farther sites. Trash was piling up around the fringes, and there were lines at the water buffaloes for purified water.

The evacuees themselves were just getting over the shock of being dispossessed. Most had been rousted from their homes and managed to take only what they could lay their hands on. As a result, unneeded and sentimental items were being abandoned or traded away for food and warm bedding. Now, at rest for the first time in days, the evacuees had time to take stock of their situation, and assign blame.

Unsurprisingly, the Confederacy came in for most of the blame. After all, they were the only ones on hand, with their Goliath walkers and combat-suited marines a very visible presence. The Protoss, on the other hand, were a rumor, the only proof of them reports from the Confederacy itself. Mar Sara had been on the other side of the sun, so its people missed much of the light show that had destroyed their sister planet.

Mike cataloged the evacuees' plight and listened to the complaints. There were stories of separations and of valuables left behind, reports of farms and homes commandeered by the Confederate forces, and all manner of complaints, major and minor, against the military forces that had replaced all the civilian authorities. The local magistrate had become a refugee himself, leading one pack of refugees to another concentration point. No one was willing to stand up to the Confederates, but the refugees were angry enough to complain to a reporter about it.

Yet under the complaints and bluff talk, there was noticeable and definite fear. There was fear of the Confederate forces, natch, but also fear that arose from the realization that suddenly mankind was no longer alone. The Mar Sarans had seen the reports of the destruction of Chau Sara, and they were afraid that it would happen here. There was a lot of anxiousness in the camp, and a great desire to be someplace—anyplace—else.

And there was something else there as well, Mike discovered as he moved among the uprooted populace. The sudden knowledge of the Protoss was followed by a wave of mysterious sightings. Lights were reported in the sky, and strange-looking creatures on the ground. Cattle were found slain and mutilated. Add to that the blanket admission that the Confederacy was definitely herding the populace out of certain areas, as if they knew something they weren't telling people.

The stories of aliens and undiscovered xenomorphs on the ground came up again and again. No one had actually seen them, of course. It was always a friend of a friend of a relative in another camp who saw them, or at least heard of them. The stories were more along the lines of bug-eyed monsters than creatures in shining ships, but then, if someone had seen the Protoss ships, the military would be all over the report in minutes.

After about two hours (and the last of Rourke's cigarettes), Mike padded back to the jeep. Lieutenant Swallow was as he had left her, alert, standing next to the driver's side.

"We have enough," he said. "Thanks for the chance to get out here. We can go."

Swallow didn't move. Instead she was staring at something.

"Lieutenant Swallow?"

"Sir," she said, "I've been watching something curious. May I share it with you?"

"And this curious thing would be?"

"You see that woman over there, the red-haired one in the dark outfit?"

Mike looked. There was a woman, young, dressed in what looked like night-camo pants, dark shirt, and a multipocketed vest. She had brilliant red hair that was bound in a ponytail at the nape of her neck. She looked quasi-military, though not from any unit that Mike had ever seen. Maybe some planetary militia or law-enforcement organization. Marshals, that's what the locals called the lawmen, but she didn't look much like one. Mike suddenly realized that he hadn't seen anything of the local law since the marines landed, and had just assumed they had been sucked into the general evacuation.

"Yeah?" he said.

"She's suspicious, sir."

"What's she doing?"

"The same thing you've been doing, sir. Talking to people."

"Well, *that's* definitely suspicious. Shall we go talk to *her*?"

The red-haired woman rose from her most recent conversation with an elderly man and crossed the compound. Swallow strode off toward her, Mike in tow.

As they closed, Mike noticed something else suspicious about the woman: she looked significantly less dusty than the rest of the refugees. And less worried.

"Excuse me, ma'am," Swallow said.

The red-haired woman hesitated in mid-stride and looked around. "Can I help you?" she asked. Her jade-green eyes narrowed just a hair, and Mike noticed that her lips were just a tad too wide for her face.

"We have a few questions," the lieutenant said, perhaps more bluntly than Mike would have liked.

The wide lips pursed, and the woman asked, "And *who* would be asking these questions?" A cold wind seemed to pass between the women as she spoke.

Mike interposed himself between the two. "I'm a reporter for the Universe News Network. My name is Michael . . ."

"Liberty," finished the red-haired woman. "I've seen your reports. They get things right more often than not."

Mike nodded. "They're always right when I finish them. If something went wrong, I blame my editors."

The woman gave Mike a piercing stare, and he was positive she could turn those green eyes into sharp blades that could carve deep into his soul. "I'm Sarah Kerrigan," she said simply, to Mike, not to the lieutenant.

Okay, thought Mike. *Not local law at all.*

"And where are you from, Miss Kerrigan?" asked Lieutenant Swallow. She was still smiling, but Mike could now feel a bit of tension in that smile. Something about this Miss Kerrigan rubbed the lieutenant the wrong way.

"University of Chau Sara," said Kerrigan, looking intently at the officer now. "Part of a sociological team stationed here when the attack came."

"That's a convenient origin," Swallow said, "considering that no one can check on it right now."

"I'm sorry about your planet," put in Mike suddenly. He intended simply to blunt Swallow's tacit accusation, but for the first time he realized that he *was* sorry for the destruction he had seen from orbit. And embarrassed, because he hadn't really thought of it earlier.

The red-haired woman swung her attention back to the reporter. "I know," she said simply. "I feel your sorrow."

"And what are you doing here, Miss Kerrigan?" Swallow was being as blunt as Anderson's favorite letter opener.

Kerrigan replied, "Same as everyone else here, Corporal . . ."

"Lieutenant, ma'am," interrupted Swallow, sharper now.

Kerrigan managed an amused smile. "Lieutenant, then. Trying to find out what's going on. Trying to find out if there's really a plan for evacuation or if the Confeds are running a huge human shell game, here."

"What do you mean by that?" snapped Swallow, but Mike was already rephrasing the question.

"Do you feel there is a problem with the current evacuations?" he put in.

Kerrigan gave a snorting laugh. "Isn't it obvious? You've got bands of people shunted out of the cities and into the hinterlands."

"The cities are not defensible," Swallow noted.

"And the wilderness is?" Kerrigan shot back. "It seems the Confederacy has mistaken activity for progress. They're content to move the refugees around like checkers on the board, without any real plan to evacuate."

"Such plans are in the works, I understand," Mike said calmly.

"I've read the official reports, too," Kerrigan said. "And we both know how much truth there is to them. No, the Confederacy of Man is just chasing its tail right now, moving people around in the hopes that they'll be ready."

"Ready for what?" Mike asked.

"Ready for when the next attack comes," Kerrigan said dryly. "Ready when the next thing goes wrong."

"Ma'am," Swallow said. "I must tell you that the Confederacy is doing as much as is humanly possible to aid the people of Mar Sara."

Kerrigan interrupted hotly. "They are doing as much as is humanly possible to protect themselves, Soldier. The Confederacy has never given a damn beyond the limits of their own bureaucracy. It particularly has never given a damn about its people, and most of all it's never given a damn about anyone not on Tarsonis."

"Ma'am, I must inform you . . ." Swallow began, her smile as brittle as glass.

"I must inform *you* that the Confederacy's history damns it as surely as its current actions do. It's willing to write off the Sara system, just like it wrote off the colonies in the Guild Wars and Korhal itself."

"Ma'am," Swallow said. "I must *warn* you now that we are in a military zone, and dangerous talk will be dealt with swiftly." Mike noticed that Lieutenant Swallow's hand had drifted to the grip of her slugthrower.

"No, Lieutenant," Kerrigan responded, her eyes blazing, "I must warn *you*. The Confederacy is leading you to the slaughter, and you won't realize it until the knives come out."

Color flushed along Swallow's face. "Don't make me do something you'll regret, ma'am."

"I'm not *making* you do anything," Kerrigan hissed. "It's the bastards in the Confederacy that *make* people do things. They reach inside you and twist you apart until you're their plaything! So the question is: Are you going to follow the programming they gave you, or not?"

Mike stepped back, suddenly aware that the two women were about to come to blows. He looked around, but it seemed that the rest of the camp was paying them no attention.

For a long moment the two women stood, their eyes locked. Finally, Lieutenant Swallow blinked, stepped back, and pulled her hand from the gun butt.

"I *must* assure you, ma'am," said Lieutenant Swallow, her face now ashen, "that you are in error. The Confederacy is only thinking of its people."

"If you *must* assure me, then you *must*," Kerrigan said, snapping off the words. "Will there be anything else, or am I free to engage in an illusion of freedom?"

"No, ma'am. You can go. Sorry to have disturbed you."

"It's nothing." Kerrigan's sharp green eyes softened for a moment. She turned to Mike. "In answer to your next question, you'll find some answers at Anthem Base. It's about three klicks west of here. But don't go alone." She shot a look at the lieutenant.

And then she was gone, striding across the compound and quickly losing herself among the tents.

"The woman was under stress," Swallow said through clenched teeth. She reached up with one hand and pulled a stimpack from her belt.

"Of course," Mike agreed.

"It's not surprising for people to blame their rescuers for their problems," she continued, pressing the pack against the knobby flesh at the back of her neck. The stimpack hissed softly.

"Right."

"And this was not the place or time for an incident." Slowly the color returned to her face, and she started breathing regularly.

"Not the place at all."

"And it would be best not reported," she said firmly.

Mike thought of Swallow's former hobby. "Of course," he said.

"We should go now," said Lieutenant Emily Jameson Swallow, turning back to the jeep.

"Uh-huh," Mike said, scratching his chin and looking at the place where Kerrigan had disappeared. He thought of chasing after her but realized that he would probably not even find her again, unless she wanted to be found. He wanted to ask her about a lot of things.

Particularly about how she knew what his next question was.

He *was* going to ask about the xenomorph sightings. *That* was the next question he was going to ask. This Kerrigan could have known that from talking to the same people that he had been interviewing.

Or it could have been something else about Kerrigan that let her know what he was thinking.

Regardless, as he loped to catch up to Lieutenant Swallow, he resolved never to get into a card game with Sarah Kerrigan.

CHAPTER 5

ANTHEM BASE

Nature abhors a vacuum, and human nature hates a lack of information. Where we can't find it, we go looking for it. In some cases we just invent it.

That was the case on the Sara system. Willfully ignorant, we charged into the hinterland looking for answers—answers that we soon realized we didn't want to find.

We were stupid to assume that we would be all right. We were stupid to go off half-cocked. We were stupid to go in undergunned. We were stupid to think that we understood what we were getting into.

And we were most stupid of all to assume that the Protoss were the first alien race that humanity had met.

—The Liberty Manifesto

IT TOOK SOME CAJOLING TO GET LIEUTENANT Swallow to detour to Anthem Base. He told her what he had learned in the camp from the other evacuees, couched in neutral terms so as not to rattle her further.

Even so, the Kerrigan woman had shaken the soldier badly,

and now Swallow drove with a wordless intensity across the back roads beyond the camp. The stimpack had given her control over her anger but did not eliminate it entirely.

A rooster's plume of dust churned in their wake, and Michael Liberty was sure that the inhabitants of Anthem would see them coming.

Yet when they got there, the town was empty.

"Looks like they've evacuated," Mike said, dismounting.

Lieutenant Swallow just grunted and moved to the back of the jeep. Opening a hatch, she pulled out a gauss rifle.

"Want one, sir?" she asked.

Mike shook his head.

"Pistol, at least?"

He shook his head again and headed for the nearest building.

It was a mining town, nothing more than about a dozen buildings made of local wood and preformed construction pods. It had become a ghost town. No livestock, no dogs, not even birds.

So why, wondered Mike, did he get the feeling he was being watched?

The first building was a claims office. Wooden floor, quarters in the back. The place looked as if its occupants had just left it. There were still blue crystals resting on the scales on a countertop.

Mike walked in. Swallow lingered at the door, her oversized weapon at the ready. There was an acrid smell in the air.

"They've evacuated," she said. "We should do the same."

Mike picked up a coffeepot. It had been boiled to a solid sludge, and the pot itself was warm to the touch.

"This is still on," he said, pulling the plug from the hot plate.

"They left in a hurry, sir," Swallow said, a nervous tone now creeping into her voice. "You said the evacuees were complaining of being shuttled off."

Mike walked behind the counter and pulled open a drawer. "There's still money in the till. Can't imagine any assayer leaving his cash behind. Or the marines not giving him a chance to recover it. Odd." He disappeared into the back room.

Swallow shouted after him, and he reappeared.

"Somebody's quarters. Looks like there was a struggle there," he said.

"Unwilling evacuee," Swallow said, looking hard at Mike. "They probably dragged him off before he had a chance to close up his shop."

Mike nodded. "Let's check the other buildings. You take one side. I'll take the other."

Lieutenant Swallow took a deep breath. "As you wish, sir. But stay in the doorways where I can see you."

Mike crossed the street to the opposite line of buildings. A fresh breeze kicked up, and dust devils swirled down the main street of Anthem. The place was completely deserted by both man and beast.

Then why, wondered Mike, did the hairs on the back of his neck still bristle?

Across from the claims office were a pair of residences. Like the assayer's office, they seemed only recently deserted. A video screen was active in one, flickering soundlessly with a bad transmission of a news report. Stock footage of a battle-cruiser, identified as the *Norad II*, cruising effortlessly through space.

There was a spilled can of beer next to the easy chair in front of the video. Despite himself, Mike found himself checking to see if any cigarettes had been left behind. No such luck.

The third building was a general mercantile, and it looked as if it had been ransacked. Bins had been overturned and products pulled from the racks and strewn across the floor. Behind the register a large glass gun case had been smashed open. The guns were missing.

Perhaps this was what Sarah Kerrigan wanted him to find,

thought Michael. The signs of an armed struggle. Against the Confederacy's evacuation? Or against the Protoss?

Mike looked over his shoulder to see Swallow crossing to a two-story tavern on her side of the road. He stepped into the mercantile, and his foot struck something crunchy.

Mike knelt down. The floor was covered with some type of mold or fungus. It was a dark grayish substance, its edges crusty but slightly elastic to the touch. It contained a spider-web pattern of darker bands, almost like arteries.

Something had spilled here, and some type of native mold had taken quick advantage of it. Very quick, he realized—it could not have happened more than two days ago.

There was something else about the mercantile. There was a sound from the back of the store, the sound of something sliding over the wooden floorboards. It shifted once, then was silent.

A wild animal? Mike wondered. A snake? Or perhaps a refugee who had escaped the initial evacuation, or returned later. Mike took another step into the room, the fungus crunching under his boots.

He was suddenly very aware that he didn't have a weapon on him.

Swallow gave a shout from across the street. Mike looked at the door to the back room once, then back to Swallow. He backed out of the general store and crossed over to the bar. Swallow was plastered against the wall outside the door.

"I think there's something over in the store—" Mike said.

"I found the inhabitants," Swallow hissed. The veins were pounding along the scars in her neck and thundered at her temples, and her eyes were wide. She was terrified, and the fear was eating into her resocialization programming. It was clear that she had hit the stimpack again, as the discharged unit now lay on the porch floorboards.

Despite himself, Mike looked through the open doorway in the bar.

It had been transformed into an abattoir. Once-human forms hung by their feet from thick ropes attached to the ceiling. Many had been stripped of clothing and flesh. Others had had limbs removed, and three had been decapitated. The three skulls were set along the bar, and had been neatly carved open to reveal the brains beneath. Something had been gnawing on one of the brains.

As he watched, something like a gigantic centipede writhed around on one of the bodies. It was like a huge, rust-colored maggot. And it was feeding on the flesh.

Mike suddenly found it very hard to breathe, and wished he had a stimpack. He took a step into the room.

His feet crunched on the crusty fungus that covered the room. And he realized that he was not alone.

He felt its presence before he saw it. The sudden feeling of being watched returned.

He started to step back, out of the doorway. He started to turn. He started to say something to Swallow.

Something blurred from behind the bar, bolting forward in a single impossible leap, barreling for the doorway.

It didn't hit Mike. Instead, something larger slammed him to one side.

Mike hit the porch floorboards with a thump and twisted to see Lieutenant Swallow, who had struck him, firing at a large dog in the street. No, it wasn't a dog. It had four legs, but the similarity ended there. Patches of orange-shaded flesh were skinless, muscles showing through. Its head was adorned with a pair of huge, underslung tusks.

And it was screaming under the barrage of metal spikes from the gauss rifle. The hypersonic rounds riddled it in a dozen places, and it flailed in the dirt as Swallow kept her finger clenched on the trigger.

"Swallow!" shouted Mike. "It's dead! Lieutenant Swallow, quit firing!"

Swallow let go of the trigger housing as though it were a live snake. Sweat rolled down her face, and the sides of her mouth were flecked with foam. She was breathing hard, and despite herself, her free hand went for her knife.

Mike realized that her resocialization had been stressed to its utmost, and she was about to lose it.

"Sweet Mother of Christ," she said. "What *is* that!"

Mike didn't care. Instead he shouted, "Back to the jeep! We'll send armored troops! Come on!"

He took two steps, then realized that Swallow was still in the doorway, staring at the skinned dog-thing in the street.

"Lieutenant! That's an order, dammit!" bellowed Mike.

That did it. The beauty of resocialization was that it made its subject vulnerable to orders, particularly under the effect of stims. Swallow suddenly was back in control, running toward the jeep, passing Mike. There was movement from the mercantile as they ran. More of the dog-things were coming through the doorway. They could leap prodigiously, Mike realized, and could strike them in the back as they fled.

The dog-things didn't. Instead the creatures waited for them almost to reach the jeep when *something else* rose up behind the vehicle.

To Mike it was a snake, a cobra rearing to strike. A snake with an armored head that flared out backward in a broad frill of bony chitin like a prehistoric lizard's. It was a snake with two arms jutting from its body, arms that ended in wicked-looking scythes.

Scythes that now drove into the hood of the jeep, pinning it to the street. The snake-creature let out a hissing cry of victory.

Swallow cursed. "They've got us surrounded!"

Mike grabbed her by the sleeve. "The claims office. It has one entrance! Make for it!"

He headed in that direction, the soldier hot on his heels. Behind him he heard more gunfire and the screams of the dog-things. Swallow was backpedaling and firing at the same time, covering their butts as they fled.

He paused in the doorway of the office and quickly scanned the room. Nothing had changed since he had been there moments before. He ran for the counter and came up with a primitive shotgun. He broke it open and found a pair of rounds chambered.

Yeah, the office had been left as if its owner had been called away suddenly. Or dragged away.

Swallow was in the doorway, firing bursts. There were more inhuman screams, then silence.

He looked out the doorway to see a half-dozen bodies in the street, all of them dog-things. Now they looked even less like normal animals than before, the uninjured portions of their bodies riven with pustules and knotted muscles. One of them still twitched a leg in a pool of gelatin that could have been its blood.

Of the snake-thing with the scythes there was no sign. The jeep was a crumpled husk at the end of the street, its leaking fuel darkening the sand beneath it.

"Those were the things that killed Chau Sara?" Swallow hissed the question, her voice a strangled whisper. Her eyes were practically orbs of pure white.

Mike shook his head. The things they had seen in space had a frightful beauty about them. They were gold and silver and seemed to be made of lightning and elemental power itself. These things were nothing but muscle and blood and madness. It hurt him even to look at them.

"Oh Christ, where is the big one?" Swallow asked.

Mike choked back the dust and the fear. "We have to get out of here before they regroup."

Swallow turned toward him, wide-eyed and panicked. "Out of here? We just got here!"

"They're going to regroup and try again."

"They're animals," she snapped, and the tip of her gauss rifle rose slightly toward Mike. "Shoot a few, the rest will run."

"I don't think so. Animals don't hang up their kills. They don't take trophies."

Swallow gave a short, strangled cry and stepped back into the office. "No, don't say that."

"Swallow. Emily, I . . ."

"Don't say that," she said, stepping back again. "Don't say that they're intelligent. Because if they are, they know we're trapped, and they know they can take us whenever they want to. Dammit, we're fu—"

She took another step backward, and the floorboards gave way beneath her. She let out a strangled scream, and the gun fell from her hands as a pit opened beneath her feet.

From deep within the pit, there was the sound of angry chittering.

Swallow twisted as she fell, grabbing the floorboards to break her fall. The chittering grew louder.

Mike stepped forward, almost dropping his own weapon. "Emily, grab my hand!"

"Get out of here, Liberty!" Swallow snarled, her eyes almost all white from fear. With her free hand she grabbed her combat knife. "Oh God, they're right underneath us!"

"Emily, grab my hand!"

"Someone has to get back," she said, pulling her knife free and hacking at something unseen within the pit. "They're going to attack from above as well. Get going! Hump it back to the camp. Warn people!"

"I can't—"

"Move! That's an order, dammit!" Swallow was snarling as the last of her resocialization shattered beneath the creatures' assault. She let out a feral scream and started flailing with her knife.

Mike turned back to the door, and there was a shadow there. Without thinking, he pulled both triggers on the shotgun and was splattered by ichor of the exploding dog-thing.

Then he ran. Not looking back, he ran, throwing the spent shotgun aside as he fled. Toward the jeep. Lieutenant Swallow had pulled the rifle out of a hatch in the back. She had offered him one. It had to be there still. Other weapons as well.

He nearly made it when the ground erupted beneath the jeep.

The armor-headed snake-thing, with the scythe arms. It had been waiting for him.

Mike sprawled out of the way of the eruption and started crawling backward, away from the serpent-thing. He was trapped in the creature's eyes, luminous yellow eyes set deep beneath its armored carapace.

There was intelligence in those eyes, and hunger. But nothing that resembled a soul.

The creature rose on its tail, towering over the shattered jeep, ready to leap forward. Mike threw his arm over his face and screamed.

His cries were drowned out by the sound of a gauss rifle on full auto.

Mike looked up to see the huge serpent-beast twist and shudder under a relentless volley of rifle spikes. As it writhed, it shot spines from its armored body that peppered the surrounding ground like deadly rain.

Then a round found the remaining fuel in the jeep, and the entire vehicle went up, taking the serpent-thing with it. It bellowed something that might have been a curse and might have been a cry to some unknown god.

The explosion pressed Mike backward against the ground, and the warmth of the fire beat against his exposed face and arms. He looked down the street. No sign of the dog-creatures. Only corpses.

There was a sound behind him, and he spun in place, still on the ground. He expected more dog-things, but he knew he was wrong even as he turned. It was the sound of booted feet, not callused paws.

A large, thankfully human figure blocked the sunlight. Broad-shouldered, and packing a heavy slugthrower from a belt holster worn low on his hip. Dizzily, Mike thought at first the shadow belonged to another of Swallow's unit, that the lieutenant had somehow managed to call in reinforcements when they had split up.

As his vision cleared, Mike realized the figure wasn't in

marine uniform. His pants were buckskin leather, well-worn and rough. He was wearing a denim shirt, neat but faded, rolled up at the sleeves. A lightweight combat vest, made of some open, leathery weave, pegged him as some kind of military. So did the gauss rifle he was packing. His boots were well-made but as worn as the rest of his outfit.

"You all right, son?" The silhouette held out a hand.

Mike grabbed the hand and gently rose to his feet. He felt like one great bruise, and the figure's voice sounded distant and tinny in his ears.

"Fine. Alive," he gasped. "You're not a marine."

He could see his rescuer's face now. A head of sandy blond hair and a neatly trimmed mustache and beard.

The figure spat into the dust. "Not a marine? I guess I'll take that as a compliment. I'm the local law in these parts. Marshal Jim Raynor."

"Michael Liberty. UNN, Tarsonis."

"Newsman?" Raynor asked. Mike nodded. "Kind of far from home, aren't you?"

"Yeah. We were checking out a report. . . . Oh God."

"What?"

"Swallow! The lieutenant! I left her in the claims office!" Mike staggered toward the assayer's office. The lawman followed close behind, his weapon ready. In the aftermath of the explosion, there was no further sign of the dog-things.

Mike found Lieutenant Swallow facedown, still half in the pit, one hand still gripping her combat knife, the other clutched tightly to a loose floorboard.

The marshal looked at the room and said, "Son." It had a warning tone.

"Give me a hand here," Mike said, grabbing Swallow's knife arm, "We can haul her up and . . . Oh God."

Lieutenant Emily Jameson Swallow no longer existed below the waist. Her flesh ended in stringy tatters of meat, and a few vertebrae dangled from a torn spinal cord like beads on a broken string.

"Oh God." Mike let go of the body. It slid back into the pit with a sick, slithering sound. There was a squishy thump, and the sound of something else moving below.

Mike fell to his knees, leaned forward, and puked his guts out. Then a second time and a third, until all he had was dry heaves. His head spun, and he felt as if something had sucked all the blood out of his brain.

"Not to interrupt," said Raynor, "but I think we need to go. I think all I did was take out one of their officers. Fragging the captain, if you take my meaning. They're regrouping. We'd better go. I got a bike outside." He paused for a moment, then said, "Sorry about your friend."

Mike nodded, and felt his stomach make one last attempt to empty itself.

"Yeah," Mike gasped at last. "Me, too."

CHAPTER 6

CREEPS

War is easy to understand on paper. It seems so distant and academic in black and white. Even the vid reports have a cool, detached manner that keeps the viewer from understanding how horrible it really is.

This is nothing more than a sanity filter, allowing those who take in the information to separate the reports and numbers from the awful reality. It's why those who lead armies can do all sorts of terrible things to their troops that no sane man would think of if he had to look them in the eye. Which is one reason they don't.

But when you're confronted with death, when you're confronted with having to deal out death or die yourself, then everything changes.

The filters drop away, and you have to deal with the insanity directly.

—The Liberty Manifesto

"THEY CALL 'EM THE ZERG," SAID MARSHAL RAYNOR, climbing onto his hover-cycle. "The little ones are called zerglings. The snaky one we blew up is called a hydralisk. They're supposed to be slightly smarter than the small ones."

Mike's mouth still felt as if he had been gargling garbage water, but he said, "Who calls them those things? Who named them the Zergs?"

Raynor replied, "The marines. That's where I heard it from."

"Figures. Those marines mention anything about something called the Protoss?"

"Yep," Raynor said, strapping the reporter in. "They have shining ships and blew up Chau Sara. May be coming here, too, I understand. That's why everyone is beating feet for the exits."

"Think they're one and the same?"

"Don't know. You?"

Mike shrugged. "I saw their ships over Chau Sara. I'd be surprised to discover that these . . . things . . . were at the helm. Maybe their allies? Maybe slaves?"

"Possible. It's better than the alternative."

"And that is?"

"That they're enemies," said the lawman, firing up the hover-cycle's main plant. "That would be much worse for anybody caught between them."

They circled the dead town of Anthem Base one last time. Liberty recorded the devastation on his comm unit as Raynor fired fragmentation grenades into the wooden structures. They left a pillar of smoke behind them.

Raynor explained that he was riding scout for a group of refugees. Local government types. They were another few klicks farther along, heading for a place called Backwater Station.

"There's a refugee camp about three klicks back that way." Mike motioned toward the rear. "Aren't you heading that way?"

"Nope. There was a report of trouble up at Backwater, and we went to investigate it."

"No mention of a refugee camp at all in your report?" Mike asked.

"Nope. Of course, it *does* seem like the Confederacy wants to have most of the planetary population running around like chickens with their fool heads cut off."

"Somebody else said that to me just before we came here."

"Whoever told you that," Raynor said approvingly, "has his head screwed on right."

They flew smoothly over the rough terrain, Raynor changing course only to veer around the larger obstacles. The Vulture hover-cycle was a long-nosed bike with limited gravity hover technology that kept it a foot above the ground. The onboard computer and sensors in the nose kept it at a steady pace, ignoring the smaller boulders and scrub trees.

Strapped in on the back, Mike thought, *I gotta get one of these . . . and a decent set of battle armor.* He thought again of Lieutenant Swallow and wondered how she would have fared had she been wearing her insulating cocoon of neosteel.

They caught up with Raynor's pack of refugees within the hour. The marshal was right: this particular gathering had been the local government types, conveniently sent into the wilderness on marine orders. Mike could imagine Colonel Duke's delight in issuing *that* particular communication. The march had been brought to a halt, and Raynor accosted one of the rear guard.

"Something ahead we hadn't counted on," said the soldier, one of the colonial troops in CMC-300 armor. "Looks like an old command post."

"One of ours?" Raynor asked.

"Kinda. It wasn't on any maps of the area. We sent the rest of the scout unit up to check it out."

Raynor twisted around in his seat. "You want off?" he asked Mike.

"Off the planet, yeah," Mike said. "But as long as I have to be here I want to take a look. It's the job. Duty." He thought of Anthem Base and didn't trust old buildings all of a sudden.

Raynor grunted an agreement and gunned the bike forward. They crested a low hill and found the command post on the other side.

Michael knew what to expect from command posts. They were ubiquitous, even on Tarsonis. Half-domes filled with sensor equipment and computers, they were little more than small automatic factories that ground out construction vehicles to work the local mines, and would not have much in the way of either a staff or a defense. Some brilliant developer along the way put jumpjets on the bottom of the structures to move them where needed, but if you ever had to move them, you had to shut everything else down.

This one was, well, different. It seemed a bit mashed along one side. Not damaged from without, but rather shrunken from within, like an apple that had been left in the sun too long. The sides were overgrown with briers and tangles. In a half-circle around it, the colonial forces, green local troops in worn combat armor, were cautiously approaching.

"Never saw anything like that before," Raynor said. "All overgrown and such. For it to look that bad, it would have to have been here before the colony was settled."

Mike looked at the ground around the base of the command post. He pointed. "Look there!"

"What?"

"The ground. It's got that creeping gray stuff around it. We found it in Anthem before the Zergs attacked."

"Think it's connected?"

"Oh, yeah." Mike nodded in agreement.

"Good enough for me," said the marshal, flipping over the comm mike on his bike. "That building's been infested with Zerg, boys. Let 'em have it!"

Mike kept his own recorder open and said, "Tell them to look out for the zerglings. They like to burrow."

He didn't need to give the warning. The ground in front of the command center opened up and spilled forth a double-handful of the skinned-dog creatures. The colonial forces were prepared, and mowed them down as soon as they appeared. The zerglings didn't stand a chance, and were reduced to pulpy husks in the first volleys. Having dealt with the initial threat, the local militia then fired incendiary rounds into the command post itself. The building started to burn.

Raynor stayed on the bike, firing fragmentation grenades from a stubby launcher until the roof cracked open like a shattered eggshell. Mike got a good look within: the entire structure was nothing more than a tangle of pestilent vines, a riot of orange, green, and violet. Sacs of messy proto-*somethings* were hanging along one wall. They screamed as the fire reached them.

"You're getting all that?" Raynor asked as the roof caved in, burying the smoking relics of the infested building beneath it.

"Yeah." Mike closed his recording unit. "Now I need someplace to patch in for a report."

Raynor smiled. "I told you, this band of refugees are government types. If anyone has a decent comm system, it'll be them."

Marshal Raynor was right. The refugees did have a more-than-adequate comm link, and in normal times it would be a smooth link. But as he logged on, it was obvious to Mike that parts of the system were going down worldwide. There were obvious holes in the net, and a high level of background noise. Like the farms, the communications network was being forcibly ignored, with immediate ramifications.

He crafted the tale as best he could, wondering what the military censors would pull out before giving it to UNN, and what Handy Anderson would change. The viewing populace, and all the steps in between, needed to know what was going on, regardless.

He packed most of the material from the refugee camp as a sidebar, but said nothing of the altercation between Swallow and Kerrigan. He went into detail about the situation at Anthem Base and provided footage of the firing of the command post. He closed with a note that the command post was not on any colonial maps, confident that the censors would pull that line, if they felt they had to pull anything.

He was also sure they would let run the shots of the brave colonial forces mowing down the zerglings. Triumphant actions like that always played well with the military censors.

As the report percolated through the buffer into the general net, Mike pounded the orange dust out of his coat. Then he hunted down Raynor in the mess tent. The sandy-haired man offered him a cup of coffee. It was military-style "B"—boiled to a thickened sludge and allowed to cool. It was like drinking soft asphalt.

"You get off your report?" asked the lawman.

"Uh-huh," Mike replied. "Even remembered to spell your name right." He flashed a brittle grin.

"You okay?" Raynor asked. It came out "yokay."

Mike shrugged. "I'll hold up. Writing helps me work through it."

"You've seen death before, right?"

Mike shrugged again. "On Tarsonis? Sure. Random shootings. Suicides. Gang hits and auto accidents. Even some things that would rival those bodies hung up in the tavern." He took a deep breath. "But I'll admit, never anything like this. Not like the lieutenant."

"Yeah, it's tough when you were talking to the victim moments before it happened," said Raynor, taking another slug of asphalt. "And when it's sudden. And just so you know, the answer is no, it wasn't your fault."

"How could you know that?" Mike asked, suddenly irritated. He had been thinking exactly that: that he was responsible for bringing Swallow to Anthem and to her death.

"I know because I'm a marshal. And while I've never seen anything quite like Anthem Base, I've been in situations where some people live, and some die. And the living feel guilty about still being alive. Afterwards."

Mike sat there for a moment. "What do you recommend, then, Doctor Raynor?"

Raynor shrugged. "Pretty much what you're doing. Get on with your life. Do what you have to do. Don't get strung out. You got rattled, but you're shaking it off."

Mike nodded. "You know, speaking of getting on with life, there's one thing I've been meaning to do."

"And that is . . .?"

"Learn to use that combat armor. I passed on the chance when I was flying around with the fleet, and I've been regretting it ever since. Seems like it might be a survival skill around here."

"That it is." Raynor looked over his mug at the reporter. "Yeah, I think we got a spare two-hundred-level suit. And we're going to be encamped here until we hear from the marines. It might be a good time to learn."

A half hour later Mike was suited up outside the mess tent. It had taken ten minutes to scare up the suit from all the cargo that the evacuees had brought along, and another twenty to suit him properly. He knew that Swallow could slip into her suit in three minutes, tops. *Crawl before you can walk,* Mike told himself.

The suit itself was similar to the powered combat suits used by the *Norad II* crew. It was invulnerable to small-arms fire, had limited life-support (as opposed to the full space-traveling suits of the marines), and packed basic nuclear/biological/chemical shielding. Still, it was an earlier model than standard marine issue, practically an antique. Apparently the local law got hand-me-downs from the Confederate government.

The complete suit raised Mike's height by a full foot, the oversized boots containing their own stabilization computers to keep him upright. The suit also rode a little high in the crotch, as well, until Raynor showed him where the lever was to raise the foot supports. The suit could be sealed, and it would run for seven days on its own recycled waste. That was a thrill that Mike could pass on for the moment.

The shoulders were oversized as well, housing ammunition reloads and sensor arrays. The backpack was an oversized air conditioner, shunting away heat from the body. The more advanced models carried mufflers to cut down the noise and heat signature, but this was an ancient model, battered and repatched numerous times.

Parts of it seemed a bit tight, snug around the arms and legs in wide bands. Other places seemed loose and open.

"The tight spots are part of the salvage system," said Raynor, strapping him in. "You take a big hit to an arm or leg, the suit seals off in a tourniquet. One piece goes but the rest survives."

"Feels like a hollow spot under the arms," said Mike.

"Yeah, well, this is marine surplus. That's where the stim-packs would be. We don't use them in the colonial militias. Too many people get addicted to the drugs in them." He closed the last latch and sealed Mike in. The reporter swayed back and forth, feeling like a turtle on stilts.

Raynor was in his own suit, looking equally battered and worn. The lawman nodded behind his open visor and said, "The armor will stop most common slugthrowers, though a good needle-gun can still punch through. That's why most front-line troops carry C-14 Impalers, gauss rifles that fire eight-millimeter spikes."

"What now?"

"Now you walk," said Raynor. Several other soldiers were now watching as well, and a small crowd was forming at the entrance to the mess tent. The lawman nodded again. "Go ahead."

Mike looked at the telltales along the rim of his visor. He *had* read the manuals earlier, on the ship, and knew that the small lights meant that everything was hunky-dory. He took a step forward.

He expected the step to be like pulling out of mud, since he was lifting the huge weight of a booted foot. Instead the foot, tethered into sensors and backed by a ton of cabled ligature, came up almost to his waist. High-stepping, Mike overbalanced, leaning backward. The servos whined in response, and he twisted, falling on his side with a resounding thump.

Raynor put a hand to his face, trying to look sage but barely covering the grin that blossomed beneath his fingers. Mike saw that several of the other militiamen were trading money back and forth. *Great, they're betting on this*, thought Mike. The telltales along his visor flashed a warning yellow. He looked at them, consulted the manual in his memory, and decided that they all meant "Hey, dummy, you've fallen over."

"A hand here?" Mike said.

"You're better doing it on your own." There was a smile in Raynor's voice.

Wonderful, thought Mike, slowly rolling onto his belly. He found he could push himself up on one hand, but moving the oversized legs underneath him was a tight fit. At last he pulled himself up to a near-vertical position.

"Good," Raynor said. "Now walk. Go ahead."

Mike tried shuffling this time, and the armor responded by slogging forward, churning up a cloud of orange dust. He shuffled ahead ten feet, then turned, and shuffled another ten. By the second turn he was confident enough to take real steps, and when he didn't fall down, started moving normally. The telltales winked green at him again, and he was relieved that he hadn't damaged the suit. He was also glad he hadn't laughed too hard at the new crewmen during the drills on the *Norad II.*

Raynor went over to the colonial militia and came back with the gauss rifle. He handed it to Mike, and his armored hand closed over the larger of two grips. The smaller grip, used by nonarmored shooters, required the firer to use both hands to steady its long barrel. In the armor, Raynor could heft it easily.

"Take a shot at that boulder," he said, trying valiantly to keep a smile from his face.

At first Mike thought the marshal was only amused by his performance, but as he leveled the gun, he thought about what he was doing. The armored turtle on stilts was about to fire a gun.

"Hang on," he said. "How does this thing handle recoil?"

Raynor turned to the other militiamen. "See? I told you he was smarter than he looked!" Some of the colonial soldiers reached for their wallets.

To Mike he said, "You brace, go into a broad-legged stance. The suit knows the maneuver. It compensates along the gun arm."

Mike turned back toward the boulder, braced himself, and let off a burst. A volley of spikes erupted from the muzzle of the rifle and peppered the boulder. Splinters of rock flew everywhere, and Mike saw that he had carved a white scar across the surface of the stone.

"Not bad," said Raynor, smiling fully now. "That's one rock that's going to think twice about attacking good God-fearing people."

Mike felt as though a load had been lifted from his shoulders. Swallow was dead, and there were strange xenomorphs all over a wilderness filled with refugees. But at least he was doing something about it.

As far as he was concerned, he had made an important, armored, first step.

Raynor's evacuees were supposed to hold tight until the marines contacted them. Mike figured he could hang with Raynor's crew for about a day, maybe two, then either catch a lift back to the city with the marines or find his own ride back. Heck, once news of the colonial marines fighting the Zerg got on the local news, their group might even be bumped forward in the queue.

He didn't worry about the report until late the next day, when the real marines arrived.

They howled down out of the orange sky like steel-shod furies. The Confederate dropships deployed at the cardinal points around the refugee camp, preventing easy escape. As soon as they landed, heavily armored marines in full, modern combat gear piled out, accompanied by firebats, specialty troops armed with plasma-based flamethrowers. A single Goliath strode out of the belly of one of the dropships and stood guard over the far end of the camp.

The marines quickly surrounded the encampment and advanced into the refugees' midst. Wherever they met colonial troops, they called for their disarmament and surrender. Surprised and unsure, the colonials complied.

Mike, now dressed in his civilian gear and long duster, headed for Raynor's tent. He got there just as the marshal was shouting at his vidscreen.

"Are you out of your mind? If we *hadn't* burned that damned factory this entire colony could have been overrun! Maybe if you hadn't taken your sweet time in getting here . . ."

"Now I asked you nice the first time, boy," came a familiar voice over the screen that froze Mike's soul. He could not see the face, but he knew that Colonel Duke was at the other end of that vid-link. "I didn't come here to talk with you. Now throw down them weapons!"

Raynor muttered, "Guess you wouldn't be a Confederate if you weren't a *complete* pain in the ass." Only then did he toggle the link off. To Mike he said, "Typical Confed thinking. We do their jobs for them, so naturally they're peeved at the competition."

A pair of marines in full kit appeared in the doorway. "Marshal James Raynor, we have a warrant for your arrest for treasonous activities—"

"Yeah, yeah." Raynor sighed. "I got the love note from your colonel." He placed his sidearms on the table. They vanished into the possession of the marine.

"There was also a Michael Liberty of the Universe News Network present at the time of the assault on the command post," said the marine, turning toward Mike.

"Well, he's—" Raynor began.

"Gone," said Mike, holding up his press tags. "Name's Rourke. Local press. Mickey booked out yesterday after filing his report."

The marine swiped the swapped ID card across a reader, then grunted. Mike hoped that the patchiness of global communications prevented Rourke's picture from coming up.

The marine said, "Mr. Rourke, you are as of this moment in a restricted area. You must leave at once."

Raynor said, "What the—"

Mike interrupted him. "Of course, sir. I'm gone."

The marine continued. "I must remind you that under martial law, anything you report of this will be reviewed by military censors. Any treasonous writings will be reported, and the writer will be punished to the full extent of the law."

"Right you are, man. I mean, sir," said Mike.

Raynor shouted at Mike, "Hey, 'Rourke,' you'd better take my bike." He tossed the reporter the keys. "It doesn't look like I'm going to be needing it for a while."

"Sure thing, Marshal," said Mike.

The lawman looked hard at Mike. "And if you see that Liberty jasper," he said in a stony voice, "tell him I expect him to do something about this mess. You hear?"

"Loud and clear, man," said Mike. "Loud and clear."

Even so, Mike didn't let himself relax until he was a good five klicks from the refugee encampment. When he left, Raynor's men were being herded into the dropships. If Duke followed standard Confederate military procedure, they would be lifted to a prison hulk in high orbit.

Mike consoled himself with the fact that at least in orbit they would have some protection from the Zerg and the Protoss.

Originally Mike's plan was to get back to the city, catch a ship off-planet, and then let Handy Anderson sort out the details of his unauthorized sojourn once Mike got back to Tarsonis. But the idea of leaving Raynor to rot in some marine prison churned at him. The marshal was one of the aw-shucks good-old-boys who seemed to thrive out here on the Fringe Worlds, but he wasn't a bad sort. And he had saved Mike's bacon at Anthem.

Briefly the face of Lieutenant Swallow rose in his memory. She had helped him, and he had failed her. Despite what Raynor had said, he felt responsible. Would he fail Raynor as well?

"Fail is such an ugly word," he muttered, but he knew he couldn't leave the lawman to Duke's tender mercies. By the time he hit the city limits, he knew he had to get a shuttle to the *Norad II* and have it out with the colonel.

Hell, maybe we'll get adjoining cells, he thought.

The city was completely evacuated now, and there wasn't even a cordon at the main entrances. The streets were abnormally empty, and not even other Confederate troops were present. Flying down the empty streets, Mike wondered what had happened to the café crowd at the press pool. Were they still there, or had they been evacuated to some dump in the wilderness as well?

There was a *whump*, and the Vulture hover-cycle rocked beneath him. Looking back, he saw that another Vulture had crept up on him and nudged his left rear bumper. Behind the polarized window, Mike saw the silhouette of the driver point to his ear. The universal symbol for "Turn on your radio, idiot."

Mike toggled on the comm unit, and Sarah Kerrigan's face appeared on the screen. "Follow me," she said.

"You trying to get me killed?"

"That's a stupid question, considering you're already dead."

"What?!" Mike sputtered.

"A report went out an hour ago. Said that some terrorists in stolen firebat armor strafed a bus full of reporters. They identified the victims by their badges. Congrats, you got top billing in the obituary."

"Oh God." Mike felt the weight shift in his stomach. Rourke had his press badge. The idea that the construction scandal had finally caught up with him, this far out, crossed his mind.

Kerrigan laughed. "This is no building-supplies scandal

back on Tarsonis, newshound. Somebody here wanted you dead. You know too much, Mr. Liberty."

Mike's stomach churned. "What do you mean?"

Frustration crackled over the link. "I mean that your report from the field brought the house down on the local forces. The fact that they are fighting the Zerg and the marines aren't is painfully obvious, so Duke had the local troops arrested and shipped off-planet. He wants the place defenseless. Isn't it obvious? If you really want to help the locals, follow me."

Mike shook his head. "And if I refuse?"

"I'll run you off the road and drag you off," crackled the comm link. "Jeez, you drive like someone's grandmother."

With that Kerrigan pulled her Vulture ahead and took a quick left. Liberty followed, suddenly painfully aware that he took the corners much too wide.

They headed for a district full of warehouses, some of them now nothing more than empty husks. Kerrigan's Vulture slipped into the open door of one of them. Mike pulled his inside as well, and Kerrigan ran down the door behind him.

"Bumping me like that was pretty dangerous," Mike said, dismounting from the Vulture. "You must think yourself a pretty good driver."

"I am. I'm *also* very good with knives. And guns, too. You steal that?" she asked, looking at the bike.

"Got it from a friend."

"Your friend is hard on his equipment. This is a safe house. There's one more thing before we go on."

Before Mike could react, Kerrigan snaked out a hand and grabbed his press tags. With a single smooth motion she tossed them in the air, pulled a handheld laser, and fried the tags at the top of their arc. The melted remains landed with a sodden *splot* on the concrete floor.

"We think the press tags can be traced. That would explain why bad things happened to the guy with your original tags. Eventually they'll figure out that they left a reporter alive, and they'll come after you then. Now come back here. I have to set up some equipment."

She turned, leaving Mike sputtering. She started moving some equipment in the back.

"Look, you know you can't trust Duke's forces right now, so will you listen to my side, at least?" She bent over to check some plugs.

Mike recognized the equipment. "That's a full holo setup."

"State of the art," Kerrigan said with a smile. "My commander has been fortunate enough to get the best."

"The best indeed, if he can afford to keep his own telepaths."

Kerrigan froze for only a fraction of a second, but enough to make Mike smile. "Yeah, well," she said. "I don't do enough to hide *that*, do I?"

"I was willing to buy your being a big fan of mine," Mike said, "but just *happening* to find me while I was coming into the city, well, that was a bit *too* much to believe. I thought that only Confederate Marine ghost-troopers were telepaths."

"Well, I did that job once. Got tired of it and left."

"I don't need to be a telepath to know there's more to the story than that." Mike shrugged in a disarming way, then added, "It's not a job you retire from. I also thought that telepaths had inhibitors on them to protect us normal folk."

"It's the other way around," said Kerrigan, a taste of bitterness in her voice. "The inhibitors also keep your nasty little thoughts out of *my* mind. It's tough when you know everyone around you is untrustworthy at some level." She looked hard at Mike, her green eyes flashing. "The bathroom's in the back corner. No, it doesn't have a window you can sneak out of. I don't want to shoot your knees out to keep you here, but you know I will."

"Why me?" muttered Mike as he headed for the john.

"Because, you idiot," shouted Kerrigan from across the room, "you're important to us. Now powder your nose and get back here."

When Mike returned she had finished the setup for the holographic rig. It had a full projection plate, but could fit into a couple of suitcases.

"It's not, you know," she said as he approached.

"Not an advantage to a reporter to read minds?" Mike was catching on to the odd shorthand of talking to a telepath.

"No." Kerrigan shook her head, "Most of what I get is off the surface, and even that is usually pretty slimy. Animal needs and all that crap. And secrets. Dammit, my entire life has been filled with secrets. It gets real old, real fast."

"Sorry," Mike said, suddenly realizing he didn't know if he meant it or not.

"Yeah, you meant it. You just don't know you meant it. And no, I don't have any cigarettes. Here we go."

She stroked a switch and spoke softly into a microphone. The lower plate of the holographic transmitter whirred softly, and a humanoid aura took form in the light. It seemed to be carved out of the light itself, a massive man, broad-shouldered, in quasi-military uniform. His face resolved into bushy eyebrows, a craggy nose, a huge mustache, and a prominent chin. His hair was black with gray stripes, but still was more black than gray.

Mike recognized him at once from dozens of wanted posters across the Confederacy.

"Mr. Liberty, I am so glad you could join us," said the glowing figure. "I am Arcturus Mengsk, leader of the Sons of Korhal. I would like to ask you to join us."

CHAPTER 7

DEALS

Arcturus Mengsk. There's a name that is synonymous with terror, betrayal, and violence. A living example of the ends justifying the means. The assassin of the Confederacy of Man. The hero of the blasted world of Korhal IV. King of the universe. A savage barbarian who never let anything or anyone get in his way.

And yet, he is also charming, erudite, and intelligent. When you're in his presence you feel that he's really listening to you, that your opinions matter, that you're someone important if you agree with him.

It's amazing. I have often wondered if men like Mengsk don't carry around their own reality-warping bubbles, and all who fall in are suddenly transported to another dimension where the hellish things he says and does suddenly make sense.

At least, that's the effect he always had on me.

—The Liberty Manifesto

THE GLOWING FIGURE PAUSED FOR A MOMENT, THEN said, "Is there something wrong with our connection, Lieutenant?"

Kerrigan responded, "We read you loud and clear, sir."

"Mr. Liberty, can you hear me?" Arcturus asked.

"I can hear you," said Mike. "I just don't know I can believe what I'm hearing. You're the most hated man in the Confederacy."

Arcturus Mengsk chuckled and folded his hands over his broad, muscle-flat belly. "You honor me, but I must reply that I am only the most hated man among the Confederacy's elites. Those elites who make it their mission to keep everyone else under their thumbs. Those who choose to think otherwise are cast out. I have survived that casting out, and as such I am a danger to them."

Mengsk's words washed over Michael Liberty like warm honey. The man's manner and voice screamed "politician" at every turn. Here was a creature who would be at home in the Tarsonis City Council, or among the confabs and social retreats of the Old Families of the Confederacy.

"I know a lot of reporters who would like to talk to you," Mike said.

"You among them, I hope? I've been a fan of your work for many years. I must admit my surprise at seeing your illustrious name attached to mere military reporting."

Mike shrugged. "There were extenuating circumstances."

"Of course," said Mengsk, another smile appearing beneath his bushy salt-and-pepper mustache. "And similarly, I fear my own vagabond lifestyle has prevented a suitable interview from being set up. The few that have been managed were quickly spoiled by the Confederacy. I think you understand what I mean."

Mike thought of Rourke, dying with Mike's press tags, and of Raynor's people, locked up in orbit, and the refugees waiting for dropships that didn't seem to be appearing. He nodded.

"I know my reputation precedes me, Michael." Mengsk brought himself up short. "May I call you Michael?"

"If you want to."

Another half-concealed smile. "And I must tell you that

this reputation is fully deserved. I am, by Confederate lights, a terrorist, an agent of chaos against the old order. My father was Angus Mengsk, who first led the people of Korhal IV in rebellion against the Confederacy."

"And paid for it with the death of the planet."

Arcturus Mengsk turned somber. "Yes, and I carry their ghosts with me every day of my life. They were branded rebels and revolutionaries by the Confederates, but, as you well know, it is the victors who are given the luxury of writing the histories."

Mengsk paused for a moment, but Mike didn't leap in, either to agree or disagree. At length Mengsk said, "I make no apologies for the actions of the Sons of Korhal. There is blood on my hands for my actions, but I have yet to reach the 35 million lives that the Confederacy claimed on Korhal IV."

"Is that a target number?" Mike asked, looking for a chink in the politician's armor.

He expected a flash of anger, or a quick rebuttal. Instead, Mengsk gave a brief chortle. "No. I cannot hope to compete with the merciless bureaucracy of the Confederacy of Man. They wave the banners of Old Earth, but no ancient government would have tolerated the inhumanity that the Confederacy considers business as usual. And those who would raise the alarm are either silenced by violence or shamed into complicity through comfort."

"That would be us in the press," stated Mike, thinking of Handy Anderson's nosebleed office.

Arcturus Mengsk shrugged. "The shoe very well may fit, though I will not press the point. I know that you, for one, are a rare individual who has not shrunk from always seeking the truth."

"So, all this"—Mike waved at the equipment and Kerrigan—"is to set up an interview opportunity?"

Again the easy laugh. "There will be time for interviews later, but there are more pressing matters at the moment. You know the refugee situation in the hinterlands?"

Mike nodded. "I've visited a few of them. They've emptied the cities, and the people are now waiting in the wilderness for the Confederacy dropships to come for them."

"And what would you say if I told you there would be no such ships coming?"

Mike blinked, suddenly aware that Kerrigan was looking at him. "I'd have a hard time believing that. They may be delayed, but they wouldn't abandon the populace here."

"It's true, I'm afraid." Mengsk sighed. Mike wished for some long-distance telepathy himself to dig underneath the man's well-mannered outer mantle. "None are en route. Indeed, Colonel Duke has been very busy for the past few days uprooting the Confederate military structure here, preparing to retreat at the first appearance of the Protoss, or the overwhelming success of the Zerg."

"What do *you* know about the Protoss and the Zerg?" Michael asked sharply.

"More than I want to admit," Mengsk said with a grim smile. "Suffice it to say that they are ancient races, and that they hate each other. And they have little or no use for the human race, either. In that way they are very much like the Confederacy."

"I've seen both the Zerg and the Protoss at work," Mike said. "I have a hard time believing that they are like anything human."

"Even though the Confederacy plans to abandon the population of Mar Sara? To let the Zerg overrun them from below, or the Protoss vaporize them from above? This system is nothing more than a giant petri dish to the bureaucrats on Tarsonis, where they can watch these alien races duel and plan how to save their own hides. Can you, as a man, stand aside and watch this happen?"

Mike thought of the deadly, radiant rainbows on the surface of Chau Sara. "You have a solution," he said, making the words a statement, not a question. "And this solution somehow involves me."

"I am a man with great but not unlimited resources," said Arcturus Mengsk, suddenly with the intensity of a gathering storm. "I have my own ships en route to ferry as many people as I can out of the system. Kerrigan has located the bulk of the camps and spread sufficient anti-Confederate ideas that we may be welcomed as heroes. I have been in contact with the fragments of this planet's government. But I need a friendly face to reassure them that we do indeed come in peace."

"And that's where I come in."

"That's where you come in," Mengsk repeated. "Your reputation precedes you as well."

Mike thought about it, conscious of both the Protoss above and the Zerg below. "I won't fashion propaganda for you," he said at last.

"I'm not asking you to do so," said Mengsk, spreading his hands wide. Welcoming him.

"And I report what I see."

"Which is more than the Confederacy allows you now, under their military strictures. I would expect no less from a reporter of your caliber."

Another pause. Mengsk ended it by saying, "If there's anything I can do to help you further . . ."

Mike thought of Raynor's men. "I have some . . . associates . . . in Confederate custody."

Mengsk raised an eyebrow at Kerrigan. She said, "Local militia and law-enforcement officers, sir. They were captured and secured in a prison ship. I can find the location."

"Hmmm. Ask no small favors, eh, Michael?" Mengsk scratched his chin, but even over the connection, Mike knew the man had already made up his mind. "All right, but you have to help with it. But first . . ."

"I know," Mike said with a shrug. "I have to write your bloody press release."

"Exactly," confirmed Mengsk, his eyes twinkling. "If we're agreed, then I'll let Lieutenant Kerrigan take care of the details."

And with that the light-wrapped figure evaporated.

Mike let out a deep breath. "You still reading my mind?" he asked at last.

"It's hard not to," Kerrigan said levelly.

"Then you know I don't trust him."

"I know," answered Mengsk's lieutenant. "But you trust that he'll live up to his side of the bargain. Come on, let's get started."

The prison ship *Merrimack* was an old relic, a Leviathan-class battlecruiser that had been stripped of everything useful, save for life support, and even that was quirky and unreliable. Even its drive had been disengaged once it had warped in, and it had been towed to its station high above Mar Sara's northern pole. Its holds were filled with unarmed men, prisoners who had been seized for various reasons and who were considered too dangerous to leave on the surface. There were a lot of the homegrown planetary militia up here, along with the marshals and not a few outspoken local leaders.

What the collection of prisoners, stashed away behind locked bulkheads, did not know was that they were being overseen by a skeleton crew, a fraction of the normal staff of such a prison hulk. Most of the important ranking officers had already been shuttled off, and of the major ships that had visited Mar Sara in the past few days, only the *Norad II* still remained in orbit.

Captain Elias Tudbury, the remaining ranking officer on board the *Merrimack,* growled as he scanned the docking ring monitors. The last shuttle was overdue by at least an hour, and if the radio scuttlebutt was correct, the Protoss with their lightning weapons were due any time now.

And Captain Tudbury had not survived long enough to command a prison ship by exposing himself to danger of any stripe. Now, as the shuttle edged its way toward the dock, he shifted uneasily from one foot to the other. Beside him the comm officer was monitoring frequencies.

The sooner the shuttle arrived, Tudbury thought, the sooner he and his few stragglers could get away from here, leaving the prisoners to their fate.

The speaker crackled over his head. "Prison Shu . . . port five-four . . . requ . . . sting clear . . . for docking. Passphrase . . ." The rest was lost in static.

The comm officer tapped his headpiece and said, "Repeat transmission, five-four-six-seven. I say again, repeat transmission."

The speaker continued to crack and spark. ". . . ison shuttle . . . six-seven. Requesting clearance . . . king. Pass . . ." More static.

"Come again, five-four-six-seven," said the comm officer. Tudbury was practically exploding with anxiety, but the comm officer's voice was soft and mechanical. "Please repeat."

"Interferen . . ." came the response. "We wi . . . pull off and tr . . . gain later."

"No you don't," said Tudbury, reaching past his officer and flicking a switch. "Shuttle five-four-six-seven, ya'll are cleared for docking. Get your ass in here and get us off this tub!"

The hydraulics hissed as the two ships linked, while the communications officer pointed out the violation of standard protocol.

"This is a nonstandard situation, son," said Tudbury, already halfway to the dock, his duffel already packed and swinging behind him. "Grab your gear and spread the word. We're off this here wreck!"

The airlock slid open, and Captain Tudbury was looking down the barrel of a large-bore slugthrower. At the operating end of the slugthrower was a lean man with a ponytail who looked like someone Tudbury had seen on UNN.

"Boo," said Michael Liberty.

It took a mere ten minutes to overpower the rest of the crew, most of whom were armed only with their duffels and a great desire to leave, and another twenty to convince them to reengage the warp engines and limp the *Merrimack* out of planetary range. Raynor and his men took the shuttle with Liberty.

"I'll admit," said former marshal Raynor, "that when I told you to do something, I didn't expect this."

Mike Liberty blushed. "Let's just say I made a deal with the devil, and it worked out to our benefit."

As if on cue, Mengsk's broad face filled the shuttle's viewscreen. "Congratulations, Michael. We must report success as well with our endeavor. We have been welcomed with open arms by the people of Mar Sara and even now our ships are evacuating the refugees. I have come to understand that even Colonel Duke is unwilling to fire on ships filled with innocents, and the turn of events has vexed him dearly."

Raynor leaned toward the screen. "Mengsk? This is Jim Raynor. I just want to thank you for your help in getting us off that hulk."

"Ah, Marshal Raynor. Michael apparently thinks very highly of you and your men. I was wondering if you would be willing to help me in a small matter." Mengsk's smile filled the screen.

"Now wait a minute, Mengsk," said Mike. "We made a deal here, and we both did our part."

"And that bargain is done, Michael," continued the terrorist leader who had saved the population of a planet. "But now I want to offer a similar arrangement to the former marshal and his men. Something that, I hope, will be beneficial to *all* our peoples."

CHAPTER 8

ZERG AND PROTOSS

It would be easy to declare that Arcturus Mengsk was a master manipulator, which he was, or that he regularly deceived others, which was true as well. But it would be a mistake to deny all personal responsibility in falling into his web.

It seems now the height of folly ever to have dealt with the man, but think of the situation when the Sara system died. You had the mindless beasts of the Zerg on one side, and the unholy fury of the Protoss on the other. And in the middle you had the criminal bureaucracy of the old Confederacy of Man, which was willing to write off the population of two planets in order to learn more about its enemies.

With such a surplus of devils in the universe, what did it matter if there was one more?

—The Liberty Manifesto

THE JACOBS INSTALLATION WAS BUILT INTO THE SIDE of a mountain on the far side of Mar Sara from its major cities. It wasn't listed in any planetary archive that Michael Liberty had found, but Mengsk knew about it.

Somewhere in the Jacobs Installation there was a computer with data in it. Mengsk said he didn't know what the data was, but he knew it was important. And he knew that he needed it. And he knew that Raynor would go get it for him.

All of this made Mike wonder what else Mengsk knew. It also made the reporter think about other deep craters on Chau Sara. Had there been similar locations on the other planet, unknown to most humans but beacons to the Protoss? Had Mengsk known about these as well?

Liberty suddenly felt as though he were at the epicenter of a bomb site, and the countdown had already begun.

The planet was already unraveling. He could see the devastation from the screens on the dropship that brought Raynor and his combat troops in. Miles of former farmland was now overrun with the creep, a pulsing living organism that covered the earth and sent tendrils deep into the rock beneath. Odd constructs dotted the landscape like twisted mushrooms, and scorpionlike creatures pulled down and consumed anything in their path. He could see packs of the skinned-dog zerglings, herded by the larger snake-beast hydralisks. And once, on the horizon, there was a flight of things that looked like winged organic cannons.

The creep had not reached the Jacobs Installation yet, but the strange Zerg towers were already on the horizon. The front gates were open, and men were trying to flee the complex. The dropship came under fire as it deployed Raynor and his troops. Even in the relative safety of a low-grade technician's combat suit, Liberty hung back.

I'm not doing this for Mengsk, he told himself. *I'm doing it for Raynor.*

The guards were more interested in flight than fight, and Raynor's troops scattered them easily. Michael Liberty followed the hulking armored forms into the base itself.

The resistance stiffened as soon as they entered. Defensive guns were mounted in the wall, and pop-up turrets erupted at every corner. Raynor lost two men before he got cautious.

"We need to find some control computer," said Mike.

"Yeah," Raynor agreed. "But I'm willing to bet it's on the *far* side of those guns."

And with that he was out in the corridor, spraying spikes in a wide arc, hitting targets that had been unseen a moment ago. Mike followed as close as he dared, his own gauss rifle at the ready, but by the time he rounded the corner Raynor was standing in a smoking hallway. Charred emplacements scorched the walls and floor.

Another hundred feet and another intersection. And another turret popping up from the floor like a mechanical gopher, spraying the hallway.

Raynor and Liberty dodged into one doorway, three others of the squad into another. One man wasn't fast enough and was caught in the stream of bullets, his fall forward slowed by the continual impacts of the spikes against his helmet and shattered chest plate.

"Okay, we need to take this one out," said Raynor.

"Hold on," said Mike. "I think I found something."

It looked akin to a typical comm center, with zooming screens on either side and altogether too many buttons. But the screens showed what looked like a diagram of the installation itself.

"It's a map," said Raynor.

"Full marks," said Mike. "Better yet, it's a map that we can use."

Several areas already flashed red, marking where the assault team had already passed. Other regions were flashing green pips, including the one outside the door. Probably active defenses.

"Right," said Mike. "You know anything about computers?"

"Had to replace a memory board on my Vulture once," said Raynor.

"Dandy." Mike's own experience consisted of repairing persnickety comm units in the field, but he didn't say anything. He scanned the various buttons and toggles. All were numbered, but there was no master listing.

He hit a toggle, and one of the green lights went out. He hit another and another vanished. He started flipping the toggles and mashing the buttons wildly. About fifteen seconds later the staccato in the hallway stopped.

"Nice job," said Raynor.

"Let's see what the others do." Mike grabbed a small dial and turned it. Somewhere deep in the complex a Klaxon sounded, and there was a vibration under their feet.

"What the Sam Hill was that?" said Raynor.

"The sound of me pushing my luck too far," said Mike.

"So why did you do that?"

"It seemed like the right thing to do at the time."

Raynor let out a frustrated sigh, then said, "Can you get the data we're looking for off this terminal?"

Mike shook his head, running a finger over the installation schematic. "Here," he said. "There's a separate system, not linked up to the mainframe."

"Think that's it?"

"Has to be. The best way to protect information from hackers is to completely separate the machine that it's on. Basic computer security one-oh-one."

"Then let's go whack some varmints," said Raynor, signaling to the survivors of the squad.

"Yeah," Mike said with a laugh. "Let's git them 'varmints.'"

They stepped out, then dodged back immediately as another volley of spikes ricocheted down the hallway.

"Liberty!" Raynor bellowed. "I thought you got all the gun emplacements!"

"Those aren't emplacements, Jim," Mike shouted back, squatting in the doorway. "Those are live targets."

Indeed, there was a pair of white-armored forms now at the crossroads, their combat armor similar to Mike's own save for color. They carried their own gauss rifles and were spraying the corridor.

Mike brought his own weapon up and leaned forward for a shot. A white-armored specter hovered in his crosshairs.

And Mike found he could not shoot. His target was a man, a living human. He could not shoot.

The target in white armor harbored no such compunctions, and let loose a burst. The doorframe splintered under the assault as Liberty rolled back into the room.

"What happened?" Raynor shouted. "They in cover?"

"They . . ." Mike began, then shook his head. "I can't shoot them."

Raynor frowned. "You took out a Zerg with a shotgun. I saw you."

"That was different. These are humans."

Mike expected the admission to disgust the lawman, but instead Raynor merely nodded and said, "That's okay. Lots of folks have a problem with shooting other people. The good news is that *they* don't know you don't want to shoot them. Fire a little over their heads. That will spook 'em."

He pushed Mike back toward the door. Across the hallway the other two marines were trading shots with the white-armored forms.

Mike rolled out of the doorway, targeted the one on the right, raised his gauss rifle just a hair, and let off a burst. The white form dropped into a crouch, while his companion brought his own weapon around and dropped to one knee.

Despite himself, Mike smiled. Then the chest of the soldier he had fired above blossomed in a fountain of blood. His companion brought his own weapon around, but too slowly. His head vaporized in a red mist as visor and helmet shattered.

Mike looked up to see Raynor standing above him, leaning out of the doorway. He had taken the two enemy troopers out with single shots.

Raynor looked down and said, "I understand if you have a problem shooting people. Fortunately, I don't. Now let's go."

The wall and floor guns were silent now, and the team was

practically running through the halls. In his lighter armor, Mike was in front.

He suddenly realized that this was not the smartest place to be.

Then he rounded the corner and sprawled over a zergling.

In one graceless swoop Mike skidded forward, tumbling over the top of the skinless beast. He could feel the creature's muscles pulse and shudder beneath him as he inadvertently vaulted over it. He landed on his shoulder and felt pain ratchet through the right side of his body.

"Zerg!" Mike shouted. "Kill it!" He ignored the pain and twisted his rifle around, praying it hadn't been damaged in the fall.

"Crossfire!" Raynor bellowed. "We'll hit each other!"

There was a silent moment in the hallway—Raynor's troops on one side, Mike on the other, the Zerg in the middle. This close, Mike could smell the creature's fetid breath. Its very skin seemed to exude decay and rot.

The zergling turned toward the squad, then toward the reporter, as if trying to determine which to attack first. Finally some organic circuit closed in its twisted mind and it came to its decision.

It leaped at Liberty with a chittering cry, its claws extended.

Mike dove forward, underneath the leap, and raised his gauss rifle. He caught the creature in the belly, spearing it and catching the beast's own momentum. Beast and barrel rose in a slow arc above him.

At the top of the arc Mike pulled the trigger, and a volley of spikes splattered the zergling. Those that passed through its body embedded in the metal ceiling of the hallway.

Mike sputtered as he was drenched in the beast's ichor. Raynor ran up.

"What are Zerg doing here?" Raynor asked.

"Maybe they're after what we're after?" Mike suggested.

"Let's find that information, now." Raynor waved the remains of the team forward.

"Let's find a shower," Mike muttered, wiping the Zerg's guts off his stained armor.

The complex had a few surprises left. The passage widened into a larger room. Three more zerglings were within, brought down in rapid fire before they could react. Along one wall was a line of cages, all open. They gave off the fetid smell of the zerglings.

"They were keeping them here," said Raynor. "Pets? Studies?"

"And for how long?" Mike reached the isolated computer station and started hitting buttons. "Christ. Look at this."

"The information?"

"That, and more. Look at this. These are readings on the Zerg going back months."

"But that's impossible," said Raynor. "Unless . . ."

"Unless the Confederates knew about the Zerg all the time. They knew they were here. Hell, they may have *brought* them here."

"Samuel J. Houston on a bicycle," said Raynor. Mike assumed that was a curse. Then Raynor added, "Get the disk and let's move out."

"Working," said Mike. The disk burner chugged for a few minutes, then ejected a silvery wafer. "Got it. Let's go!"

The moment Mike plucked the disk from the machine, the lighting suddenly went red. From above them a female voice intoned, "Self-destruct sequence initiated."

"Crap!" cursed Mike. "It must have been booby-trapped!"

"Let's move!" said Raynor. "Don't make any wrong turns!"

Mike, in his lighter armor, led, now unafraid of running into any other surprises. They encountered nothing but the dead on their way out, the soft tones above them warning them, "Ten seconds to detonation," then "Five seconds to detonation."

Then they were outside, beneath the rotten-orange sky. Mike kept running, intending not to stop until he reached the dropship.

Raynor caught up with him and threw him to the ground.

Mike bellowed a curse at the marshal, but it was drowned out by the explosion.

The entire side of the mountain rippled from the detonation, focusing a single blast from the mouth of the installation. A blistering hot wave washed over Liberty and the prostrate marines, and the top of the mountain fell in on itself. Mike hugged the bucking earth and prayed. And once it stopped, he realized that if he had been standing, he would have been blown away in the blast.

"Thanks," he said to Raynor.

"Seemed like the right thing to do at the time," said the former lawman. "Come on, let's get back before the Zerg find us here."

Mengsk was waiting for them on the bridge of his own command ship, the *Hyperion*. Compared to the bridge of the *Norad II*, this bridge was smaller and cozier, more of a den/library than the nerve center of a fleet. The perimeter of the room was dotted by technicians speaking softly into comm units. A large screen dominated one wall.

Of Lieutenant Kerrigan, Mike noticed, there was no sign.

"There were Zerg there!" said Raynor, handing over the disk. "The Confederates have been studying the damned aliens for months!"

"Years," said Mengsk, unsurprised. "I saw Zerg in Confederate holding pens myself, and that was over a year ago. It's clear the Confederates have known of these creatures for some time. For all we know, they could be *breeding* them."

Mike said nothing. The bottom had dropped out of the Confederate secrets market. There was nothing that they did that would surprise him now.

Raynor's jaw dropped open. "You mean, they've been using my planet as some sort of laboratory for these . . . things?"

"Your planet and your sister world," said Mengsk. "And gods know how many more Fringe Worlds. They've sowed the wind, my friends, and now they are reaping the whirl-wind."

For the first time, Raynor was stopped in his tracks. The enormity of the crime, Mike thought, was just too much for his local law-enforcement brain. Who do you arrest when the crime is genocide? How do you punish for such crimes?

Mike spoke up. "I've got a report to file. Summarizes everything we've found so far."

"We have a scrambled comm setup for your use," said Mengsk. "But you know they'll never run the story."

"I have to take that chance," Mike admitted, but inwardly he had to agree with Mengsk. If the Old Families of Tarsonis were paranoid enough to threaten a scandalmonger like him over a construction scandal, how willing were they to admit to dealing with planet-devouring aliens?

Mike was suddenly glad that the mind reader wasn't present.

A soft bell chimed, and one of the technicians announced, "We're getting warp signatures at mark four-point-five-point-seven."

"Pull back to a safe distance, scan on maximum," said Mengsk. "Gentlemen, you may remain if you want to see the last act of this particularly tawdry passion play."

Neither Mike nor Raynor moved, and Mengsk turned back to the screen. The huge orange ball of Mar Sara loomed over them, a few white clouds scattered high across its northern hemisphere. Yet most of that orange surface was now mottled, spoiled. Overrun by the creep, and the things that lived in it.

The very surface of the land seemed to pulsate and bubble, heaving like a living thing. The creep had even spread over the oceans in broad mats, writhing like living carpets of algae.

There was nothing human left on the planet. Not alive, at any rate.

A flash blossomed to one side of the planetary disk, and Mike knew that the Protoss had arrived. Their lightning ships warped into being. A flash of blue-white electricity, and then they were there. The golden carriers with their moth attendants, and metallic bat-winged creations that wove among the larger ships. They were breathtaking and deadly, forces of war raised to the level of an art form.

Mengsk spoke softly into his throat mike, and Mike could feel the engines engage. The terrorist leader was prepared to get out at the first sign that the Protoss had noticed them.

He need not have worried. The Protoss were completely intent on the diseased planet beneath them. Hatchways opened up in the bottoms of the larger ships, and great beams of energy, so intense as to be colorless, lanced downward toward the surface. The aliens laid down a withering barrage against the planet beneath.

Where the energy beams struck, they burned. The sky itself curdled as the beams pierced through the atmospheric envelope. Air itself was torn away from the planet by the force of the blows.

And where the beams struck the surface, they erupted, boiling the ground where they struck, uprooting both the creep-infested lands and those that had not yet been infected. Deadly rainbow radiation, more brilliant than Mike had ever seen, spiraled out from the impact points, churning earth and water mercilessly, distorting the matter of the planet itself.

Then other ships began firing thinner beams with surgical accuracy, adding to the barrage in places. The cities, Mike realized. They were targeting the cities and making sure that nothing could survive there. Any place of human settlement. Including, he knew, the Jacobs Installation itself.

They had cut their timing very close indeed, he thought, and his stomach gave an uneasy lurch.

One of the pulsing beams punched through the crust itself, and the ground erupted in a volcanic upwelling. Magma pushed to the surface, consuming everything that had been uprooted by the energy beams. Most of the world's atmosphere was burning now, torn away from the orb in a veil that trailed it in orbit, and what was left spiraled in hurricanes and tornadoes, until destroyed by more beams.

Now red volcanic glows covered the northern hemisphere of Mar Sara like welts. The remainder of the land heaved in a deadly rainbow. Nothing could survive the assault, human or otherwise.

"Exterminators," said Mike softly. "They're cosmic exterminators."

"Indeed," said Mengsk. "And they *can't* or *won't* tell the difference between us and the Zerg. Maybe to them there is no difference. We should prepare for departure. They may notice us at any time."

Mike looked at Raynor. The former marshal was stone-faced and grim, his hands clutching the railing in front of him. In the light of screens that showed the blue lightning of the Protoss ships, he looked like a statue. Only his eyes were alive, and they were filled with infinite sadness.

"Raynor?" said Mike. "Jim? Are you all right?"

"No," said Jim Raynor softly. "I mean, can any of us be all right after this?"

Mike had no response, and sat there as the planet died and Arcturus Mengsk spoke softly into his throat mike. After a moment, the terrorist leader said, "We are ready for departure."

"All right," said Raynor, his eyes never leaving the screen. "Let's go."

CHAPTER 9

MARSHAL AND GHOST

James Raynor was the most decent man I ever encountered during the fall of the Confederacy. Everyone else, I can safely say, was either a victim or a villain, or quite often both.

At first wash, Raynor seems like a backwoods cowboy, one of those good old boys that you see in the bars swapping lies about the days gone by. There's a cocksureness, an overconfidence about him that just makes you bridle initially. Yet over time you come to see him as a valuable ally and—dare I say it?—a friend.

It all comes from belief. Jim Raynor believed in himself, and he believed in those around him. And from that belief came the strength that allowed him and those who followed him to survive everything else the universe threw at him.

Jim Raynor was a most decent and honorable man. I suppose that's why his is the greatest tragedy of this godforsaken war.

—The Liberty Manifesto

MENGSK STRUCK LIBERTY AS JUST ANOTHER politician. For all the ghosts that supposedly haunted the man, his motivations were as apparent as those of the lowest ward heeler on Tarsonis. He was still gathering his power, and unwilling to pass on any potential ally. It was, Mike realized, why he knew the man would keep his word—he was still in a position where it would be dangerous for him if it got around that he did not.

Mengsk made Raynor a captain for his troubles, and Liberty was granted a series of one-on-one interviews. Mike avoided the level of propaganda that Mengsk apparently desired, but that made the charismatic leader even more available to Mike's questions. Mike's own resistance made his approval more desirable to the rebel commander.

Slowly, Mike found himself agreeing more and more with Mengsk's opinions of the Confederates. Hell, he himself had said many of the same things, though in a more cautious fashion, in various reports over the years. The Confederacy of Man was a criminal bureaucracy, filled to the brim with career politicos and grafters whose battle cry was "Where's Mine?"

And Mengsk was right about another matter. UNN never ran anything of his report on the destruction of Mar Sara, or of the Confederate culpability in the attack. They did get around to telling the people that there was not one but two hostile enemy threats out in the universe, the subversive Zerg and the sky-blasting Protoss. Both were presented as implacable foes of humanity, and the only solution was to group together beneath the Confederate flag to repulse them.

"Such is the nature of tyrants," said Mengsk late one evening on the *Hyperion*'s observation deck, his snifter of brandy untouched on the table between them. Liberty's glass had long since been drained and set down empty beside a chess set of which the white king had been toppled. Mengsk played black as habit, Liberty usually lost as white. An unused ashtray rested at the far end of the table. Michael had given up smoking again, but Mengsk made it available to him nonetheless.

Mengsk continued, "Tyrants can only survive by presenting

a greater tyrant as a threat. The Confederacy does not realize the danger of the other tyrants that it has now called down upon all of us."

"Before the Protoss and Zerg," Mike noted, "their favorite threat was *you*."

Mengsk chuckled. "I must admit that I feel that the best form of government is benevolent despotism. I don't think the oligarchs in charge agree with that."

"And are *you* pointing at greater tyrants to cover your own abuses?" Mike asked.

"Of course I am," said Arcturus Mengsk. "But it does help that our foes *are* greater tyrants than we are. Or ever intend to be." He picked up Mike's toppled king from the board. "Another game, perhaps?"

Mike saw nothing of Kerrigan, and when asked, Mengsk only said, "My trusted lieutenant works best in the field." Mike took that to mean that she was out sizing up another planet ripe for rebellion.

He was right. Two days later Mengsk called both Liberty and Raynor to his observation deck. A graphic display showed another world, this one a ruddy brown. Behind it a gas giant loomed like an overprotective parent.

"Antiga Prime," said Mengsk, tapping the screen. "Border colony of the Confederacy of Man. Its people are very, very tired of the Confederate military, which has gotten a bit heavy-handed since the Protoss and Zerg first appeared. I want Captain Raynor to help the Antigans get their revolt off the ground. That means dealing with a unit of Alpha Squadron they've got baby-sitting the major road on the ground."

"My pleasure, sir," said Raynor. Mike noted that Raynor seemed calmer, more controlled now than he had when they left the Sara system. Incorporating his own unit's survivors with Mengsk's Sons of Korhal apparently helped see him through the loss of Mar Sara, and his bold, brazen nature was bubbling once more to the surface. He was itching for action.

Mengsk turned. "And Mr. Liberty, if you want to accompany his unit?"

"You may have overlooked this fact, Arcturus," said Liberty, "but I'm still not working for you."

"You're not working for anyone at the moment, it seems," replied Mengsk. "The UNN has been noticeably devoid of your illustrious presence. I only thought you would be professionally interested . . ."

"And . . .?" prompted Liberty.

"And your glib tongue and clever notepad might be enough to encourage the Antigans to cast off their shackles." He smiled a slightly shamefaced grin, and Mike knew that he was going planetside.

Antiga Prime had once been a water world, but the oceans had left without leaving a forwarding address. All that remained were hard mudflats and low, flat mesas covered with a native shrub with purple blossoms. Occasionally the whitened bones of some fossilized sea creatures rippled out of the surrounding strata, the only reminder that life larger than humans had once been here. Pretty in an arid, lifeless sort of way.

The dropship brought them down on a low plateau that looked like every other low plateau on Antiga.

Mengsk had mentioned that his scout would contact them once they were on the ground. Mike had no doubt who that scout would be. As the rebels set up a perimeter around the ship, he kept the comm link open to Mengsk and the regional commanders.

Kerrigan appeared out of nowhere, despite the fact that there was no cover around. She was dressed in ghost armor— a hostile environment suit—and had a canister rifle slung across her back. Her helmet was off, and her red hair flashed in Antiga's too-bright sun.

Kerrigan snapped off a quick salute. "Captain Raynor, I've finished scouting out the area and . . . You pig!"

Mike quickly turned down the volume on his comm unit. Raynor lurched backward as if struck.

"What?" he said. "I haven't even said anything to you yet!"

Kerrigan's too-wide lips turned into a nasty sneer. "Yeah, but you were *thinking* it."

"Oh yeah, you're a telepath," said Raynor, shooting Mike a look that even the reporter could read. *And why didn't you warn me about this?* To the lieutenant he said, "Look, let's just get on with this, okay?"

Kerrigan snorted. "Right. The command center is a couple klicks due west, up on one of those mesas. Alpha Squad, but no Duke. Sorry, boys. We take them out, and the indigenous forces would be willing to rise in rebellion. There are some towers that need to come down if I'm to get in."

"Right," said Raynor, frowning. "I don't *need* to tell you to move out."

"No, you don't," said Kerrigan, a touch too hotly. "But there's another thing."

"Go ahead, Lieutenant," said Raynor. "I *don't* read minds."

"There have been increasing reports of xenomorphs in the area." Kerrigan almost smiled at the reaction to her words.

Raynor frowned deeply.

Mike nearly jumped in his seat. "Xenomorphs? Zerg? Here?"

"Cattle mutilations, mysterious disappearances, bug-eyed monsters," confirmed Kerrigan. "The usual suspects. Not a lot, but enough."

"Crap," muttered Raynor. "Confederates *and* Zerg. They seem to go hand in hand. Okay, *now* let's roll out."

The wide, dried mudflats of Antiga Prime were ideal for speed and lousy for cover. Twice marine scouts appeared to the south, distracting Raynor in his Vulture to deal with them as Kerrigan, Raynor's troops, and Mike slowly crept up on the mesa. They were about three hundred yards shy when a tower cannon opened up on them.

Mike's comm link crackled. "Dammit," said Kerrigan. "They've got sensors out the buttcheeks on that thing. I can't even sneeze without it picking me up. Can you get reinforcements on that blower?"

"Working on it," snapped Mike as another shell bounded into the outcropping above him. "Raynor! It's Liberty! We're pinned down! Need your firepower, *muy pronto*."

Mike was unsure that the former marshal had gotten the message, until he heard the high-pitched whine of Raynor's Vulture engines. The captain topped a nearby rise in a single hop, closing as the tower tried to traverse its gun to the new target. It was too slow, and with a resounding thump a volley of frag grenades shot from under the vehicle's front hood. Blossoms of flame erupted at the base of the tower.

Kerrigan gave a cry, and the remaining pinned troops rolled out of their hiding places and lacerated the tower with spike fire. Raynor passed for another blitz, but it was overkill: by the time a second string of explosions blossomed at the base, the tower was already listing, and as Raynor sped off, it toppled completely in his wake.

Mike's private line crackled. "Next time, make it something important, buddy!" said the captain.

"What did he say?" Kerrigan asked, then added, "Never mind. He's a pig, but he's a pretty competent pig."

Mike shook his head. "Captain Raynor is one of the most upright, moral men I've met since leaving Tarsonis."

"Yeah, he's that way on the surface," said Kerrigan. "Everything's under real tight control. It's underneath that he's a pig, like most people. Trust me on this."

Mike didn't know what to say. Eventually he managed, "He has been under a lot of stress lately."

Kerrigan snorted again. "Yeah, like who hasn't?"

They were within sight of the command center, another standard-issue half sphere, a portable setup. This one glistened in the sun, though: the Zerg hadn't corrupted it yet. Somehow that made Mike feel both better and worse at the same time.

Another call came in. This time Raynor was looking for

reinforcements. Could Kerrigan send down the troops still with her?

"He says—" Mike began.

"Send them," said Kerrigan.

"But you've got to—"

"I've got to get inside. And I can do that either with or without the support troops. They're just extra targets. Send them off, and follow when you can."

Mike relayed the orders, while Kerrigan put up the hood and helmet of her ghost suit. Mike watched her fasten the helmet, touch a device at her belt, and . . .

Vanish.

No, not quite vanish. There was a ripple around her, one that you could follow if you knew what to look for, and looked very hard. The guards at the front of the command center did not know what to look for, and were not looking hard enough. There was a burst of unseen canister fire, and the guards blew apart in a couple of pieces each. Then an explosion at the main gates, which suddenly yawned wide. There was a silhouette among the smoke for a moment, a female figure with a large gun. Then she was gone, into the depths of the enemy command center.

Mike followed slowly, very much aware that he lacked the cloaking technology and psionic talent that made the telepathic ghosts possible. He paused briefly near the dead guards. They wore Alpha Squadron uniforms, but their bleeding heads were covered with helmets polarized in the Antigan sunlight. He decided not to remove the helmets: these might be people he knew. People who still owed him poker money.

Mike sneaked into the devastation of the command center.

It was easy to know where Kerrigan had gone; Mike just followed the path of broken and bleeding corpses. Men and women in full combat rig had been tossed around like rag dolls and now lay crumpled in pools of their own blood.

Michael Liberty thought briefly of Lieutenant Swallow and realized that he was now getting used to freshly dead bodies.

Maybe he was growing the necessary emotional armor to survive in a universe at war.

He found Kerrigan's canister rifle, rammed through the front plexishield of a toppled Goliath walker. From up ahead came the sounds of battle. Despite himself, he cradled his own gauss rifle and pressed forward.

And he was rewarded with the privilege of watching Sarah Kerrigan fight.

It was blood poetry, war ballet. She had reached the center of the command center now, armed with her knife and a slugthrower. She would wink into existence, slit a throat, then wink out again. Marines would rush to that location, and she would appear a few feet away, firing a burst point-blank into the helmet of her target. Then gone, then back again, this time with a spinning kick that broke the neck of a bellowing officer.

Mike brought his weapon up but found he could not fire. It was more than just a reluctance to take human life. He could not tell where she was at any one time. And through it all she moved with a catlike grace and determination that shredded every opponent she encountered.

She *was* very good with knives. More important, she was like the Protoss—glorious and deadly.

He stood in the entrance for only a minute, but it was enough time for Kerrigan to dispatch every enemy in the command center. The only survivors were the ones who chose to flee at the outset.

Only then did Kerrigan come fully into view, sinking to her knees in exhaustion, her back to Liberty.

Mike walked up behind her and moved to put his hand on her shoulder.

His hand never reached her. Without hesitation, she spun in place, grabbed his outstretched wrist with one hand, and brought up her combat knife with the other.

Only when the tip of the knife was inches from Mike's face did she freeze. Her face was a mask of rage. Fear flooded

Mike's mind, and in an instant he knew she was aware of that fear.

"Don't. *Do.* That," she said, biting off each word. Then she dropped her knife and put her face in both hands, "You're afraid of me."

Mike hesitated for a moment, then settled on "You betcha."

"I'm sorry," she said. "Sorry you had to see this."

Mike took a deep breath. "I just never visited you at work before. You rest for a moment. I've got to kick off a revolution."

He shoved a broken body from the communications console, inserted the prerecorded disk, set the levels, and put out a general signal on all bands.

"This is Michael Liberty, broadcasting from Antiga Prime, with a report that the master command center for this world has been disabled by rebel forces. Repeat, the master command center has been disabled. The power of the Confederacy has been interrupted, and there is a strong possibility that it can be shattered entirely if the people of Antiga rise up to take control of their own destiny. The Confederate Marines in charge of the command center are either dead or in full retreat, while rebel losses have been . . ." He looked at Sarah Kerrigan, exhausted, weeping into her hands. ". . . been minimal. We have a message here from Arcturus Mengsk, leader of the Sons of Korhal. Please stand by."

Mike popped the preprogrammed cartridge into the player and let the smooth, melodious tones of the terrorist leader rouse the people to action. Mike went back to Kerrigan, this time circling her so she knew he was coming.

Her eyes were dry now, but she was shuddering, her arms crossed in front of her, her breathing in short gasps.

"It's okay," said Mike. "You got them all."

"I know," she said, looking at Mike. "I got them all. And as I killed each and every one of them, I knew what they were thinking. Fear. Panic. Hatred. Hopelessness. Breakfast."

"Breakfast?"

"One of the techs had skipped breakfast, and he was really regretting not having had waffles." Kerrigan gave a sniffling giggle. "He was about to have his throat slit, and he was worrying about waffles." She put her hands along the sides of her head and ran her fingers through her red hair. "It sucks being a telepath."

"I'll bet," said Mike, aware that the fear was still with him. The fear that Kerrigan could cut open his belly before he could even react. And that she knew he was thinking that.

"I know you're afraid," said Kerrigan. "And you can admit it. That makes you smarter than most. God, what I went through to become this, what the Confederates did to me. Do you know?"

"I know that the Confederacy has a lot of deep holes to hide their secrets in. Deeper and blacker than I ever imagined. Ghost training was for an elite group of carefully controlled telepaths. . . ."

Kerrigan was nodding as he spoke. "Controlled through drugs and threats and brutality, until they owned you body and soul. They are no better than these Zerg creatures, creating warriors for a larger empire. We have no lives but the ones the Confederacy allows us, until we are no longer useful, and then we are discarded, lest we create future problems. Unless . . ."

"Unless you escape," said Mike. "Or someone helps you escape." And he suddenly realized why this former ghost was working for Arcturus Mengsk. She owed him her life.

Kerrigan just nodded in response. "There's more to it, but yes."

There were heavy footfalls at the entrance, and Mike rose with his gauss rifle ready. Raynor's armored form appeared in the doorway.

"You children okay?" he shouted.

"We're done here," said Mike. "Center captured, message delivered."

"Good," said Captain Raynor, "'cause we've got a chunk of

Alpha Squad coming up from the south, and we're going to need all the help we can get handling them. She okay?"

"I'm fine," said Kerrigan, rising to her feet. "You can talk to me directly, you know."

"Maybe I'll just *think* it at you," said Raynor.

"Jim!" Mike said sharply. "That's enough."

"What?" Raynor looked surprised by Mike's tone.

"That's *enough*," repeated Mike, his tone less heated but still grave. His serious voice.

The large captain looked at Mike, then slowly nodded. "Yeah, I suppose it is." To Kerrigan he said, "Sorry to offend, ma'am."

"Used to it, Captain," said Kerrigan. "You said we had more Confederates to kill. Let's get a move on."

She forced her way past both men, phasing invisible as she went.

Captain Raynor shook his head. "Women."

Mike softened his tone. "She's been under a lot of stress lately."

Raynor snorted. "Could have fooled me."

Mike followed Raynor out of the building. Along the horizon there were small flashes of battle as the Antigans and Confederates met in combat.

Above them, in the darkening sky, there were other flashes, of another battle. They danced across the sky like new stars and ended only when a brilliant meteor streaked across the sky, splitting the screaming atmosphere in its wake.

CHAPTER 10

THE WRECK OF THE NORAD II

There's an old Earth word. Its called schadenfreude—*the feeling of elation that comes from learning of the suffering of others. Like when you hear that a rival newsman suddenly was caught cursing in front of a live mike, or that a particularly corrupt alderman just stepped in front of a garbage truck. It's elation accompanied by that twinge of guilt for feeling so good, and the quiet, fervent prayer that something that bad never happens to you.*

With the Protoss and Zerg biting deep into Confederate territory, we had schadenfreude *in buckets.*

—The Liberty Manifesto

OTHER MEN AND WOMEN WENT TO WAR. MIKE returned to Mengsk's base and monitored the flow of communications. There was the blind panic he had come to expect during warfare—units suddenly cut off and demanding, then pleading for, reinforcements, then relief and finally rescue. Other messages from units that suddenly evaporated in a haze of radiation. And still other messages, these from civilians, asking for help from anyone, on any side.

And then there were the anomalous reports, the ones of monsters suddenly appearing in the countryside, ascribed to the Confederates, or the rebels, or to invasions from beyond. These reports were growing more numerous by the hour, and they convinced Mike that Kerrigan was right: the Zerg were on Antiga.

He wanted to hit the console when that realization sank in. Zerg presence was as good as a cancer diagnosis, and much more fatal. Until they figured out how to defeat them, the Zerg would eat this world alive. Or the Protoss—fatal chemotherapy—would sterilize it to keep the Zerg from spreading.

"But it doesn't work that way, does it?" said Mike to the comm unit. "A few cells always seem to escape, and the cancer keeps growing."

The fury he felt in his belly lasted only a moment, then was replaced with amazement as the next message rattled through his earpiece.

"*This is General Duke, calling from the Alpha Squadron flagship* Norad II*! We've crash-landed and are being hit hard by the Zerg! Request immediate backup from anyone receiving this signal! Repeat, this is a priority one distress call. This is General Duke. . . .*"

The distress call went into a loop, and Michael listened to it three more times before checking the other channels.

There were a couple calls asking for confirmation, and a plethora of other responses, describing attacks by the Zerg and Antigan rebels, and in one case, an assault by other Confederate forces. And there were now reports of Protoss ships in-system, fighting something themselves, probably Zerg similar to the ones that brought down the *Norad II*, out in the outer rim of ice worlds. There were even some reports of Protoss ground forces appearing. There was a lot of noise, but nothing that resembled an honest, solid offer of help.

He's cooked, thought Michael. *Old Duke's goose is finally cooked.*

Raynor stormed in about ten minutes later. "Mike, you're with me. Suit up."

"What's up?" Mike asked, reaching for his combat armor.

"You didn't hear the news in here?" Raynor looked as though lightning bolts would spring from his brow at any moment.

"The normal panic and despair," said Mike, waving at the board. "Oh, yeah. I heard Duke finally got promoted to general. Should we send a fruit basket?"

"Funny, newshound. Mengsk wants us to go in and rescue him. He thinks Duke would make a good ally."

Mike blinked at the captain. "I'm hearing things, right?"

"That's what I said," Raynor said, holding out Mike's helmet.

"He's crazy!"

"It's been noted," Raynor said grimly.

"And Mengsk wants *me* to go? It's news I can cover from here."

"*I* want you to come along. That bastard locked me and my boys up. I'm going to want someone there who he's willing to talk to."

"Did I mention that the last time I talked to him he had me forcibly ejected from his bridge?" said Mike, taking the helmet.

"It's come up, but at least I'm sure you're not going to shoot him right away."

Mike locked down the helmet and followed Raynor out of the comm area. "I suddenly have a craving for a cigarette."

"Maybe you can bum one off Duke."

Only when they were on the road did Mike think to ask, "Does Kerrigan know about this?"

"Uh-huh."

"And she thinks it's a good idea?"

"Actually," said the former lawman, "she's the one who called Mengsk crazy."

"So you two agreed on something. I'm amazed."

"Yeah," said Raynor. Then there was a pause. "Yeah, I guess we did."

Arcturus Mengsk was starting to rally troops now to his

banner, and when Raynor and Mike arrived on the surface, the assault to rescue the downed battlecruiser was already under way.

The units that barreled across the flats now included Antigan rebels, Sons of Korhal, and Confederate stragglers that had discarded their loyalties and kept their weapons. Raynor rode at the left flank of a flight of Vulture hover-cycles, while overhead a squadron of A-17 Wraith fighters tore through the sky. Huge Goliaths left great splayed footprints in the soft mud, and they soon overtook a unit of Arclite siege tanks, churning across the bottomlands, their support frames pulled up for movement.

The combined forces met resistance almost immediately. Zerglings and hydralisks spattered on all sides of them, like bugs on a windshield. The air was filled with both the organic cannons (now known to Mike and the rest of human space as mutalisks) and creatures that looked like jellyfish brains with lobster claws; they drifted over the alien forces like storm-clouds in the desert.

There was a cluster of marines off to Mike's right, swarming up the sides of what looked like a giant upright zergling, a titanic creature with front claws like huge, hooked sabers. On the horizon, something that looked like a cross between a flying squid and a giant starfish fled from the assault of the Wraith fighters.

They plowed through the Zerg forces, routing some, eliminating others. A group of zerglings erupted from the ground and took out a full unit of marines before the Vultures arrived and laid down a blanket of withering fire.

The Zerg fell back, returned in greater numbers, then fell back again. Mike felt he was fighting the sea. The waves were being beaten back, but he was sure that it was an illusion. The tide was coming in, and it would return in greater force.

In his gut Mike knew that Antiga Prime was damned, as damned as Chau Sara and Mar Sara had been. These things were burrowing through the heart of the world, and either they would be successful or the Protoss would burn them from space.

The Zerg line stiffened for a moment, then broke again, and the humans were through, heading for the uplands where the *Norad II* went down.

With one glance at the starship, Mike could see that the old behemoth would never fly again. Its rear engine pods had been twisted at a forty-five degree angle to the rest of the structure, and the lower landing struts, if they had even been deployed, had been mired totally in the mud. The ship's forward bridge hung precariously over the edge of the mesa, with a view of the devastation beneath it.

Mike and Raynor gunned their engines for an open hatchway and drove their Vultures on board. They sealed the hatch behind them manually, while outside another wave of muta-lisks popped up over the horizon.

"Which way?" asked Raynor, pulling off his helmet.

"Come on," said Mike, tearing off toward the bridge. He moved through the tight spaces of the *Norad II* effortlessly, despite his combat armor. He had noticed that Mengsk provided larger hallways on his ship than the Confederacy managed.

It was as if Duke had never left the bridge. The silverbacked gorilla was still hunched over his station in his armored hide. The only change was the number of screens around him that showed nothing but static, and a cascade of fiber-optic cables draped along one bulkhead. He turned to the newcomers and scowled.

"You're about the last folks I expected to show up," he growled.

"Yeah, we love you, too, General," said Mike, pushing his way to the ship's comm unit. He punched in the communication code for Mengsk's base.

"What's all this about?" Duke barked.

"A word from our sponsor," said Mike. "It feels like years since I last said that. Anyone got a cig?"

On the screen, the static-scarred form of Arcturus Mengsk formed. Mengsk, thought Mike, safe in his secret redoubt while the rest of us did the fighting and bleeding.

Mike didn't think it possible, but Duke's scowl deepened. "What's your angle, Mengsk?" he asked.

"Our angle?" Raynor snarled. "I'll give you an *angle,* you slimy Confederate piece of . . ."

"Easy, Jim," said Mike.

"In case you haven't noticed," said Mengsk, "the Confederacy is falling apart, Duke. Its colonies are in open revolt. The Zerg are rampaging unchecked. What would have happened here today if we hadn't shown up?"

"Your point?" Duke kept a stone face.

Mike checked the other screens. Another Wraith attack had dispersed the mutalisks, but the flying starfish looked to be made of tougher stuff.

"I'm giving you a choice," Mengsk said smoothly. "You can go back to the Confederacy and lose, or you can join us and help save our entire race from being overrun by the Zerg."

"You expect me to answer that?"

"I don't think it's a difficult decision." A small smile appeared beneath Mengsk's gray-spattered mustache.

"I'm a *general,* for God's sake," Duke exploded.

"Oh yeah," said Mike. "Congratulations. Shall we put it on your tombstone?"

"Michael, please," said Mengsk. "Duke, you're a general without an army. I'm offering you a position on my staff, in my cabinet, not just some backwater post where they shelved you before the war."

"I don't know . . ." said Duke, and Mike saw the warrior waver for a moment. Mengsk had him. Poor Duke, he had been hooked. He just didn't know it yet.

"Don't test my patience, Edmund," said Mengsk. Somewhere beyond the bulkheads, something exploded near the ship. Almost as if it had been planned to punctuate Mengsk's comment.

Duke held the moment for a decorous beat, then said, "All right, Mengsk. You've got a deal."

"You've made the right choice . . . *General* Duke," said Mengsk. "Captain Raynor?"

"Yes, sir?" Raynor was scowling now.

"Escort the general's supporters and equipment to a safe location." As Mengsk spoke, Duke enabled the ship's self-destruct. In twenty minutes they would be klicks away, and the *Norad II* would be a thermonuclear fireball.

"I hope it takes a lot of Zergs with it," said Mike, as the bridge started to clear very, very fast.

Later, Mike was back at Mengsk's communications center. With the explosion of the *Norad II*, there had been a lull in the fighting. Confederate troops, including the neurally resocialized ones, had switched sides easily with official permission, and now the only enemies to deal with were inhuman.

The downside was that there was no shortage of these.

Mike wrapped up a report on the *Norad II* rescue and shot it into the net. He leaned back and ran a hand through his hair. It felt thinner than before.

A pack of cigarettes, slightly crushed, dropped onto the console, followed by a foil container of matches. Raynor said, "One of the crew of the *Norad* says you're even now."

"Excellent," said Mike, drawing out a coffin nail.

"Sending another report to nowhere?"

"I thought Kerrigan was the mind reader. But yeah. Old habits die hard, though I have the fantasy that someone finds these reports years later and appreciates all the sacrifice of men and women against these things. And all the stupidity as well."

Raynor settled down into a chair across from him as Mike lit up. "Unlikely. Like Mengsk says, the victors write the histories. Losing memoirs are deleted like yesterday's data."

Mike took a deep draw and coughed, making a face. "What did they marinate these in, cat urine?"

Raynor raised his hands. "Best I could find, under the circumstances. Story of our lives."

"You betcha," said Mike. "Speaking of the uber-Mengsk, how did your talk with Arcturus go?"

"I told him that Duke was a snake." Raynor sighed. "And he said . . ."

"That he was *our* snake, right?"

Raynor shook his head in disbelief. "I believe in Mengsk's cause, that the Confederacy has to go, and he did get me out of stir, but, man. Some of the deals he's making. Some of the things he's asking us to do . . ."

"Don't go following causes," said Mike, taking a painful puff. "They'll just break your heart. When idealism meets reality, it's rarely reality that backs down. I've seen more good government types turn into political hacks than I've seen zerglings. And I've seen a lot of zerglings."

There was a silence between the two men. In the background the muted comm units spoke of mutalisks and Wraiths, of Goliaths and hydralisks, and the starfish things, which they were calling Zerg queens. And death. They spoke incessantly of death.

"I tell you I was married once?" Raynor volunteered.

The chasm of personal interaction yawned wide and deep at Mike's feet. "It hasn't come up," he said calmly, hoping that he was not expected to share back.

"Married. Had a kid. He was 'gifted,' they said."

"I heard the quotation marks around that. Gifted like in ghost material? Psionic powers? Telepathic?"

"Uh-huh. Sent him off to a special school. Government scholarship. A few months later, we got a letter. There had been an 'incident' at the school."

Mike had heard of such letters. They were unfortunately as common as grass when dealing with telepaths. Another of the Confederacy's dirty little secrets, rarely broadcast. "I'm sorry," Mike said, because that was all he could say.

"Yeah. Liddy never recovered. She just sort of wasted away, that winter she went down with the flu. And afterwards, I threw myself into my work. Found out I liked working alone."

"It's an easy trap to fall into, hiding in your work," said Mike, looking at the *transmit* light of his comm link, which meant his report was being sent out into the void.

"Anyway, I wanted you to know," said Raynor. "You may have thought I was being hard on Kerrigan for being a telepath. Maybe I was. But I have my reasons."

"She's got her own problems, you know. Like everybody else, and like no one you've ever met. You might want to cut her a little slack."

"It's kind of hard, when she knows what you're really thinking."

"Kerrigan seems to be a good soldier," said Mike, the image of her as a death-dealing dervish rising unbidden to his mind. "She may be wound a little tight, that's all."

"I think she's dangerous," said Raynor. "Dangerous to the troops around her. Dangerous to Mengsk. And dangerous to herself."

Mike shrugged, unsure how much he could comfortably reveal to the ex-marshal. He settled at last for "She's had a tough life."

"And we've had it easy so far?"

"All the more reason to keep an eye on her. Watch her back. Whether she knows it or not, though she probably will. We all need guardian angels."

The conversation shifted after that to questions of what worlds were in rebellion and what effect Duke's defection would have on other military leaders. Finally Raynor took his leave and abandoned Mike to the soft urgency of the communications room.

Mike looked at the half-empty pack of cigarettes. The taste of the first one was still pungent in his mouth.

"Hell," he said, reaching for the pack and the matches. "I guess, around here, you can learn to tolerate just about *anything*."

CHAPTER 11

CHESS

I played chess with Arcturus Mengsk. I lost regularly, by the way. Someday I'll probably be dragged before some high justice and told that this was a crime against the state, but I will have no defense. Other than losing more times than I won. More often than not, Mengsk would dangle some bait in front of me in a game, and I would snap at it, only to discover too late that I had been distracted from the trap he was setting.

The entire human campaign against the Zerg was similar, consisting of a series of defeats, each one more galling than the last because each time we ignored what was really going on. Our first warning that the Zerg were planetside came usually too late, when the creep appeared at our doorsteps or the Protoss warped in with the thunder-god ships.

We thought we could escape it. Some of us, including Mengsk himself, thought we could control it. But we were all pawns in a greater game.

No, not pawns. Dominos. Each falling in turn, planet after planet, person after person, until we reached the biggest domino of them all, the one called Tarsonis.

—THE LIBERTY MANIFESTO

"THE COMPARISON HAS BEEN MADE BETWEEN WAR and chess," said Arcturus Mengsk, forking his knight to threaten both Mike's queen and his bishop.

"You're very good at both," said Mike, moving his queen to take Mengsk's rook.

"Actually, I find the comparison to be false," said the terrorist, moving his knight to take the bishop. "Checkmate, by the way."

Mike blinked at the board. Mengsk's strategy was obvious now, in the same way that it had been totally opaque mere seconds before. The reporter mentally kicked himself and reached for his brandy snifter. In the background, the lost tunes of ancient Miller and Goodman warbled out of the comm unit. The ashtray to one side of the board was filled with butts, all of them Mike's. They smelled faintly of cat urine.

They were on board the *Hyperion*, resting in a hidden hanger on Antiga Prime. Duke was off reorganizing the rebel troops into something that was more Confederate in nature. Raynor was off trying to keep Duke from making a complete mess of things. Mike had no idea where Kerrigan was, but that was normal for Kerrigan.

"Chess is not like war?" Mike asked.

"Once, perhaps, it was," said Mengsk. "On Old Earth, back in the mists of time. Two equal opponents, with equal forces, on a level playing field."

"And that's not the case. Not anymore."

"Hardly," said the terrorist, warming to his own discussion. "First, the opponents are hardly ever truly even. The Confederacy of Man had Apocalypse-class missiles and my homeworld did not; the Confederacy played that card until Korhal IV was a blackened glass sphere hanging in space. Hardly even. Similarly, our little rebellion seemed at first to be undermanned and underfunded, but with each new revolt the Confederacy loses more of its will to fight. It is ancient and rotten, and all it needs is a good push to cave it in. You don't see that in chess.

"Second," Mengsk continued, "is the idea of equal forces. I mentioned the missiles, so effective in my father's time, yet mere pinpricks in the light of the forces being wielded today. Forces continue to evolve—nukes, telepaths, now Zerg being raised by the Confederacy."

"War is supposed to increase development," said Mike.

"Yes, but most people use the guns and armor analogy: one side gets a better gun, the other side gets better armor, which inspires a still-better gun, and so on. The truth is that a better gun inspires a chemical counterweapon, which then inspires a telepathic strike, which then brings about an artificial intelligence guiding the weapon. The pressure of war does bring about growth, but it is never the neat, linear growth that you learn about in the classroom."

"Or read about in the papers."

Mengsk smiled. "Third is the idea of a level playing field. The chessboard is limited to an eight-by-eight grid. There is nothing beyond this little universe. No ninth rank. No green pieces that suddenly sweep onto the board to attack both black and white. No pawns that suddenly become bishops."

"A pawn can become a queen," Mike noted.

"But only by advancing through all the spaces of its row, under fire the entire time. It doesn't suddenly blossom into a queen by its own volition. No, chess is nothing like war, which is one of the reasons I play it. It's so much simpler than real life."

Not for the first or last time, Mike thought about Mengsk's almost-supernatural ability to warp reality around himself. "You think that the Confederacy is going to be able to come up with a weapon against these latest attacks? Against the Protoss and the Zerg?"

"Unlikely, though they are pulling out all the stops. Doing what they do best right now: propaganda and silencing those who speak out. Those are their best weapons, and they have never hesitated to use them before. But they're just throwing spitwads at a bull elephant that's bearing down on them. Hang on, I've got something here I wanted to show you." Mengsk pressed numerous buttons on a remote control. He stared at it, as if trying to remember a secret code.

"I thought you once said that the Confederacy was breeding the Zerg. Doesn't that make the Zerg their weapons?" Mike asked.

"Originally I thought so as well." Mengsk pressed a few more buttons, then paused. "And though I may be incorrect in the assumption, as far as *our* propaganda is concerned, that's our story, and we're sticking with it. Nothing undermines faith in the government faster than realizing that they've been developing deadly alien menaces in their spare time."

"But the truth really is?" Mike prompted.

"The truth is as malleable as ever." Mengsk grinned. "Yes, the Confederacy has been studying the Zerg for years, and the ones in the Sara system were deliberately brought there by Confederate agents. Yes, they were a big weapons test. But no, they didn't create the Zerg. No, they had a much worse plan in mind. It was on those disks that you and Raynor brought back from the Jacobs Installation. Here we go. You'll appreciate this."

He hit a button, and the screen sprang to scratchy life. When the distortion had cleared, Mike could see a string of low buttes and mesas beneath an orange-brown sky. The scene could have been anywhere on Antiga Prime. The familiar UNN logo perched along one side, and multiplanetary stock prices crawled across the bottom of the screen.

Then a frighteningly familiar voice spoke over the panorama. "This is Michael Liberty, reporting from Antiga Prime."

Mike blinked. That was his voice, part of his last transmission out. But he had never sent this particular footage. Had they pulled it from a file somewhere?

The camera continued to pan, then settled on the speaker. He was dressed in a neat duster (much neater than the one that currently hung in Mike's locker), his blond hair pulled back to cover a bald spot, his features hard-chiseled and experienced, his eyes deep and soulful.

It was Michael Liberty, but not Mike. This Michael Liberty looked almost like an idealized version of Mike himself.

The figure on the screen continued. "This reporter has just escaped captivity at the hands of the infamous terrorist Arcturus Mengsk. I was captured on Mar Sara by the rebels shortly before the reptilian Protoss destroyed the planet, and have only made it to safety now."

"That's not me," said Mike.

"I know," said Mengsk. "And the Protoss aren't reptiles, as far as we know. But keep watching."

"During my captivity I learned that Mengsk and the Sons of Korhal are in control of powerful mind-control drugs, which they have been using freely on the populace," continued the flat-screen Mike Liberty. "Hundreds have died as a result of indiscriminate spraying, which can only be described as chemical attacks against innocent citizens. Others have been warped into strange mutagenic shapes as a result of side effects of these drugs."

Mengsk made a rude noise, but the figure on the screen continued. "Mengsk sent a saboteur aboard the *Norad II* and exposed the crew to a virulent toxin. The result was the recent crash of that ship. Agents of the Sons of Korhal captured those affected by the mind-control drugs, and left the rest to die at the hands of their Zerg allies."

"Zerg allies? Who's writing that crap?" Mike snapped at the screen.

"It *is* much of muchness," Mengsk said calmly. "Laying it on a bit thick and all."

"I believe that General Edmund Duke, scion of the Duke Family of Tarsonis, has fallen prey to these mind-control devices, and now has been reduced to a mentally reprogrammed zombie in the service of the terrorists. In this way Mengsk and his inhuman allies hope to confuse the brave warriors of the Confederacy and cause them to lose faith in their leaders."

"Brave warriors of the . . . I used that line in a filler piece I did on the *Norad II*!" said Mike. "And the bit about 'virulent toxins.' That rings another bell."

"Groundwater pollution outside a middle school," said Mengsk. "One of your better early pieces, if I remember right."

"Only by eternal vigilance can we root out such terrorists as Mengsk and his mind-controlled minions," said the figure on the screen. "As I speak a massive Confederate blockade is surrounding Antiga Prime, and the terrorist should be destroyed within a few days. This is Michael Daniel Liberty for UNN."

Mengsk hit another button. Michael Daniel Liberty froze into silence on the screen.

"Did you see that!?" Mike shouted, jumping up from his seat. "That wasn't me!"

"I hope not," Mengsk said with a calm grin. "You seem like such a rational and truthful reporter, most of the time."

"What did they do?"

"You've never been edited before?" Mengsk raised an eyebrow.

"Of course!" Mike snapped, then added quickly, "I mean for time, or if the facts couldn't be confirmed, or the legal department had a problem, or a sponsor raised a stink. I mean, I've had things cut before, and sometimes they've slid in images that took the tone of the story in a different direction. But this is a . . . a . . ."

"Lie?"

"Fabrication," Mike said, frowning.

"Indeed. Clipped together from bits of previous reporting, using another actor as a stand-in, a shuffling of pixels. Mind you, it's easy enough on a flat screen—damned impossible with a true hologram. That's why I prefer the latter, you know. This is just enough to fool someone just catching the news, to remind them that you're alive and well and fighting the good fight for UNN and the Confederacy."

"But my reports . . ." Mike sputtered.

"Grist that they took apart and reassembled as they saw fit."

Mike slouched back into his chair. "I'm going to *kill* Anderson."

"Your Anderson may already be dead, I'm afraid," said the terrorist. "If he's as devoted a reporter as you."

Mike snorted.

"Or," Mengsk reconsidered, "he may be acquiescing to the current power structure, though he knows it's a horrible idea. Maybe that's why the 'toxic poisons' line is in there—a bit of internal sabotage, a desperate cry for help. I mean, it doesn't make a whole lot of sense: Why would mind-control drugs be poisons? Of course, it did let them lift an entire sentence verbatim."

"Yeah, that's a shortcut Handy Anderson would take."

"I just wanted you to know that your own network has turned its back on you. I didn't want you to find out at a bad time. Like on the battlefield, for example." Mengsk refilled Mike's snifter.

"But why this?"

"Propaganda is a weapon that the Confederacy wields best, and wields heaviest. It is their hammer. And when all you have is a hammer, then everything looks like a nail."

"You'd think they'd have better weapons than a reporter to throw at you," Mike muttered. He shook his head at the screen. "What happened to all their Zerg research, the material we got out of that installation?"

"Ah." Mengsk hit another series of buttons. "The Jacobs disk. I'm glad you remembered that—it shows that my mind-control drugs have not had a complete effect on you. Don't look at me that way, it was meant as a joke."

"I'm a little sensitive about that right now. It'll pass."

"I expected weapons data—something to keep them ahead of the technological curve. Instead I found something much more interesting. Here we go. You know about ghosts, of course."

Mike thought of Kerrigan, the merciless fighter who felt the death of each of her victims. "Telepathic warriors. A specialty of the Confederates, and an example of your technological curve."

"An interesting example, if I may digress. The original inhabitants of the colony ships were Earth people, but the long voyage apparently put a twist in their genetic code, enough to bring out more psionic abilities than were common in the original Terran populace. An interesting happenstance."

"I think we've both gotten to the point where we don't believe in happenstance." Mike took a pull on his brandy.

Mengsk gave a good-natured shrug. "By design or accident, the humans of what would become the Confederacy tended toward psychic abilities. Again, through design or accident, we found this out and created the ghosts—superior assassins with mind-reading powers. It's a horrible process—only a few children make it out of the process in any usable state. And, until recently, the Confederate's control over them seemed unbreakable."

"Lieutenant Sarah Kerrigan. How did you break their control over her?"

"That's a case where one side gets better armor, and the other side gets a bigger gun," Mengsk said with a smile. "Suffice it to say that the control over her was broken, and broken in such a way that she was left amazingly intact and generally useful."

"And grateful."

"And grateful," Mengsk admitted. "And she has appeared often enough that the Confederates are in a tizzy about it."

"Which suits you just fine," said Mike. "But you were busy digressing?"

"Yes. Now we get to the Jacobs disk. It turns out that our pestilent friends the Zerg are attuned to psychic emanations. Apparently the wavelengths that the ghosts function on are similar to those that the higher-level Zerg use to control the lesser ones. So they can zero in on them at close range."

"How close?" Mike asked, thinking suddenly of Kerrigan's activities in the Sara and Antiga systems.

"For a normal telepath, very, very close. Tens of yards at best. By that time a hydralisk can smell them anyway. But that's part of the technology the Confederates have used in their tower defenses and other anti-ghost detectors."

"Guns and armor. Can the ghosts read Zerg minds like they do humans'?"

"It's much more painful. And yes, the Confederates tried. They came away with the idea that the Zerg are an ultimate evolutionary success story: everything is either genetic material for their creations or meat to be fed to their children. They operate off a hierarchy of hive minds, each greater than the ones below it, growing up to near-planetary consciousnesses."

"Sounds appealing." Mike took another long sip of his brandy. It burned the back of his throat and reminded him he was human.

"Nasty. The Protoss are as bad," said Mengsk. "Mind you, this is all from the Zerg viewpoint that's recorded on the disks, but the Protoss are the ultimate genetic purists. They see themselves as the judges of the universe, eradicating any life that gets out of hand and does not meet their standard of perfection."

"Genetic Survivors versus Genetic Xenophobes. A match made in hell."

"Very much so. So the Confederates discover the Zerg and discover the telepathic attraction. They want more Zerg available."

"More? Why in the name of God would they want more?"

"The nonlinear nature of war, son. They were looking for a weapon with all the advantages of nukes and none of the downside, like radiation or bad press. The Zergs were perfect—they were ugly-buggy aliens that the Confederates could unleash on anyone, and then come in afterwards and eliminate. A pocket plague of monsters."

"You said you thought they were breeding them."

"And I was wrong about that," Mengsk said smoothly, "Breeding them is much more complex than just capturing a bunch of zerglings and putting them in the same cage. So they needed to lure more into their traps, and that's where the telepaths came in."

"But the telepaths have limited range."

"Yes," Mengsk agreed. "So they worked on improving that range. What you pulled out of the Jacobs Installation was the plans for a Transplanar Psionic Waveform Emitter. Nice name, and fairly self-descriptive. With it they could boost the power of a telepath and make it an interplanetary beacon for the Zerg, drawing them in like moths to a lantern."

Mike was silent for a moment, then said, "The Sara system."

"Exactly. That's what I mean when I say they were using those planets as a testing ground for their weapons. They brought the Zerg to Sara, and the Protoss came after them. But they brought more than just a couple zerglings—they brought the whole Zerg ecosystem and power structure into play, which they *didn't* expect. And now the Zerg are moving from system to system at will, directed by their own intelligence, intent on either transforming humanity or consuming it."

"So you know how to defeat them?" Mike asked.

"Other than blasting each and every one of them into bits and burning their nests, no." Mengsk leaned forward. "But I do know how to send them in the directions I want them to go."

"How does that help?" Mike shook his head. Had the brandy made him suddenly stupid?

Mengsk leaned back. "There was one piece of truth in that news report your doppelgänger delivered. There is a serious blockade forming around Antiga. The Confederates are hoping to keep us penned up until either the Zerg or the Protoss destroy us."

"And we're just sitting here?"

"No. I'm already doing something. We built an emitter, based on the plans you liberated. We're going to take it into the heart of Confederate territory and set it off. Every Zerg from as far away as ten light-years is going to come here. They're going to fall among the blockaders like falcons on doves. The crash of the *Norad II* will be a simple fender bender in comparison."

"But the emitter will only amplify. You need a telepath to . . ." The final circuit closed in Mike's brain. "Kerrigan. You're going to use Kerrigan to bring in the Zerg."

"Very good."

"You can't do that!" Mike objected. "You want her to break into a Confederate camp? They'll have detectors. She'll never make it!"

"I have a high degree of confidence in the lieutenant."

"You can't do that!" Mike repeated.

"You have your tense wrong. I gave the orders for the operation before we sat down for our first game. The good lieutenant should be picking up the emitter in the shops below right about now. If you hurry, you can catch up with her."

Mike cursed and launched himself from his seat.

"And wish her luck from me!" Mengsk shouted at Mike's back as the reporter bolted out of the terrorist leader's quarters. Then Mengsk leaned back, lifted his own brandy snifter, and offered a silent toast to the frozen figure of the false Michael Liberty on the screen.

CHAPTER 12

BELLY OF THE BEAST

Aliens were pressing in on human space, and the humans reacted by turning on one another. I can only imagine what the Zerg and the Protoss thought as they landed on planets that consisted of nothing but rebels and Confederates whaling the tar out of each other. They probably thought it was the normal behavior pattern for our race. And I suppose they would be right.

Mengsk's successes, spread in part by bootleg copies of my own reports, sparked dozens of brushfire wars. Every crank with a gripe took up arms against the ancient Confederate regime. The Confederacy in turn reacted as it always had to armed dissent—with harsher and harsher oppression that in turn spawned other revolts.

And through it all, the Zerg were infiltrating more planets, and the Protoss were turning them to dead lumps. The humans didn't have so many worlds that they could afford to lose them at this clip. If the two sides had been thinking, they would have joined forces to fight the true menace.

I think everybody was so busy planning and fighting that no one really had time to think.

—THE LIBERTY MANIFESTO

"KERRIGAN!" MIKE SHOUTED IN THE LANDING BAY. The lieutenant was just putting on her helmet. He had no time for armor, but he did grab his duster.

"Liberty," she said grimly. Mike saw a large device mounted to the side of her Vulture bike. "I'm just heading out."

"Ride shotgun?"

"Look, normally I'd . . ." she began, then looked at Mike with her deep jade-green eyes. The hairs on the back of Mike's neck stood up, and he knew that she knew.

Her too-wide lips twitched for a moment. Then she shook her head and said, "It's your funeral. I'll need someone to lug the gear anyway. Come on."

The pair roared out of the hangar, making for the rendez-vous point.

Antiga Prime had suffered under the relentless assault. The sky was darker now from the smoke of continuous pyres, and the great bloated figure of the world's gas giant primary hung like a sorrowful god behind a shroud of mourning. In the distance there was the thunder of Arclite artillery, though who was firing, and who they were firing at, was unknown.

They passed abandoned bunkers, cracked open like egg-shells, surrounded by the partially buried detritus of war: broken weapons and shattered men. The thunder grew louder, and Liberty realized they were heading into the heart of the storm.

"We've got siege tanks and Goliaths," Kerrigan said over the comm link, "trying to punch a hole in their lines. We slip through and into Confederate territory. Regret coming now?"

"Maybe a little." Mike knew that the ghost knew his answer even before he spoke.

"So Mengsk gave you the whole song and dance," she continued. Mike frowned, concerned that the telepath was rummaging through his thoughts so easily. "Got you to come along."

"Check my mental replay again, Lieutenant," said Mike. "Mengsk never asked me to go."

"He didn't have to. He knows the buttons to press on people. Probably he felt that if he ordered you to come help, you'd probably just dump him then and there."

"He's probably right."

"He usually is. That's why it's probably a good idea you're along."

Up ahead, a pile of boulders vaporized in a massive explosion. Kerrigan brought the cycle up short.

"That shouldn't happen," she said. "Our siege tanks know we're coming this way. Did Duke screw up his artillery spotting on purpose, or . . ."

Mike heard the whistling of another set of incoming rounds. "It's their tanks!" he shouted. "They've broken through *our* lines!"

Kerrigan gunned the engine the moment he said it, tearing the Vulture at a sharp angle to its original course of travel. The road ahead vanished in a crescendo of flying earth and rock as another round tracked closer. The shattered earth was too much for the limited grav units, and the entire bike shook.

"It's a bit—" Mike began.

"Sorry for the rough ride," Kerrigan snapped over the comm link. "Just hang on!"

Next time let me finish my sentence, thought Mike, and felt Kerrigan shrug on the bike.

The Confederates must have had a spotter. The missile fire tracked them mercilessly, staying about a hundred yards behind them. Kerrigan took them into a ravine that had long since lost anything that looked like water.

"Let's see them follow in here," she said.

Mike heard the high-pitched whine of metal slicing through air, "Wraiths!" he yelled into the comm link.

The fighter spacecraft came in low and hard, blasting both sides of the ravine with their 25-millimeter burst-lasers. The scrub was incinerated at a touch, and the fighters pulled up, unable to see their prey through the smoke they had generated.

"They're herding us," Kerrigan's voice crackled over the comm link. "But to where?"

The ground beneath the hover-cycle suddenly changed in texture, from red clays and brownish slates to a mottled clumping of gray-black moss.

"Creep!" said Mike, as soon as he had recognized it. "They're herding us into Zerg territory!"

Kerrigan cursed and threw on the brakes, but the creep beneath the grav-fields provided no traction for the bike's transducer coils. The thin bike started to fishtail, then skewed horribly to one side, plowing up a thick crust of the creep like foam on a wave.

Mike shouted, and Kerrigan yelled something. The reporter clutched the container of the psi emitter, half hoping that it would provide some protection. He was sure that if anyone could get them through this, it would be the ghost lieutenant.

Then the ground opened up beneath them, and they both tumbled into the darkness.

Sometime later, Mike heard Kerrigan's voice, as if from a distance, "Liberty?"

"Urg," was the best Mike could reply. *Hell, she can read my mind, let her read this.*

"Is the psi emitter all right?" she asked.

"Oh yeah. I cushioned its fall with my body."

He opened his eyes and discovered he was lying in soft, recently churned earth. That must have been what broke their fall as they pitched down the rabbit hole.

He looked up. There was a jagged hole in the ceiling, probably where they tore through the creep matting. Already the thick webbing was reknitting across the opening.

Mike spat out some blood. He had bitten the inside of his mouth in the fall. The rest of his body seemed battered but generally unharmed. His duster was caked with soft earth. He would feel the bruises tomorrow.

If I'm lucky, he thought.

"If we're both lucky," said Kerrigan. She was already on her feet, sweeping the area with a wrist-mounted light. She had slung her canister rifle over her shoulder.

Mike stood up, and found himself wobbling but unhurt. "Y'all right?" he managed.

"Not bad," said the ghost. "I landed on my pride, which is, I'm afraid, a lost cause. Had to shoot it, put it out of its misery. We're patsies. Fools. Mooks. Rubes."

"No one expected the Confederates—" Mike began.

"To use the terrain and situation to their advantage? Exactly. Which is why we're patsies. They came out to meet our attack, and then flushed us into the one place we don't want to be."

"You know, this would be easier if you—"

"Let you finish your sentences. Sorry. Nervous habit right now. You're practically broadcasting your fear, and that's irritating *me.*"

Like anybody wouldn't be afraid in this situation, Mike thought, walking over to the remains of the Vulture bike.

"The bike is shot," Kerrigan said, without looking, and of course she was right. The frame was bent in three places, so that the long, lean vehicle had been turned into a twisted corkscrew. Something important had been punctured and was leaking into the ground. The bike, in spite of all its metal and shaped ceramic, had taken the fall worse than he had.

"This way," said Kerrigan, pointing sharply one way along the corridor.

"Any clue why?"

"No, but something large and foul-thinking is in the other direction. You get to carry the emitter."

Mike hoisted the emitter in its container and followed. He thought about the lieutenant's mood. After a few minutes Kerrigan said, "It's a feedback loop."

"Stop *doing* that."

"But it is. Your fear is sent to me, and I'm in turn taking it out on you. Which increases *your* anger." She paused for a moment. "Something's real strange here. Wrong. I can handle this kind of thing normally. Most of the time."

Mike thought of the Zerg's supposed connection with telepaths, then wished he hadn't.

Kerrigan's too-wide lips twisted in a grim smile. "Yeah, I know. Raynor already gave me grief about it at the briefing with Arcturus, thank you very much. It does explain the Confederacy's interest in telepaths. And also there have been a lot of MIAs among the Confederate telepaths. Even outside the ghost units, I hear things."

"Think the Zerg are collecting their own telepath subjects?" Mike asked, then realized that Kerrigan had let him finish his sentence.

"Uh-huh. Hang on, something's up ahead." She pulled out her side arm and edged forward, her other hand, the one with the wristlight, pointing ahead.

The something was hanging across the passageway like a great spider. Her light flashed against it, and it shrank away from the beam. It was a great eye, human in appearance, its pupil contracting under the harshness of the wristlight's beam.

Mike felt a wave of revulsion and nausea sweep over him. Apparently Kerrigan felt it as well, and her emotions were compounded through Mike's mind. She let out a loud curse and fired a short burst into the twitching orb.

The eye-thing let out a screech that sounded like glass and blew apart, the muscular strands of its web peeling back toward the wall like broken rubber bands.

"What was—?" Mike began.

"Observer? Sentry?" Kerrigan guessed, and for the first time Mike caught a bit of fear in the unshakable Sarah Kerrigan's voice. Feedback loop, he reminded himself. He willed himself to calm down. Otherwise they would get themselves killed.

"What does it feel like?" he asked, as they edged past the shredded meat of the eye-thing. Mike noticed that there was creep along the floors and walls of the passage.

"What?" said Kerrigan, distracted by the ichor.

"You said it felt strange down here. Strange?"

Kerrigan was silent for a moment, and Mike felt she was trying to regain her emotional strength. "It's tough to describe to a hard-shell, sorry, a nontelepath. It's like you're in a hotel hallway and there's a party in one of the rooms. As you pass it, you hear that there's a party, but it's not yours. You don't make out anything distinct, but there's a babble of voices. That's what it feels like."

"Maybe psionic power on a different channel?" Mike suggested.

"Maybe, but it's larger. Like standing on a street outside a theater where there's a concert. You hear something organized, but all you make out is blather. It's maddening." She paused for a moment. "Oh my God. Mike, come here."

The passage opened out to the right, into a larger cavern, before continuing upward. Mike could feel fresher air on his face from the passage across the way. They must be near the surface.

The larger cavern was filled with creep. Vague pouches hung from the walls, and things that might have been organs dotted the grayish fungus. Along the wall was a scattering of centipedelike creatures moving among a field of toadstools.

"Maggots," said Mike. "I saw them at Anthem Base, on Mar Sara." He shot an image of the bar there to Kerrigan, and noticed her shudder. "Is this a garbage dump for the Zerg? What are they eating?"

"They're not eating. They're nursemaids. They're tending the eggs."

What Mike had first thought of as toadstools were really eggs, green with reddish speckles, that sat on stands of piled creep. The eggs pulsed with their own heartbeats. As Mike watched, the skeletal face of a hydralisk appeared beneath the murky surface of the nearest egg, like a drowned creature in a tidal pool. The egg quivered a little, as if the beast within knew of their presence.

The maggots were busy building up piles of the creep. Then one climbed the pile, curled in on itself, and wove a thick spider-silk cocoon around itself. The cocoon hardened, and the maggot became an egg.

"Crap," said Mike, suddenly realizing what the maggots were.

"Larvae. They're the basic building units of the Zerg. Larvae to eggs to monsters. That's why the Confederates never got anywhere breeding the suckers, despite what Mengsk said. The zerglings and hydralisks *can't* breed—they all come from the same genetic stock, served up to order from some higher power."

Mike nodded, and the hydralisk face in the egg turned toward him. The egg started to vibrate violently as the beast within tried to force itself out.

"Head toward the fresh air," said Kerrigan, unslinging her canister rifle. "I'll be along in a moment."

Grunting under the load of the emitter, Mike continued up the corridor. When he heard the whirring noise of the canister rifle's feed and the sliding ratchet of its pump action, he started running. Behind him now was the hammering chatter of the rifle's sharp-tipped bullets strafing the egg chamber. Then there was silence.

The air grew fresher, and he saw natural light up ahead. Mike's legs felt like lead weights, but he forced them forward. Ten more yards, then five, then two. Then up to the surface, into the early-evening air, and . . .

Face-to-face with his reflection in the mirrored surface of a Confederate marine's combat visor. Despite himself, Mike yelped and almost fell backward. A sentry from the Confederate forces was posted at the entrance.

The sentry lumbered a step toward the reporter, and Mike realized that something was wrong with the man. His knees were bent oddly, and his arms seemed to belong to separate entities. One hand raised a gauss rifle uncertainly, while the other touched something at the base of its armor.

The mirrored visor slid back to reveal a face from hell. Half of it had been eaten away to the yellow-stained skull, which oozed a thick grayish creep from a useless eyehole. The other half, the greenish shade of rot, was studded with rocklike extrusions that broke the skin like short daggers.

It was a sentry, but not for the Confederates. It had once been human, but not now. It had once been sane, but not now. Now it only lived to protect the nest. It brought up its gauss rifle and let out a cry as if coins were caught in its throat. The creature's good eye seemed to weep blood.

Mike heard the whine of the canister rifle behind him and threw himself to the ground, twisting to cushion the emitter as he toppled. An instant later the air where he had been was filled with live rounds. A few of the rounds shredded the edge of his coat.

The transformed Confederate sentry was transfixed by the rifle fire, but only for a moment. Then its gauss rifle slowly spilled from its hand and it fell backward, its armor in tatters. What lay beneath the armor was no longer human, but it reacted to the canister shot in the same fashion.

Kerrigan ran up and tugged hard on Mike's collar. "Are you okay?"

Spots danced in front of Mike's eyes, but he refused to succumb to the bitter bile rising in his throat. "What *was* that?"

"The Zerg are master biologists. That's probably what they want to do with humanity. Turn it into another experiment. Another servant race."

Mike took a deep breath, looking at the lacerated, rotting meat, and said, "It doesn't look like a successful experiment."

Kerrigan gave an exhausted shrug. "Maybe if they had better material to work with. You volunteering? I'm sure they need a reporter." She managed a tight, chiding grin, and despite himself, Mike let out a chuckle.

Breaking the feedback loop, he thought. Foxhole jokes. Gallows humor in the face of the obscenity of war.

If Kerrigan read those thoughts, she did not let on. "Feel like running for a while?" she asked.

"How far?"

"As far as we can."

"You start, I'll follow," said Mike, hoisting the emitter in front of him.

They were lucky. They were on the edge of the creep. Yet even from their vantage point Mike could see a line of towers in the direction opposite their line of travel. They looked like great, misshapen flowers from some giant's garden, and the cannonlike mutalisks danced among them. There were other flying monsters as well, including the starfish squids, the lobster-jellyfishes, and the great flying crabs.

"They're winning," said Mike. "The Zerg. They're getting more powerful every damned planet they take over."

"Try not to think about it." Kerrigan touched her wrist. "I just sent out a short pulse-message. If Arcturus is listening, at least he'll know we're still alive."

Travel was easy now, for even as the sun set there was strong reflected light from the gas giant above. To their left there were more flashes along the horizon, and the sound of distant thunder.

"You say you heard about other ghosts going MIA. You hear from them?" Mike asked.

Kerrigan's lips made a firm line, and she shook her head. "Most telepaths avoid one another. I don't even talk to the ones in Duke's command. It's bad enough being around the continual chatter of normal people. Being with another telepath is a hundred times worse. People can't control their thoughts, at least not very well. Ghosts read other ghosts very well, and form their own feedback loops. Most need psionic dampers to keep them sane. That's like the neural resocialization, but much, much worse."

"But you don't have any psionic dampers."

"I still have some, but most of them are gone. Arcturus . . ." She paused for a moment, then said, "You don't like him, you know."

"Never would have guessed. But you think the world of him."

"He . . ." She paused again. "He broke me out; I guess that's the best way to put it. He rescued me, freed me, broke me of the dampers and the guards and the horror. I owe him my life. More important, I owe him my soul."

As if in response to her comment, the comm link beeped. Mike scanned the horizon for movement. Nothing. Kerrigan popped open a small screen, and Mike could envision Mengsk's smiling face there.

"Good to know you're alive," said the rebel leader. "Your position puts you a klick south of where you need to be. No bogeys between you and the Confederate camp. We're drawing off their reserves."

"We were delayed," said Kerrigan. "The Zerg. There are a lot of them already here."

"And there will be more when you set off our little surprise. They'll keep our Confederate friends busy while we escape."

A frown crossed Kerrigan's features. "They'll be wiped out, Arcturus." Static crossed the line. "Arcturus? Do you read? The Zerg don't take prisoners."

"Kerrigan!" said Mengsk, and Mike could imagine the stern-father look on the terrorist's face. "We didn't invent the emitters, but if we don't use them, we will all die, blockaded by the Confederates. And if we die, all hope of humanity dies with us."

"Yes, sir."

"Remember how much I trust you. And say hello to Mr. Liberty for me, eh?"

Kerrigan closed the screen and turned north. Mike picked up the emitter and followed.

Mike was silent for a while, then said, "I think they're afraid."

"Who? The people in charge of the ghosts?"

"Yeah. They don't want you to be able to communicate your experiences to other telepaths. Conspire against them. That's why the psionic dampers and the training."

Kerrigan shrugged. "That's likely. I think it's also to keep their investments in one piece. The casualty rate is incredibly high among the ghosts."

"I thought you'd be lionized, after all that investment. Like Wraith pilots or destroyer captains."

Kerrigan let out a horrible laugh. "Lionized? God, even the child molesters they put in the marines get better treatment than we do. The criminals in the marines are just medicated and indoctrinated to follow their leaders. We're given the living nightmare of pushing against our restraints constantly, knowing that if we break them, we'll spin out into insanity because we can't keep others' minds out of our own."

"Easy, Lieutenant. I didn't mean—"

"Of course you didn't mean anything," Kerrigan said hotly. "That's what drives us crazy. Your words mean one thing, but your mind's broadcasting something completely different. Raynor's all gung-ho, but I can feel his unease, his disgust. And I know he's watching, even when my back's turned. It's knowing what's on the tip of everyone's mind without being able to respond."

"I'm sorry."

"I know," said Kerrigan, softening a little. "That's one of the things I *do* like about you, Michael Liberty. You're all surface. Don't take that the wrong way. You think of something, and you say it. Your only defense is when you're asking questions, playing the hard-nosed reporter. It makes you easier to tolerate than most humans."

She paused for a moment as they crested a hill. In the distance rose the ruined towers of the Confederates' outer perimeter. There was no fire from the towers; Mengsk's troops had drawn them off.

"You know what the final exam is to get into ghost training?" she asked suddenly. Mike shook his head, knowing better than to interrupt.

"They have a guard with a gun," she said, and her eyes seemed to mist over. She herself was elsewhere. "The guard takes the gun and presses it against your forehead, or the forehead of someone you care about. You have to kill the guard before he pulls the trigger." Her eyes refocused, and she looked at Mike hard. "I was twelve at the time."

Mike blanched, and despite himself, thought of Raynor's son. The "gifted" child who had experienced an "incident."

Kerrigan reacted as if Mike had slapped her. She sank to one knee and gripped her forehead with her hand. After a while she said, "Christ."

Mike said quickly, "I'm sorry. I didn't mean to tell you, it just slipped out."

"Christ," she repeated. "I should have guessed. I just didn't know."

Mike shook his head. "You're a telepath. How can you not know?"

Kerrigan looked up, and there were tears at the corners of her eyes. "Telepaths don't dig down into your thoughts, at least if they want to stay sane. We hear all the surface chatter, all the stuff that's on the top. What you're thinking about. Errant thoughts. Whether that woman has a nice set of legs. All the stupid crap. Not the stuff they keep buried. Not the important crap." She was silent for a moment, then asked, "He say when it happened?"

Mike shook his head and turned away, partly to keep an eye out for Confederate patrols, partly to give the lieutenant a chance to pull herself together.

She probably knew that, but when Mike turned back she was on her feet and her eyes were dry. "Let's plant this thing. Base of one of those towers should do it."

They reached the shell of the gun emplacement without difficulty, and Mike surrendered the burden he had been lugging for the past few kilometers. With deft, practiced hands, Kerrigan began setting up the psi emitter that she had never handled before. Mike realized that she must have gotten the instructions in a burst of telepathy when she picked up the device.

It was a lash-up, and it took a few minutes for the lieutenant to uncoil all the packing material and check all the leads. Then she pulled out what looked like a starfish-shaped headset and placed it on her head. A crown of delicate copper filigree was lost among her red tresses.

"The transplanar psionic waveform emitter," explained Kerrigan, "is like the sound box of a violin. It will capture, amplify, and then propagate the psychic beacon that is fed into it. That's why we're here—it needs a ghost to activate it."

She flipped a few switches, pressed a toggle, and then took off the headset. Her face looked strained. "Okay. Let's go."

"That's it?"

"You wanted an airhorn and bright light? A chime from above? Or a big clock with a countdown? Sorry." Kerrigan's face was ashen now, and Mike suddenly realized that, even though he couldn't feel it, Kerrigan could, and it was getting "louder" all the time.

"Right," Kerrigan said. "Let's go."

Mike and Kerrigan headed along the line of abandoned tower emplacements, each one a shattered monument to the battle of Antiga Prime. She had to pause, wincing from the unheard noise. It was as if she could hear nails on a chalkboard, a grating sound that Mike was deaf to.

They made it to the fourth tower, where the pain seemed to ease. By the sixth tower she was almost normal again. She popped open the small screen on her wrist. "Psi emitter in place," she said.

Mengsk's unseen face said, "Excellent, Sarah, I knew you could do it. We've got to get you out before every Zerg on Antiga gets there. Dropship en route."

"I know," Kerrigan said, breathing hard. Her lips formed a thin line, then she said, "Promise me . . . Promise me we'll never do anything like this again."

"Sarah." Mike could imagine Mengsk shaking his head over the line. "We will do whatever it takes to save humanity. Our responsibility is too great to do any less."

And he was gone again, the great wise leader on the far side of the electronic channel, directing the war from the safety of his brandy and chess games.

"Why do you trust him?" Mike asked. The thought had crossed his mind and he said it. "Why do you follow him?"

Sarah managed a weary smile. "He saved my soul."

"And you've been killing for him ever since. Don't the scales ever balance? Aren't you due your own freedom?"

"It's . . . complex. Mengsk is a lot like you. Okay, I'm sorry, he's actually the complete opposite. You're all surface, like a sheet of newsprint. He's all depth. He tells you what he thinks, and he's so convinced of it, down to the core of his being, that the effect is very much the same. He inspires me to believe."

"He's a politician. If you look deep enough, you'll find that out. There's a bottom to that swamp of his soul."

"And will that change anything? Do I want to look?"

"Sometimes looking isn't a bad thing. If you looked a little harder, then maybe Raynor wouldn't seem like such a jackass."

Kerrigan opened her mouth to say something, then stopped and nodded. "Yeah, you're probably right. At least with Raynor. I guess I owe that much to the jackass."

"Our responsibility is too great to do any less," quoted Mike.

Kerrigan let out a laugh, a short giggle. It was unexpected and unplanned and very human.

Mike let out a long breath and wondered which would arrive first, the Zerg from the nearby colony or Mengsk's promised dropship.

CHAPTER 13

SOUL-SEARCHING

Through the lens of history, war seems to function with a frightening punctuality, like a murderous music box. Battles are no more than clockwork mechanisms of death, a drama of destruction with each act flowing naturally into the next, until one side or the other is vanquished. In retrospect, the fall of the Confederacy seems like a logical slide that, once begun, leaves no question as to its conclusion.

For those of us trapped in the middle of the war, there was nothing but raw panic broken by periods of total exhaustion. No one, not even those who supposedly did the planning, had any clear idea of the forces we were dealing with, until it was too late to change.

Clockwork? Perhaps. But I prefer to think of it as a timer on a bomb we were feverishly disarming, hoping we could finish before the damned thing exploded in our collective faces.

—THE LIBERTY MANIFESTO

THE DROPSHIP WOULD REJOIN THE *HYPERION* IN low Antigan orbit. Mengsk had left the surface as soon as the emitter was activated, but he didn't want to try to run the Confederate blockade above without gathering all his wandering, barefoot children home. At least that's how it seemed to Mike.

As they rose from the surface, Mike watched the screens. All the ship's cameras were directed toward the surface. The emitter was already having an effect on the Zerg below. They were boiling out of their nests like angry ants, moving randomly, even attacking each other in psionic-inspired madness. But soon they started descending on the tower where Mike and Kerrigan had left the emitter. A hurricane of living creatures circled the beacon like moths around a flame.

As the ship rose higher, its sensors picked up other nests, other reactions as the ever-sounding chord that came from Kerrigan's mind echoed and reverberated, growing stronger by the second. There were radioed cries from Confederate ground troops as they were overwhelmed, and the night side of Antiga Prime was now dotted with small explosions. The rebels had more warning, but those who were too slow to get off the ground were swallowed in the waves of zerglings and hydralisks.

The dropship continued to rise, and Mike could see the curve of the horizon. There was a bright flash along it, and a few seconds later the electromagnetic pulse swept over the ship. The screens went momentarily blank before countermeasures kicked in. One of the great Behemoth-class cruisers, sister ship to the *Norad II,* had gone down beneath the growing assault.

Above them the Confederate blockade was already disintegrating. Available ships with landing capability were being rerouted, while others were trying to strafe the now everpresent Zerg.

There was a triad of glowing triangles that streaked near them, and Mike blinked as they left hot patterns on his retinas. The Protoss were already present—not in force, but still in the atmosphere.

Then came reports from the ships farthest out. Warps were opening in space, and through the warps were coming hordes of Zerg. The lobster-brain-jellyfish, the queens, the mutalisks, and the strange flying crabs were all erupting from space and descending on Antiga, summoned forth and trapped by its siren call.

The dropship docked with the larger *Hyperion*, and the entire crew evacuated the smaller ship. The dropship itself was abandoned, jettisoned from the lock, and left to go spinning down toward the surface. Its presence would only slow the *Hyperion* from its escape, and there was no time to secure it.

Mengsk's ship rose like a bubble among the panicked Confederates and descending Zerg. The Zerg fought only when there was something in their way, and the Confederates did not disappoint, putting their best ships in the path of the assault. There were several more flashes, but the *Hyperion* showed the explosions as only slightest flickers, each brief dimming representing the deaths of five hundred more Confederate humans in a nuclear fireball.

Kerrigan was worn and white-faced. Mike was sure she could still hear the psionic call, even at this altitude. It worked on some level that he could not be sure of, and pulled across the depths of space to bring in the enemy. He helped her out of the landing bay.

Raynor came across them in a gangway. "Congratulations, you two," he said warmly. "You really lit a fire under the Zerg's backsides. I don't know what you said, Lieutenant, but it sure brought them running."

Kerrigan's head came up, her eyes blazing with fury, and even Raynor could see the rage and frustration behind them. Then, as suddenly as it appeared, it was gone, expended, leaving only exhaustion in its wake.

Raynor reached up to touch Kerrigan's shoulder. His voice softened, and his forehead creased in concern. "Lieutenant, are you all right?" He separated the words with slight pauses, Mike noted.

Kerrigan looked up again into Raynor's eyes, and there was no anger there. Mike thought of the feedback loop—fear breeding fear, concern breeding concern. "I'm fine," she said, pushing a stray strand of red hair out of her face. "It's just been very tiring."

Mike said, "Mengsk?"

"Up in his observation dome," said Raynor. "I think he wants to watch the battle. I left him to it. Nothing I really want to see."

"I can report to him, if you want to rest," Mike said to Kerrigan.

She paused for a moment, and almost physically wavered. "If you would, Michael," she said. She was still looking at Raynor.

"You look really beat," said Raynor to the lieutenant, his concern so obvious that even Mike could read it. "You want to grab a cuppa joe in the galley? Maybe talk?"

"Coffee would be nice," said Kerrigan, and a small smile tugged at the corners of her mouth. "Talk too. Yes. Talk would be good."

Mike held up a hand and headed for the lift, leaving the pair in the hallway. As he hit the lift doors, he put one thought at the top of his mind, where Kerrigan could easily find it.

Remember to let him finish his damned sentences, he thought, and then rose to find the architect of Antiga Prime's destruction.

Mengsk was alone on the observation deck, his hands behind his back, facing the main screen. The chess set had been set up for a new game, and a fresh pack of cigarettes sat next to the ashtray. Two brandy snifters and a still-corked bottle of cognac rested on the bar.

All the screens but the main one had been turned off, and the last screen showed a real-time display of Antiga Prime, hovering at the center. Small yellow triangles represented Confederate forces, red triangles the ever-multiplying Zerg.

A few blue-white pips that Mike had never seen before were on the surface. There were also a few circles planetside: rebel forces that had been unfortunate not to have escaped in time. As Mike watched, they were subsumed in a wave of red triangles.

It was a similar story in orbit. More red triangles, each representing tens or hundreds of Zerg fliers, all converging on Antiga Prime. The ships that bolted were untouched. Enough stood and fought to form clustering points as the Zerg swarmed over them, ripping them apart in space.

Mike remembered the image of the *Norad II* going down. This was a hundred times worse.

"We're pulling away at top speed," Mengsk said reassuringly. "I have the ship's computer compensating to keep the scale the same."

Mike crossed to the bar, pulled the cork, and poured himself an inch of cognac. He did not pour any for Mengsk.

"We calculate that, based on the strength of the emissions, we are calling every possible Zerg from twenty-five light-years out to us," continued Mengsk. "Maybe more. Lieutenant Kerrigan is quite the siren, luring these sailors to their doom."

"It took a lot out of her," Mike said, taking a long pull on his snifter.

"But not more than she could handle. I am glad you were there for her. She might not have made it, otherwise."

Mike felt his face flush, and for a moment thought it only the brandy. "You didn't leave me much choice, did you?"

"Not really." Mengsk shrugged sheepishly and turned toward Mike. Behind him, the red triangles multiplied. There was almost nothing left of the Confederate forces on the ground. "But I'm still glad you were there for her."

Mike snorted and took another drink. Mengsk poured himself one. Blue-white triangles were appearing now at the edge of the screen. The Protoss had arrived in force.

Mengsk looked at the screen and said, "Interesting report

while you were gone." Mike said nothing, and Mengsk continued. "Protoss ground forces pitched in to engage the Zerg we encountered. Their leader's name is Tassadar. He calls himself the High Templar and Executor of the Protoss Fleet. His flagship's name is the *Gantrithor.*"

"Maybe they were impressed with your work and decided to lend a hand. You must have a good press agent."

Mengsk gave Mike a withering look. "Come now, Michael. I expect better from you. Work out what I just said."

Mike was silent for a moment, then said, "Ground forces?"

Mengsk brightened. "Exactly. Individual warriors in very ductile power suits. Strange buglike vehicles. Spell-casters that I can only assume are psionicists of some type. Tougher than the Zerg, man for man, though the Zerg have it all over them in raw numbers. Very intriguing, watching them battle. You might want to review the tapes later."

"Hang on," said Mike.

Mengsk's smile broadened. "I'll wait. You'll get it. I believe in you."

"If the Protoss have ground forces . . ."

"Quite good ones, I think I just said."

"That means they've fought the Zerg on the ground before. And more important, they've won those battles."

"Or why maintain a ground force in the first place? Yes! Take it to the last step."

Mike's eyes opened wide. "Which means the Zerg can be destroyed without blowing up the planet they're on!"

"Full marks!" Mengsk took a sip from his snifter. "It may be a difficult task, and I think that the Protoss are overmatched in this case, but yes, the Zerg can be beaten on the ground." He chuckled. "I had to explain it to Raynor three times, you know."

"But," said Mike. "But then all we've done is to just set the Protoss up to blow up Antiga Prime!"

"And a large piece of the Zerg forces with it. It should rock them back on their heels for a while. Long enough to let us get the upper hand against the Confederacy."

"They'll blow up Antiga Prime, and with it any surviving humans!"

"No humans would survive that many Zerg. We will do whatever it takes to save the greater humanity," Mengsk said solemnly.

"Even if we have to kill all the humans in order to do it," Mike snapped. Mengsk said nothing, and Mike just let the silence expand to fill the dome. On the main screen, Antiga was nearly covered with red triangles, and a perimeter of blue triangles was in orbit around it. There were no yellow triangles left.

After a moment, Mengsk said, "I know what you're thinking."

Mike set his glass down. "You're a telepath, too, now?"

"I'm a politician, as you're wont to tell me. And that means that I'm sensitive to other people. Their needs, their desires, their motivations."

"So what am I thinking?" Mike suddenly felt like a bug under a microscope.

"You're asking yourself if I would sacrifice you for the good of all humanity. The answer is yes, in a heartbeat and without remorse, but I really don't want to. Good help is, as they say, hard to find. And you're very good, at more than just being a reporter."

Mike shook his head. "How do you do it?"

"Do it?" Mengsk canted his head.

"Find everybody's button and press it. You play people like they were pianos. Kerrigan would leap into a hydralisk's mouth for you, Raynor will jump through hoops for you, hell, you've even gotten that old pin-headed gorilla Duke eating out of your hand. Doesn't that bother you?"

"No. It's a gift. I find that others tend to be scattered in their thinking. I try to provide a strong center for them. Raynor is in many ways consumed by anger for the Confederates: I am but a means by which he can vent that anger. Duke looks for nothing more than political cover to let him settle old scores and create new atrocities: I provide that. Sarah? Well, Lieutenant Kerrigan has always sought approval, despite her own gifts. I provide that as well."

Mike thought of Sarah Kerrigan, down in the galley, talking with Jim Raynor over coffee. He asked, "And me?"

Mengsk gave a great smile and shook his head. "You want to save souls, dear boy. You want to make a difference. Whether you're covering some traffic tie-up or rooting out some alderman's corruption, you're trying to make things better. It's practically in your genetic code. And you believe in it. *That* makes you very valuable. It makes you an incredible resource. You keep Raynor from being too impulsive, Kerrigan from being too inhuman. They both respect you, you know. You wrote off General Duke as hopeless, I think, soon after you met him, but I do believe you still hold out hope for me. That's why you've hung around, in hopes that I will find my own redemption."

Mike frowned. "And what keeps me from leaving now, knowing that this hope for your salvation is probably misplaced?"

"Ah," said Mengsk, watching the screen. The Protoss encirclement was almost complete. "Part of it is your concern for others. But I can be honest with you, now, because the Confederacy, through its puppet the UNN, has betrayed you. It has used your face and words against you. Now you've got your own personal reason to fight them. Your own reason to commit. They have made it *personal*. You can go on your own . . ." Mengsk let his voice trail off.

"But where would I go," Mike said in a flat tone. A statement, not a question.

"Exactly. You're in for the long haul. Until victory or defeat. Ah, it begins. Will you watch with me?"

Mike looked at the screen, at the ring of blue-white triangles surrounding the doomed world. Already spearheads of red were rising from the surface, but they were repelled as the Protoss built up their weapons charge to burn the world, to sterilize it to the deepest tunnels.

"I'll pass," said Mike, his mouth like ashes. He turned and walked toward the lift, not turning back to watch.

Mengsk did not seem to notice Mike's departure. He stood, snifter in hand, and watched as the Protoss rained poisonous flame onto Antiga Prime.

CHAPTER 14

GROUND ZERO

The use of the psi emitter on Antiga Prime was a watershed event, a Rubicon, a point of no return. It was like the first appearance of ghosts in the Confederacy ranks, or the indiscriminate use of the Apocalypse bombs that leveled Korhal IV. It changed everything.

It also changed nothing. For the average citizen caught between the rebels and the Confederates, and the Confederates caught between the Zerg and the Protoss, the war was still as deadly as ever. More planets would vaporize under the Protoss's weapons, and more humans would be swallowed by the Zerg hives. Yet after the swarming of Antiga Prime, there was renewed hope among the rebels. Now, at least, we had a weapon.

And like the damn-fool humans we were, we could not resist using it.

—The Liberty Manifesto

TEN DAYS LATER, THEY WERE ON TARSONIS ITSELF, blockbusting through the densest of the downtown districts.

The city had taken the assault hard. The western precincts were still in flames caused by a battlecruiser that had gone down in their midst, and a fountain of hot dust, laden with phosphoric heavy metals, plumed southward in the strong wind. The upper windows of most of the major buildings were shattered, and in some cases entire facades had slid from the metal skeletons beneath, leaving hills of broken glass at the titanic tower's feet.

The elegant spires of Tarsonis were nothing more than jagged, twisted remains, their fractured edges scratching the bleeding sky. The atmosphere itself was torn by the shrieks and booms of battling craft, and streaked with the smoke of downed fighters.

Most of the streets were jammed with the amorphous, burned wreckage of ground cars. Their shining paint jobs had been baked by fire and heat to a uniform gray, and the once-tinted windows were shattered, jagged holes. Initially Mike looked into the vehicles to see if he could identify those within, but after the first hour he just ignored the blackened corpses, with their burned-stick limbs and withered, scream-ing faces.

The only things left alive on the streets were the warriors, striving hard to kill each other.

The wreck-jammed side streets kept Raynor's unit to the main boulevards, wide streets once dominated by parklike traffic islands in the center. The trees there were toppled and burned now, and what statuary to famous Confederates remained had been amputated to mere nubs.

Raynor's unit was pinned down near one of the tri-level fountains along the central plaza. A discarded, bent brass plaque identified it as a memorial placed there by the Daugh-ters of the Guild Wars Veterans. The fountain itself was now no more than a mound of damp debris, the only hint of its pre-vious incarnation a stone cannon jutting from the shattered stone. Mike found himself wishing the cannon were real.

Across the plaza, past a hastily erected barricade of dead cars, an Arclite siege tank had planted itself firmly between two buildings. It sat square in their path, fully deployed, its side pontoons firmly set in the asphalt. The shock cannon sent blistering rounds overhead, and its twin 80's raked the debris of the fountain. The siege tank had become a rallying point for the Confederate Security Forces, most of them the remains of the Delta and Omega Squadrons. Now the recombined units, safe under the heavy fire of the Arclite, laid down continual suppression fire on Raynor's position.

Behind the stone cannon, Mike kept his head down and desperately slammed the side of his comm unit. It burbled frustratingly at him.

"I have *got* to think about a major career change," he muttered, then ducked instinctively as another round of fire thundered through the city's stone canyons.

Raynor slid down the debris pile toward Mike, pushing a small avalanche ahead of his heavy boots. "Any luck?" he asked.

Mike shook his head. "It's probably a general jammer unit they have in operation, as opposed to an EMP pulse that would knock out the unit. That means the radio is still working, I just can't punch through the interference. Something with more power could."

"Just freaking great. We're chewed up as it is. We can't go back, and we can't get past the tank. We need to call for an evac, but it's not going to happen if we can't get in touch with the *Hyperion*."

"You boys need a hand?" Sarah Kerrigan warped into being near them. She was dressed in her environmental suit and carried the bulky canister rifle on her back. There were dark red stains on her pants cuffs, as if she had been wading through a river of blood.

Her eyes were bright and very, very alert.

"It's good to see you, Lieutenant," said Raynor. "We were just bemoaning our fate."

"I was in the neighborhood and heard gunfire," said Kerrigan. "What's the sitch?"

"Arclite, hull down, between the buildings," said Raynor, "supported by a full squad of marines."

"That all? I thought you were having trouble."

"Anything you can do to help would be appreciated, ma'am," Raynor said, grinning.

"Piece of cake," said Kerrigan, reaching up over her shoulder and pulling the canister rifle like a sword from its sheath. "Lay down some suppression for me while I sneak up on them, will you?"

"Left or right flank?" asked Raynor.

"Left, I think," said Kerrigan, and smiled again. The smile just accented the wildness in her eyes. "That's *your* left, Jimmy."

"You got it, Sarah," said Raynor.

Kerrigan touched a device at her belt. Her cloaking device activated and she faded from view as Raynor bellowed orders at the remainder of the squad. The gauss rifles coughed as they laid down their own devastating layer of spikes in response to the Confederate fire. Their sudden assault silenced the marines, but the Arclite's shock cannon continued to boom heavy shots over the rebels' heads.

"So you think she can do it, 'Jimmy'?" Mike asked.

James Raynor flushed and shrugged beneath his armor. "Probably. But it won't mean a damn unless we can flag a lift out of this dump."

A curtain of dueling impaler spikes flew between the two camps, and Mike wondered how Kerrigan could dance across such a battlefield. One stray shot could take out her cloak, and she would bleed under the gauss rifle's spikes like any other soldier.

Then the far flank of the Confederate flank started to collapse, accompanied by the high-pitched whine of the canister rifle. One after another the Confederate Marines twitched and fell under an unseen sniper. The flank was vulnerable, as marines started firing randomly at their suspected assailant.

There was a flicker, and Sarah Kerrigan appeared, briefly, atop the barricade of wrecked cars. She flickered out again, and the air around her was filled with spikes.

Raynor bellowed for a charge, and the remnants of the squad rose from their hiding places and ran across the plaza, their heavy boots shattering the faux granite of the walkways.

The siege tank's protective screen of Confederate marines was thrown into disarray, though the Arclite they were protecting continued to hammer the rebels' position. The 80-millimeter cannons quickly found the range of the charging rebels, while the main shock cannon brought itself around smartly, firing heavy 120-millimeter shells as it did.

Kerrigan appeared again, this time on the main deck of the siege tank, right beneath the cannon. She shoved the barrel of her canister rifle into the turret ring, then somersaulted away as the Confederate rifle fire closed in on her.

Mike imagined he could hear the rising charge of the canister rifle set to overload, and shouted out a warning. Raynor and his men needed no warning, and they dropped in place.

A red flare blossomed at the base of the tank's turret, and the blast scattered the remaining Confederates. The lesser guns were silenced, but the large shock cannon continued its traverse, firing round after round as it swung around, its programming jammed.

The shock cannon took a bite out of the corner of one of the two flanking buildings, and the ground rumbled beneath them. The cannon kept going, its barrel now glowing a dull red as it tried to swivel around, but was trapped by the structure. It continued to fire, and the great structure shook from the assault. The top of the tank popped open, and the crew within tried to scramble out, like clowns spilling from an overstuffed car in a circus act.

They never made it. There was a tremor that ripped through the entire plaza, and the pummeled building collapsed on the tank at its feet, tons of steel and masonry falling in on itself, raising a hot cloud of dust. Only in the quake of the building's collapse did the Arclite finally stop firing.

Raynor picked himself up off the shattered pavement, along with the remains of the squad. Mike pulled himself up as well and shouted, "Kerrigan? Lieutenant?" His voice sounded small and lost in the wake of the explosion.

Kerrigan wafted up alongside them, gray as the ghost she was supposed to be. Mike realized it was dust adhering to the cloaking field itself, forming a shell surrounding the telepath. She hit another control on her belt and turned tangible again. The lines of wear and exhaustion were now tight around her face, but her eyes were still bright. The cloak took something out of her, but she didn't want to admit it.

"Target neutralized, Captain," said Kerrigan. "But I'm afraid we can't go that way now."

"It doesn't matter," said Raynor. "The Confederates have to be regrouping by now. They should be mounting a counteroffensive soon enough. We just can't hold this area. What we need is a way to punch through the jammer."

"Jim," said Mike. "Three blocks west of here is the UNN broadcast building. Its circuits have been shielded, and it has generators in the basement. They may still have enough juice to overcome the interference."

Raynor nodded. "It might just be wreckage now, but it's worth a shot." He motioned the patrol forward. Kerrigan fell in line alongside Mike.

"So you were just in the neighborhood," Mike said to the telepath. "You just *happened* to be around?"

"I go where Arcturus Mengsk thinks I am needed most," said Sarah Kerrigan, barely hiding her amusement at Mike's thoughts.

"And what's our fabled leader up to *this* time?" Mike asked. "Jim's right. I'm getting fragmentary reports of reinforcements rolling in from the suburbs. Walkers, tanks, and bikes. It's going to get real hot here real soon. Has he got a plan for this?"

"He's told me he has."

The Universe News Network Building had fared pretty

badly but was still intact. The windows along the east side were nothing more than empty holes, and one of the great letters had fallen hundreds of feet to impale itself in the twisted wreckage of the concrete beneath.

Raynor looked up at the building. "I hope the equipment you're thinking of isn't in the penthouse."

"Upper levels are for management," said Mike. "The worker bees toil on the fourth floor. And the broadcast booth and generators are in the basement."

Though his tone was glib, his heart sank. This had been his base of operations for years, his home away from home. He had grabbed a dog and soda where the huge "N" now rested, arguing planetary politics and local ordinances with the copywriters and stringers. There had been a pretzel stand next to the honor boxes. Now there were just twisted reinforcement bars jutting out of the concrete, and no sign of survivors.

The patrol moved inside. Mike didn't expect any inhabitants, but the ghostly stillness covered the lobby like a shroud. Even on weekends there was a continual hubbub here. Now there were only scattered paper and asbestos dust shaken loose from the ceiling tiles.

It was quiet, save for the crunch of their own boots. Mike glanced up the broad stairs to the mezzanine and arcade levels (quicker than the elevators even when the lifts were running), and thought about finding his old desk. Wondered if his stuff was still there.

He wondered if there was anything there he really needed.

Raynor caught him looking up. "I thought you said the equipment was downstairs."

"Yeah, just dealing with my own ghosts," said Mike, a grim tenor in his voice. He led the squad through the debris, downward, into the building's primary basement.

Whatever else Mike thought of management, they were green-tag former military, and that meant they thought in terms of triple redundancy. The main power had been cut, but the broadcast studio was packing its own batteries, and if need be, old gasoline generators for power. The link to the tower was still solid, despite all the fighting, and UNN kept underground lines to various outposts through the globe-girdling metropolis. Many of these had been cut, and their red telltales winked evilly on the primary board.

Even the air-conditioning was still working, and their visors frosted at the sudden temperature change.

Raynor looked around uncomfortably. It was too easy for a stray shot from the outside chaos to bring the building down on top of them, to make this their tomb. To Mike he said, "This going to take long?"

Mike shook his head as he ran leads from the field comm unit into the main board. "Just need to boost the signal. Piece of cake. Here we go." He flipped a toggle and said, "Raynor's Rangers to Mother Ship. Do you read? Rangers to Mother Ship. *Hyperion*, you there?"

The speakers crackled and spat, and a balding female face appeared on the miniscreen. "Mother Ship. Crap, Liberty, you almost blew out my eardrums. What are you broadcasting on?" The voice was vaguely familiar.

"Old UNN surplus. Power of the press," said Mike. "We're at the Network offices. Unit's pretty shot up, and the uglies are regrouping. Need an evac."

"Working," said the voice on the other end, and Mike placed it. The tech from the bridge of the *Norad II*. One of Duke's people. "There's a park four blocks south of you. Can you pull back that far?"

Mike looked at Raynor and Kerrigan. Both nodded. "Affirmative," he said. "See you there, thirty minutes ETA."

"Roger that," said the tech. "Hold on. Patching you through to headquarters."

Mike's brow furrowed at the delay, then Mengsk's graying face materialized on the screen. "Michael," he said, his voice grim, and Mike noticed lines of concern at the corners of his eyes. "Are Kerrigan and Raynor there?"

"Still with you," said Raynor. "The lieutenant's here as well."

"Excellent, report when you get back." Something beeped to the terrorist's right and he reached over. General Duke appeared on another screen.

"This is Duke." He looked more than ever like a foul-tempered gorilla. "The emitters are secured and on-line. Returning to the command ship."

"Emitters?" Mike asked. "Psi emitters?"

Kerrigan leaned on the console over Mike's shoulder, her face close to the screen. "Who authorized the use of psi emitters?"

Mengsk's face grew stony. "I did, Lieutenant."

"You going to bring the Zerg here? Siccing them on the Confederates on Antiga was bad enough. This is insane!"

Raynor broke in as well. "She's right, man. Think this through."

Mengsk let out an angry exhalation. "I have thought it through, believe me." He paused and watched the three of them through the network feed cameras. On another screen, General Duke looked like the cat that swallowed the canary. "You all have your orders. Carry them out."

Then the screen went dead.

"He's lost it," said Raynor. "He's gone over the edge."

Kerrigan shook her head. "No. He has to have a plan."

Raynor said firmly, "Yeah, he has a plan. He plans to let the Protoss and the Zerg burn up the Confederacy one planet at a time, and take over what's left."

Kerrigan shook her head again. "He's always had a way to take care of things. He's not afraid to sacrifice, but he's no fool."

"He's not afraid to sacrifice," said Raynor grimly. "Confederates. Zerg. Protoss. When is it going to be our turn?"

"I'll talk to him when we get back," said Kerrigan.

Mike sat there, staring at the now-dead screen. "He's a politician," he said. "He weighs every decision on how far it advances him on his personal path to power. Never forget that."

Raynor opened his mouth to say something, but there was the sound of rifle fire above.

"Visitors," said Kerrigan.

"We've been rumbled," said Raynor. "Probably they caught some of the signal we pushed out. Let's go."

"Right. One more thing," said Mike, pushing himself away from the console and heading deeper into the basement.

"Liberty?" said Raynor. "What the hell?"

"He's after something else," said Kerrigan. "I'll go after him. You take care of the visitors. I read only a handful of marines. You can handle it. Watch out, one's a firebat." And she was gone as well.

She tracked Mike to another staircase, this one spiraling into the dimly lit darkness below. Pumping her canister rifle, she carefully climbed down after him.

Mike was in front of a steel door, bashing at the padlock with the butt of his gun.

"We should go," said Kerrigan.

"In a moment. This is Handy Anderson's secret stash. His secrets. I hadn't thought about it until just now. No one was usually allowed down here. It's supposed to be the records backup, the records morgue, but it's also where Anderson kept his dirt on everybody in the city."

"It's data you can use," said Kerrigan calmly, picking up Mike's surface thoughts. "You can look through it and see if there were any warnings, anything that was kept hidden, about the Zerg and the Protoss. Stuff that might have made a difference, if only people had known about it."

"Hindsight is twenty-twenty," said Mike.

"Stand aside," said the ghost. The canister rifle whined under a charge, and she fired a bolt into the lock. Fragments of metal flew in all directions.

The cache, no bigger than a broom closet, was lined with thin shelves. There were boxes of disks on all the shelves.

"We can't take it all," said Kerrigan.

"Take as much as you can." Mike opened his own pack and pulled out supplies and spare ammo, replacing them with the disks. "If Mengsk is really going to kill this planet, I want some of our reports to survive. And maybe we can figure out what really happened here."

Kerrigan opened her own pack and started shoving disks in as well. They would still have to leave the bulk of it behind.

"Don't sweat the earlier stuff," said Mike.

"You think Mengsk is really serious about the psi emitters?" Kerrigan asked, getting Mike's answer as soon as she asked.

Mike spoke anyway. "Like I said, he's a politician. If he can force the Confederates to back down with a threat of the emitters, he'll do it. If he doesn't, well, Tarsonis is one more casualty in his war. He can justify it. Someone on Tarsonis gave the order to kill his homeworld."

"But this is the heart of the human worlds. The biggest and the brightest. The center of humanity."

"This is Mengsk. With the psi emitters, he's bigger than worlds."

"I can't believe he'd do this. I've read his thoughts, like yours and Jim's. He wouldn't do this."

"You said yourself that when you're with him, he believes in every word he says, deep in his heart."

"Yeah."

"Then, next time you're with him, look deeper. There. That's as much as we can take. What's the story topside?"

Kerrigan said nothing, and Mike wondered if she was thinking about his question or his earlier suggestion. Finally she said, "They're fine. More Confederates on the way. Let's go."

Mike pulled up his pack and started out of the room. "Think about what I said, okay?"

"Thinking," said Kerrigan with a grim smile, "is the one thing a telepath *can't* avoid."

CHAPTER 15

THINGS FALL APART
(IT'S SCIENTIFIC)

Everyone hates surprises. In the final days of Tarsonis, surprises were the nature of the campaign. Units appeared where none had been reported, secret transmissions threaded between allies, battle plans were activated that we had no idea were in place. We found out how many moves out those plans had been laid. In a word, we had been foxed.

But even those in charge got their own surprises. As any operation gets larger and larger, more pieces slip between the fingers, more pieces are ignored, until things start happening that you have no idea were about to occur. That's what happened to Mengsk at the end, when suddenly some of his loyal soldiers had second thoughts and the chess pieces weren't moving around the board the way he wanted them to.

And that's probably why he kicked the board over. Heckuvan end-game strategy, but it works.

Supposedly if you are in control of everything, you hate surprises. But I'll tell you, when you are not in control, you hate them even more.

—THE LIBERTY MANIFESTO

THE DROPSHIP MET THEM IN ATKIN'S SQUARE. AS the remains of Raynor's team boarded, a group of techs in lightweight armor disembarked. With them was one of Duke's ghosts, the telepath's face hidden behind an opaque visor.

"This ain't no place for soft targets," said Raynor. "You boys don't even have decent armor."

"Yeah, but we got orders," snarled the captain in charge, and they pushed through Raynor's men and out into the city, heading in the direction from which the rangers had come.

Mike supposed that Mengsk had figured out there were things to loot from the UNN building. He suddenly felt very good about the backpack full of stolen secrets he had brought with him. Something he could use as leverage with the rebel leader.

Then he looked at Kerrigan. Kerrigan was looking at Duke's ghost. The blood had drained from her face.

"What's wrong?" Mike asked.

Kerrigan just shook her head and said, "We'd better get back to the command ship."

As soon as they returned to the *Hyperion*, Raynor was summoned into General Duke's wardroom to discuss strategy, "at his soonest convenience," as the message said. Muttering a string of obscenities, the former marshal lumbered forward, not even shucking his battle armor. Mike popped his own visor and seals and climbed out of the suit. Kerrigan, stripping her lighter armor with practiced ease, was already heading for the exit.

"Hang on," said the reporter. "The uber-Mengsk wanted both of us to report in when we got back. I'll go with you."

Kerrigan said, "Let me talk to Arcturus on my own. He'll be more forthcoming with me." She strode down the halls of the *Hyperion* toward the lift to his observation post.

Mike considered going after Kerrigan, but she was right. The rebel leader and the ghost had a history, and Mengsk would be more willing to open up to her.

And maybe, Mike thought, she'd be able to pull something useful out the terrorist's mind. Like what he was thinking in planting more psi emitters.

Mike looked around. Most of the rest of the unit had stripped and were heading for the showers. Raynor himself would be with the general in the wardroom. Not that the general would be the best company right now, but talking to him beat cooling his heels until Mengsk rang him up.

And he didn't want to be caught stuck in the shower if Kerrigan needed him.

As Mike moved through the ship, he thought about the tech he had spoken with over the comm unit. Now that he noticed, most of the crew on the *Hyperion* were strangers: members of the Alpha Squadron as opposed to Mengsk's original rebels from before Antiga Prime. One by one, those original revolutionaries had fallen by the wayside or been promoted to other ships. Part of a plan by Mengsk to spread his agents among all the ships of his fleet, or part of a plan by Mengsk to move the old guard aside in favor of professional soldiers?

Whichever it was, Mike was sure that it was part of a plan by Mengsk.

Mike was almost to the wardroom when the door exploded, and two men in combat armor tumbled out.

It was Raynor and Duke, locked in each other's arms. The former lawman had already ripped off the shoulder plate of the general's suit and spiderwebbed the man's visor with a steel-shod fist. Duke was no slouch, however, and there were several new dents in Raynor's already-rumpled chest plate.

"Jim!" shouted Mike. Despite himself, Raynor turned toward the reporter.

General Duke did not miss the opportunity, slamming both fists into the side of Raynor's helmet. The former marshal staggered back a step, but did not fall.

Now free of his opponent's neosteel embrace, Duke went for his side arm, a nasty needle-gun that could penetrate bulkheads. Raynor recovered as the general brought the weapon up and grabbed the older man by the wrist. Then, the servos in both sets of armor squealing, Raynor slammed Duke's arm against the bulkhead.

Once. Twice. On the third time something cracked in Duke's gauntlet and the general screamed. He dropped the gun and sank to the deck. The needler went skittering across the floor. Mike knelt down, grabbed it, and rose, clamping it to his own belt for safekeeping.

Only then did Mike become aware that they were not alone in the hallway. Ahead and behind them were armed marines, their weapons leveled on Raynor and himself.

"Y'all just signed your own death warrant, boy!" Duke snarled. There was blood at the corner of his mouth, and he cradled his pistol hand. More than metal had been shattered by Raynor's blows.

"You just signed the death warrant of your home planet, General!" Mike snapped. To the marines he said, "He just set off the emitters. He called the Zerg here! Dammit! He and Mengsk didn't even give the Confederates a chance to surrender! The Zerg are coming here, and this bastard is the one who rolled out the welcome mat!"

Some of the marines lowered their weapons. They seemed suddenly to be having second thoughts about the revolution, or were suddenly worried that the Zerg were going to show up on their doorstep. Others kept a flinty-eyed, neutral glare, and their weapons remained aimed at Raynor's chest.

Mike figured the ones who were hesitating were the ones who weren't neurally resocialized. The others were waiting for the kill order.

"I'll have you court-martialed!" said the general. Mike let out a thin breath. Duke was threatening, not ordering Raynor's death. He was concerned that Mengsk might not approve.

"You want my rank, you can have it," Raynor said hotly. "And I'm not in your chain of command. I answer to Mengsk, same as you. You can't do squat without Mengsk's say-so."

"And whose orders do you think I was following when I

activated the emitters, boy?" said Duke, smiling despite his pain.

"You set off a dozen emitters on Tarsonis!" said Raynor. "The populace will be swarmed!"

"We set them off in strong Confederate locations," said Duke, "and evacuated most of our regular troops. Hell, boy, didn't you realize that we were planting one more when we picked *you* up?"

Mike suddenly thought of the ghost and the tech crew, and the way Kerrigan had reacted. Of course Mengsk wouldn't care about information. He was after control of the entire realm of human space.

Raynor spat. "You son of a . . ." He took two steps toward the general.

General Duke, in his armored battle suit, held up his good arm. Not to attack, but to ward off a blow. The general was afraid, an old man quailing in a neosteel shell.

Raynor paused for a moment, then spat again. He wheeled and headed for the lift to the observation dome.

None of the marines in the hall stopped him. Some didn't have the guts to open fire on one of their own. Some didn't have the orders. And some didn't know which man was the true criminal.

Mike followed Raynor. Behind them General Duke bellowed for the soldiers to get back to their stations.

Mike laid a hand on Raynor's shoulder, and the big man turned. For a moment Mike was afraid that Raynor was going to take a swing at him, but the fire in the man's eyes was replaced with deep, bitter sadness.

"They didn't even give them a chance," he said. "They could have used it as a threat, but they just set them off. No warning, nothing. While we were en route back to the ship. They set them off."

"So what are you going to do?" Mike asked.

"I'm going to have it out with Mengsk himself," said Raynor. "He's got to be made to see reason."

"You're not going up there. Right now Duke is probably

on the blower with him, calling for your hide. You've got about ten minutes before he convinces some of his followers to arrest you. With or without Mengsk's permission."

"Yeah," Raynor said bitterly. "And the way I feel right now, I'd probably take a shot at Mengsk as well."

"Well, there's that. And Mengsk *will* have you killed if you do that."

"So your prescription is, Doctor Liberty?" said Raynor.

"Go find some allies. The rest of your unit from planetside. Any of the old colonial militia from the Sara system, if any of them are left on board. Go there and stay there until I call for you. And here." He passed the pack to him. "Hold on to these. There's juicy gossip on those disks."

"Where are you going?" Raynor asked.

"*I'm* going up to the observation deck. I need to talk to the great man himself. I'll try not to hit him."

Raynor nodded and stomped off, the bag of secrets looking small and insignificant in his heavy hand. Mike took a deep breath, closed his eyes, and repeated the mantra.

"I am *not* going to hit him," he said softly. "I am *not* going to hit him."

The doors to the lift opened, and Kerrigan stalked out. Her face was a roiling storm cloud of anger and doubt.

Mike jumped back as if she had been General Duke swinging an armored fist.

"Lieutenant," he said. "Sarah, what's wrong?"

"I spoke with Arcturus," said Kerrigan, and for the first time that Mike could remember, she stammered, unsure of how to phrase her next words. "He . . . he explained himself. And his explanation was full of examples and buzzwords and quotes and omelets and breaking eggs and freedom and duty and everything else. And he had me believing, Mike. I really wanted to believe that he had information we didn't, like there were Zerg queens in the heart of Tarsonis itself, calling the shots through puppet rulers, sacrificing the populace, and eating babies in the streets."

She took a deep breath. "But as I listened, I watched the map of Tarsonis on the planet behind him."

Mike said, "I know the screen. It's his favorite toy."

Kerrigan gave a derisive snort. "As I watched, that screen turned red. All of it, red from the Zerg arriving." She looked at Mike, looking for confirmation in his eyes.

"There were no Zerg on Tarsonis until he set off the psi emitters," she said in a small voice. "None at all. It wasn't like the Sara planets, or even Antiga Prime, where there were some already there and we had already lost the world. *There was nothing there* to threaten us but other humans."

She took a deep breath and closed her eyes. "And now the Zerg are coming from everywhere. They're on the planet. Arcturus didn't recall any of the units currently in combat. He didn't even bother to get the teams that placed the psi emitters off-planet. He left them there. 'Sacrifices must be made,' he said, and he said it in that calm, pleased voice as if he were ordering coffee."

Mike thought of the team that landed at Atkin's Square, and hoped that Kerrigan was too upset to pick up his suppositions. Instead he said, "All right. He told you this. And then what happened?"

"And then word came up from the bridge about a fight between Jim and Duke." Kerrigan's face was a storm cloud again. "And he dismissed me. Just told me I had to go, just like that. And I . . . I lost my temper with him."

"There's been a lot of that going around. And for good reason."

"Mike, there was no rationale for him to do this. I thought it was a bluff, or that Tarsonis was already infected, or that there was a master plan. It was just that Arcturus has a hammer, and when you have a hammer, every problem seems to be a nail."

Mike remembered Mengsk making the same quote earlier. It seemed like half a lifetime ago.

"It's okay," Mike said, reaching up to hold her by the shoulders. She did not turn away.

"And Mike"—her voice was a whisper—"when I got mad at him, I *looked*. I mean I really *looked* into him."

Michael waited for her to continue, but she just shook her head. When she spoke, it was in a low hiss. She spat, "That *bastard*."

Mike said, "Look, I sent Jim down to his quarters and told him to keep his friends around him. I think you qualify."

Kerrigan looked up at Mike, and for the briefest moment she looked unsure. Then a wry smile tugged at the corners of her lips and she said, "No, I don't think so. I'm so upset right now . . . Jim would just make me feel . . ." She let out a long breath and shook her head. "I need to be alone for a little while. I need to know that I can still rely on myself. To make sure I know that I can do what needs to be done. Despite this, I'm still a good soldier, and I have a job to finish. Maybe some good will come out of this. Okay?"

Mike disagreed, but he said, "It's okay."

Kerrigan grinned. "Even if I weren't a telepath, I'd know you're lying. Mengsk is right about that. You want to save everyone from themselves. I want you to know that it's . . . appreciated."

"You watch out."

"I can take care of myself." Kerrigan managed a sure, wide-lipped smile. "I'm no one's martyr. Hell, some days I even believe that. Just tell Jim . . ." She paused and shook her head again.

"What?" Mike asked, expecting her next words.

"Nothing," she said at last. "Tell him to just watch out, too, okay? For me."

And she was gone, heading down to the dropship bays. Mike watched her stride down the hall, shedding unease and unsureness like a butterfly leaving its chrysalis behind.

Mike just wished that his stomach didn't hurt so much, and he was sure that it would be a long time before he saw her in the flesh again.

Mike took the lift up to the observation deck. Arcturus

Mengsk was there, his hands behind his back, watching the screen of Tarsonis fill up with red triangles. They were nearly a blur on the screen itself, broken by the hot yellow marks of Confederate troops.

Mike noticed that the chessboard had been thrown across the room, and the pieces were scattered about. Kerrigan had definitely lost her temper.

Mengsk turned away from the map, his salt-and-pepper beard now looking more white than black. "Ah, the third of my brilliant rebels," he said. "I was wondering when you were going to turn up. Actually, I expected you to be the first one to march in here with demands and insults, not the good lieutenant. You must have really gotten to her."

"I didn't do anything," said Mike, "but stand by her while you consigned another planet to its death."

"One death is a tragedy, a million deaths is a statistic."

"Do you keep a database of quotes to justify your excesses?" Mike asked, his eyes narrowing.

Mengsk smiled grimly. "I take it that this means you've finally given up trying to save my soul? I hope not, because after we succeed, I'll need men like you more than ever, to help form the new universal order. To help form the needed order to repel the alien menace."

"Alien menace?" Mike sputtered the words. "That would be the menace that you yourself brought down on this world? Is *that* the alien menace you mean?"

Mengsk tilted his head and pursed his brows, as if disappointed in Mike's response. Behind him, the screen continued to throb and glow, and now blue-white triangles were moving in from the edge of the screen.

What Mengsk said was, "I didn't anticipate Sarah coming up here. And I didn't expect Raynor to pick a fight with a general. That was foolish. And inconvenient. I'm going to have to smooth over some harsh feelings there."

"Harsh feelings? They nearly killed each other just now."

Mengsk shook his head again, and Mike realized that the

man was minimizing the problems, just as he was minimizing the situation on Tarsonis. Minimizing them to the point where they could be ignored, glossed over, forgotten.

His own reality-warping field, thought Mike.

"General Duke is," the rebel leader said, "at heart a coward. I provide him with the spine he needs to go forward. James, on the other hand, is all courage and honor looking for a place to explode. A loaded gun looking for targets. I've given him direction. I've given him targets. Both men are very useful at what they do, and once we've taken Tarsonis, all this will wash out. Neither man can really survive without me, and to stay viable, they'll realize they will have to follow my directives."

"Are they just chess pieces to you?" Mike asked.

"Not chess pieces. Tools. Talented, useful tools. And yes. Raynor, Duke, the Zerg, the Protoss. Yes, even you and dear Lieutenant Kerrigan are all tools to achieve a greater good, a better future. Yes, things look dark right now, and I'll admit my culpability. But think of this: if things are terrible now, think how good we'll look when we take over, eh?"

"Don't look now," Mike said, looking past Mengsk, up at the screen, "but I think some more of your tools are attacking your other tools."

"Eh?" Mengsk spun in place and looked at the board. Already the first blue-white triangles, the symbols of the Protoss, were making planetfall. The red Zerg triangles were dispersing in their wake in ripples. It was as though the Protoss were stones thrown into a crimson pond.

"This is bad," Mengsk said softly. "Very bad. I did not expect them to arrive so quickly. This is very bad indeed."

"Oh my God. You *really* didn't expect this," Mike said, blinking in surprise. Then the nervousness in his stomach turned to chill fear, and he added, "Why doesn't that make me feel any better?"

CHAPTER 16

FOG OF WAR

Let's not kid ourselves, we got our heads handed to us by the Zerg and the Protoss. Yes, they were like nothing we had ever seen before. Yes, their biology was different. Yes, their technology, or what we would call their technology was more advanced than ours in dozens of areas. And of course, they were belligerent and aggressive in the extreme, they knew where we were, and they had the advantage of surprise.

But (and this is a rather large but) we humans are about the most ornery cusses in the galaxy. We had been fighting among ourselves for as long as we've been in the sector, and we had honed our own battle technologies to the point where we were their equal in many ways. We had the advantages of interior lines of supply (that's military for "surrounded") and native terrain (that's military for "we're fighting them in our living rooms"). We could have taken them if we had gotten our act together.

So what happened? The very thing that made us good warriors—the fact that we had fought among ourselves—also made us horrible at banding together in our hour of crisis. We could not unite under one banner or even form a coalition. In fact, every time there was a chance for that, one faction or another did something to enhance the advancement of their own political agenda over the other factions. Often at the expense of the rest of humanity. I can't imagine the hive-minded Zerg or the glowing Protoss falling prey to such basic human drives as greed and power and raw pigheadedness.

Of course, those are all basic human drives, and that's why nonhumans were cleaning our clocks.

—THE LIBERTY MANIFESTO

"YOU REALLY DIDN'T KNOW, DID YOU?" MIKE ASKED. "You didn't know the Protoss would get here? How could you not know?"

"Impudent pup," said Mengsk, stalking to his console and scanning a dozen screens at once. "Of *course* I knew the Protoss would get here. They follow the Zerg around like housewives chasing flies with a rolled-up newspaper, looking for them to alight so they can swat them. I just didn't expect them to get here so *soon*."

Despite himself, Mike smiled. Anything that disturbed the great Arcturus Mengsk was enough to make him happy. And, upon consideration, if the Protoss had been in contact with Mengsk, they probably saw him for the two-faced politico he was, and they were just hanging out in warp space waiting for him to do something like this.

Mengsk cycled through a number of screens, then cursed under his breath. Finally he opened a toggle and said, "Duke!"

The battered face of the general appeared on the screen. "Sir, have you considered my request regarding Captain Raynor?"

"Spare me your petty bickering," Mengsk snapped. "Get the local commanders on-line. The Protoss are here."

"Yes, sir, we know," Duke said proudly. "But they're avoiding our forces, concentrating primarily on the Zerg hives." He paused and blinked, completely unaware that this might be a bad thing.

"If the Protoss forces engage the Zerg," Mengsk said, enunciating each word, "then the Zerg are fighting *them* instead of the Confederates. If the Protoss engage the Zerg, the Confederates may escape. The Old Families may get away, and with them the heart of Confederate power!"

Duke blinked again, then his face fell. "We need to stop the Protoss, then. I can send them a transmission telling those glowing buzzards to back off."

Mengsk ignored him and hit some other toggles. "Send Lieutenant Kerrigan with a strike force to engage the Protoss advance party. Captain Raynor and General Duke will stay behind with the command ship."

Raynor's angry face, as red as the surface of Tarsonis, popped up on another screen. "First you sell out every person on this world to the Zerg, and now you're asking us to go up against the Protoss? You *are* losing it. *And* you're going to send Kerrigan down there with no backup?"

Mengsk's face had already changed from surprised agitation to calm reassurance. The reality bubble was disrupted, but not broken. Mike wondered how much more would be needed to bring down the entire facade the man projected. And what would happen once the mask dropped? Was there any center at all to the man to be revealed?

Mike realized he could stay, poking and arguing, and maybe even getting an angry response out of the terrorist. Mengsk was starting to look as though he might be at the end of his tether, but he was right about one thing: Michael Liberty had given up trying to save Arcturus Mengsk's soul.

And there were other, more deserving recipients of his aid.

Mike started for the lift. Behind him, Mengsk was saying calmly, "I have absolute confidence in Kerrigan's ability to hold off the Protoss."

The lift doors closed as Raynor's voice said, "This is bullsh—" And then Mike was dropping down to where, he hoped, Raynor had gathered some allies.

And despite himself, he hoped that Kerrigan had changed her mind and would be there as well.

There were about two dozen men in Raynor's barracks. Some were already strapped into their battle armor. Others were hastily suiting up. Raynor was at the comm unit.

Kerrigan was not there in body. Instead her voice, tinny over the wrist-mounted receiver, bounced upward through the room.

"But you don't owe him this!" said Raynor. "Hell, I've saved your butt plenty of—"

Kerrigan interrupted him. "Jimmy, drop the knight-in-shining-armor routine. It suits you sometimes. Just not . . ."

She paused for a moment, as if reconsidering her words. ". . . not now," she said. She sounded tired and worn. Almost defeated. "I don't need to be *rescued*. I know what I'm doing. Once we've dealt with the Protoss, we can do something about the Zerg."

She took a deep breath. "Arcturus will come around," she said, but she sounded to Mike as though she didn't hold out much hope. "I know he will."

Raynor's lips were a thin line framed by his sandy blond beard. "I hope you're right, darlin'. . . . Good hunting."

He closed the link and looked up at Mike.

"We're going after her," said Mike. A flat statement of fact.

"You bet your ass we are. Suit up. Bring your gear. We may not be welcome back here afterwards."

Mike slipped into one of the empty combat suits. "Mengsk screwed up in one other place," he said, his hands now flying automatically over the fittings and seals. "Once Kerrigan engages the Protoss, they're going to treat us as hostiles. All of us. And there's a lot of Protoss hardware floating around in the system right now, orbiting Tarsonis."

Raynor grunted agreement as he ran the check systems on his own suit. He had patched up most of the damage inflicted by Duke earlier, but Mike noticed that some of the telltales were still flashing a nasty yellow warning beneath his visor.

"So we have to dodge Protoss birds as well as Zerg," said Raynor. "It's never easy around here."

"That's why we love the challenge," Mike said, more to himself than to anyone else. He hefted the knapsack of stolen data and, on the spur of the moment, shoved his old coat, the gift from the newsroom, on top. It had been singed by laser fire and spattered with blood and less recognizable fluids, and baked under foreign suns. It was tattered and ragged and bleached.

A lot like myself, Mike thought, shoving the coat down hard into the backpack, making everything fit. There was nothing else he wanted from the locker. He hoisted the sack, slung it across the back of his armor, and followed Raynor out.

The ship had gone to red alert with the first appearance of the Protoss, and now Raynor's men moved through crimson-lit hallways to the dropship bays. Mike could feel the g-forces through the deck plates; the big command ship was weaving through something, but he could not tell if it was debris or enemy fire.

"Think we can get off the ship?" Mike asked as they stepped into the landing bay.

"Yeah," said Raynor. "The dropship pilots are good old boys. They aren't afraid of Duke's wrath, or anything else for that matter. They can always say I threatened them into bringing us down."

"They may not be afraid of my wrath, but you should be," said General Duke from the shadows to one side.

The lights flashed from red to yellow, and Mike saw Duke standing there among the dropships with two squads of marines. They had their weapons aimed at Raynor's men. Duke was cradling his own weapon, a borrowed gauss rifle, in his off hand, his right hand hanging uselessly at his side.

"Going somewhere, boy?" said Duke, a hearty smile appearing above the sealing rim of his helmet. There was still dried blood at the corner of his mouth. Perhaps he thought it was a badge of honor, Mike thought, or a slight to be avenged.

"We're going after Kerrigan," said Raynor. "She needs backup, regardless of what Mengsk says."

"That girl needs what Mengsk *says* she needs," Duke drawled. "But it's nice of you to go to the effort. Now I have solid proof of mutiny, and I can provide the traitors to go with it."

Mike scanned the marines. They were all neurally resocialized and, worse yet, already pumped to the gills with stims. Their eyes were practically pupilless. In this state they were effectively hardwired into Duke's nervous system. Once the general gave the command, they would automatically jump, or fire, or drop for twenty push-ups, without thinking twice.

So the solution would be to keep the general from giving that order.

"Mengsk would be very disappointed if you killed us," Mike said.

Duke laughed. "I'll just throw one of his old quotes back at him: 'It's easier to seek forgiveness than to gain permission.' Now, you boys with Raynor, you drop the weapons now and surrender. I might even let you live if you do."

Raynor didn't move. Behind him, Mike could hear some of their rangers slowly laying their rifles on the deck.

Then the *Hyperion* pitched to one side, hard. Something big had slammed into its side. The marines, in their bottom-heavy boots, rocked in position, and Duke's aim was thrown off for a moment.

When he could bring his weapon back around, Raynor had his own rifle unslung and ready.

"This just gets better and better," Duke said, smiling through yellowed, peglike teeth.

"I don't think you have the guts," said Raynor.

"You so much as blink, boy, and my men will fill you with so much metal you can run a scrap drive. Now drop your weapon by three. One . . . Two . . ."

There was a high-pitched whine, and Duke's left shoulder exploded in a shower of molten metal. Duke's marines all jumped and brought their weapons around, but did not fire. They had been ordered to wait for the command.

The general slowly dropped to his knees, his own weapon clattering to the ground. His armor hissed as locking rings isolated the wounded shoulder and medpacks pumped narcotics into the general's bloodstream.

Smoke curled from the barrel of the needle-gun. Mike thumbed the hammer of the weapon back, and another round clicked into place.

"I think it's time you just shut up," Mike said to the general.

"I can have you burned where you stand," said Duke. The meds in the armor were already taking effect, and his voice was slurred.

Mike took two steps forward and said, "Go ahead. You'll go first. Give the order, General."

Duke hesitated, his eyes unfocusing for a moment as the drugs hit his system hard. He was striving to stay awake on sheer cussedness.

"You don't have the guts," he managed.

"Try me," said Mike. "I've finally learned to shoot a human target."

There was silence in the landing bay for a moment; then Raynor said, "Men, pick up your weapons. We're moving out."

Raynor's men picked up their guns and threaded their way through the rebel marines. Without Duke's specific orders, they would not fire on possibly friendly targets. Raynor paused by Mike and the kneeling Duke.

"Go ahead," said Mike. "I'll catch up."

Duke's face was ashen, and his eyes were milky and pupilless. No rational thought was left, only hatred and cowardice warring in his mind. He hissed, "If I ever see you again, I'll kill you."

"Then get a good look at my back," said Mike, "because that's the only way you'll get a shot off in time."

Then the drugs took full control and Duke pitched backward.

Mike turned to the zombie-faced marines. "Get him to sickbay pronto, and clear the bay for liftoff." The marines managed a grunt and left, taking their fallen leader with them.

Mike ran for the dropship. The engines were already start-ing to whine as he charged up the gangplank.

Raynor had been right about the dropship pilots. The pilot had the coordinates punched in and clearances made before Mike had gotten on board. Now the atmosphere was evacu-ated and the dropship pitched out of the *Hyperion* and into the chaos beyond.

Space was being ripped apart all around them. The *Hyper-ion* was flying through a debris field, pieces still burning as the air bled out of a pierced hull, the remains of some other human ship that had fallen in the path of the Protoss. Energy beams sliced through the vacuum, blistering the retinas of observers.

Mike slid into the nav/comm console behind the pilot's rig.

"I'm going to try to raise Kerrigan's unit," Mike said.

"She's not going to like it," Raynor said grimly, then added, "Do it anyway."

The huge carriers of the Protoss slid like great beasts through space, their attendant flocks of fighters dancing around them like golden flies. Crescent-shaped ships corkscrewed toward the planet, and needlelike fighters and scouts made of silver and gemstones lanced through the debris field.

Behind them, the *Hyperion* itself was burning in a half-dozen spots. Nothing major, but at the moment Mengsk would be worried about more than just a group of AWOL former sup-porters. The battlecruiser's Yamato cannon split the sky with repeated shots, breaking up units of Protoss fighters.

"We got more company!" said the dropship pilot. "Strap in and hold tight!"

Now the Zerg were rising from Tarsonis. The great flying cannons, orange with purplish wings, came aloft and splat-tered in the hundreds against the Protoss carriers. They were followed by the larger flying crab-things, which seemed less affected by the small fighters than the mutalisks were. As

Mike watched, one of the crab-things flew into the intake of a carrier, and the entire Protoss ship went up in a ball of blue-white flame.

A pair of the winged mutalisks noticed the dropship and banked toward them, their gullets vomiting forth coiling globules of bilious matter.

The rebels had precious little in the way of defense on the dropships, and the pilot cursed and tried to bank away from the intercept course.

They weren't going to make it, Mike realized, and braced for the impact with the Zerg acid-spittle.

A trio of bolts ripped the attacking mutalisks into organic tatters, shredding their wings with laser fire. A trio of A-17 Wraiths swooped through the remains of the Zerg, and Mike caught a glimpse of Confederate insignia on the pylons of the ships. Then they were gone as well, looking for new allies and new targets.

"Any luck?" Raynor asked, leaning over Mike's shoulder.

"Lots of traffic right now," Mike snapped. "Hold on. Got a lock. She's broadcasting. I'm putting it on the screen."

"This is Kerrigan." Her face on the screen was now drawn and haggard. Frightened, Mike thought, and a cold chill ran through him. "We've neutralized the Protoss ground units, but there's a wave of Zerg advancing on this position. We need immediate evac."

Another screen winked into existence, and Mengsk's face fluttered into view. Something was sparking erratically near that face, causing him to appear and disappear like a Cheshire cat. "Belay that order," the rebel leader spat. "We're moving out."

Raynor punched the microphone button. "What? You're not just going to leave them?"

If Mengsk had heard Raynor's comment, he gave no outward sign. Given the interference, it was likely he hadn't heard. Instead he said, "All ships prepare to move away from Tarsonis on my mark."

A burst of static broke up Kerrigan's signal. Something big had hit near her. Then she was back. "Uh, boys? How about that evac?"

"Damn you, Arcturus," Raynor said through gritted teeth. "Don't do this."

Mengsk continued to fade in and out. Finally he came in, crisp and clear. "Signal the fleet and take us out of orbit. Now!"

"Arcturus?" said Kerrigan, in comparison to Mengsk now nothing more than a ghost on the screen. "Jim? Mike? What the hell's going on up there . . . ?"

Then the fog of war swallowed her entirely, and the screens registered nothing but static.

Raynor pounded the nav/comm console in frustration.

"You break it, you bought it," said the pilot, throwing the dropship into a tight spiral to break off pursuit by a pair of crab-things. With steel nerves the pilot dropped the fleeing shuttle beneath a Protoss scout, and the crab-things set up to attack it instead.

Mike tracked the location of Kerrigan's broadcast and fed the coordinates into the helm. The ship rocked and swayed onto its new course.

Around them a hundred new stars were born and died in a matter of instants. The greatest danger now was debris from the stricken ships, and the pilot cursed a couple times as he had to lurch suddenly to avoid catching a large piece in the hull.

Finally they were in the atmosphere itself, the screens tinged orange from the reentry fires. Most of the battle was now above them. They only had to worry about surface units now.

But as above, so below. They were coming in low across the rubble-strewn surface of the planet itself. The great cities of Tarsonis were burning, the broad plazas filled with debris and the sunward spires now nothing more than a set of jagged, erratic teeth. The glass of the great buildings had been completely shattered, leaving only the twisted wreckage of

the steel skeletons beneath. One great swath had been leveled through three blocks, ending in the crippled wreckage
of a Protoss carrier, venting unearthly radiation from every
broken seam.

The buildings decreased in size as the rebels flew toward
the farmlands and suburbs, but the devastation was still
severe. Mike could see craters where ships had augured into
the surface. There were sweeping fires here as well, consuming homes and fields, and moving among them there were
warriors from all sides.

Now there were new buildings as well along the scorched
landscape—those of the alien invaders. The creep was everywhere, and deadly poppy-headed structures uncoiled toward
the sky. Nests surrounded with pulsing eggs dotted the landscape.

There were other structures, too, among the debris. These
were golden, with impossible buttresses and sweeping shells,
and mirrored surfaces of unshatterable glass. The Protoss were
setting up their defenses on Tarsonis.

Perhaps they thought there was something here worth saving,
Mike thought. That means they had more faith in humanity
than Mengsk did.

The ground beneath them roiled with the Zerg, and among
them, like shining knights, the Protoss warriors strode, leaving
a wake of dead, oozing bodies. Four-legged mechanical spiders crawled through the ruins, and huge things that looked
like armor-plated caterpillars assaulted the Zerg hives. Lance-
thin fighters strafed the hulking scythe-Zergs that swept the
Protoss warriors aside like a farmer threshing wheat.

Mike said, "We should be close now."

The radio scratched and spat, and a male voice, young and
frightened, came on, ". . . looking for an evac. We got civilians
and wounded. We can see your craft. You got room on that
tub?"

Raynor was on the radio. "Lieutenant Kerrigan, are you
there?"

"No Kerrigan, sir," came the crackling response. "But we're really hurting. The Zerg are everywhere, and coming in with another assault. If we don't leave now, we're not leaving." There was a tremor of fear in the voice.

Mike looked at Raynor. The large man's face was unreadable, a clay sculpture of the real thing. Finally he said, "We're going down. Tell them we're coming."

Mike nodded and said, "But Kerrigan . . ."

"I know," said Raynor, and over the background hiss of the comm unit Mike could swear he heard the sound of a heart breaking. The former lawman took a deep breath and added, "Mengsk would abandon these people like the rest. We won't. I hope that's why we're better than he is."

The dropship grounded itself at the edge of a school-turned-bunker, and refugees had begun streaming out even as the pilot hit the retros. They were led by a lanky kid who wore the tatters of a combat suit. Some volunteer from a Fringe World for Mengsk's rebellion. Mike had never seen him before.

The kid saluted Raynor and said, "Damn glad to see you. Heard the bug-out order, but no one came for us. There are Zerg all along the northern flank. Some Protoss hit them a while back, bought us a breathing spell, but I think the bugs are coming back. The creep's halfway here already, and there's nothing we can do about it."

Raynor just said, "What unit is this?"

The youngster blinked. "We're not any unit at all, sir. There are about a half-dozen units, or what's left of them, that holed up here. Confederate and rebel both, sir. When the Zerg started swarming and the Protoss started blasting, it was every human for himself."

"Have you heard anything about a Lieutenant Kerrigan?" Raynor snapped. "She was engaged in fighting the Protoss near this location."

"No, sir," said the kid. "One of the stragglers said there was a unit fighting Protoss up on the ridge." He waved in the direction of the Zerg. "If'n that's true, Zerg got 'em, I'm afraid."

Raynor took a deep breath, then said, "Get your people on the dropship. Don't worry about heavy ordnance. Leave it. It's not like the Zerg or the Protoss can use it. We lift in two minutes."

Mike came up alongside Raynor and said, "We can still search for her."

Raynor shook his head. "You heard the kid. There's more Zerg coming. With Mengsk's rebels pulling back, the entire planet's going to be awash in aliens in no time at all. The dropship has no defense, and we've got noncombatants on board. We have to get out now and hope we can bum a lift out of the system before everything goes up."

Mike put a hand on Raynor's shoulder. "I'm sorry."

"I know," said Raynor. "God help me, I know."

CHAPTER 17

ROADS NOT TAKEN

*The Confederacy died with Tarsonis. So much of the power and prestige
had been locked up there for so long that with its collapse the rest of the
Confederacy went with it.*

*Arcturus Mengsk played coroner, of course, performing the autopsy and
declaring that the patient had died of massive Zerg poisoning, compounded
by Protoss trauma. The irony that Mengsk's fingerprints were all over the
Confederacy's murder weapon mattered little to many and was ignored by
most. As you might expect, it was not something UNN covered in those days.*

*Before the last Confederate trooper was digested in a Zerg hive, Mengsk
declared the Terran Dominion in order to unite the surviving planets, a
shining new phoenix that would rise from the ashes and gather together all
of humanity. Only by standing together, the former rebel declared, could we
come to defeat the alien menaces.*

*The first ruler of this bright, shining new government was Emperor
Arcturus Mengsk I, ascending to the throne by popular acclamation.*

*The irony of this last little fact, that most of the acclamation was Mengsk's
own, was also missed by most of the general populace.*

—THE LIBERTY MANIFESTO

EVEN AS TIME TICKED AWAY, THEY CIRCLED FOR another twenty minutes, looking for stragglers on the ground. All they found was a lot of Zerg and a lot of land already swallowed by the creep. Finally, listening to the repeated protests of the dropship pilot, they lifted off. Beneath them, the ground churned with Zerg building new structures of gothic flesh. There were flashes of Protoss weapons crackling over the horizon like heat lightning in the summer.

Mengsk contacted the dropship on the way up, a general call to all ships within the area. The terrorist's face was calm, but it was a stone-faced calm, one that didn't project across the screen. His eyes were bright and avaricious.

"Gentlemen, you've done very well, but remember that we've still got a job to do. The seeds of a new empire have been sewn, and if we hope to reap—"

Raynor leaned forward toward the comm-mounted camera and toggled a switch. "Aw, to hell with you!" he snarled.

Mengsk heard that one. The great brow lowered between the rebel leader's eyes. "Jim, I can forgive your impulsive nature, but you're making a terrible mistake. Don't cross me, boy. Don't ever *think* to cross me. I've sacrificed too much to let this fall apart."

"You mean like you sacrificed Kerrigan?" Raynor snapped.

Mengsk recoiled as if Raynor had reached out through space and slugged him. His face reddened. "You'll regret that. You don't seem to realize my situation here. I will not be stopped."

Raynor had finally broken through the thick, deep patina that covered the leader of the rebellion and found the man beneath. Mengsk was angry now, and veins were standing out at the base of his neck. "I will *not* be stopped," he repeated, "Not by *you* or the *Confederates* or the *Protoss*, or *anyone*! I will *rule* this Sector or see it burned to ashes around me. If any of you try to get in my . . ."

Raynor hit the kill switch for the sound and watched Mengsk spit and bellow silently on the screen.

"You got under his skin," said Mike. "At last."

"Must have been something I said," Raynor said, but he didn't smile when he said it.

In the humming silence of the dropship, Mike said, "I'm sorry about Sarah." It didn't sound any better now than it had before, on the surface.

Raynor sat down next to Mike and looked at the deck for a while. "Yeah, me too," he said at last. "I shouldn't have let her go alone."

"I know what you're going through."

"What, you're a telepath now?"

Mike shrugged. "I'm a human. That's what's important. It's been a long war. We've all had losses. We've all seen things we don't want to have seen. A smart man once told me that the living feel guilty about still being alive. And no, it's not your fault."

"Sure feels like it," said Raynor. There was a silence in the dropship cabin. Finally the ex-lawman shook his head. "It's not over," he said. "The Protoss and the Zerg aren't going to give a rat's ass that Mengsk is running things now. They don't care about human wars or human leaders. They're battling throughout humanspace. It's not over."

"I think it's over for me," said Mike. "I'm not a warrior. I've played at it, but I'm a newsman. I don't belong on the battlefield. I belong behind a keyboard or in front of a holo camera."

"The universe has changed, son. What are you planning on doing?"

It was Mike's turn to take a long pause. "I don't know," he said at last. "Something to help out, I suppose. Can't help myself there. But it has to be something other than this."

The dropship had limited range, but they managed to flag down a lift out–system on the *Thunder Child*, an old Leviathan-class cruiser that only four hours and one mutiny earlier had been in the service of the Confederacy. Now it and most of the human ships were pulling back out of combat, leaving Tarsonis to the Zerg, the Protoss, and whatever poor fools who thought underground bunkers were a good idea.

The comm officer of the *Child* met them at the gangway. "I have a message for you from Arcturus Mengsk."

"Mengsk!" spat Raynor. "Is he looking for me to rip him a new orifice?"

"It's not for you, sir," said the comm officer. "It's for a Mr. Michael Liberty. Emphasis on the Mister. You can take it in the communications room, if you want."

Raynor raised a tired eyebrow. Mike waved him to come along. The former planetary marshal, former rebel captain, former revolutionary settled himself in a chair out of view of the comm console's camera. Mike toggled the reply switch and waited for the message to come through space from the *Hyperion*.

Arcturus Mengsk warped into view on the screen. Every hair was back in place, and every action mannered and rehearsed. It was as if the earlier incident had not happened.

"Michael," he beamed.

"Arcturus," said Mike, not even giving him a smile.

Mengsk looked down briefly in sorrow, as if thinking carefully about his next words. Once it would have worked, but now it was a shallow, emotionless mannerism, one that the rebel leader clearly had rehearsed. Michael almost expected him to come around and sit on the edge of the desk. "I'm afraid I can't express sufficiently my regrets about Sarah. I just don't know what to say."

"Captain Raynor had a few choice words," said Mike, his own eyes now blazing.

"And someday, I hope that Jim and I can talk about it." Mengsk's smile was forced and strained. Something had happened, and the great bubble around Mengsk had been shattered. "But that's not why I called you. I have someone who wants to talk to you."

Mengsk reached offscreen to flip a switch and a new face replaced that of the future emperor of the human universe. A balding head dominated by a pair of bushy eyebrows.

"Handy?" said Mike.

"Mickey!" said Handy Anderson. "It's good to see you, buddy! I knew that if anyone in the stable survived this mess, it would be you! You're the lucky coin, always turning up when needed!"

"Anderson, where are you?"

"Here on the *Hyperion*, of course. Arcturus had me shuttled over from a refugee ship. He's been telling me how great you've been through all this. A real trooper. Why no reports for a while?"

"I sent reports. You changed them, remember? Said Mengsk had captured me? Ring any bells?"

"A small bit of editing," said Anderson. "Just enough to make the powers that be, God rest their eternal souls, content. I knew you'd understand."

"Handy—"

"Anyway, I hear you've done a bang-up job. And I knew you'd want to know that, despite the present situation, you can have your old job back."

"My old . . ."

"Sure. I mean, the people who wanted you dead are now no longer in the business, one way or another. I was talking with Arcturus, here, and we could make you the official press liaison to his government. He thinks the world of you, you know. Apparently you grew on him with your winning personality."

"Anderson, I don't know if . . ." Mike said, tapping his forehead with the palm of his hand.

"Just listen. Here's the deal," said the editor-in-chief. "You'd get your own office, just down the hall from Arcturus's. All access, all the time. You do the trips, cover the dinners, get the awards. Lotsa perks. Lotsa security. It's a cush job. Hell, I can get a stringer to type up your reports for you. I tell you—"

Mike thumbed the sound off. Anderson kept talking, but Mike was no longer looking at him.

He was looking at his own reflection in the smooth surface of the screen. He was leaner than when he had last been in Anderson's presence, and his hair was more rumpled. But there was something else as well. It was in his eyes.

His eyes seemed to be looking beyond the console, beyond the walls of the ship itself. It was a distant look, a hard look, a look that he once thought of as being one of despair, but now realized was determination. He was seeing a bigger picture than the one he was immediately involved with.

A look he had seen before on Jim Raynor's face, when Mar Sara died.

"How long will he go before he notices you're not listening?" Raynor grunted.

"He's never noticed before," Mike said. He sucked on his lower lip for a moment, then said, "I know what I want to do. I should start using my own hammer."

Raynor sighed. "Try that once more, in English."

"When all you have is a hammer, everything looks like a nail," quoted Mike. "I'm not a warrior. I'm a newsman. And I should start using my newsman tools for the good of humanity. Get the story out. Get the *real* story out."

Mike hooked a thumb toward the screen. Handy Anderson had finally noticed that he wasn't being heard. The balding editor-in-chief tapped the screen and mouthed an unheard question.

"I want to get as far away from Arcturus Mengsk as possible," said Mike. "And then I want to start telling the truth about all this. Because if I don't, people like *him* are going to determine what really happened." He jerked a thumb at the screen. "Him and Arcturus Mengsk. And I don't think humanity could survive those lies."

Raynor smiled, and it was a broad, earnest smile. "It's good to have you back," he said.

"Its good to be back," said Mike, looking at the far-eyed stranger reflected in the monitor. He shook his head and added, "I could *really* use a cigarette."

"So could I," said Raynor. "I don't think there are any on this tub. But look at the bright side: at least you still got your coat."

POSTBELLUM

BATHED IN LIGHT, THE MAN IN THE TATTERED COAT stands in a room of shadows. The smoke from the last of a series of cigarettes snakes around him, and the ground at his luminous feet is scattered with butts that look like fallen stars.

"So what you're seeing," says Michael Liberty, the luminous figure speaking to the surrounding darkness, "is my own private little war, fought on my turf, and with my weapons. Not cruisers and space fighters and marines, but just words. And the truth. That's my specialty. That's my hammer. And I know how to use it."

The figure takes another long puff, and the final coffin nail joins the others on the floor. "And you people, whoever you are, need to hear it. True and unfiltered. That's why the holo transmissions: they're harder to fake. And I'm spreading this as far as I can, over the open wavelengths, so everyone knows about Mengsk, and the Zerg, and the Protoss. And knows about men and women like Jim Raynor and Sarah Kerrigan, so they and others like them may not be forgotten."

Michael Liberty scratches the back of his neck and says, "I went into the military thinking it was just another bureaucracy filled with craven cowards and corporate stupidity.

"Well, I was right, but I was also wrong."

He looks at the viewers with unseeing eyes. "But there are also people really trying to help others. People really trying to save others. Save their bodies. Save their minds. Save their souls."

His brow furrows, and he adds, "And we need more people like that, if we're going to survive the dark days ahead."

He shrugs again. "That's it. That's the story of the fall of the Confederacy, of the Zerg and the Protoss invasions, of the rise of Emperor Mengsk of the Terran Dominion. The battles are still being fought, planets are still dying, and most of the time, no one seems to know why. When I find that out, I'll get you that information, as well.

"I'm Michael Daniel Liberty, no longer of UNN. Now I'm a free man. And I'm done."

And with those words the figure freezes in place, trapped in its prison of light. He is caught with a tired smile on his face. A satisfied smile.

Around the hologram the lights come up, luminous bulbs that have been bred specifically for the purpose. The walls pulse and sweat, and thick, viscous fluid drips from weeping sores along that wall to keep the air moist and warm. The cable of the human-constructed hologram projector merges in a gooey lump into the organic power constructs of the main structure. The connection between the two worlds was once a colonial marine, but now serves a higher purpose for its new masters.

On semiorganic screens around the perimeter, the better brains of the Zerg discuss what they have seen. They are morphic constructs, bred only to think and direct. They too serve their higher purpose within the Zerg hive.

In the projection room a hand reaches up and touches the rewind button. The hand was once human, but is now transformed, the product of the Zerg's mutagenic capabilities. The flesh of the hand is green and dotted with chitinlike extrusions. Beneath the surface of the skin strange ichors and new organs twist and slide. Once she was human, but she has been transformed and now serves a higher purpose. She was once called Sarah, but now is known as the Queen of Blades.

The other organic minds, leaders of the Zerg, make noise in the background. Kerrigan ignores them, for they say nothing, at least nothing that matters. Instead she leans forward to study the weathered face in the holo, the face with the deep transfixing eyes. Deep within her restructured heart something stirs, a ghost of a memory of a feeling for this man. And for other men. For those who would sacrifice all for their humanity.

As opposed to merely sacrificing their humanity itself.

Kerrigan shudders for a moment as the old feeling washes over her, that now-alien feeling of her once-human nature. Yet as quickly as it appears, the emotion is suppressed, so that none of the other Zerg notice it. At least that's what Kerrigan assumes.

Kerrigan nods. She blames the reporter's words for the uncomfortable emotion. It has to be the report itself, not the memories it brings, that disturbs her. Michael Liberty always was a master of words. He could make even a queen long for her days as a simple pawn.

Still, there is much in Michael Liberty's broadcast, and much that is not realized by the nonhuman minds that are now her compatriots. There is much valuable data here. Much that can be divined from Michael Liberty's words. What he says and how he says it.

The projector chimes, signaling the rewind complete, and the inhuman hand presses the play button, then raises a finger to her very wide lips.

Kerrigan, the Queen of Blades, permits herself a small smile and concentrates on the man wrapped in light. She wants to see what else she can learn from her new enemies.

SHADOW OF
THE XEL'NAGA

GABRIEL MESTA

ABOUT THE AUTHOR

Gabriel Mesta is a pseudonym for the husband-and-wife team of KEVIN J. ANDERSON and REBECCA MOESTA. They have written two dozen books together and dozens more separately. They have worked in many "universes," including *Star Wars*, *The X-Files*, *Star Trek*, *Titan A.E.*, and *Dune*, as well as their own original universes. For more information on their work, please visit them on the web at

www.wordfire.com

or

www. dunenovels.com

or write to them care of

AnderZone
PO Box 767
Monument, CO 80132-0767

This one is for Scott Moesta,
for his expert advice in the StarCraft arena (we couldn't
have done it without you). All those long, hard hours
of playing games finally paid off!

And for his wife, Tina Moesta, for understanding that
sometimes a guy has to go kick some alien butt.

ACKNOWLEDGMENTS

Special thanks to Chris Metzen and Bill Roper at Blizzard for their valuable input; Rob Simpson and Marco Palmieri at Pocket Books for their support and for insisting on having us do the project; Kevin J. Anderson and Rebecca Moesta, without whom Gabriel Moesta wouldn't exist; Matt Bialer of the Trident Media Group for his encouragement on this project; Debra Ray at AnderZone for cheering us on; Catherine Sidor, Diane E. Jones, and Sarah L. Jones at WordFire, Inc., for keeping things running smoothly; and Jonathan Cowan, Kiernan Maletsky, Nick Jacobs, Gregor Myhren, and Wes Cronk for being our *StarCraft* "tour guides" and for their unquenchable enthusiasm for the game.

CHAPTER 1

AS A SMOTHERING BLANKET OF DARKNESS DESCENDED over the town of Free Haven, the rugged settlers scrambled to avoid the storm. Night came quickly on the colony planet of Bhekar Ro, with plenty of wind but no stars.

Pitch-black clouds swirled over the horizon, caught on the sharp mountainous ridge surrounding the broad valley that formed the heart of the struggling agricultural colony. Already, explosive thunder crackled over the ridge like a poorly aimed artillery barrage. Each blast was powerful enough to be detected on several still-functioning seismographs planted around the explored areas.

Atmospheric conditions created thunder slams with sonic-boom intensity. The roar itself was sometimes sufficient to cause destruction. And what the sonic thunder left unharmed, the laser-lightning tore to pieces.

Forty years earlier, when the first colonists had fled the oppressive government of the Terran Confederacy, they had been duped into believing that this place could be made into a new Eden. After three generations, the stubborn settlers refused to give up.

Riding in the shotgun seat beside her brother Lars, Octavia Bren looked through the streaked windshield of the giant robo-harvester as they hurriedly trundled back to town. The rumble of the mechanical treads and the roar of the engine almost drowned out the sonic thunder. Almost.

Laser-lightning blasts seared down from the clouds like luminous spears, straight-line lances of static discharge that left glassy pockmarks on the terrain. The laser-lightning reminded Octavia of library images she had seen of a big Yamato gun fired from a battlecruiser in orbit.

"Why in the galaxy did our grandparents ever choose to move here?" she asked rhetorically. More laser-lightning burned craters into the countryside.

"For the scenery, of course," Lars joked.

While the bombardment of hail would clear the air of the ever-present dust and grit, it would also damage the crops of triticale-wheat and salad-moss that barely clung to the rocky soil. The Free Haven settlers had few emergency provisions to help them withstand any severe harvest failure, and it had been a long time since they had asked for outside help.

But they would survive somehow. They always had.

Lars watched the approaching storm, a spark of excitement in his hazel eyes. Though he was a year older than his sister, when he wore that cocky grin on his face he looked like a reckless teenager. "I think we can outrun the worst of it."

"You always overestimate what we can do, Lars." Even at the age of seventeen, Octavia was known for her stability and common sense. "And I always end up saving your butt."

Lars seemed to have a bottomless reservoir of energy and enthusiasm. She gripped her seat as the big all-purpose vehicle crunched through a trench and continued along a wide beaten path between plantings, heading toward the distant lights of the town.

Shortly after their parents' death, it had been Lars's crazy suggestion that the two of them expand their cultivated land and add remote automated mineral mines to their holdings. She had tried, unsuccessfully, to talk him out of it. "Let's be practical, Lars. We've already got our hands full with the farm as it is. Expanding would leave us time for nothing but work—not even families."

Half of the colonists' eligible daughters had already filed requests to marry him—Cyn McCarthy had filed three separate times!—but so far Lars had made plenty of excuses. Colonists were considered adults at the age of fifteen on this rough world, and many were married and had children before they reached their eighteenth birthday. Next year, Octavia would be facing the same decision, and choices were few in Free Haven.

"Are you sure we want to do this?" she had asked one last time.

"Of course. It's worth the extra effort. And once we're established there'll be plenty of time for each of us to get married," Lars had insisted, shaking back his shoulder-length sandy hair. She had never been able to argue with that grin. "Before we know it, Octavia, it'll all turn around, and then you'll thank me."

He had been certain they could grow crops high on the slopes of the Back Forty, the ridge that separated their lands from another broad basin and more mountains twelve kilometers away. So the brother and sister had used their robo-harvester to scrape flat a new swath of barely arable farmland and plant new crops. They also set up automated mineral mining stations on the rocky slopes of the foothills. That had been almost two years ago.

Now a gust of wind slammed into the broad metal side of the harvester, rattling the sealed windowports. Lars compensated on the steering column and accelerated. He didn't even look tired from their long day of hard work.

Laser-lightning seared across the sky, leaving colorful tracks across her retinas. Though he couldn't see any better than his sister, Lars didn't slow down at all. They both just wanted to get home.

"Watch out for the boulders!" Octavia said, her piercing green eyes spotting the hazard as rain slashed across the windows of the impressive tractorlike vehicle.

Lars discounted the rocks, drove over them, and crushed the stone with the vehicle's treads. "Aww, don't underestimate the capabilities of the machine."

She snorted indelicately. "But if you throw a plate or fry a hydraulic cam, *I'm* the one who has to fix it."

The multipurpose robo-harvester, the most important piece of equipment any of the colonists owned, was capable of bulldozing, tilling, destroying boulders, planting, and harvesting crops. Some of the big machines had rock-crusher attachments, others had flamethrowers. The vehicles were also practical for traversing ten- to twenty-klick distances over rough terrain.

The hull of the robo-harvester, once a gleaming cherry red, was now faded, scratched, and pitted. The engine ran as smoothly as a lullaby, though, and that was all Octavia cared about.

Now she checked the weather scanner and atmospheric-pressure tracker in the robo-harvester's cabin, but the readings were all wild. "Looks like a bad one tonight."

"They're always bad ones. This is Bhekar Ro, after all—what do you expect?"

Octavia shrugged. "I guess it was good enough for Mom and Dad." *Back when they were alive.*

She and Lars were the only survivors of their family. Every family among the settlers had lost friends or relatives. Taming an uncooperative new world was dangerous, rarely rewarding work, always ripe for tragedy.

But the people here still followed their dreams. These exhausted colonists had left the tight governmental fences of the Confederacy for the promised land of Bhekar Ro some forty years before. They had sought independence and a new start, away from the turmoil and constant civil wars among the inner Confederacy worlds.

The original settlers had wanted nothing more than peace and freedom. They had begun idealistically, establishing a central town with resources for all the colonists to share, naming it Free Haven, and dividing farmland equally among the able-bodied workers. But in time the idealism faded as the colonists endured toil and new hardships on a planet that did not live up to their expectations.

Nobody among the colonists ever suggested going back, though—especially not Octavia and Lars Bren.

The lights of Free Haven glowed like a warm, welcoming paradise as the robo-harvester approached. In the distance Octavia could already hear the storm-warning siren next to the old missile turret in the town plaza, signaling colonists to find shelter. Everyone else—at least the colonists who had common sense—had already barricaded themselves inside their prefabricated homes to shelter from the storm.

They passed outlying homes and fields, crossed over dry irrigation ditches, and reached the perimeter of the town, which was laid out in the shape of an octagon. A low perimeter fence encircled the settlement, but the gates for the main streets had never been closed.

An explosion of sonic thunder roared so close that the robo-harvester rattled. Lars gritted his teeth and drove onward. Octavia remembered sitting on her father's knee during her childhood, laughing at the thunder as her family had gathered inside their home, feeling safe. . . .

Their grandparents had aged rapidly from the rigors of life here and had the dubious distinction of being the first to be buried in Bhekar Ro's ever-growing cemetery outside Free Haven's octagonal perimeter. Then, not long after Octavia had turned fifteen, the spore blight had struck.

The sparse crops of mutated triticale-wheat had been afflicted by a tiny black smut on a few of the kernels. Because food was in short supply, Octavia's mother had set aside the moldy wheat for herself and her husband, feeding untainted bread to their children. The meager meal had seemed like any other: rough and tasteless, but nutritious enough to keep them alive.

Octavia remembered that last night so clearly. She had been suffering from one of her occasional migraines and a dire sense of unreasonable foreboding. Her mother had sent the teenage girl to bed early, where Octavia had had terrible nightmares.

The next morning she had awakened in a too-quiet house to find both of her parents dead in their bed. Beneath wet sheets twisted about by their final agony, the bodies of her mother and father were a quivering, oozing mass of erupted fungal bodies, rounded mushrooms of exploding spores that rapidly disintegrated all flesh. . . .

Lars and Octavia had never returned to that house, burning it to the ground along with the tainted fields and the homes of seventeen other families that had been infected by the horrible, parasitic disease.

Though a terrible blow to the colony, the spore blight had drawn the survivors together even more tightly. The new mayor, Jacob "Nik" Nikolai, had delivered an impassioned eulogy for all the victims of the spore plague, somehow rekindling the fires of independence in the process and giving the settlers the drive to stay here. They had already lived through so much, survived so many hardships, that they could pull through this.

Moving together into an empty prefab dwelling at the edge of Free Haven, Octavia and Lars had rebuilt their lives. They made plans. They expanded. They tracked their automated mines and watched the seismic monitors for signs of tectonic disturbances that might affect their work or the town. The two drove out to the fields each day and labored side by side until well after dark. They worked harder, risked more . . . and survived.

As Octavia and Lars passed through the open gate and

drove around the town square toward their residence, the storm finally struck with full force. It became a slanting wall of rain and hail as the robo-harvester ground its way past the lights and barricaded doors of metal-walled huts. Their own home looked the same as all the others, but Lars found it by instinct, even in the blinding downpour.

He spun the large vehicle to a halt in the flat gravel clearing in front of their house. He locked down the treads and powered off the engine, while Octavia tugged a reinforced hat down over her head and got ready to jump out of the cab and make a break for the door. Even running ten feet in this storm would be a miserable ordeal.

Before the robo-harvester's systems dimmed completely, Octavia checked the fuel reservoirs, since her brother never remembered to do so. "We'll need to get more vespene gas from the refinery."

Lars grabbed the door handle and hunched his head down. "Tomorrow, tomorrow. Rastin's probably hiding inside his hut cursing the wind right now. That old codger doesn't like storms any more than I do."

He popped open the hatch and jumped out seconds before a strong gust slammed the door back into its frame. Octavia exited from the other side, hopping from the step to the broad tractor treads to the ground.

As she ran beside her brother in a mad dash to their dwelling, the hail hit them like machine-gun bullets. Lars got their front door open, and the siblings crashed into the house, drenched and windblown. But at least they were safe from the storm.

Sonic thunder pealed across the sky again. Lars undid the fastenings on his jacket. Octavia yanked off her dripping hat and tossed it into a corner, then powered up their lights so she could check one of the old seismographs they had installed in their hut.

Few of the other colonists bothered to monitor planetary conditions or track underground activity anymore, but

Lars had thought it important to place seismographs in their automated mining stations out in the Back Forty foothills. Of course, Octavia had been the one to repair and install the aging monitoring equipment.

Lars had been right, though. There had been increasing tremors of late, setting off ripples of aftershocks that originated deep in the mountain range at the far side of the next valley.

Just what we need—another thing to worry about, Octavia thought, looking at the graph with concern.

Lars joined her to read the seismograph strip. The long and shaky line appeared to have been drawn by a caff-addicted old man. He saw several little blips and spikes, probably echoes of sonic thunder, but no major seismic events. "Now that's interesting. Aren't you glad we didn't have an earthquake tonight?"

She knew it would happen even before he finished his sentence. Maybe it was another one of Octavia's powerful premonitions, or just a discouraged acceptance that things would get worse whenever they had the opportunity.

Just as Lars formed another of his cocky grins, a tremor rippled through the ground, as if the uneasy crust of Bhekar Ro were having a nightmare. At first Octavia hoped it was merely a particularly close blast of sonic thunder, but the tremors continued to build, lurching the floor beneath their feet and shaking the entire prefab house.

Lars tensed his powerful muscles to ride out the temblor. They both watched the seismograph go wild. "The readings are off the scale!"

Astonished, Octavia pointed out, "This isn't even centered *here*. It's fifteen klicks away, over the ridge."

"Great. Not far from where we set up all our automated mining equipment." The seismograph went dead, its sensors overloaded, as the quake pounded the ground for what seemed an eternity before it gradually began to fade. "Looks like you're gonna have some repair work to do tomorrow, Octavia."

"I've always got repair work to do," she said.

Outside, the storm reached a crescendo. Lars and Octavia sat together in weary silence, just waiting out the disaster. "Do you want to play cards?" he asked.

Then all the lights inside their dwelling went out, leaving them in pitch blackness lit only by flares from the laser-lightning.

"Not tonight," she said.

CHAPTER 2

THE QUEEN OF BLADES.

Her name had once been Sarah Kerrigan, back when she'd been something else . . . back when she'd been human.

Back when she'd been *weak*.

She sat back within the pulsing organic walls of the burgeoning Zerg hive. Monstrous creatures moved about in the shadows, guided by her every thought, functioning for a greater purpose.

With her mental powers and her control over these awful and destructive creatures, a transformed Sarah Kerrigan had established the new hive on the ashen ruins of the planet Char. It was a gray world, blasted and still smoldering from potent cosmic radiation. This planet had long been a battlefield. Only the strongest could survive here.

The vicious Zerg race knew how to adapt, how to survive, and Sarah Kerrigan had done the same to become one of them. Raised as a psi-talented Ghost, a telepathically powered espionage and intelligence agent for the Terran Confederacy, she had been captured by the Zerg Overmind and transformed.

Her skin, toughened with armor-polymer cells, glowed an oily, silvery green. Her yellow lambent eyes were surrounded by dark patches of skin that could have been bruises or shadows. Her hair had become Medusa spines—jointed segments like the sharp legs of a venomous spider. Each spike writhed as plans continuously burned through her brain. Her face still had a delicate beauty that just might lull a human victim into a moment of hesitation—giving her enough time to strike.

When she caught a reflection of herself, Sarah Kerrigan occasionally recalled what it had been like to be human, to be lovely—in a human sort of way—and that she had once even begun to love a man named Jim Raynor, who was also very much in love with her. *Human emotions and weaknesses.*

Jim Raynor. She tried not to remember him. She would have no scruples now against killing the burly, good-natured man with his walrus mustache, if such was required of her. She did not regret what had happened to her, since she had a more important mission now.

Sarah Kerrigan was much more than just another Zerg.

The various Zerg minions had been adapted and mutated from other species that they had infested during their history of conquest. Drawing from a sweeping catalog of DNA and physical attributes, the Zerg could live anywhere. The swarms were as much at home on bleak Char as they had been on the lush Terran colony world of Mar Sara.

A truly magnificent species.

The Zerg swarm would sweep across the worlds in the galaxy, consuming and infesting every place they touched. Because of their nature, the Zerg could suffer overwhelming catastrophic losses and still keep coming, keep devouring.

But in the recent war against the Protoss and the Terran Confederacy, the almighty Overmind had been destroyed. And *that* had nearly spelled the end for the Zerg swarms.

At first, their victory had seemed secure as the Zerg infested the two Terran fringe colony worlds of Chau Sara and Mar Sara. Their numbers grew while the rest of the Confederacy remained oblivious to the danger. But then a Protoss war fleet—never before seen by humans—had sterilized the face of Chau Sara. Though the unexpected attack obliterated the Zerg infestation there (and also slaughtered millions of innocent human colonists), the Terran Confederacy had responded immediately to this unprovoked aggression. The Protoss commander had not had the stomach to destroy the second world of Mar Sara, and so the Zerg infestation grew there unchecked.

Eventually, the Zerg minions had wiped out the Terran Confederate capital of Tarsonis. And Sarah Kerrigan, human Ghost, a covert psi-powered operative, had been betrayed by her fellow military comrades and infested by the Zerg. Recognizing her incredible telepathic powers, the Overmind had decided to use her for something special. . . .

But then, on the nearly conquered Protoss home planet of Aiur, a Protoss warrior had killed the Overmind in a suicidal explosion that made a hero of him and decapitated the Zerg hive.

Leaving Sarah Kerrigan, the Queen of Blades, to pick up the pieces.

Now the control of the vicious, swarming race lay in her clawed hands. She faced the tremendous challenge of transforming the planet into a new nexus for the perfect Zerg race. The swarms would rise again.

Under her guidance, a few surviving drones had metamorphosed into hatcheries. Kerrigan's Zerg followers had found and delivered enough minerals and resources to convert those hatcheries into more sophisticated lairs . . . and then into complete hives. With the numerous new larvae generated by the hatcheries, she had created creep colonies, extractors, spawning pools. Before long, the organic mat of Zerg creep spread over the charred surface of the planet. The nourishing substance offered food and energy for the various minions of the new colony.

It was everything she needed to restore the wounded, but never defeated, Zerg race.

Kerrigan sat surrounded by the light. Her mind was filled with details reported to her by the dozens of surviving overlords, huge minds that carried separate swarms on missions dictated by their Queen of Blades. She did not relax, she never slept. There was too much work to do, too many plans to lay . . . too much revenge to achieve.

Sarah Kerrigan flexed her long-fingered hands, extended the rapierlike claws that could disembowel an opponent— *any opponent*, from the treacherous rebel Arcturus Mengsk, who had betrayed her, to General Edmund Duke, whose ineptitude had led to her eventual capture and transformation.

She looked down at one claw, thinking of how she could draw it across the throat of the jowly iron-edged general and watch his fresh hot blood spill out. Though they had not intended it as a favor, Edmund Duke and Arcturus Mengsk had made it possible for her to become the Queen of Blades, to reach the full power and fury of her potential. How could she be angry with them for that?

Still . . . she wanted to kill them.

In the hive around her, zerglings moved about, each the size of a dog she had once owned as a young girl. They were insect-shelled creatures shaped like lizards, with clacking claws and long fangs. Zerglings were fast little killing machines that could descend like piranha onto an enemy army and tear the soldiers to pieces.

Sarah Kerrigan found them beautiful, just as a mother would view any of her precious children. She stroked the gleaming greenish hide of the nearest zergling. In response, it ran its claws over her own nearly indestructible skin, then dusted her with the feathery touch of its fangs, a caress that might have been fondness. . . .

Hideous hydralisks patrolled the perimeter of the colony, some of the most fearsome of the Zerg minions. Flying, crablike guardians soared overhead, ready to spew acid that would destroy any ground-based threat.

The Zerg swarm was safe and secure.

Sarah Kerrigan wasn't worried, and certainly not afraid, but she was careful. She moved about restlessly on powerful muscles, though she could see everything through the eyes of her minions if she chose.

Along with her remaining human ambition and the emotional sting of betrayal, she also felt the relentless conquering urge that came from her new Zerg genetics.

In aeons long past, the mysterious and ancient race of the Xel'Naga had created the Zerg race, their perfect design relentless and pure. Kerrigan smiled at the delicious irony of it. The Zerg had been so perfect they had eventually turned on their creators and infested the Xel'Naga themselves.

Now that the leadership of all the swarms was in her own hands, Kerrigan promised herself that she would lead the Zerg to the pinnacle of their destiny.

But when she sat back in her hive and watched the swarming creatures going about their business, gathering resources and preparing for war, the Queen of Blades felt the tiniest remnant of human sympathy stirring in her heart.

She felt sorry for *anyone* who got in her way.

CHAPTER 3

AS IF TAUNTING THEM WITH THE WEATHER'S capriciousness, the next morning on Bhekar Ro dawned bright and clear. It reminded Octavia of the photo-images the original survey crew had shown her grandparents to lure them and the first group of desperate settlers here.

Maybe it wasn't all lies after all. . . .

As she and Lars cracked open the door seal of their dwelling, a trickle of rainwater ran down from the entryway, pattering onto the soft ground. High overhead, the angular shape of a glider hawk cruised along, searching for the flooded-out bodies of drowned lizards.

Octavia trudged across the drying muck to the robo-harvester. With a shake of her short brown curls, she set to work. She ran an experienced eye over the hull and noticed dozens of new hail craters pounded into the metal, making it look like the rind of a sourange. Of course, nobody on Bhekar Ro cared much about shiny paint jobs, as long as the equipment worked. She was relieved to find that the storm had done no serious damage to the machinery.

Up and down the town streets, ragged colonists woke up and emerged from their houses to assess the damage, as they had done so many times before. From a nearby dwelling, Abdel and Shayna Bradshaw were already squabbling, dismayed at the amount of repair work they would have to do. From across the street Kiernan and Kirsten Warner waved to Cyn McCarthy, who trotted toward the mayor's house at the center of town, an optimistic smile on her freckled face in spite of the disaster. Good-natured Cyn had a habit of offering her help wherever it might be needed, though the copper-haired young woman often forgot to do what she had promised.

Because the rough weather came at unpredictable times, with no identifiable storm season, the settlers had a continuous battle to repair what was broken. They constantly planted the cleared fields, rotating crops from whip-barley to triticale-wheat to salad-moss, hoping to harvest more than they lost, striving to get two steps ahead before they had to take one step back again.

Among the casualties of the devastating spore plague had been four of the colony's best scientists. Cyn McCarthy's husband, Wyl, a second-generation chemical engineer, had been one of them. For the first decades, the scientists had worked with the planet's resources and environment, concocting biological modifications of the crops and animals to increase their chances of survival. Free Haven had been stable for a while, the arable land slowly increasing.

But the deaths of these educated people left the rest of the untrained settlers too busy with simple survival to learn any new specialties. The colonists went about their tasks as farmers, mechanics, and miners, their daylight hours filled with urgent matters that left no time for exploration or expansion. The general consensus, voiced by Mayor Nikolai, was that investigation and scientific pursuits were a luxury they could return to at some later date.

"Any real damage?" Lars asked his sister as she finished her inspection of the big robo-harvester.

Octavia rapped her knuckles on the pitted and scarred door. "A few more scrapes. Just cosmetic."

"Beauty marks. Adds character." Lars opened the door, and melted hailwater ran out of the cab and down through the flat metal treads. "We need to get out to the Back Forty and check on those seismographs and the mining stations. That quake hit them pretty hard."

Octavia smiled, knowing her brother well. "And, since we're out there, you'll want to see if the tremors uncovered anything."

He gave her that grin again. "Just part of the job. We registered some pretty hefty seismic jolts. Could be significant. And you *know* none of the other settlers is going to bother taking a look."

The decades-old weather stations and seismographs the scientists had set up at the valley perimeter continued to take readings, and occasionally Lars would retrieve the data. For the most part, the settlers stayed within their safe cultivated valley, growing enough food to stay alive, mining enough minerals to repair their facilities, but never expanding beyond their capabilities.

In the past, other colonists had tried to establish settlements beyond the main valley. Some had moved away from Free Haven, searching for better farmland. But one by one each of those distant farms had fallen to blight, plague, or natural disaster, and the few survivors had made their way back to the colony town in defeat.

Octavia climbed aboard the robo-harvester with Lars as he powered up the engines. She swung the door shut just as the thick treads began to move. Other settlers set out in their own vehicles to inspect their fields, clearly anticipating the worst.

Octavia and Lars took the robo-harvester far out toward the foothills. Lars had the true pioneer spirit, always wanting to find new mineral deposits, productive vespene geysers, fertile land. He would be happy just to *make* discoveries, while Octavia hoped to fulfill her parents' dream and actually transform Bhekar Ro into a place where they could be proud to live. Someday.

As the big vehicle trundled across the valley floor, she could see that many of the fragile crops had been hammered by the storm. The hail and sonic thunder had battered tall stalks to the mucky ground or bruised unripened fruit; the laser-lightning had set stunted orchards on fire.

A few hardy farmers were already out trying to salvage what they could. Gandhi and Liberty Ryan, sweating in their overalls, worked hard to erect protective bubbles over the seedlings, assisted by their adopted hand, Brutus Jensen, and three children of their own. The family members were too tired even to talk to one another as they went about their labors. Brutus Jensen managed to give them a halfhearted wave, while the Ryans could barely nod.

Kilometers farther along, the road dwindled to little more than a path marked on a navigation screen. They paused briefly at the far edge of the officially settled area.

Lars kept the robo-harvester's engine running as he called out in the direction of a shack and some storehouses. "Hey, Rastin! Get out of that puttering refinery and hook us up so we can fill our tanks. Or have you been sniffing too much vespene gas?"

The lanky old prospector strode around the hissing and throbbing stations he had built around the cluster of chemical geysers where he had staked his claim. Old Blue, his mastiff-sized dog, came out from his sleeping hole under the corrugated metal porch.

The dog's lips were curled back and his sky-blue fur bristled as he growled, but Octavia climbed out of the robo-harvester and clapped her hands. "You don't fool me, you grouch of a dog."

With a happy bark, Old Blue bounded toward her, his thick tail wagging. She patted his head and high shoulders, trying unsuccessfully to keep his muddy paws off her jumpsuit.

Rastin and Lars exchanged complaints and insults—because that was the way the old prospector conducted business—but Rastin wasted no time filling up their vehicle. Octavia had never been able to decide whether the codger was an efficient worker or just anxious to get rid of any visitors so he could go back to his solitude.

One of the few surviving original settlers, Rastin had been independent and alone on Bhekar Ro for forty years. He had always wanted to get away from the Terran Confederacy, and might actually have preferred an empty habitable world all his own; the small group on this planet had been the best he could do.

Rastin lived in an often-repaired shack made out of spare components. He had erected his refinery over a cluster of four vespene geysers, one of which was already played out. The remaining trio of geysers produced enough of the fuel to meet the colony's modest needs.

Having fueled the robo-harvester, the old prospector sent them off with a gruff wave that looked very much like a gesture of disgust. Octavia patted Old Blue's big head again before she stepped back up onto the vehicle's muddy treads. The dog bounded off with the grace of a jumping mule as it spotted a hairy rodent dashing between broken rocks.

Rastin went back to tinkering with his equipment, grumbling because after the earthquake another of the geysers had stopped producing. He delivered a swift kick to the pumping station, but even this tried-and-true repair procedure did not wake the geyser.

Leaving Rastin's homestead, Lars and Octavia ascended into the steep foothills toward the boundary ridge. The terrain became much rougher. Their Back Forty extended far past where the potential cropland had been demarcated by the cooperative families. Out here, the mineral and resource rights had been up for grabs to anyone with the spare time or ambition to increase their acreage. So Lars and Octavia had staked out a claim, in addition to the fields their parents and grandparents had tilled.

As the morning grew warmer and the orange sun climbed into the sky, bleaching away shadows, the robo-harvester clawed up a steep ridge, following paths that only Lars had ever driven. "Our mining stations are still off-line," he said, his voice flat. "And that's the most I can say."

As he brought the robo-harvester to a halt, Octavia could see to her dismay that the automated installations were tilted on their anchor pads, obviously damaged and unable to function.

"Go to it, Octavia—you're the expert."

With a sigh, she descended from the vehicle and hunkered down to see how much repair the mining stations would require. She studied the control panel of the processing turret, surprised at how many red warning lights were illuminated at the same time.

Under normal operation, the clunky machines would wander over the rocky slopes, taking mineral samples and marking desirable deposits. Then processing turrets would be erected so that the mining and extraction activities could continue until a valuable vein had been processed, while the mechanized scout continued to search for more sites.

Lars left his sister to her work. "I'm going up to the top of the ridge to see about those seismographs. Maybe I can fix them myself."

Octavia suppressed a disbelieving snort. "Be my guest."

Her brother climbed up the slope from boulder to boulder, until he topped the saddle and stared across the next valley. She didn't notice how long he stood in silent awe before he started yelling for her. "Octavia! Come up here!"

She looked up, slammed the service door shut on the mining turret, then stood. "What is it?"

But Lars bounded up onto a higher rocky outcropping, from which he could get a better view. He gave a low whistle. "Now *this* is interesting."

Octavia scrambled after him while the back of her mind ran through the different tricks she'd probably have to use to get the mining stations functional again. She knew Lars got distracted easily.

From the top, she got a good look into the next valley, quickly seeing the changes the previous night's earthquake had wrought. Numerous new vespene geysers steamed into the air, curls of silvery-white mist that could provide the colony with more than enough fuel for the next several decades.

But that wasn't what had caught her brother's eye.

"What do you think it is?" He gestured wildly toward the next rugged ridge across the bowl-shaped valley, twelve kilometers from Free Haven.

Before the quake, a prominent conelike peak had jutted into the sky, a distinctive landmark on the continent. But that was yesterday.

The terrible storm and severe tremors had sparked a huge avalanche, breaking off an entire side of the mountain. The stones had fallen away, split off like a scab ripped from a ragged wound, to expose something very strange—and completely unnatural—inside the mountain.

And it was glowing.

The two of them rushed back to the robo-harvester. The big vehicle crunched across the rough terrain and over the mountainous saddle, then toiled headfirst down the easiest switchbacked path into the adjacent valley. Lars drove faster than she had ever seen him try, but Octavia didn't complain. For once, she felt as eager to investigate as her brother did.

He raced past the hissing geysers and clouds of eye-stinging gases, leaving deep tracks in the soft valley floor. Small animals of species Octavia had never seen—they probably weren't edible anyway—scampered out of the way.

Finally, the vehicle crunched to an abrupt stop at the base of the avalanche field where the mountainside had collapsed. Octavia peered up through the dusty windshield at an enormous structure. She and Lars both stared at it in fascination and confusion, before jumping simultaneously out of the robo-harvester for a better look.

Neither of them had any idea what the object could be.

Once buried deep within the mountain, the amazing artifact now pulsed like a huge resinous beehive. Its swirled walls and curved faces were lumpy and pocked with open air vents or passages. There seemed to be no functional design, no sensible blueprint, no purpose that Octavia could fathom.

But the thing was obviously of alien origin. Possibly organic.

"I guess we're not alone here on this planet," she said.

CHAPTER 4

THE ABANDONED WORLD HAD NO REMEMBERED name. The planet was so obscure that it did not show up on even the most detailed of Protoss charts.

The scholar female Xerana stepped on the dusty, time-worn remnants of what must once have been a Xel'Naga outpost, probably the first living being to stand here since the ancient progenitors had vanished into history and legend. She marveled at the idea and felt a stab of disappointment that she could never share this with the rest of the Protoss race.

Her broad, knobbed feet crunched on tiny pebbles and rubble. No doubt, all of this had been a magnificent city, ages ago. The smell of dust and mystery hung thick in the still air.

Xerana, like the others of the Dark Templar, had been banished from Protoss society, exiled from their beloved homeworld of Aiur. When the Protoss Judicator class had commanded that all members of their race must join the way of the Khala, a telepathic union that connected the Protoss in a sea of thought, the Dark Templar had refused to follow. They became outcasts, persecuted because they feared the Khala would strip away their individuality, melding them into an overall subconscious mind.

Although the stern Judicators had driven them off and even now continued to hunt them down, the exiles bore the Protoss no ill will. The fabled Xel'Naga race had created all of them. The followers of the Khala disagreed with the Dark Templar on fundamental issues, but Xerana and her comrades still considered the First Born—the Protoss—their brothers and sisters.

And because they strove to better themselves in ways that the other Protoss refused to consider, the Dark Templar had discovered new sources of information. Xerana herself had unearthed many artifacts of the Xel'Naga and secrets of the Void. The other Protoss did not have such things, and they might never learn unless they stopped hating the Dark Templar. . . .

On the silent, haunted landscape, Xerana stepped out under an orange sky and continued to walk among the powdery ruins. Even among the Dark Templar, she was a loner, a scholar. She was obsessed with finding any information about the ancient race that had created the Protoss, and much later the hideous Zerg.

But the ruins on this abandoned planet had been worn down by erosion, erasing the most dramatic of remnants. Xerana did not give in to discouragement. She continued to dig.

She looked up, saw a gauze of grayish clouds crawl over the orange sky, and wondered if a storm was coming and if she might be in danger. But the gray clouds, like visual static or smoke, soon dissipated. Xerana bent back to her work, searching the rubble.

As twilight came, she allowed herself to imagine the evening activities that the Xel'Naga must have enjoyed. She knew the ancients had walked here in the shadows, and she now followed in their footsteps.

The Xel'Naga, also called the Wanderers from Afar, were a

peaceful and benevolent race, driven by the goal of studying and then spreading sentient evolution throughout the universe. After many experiments on other worlds, the Xel'Naga had come to the jungle world of Aiur and concentrated their efforts on the indigenous race there, secretly guiding them through evolution and civilization until they became the Protoss, the First Born.

But when the satisfied and triumphant Xel'Naga finally revealed themselves, they unwittingly caused world-spanning chaos. The Protoss tribes split apart, each finding different ways to advance themselves. Some even turned upon the ancient Xel'Naga, finally driving away the Wanderers from Afar and then attacking each other in a protracted and bloody civil war known as the Aeon of Strife.

Eventually, the Protoss healed their civilization by bringing the race together in a religious and telepathic bonding known as the Khala. For many centuries, the Khala allowed the Protoss to grow strong again, although it engendered a rigid caste system, limited independent thought, and blurred the distinction between individuals. Adherence to the path of the Khala was strictly enforced by unwavering religious-political leaders called Judicators.

A few Protoss tribes refused the Khala, separating themselves from it and holding to their precious individuality. For a long time, the existence of these rebels remained a dark secret. And then came the persecution, until finally the Judicator Conclave banished all of the Rogue Tribes, placing their members aboard a derelict Xel'Naga ship and sending them off into the Void.

These exiled rebels had become the Dark Templar, like Xerana, still loyal to the race that had driven them out but voraciously inquisitive, burning to understand their origins. Xerana needed to know why the Xel'Naga had considered the Protoss failures, why they had never returned, and why they had later devoted their efforts to creating the vicious Zerg.

Like the others of her group, Xerana was a warrior as well

as a researcher and scholar. So far, she had deciphered a great deal of Xel'Naga lore. Other Dark Templar had also tapped into the powers of the Void, learning secret psi techniques that the rest of the Protoss race did not understand. . . .

Even when darkness fell on this unnamed world, Xerana still did not return to her large ship in orbit. Her golden gem-fire eyes adapted to the dark, her telepathic senses extended, and she continued to search. Her slender, muscular body was covered by dark robes held in place by a wide hieroglyphic-inscribed sash that signified her scholar's profession. She wore her clothing as a matter of formality and function, never for comfort. Affixed to her wide collar was a thin, etched tablet, a fragment she had found on an earlier excavation, displaying indecipherable words that had been inscribed by the hand of a long-forgotten Xel'Naga poet. It was her most prized possession.

Traveling farther, Xerana found broken pillars, weathered columns of stone that time had polished smooth. She could make out the arrangement, though, similar to that of temples she had seen on other worlds. The pillars of rock had been placed in a precise pattern, as if to focus the energies of the cosmos.

The columns had slumped under the weight of ages, battered by cosmic rays and pounding heat, scoured by millennia of wind that, on this world of unexpected colors, was as faint as a baby's breath. All around her in this place, Xerana could sense their presence with her psionic powers. She felt the whispers acknowledging her, guiding her.

She kicked over a crumbling boulder on impulse, and there, underneath the protective barrier of rock, saw a curved light stone, facedown in the ashy earth.

Ah . . .

Xerana pried it up and found a small fragment of an obelisk. A few faint pictographs still remained on the weathered and burned chunk of stone. This was what she had come here for. She could feel it.

Before dawn, pleased with her prize, Xerana returned to her wandering ship and began studying her treasure as she set off into the lonely darkness again.

Keeping to herself, for she had no companions, Xerana sat among all the artifacts she had collected. As she roamed the stars in her ship in search of answers, she had compiled a repository of Xel'Naga artifacts. She did not hoard these treasures or keep them merely as her personal possessions. They were for research, and each tiny item held one small part of the key to the understanding that the Dark Templar so desired.

Xerana spent hour upon hour meditating, trying to piece together what was known of the ancient lost race so that she could derive fresh insights. She had already spent nearly a century digging up answers in the cold Void and in the vibrant genes of her race. In a separate chamber, where she went when she allowed herself to feel lonely, Xerana also kept many mementos of her beloved planet, Aiur, which she would probably never see again.

As her ship cruised along, Xerana studied the worn, broken piece of the obelisk. After studying it almost to the point of putting herself into a trance, Xerana finally found a comparison among her other tiny specimens, and was able to decipher a set of runes. She translated a fragment, perhaps a bit of poetry or a legend that the Xel'Naga progenitors would have told each other as darkness gathered.

Maybe with this additional piece of data she could add to the history the Dark Templar already knew. She might use it to make a connection with other seemingly disparate artifacts.

She felt excitement and pride build within her, though she knew there were many secrets left to uncover. As her ship moved along, continuing its search, Xerana felt that a breakthrough was near, that the answers to her most important questions were so close she could almost touch them.

CHAPTER 5

UNDER THE COMMAND OF GENERAL EDMUND DUKE, the warships of Alpha Squadron were always ready for battle. In fact, the troops were eager for it.

The devastating first conflict with the Zerg and the Protoss had obliterated the fringe colony worlds of Chau Sara and Mar Sara, the Confederacy government world of Tarsonis, and the Protoss home planet of Aiur.

Duke hated aliens—of any flavor. He woke up at night in his flagship cabin trying to strangle the sweaty sheets on his bunk.

In the upheavals of the recent war, the charismatic rebel Arcturus Mengsk, leader of the violent Sons of Korhal, had seized command of what had been the Terran Confederacy and crowned himself the new emperor. Duke didn't think the man was particularly honorable or trustworthy or even talented. Mengsk was a politician, after all.

Different government, same military. General Duke just did his job.

Since he wanted to keep his command, Duke had no compunction about obeying whatever Emperor Arcturus Mengsk told him to do. The general knew who issued his orders.

Many of the vessels had been damaged in the conflict, including his flagship, the *Norad II*. Since then, however, the new Emperor Mengsk had spent a lot of money to pump up the military. Alpha Squadron's damaged ships had been refurbished, their weapons had been reloaded, and they had been sent out into space again.

His fleet consisted of battlecruisers, Wraiths, science vessels, and dropships, a full-fledged force ready for a dangerous galaxy. The cursed Protoss and Zerg were still out there somewhere.

Alpha Squadron had left Korhal, the emperor's new capital planet, which had been damaged by Confederacy vengeance many years before. But Arcturus Mengsk had had the last laugh . . . and General Duke still had his military command. Nothing else mattered much to the general.

For months, the ships of Alpha Squadron had been out on routine survey missions, mapping potential colony worlds, reestablishing contact with others that had fallen by the wayside. Duke could not have imagined a more boring assignment—not for a brilliant strategist like himself, and not for his loyal soldiers either.

But the political situation with the newly formed Terran Dominion was still unsteady, and Mengsk had picked his own men to form the Imperial Guard close to home. Presumably, General Duke had not yet convinced the emperor of his loyalty, so he and Alpha Squadron were dispatched far away, where they could cause little trouble.

Duke preferred to avoid politics anyway, and if those two malicious species wanted to come back for another dogfight, he'd be happy to give it to them, all right. Damned aliens! In any case, the general expected to uncover more information and more strongholds of the evil Zerg or the treacherous Protoss—he didn't care which—out here in the uncharted areas than he would ever find back home in the civilized sectors.

After so much time on patrol, General Duke had assessed the fleet's resources, looked at their military capabilities, and given orders for Alpha Squadron to stop at the next vespene-rich asteroid field. He intended to stuff his ships to the gills with more resources than the emperor had allowed him. Now he stood on the flagship, the rebuilt and completely repaired *Norad II*—now named *Norad III*—a battlecruiser with all the punch General Duke could ever wish for.

Ready to go.

He just wished he had something to *fight* against, rather than doing this continuous . . . social studies homework assignment. Did Emperor Mengsk really want to know about the status of podunk colony worlds? Surely the new ruler of the Terran Dominion had more important things on his mind.

Duke looked out the portholes of his flagship and watched the activity around him in space. All his soldiers moved efficiently—not because they were trying to impress their commander, but because they were truly that *good*. He had seen to that himself.

On vespene-rich asteroids in the belt, faint wisps of the silvery gas escaped into space from the low gravity, making the floating rocks look like played-out comets. Mobile Space Construction Vehicles found the most powerful geysers and set down, using asteroid materials to build impromptu refineries, which captured and distilled the gas into usable form. The SCVs bustled about like honeybees in a field of flowers, harvesting the gas and returning to the fleet with clear barrels of the fuel.

Soon Duke's ships would be more than ready for anything . . . and, again, with nothing important to do.

The task took no longer than necessary, following standard operating procedures. Still Duke paced the deck, glancing at status screens, barking orders to his officers, prowling about looking for something useful for his ships to do. Scouts in powered suits retrieved other valuable minerals from the asteroids in order to bring all of Alpha Squadron's ships and supplies up to optimal levels.

During a lull, his helmsman and weapons officer, Lieutenant Scott, chose to speak up. "General, sir, might I ask you a question? Permission to speak freely?" Tall, handsome, and forthright, Scott was well respected by the other marines.

"I assume all my officers have brains in their heads, Lieutenant. Otherwise, I'd just commission a crew of robots." Duke was bored enough to give the young man his permission, though normally such boldness would have earned him a reprimand.

"I assume you have a plan, sir?" Lieutenant Scott said. "Are we waiting to make our move?"

"I always have a plan," Duke said gruffly.

"What kind of plan, sir? Are we going to strike back at the unlawful Dominion and overthrow Emperor Mengsk? Are we going to help establish a government in exile for the overthrown Terran Confederacy?"

"Enough, Lieutenant!" General Duke said, raising his voice to a roar. "If the emperor hears such words he will convict you of treason."

"But, General, sir—they are *rebels*." Scott seemed dubious. "Sons of Korhal. They were our enemies."

Duke pounded his fist on the command console of the *Norad III*. "They are *currently* the lawful government of all Terrans. Would you have me become a rebel myself, just so that I can wreak vengeance on another pack of rebels? May I remind you that our duty is to follow the orders of our commander in chief. After the destruction of Tarsonis, and now that we've finally driven back the Zerg, our legal political leader just happens to be Emperor Mengsk. You would do well not to forget that, son."

Lieutenant Scott realized it was time to hold any further comments in check.

Duke lowered his voice, knowing that all of his marines were impatient to strike against the vile aliens. "We are engaged in a fight for the human race, Lieutenant. Let's keep our priorities where they belong."

The other officers on the bridge, many of whom probably felt the same as Lieutenant Scott, took the reprimand to heart and very quickly found urgent duties with which to occupy themselves.

The general sat back in his command chair, watching the remaining tedious operations taking place out in the asteroid belt. A military leader must always remain focused on his goal. He did not neglect attention to details. A conflict could be won or lost because of a tiny item that someone had overlooked.

Alpha Squadron had always prided itself on being the first military unit into a fight, and also the first group out. Right now, though, there was no place to go. Even when the mineral and vespene operations were completed in the asteroids and the ships withdrew to begin their slow journey through space again, General Duke knew that nothing exciting would happen.

He retired to his quarters after turning over command to a surprised Lieutenant Scott. He saw no tactical advantage to their current mission and decided to take some time to hone his skills.

General Duke spent the next three days at his own computer screens, challenging himself with exciting tactical war games in order to sharpen his edge. He played scenario after scenario, beating the computer every time.

Still, he was getting tired of nothing happening. He was, after all, a man of action.

CHAPTER 6

OCTAVIA AND LARS STOOD AT THE BASE OF THE steep, crumbled slope where great rocks and cascades of soil had broken away and tumbled down to expose the alien object.

Octavia leaned against the robo-harvester. Brownish gray dirt fell away from the side of the gigantic tractor. Running a hand through her brown curls, she continued to assess the ominous, pulsing construction from a distance. But Lars, as usual, bounded ahead, his eagerness and curiosity overwhelming his common sense.

Her brother had always wanted to be first, to run the fastest, to build the tallest structure, to reach the top of the hill before Octavia or their few other young settler companions could. Now Lars used hands and feet to clamber up the sharp, raw edges of rock that had fallen down during the previous night's storm and earthquake.

She followed him, her breath coming heavy in the sour-smelling air. The freshly overturned dirt had an odd taint, as if it had spoiled long ago. The colonists knew from experience that only a few crops could survive in Bhekar Ro's soil. Octavia was used to the smell, of course, and rarely noticed it except after a hard rain. In filmbooks, she had seen lush agricultural worlds, verdant fields heavy with crops. She never knew whether to believe such fantasies.

Now she climbed after her brother, her hands and clothes growing dirty. Dirt was just another part of their harsh daily lives as farmers.

"Hey, look at this!" Lars called, and in a few moments she had clambered up closer to the smooth, curving walls of the bizarre structure.

Protruding from the newly exposed area were giant snowflake crystals, shards of transparent material that seethed with strange energy, each fragment longer than her arm. Octavia pressed one hand against the slick surface, finding it achingly cold, but not icy. A strange sensation like an electric tingle ran through the whorls of her palm and fingertips as if some energy were mapping her cellular structure and studying it.

"Now *these* are interesting," Lars said, his hazel eyes alive with wonder. "What do you think we could use them for? I bet we could take a full load of these crystals back on the robo-harvester."

"Why? To make giant necklaces for the old farmwives?" Octavia said, pulling her hand away from the crystalline formation. Her fingers continued to tingle.

Lars grinned his cocky grin. "I don't know about those farmwives, but I have a feeling Cyn McCarthy might like one."

Octavia raised her eyebrows. So, her independent brother had actually noticed that the pretty young widow was interested in him romantically. Far be it from Octavia to discourage him. Maybe he wasn't as dense as she had thought!

"All right, Lars, I admit the crystals *might* be useful. But before you start making grandiose plans, let's be practical, here—just for a few minutes, please? I suggest we look around.

And be careful not to change anything until we understand more."

Lars grinned at her and climbed up the slope again toward the gleaming, labyrinthine structure. "Well, the way to find out more is to do some poking around. Let's split up and we can cover more ground."

"Splitting up is never a good idea," Octavia said, knowing the warning would be ignored by her enthusiastic brother.

"You be careful, and I'll be careful," he said, "and we'll be back in time to fix the seismographs by midday."

Octavia clamped her lips together and didn't bother to contradict him. She wasn't worried about the seismographs in the least.

The beautiful crystalline protrusions stuck out all around them at odd angles like the spines of a ruffled urchin lizard. Lars moved toward the eerie facade of the object itself, fascinated by the mysteries that drew him.

Octavia moved more slowly, pausing to study the crystals, trying to understand how they grew, where they came from. It seemed as if they had been planted around this buried object as . . . markers? Defenses? Some sort of message?

Puffing and sweating, though the effort did not diminish his exuberant grin, Lars reached the strange swirling shapes that formed the walls and openings of the giant object. The structural material was a pearlescent green, lit from within like some sort of hardened bioluminescent slime. He stood back, appraising the enormous structure. From his furrowed brow and quickly moving eyes, Octavia could tell that her brother wasn't trying to understand the artifact, but was merely trying to choose the best means of getting inside.

Lars touched the exposed material. All of the soil and dust had flaked off, as if the object had a kind of static charge that repelled grime and dirt. He rapped against the wall with his knuckles, then held up his hand. "It sort of tingles. I can't tell if the material is plastic or glass or some kind of organic extrusion. Interesting."

"You promised to be careful," she called. "And I've got a bad feeling about this."

He looked down at her with raised eyebrows. "You always have bad feelings, Octavia."

Her brother dismissed her concerns, but then Lars had never been as sensitive as she was. Octavia often had a knack for foreseeing events, for feeling when to avoid a certain situation. She had no hard proof, of course, but she was confident that her premonitions were correct. "And when have I ever been wrong, Lars?"

He didn't answer.

She knelt by one of the largest crystals and touched it again, running her hands over the slick surface. The odd cold tingle of energy called out to her, trying to communicate something that she couldn't comprehend. Overall, around this entire structure, Octavia felt a brooding, sleeping presence, something indescribable, buried and not yet awakened.

A frisson of inexplicable energy touched her mind, but she didn't know how to pursue the feeling, to explore it. It was an odd probing sensation, but whatever produced the feeling clearly didn't understand her or recognize her humanity.

Octavia swallowed hard in a dry throat and withdrew from the powerful crystal. The connection in her mind faded, but did not go entirely away.

Lars happily continued his explorations, poking his head into the smaller openings and then finally walking into a large, curving orifice that led deeper into the structure.

Octavia moved slowly, reaching the top and looking into the dark, cool opening where her brother had disappeared. Odd odors wafted from inside, like a rich mulch, something sizzling and alive. Though the power contained within the artifact intimidated her, she didn't feel that it was particularly evil or threatening. Just . . . unlike anything she had ever encountered before.

His voice called back to her, echoing yet damped by the solid walls of the structure. "Octavia, come in here! You won't believe the amazing things."

She stepped forward, peering into the shadows. She heard footsteps as he came hurrying back toward her. His eyes were aglow. "These passages are studded with more crystals and other strange objects, treasures, resources! We could use a pickax or a laser cutter to chop them out of the walls."

"You don't even know what they are, Lars," she said.

"I'll bet they'll bring a lot of credits once we sell them."

She didn't enter the artifact, but instead put her dirty hands on her hips. "Who would you sell them to, Lars? For what? Crops? Equipment? Nobody in Free Haven has anything to spare. And our colony hasn't traded with anybody since before you and I were born."

Grinning, Lars lowered his voice as if afraid someone might be eavesdropping. "This goes far beyond what Bhekar Ro can handle, Octavia. I think as soon as we get back, we need to contact the Terran government. We'll be rich! Imagine what we can sell this for. Even you have to admit that this is interesting—the find of a lifetime. Our colony can acquire new equipment, new seed stock, maybe even new workers to bolster our population. We've lost so many families in the past few years."

Octavia felt her heart sink as she remembered their dead parents and all the specialists and just plain good people who had died in the spore plagues or in natural disasters or in any number of other tragedies that had beset Bhekar Ro since its formation. She felt her brother's optimism and imagined all the wonders he had described, realizing that—for once—Lars might actually be right in his ambitions.

Then she made a disbelieving sound. Even if this artifact turned out to be something truly remarkable, meeting all of the hopeful criteria Lars envisioned, the colony's communication link with the Terran Confederacy had been left unused for thirty-five of the forty years Free Haven had existed as a human settlement. The colonists had come here to get away from Terran governments, to live for themselves and be self-sufficient. Their parents and grandparents had hated any interference or oppression, and few of the colonists would choose to call attention to themselves again.

"I don't think the others would agree, especially not Mayor Nik," Octavia said. "I'm not convinced that even something like this is worth bringing the Confederacy back to breathe down our necks. You've heard the stories Grandfather used to tell. It could damage our way of life."

Now Lars looked at her in astonishment. "Our *way of life*? Could it get any worse? Do the list of pros and cons for yourself, and you'll be convinced." He turned around and quickly moved deeper into the glowing corridors.

Octavia followed him, still sensing the oppressive mental presence around her, feeling it grow more powerful. Lars hurried farther along, stopping to rap against walls with his fist, listening to the echo, trying to discover differences.

Striations of color ran through the walls like veins of ore . . . or maybe like the blood vessels of an alien creature. He sniffed, then studied the wall carefully. He tried to scratch it with his fingernails, but could make no mark. He shook his head and moved on.

Lars had always dreamed of being a prospector, an archaeologist, an explorer here on this largely unmapped world. But nobody on Bhekar Ro had much chance to be more than a simple farmer, working through every hour of gloomy daylight just to keep the colony functioning. Octavia didn't have the heart to drain away her brother's enjoyment right now. He had been waiting for an opportunity like this all his life.

Octavia felt a sudden reluctance to go deeper into the chambers of the artifact, as if the air were thickening around her. The odd psychic energy formed a wall, slowly pushing her back.

Lars didn't seem to feel it at all. He turned to examine an arch in the tunnel where it hooked to the left, and saw a cluster of beehive-shaped objects made of something smooth and translucent. They looked almost like large, faceted jewels that grew out of the walls.

"Come on!" Standing in the arched opening of the side tunnel, Lars reached up with one hand to the cluster. As soon as he grasped one of the brightly colored protrusions, though, the entire light and atmosphere in the artifact changed slightly. It was as if he had triggered something.

His hand remained fastened to the nodule. His face fell, and an instant later, he froze. Octavia sensed a crackle of energy flowing through him. All of the crystal shards protruding from the walls and those outside the artifact glowed brighter, as if they had been switched on.

"Lars!" she shouted.

But he couldn't move, couldn't even make a sound.

Sizzling beams shot out like lightning bolts, linking one crystal after another in a webwork. Bright light ricocheted down the corridors, blinding Octavia. She tried to move, but it all happened so fast.

Lars stood within the arched opening like an insect trapped on a microscope slide, and the brilliant beams from the crystals flooded over him like spotlights, scanning him, crashing into his body. In a flash, his skin turned completely white. His bones and his muscles glowed from inside, as if he had become a luminous substance through and through, every cell converted to pure energy.

Then the walls themselves took on the same blinding white glow, as if they were absorbing Lars down to the last atom. Suddenly the lightning stopped. All the lights faded to their former eerie dimness.

And Lars was gone. Not even a shadow remained.

Two of the large crystals outside the artifact shattered, and sparks flickered down the corridors, bursting other crystals in a chain reaction, as if Lars had been something unpalatable, a substance this artifact could not digest.

Smoke curled through the tunnels. The deafening sounds quieted, leaving only the faint echo of a scream. Octavia couldn't tell if it was the last sound made by her brother or her own wordless cry.

After a lull of less than a second, the walls brightened again, the larger crystals shimmering. Lightning bolts crackled. Lars had awakened something ominous, and Octavia wondered if his death might bring about the destruction of them all.

Octavia turned and scrambled down the smooth tunnel to the opening. Toward daylight. She ran faster, terror making her eyes wide, her mind numb. Too many things were happening. She wanted to go back and search for her brother, to see if anything of his body remained.

But her drive for self-preservation kicked in. She knew the artifact wasn't done yet.

Octavia bounded out of the opening and down the boulder-strewn slope, somehow keeping her feet under her, dropping from one rock to another, steadying herself with her hands and spreading her arms to keep her balance.

The hillside vibrated harder. Now all the large crystals that had seemed so beautiful a moment ago looked like loaded weapons, tapping energy reservoirs that summoned lightning from within their atomic structure.

Her retreat was a blur. Somehow, faster than she had ever imagined she could move, Octavia found herself back at the robo-harvester, leaning against the mud-encrusted treads. Behind her, on the steep hillside, the tall crystals ignited. Lightning bolts that sparkled like blue spiderwebs connected them all, drawing their power together and weaving it into a knot of energy until all the stray threads converged.

Finally, a beacon of sound and light—some sort of giant transmission—speared upward into the sky and far out into space. It was not directed at her at all, but somewhere distant. To something *not human*.

The shock wave knocked Octavia flat, sending her sprawling on the broken ground. She could barely hold on as the pulsing signal rippled and tore through the air.

Out of breath, frantic, she crawled up the treads of the robo-harvester. As she grabbed the door of the armored cab, her head throbbed and her ears rang. She threw herself inside, slammed the door, and collapsed on the seat. She could barely hear anything.

For the moment she felt protected, but not enough. Moving blindly, she started the engine of the enormous vehicle, wheeled it around on its treads, and crunched over the broken ground at top speed, sending rocks and dirt clods flying as she raced across the valley. She had to get back to Free Haven.

Octavia couldn't think straight, could not yet address in her mind what had happened to her brother, what she had seen with her own eyes.

But she knew she had to warn the other colonists.

CHAPTER 7

OUT IN DEEP SPACE, SURROUNDED BY THE MOST powerful warships of the Protoss expeditionary force, Executor Koronis sought the privacy and refuge of his own quarters aboard the flagship carrier *Qel'Ha*. There he could contemplate his mission, his destiny, and the fate of his race.

He could sense through his nerve appendages all of the loyal Protoss who served aboard the ships in his fleet: the industrialists, scientists, and workers in the Khalai class; the ferociously dedicated zealots and other soldiers in the determined warrior class, called the Templar. He even sensed the stern governmental-religious caste of Judicators, who oversaw the prosecution of this mission and maintained focus on the Khala.

But as he tried to find peace and contemplation, Koronis could feel the utter misery and failure of his entire crew. The Executor's shoulders slumped, causing the stiff pointed pads of his uniform to sag. The Protoss homeworld of Aiur had suffered a devastating attack by the Zerg and had very nearly been destroyed, but Koronis's expeditionary force had been far from the scene of carnage, far from their families and homes. They had not helped at all. They had failed. And the entire Protoss race had teetered on the brink of extinction.

It was a difficult burden to bear.

Koronis sat in his polished curved meditation seat and held in his scaly hands a small fragment of a worn but still-glittering crystal. The gem merchant had told him that the ancient prophet Khas had used this shard when he discovered the telepathic Way of the Khala. The Khala had finally unified the Protoss, brought them together through their mental abilities, and ended the Aeon of Strife that had torn their civilization apart for so long.

Koronis did not know if the myth surrounding the origin of this Khaydarin crystal was true or merely a story concocted by a trader wishing to get a better price, but the Executor took comfort from the possibility. He stared into the crystal, concentrating his mental energies. His depthless golden eyes burned like small suns, looking deep within the crystal structure, far into the corners of the universe. His textured gray face rippled as he concentrated, brow ridges furrowing, ornamented shoulders hunched. His mouthless chin remained firm.

Many decades ago the Protoss Conclave had sent out Koronis and his expeditionary force on a long-term mission far beyond the fringes of the Koprulu Sector. Since the Protoss were a long-lived race, they did not worry about decades or even centuries, and he had been proud to be chosen. Before departing, Koronis had been named Executor, a high rank held by very few, for his mission had been considered extremely important.

He and his crew had been dispatched to search for any sign of the heretical Dark Templar, who had refused to join the Khala and kept themselves separate from the unified mental presence of the Protoss. The Judicators in the Conclave could not accept such a blight on Protoss society. They commanded that the Dark Templar must be either brought into the fold or destroyed. Koronis had never considered the Dark Templar to be a great threat and would have preferred to leave the exiles alone, but the fanatical Conclave politicians made such decisions, not he.

Koronis was far more interested in the second part of his mission: to search for any remnants of the ancient progenitor race, the Xel'Naga, who had created the Protoss as their special children, their First Born.

Recent discoveries proved that the Xel'Naga had created the hostile Zerg as well, perhaps intending the Zerg to supplant the First Born. Executor Koronis did not know what to think of that, but it seemed to bespeak the continued failure and disappointment of his people.

As he contemplated, the Khaydarin crystal began to glow with a warm humming. At first Koronis took strength from it, until the power of the crystal artifact also amplified his ability to sense the anguish and despair that ran rampant through his crew.

He closed his gleaming eyes and withdrew his mind from the Khaydarin crystal. So far, after decades of searching, the *Qel'Ha* had uncovered no evidence of the Xel'Naga. Nor had they found any of the Dark Templar.

His expeditionary force was a mighty fleet that could have made a difference in the defense of Aiur against the Zerg; instead, for years they had wasted their time out here on the fringes of inhabited space. Koronis had nothing to show for it. With his three-fingered hand he held the long, colorful sash that designated his rank and office, a proud symbol that now seemed meaningless to him.

The shield door at the entry to his quarters slid upward, and the imposing figure of Judicator Amdor stood in the corridor, his red-orange eyes blazing. A deep purple robe was draped around him, flowing as if in reflection of his moods or mental energies. Jeweled shoulder pads and metal-scaled headgear made Amdor look ominous and impressive. On purpose.

As a powerful political representative of the Conclave, Judicator Amdor did not feel the need to show Koronis courtesy. There would have been some friction between the two of them if the commander had allowed it, but he was loyal to his race and to his mission and did not rise to the occasional criticisms that the stern Judicator heaped upon him. Amdor seemed to think the expedition's failure was the Executor's fault.

With no lips to move, no mouths to form words, all Protoss communicated through tight, telepathic bursts. The Judicator focused his conversation closely enough that no eavesdroppers could pick up even a hint of his sentences, though at times the mental spike was so sharp that it caused Koronis a faint twinge of pain. He showed none of it, however, simply turned and listened to what the Judicator had to say.

"This disgrace has gone on long enough, Executor. Our expeditionary force must return to Aiur. We are too late to help with the great battle against the Zerg, but we can assist with rebuilding. Turn the *Qel'Ha* around, and we will voyage back home. We must salvage what we can."

The Zerg Overmind had been obliterated, and Aiur was saved, though at the cost of devastating much of the land. Tassadar, the accused traitor, had combined the powers of the Khala with secrets learned from the Void. Judicator Amdor called Tassadar's actions a despicable heresy taught him by the Dark Templar, but Koronis could not fault the hero for his results.

He wished he had been there to see the end. It would have been a marvelous sight. . . .

Without hurrying, the Executor put away his crystal fragment and rose from his meditation chair. He straightened his sash and adjusted his extravagantly pointed shoulder pads.

Koronis's mental control was not as precise as that of the Judicator's, and Amdor caught some flicker of his musings. "Tassadar was no hero!" he said, his thought-words sharp.

"He sacrificed his dedication to the Khala in order to achieve glory for himself and short-term gain."

Surprised, the Executor faced Amdor in the ship's corridor outside of his quarters. "But he saved the Protoss and sacrificed himself in the process. I hardly believe you can ascribe selfish motives to what Tassadar achieved."

"The greatest thing he achieved," Amdor snapped in return, "was that by eradicating the Zerg and devastating Aiur, he cleansed the Protoss race! In the aftermath of this disaster, we now have the opportunity to rebuild, to burn out the cancerous heretics that have corrupted our dedication to the Khala. I am eager to return home so that I can help the Conclave to ensure that we do not slip down this dark and ill-advised path."

Seeing no point in arguing, Koronis acquiesced. He, too, wanted to return home, even without Amdor's insistence. "I exist to serve the Khala."

When the two of them reached the bridge, the Executor took over the *Qel'Ha*'s egg-shaped command chair. Judicator Amdor stood beside him like a grim parent, as if not convinced the commander would do as he had promised.

With the psychic booster, Koronis sent a message to all the Protoss minds in his fleet. "We will go home. We have work to do with our families and our cities and our world. Since we could not help when Aiur needed us most, we must be willing to give our lives and our minds to assist now . . . to make up for not being there."

Through the mental link of his nerve appendages, Koronis felt a surge of relief and enthusiasm ripple through the crew, a hope that raised them above their gloom. The engines of the fleet's carriers and flanking ships powered up. The navigators calculated a course that would take them back to the heart of Protoss space.

But before they could embark, the psychic communication loops—broad spiderweb transceivers woven into the hulls of the ships—received a powerful message pulse. A distant, alien signal.

The eerie notes vibrated through Koronis's mind, through the ships, through the entire crew. A cry, a shout, an indecipherable message.

The throbbing signal continued to pound, grating on the Executor's nerves, haunting yet somehow familiar. Judicator Amdor stood stiffly, confused at first, then startled.

When the distant call finally stopped, all the Protoss remained stunned. The Executor directed his thought-speech to Amdor, although others in the vicinity caught the fringes of his excited thoughts. "There is something of the Xel'Naga in that signal! I recognize the symbols and the tones. Do you not hear it? The message is . . . urgent."

"And quite powerful," Amdor said. "But what Xel'Naga device could broadcast a signal so strong and clear as to reach this far?" The Judicator turned his sharp gaze to the technical Khalai working at the communications equipment on the *Qel'Ha*'s bridge.

One of the officers sent a quick mental burst. "We have tracked the signal back to a small planet. Uninhabited, as far as we know."

Koronis studied the coordinates, quickly calculated how long it would take the expeditionary force to go there. He sent his thought clearly to Amdor. "Judicator, this signal offers us the opportunity to return to Aiur with some measure of honor and success—not as complete failures. If we can indeed find an important Xel'Naga device, we will accomplish our mission of discovery and return to Aiur as heroes. We can bring hope to our people."

The Judicator nodded. "If the signal came from the Wanderers from Afar, it may well be an omen. We are the First Born, and our destiny is to retrieve our race's lost glory. Finding whatever sent this signal could be a huge step toward achieving that goal."

"En taro Adun," Koronis said, using the honor salute that meant "in honor of Adun," a great Protoss hero.

"En taro Adun," the Judicator responded curtly, as if distracted and already making plans.

Feeling confident for the first time since he had received the terrible news about Aiur, Executor Koronis summoned a robotic observer and commanded that it be dispatched immediately to the source of the mysterious Xel'Naga signal.

CHAPTER 8

GONE. LARS WAS GONE.

The thought beat at Octavia's mind in rhythm with the thumping treads of the robo-harvester as she careened across the long, rugged kilometers toward the settlement. Her hands and feet operated the heavy equipment without any help from her conscious mind, for she had room for only one thought there: *Lars is dead!* She could hardly wrap her mind around it.

The robo-harvester lurched and bounced, crashing over dirt piles and mounds of rock debris. The rocking motion twisted her neck and shoulders, but she gritted her teeth.

Overhead, the same glider hawk still rested on high breezes, scanning the ground in a fruitless search for food. . . .

The massive vehicle ground its way up the steep slope, back and forth against the grade as boulders and loose dirt sprayed beneath the flurry of treads. Octavia's view of the stark landscape in front of her dimmed and grew blurry, as if a fog had rolled into the broad valley. She tried to clear the windshield but soon realized that the problem was with her own eyes.

Octavia was not given to bouts of weeping, and she didn't have time for it now. She had to get back to Free Haven to sound the alarm. To tell the other settlers about the ominous, murderous artifact that had been uncovered by the storm. She had always been far too practical to waste time on useless displays of emotion—not because she didn't care when a friend or family member died. It was a survival mechanism. Those colonists who allowed themselves to become easily depressed by the cruel vagaries of life here soon became listless, careless. And carelessness on Bhekar Ro usually meant a speedy death.

As far as Octavia could recall, she had cried only a few times before: once after the death of her grandparents, another time about a week after her parents' deaths from the spore blight, during the next thunderous storm when the realization had hit her like a slap in the face that her father would never be there to comfort her again. Tears were such an unaccustomed sensation that she hardly recognized it. *Lars is gone!*

But then, as salty drops flowed down her cheeks, her anger began to flow as well. What a ridiculous waste! It didn't make any sense. And what *was* that thing out there on the ridge? It obviously wasn't of Terran origin.

Why had she allowed Lars to talk her into going out there? What had they stood to gain from it? Yet Lars, with his insatiable curiosity, had felt the need to go. He had only been exploring.

And the thing had murdered her brother. *Murdered.* Stolen Lars from her forever—and for what? Who could say?

One thing she did know, however. She had to warn the other colonists before the artifact could claim any more lives.

The village meeting hall was filled to overflowing with nearly two thousand grumbling settlers. Octavia could hear snatches of conversation from around the hall.

"What kind of emergency? Wasn't the storm emergency enough?"

"I have crops to replant. Couldn't this wait?"

"I heard Lars Bren found something."

"I heard he's disappeared!"

". . . better hurry it up or I'll be leaving."

At last, Mayor "Nik" Nikolai took his place on the low platform at the front of the room and called the meeting to order. He was a distractible and not overly charismatic person under normal circumstances, but at the age of twenty-eight he was already considered an established, respected administrator, more or less. He banged on his podium, trying to get the audience to settle down.

"Excuse me! Hello? Octavia Bren has some serious news for us." He paused a moment, looking around. "Serious enough that I thought we might need to take a vote about what to do after you hear what she has to say."

"Can't you just sum it up and we'll take a vote and get out of here?" Shayna Bradshaw yelled from the audience. "My irrigation system is clogged again, and—"

The mayor shook his head. "I think it'll be best if I let Octavia tell you in her own words."

Octavia gritted her teeth at the grumbling in the room and stepped onto the platform. She clung to her anger instead of her grief. How hardened they had all become to news of tragedy or calamity. Somehow she had to make them understand how important this was. She cleared her throat and put as much volume and authority into her seventeen-year-old voice as she could. "I know most of you believe there's nothing important enough, nothing *urgent* enough to justify calling all of you here. Shocks and disappointments, even death, have become part of our everyday life."

"So get to the point!" old Rastin called from the center of the room.

"Where's your brother?" called Cyn McCarthy, looking hopeful.

Octavia drew a deep steadying breath and started again. "Lars is dead." She held up a hand to forestall the automatic murmurs of sympathy from the gathered crowd. "He was killed by something out on a ridge about twelve klicks from here. An alien artifact that was buried inside the mountain. Something huge."

"Did you say alien?" Mayor Nikolai was surprised.

"Yes, *alien*! We are not alone here on Bhekar Ro!"

Octavia described what had happened. Haltingly, she told about their exploration of the artifact, and when she got to the part with the bright beams of light spearing across her brother's body, flashing around him as he disintegrated, her throat seized up and refused to work. She felt a hand on her arm and looked up to see Cyn McCarthy standing next to her, a stricken look on the young widow's freckled face.

"Seems to me the answer's simple," old Rastin said dismissively. "Nobody in the colony goes near that thing again. Leave it alone. If we expand, we just go th' other direction."

Octavia gritted her teeth again, and anger gave her back her voice. Unless she convinced the settlers that this was serious, they might all die.

"Ignoring it isn't good enough. Something else happened out there. As I was leaving that *thing*, it sent a signal up into space. Some kind of transmission, or alarm, or homing beacon. The light was so bright it almost blinded me, and the sound shook the ground and threw me off my feet."

"Hey, was that right before noon for about two minutes?" asked Kiernan Warner from the front row. "I think I heard that! If it was twelve klicks away, it must've been really loud."

"Do you think the artifact was trying to communicate with us?" Lyn's younger brother Wes asked in an alarmed tone.

Octavia shook her head. "The beacon went straight up into space, as if it thought someone was out there waiting to get its signal. It might have been trying to communicate with someone, but definitely not *us*."

The room erupted with exclamations, questions, and suggestions, and Octavia knew she had gotten their attention.

Mayor Nikolai took the stage again and held up his hands for quiet. When the room settled down slightly, he said, "Octavia believes we should contact the Terran Confederacy. Let them know what we've found here."

A few of the colonists began to voice objections, but were quickly shushed by their neighbors.

"We don't know if that was a comm beacon or not, but if more of those things show up on Bhekar Ro, we may not be able to handle the situation ourselves," Mayor Nikolai said.

"This is our planet!" Wes's cousin Jon said.

Octavia spoke up again. "Even if the artifact is the only one of its kind, we don't know what it can do. Now that it's been unearthed, it might become aggressive and go after our settlement. It might even cause earthquakes that could wipe us all out."

"Put it to a vote," Jon yelled.

"Yeah, we've heard enough," Kiernan added.

"My irrigation system is still leaking," Shayna Bradshaw grumbled.

To Octavia's relief, with the exception of three colonists, the vote was unanimous. A message would be sent to the last-known Terran government. Maybe the Confederacy had experience with such matters.

Octavia paced anxiously outside the communications turret that stood at an intersection across from the plaza at the center of the village. The comm system was like the antique missile turret at the center of the plaza in that no one knew if the equipment still worked. It had not been used for long-range communication in dozens of years, only for contacting outlying farms and settlements during emergency situations.

The mayor had insisted on complete privacy inside the turret while making the transmission attempt. He had been shut inside the tower for forty-five minutes now. Octavia hoped that was a good sign. Or maybe he couldn't figure out how to operate the transmitter.

Finally, Mayor Nikolai emerged wearing a bemused expression. He ran a hand through his spiky blond hair, looking very satisfied with himself.

"Did you get through?" Octavia asked. "Did you talk to the Terran Confederacy?"

"Well, not exactly. It seems the Confederacy fell apart and now the government is called the Terran Dominion. The guy I talked to called himself the emperor—pretty impressive, I suppose. Name of Arcturus Mengsk. He seemed interested in what we found, asked a lot of questions. Told me they'll probably send a military force out to investigate immediately."

Octavia heaved a sigh of relief. "Good. Then help is on the way."

Their troubles were over.

CHAPTER 9

AS HE LOUNGED BACK ON THE THRONE, NEWLY installed in the restored capital of Korhal, Emperor Arcturus Mengsk felt vindicated for all the years he had spent in guerrilla activities, scheming against the repressive Terran Confederacy.

The throne felt *right* to him, as if he had always deserved it. And he felt powerful.

In the background, a holoprojection was playing, repeating the magnificent speech he had given to all human beings on the event of his self-coronation. Mengsk never got tired of hearing the words.

"Fellow Terrans, I come to you, in the wake of recent events, to issue a call to reason. Let no human deny the perils of our time. While we battle one another, divided by the petty strife of our common history, the tide of a greater conflict is turning against us, threatening to destroy all that we have accomplished."

Very dramatic. Very compelling. Mengsk had practiced the speech many times in front of numerous advisors.

It had been months now since the overthrow of the Terran Confederacy, when Mengsk himself had arranged to lure the evil Zerg minions to the capital planet of Tarsonis. There, the voracious aliens had done Mengsk's destructive work for him. And better still, he had managed to make it appear that he was the hope of all humans, a knight in shining armor.

His image continued to speak. "It is time for us as nations and as individuals to set aside our long-standing feuds and unite. The tides of an unwinnable war are upon us, and we must seek refuge upon higher ground lest we be swept away by the flood.

"With our enemies left unchecked, who will you turn to for protection?"

Good words, he thought, *a nice slogan.* Worth repeating.

Much remained to be done, though. Emperor Mengsk had worlds to subdue, governments to reestablish, figureheads to put into place.

And now he had received this odd message from the forgotten colony of Bhekar Ro.

Mengsk shifted in his throne, looking at a transcript of the communiqué. He wanted to review every word of his conversation with the colony's mayor, Jacob Nikolai. *Never heard of him before.*

Running his well-manicured fingers down his bushy whiskers, Mengsk frowned, wondering what to do about the situation. His initial instinct had been to ignore the request for assistance. Bhekar Ro was not on the list of important worlds on which the new emperor needed to secure his grasp. Even the Confederacy had left them alone. Why should he really be concerned about a bunch of dirt farmers from a backwater world nobody had ever noticed?

Distracting sounds drifted to him from the rooms surrounding the throne chamber: loud hammering, buzzing diamond cutters, and sparking laser welders. Now that he had control of the Terran government, Mengsk had ordered construction on a vast scale to begin on the devastated worlds, such as the restoration here on Korhal, which remained scarred from previous Confederate atrocities.

Over the din, his holo speech continued. "The devastation wrought by the alien invaders is self-evident. We have seen our homes and communities destroyed by the calculated blows of the Protoss, we have seen firsthand our friends and loved ones consumed by the nightmarish Zerg. Unprecedented and unimaginable though they may be, these are the signs of our time."

Infrastructure damaged by the Zerg invasion and the Protoss strikes on Mar Sara and Chau Sara needed to be healed and rebuilt—but those unimportant places could come later. First the emperor had to figure out how to squeeze more taxes from the populace so that he could restock his imperial treasury. Any planet that did not cheer Mengsk's presence loudly enough would find it far more difficult to receive funding and civil engineers for their construction projects.

"The time has come, my fellow Terrans, to rally to a new banner. In unity lies strength. Already many of the dissident factions have joined us. Out of the many we shall forge an indivisible whole, under the authority of a single throne. And from that throne I shall watch over you."

He decided to make sure that this coronation speech was taught to all young students in the new Dominion. Revising history could well become a full-time job. . . .

Mengsk poured himself a glass of rich purple klavva wine, drank it down quickly, then poured a second glass that he could savor. The decision about the strange alien object on Bhekar Ro rested squarely on his shoulders. He couldn't pass it off to anyone else—that was the *dis*advantage of being emperor. But Arcturus Mengsk had earned the right, earned this position, and he chided himself for complaining about the minor duties of a great ruler.

What exactly had those backwater settlers found? He had agreed to send assistance, but was it really worth his while to investigate?

One of his uniformed aides marched briskly into the opulent throne room and gave him a smart raised-fist salute that had been used by the Sons of Korhal. If Emperor Mengsk had his way, the salute would soon be accepted throughout the Terran Dominion.

The aide handed him a rolled document, which Mengsk opened and studied. Ah, the daily list of scheduled executions! The emperor ran his fingernail down the numerous names and recognized few of them. He didn't remember what their crimes were, and right now he didn't have the time to check up on everything. Too many annoying details. Most of them must have been political prisoners or mutineers who refused to give up the old reins of the Terran Confederacy.

He began to check the cases one by one, but then decided he had more pressing matters to attend to. Mengsk simply stamped the entire list "Approved" and handed it back to the aide, who raised his fist in the Dominion salute again and hurried off to present the duly-signed document to the Executioners Guild.

Another job done for the day.

His holo speech wound toward its conclusion. "From this day forward let no human make war upon any other human. Let no Terran agency conspire against this New Beginning. And let no man consort with alien powers. And to all the enemies of humanity: Seek not to bar our way. For we shall win through, no matter the cost."

Mengsk stared again at the summary of the conversation he'd had with Mayor Nikolai. *What to do?* he mused. There was no point in being suspicious that these settlers were lying to him or overblowing their discovery, since they were so far out of galactic politics that they hadn't known who Emperor Mengsk was, had not even *heard* of the Terran Dominion.

Still, who really cared if some clodhoppers dug up a big shiny rock and didn't know what to make of it?

Unless the thing had some value to it. Emperor Mengsk never reacted too spontaneously. What if this alien "thing" was actually something important, something he shouldn't ignore? It could be a new threat, something sinister left by the Zerg or the Protoss, strange races that still brought fear to his heart, even though he had used them to his own ends in order to crush his former rivals.

Did he dare dismiss this discovery without investigating it? What if the pulsing artifact were a powerful repository of knowledge? What if it contained valuable resources . . . or even a weapon? Alien artifacts were exceedingly rare. Emperor Arcturus Mengsk knew he needed all the help he could get while he cemented his hold on power.

He went into his war room and called up the glowing three-dimensional star maps that showed the Koprulu Sector. He glanced at the familiar stars and planetary systems, then had the computer add a tiny dot to mark the Bhekar Ro colony, using coordinates backtracked from the communications signal. The colonists had been quiet for so long that they had fallen off regular Confederacy records. Mengsk muttered at the incompetence of his predecessors.

He studied the surrounding area, then called up a tactical display that showed where all of his ships in the sector were currently stationed. With a smile on his bearded face he decided to dispatch General Edmund Duke and his Alpha Squadron to investigate. They needed something to do anyway.

The gruff general, who was already in the vicinity, was expendable at this point. The mission would keep the man and his marines occupied, and Mengsk doubted the colonists would complain overmuch to the hard-as-nails officer. The emperor didn't mind giving General Duke a more interesting assignment—as long as it kept him safely away from Korhal for the time being.

Though Duke had taken an oath to the new Dominion, he had fought on the side of the Confederacy for many years. Mengsk remained uneasy about having such a forceful military leader with so much firepower at his disposal just sitting around and getting bored.

The general was a hardened military leader who had sworn to defend his new government—and such men did not take oaths lightly. Still, he didn't distrust the commander entirely. The emperor decided to give Duke and Alpha Squadron a chance to prove themselves.

The holoprojector reset itself and began to play the coronation speech again. "Fellow Terrans, I come to you, in the wake of recent events, to issue a call to reason. . . ."

He considered shutting it off, but decided to listen just one more time.

Mengsk wrote out orders and transmitted them to the communications facility, dispatching Alpha Squadron with all due haste to Bhekar Ro.

CHAPTER 10

AT DAWN OVER THE GREASY GRAY SKIES OF BHEKAR
Ro, thin clouds swirled and then rippled like a tainted oil
stain atop stagnant water. The wastelands were quiet . . .
too quiet.

With a crack of thunder in the dry air, the fabric of space
tore and a warp-rift opened. A glider hawk reeled about, disrupted in its endless search for food.

As the echoes of the boom rippled across the valley, startling
small rodents that eked out an existence among the hardy scrub
brush, a Protoss observer from the *Qel'Ha* appeared and hovered
high in the sky. Observers were reconnaissance vessels sent out
to gather information, but not to participate in actual combat.

Automatically following its programming, the observer
switched on a micro-cloaking field and vanished from view.
The drone craft descended, activating the complex sensor array
that drained most of its operational energy, leaving nothing
for system defenses. Three-fold wing shields opened, guiding
the single, cyclopean eye.

Then it began to search.

The observer proceeded across the uninhabited areas of Bhekar Ro, unchallenged and unnoticed. While flying head-long across the vast distance of space, it had not been able to pinpoint its coordinates precisely. But now, as the observer homed in on the location of the artifact's transmitted signal, it planted navigational beacons so that the *Qel'Ha* and the rest of the Protoss expeditionary force could arrive precisely on target.

The observer spent hours circling overhead, approaching the broken mountainside where the half-uncovered organic oddity lay exposed in the morning light. Sending regular real-time reports back to Executor Koronis, the reconnaissance drone imaged and analyzed the artifact protruding from the mountainside. After its initial transmission, the object had lain quiet. Waiting.

Once the small drone had inspected every angle and approached as closely as its programming allowed without risk of disturbing the artifact that had sent the signal, it proceeded to make a wider reconnaissance. In compiling its over-all tactical survey, the drone acquired images of the mountain ranges and detected—with no hint of surprise in its robotic mind—cultivated fields and outlying settlements of prefabri-cated buildings.

Assessing the situation, the observer closed in, still cloaked, until it hovered over the central colony town on Bhekar Ro. It began to collect data on the human settlers, the resident population, and their defenses. . . .

It was a morning like any other morning, but Octavia Bren had to face the day without her brother Lars.

The other colonists left her alone, even Mayor Nikolai, who was better known for talk than for practical action. She sat in the octagonal town square remembering Lars and their time together, how they had often discussed which unmarried colonists they each might consider as a mate, how hard they had worked, what they had hoped to accomplish, how the two had teased each other as young children. . . .

It had been long enough now that the scars of her parents' deaths had healed. The other colonists were so familiar with unexpected tragedy that they sympathized with Octavia, but were not paralyzed with grief. Free Haven had suffered enough before, and would continue to endure the pain. It was their lot in life. But Octavia's grandparents had been convinced that this was a better existence than living under the Terran Confederacy. Here they were free—though at the moment Octavia could not be entirely sure that she preferred the constant uncertainty and brevity of life on Bhekar Ro.

Octavia wished she and her brother had never gone out to inspect the seismographs and automated mining stations, but Lars had been so excited about the discovery. She wished he could have been like the other colonists, never curious, never striving for more, just holding on to life as long as he could manage.

But then he wouldn't have been Lars.

As the morning brightened, Octavia stayed near the ornamental old missile turret, constructed there over an abandoned bunker by the first colonists. It was meant to be a sentry station, an automated defense that would watch the skies and protect Bhekar Ro—though from what, she didn't know. The missile turret had sat there silently for more than forty years. Nobody even believed it worked anymore.

Now, instead of being seen as a defense, the turret served as a reminder and a monument to what they had left behind in the Confederacy. Occasionally some colonists proposed dismantling it for parts, power cells, and materials, but the mayor had never gotten enough ambition to gather a crew.

Now, as Octavia sat there alone, thinking of her brother and staring up into the unpleasant, featureless sky, the missile turret suddenly clicked, hummed, and moved. System lights winked on, sputtered, then glowed bright.

She leaped to her feet and scrambled away with a shout.

A few colonists came out of their homes to look at her, then saw the activation lights on the clunky metal structure and saw the turret move.

Its hydraulics hummed as components opened, rattled, and locked into place. A brilliant light shone from its top as the turret's tracking scanner swiveled. The automatic sensors centered in and targeted something invisible in the sky. Missile turrets were designed to automatically target and fire on incoming enemy aircraft, but they also served as sentry stations; their powerful sensors could detect even cloaked vessels.

This turret had not stirred in decades, but now it locked on, selected a missile, and loaded it into the launch rack, its mechanisms clattering and groaning. Its detector systems flickered and sparked, not working properly. But it had detected something.

With a pulse of energy, the turret fired its missile into the sky. Smoke streamed from an access hatch on the missile turret as its long-dormant systems began to fail.

Other colonists, rushing out in response to the strange noise, were astonished to see that the military hardware still functioned at all.

"Could've been a misfire," the mayor said. "We should have deactivated that a long time ago."

The projectile shot upward like an exploding javelin, cruising in a smooth, perfect arc until it struck something that looked like a ripple and a halo in the air.

But Octavia stretched her forefinger toward the sky. "No, look! It's hit something."

With a flicker, the observer's cloaking field broke down, and the damaged drone wavered through the sky, its hull split open, one of its three wing covers blown away. Losing altitude, the device spun and sputtered until it crashed like an unwieldy bullet into one of the roughly tilled fields outside of town.

Without even looking to see if the other settlers were following, Octavia ran out to the crash site, where she found a bowl-shaped crater gouged into the dirt. The twisted, blackened wreckage had slammed into the ground. There was very little of the observer left to examine.

Studying what was left of the object while the colonists rushed to join her, Octavia noticed the strange alien markings on the outer covering of the drone, the broken angled panels over the sensor arrays, the large central eye.

"Either the Confederacy has changed its designs an awful lot, or that's nothing a Terran ever built," Mayor Nik announced, stating aloud what everyone else had already realized.

Octavia felt a stab of ice inside her. First the storm and earthquake had exposed the huge buried artifact. Now, from out of the sky, an invisible alien device had been shot down—though what its purpose might be she could only guess.

The colonists began to mutter uneasily, looking down at the crashed object. Octavia turned away from the alien wreckage and bit her lower lip, wondering what could possibly be going on here. And what could possibly happen next.

CHAPTER 11

WHEN THE DISTANT ARTIFACT'S INSISTENT SIGNAL reached the Zerg swarms on Char, it sent a shockwave like a mental avalanche through the Queen of Blades. As she sat in her growing hive, the pulsing transmission hammered Sarah Kerrigan's temples with an electromagnetic shriek. Somehow this blaring call was attuned to the new resonances in her head, the genetic reception signal that had been incorporated into the Zerg from the primal foundation of their DNA.

The thrumming signal caused her hive's organic shell to shimmer, as it too received the long-forgotten awakening call. The exoskeletal material that made up the hive walls began to resonate in response.

Around her, Zerg minions reacted with frenzy as the signal triggered some instinctive memory deep inside. The monstrous hydralisks reared up, hissing and slashing with their claws, their pointed spines extruded, ready to fire a rain of deadly darts at any creature they perceived as an enemy.

The doglike zerglings went wild, streaming about and attacking drones and larvae, tearing them to shreds. The alien signal pounded in Kerrigan's head, but she gritted her teeth and imposed order upon her mind. With all of her psi power, she reached out and attempted to control the instincts of her zerglings. She needed to stop them from killing more members of her hive.

In her earlier life, she had been trained in the Confederate Ghost program. The Terrans had given her agonizing neural processing treatments to pacify her latent psi powers. They had surgically implanted a Psychic Dampener to control her, to make her into a good espionage and intelligence agent. Sarah Kerrigan had been forced to murder countless enemies and learned to treat life itself as a fleeting, disposable commodity.

It had been good training for her. But Kerrigan had been betrayed by the humans she served, who had left her for dead on the Zerg-infested battlefield of Tarsonis. The woman who had been Sarah Kerrigan became the Queen of Blades, and she alone held the future of the Zerg.

If she could control them.

The signal continued, relentless. From the outer regions of the spreading hive, she could hear the vibrating bellows of an ultralisk as it roared its confusion and fear. She calmed the mammoth-sized monster, then moved on to other minions that were causing too much destruction. With an iron hand, she forced discipline upon her hive again.

Finally the pulsing signal-scream stopped. Blessed, frightening silence fell like an avalanche onto the hive. Kerrigan drew a deep breath, letting her biological systems settle, feeling the hive return to a normal, but still agitated, state. Then she began to think.

The transmitted siren song spoke to some involuntary instinctive memory that the Xel'Naga had planted inside them. The Queen of Blades knew deep within her own mutated body that the origin of this signal must be incredibly ancient, designed by the same race that had created the Protoss and the Zerg.

Though she used much of her mind to keep watch on the restless race of the Zerg—billions upon billions of creatures— she let part of her thoughts ponder what she had experienced. She knew that the Zerg must investigate—must *possess*— whatever had sent this powerful signal.

Finally reaching a decision, Kerrigan summoned all the components of the finest new brood she had assembled after the destruction of the Overmind. She had a mission for Kukulkan Brood, which she had named after the powerful Mayan feathered serpent god from the ancient Terran legends. She considered the title to be fearsome and fitting. Kukulkan Brood was one of the most fearsome assault swarms in the scattered Zerg race. She could depend on them.

When Kukulkan Brood was assembled, with all its over-lords, mutalisks, hydralisks, zerglings, ultralisks, queens, and drones—everything necessary for an impressive assault force—Kerrigan dispatched them from the smoking ruins of Char to fly across space like deadly insects.

Her orders, made perfectly clear even to the murky minds of the various Zerg minions, were to find the object that had sent the signal—and take possession of it at all costs.

CHAPTER 12

THE FREE HAVEN MEETING HALL WAS CROWDED once again with confused and disgruntled colonists. This time, though, they needed no one to tell them that things were changing on Bhekar Ro. Things that could affect their lives. Things over which they had no control.

And this time, with the exception of a few children too young to understand what was going on, every colonist was there, even families from outlying farmsteads.

Octavia sat in the front row close to the speaking platform. Many of the younger colonists had chosen to sit near her for support, including Jon, Gregor, Wes, and Kiernan and Kirsten Warner. On Octavia's right sat Cyn McCarthy. The young woman's copper hair hung limply around her somber face as if she had not washed it for several days. And the usual optimism had faded from her dark blue eyes; that scared Octavia the most.

Octavia could sense that the worst of the crisis was yet to come. The Bhekar Ro colonists would need every gram of stubbornness and determination they could muster to get through it. When Mayor Nikolai hopped onto the speaking platform, Octavia was surprised at how quickly the room quieted.

"Now then, we're tough people, and we've been through a lot," he began. "And for a long time we've prided ourselves on being just about unshakable. We deal with weather disasters, tectonic disturbances, plagues, and unexpected deaths, taking it all in stride and moving on. But in the last few days we've seen some things that fall completely outside our understanding. In all our years on Bhekar Ro, we've never had the need to deal with hostile aliens. In other words, we need to prepare for the unexpected."

Rastin the prospector stood up. "Kind of ridiculous to say that, don't you think, Mayor Nik? How can we prepare if we don't know what we're preparing for?"

Shayna Bradshaw spoke next. "If you mean we need to defend ourselves, we don't have any decent weapons. We're colonists—we've got field implements and the occasional projectile gun for shooting game." She gave an emphatic nod of her head. "Not that this planet has any game worth shooting!"

Anger flared in Octavia. "First a huge artifact disintegrates my brother and then sends a beam out into space. Then our missile turret comes to life and shoots an alien object out of the sky. It could be a message, a weapon, or a spy. We need to prepare for an emergency. That weird transmission has attracted some attention, and we don't know what's coming next. So I suggest we start thinking about what we *can* do and stop whining about what we don't know or don't have."

As Octavia subsided onto the bench beside her friends, she was surprised to see Cyn rise to her feet. "What about those Terrans you contacted, Nik? Can we expect help from them? Aren't they coming soon?"

A perplexed frown creased Mayor Nikolai's forehead. "The Terran Dominion, ah, yes. Their emperor said he would send someone immediately." He thought for a moment and then flushed. "Of course, that was days ago. And even if they're on their way, we don't know if they'll arrive before the next alien thing shows up in the sky over our heads."

Cyn straightened her shoulders, and Octavia saw a look of fierce determination sparkling in her eyes. "In that case, we'll just have to get ready to fend for ourselves."

Kiernan Warner stood now. "What about the explosives we use for leveling fields and for mining? Couldn't we use those as some sort of weapon?"

A murmur of approval and hope rippled through the room. Wes bounced to his feet. "Hey, and most of us own pulse pistols that we use for hunting lizards."

His cousin Jon stood next. "I'm pretty good with machinery. Maybe between us, Octavia and I can do something about fixing the missile turret in the main square."

Octavia shot him an approving grin. Things were getting better by the moment. "My robo-harvester has a boulder-blaster on it, and a lot of the others have flamethrower attachments. Those could do some pretty significant damage."

Old Rastin interrupted the flow of positive suggestions. "You're all a bunch of lamebrained vespene wasters, if you ask me. Half-buried artifacts, alien ships—are you really convinced we're being invaded? Who do you think these aliens are, anyway? Truth is, we don't know what's going on, and until we do, I'm not gonna sit around here on my butt just yakkin' about it." He pushed past several people toward the exit. "And don't expect me to be givin' all of you free vespene gas just because y'all think the sky is falling." He gave a grunt of disgust, stalked to the exit, and let himself out.

Mayor Nikolai stood for a moment openmouthed at the old man's audacity before pulling himself together. "Well, of course we shouldn't panic. Mr. Rastin has a point. After all, Emperor Mengsk of the Terran Dominion has been apprised of the situation, and help is probably on its way. . . ." His voice trailed off.

Unwilling to see the settlers slip back into complacency, Octavia stepped up onto the platform beside the mayor. "Nik's right. This is not a time to panic. It's time to do something constructive." She smiled as Cyn and her other friends joined her on the platform to show their support. "We've all heard some things we can do to prepare ourselves for what might be coming."

The crowd rumbled its approval and headed back out toward their homes and farms.

CHAPTER 13

ON THE BRIDGE DECK OF THE *QEL'HA*, EXECUTOR Koronis studied the high-resolution images in fascinated silence. The observer drone transmitted view after view of the magnificent organic structure. The curves and angles gave the uncovered artifact the appearance of a cathedral built by overambitious insects. Swirls and curves, glowing lights, an obviously complex, unfathomable design.

Judicator Amdor stood beside him, radiating excitement and eagerness—a great change from the dour skepticism he had shown for the past several years of their fruitless search.

Koronis was fascinated to see the jagged shards of transparent gleaming rock that protruded from the rubbled terrain all around the exposed object. "Those are Khaydarin crystals," he said, trying to imagine the sheer power that fragments of such size would possess. He recalled the tingle of energy he experienced whenever he touched the tiny shard he kept in his private quarters. Even without the secrets of the strange artifact, massive crystals such as these would be an important weapon and resource for the Protoss.

Amdor seemed more intrigued by the strange shapes and runes marked around the outer shell. "Those clues, plus the original encrypted signal, are undeniable proof that this object had its origin with the Wanderers from Afar. We have found a legacy of the Xel'Naga."

The Judicator shed his blazing glare upon all the other Protoss on the *Qel'Ha*'s bridge. His mental being thrummed with enthusiasm, which affected the other Khalai, inspiring them to greater fervor. "We must retrieve this treasure left by our forefathers, the Xel'Naga." Acting as if he were the commander of the fleet, Amdor gestured forward. "Proceed with all possible haste! We must take possession of this artifact and preserve it for our people."

Executor Koronis stiffened. Amdor had no place in the caste hierarchy to give such an order. So he repeated the order himself, as if the instructions had come from him all along. "We will not be going home immediately. Yes, even though Aiur has suffered in a terrible war, a discovery such as this may help the First Born rise again."

Amdor stared down at the images once more. "The Zerg infestation encroaches upon Protoss space, and though they share our origin with the Xel'Naga, we First Born can never accept them as brethren. We dare not allow the Zerg to capture this artifact or any knowledge it contains. The legacy of the Xel'Naga must belong to us."

The distant observer continued its survey, sending fresh images of the unremarkable world of Bhekar Ro. Executor Koronis was surprised to see the organized Terran colony and the structures erected by the small group of human settlers trying to scrape out an existence there.

However, when the old missile turret activated itself and shot the cloaked drone out of the sky, the Executor reared back in his command seat as if the shot had been fired at him personally. The blast incinerated the delicate sensors on the observer's wide arrays, and the reconnaissance drone crashed.

The loss of the observer annoyed Judicator Amdor—not because of any insignificant Terran threat, but because he would receive no more images of the Xel'Naga artifact until their ship arrived at the colony world.

"Once we reach the planet, perhaps we should proceed with caution," Koronis said. "We do not know how much military prowess these Terrans have, or what sort of defenses they can mount against us. I suggest we drop our fleet back and enter the system more slowly so that we can reassess the situation."

Now the Judicator turned his ire on Koronis. "Unnecessary! You saw the images. It's a fledgling colony, with only a few scraps of technology. Besides, they are human. Terrans are irrelevant."

Koronis conceded the point, and the *Qel'Ha* launched forward along with the rest of the expeditionary force, streaking through space at the highest speed possible.

The Executor reviewed the images the observer had transmitted, staring down at the haunting, fascinating Xel'Naga structure. After missing the great battle to protect Aiur and failing in their search to find the Dark Templar, Koronis believed that this artifact could accomplish the third part of their mission. Perhaps this would be a redemption for him.

CHAPTER 14

OVER THE NEXT COUPLE OF DAYS, WHILE THE colonists prepared for another impending emergency, Octavia found herself growing more and more restless. The tension at the back of her mind kept building. She felt a presence there, as if something alive were trying to communicate with her.

Another premonition? Or just her imagination?

If not for the strange events of the past week, she might have dismissed the uneasy feeling, but she knew it was more than that. She still mourned the loss of her brother Lars, but it was not his ghost or his presence that hovered so insistently at the edge of her awareness.

The tension continued to build like slow psychic pressure until it became unbearable. She worked her fields alone. She had already gathered her small hand weapons and donated what spare food supplies she had to the community kitchen Abdel Bradshaw was organizing.

There had been no sign of reinforcements from the Terran

Dominion, and no one in the colony had reported any alien ships or artifacts.

But still, the dread and uneasiness hammered at her mind, making her jump at shadows.

Finally Octavia could take it no more. Hardly knowing what she intended to do, she climbed into the robo-harvester and set off toward the artifact. She needed to see it again, confront it somehow, and find some answers.

All the way there she felt a thread, a growing connection to the thing at a subconscious, almost-telepathic level. *Could the artifact itself be alive?*

With each clank of the robo-harvester's heavy treads, she could feel it, hear it. Something sleeping, stirring. Something enormous and alien.

It had seemed to devour Lars—absorb him, perhaps—and then it had seemed to find him wanting. *Yes,* the presence in her mind seemed to say. It hungered. It needed to feed on life.

But not Terran life. Something . . . different.

As the robo-harvester descended into the second valley and rolled across the basin toward the slope where the artifact lay half unburied, the feeling of hunger grew stronger, more insistent. Hunger for life.

Angrily, Octavia tried to push the presence out of her head. If it didn't want Terran life, why had it killed her brother? The thing had casually murdered him and then—what? Discarded his essence? She didn't know, and it no longer mattered to her. All that mattered was that Lars was dead because of this thing.

She brought the robo-harvester to a halt at the base of the slope and stared at the enormous, eerie artifact with a hard, calculating gaze. Hungry, was it? Well, she had a hunger too— for vengeance. And she needed to do something practical for a change.

From the cockpit of the robo-harvester she powered up the boulder-blaster. She herself had suggested at the town meeting that it could be used as a weapon. Well, now she was going to find out.

Octavia took careful aim and triggered the small explosive launcher that was normally reserved for clearing boulders from fields. She held on and watched, already feeling satisfied.

The blast struck its target dead on. The familiar explosion was loud and powerful, smashing many of the tall crystals that grew like weeds in the rubble. A rain of pebbles and dirt pattered around the robo-harvester for nearly a full minute.

When Octavia was sure the shower of dirt was over, she cleared the robo-harvester's windshield and peered out to survey the damage she had done.

There was none. Not a scratch.

If anything, the artifact appeared glossier . . . *healthier* than before. Octavia had only succeeded in clearing more caked soil from its exterior. As she stared in frustrated fascination, the artifact began to pulse. The forest of surrounding crystals lit with an inner fire. Crackling energy skittered across the smooth, sinuous surface of the thing, flashing and growing in intensity until threads of lightning wove themselves together into a solid beam that speared out at the robo-harvester.

She yelled and ducked, covering her eyes.

The retaliatory bolt hit the heavy vehicle like a meteor. Octavia grabbed the seat inside the cab and held on as the robo-harvester rocked on its treads. She wanted to dive outside for cover, but decided that might be even more dangerous.

The vehicle's control panels sparked and sizzled. The alien artifact continued its pummeling lightning blast, as if to make certain its message was received. Octavia's hair lifted away from her head, alive with static electricity. She let out another loud yell, halfway between a panicked scream and a curse, at the towering object in the cliffside.

Finally the blast ended, leaving her half deafened and the big machine completely dead. Her eyes swam with brilliant smears of color from the dazzling lights. Ozone and smoke filled the cabin, and crackling steam drifted up from the harvester's engine compartment.

Octavia scrambled out of the cab, burning her hands and the side of one leg on the hot metal. In awe, she backed away from the damaged vehicle. She could tell by looking at it that there would be no way to repair the behemoth. The electrical systems were completely gone, and many of the moving parts had fused. The vehicle would never start.

But at least she was alive.

The artifact had destroyed the robo-harvester, though it had not harmed her, even after she had knowingly attacked it. What did it mean? Octavia shook her head and chided herself for having tried something so foolish.

Running a hand through her brown curls, she looked behind her at the sun lowering toward the horizon. It would be a long, long walk home.

CHAPTER 15

AS HER SHIP MOVED THROUGH THE VOID OF SPACE, the Dark Templar Xerana sat surrounded by her intellectual resources, the library and museum she had compiled. Her treasures.

She had no need for sleep now that she had a mystery in her grasp.

Xerana had received and recorded the loud signal from the distant and unremarkable world. She had studied the transmission, searching for nuances, trying to decode it. She took the ancient, incomprehensible electromagnetic patterns and organized them into layers of subtle meaning. She doubted many others alive in the entire galaxy would be able to fathom such things.

But the Dark Templar scholars had access to resources and arcane Xel'Naga texts. She knew scraps of history that the rest of the Protoss had forgotten long ago. Xerana alone, among all her race, had the best chance of deciphering the true meaning and origin of this alien transmission.

She let her ship drift, allowing the currents of the Void to carry it wherever the vagaries of gravity and solar wind and space might direct it. She played the signal over and over until every cell of her body was awash with the pulsing rhythms, until her mind was filled with the hypnotic tone—and finally, using every shred of knowledge she had in her archives, Xerana was able to comprehend the deep secret of the strange awakening object.

Roused at last from her obsessive concentration, the Dark Templar scholar felt the thrill of understanding surge through her body. But as she made her way toward the bridge of her wandering vessel, she felt weak and shaky. Xerana paused a moment to marshal her energies. She had so much to do, a mission to accomplish. Then she hurried to her controls and sank into the guidance chair, feeling as if she had become one with her craft.

Though she had translated the mysterious signal, Xerana also knew that other Protoss—and perhaps even Zerg—would have heard the beacon, too. But none of them would understand what the artifact *was*.

She had no choice but to do her duty.

Long ago, the Judicator Conclave had ostracized the Dark Templar. Although her people had been exiled from Aiur, driven away from the rest of their race and persecuted, Xerana and her comrades maintained their loyalty. Even now, honor required her to bear a warning, no matter the cost to herself.

Xerana powered up the engines of her scout vessel and set off at reckless speed into the emptiness, navigating toward the coordinates she had traced as the origin of the signal. Aside from her knowledge and her confidence, she had few weapons.

She traveled alone, fully aware that other Protoss might even now be converging on the site. Any Judicator would be eager to capture a Dark Templar like herself. This journey would be very dangerous for her, but Xerana had no time for fear. She had no choice but to take the risk.

Her vessel rapidly closed the distance to Bhekar Ro.

CHAPTER 16

DISPATCHED FROM CHAR, KUKULKAN BROOD TRAVELED across the empty vacuum between the stars. Even out in the cold darkness, their armored bodies turned the Zerg into a fleet of monstrous living spaceships. Groups of different creatures controlled by numerous overlords, the Brood followed the directives of the Queen of Blades, who had envisioned this scheme to investigate, capture, and exploit the Xel'Naga artifact.

It would belong to the Zerg by right of conquest.

Massive behemoths flew under their own energy, like star-spanning manta rays, the largest creatures ever known in the charted galaxy. With superdense hides, the behemoths could contain many other Zerg minions within the folds and pockets of their sprawling bodies. These creatures had no weapons, not even any defenses, but they carried the full strength and horror of all the Zerg subspecies.

Ages ago, when the ancient Xel'Naga tinkerers had experimented with creating the Zerg, they had adapted the ferocious and highly competitive indigenous life-forms on the planet Zerus. These prototype Zerg had rapidly adapted and assimilated all of the native species there, and as their race grew more powerful and more intelligent, the fledgling Zerg overmind had reached a critical point, a roadblock that prevented it from expanding further. The Zerg were planet-bound—until the star-sailing behemoths had wandered into the system.

Immense and docile creatures of the airless void, the behemoths drifted close enough that the Overmind had called out to them with its great telepathic powers. After it had lured the unsuspecting life-forms within reach, the Zerg minions had attacked and infested them. Before long, the genetic plan of the starfaring behemoths had been incorporated into the Zerg DNA.

Thus, the fearsome Zerg developed the ability to travel from star system to star system. They became unstoppable.

Now, after being dispatched by the Queen of Blades, the behemoths of Kukulkan Brood carried Sarah Kerrigan's strike force to Bhekar Ro. The huge creatures converged in orbit, an organic cloud that blotted out the light from distant suns. They descended lower to the veiled fringes of the atmosphere, scraping tendrils of air as their skins opened up to disgorge the overlords, the main carriers of the Zerg forces.

The overlords were immense creatures, exoskeleton-armored carriers shaped like ridged crustaceans with enormous mandibles and dangling claws. But even so they were dwarfed by the sprawling flesh of the behemoths in the sky overhead. The overlords emerged from carrying pouches and dropped in freefall through the thickening atmosphere and buffeting winds.

Since the Xel'Naga artifact had only briefly broadcast its compelling beacon, the Zerg did not know the precise location, only a general area. But the overlords of Kukulkan Brood were patient and very thorough. Under their own power, they cruised through greasy clouds and patches of thunderstorms, scratched by lightning but unharmed.

Finally the spreading swarm arrived in the vicinity of the large artifact. Only a small portion of the Brood remained in orbit with the behemoths, a second wave prepared to descend once the first monstrous troops had accomplished their objective.

The overlords spread out, seeking to release groups of drones that would establish numerous hatcheries and then several creep colonies. The heart of the new Zerg colony, the hatchery would generate enough larvae to spawn all the minions Kukulkan Brood would need to take over this planet.

The overlords would overwhelm the mysterious artifact itself and seize what could be taken. But first, in preparation, they intended to find local victims, organisms that the Zerg could infest, and thereby increase their numbers. . . .

Though he had set up his dwelling and his gas refineries over the vespene geysers, far from the town, the old prospector Rastin had been seeing too much of people for the past week. First Lars and Octavia Bren had come by to get more fuel, then he'd been called into Free Haven for not one but two all-colony meetings.

He had grudgingly driven his only vehicle—a clunky old field crawler—into town. That was more socialization than he liked to do in a year. On both occasions he'd stayed for only a few hours before driving back to his refineries and his dog, Old Blue.

But after the last storm and earthquake, one of his three remaining geysers had given out, and no matter how much he poked and probed and kicked at his machinery, he could not get the thing functioning again. He had heard that there were several new geysers over the ridge and into the next valley, but Rastin had lived in the same place for almost forty years and just didn't have the gumption to pack up his belongings and move out there.

Although the idea of being even farther away from Free Haven had its appeal. . . .

Old Blue came out from his cool resting spot under the corrugated porch and sniffed around. The big mutated mastiff stood almost as tall as his master's chest. Rastin had originally hoped to turn the horselike canine, with its bristly blue fur and an appetite like an elephant, into a beast of burden. Man's best friend combined with a draft animal to haul mineral samples and supplies. Instead, the dog was just a companion, a big, lovable creature that drooled a lot and growled occasionally, but never meant it.

Rastin distractedly patted the dog, who galloped around looking for urchin lizards or crab beetles to chase. Once he'd gotten a muzzleful of needles from an urchin lizard, and the dog knew better than to bite when he played.

Rastin banged at the refinery equipment with his worn old tools, grumbling and cursing the engines. But the machinery was not impressed, even with his harshest language. He stood in disgust, hurled his spanner wrench off into the rocks as far as it would go, then berated himself for doing such a stupid thing, because now he'd have to go fetch it.

Beside him, he was surprised when Old Blue sat on his haunches and howled up at the sky. The big blue dog's lips curled back, exposing his teeth as he growled and then whined.

"Now what?" Rastin said. "You afraid of a little mound-hopper again, you big sissy?"

But Old Blue did not calm down. He continued to growl, then lowered himself on all fours and began to wriggle backward, as if to slink away. Rastin looked up and saw a swarm of shapes in the sky, a flock of creatures—unbelievably large creatures—descending through the clouds and moving like an armada of organic battleships. "What the—?"

With an ominous buzzing sound like a hive of infuriated wasps, the swarm of invaders came down, dozens of armored and multilegged creatures that split apart, some of them descending toward the foothills where Rastin made his home.

The vespene geysers continued to boil and steam into the air, advertising their resources. They seemed to attract the strange alien invaders. Old Blue yelped and finally ran out of canine courage. He bolted back under the corrugated porch to hide in the shadows.

Summoning his surly anger to combat a paralyzing blast of fear, Rastin lunged into his shack and grabbed an old blunderbuss projectile launcher, a pellet weapon that he used for picking off rodents that ate too many of his stores. He came out and held up the weapon, gritting his teeth in defiance.

The Zerg overlords dropped low over the foothills, approaching the vital vespene geysers. Their carapaces cracked open and released a rain of hideous monsters that seemed to be all spines and armored exoskeletons and clacking jaws. As the zerglings poured out in a stampede of vicious claws and fangs, Rastin stood his ground for a moment, then backed toward his shack.

Behind the overlords, a new type of creature descended—a mass of thrashing armored tentacles, a sinuous head, and a stretched skin membrane that extended like bat wings to connect some of the tentacles.

A queen. And it seemed intent on coming directly toward him.

Rastin discharged his first round of hot metal pellets into the oncoming swarm, reloaded, and fired again. He knew his weapon was too weak, knew that in a thousand years he could never find enough ammunition to fight off this threat, but he swore and fired again. And again. When he had no pellets left, he hurled curses as the ravenous zerglings swept toward him like a tidal wave of death.

And then they were upon him.

CHAPTER 17

OCTAVIA DID NOT LIKE TO BE OUT ON FOOT AT NIGHT, but with the robo-harvester unable to function, she had no choice but to walk. She traversed the many kilometers across the valley, climbed up over the ridge panting and sweating, skipped through the scree, and stumbled her way back down toward the colony town.

She hated every second of it.

The ground was uncertain, full of shadows and hidden potholes, crevices between rocks that seemed to reach out and grab her feet. If she twisted an ankle, she would have to limp all the way back to Free Haven.

The night was dark, the skies murky and overcast. Clouds smothered the stars, but at least they held no storms. Strange flashes of light rippled across the sky like auroras or distant lightning, but the colors and energy patterns were different from the exotic weather fronts she normally witnessed on Bhekar Ro.

Too many strange things were happening lately.

She increased her pace down through the foothills, glad to see the dim lights of old Rastin's vespene refinery. The reclusive prospector probably wouldn't welcome company, especially this late at night, but Octavia had no choice. He had a vehicle, a vespene-powered field crawler that had endured for decades. Maybe he could give her a ride into town.

If nothing else, Old Blue would be happy to see her, and after the miserable times she had just endured, it would be a relief just to pat his bristly fur and see his thick tail wag with delight.

She stumbled onto a path the hermit must have used. With relief she worked her way down toward the homestead, feeling a spring in her step from the hope that her ordeal might be over soon.

As she approached, Octavia saw only a few automatic lights burning around the refinery superstructures, lending a strange silvery glow to the vespene geysers that curled into the air. The place seemed abandoned, haunted. . . . Perhaps old Rastin had already gone to bed. She had no idea what time it was.

"Hello, Rastin?" she called. "It's Octavia Bren." She paused, but only silence answered her. Even the fiddler beetles and the throaty humming lizards were silent in the night—which was very strange. It made the darkness seem more oppressive.

"Hello, Rastin? I need your help."

Although she normally would have walked up to his door and pounded, this uncharacteristic silence made her uneasy. Reclusive Rastin was unpredictable at times, and it wasn't hard to imagine that he might come out with his weapon to "defend" his home against late-night intruders. She didn't want to get a backside full of rodent shot.

She drew closer, her eagerness dwindling. "Hello? Is anybody home?" At least she expected Old Blue to start barking at her. If anything, the silence grew heavier.

She wondered if perhaps Mayor Nik had called another

colony meeting. In that case, Rastin might have gone to the village, taking Old Blue with him. Yes, that was probably the answer.

When she saw his vehicle sitting by itself in a clearing not far from his shack, she knew her explanation was wrong. The old man never went anywhere without his vehicle, so he must be home. This didn't make any sense at all. Her stomach filled with the ice of growing dread.

Inside her head, she felt a rising static, an echoing clamor of countless alien voices, discrete entities but somehow all the same. Her skin crawled. What did it mean? She had felt something similar—the strange background hubbub of an alien presence—back at the buried artifact that had disintegrated Lars and wrecked her robo-harvester.

But this was . . . different somehow. More evil. Menacing. Hungry.

Approaching the prospector's dwelling, she saw that the broken rocky ground was now covered with a creeping film, thick and slimy like a carpet of biomass. The substance was an organic growing mat that spread out from the vespene geysers, the refinery, and the shack itself.

She bent down to touch it and was immediately sorry. Her fingers felt soiled, as if she'd never be able to wipe the feeling off. The creeping mat smelled of rot and decay, unlike any vegetation that had ever grown here on Bhekar Ro. The carpet of biomass flexed and grew and expanded even as she watched.

On bare patches of dirt where the growing mat had not yet spread, she saw scratches—sharp, clawed footprints of several varieties, as if a mob of insectlike monsters had swarmed over the site.

Concern for Rastin overcame her fear, and she tiptoed closer to the prospector's house. Silence still reigned. She called out one more time, ready to run as her deep-seated uneasiness swelled to a terror pitch.

"Rastin? Please answer me."

As she stepped on the creaking sheet of corrugated metal that formed the porch, she heard something stir beneath it and saw a large creature moving in the shadows. "Old Blue!" she called, mentally telling herself to be relieved, though she felt no decrease in tension.

She backed away when she saw a flash of matted sky-blue fur and rippling muscles as the beast hauled itself out from the shadows where it lurked. And though it had once been Old Blue, the giant mutated dog was now something else entirely.

It was *infested*.

Spines thrust from its back. Above each leg, jointed, armored limbs sprouted from its shoulders, ending in clacking claws. Old Blue's original eyes had sunken in, and a new set—four of them—protruded on waving stalks, sweeping around to focus on Octavia. It curled its lips back, showing fangs that had grown into tusks. The drool that boiled out of its rabid mouth was thick and gelatinous, like a green acidic slime.

Now Octavia heard more things stirring around the homestead, bodies moving about. The dog-thing made a deep liquid roar in its throat, and Octavia stumbled away. Old Blue's paws split open to reveal a new set of claws as large as scimitars, and its muscles coiled like well-oiled pulleys and cables.

Octavia turned to run into the darkness. Old Blue lunged after her.

CHAPTER 18

THE PLANET DID NOT LOOK LIKE MUCH AS THE *Qel'Ha* approached, flanked by the Protoss expeditionary fleet. But appearances hardly mattered. Right now Executor Koronis was interested only in the origin of the signal that had summoned the Protoss here. The Xel'Naga message.

Judicator Amdor stood beside him, glaring out the viewports with his orange-yellow eyes. He seemed to believe he could conquer the blistered brown-and-green world below through sheer force of will alone.

"I want no failures, Executor. Not this time," Amdor said sternly, his telepathic message sloppy enough that others on the flagship's bridge could hear the undertone of threat. This annoyed Koronis. Bad for morale.

Smug in their position of political and religious power, Judicators often did not understand how the rest of the Khalai responded to undercurrents and subtleties. But Koronis would not provoke a confrontation now. Such matters were better dealt with behind telepathic shielded walls, so that even the loudest arguments and mental shouts could not be picked up by others aboard the ship.

That conflict could wait until later. He had a more important mission now.

"We will maintain a defensive fleet in orbit," he said. "Three carriers will track our position from the high ground while the rest will descend to claim the Xel'Naga object. We do not know if we will encounter any resistance." He looked around the bridge, felt the excitement and loyalty thrumming through his crew.

"I will send scouts first to clear out any resistance, while shuttles will follow immediately behind to carry our zealots, dragoons, and enough reavers to maintain supremacy on the ground. Judicator Amdor and I will ride down in the lead arbiter, while other Judicators will take twenty more arbiters and provide shields and cloaking cover for our forces."

Amdor looked annoyed that the Executor had not consulted him first, but nodded his smooth, grayish head, agreeing with his own role in the important operation.

Like falcons, the scouts separated from the remainder of the fleet in space and streaked down through the atmosphere of Bhekar Ro. Aboard the high-speed fighters, dual photon blasters and batteries of antimatter missiles were armed and ready for resistance.

Executor Koronis hoped such an aggressive posture would prove to be an unnecessary precaution, since he was sure his fleet had arrived here first, before any enemies could have responded to the artifact's beacon. He moved from his command bridge, followed briskly by the tall and imposing form of Judicator Amdor. They marched down the flagship corridors to the launching bays. Koronis climbed aboard the lead arbiter.

When the ships were launched, flying in the wakes of the fast scouts, Koronis's arbiter ship dropped away from his fleet, the Executor feeling uneasy at parting with the magnificent carrier *Qel'Ha*. It looked like a long, smooth pod in space, an ellipsoid split into half-closed petals. The Executor had been aboard the giant flagship for decades in his fruitless search, and now his impending triumph, the end of their hunt for knowledge, was tempered by a dim sense of foreboding. Somehow he didn't believe this mission would be as simple as the Judicator claimed it would be.

He transmitted instructions that the descending fleet was to avoid contact with the not-too-distant Terran colony. He had no fear of any weapons or defenses the settlers might bring to bear, but he had learned not to ask for trouble. Koronis avoided distractions and conflicts, concentrating on what was necessary to accomplish his objective.

Surrounded by their blanket of invisibility, the arbiters, dropships, carriers, and scouts swooped down into the stark valley at the foot of the exposed artifact. Mineral outcroppings and a fresh field of sputtering vespene geysers showed Koronis that he'd have the resources necessary to build all the reavers, photon cannons, and local defenses he would need.

After the arbiters had landed, looking like beetles with broad carapaces, most of the Protoss remained aboard, giving Executor Koronis the honor of being the first to set foot on the soon-to-be-conquered world.

To Koronis the air smelled dry and gritty, as if too much rock dust hung in the air. He paused, just *feeling* the place. Judicator Amdor strode up beside him so that the two of them stood together at the base of the slope where the massive exposed face of the mysterious Xel'Naga artifact filled the mountainside.

"Magnificent!" Amdor said, his knobby headgear gleaming in the diluted light. "Can you feel the power? Can you sense how great our victory will be when we return to Aiur?" His three-fingered hands clenched into fists.

The Judicator stepped forward and raised his long arms, extending his hands in an all-encompassing gesture. His dark robes curled around his body like a living thing. "I claim this worthy object for the First Born. It is a triumph for the Protoss. Let no one doubt our sole possession. *En taro Adun*!"

Executor Koronis knitted his craggy brows, thinking that Amdor was premature in his celebration. *"En taro Adun,"* he responded. He ran his fingers down his long sash of office. Yes, acquiring this amazing artifact was a glorious accomplishment, but he wondered what the strict Judicator bureaucracy would do with it. And how would they excavate something so huge and bring it back to war-ravaged Aiur?

Then, from the arbiter he had commanded, Koronis heard a desperate signal transmitted on a tight telepathic band. It was Templar Mess'Ta aboard the *Qel'Ha*. "Executor Koronis! We have detected a large fleet of Zerg behemoths in orbit, coming around the rim of the planet. They were hiding on the night side! The Zerg have arrived here first."

Koronis immediately assessed the threat even as Judicator Amdor reeled with anger at the affront of the enemy invaders.

"What is the strength of the Zerg fleet?" he asked.

"A complete Brood, Executor—as many minions as we have ever seen. This is no simple scout force, but a full-scale invasion."

Koronis remained grim, and Judicator Amdor turned to him, eyes blazing. "They must have responded to the signal as well! Executor, we must not lose possession of this Xel'Naga artifact. The Protoss will defend this."

Koronis transmitted back to Mess'Ta, "You know what to do, Templar."

"Yes, Executor. Defenses mounted. Flights of interceptors prepared and targeted. I have given orders to engage the enemy."

CHAPTER 19

AS SHE STOOD FACING THE INFESTED MONSTER, Octavia hoped that some primitive part of Old Blue's brain would recognize her and hesitate. But that hope was dashed in an instant as the huge dog-thing lunged.

She ducked and rolled off the corrugated porch so that the giant slavering monstrosity leaped over her. Its additional angular limbs thrashed and flailed to grab her. The razor-sharp claws along its back clacked, slicing the air. The eye stalks protruding from its head swiveled to watch her so the blue-furred dog could see where to strike next.

Her exhaustion and despair forgotten, Octavia scrambled from the porch, tearing open her hands on the rusty corrugated metal. The dog-thing spun about on the broken rocks around Rastin's shack, long claws spraying pebbles.

She ran in the other direction, flying across the stones. "Rastin!" she shouted, but in her heart she already knew that no help would come from the old prospector.

Octavia raced for the meager shelter of the low refinery

towers that covered the vespene geysers. The hideous muta-
tion that had once been Old Blue bounded after her, and she
put on more speed than she thought she possessed. Her muscles felt tense enough to snap, but somehow adrenaline held
her together.

She reached the small refinery structure and ducked
between the laced metal bars of the scaffolding just as the
canine horror struck the superstructure. He was too large to
fit through, and she felt safe for a moment.

Old Blue crashed again against the metal framework, bending the heavy paristeel. Two of his long, spindly arms lashed
forward like striking snakes, trying to reach her. Hot spittle
and slime splattered against the framework, where it began to
sizzle, releasing corrosive foam.

Wasting no energy on a scream, Octavia backed into the
refinery piping and controls. As Old Blue tore two gird-
ers apart, she found a release nozzle and wrenched it open,
blasting the monstrous dog with a mouthful of concentrated,
superheated vespene gas.

Howling and roaring, the creature thrashed backward, ripping open its hide on a sharp metal edge.

Seeing her chance, Octavia ran again, this time toward old
Rastin's beaten-up vehicle. If only she could get inside and
start it . . .

When she was halfway across the gap, sprinting headlong
with her eyes fastened on the door latch of the field crawler,
she realized that the surly old codger might keep his vehicle
locked so that no one else could start it. It seemed impossible
and foolish on a small colony such as Free Haven, but Rastin
was unpredictable.

Her hand slammed against the door handle—it was
unlocked! She wrenched the vehicle open and nearly collapsed with relief. Octavia lurched headfirst into the driver's
seat and slammed the door after her.

Old Blue was limping now, either injured or exhausted—
or possibly dying from the horrific infestation that crawled

through his muscular furred body. The dog-thing came toward her with faltering steps. Powerful jaws snapped and slashed at the air, as if chomping on an unseen enemy. Its spiny outgrowths flailed, as if grasping for something, hungry, wanting to tear apart any object within reach.

Octavia fumbled under the field crawler's steering column and found a starter button. She pressed hard with her thumb.

The engine coughed but did not catch. The vehicle seemed to sigh, as if it had already given up. She punched the starter button again. "Come on!"

Old Blue came closer, weaving, snarling.

Just then, the door of Rastin's shack was torn open from inside, literally ripped from its hinges and thrown to the ground ten feet away. A lumbering hulk strode into the faint light that seeped through the murky darkness. But this one was a humanoid form—or at least it *had* been. The figure looked as if it had been redesigned by a madman who had too many spare parts left over from a variety of species.

Rastin!

Growths and snapping tentacles protruded from the man's ruptured, festering skin. What had been Rastin's face now hung low, sunken into his chest, and the only recognizable features were two wild eyes—agonized, even frightened. But other alien eyes, black and covered with scaly carapaces, peered out from his shoulders and from the top of his skull.

On heavy feet, Rastin plodded forward, his human arms extended, though the muscular bestial limbs thrashed, claws clacking.

Old Blue staggered to a halt near the thin-hulled field crawler. From the way the monster had torn apart the scaffolding around the vespene refinery, Octavia knew that this monster could easily peel away the scant protection. Old Blue could rip her out of the vehicle like the soft meat of a thin-skinned berrynut.

She locked the door anyway.

But the dog-thing collapsed in front of her, seeming to choose its position carefully. Beneath the dog's blue-furred hide, sores began to boil. His hulk expanded, puffing and throbbing. Old Blue raised his distorted head and let out a long, thin whine.

Octavia punched the starter button again. The field crawler's engine ground and ground, picking up speed, humming, almost catching. . . .

Rastin careened off the porch of his shack and slogged toward her, arms extended. Old Blue shuddered and let out a last animal howl of pain.

The vehicle's engine finally roared, and Octavia did not wait around. She shifted the field crawler into gear and tore off, spraying stones and gravel, racing away from the trap.

Behind her, Old Blue's infested carcass erupted in an explosion of high-powered gases, flying chunks of meat, and splattering slime. The shock wave from the explosion and the rolling fist of poisonous fumes swept outward and smashed into her vehicle, rocking it sideways and rattling the windows. Luckily, the driver's cabin remained sealed, although gouts of ichor spattered the windows and doors.

Under the onslaught, the capricious engine coughed and almost died, but she coaxed it to life again and roared ahead, escaping Rastin's homestead.

Behind her, the infested prospector stood as if in despair, his unnatural limbs thrashing, his human face wailing with grief for his dead dog.

Octavia pulled away, barely allowing herself to feel safe— and then the ground in front of her swirled and split and boiled, as if giving birth to creatures from the depths of her nightmares.

Two gigantic reptilian monsters surged up from the dry, cracked ground in front of her. They resembled enormous cobras with skeletal heads, fangs like daggers, and blazing eyes that held too much intelligence. The creatures reared back, their rounded carapaces gleaming in the starlight, and moved to flank her. They hissed and rattled as they prepared to strike, reaching out with heavily armored limbs.

Octavia swerved the field crawler from one side to another, amazed at how responsive the innocuous-looking old vehicle was. She sped past the two creatures even as the ground broke and surged behind her. More attackers rose from underground.

With a sound like a thousand air bullets, the creatures bent over and unleashed a volley of long, spearlike spines that slammed into the back of the field crawler. Some of them protruded through the metal body.

Octavia did not dare slow down to check for damage. As she raced off into the night, another volley of the deadly spines peppered the vehicle, making it a pincushion.

With every second, her distance from the vespene refinery increased. She drove blindly into the night, out of the foothills and toward the distant town, eyes wide, throat dry, heart pounding.

It did not yet occur to her that she had survived. She only knew she had to get to Free Haven to warn the rest of the colony. If there was anything left of it.

CHAPTER 20

CHEWING ON IMAGINARY STEEL NAILS—THOUGH HE probably wouldn't have noticed if he'd had actual hardware between his molars—General Edmund Duke sat upright in the uncomfortable command chair of the battlecruiser *Norad III*. He was ready for action, and so were his men. He had ordered them so.

They had an alien artifact to investigate and helpless colonists to rescue. If they were lucky, the mission might turn out to be even more than that.

He knew better than to rally his marines by making gruff and patriotic speeches in a misguided attempt to fire them up enough to put their lives on the line for Arcturus Mengsk. The general himself wasn't entirely comfortable with the politics of the situation, but he tried not to dwell on it too much. He knew the appropriate carrot to dangle when he wanted to inspire his troops to give him their personal best.

"Colony world Bhekar Ro on-screen, General," said Lieutenant Scott from the tactical station. "Approaching orbital insertion."

General Duke nodded.

"I'm extending our sensor net, General," said Lieutenant Scott. "Scanning ahead for defensive positions."

Duke gave the handsome young officer a smug look, raising both eyebrows. "I figure our fifteen battlecruisers can pretty much take care of any little farming trouble, Lieutenant."

"Sir! Enemy vessels!" the Lieutenant shouted, double-checking his tactical readouts as the battlecruiser fleet homed in on Bhekar Ro.

On the screen he displayed a full analysis of what lurked high above the colony world. The soldiers on board the *Norad III* saw the display and muttered in surprise.

Duke clenched his jaw and leaned forward. "I thought those little slimeballs might be laying an ambush for us." He recognized the smooth-shelled, split-ellipsoidal Protoss carriers. The general had never been able to determine whether the ships' mottled discoloration was intentional or just ion stains from generations of service in the rigors of space.

"Power up the fleet's Yamato guns," he said. "We'll go in and ring their bells before anybody even knows we're here."

General Duke smiled and knotted his hands together as if a scrawny enemy throat were clenched between them. "All right, men," he broadcast through the long corridors of the battlecruiser. "Let's go kick some alien butt!"

The men cheered so loudly that the metal hulls rang with their enthusiasm. Alpha Squadron had been born to fight, and Emperor Mengsk had wasted their potential on pointless busywork for far too long. The marines were as bored as the general was.

"Sir, it's unlikely that the Protoss fleet was just lying in wait for Alpha Squadron," Lieutenant Scott pointed out. "They have already engaged another opponent."

As they observed, the Protoss carriers launched waves of robotic interceptors toward a hideous swarm of insectoid aliens, monstrous creatures that survived in the vacuum of space.

General Duke had seen those awful things before. "The Zerg *and* the Protoss! By damn, they've made an alliance!"

Then the Protoss interceptors smashed into the Zerg minions. In seconds, the alien battlefield turned into a chaos of weaponry discharges and exploded hulls.

"I don't think that's much of an alliance, sir," Lieutenant Scott said.

"Fine with me if they tear each other apart," the general growled. "I hate 'em both."

The Protoss carriers launched more waves of interceptors that sought out and attacked all of the Zerg creatures within reach. At first the robotic interceptors were like a swarm of stinging insects, concentrating on the massive Zerg overlords. Nearby, they made quick work of the crablike guardians, whose ability to hurl corrosive acid would have been devastating against ground targets but who were almost defenseless in space. The interceptors moved fast, striking, destroying, then searching for new targets.

Seeing the carnage, the loss of numerous overlords and guardians, a group of flying Zerg creatures known as scourges broke through and attacked the carrier itself. Reckless but determined, the group of scourges careened into the Protoss ship and exploded on impact, sacrificing themselves to take out an opposing alien vessel.

Cheering silently at seeing the loss of each Protoss craft, General Duke said, "I've had a grudge against those alien bastards ever since Chau Sara." In their first contact ever with the human race, the Protoss had come in giant ships and without warning had killed every living thing on the Terran colony planet, exterminating millions. General Duke himself had barely escaped from its infested sister planet of Mar Sara, the first place he had ever laid eyes on the hideous Zerg. "Serves them all right."

Duke had no love for the Zerg either. In fact, he hated all

aliens on general principle. And now the Zerg and Protoss were tearing each other apart in space. He couldn't imagine a more entertaining sight.

As the alien firefight continued in orbit, General Duke narrowed his eyes. He waited a moment, watching the destruction, then a smile crept over his face. "Attention, Alpha Squadron!" His booming voice broadcast through all fifteen battlecruisers. "Battle stations! We're gonna come in with all guns blazing and let them alien bastards have it."

Lieutenant Scott watched the frenzy on his tactical screen. "Sir, shouldn't we wait, send in some reconnaissance to gather tactical data before we make our move?"

The general gestured toward the screen. "You can see with your own eyes, Lieutenant—and I've never been one to sit around on my hindquarters gathering background information when it's time for *action*."

He rose from his hard command chair, knowing that standing would give him a more powerful leadership presence. "Emperor Arcturus Mengsk has declared Bhekar Ro to be of vital Terran interest." He worked to keep a straight face, knowing that none of the marines had ever heard of the place before now.

"Therefore, it is our duty to protect the colony and all of its resources from any enemy power. The presence of these alien scumbags can only be interpreted as a threat to the Terran Dominion, and we're not gonna let them endanger a single speck of dust on this colony!"

General Duke ordered all of his ships forward. With the *Norad III* in the vanguard, Alpha Squadron plunged into the fray.

CHAPTER 21

TERRIFIED, BRUISED, AND EXHAUSTED, OCTAVIA had no time to rest or to hesitate. Free Haven was in danger, and adrenaline burned like laser-lightning through her veins.

It was after midnight when Octavia careened past the low barricade fence and down the street into the village. Sounding the alarm, she drove poor Rastin's field crawler directly to Mayor Nikolai's house at the center of town and roused him out of a sound sleep. Despite his bleary eyes and the rumpled state of his spiky blond hair, he came instantly awake as Octavia related what had become of Old Blue and Rastin.

"I don't know what those creatures are, Nik, but they're alien—and they were following me."

He groaned. "Octavia, I've never known you to have an overactive imagination. But how many times have you come running into town now, raising the alarm about aliens?"

She dragged him over to Rastin's field crawler, where he saw the dozens of poisonous spines protruding like a pincushion from the back wall. The last set of monsters had shot them at her. The man could not deny the evidence of his own eyes.

Leaving Octavia to notify the people in the village proper, Mayor Nikolai excused himself and spent the next two hours at the communications station inside his home office, trying to contact families at outlying farms via the short-range comm system.

Octavia rousted Cyn McCarthy as well as Kiernan, Kirsten, Wes, Jon, and Gregor from their beds. She sent the young men out as runners from house to house in Free Haven to let the other colonists know of the approaching danger. Then she ran to the storm siren and turned it on to alert the surrounding farms as quickly as possible, even though they wouldn't know yet what kind of danger they were in until the runners got to them.

By the time the first hundred or so colonists had gathered on the street outside the meeting hall, Octavia was pleased to find that Abdel Bradshaw was already inside. His wife, Shayna, instead of arguing or criticizing, had taken it upon herself to begin setting up cots and laying out medical supplies.

"In case we have wounded," she explained.

Octavia nodded. "Let me know if you need any help."

While Cyn and Kirsten stayed to help the Bradshaws, Octavia went out to the street to speak to the sleepy-eyed colonists. A crowd had gathered around the damaged field crawler, muttering in fear and amazement. A boy of about twelve reached forward to one of the protruding spines, but Octavia snapped at him to stop. "Those could be poisonous!" she said. The others stayed away.

Next, she organized the waiting villagers into task groups, each with a different assignment. She sent a dozen of the younger teens into the meeting hall to take care of the colony's youngest children so that their parents could go about their duties without worrying.

For what felt like hours, Octavia issued orders, answered

questions, took suggestions, made snap decisions, and directed traffic as villagers brought supplies and weapons to the central gathering area. She sent Cyn with a work crew to fortify the fences on the perimeter of the village. After a couple of hours, Mayor Nikolai came out of his house, looking very disturbed.

"Did you reach everyone?" Octavia asked.

He frowned. "Most of them, except for thirteen families. Those, I couldn't contact at all."

Octavia's stomach clenched. She had seen what had happened to Rastin and his dog, somehow infested with the alien menace. Had other colonists met the same fate already?

"Maybe a few of them heard the storm siren," she suggested, knowing it was a long shot.

Mayor Nikolai glanced around at the bustling colonists. Although dawn was over an hour away, the village was wide awake and embroiled in frantic activity. "I certainly don't see any of them."

"You've got to keep trying," Octavia said.

Just then, her runners returned from their errands and raced up to Octavia, waiting for their next instructions.

"Jon, you're good with machinery. Go to the mayor's comm station and keep trying to reach our missing families until you've raised someone. Wes, you have good eyes. I want you up in the observation turret. Kiernan and Gregor, go find all the people who brought their robo-harvesters into the village and fix any boulder-blasters and flamethrowers that aren't functioning properly. Make sure that at least one of our big farm machines is stationed on each of the main streets just inside the eight gates to the village."

The young men ran off on their separate errands. Cyn McCarthy returned to report in, addressing both the mayor and Octavia at once. "The fence around Free Haven is reinforced, but they're still using several of the robo-harvesters to dig a trench around the perimeter."

Mayor Nikolai gave a grim nod. "Good thing I was able to talk the colonists into being prepared. Yes indeed."

Octavia and Cyn exchanged a look, but before Octavia could reply, Wes gave a shout from the observation turret. "Here they come! Aliens! You'd better get up here and see this for yourself."

Mayor Nikolai, Cyn, and Octavia ran to the turret and climbed the metal-runged ladder to the lookout tower. With dawn just beginning to break over the horizon, they were able to get a good look at the approaching menace.

No more than two kilometers away, a wave of creatures marched, scrambled, skittered, and loped toward the village.

The mayor swallowed convulsively.

"It's . . . it's an army," Cyn whispered in horror.

Hard, glossy carapaces provided armor for some of the creatures. Smaller ones raced forward like lizards with red eyes, lashing long tails. Some flew in the air, spreading wide leathery wings like dragons. Every type seemed to have more claws and teeth than any reasonable living creature needed to survive.

These monsters had been bred for only one thing.

As daylight brightened, the settlers could see that a good score of the shapes approaching them were distinctly human— or once had been. The colonists were infested by the creatures, just like Rastin. They all sported extra limbs, tentacles, eyes.

Sick at heart, Octavia said, "I think we know what happened to our missing families."

In stunned horror, Mayor Nikolai watched the relentless army approach. "There must be thousands of those things out there. How can we fight against that?"

Octavia gritted her teeth. "I don't think we have any choice."

CHAPTER 22

WHEN GENERAL DUKE'S BATTLECRUISERS PLOWED into the space battle in orbit, it reminded him of an expert break in a game of billiards.

Protoss craft and Zerg minions scattered in all directions, reeling from the sudden strike of the unexpected Terran forces. General Duke broadcast no warnings and requested no surrenders, just ordered his marines to inflict all the damage possible on the aliens.

He let out a loud whoop as the first shots were fired.

The Yamato guns blasted quickly, taking out Zerg overlords and one of the damaged Protoss carriers. Before the big energy weapons could recharge, General Duke launched his full fleet of impressively maneuverable Wraiths.

He paced the bridge of his flagship, keeping an eye on the tactical displays, getting updates from Lieutenant Scott and occasionally watching the battle through the viewport windows.

"Have you ever seen so many explosions in your life, Lieutenant? Witnessed so much carnage?" Actually, Duke knew that Scott and the rest of Alpha Squadron had seen the dark and dirty side of war during their battles against the Zerg in the defense of Mar Sara. But that didn't diminish his exhilaration one bit.

He turned to the comm officer. "Contact the settlers down there. We need a tactical update from the surface. I can't imagine how it can be any worse in the colony town than it is up here, but I need to set my military priorities."

"Yes, General." The comm officer bent over his station and tried to open a channel to the colonists on Bhekar Ro.

The Wraiths launched from the Terran fleet immediately cloaked before engaging a harried group of visible Protoss scouts. The alien ships had superior air-to-air firepower, as Alpha Squadron knew from previous engagements in the recently ended war, but the scouts were obviously at a disadvantage against an adversary they could not see.

The Wraiths pounded them, damaging their shields and hulls, taking out a handful of the vessels with their Gemini Missiles. After heavy pummeling from the Terran weapons, the Protoss scouts retreated, inadvertently passing close to a mass of dragonlike mutalisks that completed the slaughter with an attack move that Duke's earlier briefings had called a "Glave Wurm," expelling waves of symbiotes that chewed and sliced their way through any hull they touched. The Protoss scouts were doomed.

Their work done, the Wraiths streaked off to engage more alien targets.

From the bridge of the *Norad III*, General Duke raised his fist with a shout, cheering the victory. The bridge officers applauded.

"Our Yamato gun is recharged and ready to fire, sir," Lieutenant Scott said. He tapped a voice receiver in his ear and acknowledged, then turned to look at the general. "Battlecruiser *Napoleon* also says their Yamato is ready to fire again."

"Good. Let's both target the same Protoss carrier," the general said. He stared at the broad selection of targets on the tactical screen. Dancing his fingers through the air, he muttered, "Eenie, Meenie, Minee, Mo," and jabbed his index finger forward. *"That* one."

"Targeting, sir," Lieutenant Scott said. He opened a link to the *Napoleon.* On cue, both Terran warships fired their powerful guns, intense magnetic fields focusing a small nuclear explosion into a cohesive beam of energy. The concentrated onslaught hammered through the Protoss shields. Within seconds, the carrier's hull failed and the giant alien vessel exploded.

General Duke let out another victorious hoot. "Who'd have thought those things could come in so many different pieces!" Next he watched the Wraiths take out four more Protoss scouts. He rubbed his stubby hands together and looked around at his bridge crew. "I think we can pretty much rest assured of a victory here, men."

Lieutenant Scott frowned. "Perhaps that would be a bit premature, General."

Two Protoss arbiters moved toward General Duke's fifteen clustered battlecruisers. Duke looked at them with a sneer. "And just what do they think they're doing? Move the fleet forward. Take the *Napoleon* and the *Bismarck* closer with a squad of eight Wraiths to mop up the mess."

But as the two battlecruisers separated from the rest of Alpha Squadron, the darkness of space suddenly wavered. The arbiter fired a stasis field, an unfolding energy blanket that captured both battlecruisers along with three of the Wraiths. Although the *Napoleon* and the *Bismarck* couldn't be attacked while seized by the stasis field, neither could they make any moves of their own.

With the stasis field in place, the five Protoss carriers and eight scouts—all of which had been cloaked by the arbiter— moved forward to attack the now-exposed Wraiths like angry hornets pouring out of a nest that a foolish child had beaten with a stick.

The Wraith pilots attempted to cloak, but remained vulnerable when a Protoss observer exposed them again, stripping away their invisibility. The human pilots had no choice but to fire all their Gemini missiles in a last-ditch attempt to drive off the alien attackers, but streaking Protoss interceptors defended their ships. Without mercy, the alien fleet destroyed the five Wraiths and moved into position, ready to open fire again as soon as the stasis field wore off. . . .

The commanders of the *Napoleon* and the *Bismarck* howled at the treachery and launched their weapons. Once the stasis field was gone, forty more robotic interceptors spilled out of the uncloaked carriers and hammered like shotgun pellets into the two separated battlecruisers. The interceptors would normally have been little more than a nuisance, but in such a concentration they managed to inflict heavy damage.

Then, before General Duke could come to the defense of his ships, the Zerg attacked Alpha Squadron's flank without so much as letting up in their offensive against the Protoss. Flying through space, the hideous living creatures struck the Terran ships.

Additional squadrons of Wraiths rallied around General Duke's ships, trying to change their tactics to deal with the new threat, but the flying Zerg mutalisks launched repeated, insidious Glave Wurm strikes. A Glave Wurm struck one Wraith, ripping into the systems, then ricocheted off to another single-man fighter, causing primary and collateral damage.

The squadron commander of the Wraiths responded immediately by cloaking. After the ships vanished, they were able to turn the tide of the strike and return fire against the mutalisks. A Zerg queen and swarms of smaller self-destructive scourges detached from the main battle against the Protoss and spread through space, searching for the rest of the cloaked Wraith squadron.

Duke was proud to see his own small fighters continue to blast the Zerg scum out of space, wreaking terrible damage. The dark vacuum was filled with broken carapaces and flash-frozen alien slime.

"Sir, the Zerg overlords are catching up with us," Lieutenant Scott said. "We know they can breach our cloaking fields. They'll expose all of our Wraiths. Should we withdraw them now?"

General Duke scowled. "Not on your life, Lieutenant. Just look at the damage we're doing to the enemy."

Meanwhile, the barrage of Protoss interceptors had managed to cripple the *Bismarck,* and the battlecruiser *Napoleon* could not find enough power to retreat to safety. When the overlords drew close to the unseen Wraith squadron, they exposed the swift Terran fighters so that a Zerg queen could close in and choose her target. Thrashing herself into position, she launched a wide, rapidly spreading web of greenish goo. The thick resin splashed into the ion intakes of the fast fighters, dramatically slowing the Wraiths' controls, overloading their detectors, and clogging their weapons. Dragonlike mutalisks attacked with even more frenzy than before.

Then the hordes of small but suicidal scourge's slammed into them. The tiny Zerg beasts were like living cannonballs, thinking bombs that chose their targets and crashed against hulls, exploding and wiping out Wraith after Wraith.

"General!" Lieutenant Scott shouted, and Duke could no longer deny that he needed to reassess the situation.

"Pull back the fleet!" he said. "We need to regroup."

Anticipating the command—or perhaps praying for it—Lieutenant Scott sent out the order before the general finished speaking. No crew member aboard would dare comment on General Duke's overconfidence, though they all must have been thinking the same thing.

With the *Bismarck* dead in space and the *Napoleon* trying to limp back under continued attack, General Duke drew together what remained of Alpha Squadron. "Send a science vessel to scan the main cluster of Protoss ships. I want to know how many more are out there hiding like spiders in a woodpile."

As two science vessels glided forward, they employed their

signature weapon, an electromagnetic pulse that rippled across space and washed over the battlefield like a tidal wave. The EMP removed the energy shielding from all the Protoss ships, leaving them vulnerable—if not to the weapons of Alpha Squadron, then at least to the Zerg.

General Duke swallowed hard and concentrated on covering his own ass, since his flagship was taking a pounding. "I want another science vessel to deploy a defensive matrix over the *Norad III*. Keep us safe!" He quickly realized his verbal blunder. "Uh, and the matrix should cover any other battle-cruiser within range, of course. We need to protect our men. All of them. We've got to stay alive even if it means retreat," he said, though the words caught in his throat like a chunk of rotten lemon.

He fumed as he stared at the tactical screen, realizing that his forces might be in for a tougher fight than he had counted on.

CHAPTER 23

THE COLONISTS' DESPERATE PREPARATIONS WERE completed none too soon. The alien monsters attacked at dawn.

Octavia stood inside the fence near the steel-walled prefabricated buildings at the perimeter of Free Haven. She was exhausted. Her eyes felt scratchy. She had not slept for two days, but could not imagine resting right now.

They might all be dead in a few hours.

A robo-harvester blocked each gateway to the village. Two of the rock-crushing mining machines could be put into service as makeshift tanks, if the situation got desperate enough.

Once she got a look at the approaching Zerg in the first rays of sunlight, heard the humming, clacking rumble of the hordes, and saw the clouds of dust they churned up while marching across the flattened agricultural plains, Octavia knew that their situation had become desperate indeed.

Next to her, Mayor Nikolai took a step back in astonishment. "My God."

The settlers had distributed their stockpile of homegrown weapons, small projectile launchers, pulse pistols, and rarely used hunting guns. Some of them gripped farm implements—large scythes and sharp-ended weeding tools. A farmer with tough muscles could use them as effectively as any warrior used a spear.

Gasping, the other colonists gripped their weapons as if they were lifelines. Although Octavia herself had sounded the warning about the aliens, the menace of this swarm was orders of magnitude more powerful than she had imagined. The monstrous creatures seemed limitless.

"The perimeter fences are our first line of defense!" she shouted. None of the settlers had military experience, but she knew they had to stop the first wave, or all would be lost. "We have to keep them from getting into the town. Don't hold back on your weapons. If our lines break and we scatter, we'll each end up fighting by ourselves. They'll pick us off one by one."

Ignoring her, two of the settlers bolted for the dubious shelter of their homes.

"Stand and fight!" Octavia yelled to the rest.

Mayor Nikolai muttered something about needing to check on the children, but Octavia grabbed his arm and held him in place.

The first scout ranks of aliens, low runners with sharp razor-limb sickles, reached the perimeter of the settlement. About the size of a dog, the aliens looked like big lizards with red eyes, sharp claws, and multiple rending arms. In a massive wave, they raced across the dirt with a pattering thunder like giant hungry crabs.

The colonists' first shots rang out, many of them going wild because the weapons were poorly aimed. But because of the sheer number of alien scouts, most of the shots struck *something*. The other scout aliens stampeded over their fallen companions, either ripping them to shreds with razor-limbs or ignoring them in their death throes. It looked like an unending wave of hideous death.

Octavia felt despair overwhelm her terror. What chance did they possibly have? She had brought a pellet blaster from home, which she fired again and again. At first she took a grim pride in watching the creatures she slaughtered, but then there was no time even to pay attention. She blazed out pellets until she exhausted her stockpile of ammunition. Many of the other colonists had also run dry of shotpacks for their projectile weapons or battery cartridges for their pulse pistols.

The first mob of small aliens attacked, breaking through the fence line and raising their scythe-claws to slash and tear. Colonists screamed. Octavia watched several people fall in bloody piles of dismantled flesh. And it was just the beginning.

Kiernan and Kirsten Warner—he a young stonemason, she a teacher and amateur engineer—fought side by side with the granite-chopping implements Kiernan used in his work. He swung the long tool from one side to the other, hacking sharp limbs off the creatures, splitting their thick leathery hides, and leaving a pile of twitching, mindless alien bodies around him. Kirsten fought just as hard, as if trying to keep up with the number of victims Kiernan scattered on the ground.

Mayor Nikolai turned and bolted. Octavia shouted for him to come back, but like a true politician, he had an excuse for his hasty retreat. "I need to send an urgent call to the Terran fleet! They should have arrived by now. I've got to tell them what's going on down here." Without waiting, Nikolai ran and barricaded himself inside the communications turret.

Octavia didn't have time to worry about it. She hurled her empty, useless pellet gun at the closest lizardlike alien with such force that it smashed open the thing's head. Ooze splattered, but that didn't seem to bother the creature a bit.

As she stood for a fraction of a second, weaponless, Octavia remembered the old missile turret, the decorative monument that had surprised them all by activating itself and shooting the observer out of the skies. Even with its automated systems burned out, the turret still had a few intact missiles.

There should be enough explosives to cause some damage.

The missile turret was made for shooting at airborne targets, but it no longer functioned as it had been designed to do. Perhaps she could launch the rockets manually.

Octavia needed only one minute. It was all the time she had.

She raced for the center of town, a place that had once been peaceful, the closest thing to a park on Bhekar Ro. Behind her, the terrified colonists were forced to fall back, their lines crumbling as the bloodthirsty alien hordes attacked them. The makeshift weapons were beginning to falter, but Octavia concentrated only on the large piece of equipment.

Although she and Jon had managed to fix the mechanical parts of the gun, the electronics were completely unsalvageable. But these comprised mostly the sensors and the automated targeting systems, Octavia realized. She climbed up the metal-runged ladder and ripped open the access panel.

All she needed were the firing controls.

Using her legs and shoulder, she pushed upward, swinging the missile launcher down and swiveling it with brute force toward the oncoming alien troops. She had only two missiles left and didn't know exactly how much damage each one would cause.

Finding the trigger controls, she did her best to eyeball a trajectory, pointing the first of the small surface-to-air missiles at the center of the slavering monsters. It would be good to watch them blow up.

Squeezing one eye shut, whispering a quick prayer, she launched the first weapon. The explosive-filled projectile roared through the air, whistling and spinning. At first she thought her shot would miss, but then she saw it plow down into a cluster of the alien scouts. Flashes of fire and smoke and broken monstrous parts flew in all directions, sending the attacking creatures spinning like a hive of maddened ants.

In the moment of stunned surprise, Octavia saw no point in waiting. She swung the missile turret slightly to the left, where the lizardlike alien creatures were regrouping, then launched her second—and last—missile. She watched the new explosion with exhilaration. She had single-handedly wiped out hundreds of the attackers!

Unfortunately, the ravenous invading forces had many hundreds to spare.

As the dust and smoke settled, a brief silence hovered for a few seconds over the battlefield. Several colonists cheered at this. Others screamed in pain. The swarm of deadly aliens gathered themselves again, making hissing and buzzing noises.

Then Octavia saw what she feared most shambling out of the carnage—hulking forms, slightly man-shaped, yet twisted and distorted. The bodies had once been human. The farmers had been strong; the women had been beautiful in a coarse sort of way. But now these infested settlers had been taken over completely by the controlling alien invaders.

They plodded forward, a mass of tentacles, slashing claws, and hideous stingers that dripped venom. They looked as if a mad dollmaker had grafted extra parts onto what had previously been perfectly normal human forms.

Several of the front-line defenders wailed as the infested colonists came forward. "It's Gandhi, and Liberty Ryan! And there's Brutus Jensen."

Octavia recognized these people with a twist of revulsion. The settlers had been her neighbors. They had all worked hard to plant seedlings, protecting and nurturing them out in the agricultural fields. Brutus Jensen had been a hardworking farm hand.

The infested colonists walked forward. Free Haven's defenders were uneasy, reluctant to fire upon people who until today had been their friends.

But now they were all monsters. Enemies. Just like the prospector Rastin.

When Octavia saw their skin begin to squirm, their bodies boil, their faces and stomachs swell and puff, she remembered what had happened to Old Blue—a buildup of toxic and explosive gases. "Get away from them!" she shouted, running toward the perimeter. "Don't let them come closer!"

But she was too far away. Some of the colonists heard her and turned to look, while others were too frozen with horror to listen.

Octavia threw herself to the ground, flinching instinctively as the infested colonists came as close as they could manage before their bodies exploded like biological bombs filled with poisonous vapors and chemicals.

The violent eruption of the Ryans and poor young Brutus Jensen knocked out the front line of the Bhekar Ro defenders. Three colonists were killed instantly. Thirty meters of fence and two entire perimeter buildings were knocked over by the shock wave. Other defenders who had stood too close fell rolling on the ground, gasping and choking, coughing blood as the poison worked its way through their systems in a quick but agonizing death.

Many alien scouts in the vicinity were also wiped out, but Octavia had seen by now that the invading forces considered each individual creature to be completely expendable.

She got to her feet and saw a new wave of monsters approaching, then glanced over to the sealed doors of the comm turret where Mayor Nikolai had barricaded himself. She hoped he'd been able to contact the Terran fleet.

If the military "rescuers" did not get down here soon, there wouldn't be any colonists left to rescue.

CHAPTER 24

IN THE PROTOSS BASE CAMP IN THE SHADOW OF the magnificent Xel'Naga artifact, Executor Koronis stood beside the curved wing of the large arbiter. With a flurry of telepathic signals, he tried to follow the complex battle among the enemy forces in orbit. He remained in contact with Templar Mess'Ta aboard his flagship, receiving tactical updates.

Koronis spoke through the all-fleet telepathic channel, knowing that none of their enemies could hear or understand the powerful mental transmission. "Show no mercy against the enemies of the First Born. You must protect this great prize for the Protoss race. Our success here will decide whether the *Qel'Ha* returns to Aiur in triumph, or as a thrice-beaten failure."

Mess'Ta responded, "We all know what is at stake, Executor. We will not falter. Our resolve will never weaken."

Koronis signed off, knowing he could not have left the *Qel'Ha* in better hands, unless he himself was in orbit. But he had another job to do here.

Flanked by four other Judicators, Judicator Amdor stood below the object, raising his three-fingered hands high and spreading his claws. They all clustered together, mentally chanting, sensing the vibrations from the Khala as they attempted to detect nuances from the glowing object.

Koronis stepped up to them, watching. Before being promoted to Executor, he had been a High Templar himself, proficient in many telepathic abilities. He could feel the emanations from the exposed object, but could not determine the origin, could not comprehend whether it was a message or a warning.

Amdor turned to the Executor and indicated the silvery clear spines of large crystal growths that rose like broken snowflakes from the rubble of the avalanche. "Look at the Khaydarin crystals! These alone are enough wealth to make the entire Conclave rejoice."

"Those crystals, Judicator, are a mark of the Xel'Naga. Their very presence proves that this object is far more valuable than we had at first dreamed."

Amdor fairly glowed with satisfaction and pleasure. "We must explore, Executor. Let us go inside with all possible haste."

Koronis had made other plans, though. "I have ordered a group of dragoons to prepare."

Amdor looked frustrated, but bowed his gray head. Despite his personal ambitions, the Judicator could not argue with such a wise precaution.

Koronis turned and sent a signal to the nearest arbiter. The wings of the big ship opened. With ponderous clanking movements that grew smoother as the cyborg warriors exercised and proceeded forward, four dragoons came down the ramp.

Encased in a spherical body core and propelled by four large spiderlike legs, the dragoons plodded along. These were veteran Protoss warriors who had been crippled or mortally wounded in combat. Rather than dying in service of the Khala, they had chosen to have their bodily remnants transplanted into these mechanical exoskeletons.

The walkers lumbered forward in their armored bodies. The brains of the shattered volunteers focused energies through the Khala in order to control the movements of dragoon limbs. Their articulated legs were able to scramble over the rough terrain and climb the broken rock wall more easily than the robed Judicators ever could.

During the *Qel'Ha*'s long and fruitless search, these dragoons had waited, unused, fearing they would never contribute to the overall mission. Their greatest concern was that their sacrifice in becoming these living mechanical walkers would be in vain.

Now the dragoons had a purpose.

The first Protoss explorers to enter the exposed Xel'Naga artifact clambered upward until they reached the opening tunnels. Koronis and Amdor stood together and watched as the brave dragoons entered the mysterious labyrinth.

CHAPTER 25

THE BATTLE FOR FREE HAVEN CONTINUED WITHOUT any glimmer of hope for the struggling settlers. Octavia had no time to plan ahead or worry about the future—only to survive for the moment, and kill as many Zerg as possible.

But the ravenous alien invaders did not need to rest.

Some of the settlers fought hand to hand, using farm implements in a desperate attempt to stem the tide of monstrous creatures. Octavia had no more missiles to fire and no hand weapon. She raced toward the nearest robo-harvester, a big lumbering vehicle that Mayor Nikolai kept for his own use. She knew the man did not maintain it as well as she and Lars had kept their own vehicle, which now lay dead near the site of the alien artifact. But the robo-harvester could still cause a lot of damage.

She bounded up the treads, stepped on the metal running board, threw herself inside the huge vehicle, and powered up the engines. A snort of vespene exhaust coughed out of the top stack like smoke from a dragon's nostril.

Across the town plaza, which now became a hunting ground for the zerglings that had broken through the settlers' first defenses, she watched the stonemason Kiernan Warner and his wife Kirsten jump into one of the ponderous, slow-moving mining machines. They sealed themselves into the armored vehicle and began to plow forward.

Octavia found the harvester controls, knocked aside some clutter and trinkets the mayor had left in the driver's seat, and surged ahead, treads clanking through the streets. Clenching her teeth tightly together, she pushed the giant vehicle forward, ready to meet the next wave of Zerg. Behind the small stampeding attackers she saw bigger monsters, including nine of the hunched serpentine creatures that had shot needle spines at her as she fled in the little field crawler from Rastin's homestead. *Hydralisks.*

The monsters' fang-filled jaws opened all the way back to their stunted leather ears, and black soulless eyes stared at her as the creatures reared up in defiance of this mechanical foe.

Before she even moved close enough to fire a boulder blaster, the first hydralisk bent its hunched, hard back and launched a volley of needle projectiles. She heard them spang and ricochet off the thick walls of the robo-harvester. Octavia flinched as one bounced against the windshield, leaving a snowflake of damaged glass. She pushed the growling engines to their limits and bore down upon the first Zerg monster as it prepared to fire again.

The creature was powerful and armed with more of the needle projectiles, but it was no match for the mass and momentum of the giant harvesting machine. It flailed its clawed arms, trying to grasp the robo-harvester and wrestle it to the ground, but she rolled over the thing with her heavy treads, squashing it into a puddle of crunched exoskeleton and spreading goo.

Next, two of the remaining hydralisks converged on her from opposite sides, each hammering the vehicle with another volley of spines. She heard the pattering clang as the projectiles crashed into the metal walls, scratching and denting the hull. A few poked all the way through, leaving bright air holes, but Octavia did not cringe.

Instead, she activated the powerful combine arm, a huge rolling basket with sharpened blades that could mow down fields of triticale-wheat. She lowered the combine arm like a blurring flyswatter onto one of the spine-depleted hydralisks. The monster flailed and thrashed even as it was chopped into a thousand pieces. Slime and blood splattered her machine's windshield.

Dizzy with her success, Octavia swung the combine arm to the left and bore down on the third hydralisk, which lurched backward as if suddenly sensing its danger. She plowed over that one as well, then careened forward as three more monsters clustered in a concerted effort to stop her.

Octavia squeezed her eyes shut and drove ahead. She didn't know if the whirring blades of the harvesting arm or the crushing treads themselves destroyed the new batch of hydralisks—but when the robo-harvester clanked past, she saw that she had left all of them dead, their few intact limbs and body parts still twitching on the crushed ground.

Kiernan Warner had brought his mining machine close enough to dig into the rocky ground at the edge of the battered perimeter fence. The boulder catapult seized hard stones and began to launch them like cannonballs into the Zerg forces.

Dozens of frantic zerglings were pulverized into bloody spray. The rock thrower struck two more hydralisks, punching boulders through their hard carapaces. In its death throes, one of the ferocious creatures sprayed a cloud of poison needles in all directions. Some of them struck the cumbersome mining machine, others flew like wild arrows into the sky, while the remainder of the spines slaughtered other enemy aliens that surged forward into the gap.

Stunned by the sudden turnabout and vehemence of the colonists' defense, the attacking forces hesitated. Octavia saw the creatures fall back, their numbers vastly diminished.

But soon the Zerg circled around the octagonal perimeter of Free Haven and approached from the northeast, where they massed, ready for a full-fledged invasion of the town.

"They're trying to break through to the fuel depot!" she muttered to herself, looking toward the industrial area where the colonists stored their tanks of refined vespene gas.

Free Haven always kept a fuel stockpile "for emergencies," Mayor Nikolai said, although Octavia was half convinced that the settlers had maintained such a large reservoir of volatile vespene so that they didn't often need to deal with the grouchy old recluse Rastin.

She felt a pang of sadness, knowing that the prospector had been one of the first casualties of the Zerg swarm. Well, now maybe his painstakingly harvested vespene could help with the defense of Bhekar Ro.

Octavia used the robo-harvester's front flamethrower to blast out a column of fire that withered the nearby zerglings. The built-in flamethrower had originally been designed for clear-cutting dense forests to make way for new arable land. Now she used it to cremate a field of enemies.

One of the hydralisks turned defiantly to face her, rising up tall and hissing, but she incinerated it with a fireball right in its ugly face.

The treads of the robo-harvester clanked over the uneven ground as she made her way toward the fuel depot. Perhaps the alien army sensed this was a weak point in the town's defenses, or maybe they just wanted the vespene for themselves. The monsters clustered near the depot and moved forward together. The Zerg passed through the town's weakened fences as if they were no more than thin strings, and piled into the open area of vespene storage tanks.

Octavia knew she would only have a few seconds, and she had to act now or her wild plan was doomed. She locked down the robo-harvester's treads and let loose with the full long-range stream of her flamethrower, trying to blanket the fuel depot. Dozens of the zerglings shriveled and crisped. Two hydralisks moved through the diluted flames, singeing their glossy hides, though the creatures did not appear to notice any pain.

Octavia's target, however, was not the hideous monstrosities.

After a few agonized seconds during which she doubted the heat would be sufficient, the first and nearest storage tank reached its critical temperature. The vespene fuel erupted in a fireball that knocked out the next tank, setting it on fire, which in turn blew up the third, like a game of incandescent dominoes.

The enormous blast rippled outward, flash-crisping all the Zerg forces within the fuel depot, knocking flat any others on the periphery. The explosion continued to build, and Octavia held on to her seat as the robo-harvester bucked and rolled.

When the smoke and flames cleared, she saw to her amazement that the bulk of the attacking swarm had been annihilated through the fiery explosions, as well as the other colonists' continued efforts. The remaining Zerg troops on the fringe backed off, either from fear or a sense of defeat.

Dazed, Octavia climbed out of the robo-harvester. The surviving colonists emerged from their hiding places, some of them pale with shock, others drenched with blood—both red blood and inhuman greenish ichor.

Kiernan and Kirsten stumbled out of their mining machine, mouths open, looking amazed. No one seemed to believe the skirmish had been won, that they had driven off the implacable invading aliens.

Mayor Nikolai emerged from the shelter of his comm turret, grinning as triumphantly as a conquering hero. "I've done it! Good news. I've contacted the Terran forces. The military will be here soon."

Some of the settlers groaned, others cheered. Octavia felt too numb to complain about the mayor's actions. She slumped against the dirty treads of the robo-harvester, heaved several exhausted breaths, then looked up in awe as she heard a new rumbling, hissing sound, much louder than the one they had heard at dawn.

The third and largest wave of Zerg marched across the plains—not just small scout creatures and a few hydralisks this time, but gigantic monsters as well, like nightmarish versions of prehistoric woolly mammoths with enormous scythe-like tusks that looked capable of slicing buildings in half.

In the skies, a cluster of twisted dragonlike creatures swept along the winds, heading toward the settlement. Dozens and dozens of hydralisks slithered along in the front row. They kept coming. In addition, Octavia saw many other minions, twisted breeds, horrifying mutations, all of them looking deadly, all of them intent on wiping out the Terran settlers.

Octavia could only stare in defeat. This wave would be unstoppable.

CHAPTER 26

IN ORBIT OVER BHEKAR RO, THE SHIPS OF ALPHA Squadron continued to be battered and pounded by the frenzied Protoss and Zerg space fleets.

General Edmund Duke paced the control bridge. "Well, men, it sounds as if we need to leave this little playground behind," he said, looking at the message his comm officer had given him. "Those colonists need our help, so we'll have to go down to the surface and take care of that firestorm right away."

Lieutenant Scott watched the flaming hulk that remained of the *Bismarck* and saw the damaged battlecruiser *Napoleon* limping along, trying to break free of the converging alien forces. "Is that tactically wise, General? Our forces are in dire straits up here."

Frowning, Duke turned his craggy face toward the tactical officer. "Lieutenant Scott, it would be quite an embarrassment if we came all this way to rescue colonists, and then let the aliens gobble them up before we could help." He had learned long ago that becoming a war hero was due as much to public relations as it was to tactical brilliance. "Don't worry. We'll leave some ships in place, though, so they can keep fighting the enemy."

The lieutenant gave combat orders, directing the main force of Terran battle vessels to break off their orbital conflict and descend to the surface. To the rest of the human ships left in space to defend against the Zerg and Protoss, it looked as if they were running away.

"This is not a retreat," General Duke insisted. "We are initiating an offensive in the opposite direction."

The vanguard of Alpha Squadron plunged through the dusty skies like a cavalry riding in to save the besieged Terrans of Free Haven. Below, Duke could see the town smoldering. A great deal of damage had already been done. But the colonists had survived so far.

The general saw the stampede of Zerg sweeping across the flat ground to surround and engulf the octagonal settlement. Some of the enemy creatures had already broken through the fence, but at the sight of the numerous alien bodies strewn around—not to mention the smoking craters and the flaming debris—General Duke was impressed that the settlers had been able to mount such an effective resistance, for a bunch of clodhoppers.

Now all he needed to do was save enough of them so he could show clips of his success on the Universal News Network. He smiled. "Alien scum." He ordered his ships to fire.

Alpha Squadron entered the dirtside fray like a bull in a china shop, striking at anything that moved, though making an effort to avoid anything that appeared human. Ranks of airborne Zerg—a subspecies that General Duke recognized as mutalisks—flew upward, spitting green acid slime through the air. For some reason, though, the mutalisks did not engage the battlecruisers. Instead, the flying monsters pulled away, ascending toward the orbital conflict. They had probably been summoned by the overlords in space to engage the Protoss forces, now that the Terran military had broken off from that particular fight.

That was fine with General Duke.

Terran dropships swooped low to the ground and delivered Arclite Siege Tanks, heavily shielded soldiers wearing Goliath combat armor, and scavenger hover bikes called Vultures. These military units advanced, prepared to engage any creatures on the ground.

The general made no attempt to reestablish contact with the political administration in the Terran colony. This was a military operation, and he would damn well do what he felt was necessary.

His men knew the drill. They spread out to build defensive perimeters while the small Wraiths and huge battlecruisers provided air support against the advancing Zerg. Using full firepower, the Alpha Squadron ships struck repeatedly, pounding even the mammoth-sized ultralisks, wiping out waves of the remaining zerglings, crushing groups of hydralisks.

"This is more like it," Duke said, and took over some of the firing controls for himself just to keep in practice.

With the flying, acid-spitting mutalisks gone and no enemy air attack imminent, Duke's assault became a one-sided rout. After hours of absolute slaughter, he ended up losing only eleven Wraiths, five Goliaths, and a handful of marines and firebats, all of whom would get honorable citations signed by Emperor Arcturus Mengsk himself—if the Dominion had new stationery printed yet.

As the *Norad III* landed outside the smoking town, General Duke disembarked with his shoulders squared, his chin held high. He expected cheers, though the surviving rescued settlers looked exhausted and stunned.

Frowning slightly, he saw that his marines and firebats had caused about as much destruction to the town buildings as the Zerg had. Unfortunate. Still, it was friendly fire, so the colonists shouldn't complain. "Collateral damage, that's all," he muttered to himself as he marched down the street of his newly conquered town.

He looked for the mayor or, if the Zerg had killed the man, somebody else who could formally turn over control to this military operation. He looked around at the colonists, imagining that they viewed him as their savior.

"I'll make this my ground base of operations now," he said as more marines emerged from a just-landed dropship. He debated whether to make a speech first or to order his marines to help extinguish some of the fires in the town. In a gracious gesture, he dispatched battlefield medics to see if they could help any of the wounded settlers.

He smiled proudly and turned to the bedraggled colonists. "You civilians can all rest easy now."

CHAPTER 27

OUT AT THE SITE OF OLD RASTIN'S HOMESTEAD, THE prospector's shack and refinery structures had *evolved*. They were now completely covered with living organic matter.

Hard exoskeletons grew up in tangled, twisted labyrinths following the genetic model of a Zerg hive, a pattern that no human could comprehend. The fleshy biomass of Zerg creep continued to spread, absorbing raw materials from the rough dirt and processing it into a nourishing substance.

While many queens had landed with the arrival of Kukulkan Brood, this one had remained in the hatchery established at Rastin's homestead. The only purpose of this place was to spawn larvae by the hundreds, each of which would evolve into one of the various minions.

Ducking her triangular head on a long, sinuous neck, the queen raised her pointed arms. She knew her part in the mission. Sarah Kerrigan, the new Queen of Blades, had planted full instructions in the minds of the Kukulkan over-lords, which controlled all the queens and their hatcheries.

The queen, in turn, controlled all the wasplike drones that moved about building the hatchery, grasping material with their clacking claws. They evolved the hatchery through the intermediary stage of a defensible lair until, finally, this conquered outpost would become a full-fledged Zerg hive.

Kukulkan Brood had a variety of minions to meet any resistance. Like giant insects, drones went about their work, following instructions, utterly loyal. The larvae continued to mutate from spiny grubs into zerglings, hydralisks, even mammoth-sized ultralisks. Newborn flying-dragon mutalisks took to the skies, ready to launch aerial attacks with hurled acid.

And there was something new. The queen, following her Zerg instincts, had absorbed the DNA of the large blue-furred dog that had been infested here. The Zerg considered the ferocious animal a potential candidate for an experimental new strain of minion.

Throughout their race's history, the Zerg had conquered other species and acquired superior traits from their genetics. When the swarm had first attacked the old prospector and his dog, the queen had seen genetic characteristics and capabilities the Zerg did not have—yet.

Though Old Blue had already succumbed to the initial infestation, the queen had catalogued and remembered the canine DNA. As an experiment, she began to incorporate the improvements in the dog's musculature—and, most important, an advanced sense of smell—into new larvae. In several test creatures, the queen designed fearsome Zerg traits into large mastiff bodies that resembled the blue-furred dog. . . .

Under the old refinery structure, her drones burrowed deep beneath the ground, moving buried boulders in crustal shafts to reawaken all four of the vespene geysers. Then a drone metamorphosed into a living extractor over the spouts of valuable energetic gas. The extractor collected the outpouring vespene and packaged it in concentrated fleshy sacks, which were brought back to the hatchery. Some of the gas was used to create other Zerg minions for the conquering force. Some was sent to Zerg soldiers, which consumed the substance, drawing power and nourishment to continue the fight against their enemies.

The newborn minions tunneled into the ground or spread across the surface, expanding outward in an unstoppable force. While the attack on the colony town had been a serious effort, it was only a small part of the overall strategy of Kukulkan Brood.

The human colonists were potential resources, but they were also life-forms that could offer resistance to the Zerg plan. Ultimately, though, the settlers were irrelevant.

The main Zerg objective was elsewhere, across the ridge and in the next valley, where Protoss forces had already landed. . . .

Walking like mechanical spiders driven by living brains, the Protoss dragoons had disappeared into the cathedral shape of the Xel'Naga artifact.

But before Executor Koronis could receive a report on their explorations, his ground troops of fanatical zealots sounded an alarm. They reeled backward as the valley surface began to ripple and crack.

Then a storm of Zerg attackers emerged from the ground, boiling up from hidden burrows. Hydralisks heaved upward, their curved backs bent forward so that their volleys of poisonous needle spines sliced the closest Protoss soldiers to ribbons.

Koronis's zealots screamed and rushed forward into the fray. Though they had not yet reached the highest levels of the Khala, the Templar warriors were ruthless and fanatically dedicated to defending their race. Enhanced with cybernetic grafts, the zealots wore sophisticated power suits complete with curved shoulder crests, breastplates, and padded greaves. On their thick forearm units they wore enhancements to channel their psionic energy, focusing it into a deadly Psionic Blade. The zealots charged into battle with full fury, slashing with shimmering Psionic Blades to mow down the alien attackers.

Reacting to the sudden Zerg offensive, Executor Koronis summoned his ground forces, calling out his High Templars and launching the sluggish but deadly reavers—armored units that looked like huge caterpillars—and more of his mobile cyborg dragoons.

Following their leader's command without question, many zealots sacrificed themselves in order to draw the Zerg together, concentrating them. Koronis saw his chance.

Standing on the rocky foothills beneath the huge pulsing artifact, the Executor summoned up the energies inside him. He used one of his greatest weapons, learned from decades of studying the most subtle nuances of the Khala by meditating on his small fragment of crystal on board the *Qel'Ha*.

A Psionic Storm.

The giant Khaydarin crystals littered around the Xel'Naga artifact reflected his telepathic energy, focusing his attack so that the mental storm continued to build, gathering power.

From higher up, closer to the fringe of the once-buried artifact, Judicator Amdor looked down with concern and amazement. Crackling, energy-saturated wind blasted his dark robes until they flapped around him like angry flames. His eyes blazed.

Below, Koronis did not hold back. He released his Psionic Storm with the most terrible blast he had ever conjured. The roiling energy roared down at the concentrated Zerg minions, and he felt a searing satisfaction when the blast incinerated dozens of the ferocious alien troops.

Weakened, the Executor fell back as the wind and the light began to fade into the sky. But the struggle was not over.

Again, his zealots charged forward, their Psionic Blades ignited. The battle had just been joined. Koronis blinked with amazement to see other sections of the ground crack open, spewing forth even more Zerg attackers.

He ordered his carriers to come down and form a solid fortification around the artifact—their prize. More help could not arrive quickly enough, as far as Koronis was concerned.

Right now he could see only more and more of the Zerg rushing forward in an unstoppable wave. . . .

CHAPTER 28

WHEN THE BLUSTERY AND DESTRUCTIVE TERRAN marines took over the town of Free Haven, Octavia Bren didn't see much of an improvement over the Zerg invasion.

While the surviving settlers rushed to put out fires, tend to their wounded, and bury their dead, General Duke commandeered the largest intact building in front of the town square and then pulled out a folding command chair from his battlecruiser. He and his men moved with practiced military precision to set up their base camp inside the town limits.

While Abdel and Shayna Bradshaw took care of the injured colonists who had been carried to the meeting hall, Octavia saw to those who still lay where they had fallen. She moved from one bleeding neighbor to another, tending their cuts and broken bones with plastiscab bandages, flexsplints, and antibiotics, rapidly draining Free Haven's already small store of first-aid supplies.

Octavia looked around for help. Everyone was either wounded or occupied on urgent business—except for the

Terran military. Indignant, she strode up to where the self-satisfied general sat in his folding command chair in the town plaza, directing military operations.

"The colonists are dying," she announced. "We need medical supplies and personnel."

General Duke hardly glanced at her. "My men are busy. We've got to set up the base camp."

"Your men—and *you*, General—were sent here to *help* us." Octavia was not about to give up. People were dying. Her *friends* were dying. She locked her gaze with the general's, refusing to be ignored.

Finally he dispatched a dozen more of his cruiser's field medics to assist in the operations and had another medic fetch an entire crate of field hospital supplies. Octavia knew Duke did it more to get rid of her than out of humanitarian concerns. For now, though, all she cared about was results.

The marines of Alpha Squadron trundled down the battlecruisers' loading ramps with a dozen SCVs to gather vital minerals and stock up on vespene gas (since Octavia herself had been forced to obliterate the town's fuel depot).

Octavia splinted Jon's broken leg and moved on to a shocked twelve-year-old boy who had lost a lot of blood. She gave him an infusion of plasma and a potent pain reliever. Then she glanced up and watched with curiosity as a ruddy-faced Mayor Nikolai marched toward Duke, bony fists balled, scrawny arms bent as if for the first time in his life he could imagine punching someone.

"General, your men are gutting our buildings. They've stolen engines and supplies from our homes, and now you've sent them out on vehicles to raid our farm dwellings! We've survived the Zerg only to be plundered by our so-called rescuers. How dare you! Explain yourself."

General Duke scowled. "You called for us to rescue you, Mayor. Alpha Squadron was in the midst of a difficult conflict in orbit, but we broke free, landed here, and saved your collective butts. I'd think you'd be a bit more grateful."

Mayor Nik spluttered. "Of course we're grateful. But if we die from the Zerg today or die from starvation a month from now, we'll still all be dead."

"Now, now, Mayor. Before Alpha Squadron departs we can leave you some of our prepackaged Meals Ready to Eat. Why, I'm sure we've got a couple thousand thermal packs of Chipped Beef Deluxe that are close to their expiration dates."

Nik protested, but the general waved him away. "I assure you, we're only doing what is necessary to accomplish our objective. Alpha Squadron has its orders, you know. We've done our best to help you and these dirt farmers out, but I've got an enemy to defeat and an alien artifact to claim in the name of the emperor." He turned a baleful look on the mayor and scratched his stubbly jowl. "I warn you, don't interfere with my men, or I'll commandeer another one of your town buildings and use it as a brig."

Two marines hauled Mayor Nik away as he struggled and squirmed like a child being taken from a favorite toy.

Once the general had been debriefed by a handful of colonists his troops acquired at random, he sent marines to look specifically for Octavia Bren, who had sounded the original alarm and apparently had more close experience with the aliens than anyone else in Free Haven.

Without offering an explanation, he had her escorted to his new command center—formerly Mayor Nikolai's home—and sat back at his desk to assess her. He didn't offer her any refreshments. She felt a renewed dislike for him.

"Now, Miz Brown," he said in a gravelly voice.

"Bren, General. It's *Bren*."

"Yes, of course, ma'am. Now, it's time for you to do your duty as a citizen of the Terran Dominion."

Octavia stood straight and gave him a small frown. "Here on Bhekar Ro we're independent, General. We'd never heard of your Dominion until we sent a message just a few days ago, so how could we be citizens of it?"

"Nevertheless, Emperor Mengsk loves and counts on all of his subjects—even the ignorant ones." He drummed his thick fingers on the desktop. "I understand that you, more than anyone else in the settlement, know about this mysterious alien artifact. You've seen it with your own eyes."

"It killed my brother, General."

"Good, good," he said. "Not about your brother, I mean, but that you've got up-close experience. Now, ma'am, tell me everything you remember. What does it look like? What are the defenses around it? What else did you observe about its potential as a *weapon*, perhaps? If this thing can help us conquer the enemy, then we can leave you and your fellow farmers in peace. Wouldn't you like to go back to doing . . . whatever it is you colonists do?"

Octavia wanted nothing more in the world, so she gave him the details. Starting with how she and her brother had found the object exposed after an avalanche, she explained how it had killed Lars and later fried her robo-harvester.

General Duke raised his eyebrows. "Interesting. Perhaps it could be adapted to putting enemy vehicles out of commission. Like a lockdown strike. Hmmm, I'll have a team of science specialists study it up close."

"I think all those aliens that arrived have the same idea," she said. "Your scientists may be in for a surprise."

"Don't worry your pretty little head, my girl. We've had experience with both the Zerg and the Protoss before." He looked around at various instruments he had rewired in the mayor's dwelling, including the seismographs taken from the Brens' own home.

Offhandedly, as if recounting his glory days, he gave her a bit of background about the first war between the Protoss and the Terrans and the Zerg. As Octavia listened to him brag, she looked over at the repaired seismographs and saw them jiggling, picking up numerous explosions, all of them centered around the artifact out in the distant valley. "It looks like there's a disturbance out there, General."

Duke quickly studied the blips and pursed his thick lips. "I can ascertain that these are weapons signatures. Must be the echoes of a big battle—and my men aren't even out there yet!" He clenched a fist and pounded the mayor's desktop. "I'd better not have lost my chance at that object while I was wasting my time here rescuing helpless colonists!"

CHAPTER 29

THOUGH FAR AWAY FROM THE BHEKAR RO BATTLE-field, Sarah Kerrigan watched the progress of Kukulkan Brood from deep within the quivering organic walls of her ever-growing hive on Char.

During the battles, she felt the loss of each one of her minions, first as the pathetic colonists fought back, then as the *Norad III* and the hated General Edmund Duke brought Alpha Squadron down to devastate her advancing forces. And then the Protoss ground troops were fighting the Zerg for possession of the Xel'Naga artifact.

She experienced neither pain nor sorrow for the loss of those creatures, however. They existed to be sacrificed. Zerg minions were designed to be expendable. That didn't worry her.

However, in her progress toward replacing the full-fledged Overmind, the Queen of Blades maintained a tally of her living resources, counting each death as a number, a statistic.

With a twinge of anger, Kerrigan sent instructions to Kukulkan Brood, to the overlords and hatcheries, commanding the production of more larvae, more minions. And more. Sooner or later, in her plans for complete conquest of the galactic sector, she would need them all anyway.

And she would need the Xel'Naga artifact.

It infuriated her that the Protoss ships had arrived and established a base at the artifact first. As her anger flowed around her, several guardians hissed and began to move up and down the tunnels, reflecting her agitation. Before they could damage the hive, which would eventually heal itself, Sarah Kerrigan calmed her thoughts and focused instead on her growing plan, developing an overall scheme of betrayal and conquest that would become an all-out brood war—the next step in her blueprint for domination and revenge.

Seeing Alpha Squadron, Kerrigan was again reminded of Jim Raynor, a man she might have loved. Raynor had been a special Terran, willing to forgive even her previous life's torment as a brainwashed telepathic Ghost. Jim Raynor, however, was part of her human past—before she had fallen victim to Arcturus Mengsk's betrayal, before she joined with the Zerg.

She did not resent Mengsk for bringing her together with the Zerg . . . though she would personally eviscerate him and rip the self-proclaimed emperor limb from limb as soon as she captured the man. For the sheer pleasure of it.

It was only a matter of time.

Kerrigan reviewed her previous encounter with the too-confident and overblown General Duke, during their rescue operation on the *Norad II*.

She did not regret that part of her life. Instead, she remembered every detail and considered how she could use it to her advantage—to the Zerg advantage.

As the war on Bhekar Ro continued, the Queen of Blades focused a small part of her expanded mind on the struggle, while devoting most of her attention to even more important matters.

CHAPTER 30

BENEATH THE CRUMBLING MOUNTAINSIDE THAT held the coveted artifact, the Protoss forces battled the Zerg minions on the rugged valley floor.

But while the preoccupied alien armies fought each other, the three dropships dispatched by Alpha Squadron streaked in, carrying their own infiltration squad.

Dropships were quirky vessels, difficult to maneuver and prone to mechanical failures, but the daredevil pilots flew above the echoing explosions of the battlefield. It required fancy maneuvering to ride the shock waves from the psionic storm unleashed by Executor Koronis.

The dropships had no weapons and relied primarily upon speed and their hull armor. They dodged low, moving fast, trying to reach their objective without being shot down.

Flying mutalisks, a few stragglers not directly engaged against the Protoss, came after them. Splitting up, the three dropship pilots engaged in evasive maneuvers. Though the acid spray of the Zerg attackers pitted and damaged their thick hulls, the ships arrived at the broken mountain range and descended to where the huge pulsing alien artifact lay exposed.

Protoss and Zerg antagonists redirected their firepower, dispatching a few fighters to attack the Terran interlopers. As the dropships hovered over the giant target object, the pilots knew they had little time.

Led by Lieutenant Scott from the *Norad III*, a group of marines, firebats, and four magnificently armored soldiers called Goliaths hurried to the deployment doors. The Goliaths looked as much like walking bipedal tanks as men. They dropped out first, their powerful armor suits absorbing the impact. Marines and thick-suited firebats spun down on rappel ropes to land on the boulders around the shimmering surface of the artifact's convoluted exterior.

"Go! Go!" shouted Lieutenant Scott, a command issued both to his men—and to the vulnerable dropships.

As soon as the last marine released his rope, the first dropship wheeled about and spun upward, racing away at full acceleration. The other four dropships followed, forming a wing in the sky.

Running across the rubble, Lieutenant Scott directed his troops to the artifact's nearest opening. "Come on, let's get inside! Our orders are to map out this thing and bring back whatever reconnaissance and intelligence we can gather."

Bent low, their eight-millimeter C-14 Gauss Impalers drawn and pointed ahead, the marines raced forward into the opening. The entrance looked less like a passageway than some kind of bubble in a biopolymer resin. One Goliath went in with the first group, his heavy firepower ready to defend the team. The firebats hustled in next, looking for something to blast with their plasma-based Perdition flamethrowers.

As Lieutenant Scott prepared to follow, he looked up and was dismayed to see the dropships fleeing from a concerted enemy attack. Mutalisks converged on two of the quirky vessels, and though the pilots dodged and put on a fantastic show of aerial combat, the Zerg attackers proved too much for them. Before long, acid cut through the engines, and the armored hulls split open.

In a last strategic move, the doomed pilots both careened into a cluster of battling alien ground troops, wiping out a handful of Zerg and Protoss as the two dropships exploded on impact. The last remaining dropship, though damaged, valiantly got away, flew over the low foothills, and limped back to the Free Haven base.

Lieutenant Scott followed his troops into the convoluted passageways, and it wasn't long before they encountered a firefight of their own. Inside the topmost tunnel three powerful Protoss zealots loomed out at them, eyes blazing, mouthless faces giving them a demonic appearance.

"Look out!" Scott shouted.

The zealots raised their strangely gloved hands and activated deadly Psionic Blades. The marines were already opening fire. Their gauss rifles sent out blasts that drove the Protoss back, even as the zealots slashed with their crackling scythes.

Lieutenant Scott hadn't had time to know all the men assigned to him for this mission, so he didn't immediately recall the names of the three marines who fell screaming. While the fallen soldiers' impalers still sputtered energy bursts into the translucent wall, the lieutenant motioned one of his Goliaths forward.

The Goliath advanced, his armor fully powered, his twin thirty-millimeter autocannons blazing. The weapon blasted without pause until the nearest zealot toppled backward, dead.

Six firebats converged on the other two enemy fanatics. Flames erupted from their Perdition weapons. In a last struggle, one Protoss zealot killed a firebat with his Psionic Blade, but then the flamethrowers crisped the surviving two aliens. They all fell dead next to the three marines they had slaughtered.

Scott tightened up his squad and ordered them forward,

sparing only a quick glance at the martyred marines. "The clock is ticking. Let's keep moving." He knew this mission depended on momentum and speed. He could not spare any time for a ceremony that would make their fallen comrades rest more easily.

Though the lieutenant's commando team was vastly outnumbered, he planned to get them in and out, causing damage to the enemy while drawing as little attention to themselves as possible. Nobody knew exactly what this alien artifact was, but he intended to find out and return to General Duke with that information.

The team wound deeper into the object, planting locator blips so they could find their way back out again. Scott glanced at his suit chronometer to see how much time remained until their scheduled rendezvous. "Stimpacks, everyone," he called. "We need the extra boost."

Inside each marine's Powered Combat Suit and each firebat's Heavy Combat Suit, the in-field chemical delivery systems injected a powerful mixture of synthetic adrenaline and endorphins. Lieutenant Scott knew of the risks and potential side effects, as well as the increased unruliness caused by the psychotropic aggression-amplifier drug, but right now his team required the increased speed and reflexes the stimpacks would allow.

They charged forward, moving deeper, spiraling downward, until they encountered four massive crablike machines. The strange alien cyborgs had four articulated claw-legs and round body cores, each encasing a brain not shaped precisely like a human's. Dragoons!

The dragoons seemed to be on their way *out* of the artifact. Scott realized that if he had been the Protoss military commander, he would have sent these cyborg warriors in as a first reconnaissance party. These dragoons might already be carrying vital information. He knew, however, that no Terran technology could ever read the alien encryption in any data-recording devices carried by the dragoons. He also knew he dared not let this intelligence fall into the hands of the Protoss commander.

"Open fire!" he shouted.

Like angry spiders, the dragoons had already drawn back, preparing their phase-disrupter weapons. The Goliaths activated their twin autocannons, targeting two of the four cyborg warriors. In the confined tunnels, the heavy ammunition caused more than enough destruction to take out one of the Protoss cyborg warriors.

The other two dragoons, though, were able to fire their bolts of antiparticles sheathed in a psychically charged field. Two firebats, three marines, and one Goliath buckled, their bodies pummeled into jelly by the force.

Shouting with anger and bloodlust, other firebats closed in. Their range was shorter than the marines' gauss rifles, but when their Perdition flamethrowers lanced out, they concentrated on the body core until the fluid containing the alien brain began to boil.

One of the tanks exploded, spraying life-support liquid and boiled chunks of gray matter onto the corridor walls. The other dragoon fell over on its side, four legs twitching and thrashing, like a bug that had been drowned in insecticide.

Covering his mouth with a protective mask to block the burning stench of death in the corridor, Lieutenant Scott blinked the stinging fumes from his eyes and guided the surviving members of his team forward.

"We've got a job to finish," he said. "Let's get to the core of this object and then go home to supper."

CHAPTER 31

AS SHE WORKED WITH THE WOUNDED IN FREE Haven, the tugging call in the back of Octavia's mind grew stronger. It seemed the more she ignored the mental call, the greater the tugging became, an insistent psychic pull that reached out—not to her, specifically, but to anyone who would listen.

Among the settlers on Bhekar Ro, Octavia somehow knew that because of her deep intuition she was the only one who could hear the weird call. She looked up and around, trying to pinpoint its source. The urgent summons whispered to her from the foothills on this side of the valley where alien forces were fighting over the giant artifact that had killed Lars.

This mental signal did not come from the artifact, though. It was much closer, and it . . . *sounded* different.

All around Free Haven, the marines bustled about, calling to each other, moving from duty to duty in a rapid takeover and total conversion of what had once been a quiet colonial town.

After the great battle the day before, the Zerg attackers had fallen back and had not attempted any new offensives. Even the strange carpet of creeping biomass that had spread to engulf Rastin's land now seemed to have retreated. The Zerg were focusing their attention on the distant valley where they fought against another group of aliens that General Duke had called Protoss. The Protoss had apparently sent the mechanical observer that the colonists' clunky old missile turret had shot down.

Until recently Octavia had thought her life was complicated, given the problems and difficulties she had to face daily. But now she realized the whole world of Bhekar Ro was just the tiniest blip on the vast galactic screen. Even with the Zerg gone from Free Haven, Alpha Squadron wasted no time in setting up full-fledged defenses.

The SCVs made quick work of creating a heavily armored perimeter where the fence had been, using pieces from existing colony buildings as well as mineral resources they ripped from the fertile ground around the settlement. They rapidly constructed bunkers and erected missile turrets—new, functional ones. Marines and firebats filled the new facilities, while others were stationed inside the homes of some of the settlers that had not survived the Zerg offensive.

Farther out, beyond the ugly erected fortifications, siege tanks patrolled the area, crushing the surviving crops, knocking down orchards for better visibility of an oncoming alien army. Massively armored Goliaths strode about in search of something to fight. Vulture hover bikes cruised over the ground, acting as scouts. Their humming whine cut the air and they looked like wasps as they zipped along, crisscrossing the terrain and dropping sinister little packages called spider-mines. These small robotic bombs scurried about once they hit the ground, searched for an appropriate place to bury themselves, and waited with a sensor net for the approach of heavy enemy forces.

Free Haven had become an armed camp, and the colonists

were prisoners inside their own village. General Duke, broadcasting his gruff voice over powerful loudspeakers mounted on the tops of buildings around the town square, instructed all civilians to remain behind the fortifications, "for your own protection."

Mayor Nikolai made a show of complaining vigorously so the colonists could see that he was defending their interests. He chastised the general for overstepping the bounds of his authority, for damaging the settlers' hard-won agricultural land, and for devastating the meager stores they had managed to put by after forty years of eking out an existence.

General Duke and Alpha Squadron ignored him.

Trying to stay out of the general's way, Octavia felt the psychic call grow stronger in her mind. She'd already had her run-in with the commander and decided it would accomplish nothing if she argued with him. But perhaps there were other answers waiting for her, answers that surpassed anything this warmonger could comprehend.

If only she could understand what the strange mental presence was trying to tell her. She felt it was something deeply important. The answers were waiting . . . if only she could get out of here.

Later, as night fell, the colonists went back to their crowded homes. Some of them shared dwellings now to accommodate the marines stationed there. Some just wanted the comfort of more people.

Octavia, though, waited outside in the shadows, looking for her chance to sneak past the Terran soldiers.

Despite their grumbling at the repressive orders of General Duke, few of the colonists would want to slip past the defensive perimeter, especially at night. The marines would be looking for a Zerg attack coming toward the town. Nobody would be watching closely for someone like her, a single young woman creeping past the boundary, skirting the new missile turrets and dashing out into the night. Even if General Duke discovered that she was trying to go into the forbidden areas, he probably wouldn't deem it worth the effort to protect her against her wishes.

At the moment, Octavia did not fear the Zerg. Their attack had been open and blatant. She sensed they would not crouch behind rocks in the darkness, hoping to snatch up one or two helpless victims like herself. Judging by the seismic traces of the major battle occurring at the artifact, the Zerg and the Protoss both had more pressing concerns.

As soon as she had accepted the tugging in her mind and moved in response to it, the call became clearer. Octavia moved across the ground, knowing this could be a trap. The mental beckoning could be a siren song luring her to her death. But she didn't think so. Why would their enemies bother? A simple colonist like her was meaningless, irrelevant to any objective the three opposing forces might have.

She hurried up the street, feeling the taut muscles in her calves and thighs. She'd been through so much stress in the past few days, had eaten little and slept even less. Even so, her body felt fully aware, fine-tuned as if the constant flow of adrenaline had given her all the nourishment she needed.

The Terran military guards did not notice her as she sneaked past. The fence did not stop her. As she jogged across the rocky ground, she was most concerned about the scattered spider-mines the Vultures had planted. But those devices had been set up to detect large enemy forces, heavy ground vehicles, or creatures. She hoped—prayed—that one young female tiptoeing through the chewed-up fields would go completely unnoticed by their sensor net.

Still, she ran as fast as she could.

CHAPTER 32

DESPITE ITS CLOSE QUARTERS AND CONVOLUTED passageways, the interior of the Xel'Naga artifact was as much a battlefield as the barren valley outside.

Directed by the overlords of Kukulkan Brood, Zerg minions had split off from the main swarm and battled their way through Protoss defenders. The monsters entered the maze of wormwood passages within the greenish biopolymer walls.

Protoss zealots were sent on vigorous suicide missions by Judicator Amdor while Executor Koronis bravely directed his ground troops in the main battle. Meanwhile, the surviving members of the Terran commando squadron led by Lieutenant Scott pushed their way through the passages, taking images and recording intelligence data so that they could return and provide General Duke with all the tactical information he might need.

During his years of training in the marines, Scott had learned to assess a situation with just a glance. Now, the lieutenant kept his instincts and senses tuned to their highest pitch, hour after hour. He hoped his squadron would sustain no further casualties, but knew that was a faint hope.

Although they were deep within unexplored and mysterious territory, surrounded by hostile aliens, they were still members of Alpha Squadron. Their motto had always been "First in and first out," and they had willingly accepted their assignment. Being nervous and jumpy wouldn't make them any more efficient, and Scott didn't want his men to act like . . . colonists.

The Goliaths bent low, barely fitting through the corridors as they clomped forward, weapons fully charged and ready to fire. The walls of this strange construction were studded with jewels, pointed crystals, and glowing inclusions. In all his years of service on numerous Confederacy planets, Lieutenant Scott had seen plenty of odd environments and mind-numbingly strange life-forms. But he had never been anyplace like this before.

With the Goliaths in the lead, the team rounded a weird rippled corner and suddenly encountered a group of Zerg already hissing and raising their spiny exoskeletons in an attack posture. Six lizardlike zerglings bounded forward, followed immediately by a lurching hydralisk that bowed its carapace and extended clawed hands.

Lieutenant Scott didn't hesitate. "Open fire!"

His men were ready for the order. The firebats rushed into the lead and opened up their Perdition flamethrowers. Gouts of fire scorched the leaping zerglings, turning them into flailing fireballs as they sprang, only to crash into the curved walls, leaving a smear of smoking organic residue.

The Goliaths launched heavy firepower of their own, using their twin autocannons to cut down the hydralisk as it shot its volley of poisonous spines.

Three more marines—now no more than bloody pincushions wearing uniforms—sprawled dead. Others ran forward, howling for revenge, opening up their gauss rifles, screaming. Lieutenant Scott raised his weapon to his armor-padded shoulder and joined the battle.

While their fury was expended on the zerglings and the hydralisk, more alien enemies moved in from behind. Through one of the slick passages came a monstrous ultralisk, a mammoth-sized beast with bony scythes that slashed from side to side, chopping through two firebats as they turned around and opened fire at it. The blast of flame didn't even make the ultralisk pause. It lumbered forward, an unstoppable juggernaut that attacked and crushed the Terran opponents.

"Defensive semicircle," Scott shouted. "Now!"

The marines unloaded hundreds of rounds, never backing away a step. The two remaining Goliaths, their clanking armor partially damaged by hydralisk spines, expended their high-caliber ammunition into the ultralisk's tough hide. The firebats moved into range and unleashed their flamethrowers.

In a rampage, the smoking and bleeding ultralisk stampeded forward, heedless of the cost to its own body. The beast swung the sharp, bonelike scythes that protruded from its back and slashed the three surviving firebats, one by one.

One of the last Goliaths hammered the creature, firing and firing with his autocannons at point-blank range. And yet, even as the powerful blasts tore a huge hole in its body core, the mammoth Zerg slashed through the body-tank armor and broke the Goliath to pieces.

Lieutenant Scott watched his team being decimated, but he did not call for a retreat. He continued to pump rounds into the ultralisk as it turned toward the final, damaged Goliath. But the powerful armored trooper and the last five marines poured weapons fire into the lumbering hulk until finally the monster dropped in a heap, crushing one of the wounded and moaning marines on the floor.

New silence sounded like thunder around them, and Scott stared in amazement at what had just happened. He drew a deep breath, forcing his fear away, and called on every scrap of self-confidence and training he had left. He paused just a moment to clear his mind and make his decision before his few soldiers could succumb to shock.

"Forward," he said, and did not look at his fallen troops.

Taking the lead, Lieutenant Scott marched down the strange corridor. He had orders to see what was at the bottom of this bizarre alien object.

But he was sure this mission would only get harder as he and the remnants of his commando force continued deeper inside.

CHAPTER 33

OCTAVIA HERSELF BARELY UNDERSTOOD WHERE she was headed. Something was calling her, drawing her. In spite of herself, she followed. The presence was alien, yes. Yet somehow she felt she could trust it—had to trust it.

And so, as the darkness deepened, she walked as if in a trance. She crossed the charred and trampled fields, the ground churned by thundering Zerg claws and tentacles. Thin trees in an orchard lay strewn about like kindling, trunks shredded by angry hydralisks and ultralisks.

Broken pieces of Zerg minions lay strewn about, severed limbs like legs torn from giant insects, jagged fragments of hard carapaces, even a few gutted zergling bodies, though the monstrous minions had turned on and devoured most of their wounded. Foamy slime had seeped into the ground, leaving sticky patches of mud; some spots had already dried as hard as cement.

It took her several hours to reach an isolated mineral station in the foothills—the source of the urgent psychic plea.

She stepped up, looking around, but the darkness was too great around her. Thin gauzy clouds had once again choked off the stars.

Octavia came to a rocky hill about two hundred meters high. This was the place! She climbed it slowly, steadily, picking her way over boulders, until she reached a huge sharp slab of rock jutting up from the ground like a gigantic ax blade chopping its way free of the dirt.

There she stopped. The mental voice had called her to this spot, but she saw no one—at first.

"All right, I'm here," Octavia said out loud, not knowing whether the alien presence could comprehend her language. "What do you want?" She needed to know if this stranger could help her, if it could give the settlers some way to fight off this three-way invasion—Zerg, Protoss, and even the Terran military.

Suddenly a surprised voice spoke clearly in her mind. *But Terrans have no psi powers.*

"No, we don't," Octavia answered, still aloud.

I'm glad you have come, the voice said.

Then a tall, gray-skinned creature stepped out from around the ax-blade slab of rock to get a good look at Octavia. Octavia looked back.

The face had blazing eyes but no mouth, simply bony plates that somehow gave it a superior presence. Octavia sensed that this creature was female, most likely one of the Protoss aliens, but not part of the alien military forces that had landed in the far valley.

"You called me," Octavia said.

Yes . . .

"I'm Octavia Bren, a colonist. Who are you and why did you call me?"

My name is Xerana. I am a Dark Templar of the Protoss. I have studied the signal that was sent, and I believe I know its origin. I have come to bring a warning—

"Really?" Octavia cut in. "Well, your warning's a bit late.

That artifact of yours already killed my brother. Hundreds of people in my town have been killed by the Zerg."

Although she could not read the change of expression on the face of this alien named Xerana, Octavia thought she detected a tone of surprise in the Dark Templar's thought-speech. *Truly? Your brother was . . . absorbed?* Xerana tilted her head and leaned forward as if to study Octavia more closely. *But it would have no use for Terrans. You are not a part of this.*

Octavia clenched her teeth. "Well, I became a part of it when that thing disintegrated my brother."

Ah. The voice was like a breath in her mind. *I did not antici-pate this.*

Octavia raised her eyebrows. "You didn't anticipate a Terran answering your call, either."

Xerana's voice in Octavia's mind grew even more agitated. *I knew that my mission here would be difficult. I have come to save my people, despite their ambitions and their ignorance. When I arrived on your planet, I reached out with my mind, searching for an ally, and found one. I called out, but I did not expect that* you *would answer.*

Octavia marveled for a moment at the idea that she and this alien being who was so unlike herself might actually become allies, that they might share common goals.

"If you're here to save the lives of your people, and if you can help me save the lives of mine, then I am your ally. I'll do anything I can to help you." Octavia looked behind her, toward the valley where the frightened people of Free Haven huddled in the darkness, dreading another attack.

We are agreed, then. We will help one another. You must believe me when I tell you that the artifact will not attempt to harm humans unless they attempt to harm it first. It is a danger only to Protoss and Zerg, the children of the Xel'Naga. Octavia thought she detected a hint of sadness in the mind voice here.

A night bird flew overhead, hooting as it swooped down to snatch a black lizard from where it prowled across a flat rock. Octavia flinched, but the bird flew off with its squirming, struggling prey. The indigenous animals of Bhekar Ro had no interest in the conflict between the three powerful races.

"So, what will you do?" she asked.

I will go to the artifact.

Octavia said, "There's another . . . *presence* there. I sensed it, sort of the same way I sensed you calling me."

The artifact spoke to you?

"Not with words. Not as you're doing. Just with *feelings*. But there's definitely something there. A computer? A mind? A recorded signal? I don't know. Just be careful."

Xerana tilted her head again and looked at Octavia from an odd angle. *You are indeed an unexpected Terran, Octavia. Thank you for your concern.* She stood, her long scholar's sash flapping in the light breeze. A thin tablet with strange markings adorned her wide collar. *But my life may already be forfeit. I am compelled to tell the other Protoss that they must beware. If I knew of a way, I would even warn the Zerg overlords, but I doubt I could communicate directly. I must go to the artifact and command all of them to leave it. Alas, I doubt that they will listen.*

And you, in turn, must persuade your Terran military that this is not their fight.

Thinking of General Duke, Octavia said, "I doubt I could get anyone to listen either. But what about the artifact? We can't avoid it forever. As long as it's here on Bhekar Ro, won't there still be a danger?"

One way or another, the artifact will be gone from your planet within a few days, Xerana said. *Until that time comes, we must both do our best to keep our people safe.* With that, the Dark Templar turned and vanished from sight. She just . . . winked out of view.

Octavia stood still in amazement for a moment. Then she called out, not with her voice this time, but with her mind. *Xerana?*

Yes?

It's good to have an ally.

CHAPTER 34

WITH FREE HAVEN'S PERIMETER DEFENSES IN PLACE, General Edmund Duke felt he had done all that was necessary to keep the civilian settlers safe. The previous day, his first infiltration crew had gone inside the alien artifact, led by Lieutenant Scott. Now Duke prepared for a full military assault.

It was time for Alpha Squadron to strut its stuff.

He mobilized his battlecruisers, Wraiths, dropships, Arclite Siege Tanks, all of the ground forces, even Vulture Hover Bikes. The general decided to hold nothing back. He hoped he could simply charge into the fray and mop up nicely, now that the Protoss and Zerg had weakened each other's forces.

Ordering his troops to move out, Duke himself remained at the command center in the mayor's former house. Scratching his chin, he watched the reconnaissance images as his forces crossed the boundary line of foothills and plunged into the beleaguered valley battlefield.

The assault began with a phalanx of marines and firebats who entered the middle of the war zone, flanked by the awesome power of Alpha Squadron's siege tanks. The tanks did not waste time by going into siege mode, which would have allowed them to use shock cannons for long-range attacks. Instead, the tanks simply pounded any aliens that moved.

Pushing forward relentlessly, the marines and firebats swept aside all enemy resistance, sliding through the combat area like a hot knife through congealed salt-pudding. The Terran ground troops picked up speed, pushing forward with enthusiasm, glad to leave behind their long and boring tour of duty, during which they had done little but map out abandoned worlds and survey asteroid belts for resources. The men of Alpha Squadron had been eager to do some damage to the alien scum.

Watching via viewscreen, General Duke clapped his hands in exhilaration. A knock came at his door, and one of the low-ranking marine guards let the civilian Octavia Bren enter. The general took one look at the young settler and said, "Can't you see I'm busy, girl? I'm directing a battle here."

"Yes, General. But I've got some information you might need to know."

He frowned, not sure that this dirt-scraper could possibly have learned anything that his own people hadn't already uncovered. Impatiently he gestured her inside, but turned back to watch the battle.

The progress of the front-line troops had left what appeared to be an irreparable hole in the Protoss and Zerg defenses, but the general soon saw that this was a grave miscalculation, that his excitement was a bit premature.

"No, no!" he yelled at the screen, watching the marines and the firebats advance so quickly that the ground support at the siege tanks and the heavy armored Goliaths could not keep up.

Duke grabbed his communications intercom and shouted into it, hoping that his orders would be heard through the cacophony of ground combat. "Close up ranks! Fall back to the protection of—"

Spiderlike Protoss dragoons marched over rocky hillocks, approaching the rear of the exposed ground troops. In front of them, fiery-eyed zealots powered up their destructive Psionic Blades and charged toward the marines, trapping the ground troops. Dragoons and zealots fell upon the marines and fire-bats from three different directions. Even though flamethrowers and gauss rifles sent a blizzard of destruction into the air, the Protoss fanatics did not stop. Dragoons mowed down the Terran infantry, and zealots waded in among them, slashing right and left, cutting the firebats and then the marines to ribbons.

"Get them some air cover! Air cover!" Duke shouted.

Belatedly, the fast Wraiths streaked in, attacking from above, followed by the slower heavy battlecruisers that closed in from behind.

The marines and firebats continued to dish out destruction in self-defense, but then one of the robed Protoss Templars climbed onto a pile of rocks. Raising his three-fingered hands to the sky, he summoned an awesome Psionic Storm that battered the Wraiths into confusion, slamming the single-man fighters together, driving several down to the ground as if they had been hit by a huge invisible flyswatter.

Massively damaged, the battlecruisers and the remaining Wraiths tried to pull away, but from the other side of the valley, a second High Templar called yet another Psionic Storm that hammered them from the east.

Only one of the battlecruisers and three Wraiths managed to pull away to the relative safety of the foothills, limping back from the dangerous valley and leaving damaged and destroyed Terran vessels strewn all across the battlefield.

While the Alpha Squadron battleships hovered and tried to assess their damage, a dozen hydralisks burrowed up from beneath the ground. Before the battlecruiser captain and the Wraith pilots could ascend out of range, the hydralisks had lashed out with wave after wave of penetrating needle spines that pierced the battlecruiser's hull and shredded its engines. The enormous ship crashed down into the rugged foothills, while the three Wraiths were turned into a confetti of metal and blood before they could even fire a shot.

"That doesn't look good, General," Octavia observed.

"Shut up!" he screamed, scanning the battlefield map and trying to decide what orders to issue.

With the remaining marines and firebats cut off from the tanks and Goliaths, they were caught in the middle of a bloodbath. Even as they turned their weapons on the Protoss that stood against them, Zerg minions closed in from the flank and fell upon them.

General Duke recognized the zerglings and guardians, but not the group of giant lumbering four-legged creatures with long canine muzzles and spiny blue fur. He had never seen anything like them. The new beasts charged in like rabid wolves, sniffing the ground, turning their eye stalks, and plunging into any weak point of the marines' defenses. General Duke had observed many types of Zerg before, but these appeared to be a new form entirely.

Octavia Bren stared at the screen, shocked. "Those look like Old Blue! The aliens must have adapted something from him."

"You know where those things come from?" the general asked, turning to her sharply.

"Those aliens . . . infested a big dog at one of our outlying homesteads. That looks like what was left of him—"

"A *dog*?" Duke gave a snort of disgust. "You colonists keep *pets* around here?" He picked up his microphone, though the marines seemed to be doing everything they could, even without his direct orders. "The Zerg are causing more damage, men. Concentrate your fire and take out those . . . those *roverlisks*."

One of the marines raised a hand in an obscene gesture,

and the General assumed he must be fending off an attack from the sky.

During the melee, eight Protoss reavers slowly made their way down from the northeast, like huge armored caterpillars intent on reaching the fray. Duke knew that the marines and firebats would lose the skirmish unless they could get more air support.

Finally, the siege tanks and the towering Goliaths arrived to engage the zealots and dragoons. The armored Goliaths used anti-aircraft missiles to pound the four-legged cyborg walkers. One marine even came forward in heavy, powered armor and smashed open the brain case that was directing a dragoon walker.

Siege tanks beyond the range of the zealots' Psionic Blades pounded and pounded again. The marines and firebats never halted in their defense, and as General Duke watched, the battle changed course and finally the Terran forces gained the upper hand.

For the moment.

But it didn't last long. The Protoss reavers at last crawled within range and released their Scarab Drones, flying bombs that zipped toward their targets and exploded. Two of the Goliaths fell. A handful of marines were slaughtered in a single explosion. The tanks and Goliaths were forced to turn their attention to the armored reavers. Then two Protoss carriers converged from the west, raining down a firestorm with their small, robotic interceptors.

"This isn't possible," General Duke said. "Not Alpha Squadron. Not my best forces!"

The blinding light of explosions hurt his eyes as he stared at the tactical screen. Smoke and chaos made it impossible to see any details. The ground was littered with so many fallen troops, the general could barely discern how many of his men remained alive.

The Protoss carriers seemed to know exactly what to do. They concentrated their aerial attack on crushing the Goliaths, and when the towering armored walkers had all been taken out, the Terran siege tanks were left defenseless, like sluggish tin cans with giant targets painted on them.

General Duke could only watch as the remainder of his assault troops got trounced.

His voice was hoarse, and he spoke as if to an empty room. "It seems I have . . . greatly underestimated the alien resistance."

CHAPTER 35

IN THE HEAT OF THE BATTLE, EXECUTOR KORONIS was too involved with directing his Protoss forces to notice the tiny ripple of disturbance in the air. A stranger, a hidden visitor.

Beside him, beneath the looming majesty of the naked Xel'Naga artifact, Judicator Amdor seethed, mentally spitting insults and fury at the Zerg and Terran enemies who were attempting to steal the ancient treasure. Amdor considered that the artifact belonged to him alone.

As the zealots attacked the ground forces and massive carriers flew overhead, dropping deadly squadrons of interceptors, Koronis finally sensed a cold presence—something familiar yet separate from the Khala, the psychic link that bound all Protoss together. He turned, curious and troubled, just as Amdor whirled around, sensing the same thing.

In the air between them, standing on a raised mound of broken rock and scabrous dirt, a figure appeared. A tall Protoss female shed a camouflage of shadows, like oil dripping off steel. She phased out of invisibility, bending light around her.

"A Dark Templar!" Judicator Amdor reeled, his face and mind squirming with revulsion and disgust. "Foul heretic!" His psychic shout attracted the attention of other Judicators and High Templar nearby.

The female Dark Templar did not flinch from the insult and mental onslaught. "I come bearing a warning for you, for all the Protoss here," she said. "I am Xerana, loyal to the First Born despite the persecution that Judicators like you have inflicted upon us." The sinewy gray-skinned female looked squarely at Amdor, who drew himself taller, as if wishing he had a powerful weapon in his hands.

Uneasy, knowing the terrible powers the Dark Templar could use, Executor Koronis signaled for backup troops. He did not hate the Dark Templar, as Amdor did, but he was cautious, especially in this battlefield crisis.

Four zealots bounded to his aid, Psionic Blades already activated and flashing. One dragoon turned on its four legs and scuttled toward where the commanders had stood.

"You do not understand what you are doing," Xerana said, looking to Koronis for understanding. "You have no inkling of the true origin and purpose behind this artifact. You must not interfere with the plans of the Wanderers from Afar. Leave here."

"We are the First Born of the Xel'Naga!" Amdor said. "You and your traitorous followers have broken from the Khala and turned renegade to our race. You have caused enough damage already. Do not intrude in this place."

Executor Koronis, though, was more interested in what could have drawn this fugitive into the den of her mortal enemies. She must have known the Judicators would want to punish her. "Dark Templar, what information do you have for us?"

Amdor glared at him, eyes blazing. "Executor, surely you don't mean to listen to the corrupted words of this—"

Koronis raised his three-fingered hand. "I am the commander of this Protoss force. I would be a fool to dismiss any vital intelligence, regardless of its source."

Xerana leaned closer to the Executor, dismissing Amdor and infuriating him further. "I have a message and a dire warning. This . . . object"—she swept her hand upward to indicate the towering face of the mysterious exposed structure—"is very dangerous. It was created by the Xel'Naga, as you have guessed, and was designed to be more powerful than either the Protoss race or the Zerg. Beware what you would awaken, lest it consume all of you."

"Lies," Amdor sneered. "We are the First Born. The Protoss were chosen by the Xel'Naga—"

"And abandoned by them," Xerana cut in. "We did not meet their expectations. The Xel'Naga made other attempts to create a perfect race. The Zerg were the most destructive and successful of their new breeds, but the ancient race began many experiments and kept many secrets."

"Then what do you expect us to do?" Koronis said as the battle continued to rage behind them. The dragoon and the zealots pressed closer to Xerana, waiting for orders. "Should we let the enemies have it?"

"You must leave this object alone," she said. "Everyone, of all races. Together, Protoss and Zerg are in the process of awakening a great peril. You must retreat, pull your forces back. You take a great risk by toying with things you do not understand."

Koronis blinked his glowing eyes in disbelief, and Amdor looked momentarily amused. Then he mentally sent loud orders. "Seize this heretic!" Waves of hatred and revulsion emanated from the Judicator.

The dragoon and zealots surrounded Xerana. The Dark Templar scholar stood silent, deeply disappointed that her own people refused to listen to her message.

"It was *your* foul brethren who corrupted noble Tassadar!" Amdor growled. "The Dark Templar were the ones who opened doorways into the Void, luring other Protoss away from the Khala."

Even as she was taken prisoner, Xerana did not struggle. The Judicator proudly turned to Koronis. "We will soon take possession of this artifact, Executor. And with this Dark Templar heretic held captive aboard the *Qel'Ha*, our great expedition has changed from complete failure to a glorious victory."

CHAPTER 36

PURSUED THROUGH THE ARTIFACT'S WINDING, creepy channels, Lieutenant Scott led his few remaining marines and firebats deeper toward the mysterious core. Though the larger battle continued to rage out on the valley floor, here inside the Terran commandos encountered numerous exploratory parties of Protoss zealots and Zerg minions, all of which seemed to have received the same reconnaissance mission as Scott's team.

It seems to be a race, he thought. *And we intend to win it.*

The light within the walls became brighter, as if some inner fire were being stoked. The jewel clusters grew larger inside the curved biopolymer structure, deep crimson gems cut in strange facets and unusual shapes, as if they were internal organs.

Scott had no idea what they would find when they reached their destination, but he doubted the Zerg or the Protoss knew any more than the Terrans did. He would secure the information for General Duke and, if possible, prevent any aliens from acquiring the same data.

They did not pause to fight a group of Zerg that slithered and clattered through the hallways. Instead the lieutenant directed his men to sprint ahead, dodging through corridors even though they heard monsters in continued pursuit. The marines and firebats were willing to keep fighting, but their bloodlust had been dampened by the severe losses their troops had already suffered. Now they preferred to complete their objective and get back out alive.

The commandos followed the glowing light ahead, descending and curving, remembering to plant "breadcrumb" locators as they raced along so they could find their way back out. Scott hoped the dropships would be there in time to pick them up. He didn't worry about that, though. The members of Alpha Squadron knew their own duties.

The throbbing light in the walls formed a hypnotic call, like a flame that drew moths out of the darkness. The Zerg and the Protoss seemed to feel the call as well. They followed different passages, but all of them converged toward the central mass as if every creature could find answers here.

Finally, with his marines and firebats rushing ahead, Lieutenant Scott and his squad emerged into the artifact's blazing core, an awesome, gigantic grotto filled with a light like a blazing sun. But the fire was cold and electric, and somehow *alive*.

The walls and ceiling of the grotto reflected the light in dazzling rainbows. Jagged crystalline shards protruded in all directions. Scott stood with his mouth open, transfixed by the grandeur and the sheer power in front of him. But though he had arrived here as ordered, he had no way to explain what he saw, could not begin to draw conclusions or provide any briefing that would be at all helpful to the general.

From other passages, dark bubbly openings in the organic resin walls, Zerg and Protoss emerged, monstrous hydralisks and heavily armored zealots. But as they all converged in the grotto, none of the alien enemies made any move to attack. The fiery core of the Xel'Naga artifact was too awe-inspiring, and all three species stood stunned and amazed.

Then the heart-glow grew brighter, as if some sort of ignition had been triggered. Tentacles of light rocketed out, reflecting like lightning from the jagged Khaydarin crystals in the walls, crackling arcs all around the grotto.

One of the firebats screamed. Lieutenant Scott knew he should call for a retreat, but could not bring himself to form words. His feet were fastened to the floor, his muscles locked in position.

The energy bolts grew more powerful. The pulsing heart of the Xel'Naga artifact blazed into a blinding white ball. Suddenly the lightning struck out, targeting each of the life-forms within reach.

The bolts crashed into the firebats and the marines, while at the same time obliterating the Zerg and Protoss spectators. Lieutenant Scott opened his mouth to shout, but the energy washed over him, too, as if it was scanning and absorbing every intruder. He watched the Zerg disappear, uploaded and erased. Soon everything in the grotto was wiped clean—the Protoss, the Zerg, and all of his squad.

Then all vision winked out of his eyes. . . .

The grotto was empty of life-forms; the Xel'Naga thing had gathered every specimen within reach. The Terrans were not necessary, but the rest of these children of the Xel'Naga were exactly what the artifact needed.

In all the chambers and the walls, the glowing light increased to a living blaze. Jewel clusters exploded with the surge of energy. More dirt and rocks fell from the mountainside as a vibrating hum penetrated the biopolymer skeleton.

Powering up, the long-buried Xel'Naga artifact at last began final preparations for its emergence. . . .

CHAPTER 37

AFTER WATCHING HIS FORCES BE COMPLETELY defeated—defeated!—General Edmund Duke was in no mood to listen to panicked rumors from an untrained, dirt-streaked colonial woman. But Octavia Bren insisted on being heard. She told the general about her encounter with the Dark Templar Xerana, a mysterious Protoss scholar who brought urgent warnings about the ancient artifact.

Not that Duke could do anything about it. How did she want him to deal with it? He had just watched his best-planned offensive get stomped into a list of casualties too long to fit on a dozen computer screens. At least now, though, he had a bit more information . . . enough to make him deeply nervous.

When Alpha Squadron had arrived here after tracking down that alien signal and the colonists' call for help, the general had assumed the exposed artifact was just another BDO—a Big Dumb Object—not particularly worth losing Terran lives over, unless he had orders to do so. Weird artifacts and mysterious structures often turned up on backwater worlds, but they usually didn't amount to anything.

In this case, though, it was clear the Zerg and the Protoss wanted possession of the artifact in the worst way—and Duke no longer had the firepower to capture it for Emperor Arcturus Mengsk.

In his professional military opinion, that was *bad.*

"Thank you for your assessment, ma'am," he growled, then opened a troop communication link. "I know exactly how to respond to the situation. Call in our best Ghost. I believe MacGregor Golding will do. Send him to me right away." He looked up to see that the distraught settler remained standing in his office. "Is there anything else, Miz Brown?"

"Bren," she said. "My name is Octavia Bren."

Duke scowled, wondering what possible difference this civilian's name could make in the grand scheme of things. "If it's not tactical information, ma'am, it's irrelevant. Now, if you'll excuse me, I have a war to win. Not easy to pluck victory from the jaws of defeat."

Before Octavia could leave, the door to Mayor Nik's commandeered quarters popped open and a slender, armor-clad man walked in. His small face appeared streetwise, and his overlarge brown eyes above high cheekbones looked incredibly old, as if the young man had already seen enough to make him weary of the entire universe. MacGregor Golding stood silent, waiting for the general to speak. Then, as if a nagging distraction tugged at him, the young man turned to Octavia.

Octavia felt as if she were under a high-powered scan beam. Inside the contours of her brain, she sensed a creeping telepathic presence, like a vandal ransacking her house.

"Never mind the civilian, Agent Golding," General Duke said, breaking Octavia's concentration.

The Ghost turned back to the general. "But she is definitely worth a second look, sir. I was quarantined by the Confederate government and trained to channel my psionic energies. I can recognize the talent. This woman here has a great deal of natural potential. She might make a good Ghost herself."

Octavia's skin crawled. "Not on your life," she said. In the brief mental link they had shared, Octavia sensed what this man, this MacGregor Golding, had been bred and trained to do. She had also gained some insight into what the commander of Alpha Squadron had in mind.

"Agent Golding," the general said. "Command decision. We originally wanted to acquire this artifact for the Terran arsenal. However, given recent events, I must admit that is not likely to happen. Therefore, I have no recourse but to activate Plan B."

"Yes, General," the Ghost said. *"Plan B*. Far worse than simply losing this skirmish would be to allow this object— whatever it is—to fall into the vile hands of the despicable Zerg or Protoss. Given the choice, we must ensure that no one has access to it."

The Ghost stood at the ready in his polished Hostile Environment Suit, packing his long C-10 canister rifle. "I'm equipped with a personal cloaking device, sir. A dropship can take me to the fringe of the battlefield, and I'll make my way in from there to paint a target."

General Duke nodded, folding his hands over the mayor's now spotlessly clean desk. "Got a battlecruiser in the high atmosphere, ready to deploy a full complement of warheads."

Now Octavia raged at them both for the calm and dismissive manner in which they discussed destruction of such magnitude. "You can't nuke Bhekar Ro! It's *our* colony world. This is our home, where we've worked and sweated and—"

General Duke motioned for marine guards to remove her from his office. Livid, Octavia thrashed and struggled. He looked at her with open disapproval.

"Would you rather have me lose the battle, Miz Brown?" he asked as if the answer were self-evident.

CHAPTER 38

FOR YEARS, THE DRIVING GOAL OF JUDICATOR AMDOR had been to hunt down and capture one of the Dark Templar heretics. Their beliefs and practices were abhorrent to him, and the very knowledge of their shadowy existence, running and hiding throughout the Void, made him feel psychically ill.

For a loyal Judicator, this passion took precedence over discovering Xel'Naga artifacts. Amdor wanted to stamp out the traitors who had led so many other Protoss away from the psychic link of the Khala. The Protoss were already failures in the eyes of the Xel'Naga, but they had learned to cooperate, to draw their minds together in a graceful, flowing stream of thought that bound the race into a single unit.

Except for the members of the Dark Templar, rebels who insisted on being independent. They tried to draw Protoss minds *away*, weakening the Khala by destroying the unity of the First Born. With his every breath, Amdor felt the need to prevent such damage from continuing.

Now this loathsome female, Xerana, had willingly surrendered herself, appearing before them in the midst of their greatest battle. Amdor wished he had time to perform a full inquisition back aboard the *Qel'Ha*.

Even held captive, though, Xerana did not seem frightened. Instead, she produced images, hauling out blasphemous scrolls filled with archaic writing. "You must look at my proof," she said, her thoughts directed toward Amdor and Executor Koronis with enough mental volume that all the others could hear her. She held up a tattered scrap of a recovered document. "See the evidence for yourselves. Before you do anything foolish, you must understand what the Xel'Naga have left behind on this world. Do not awaken the seed."

Behind her, the curling porous walls of the luminous green object glowed brighter from the mountainside, as if some buried furnace were already heating up.

Amdor snatched the fragment out of her three-fingered hand and tore it to shreds. "We have no interest in your lies. I don't know what Dark Templar trick you're trying to employ. Are you calling other heretics here to help you use this great treasure in your efforts to destroy the Khala?"

Facing him squarely, Xerana gazed calmly at him. "The Dark Templar have no interest in destroying the Khala. That has never been the case. Nor have *you* ever been interested in understanding *us*. First the Judicators ordered the extermination of our tribe because we were an embarrassment to you. Then, when valiant Protoss refused to commit such genocide, you ordered us banished, to hide us from the rest of the First Born. You drove us all from our homes, yet here I am, risking myself to warn you of the folly of what you are doing."

Xerana raised a hand to gesture toward the weird unburied object. "Do not enter this artifact. You fail to understand its nature. It is not what you think."

Judicator Amdor just sneered. "More than anything else, you have just convinced me that *I personally* must go inside and investigate." He shot a blazing-eyed glance over at Koronis. "Accompanied by the Executor, of course. We shall decide for ourselves what to do with this treasure and claim its mysteries for the good of the Khala—not for outcasts like yourself."

Goaded by the fanatical Judicator's challenging look, Executor Koronis had no choice but to agree.

Her shoulders sagging, Xerana hung her head, knowing she had failed. She had not really expected a different outcome. She had been morally bound to deliver her warning, to do her best to avert the potential disaster.

"In the midst of this battle, the heretic is too dangerous to hold," Amdor said. The Judicator called forth zealots and dragoons and had them prepare their weapons. "All Dark Templar have been already judged, their lives deemed forfeit. They have turned to the lure of the Void and ignored the call of the Khala." He made a decisive gesture. "Execute this one while Executor Koronis and I enter the glorious artifact ourselves."

He moved to stand beside Koronis. The huge glowing structure seemed to call out to them, luring them closer. In his heart, Amdor felt an urgent need to go deep within its passages and experience the awe and wonder for himself.

Xerana turned a look of profound disappointment on Koronis. "You understand so little, yet you command so much."

Then, disgusted, she called upon the energies of the Void and freed herself. Using mysterious powers that she had developed during her own search through the wildness of space, Xerana reached into the all-connecting stream of Khala, the mental link that bound all Protoss into a harmonious unit with different personalities but one linked psyche. Not harming them—for no Dark Templar ever wished to hurt one of their fellow Protoss—Xerana erected temporary invisible dams in the stream of the Khala. She cut off the Executor, the Judicator, and all the nearby Protoss forces. Xerana knew how much chaos her efforts would cause.

Severed from their precious Khala network, the Protoss felt

abandoned . . . alone . . . terrified. Some of the zealots wailed in telepathic voices. The closest dragoon staggered, unable to control his cyborg body anymore.

Judicator Amdor fell to his knees and raised clawed hands as if he could physically draw down threads of the Khala from the air. "I'm blind! I'm lost!"

Then, using the trick that had brought her into their midst, Xerana bent the shadows around her, folding light so that she vanished from view. In the ensuing confusion, she fled the battlefield, leaving her people to the fate dictated by their own misguided choices.

She had a long distance to run so that she wouldn't be trapped within the holocaust.

CHAPTER 39

THE TERRAN DROPSHIP FLEW LOW FROM THE BASE at the town of Free Haven and cruised over the barrier ridge. After dancing across the edge of the tumultuous battlefield, it paused just long enough, like a hummingbird dipping into nectar, then streaked away before the enemy alien forces could fire upon it.

It left a Ghost behind.

MacGregor Golding, wearing his special cloak-impregnated armor, touched lightly to the ground and raced along in a camouflage of wind and shadows. The fury and destruction of the Zerg and Protoss fighting forces kept the alien armies so occupied that Golding could have been carrying neon flags and they would have dismissed him.

The Ghost sprinted, his muscles pumped up by two full doses of stimpacks he had secretly taken from marine stores— much more than the recommended dosage, but it was well within the limits of what his tortured body had endured through years of training locked away in Confederacy isolation. MacGregor Golding's life had been shaped and pounded until he was a living, walking weapon, a psychic bomb who now fulfilled his life's purpose—his destiny.

If a weapon could have a destiny, that is.

As Golding traversed the edge of the battlefield, he saw the carnage that remained of the victims of Alpha Squadron. Siege tanks lay blasted open, marines and firebats—or at least their body parts—lay strewn in the blood and mud of the valley floor among blackened craters and broken rocks.

Brooding knots of clouds thickened in the skies, providing cover from long-range aerial attacks. A storm would be building. The Ghost could see that. From his brief contact with the telepathically susceptible mind of Octavia Bren, Golding had stolen memories of Bhekar Ro's massive storms with their laser-lightning and sonic thunder. Not even the worst storm would wash away all the blood and carnage left here from the battle, though.

But MacGregor Golding's mission could wash it clean and sterilize the entire area.

All he had to do was call down a nuclear strike.

As he came closer to the large, ominous artifact—the focus of so much strife—the Ghost could feel the pounding, building call within his skull. Another gigantic telepathic presence, a powerful sleeping entity that seemed vast enough to overwhelm all of the puny life-forms that were fighting below it.

The Ghost didn't know what this thing was, and though his usual job was to gather intelligence and to infiltrate when necessary, that was not his mission now. General Duke had issued orders, and the Ghost wasn't required to understand, just to carry out the objective.

This artifact must be destroyed.

The concentrations of fighters and cloak-penetrating sensors near the cliffside forced MacGregor Golding to pause. They blocked his every line of approach. He saw a large caterpillarlike reaver accompanied by an observer overhead. Those Protoss devices could detect his presence and prevent him from coming closer. He shouldered his C-10 canister rifle, lightweight but bulky like a bazooka. Golding had prepared ahead, substituting some of the high-explosive rounds with special lockdown rounds. He had a feeling they would prove extremely useful right now.

Still invisible, surrounded by the cloaking field that kept him free of casual observation, he chose his route carefully, gauging how fast he could run and what the clearest path would be. He would worry about a rapid retreat afterward. Then the Ghost lowered the canister rifle and launched his lockdown round.

He watched the arcing plume of fire and smoke travel beyond the range of his personal cloaking field. Several of the Protoss and Zerg looked up, but it was too late. The lockdown round detonated, spraying the area with a dampening field that disabled the nearest reaver. The massive unit ground to a helpless halt, its weapons systems no longer functional, its powered hatches sealed so that the Protoss fighters inside could not boil out and fight hand to hand.

Moving fast now, he fired a second round, and the observer overhead crashed, its sensors off-line. Knowing he was safe in his invisibility now, MacGregor Golding raced ahead through the chaos, dodging Zerg minions and angry Protoss. They could not see a Ghost.

At the sudden unexpected loss of Protoss mechanized firepower, Zerg minions surged forward, directed by Kukulkan Brood's overlords to take advantage of the flaw in the Protoss defenses. MacGregor ran ahead, approaching the shimmering artifact, while behind him the vicious hydralisks, guardians, and zerglings plunged into the Protoss with wild abandon.

Using the chaos to his benefit, intent only on his mission, on the pinnacle of his existence, the Ghost took up his position and powered up his special frequency-targeting laser.

Via an encoded communications link, he contacted General Duke. "All ready, sir. I'm in position. Preparing to paint the target now."

"You may proceed, Golding. Good work," the general said. "If you don't make it out in time, I'll see that you receive full commendations. Unfortunately, they'll have to be sealed in your classified personnel file."

"Of course, General. I understand."

Golding activated the laser and marked a target on the face of the giant artifact. The tactical nuclear warheads could come down with pinpoint accuracy, thanks to him. The objective was assured.

Overhead, one of Alpha Squadron's remaining battlecruisers opened its weapons bay doors, ready to drop the atomic missiles.

MacGregor Golding was sitting right on ground zero, but he had a few seconds to get out of the way.

He started to run.

CHAPTER 40

OCTAVIA UNDERSTOOD THE STAKES WELL ENOUGH. A nuclear attack was imminent. And if the Terran military attacked the ancient alien artifact, the object itself would strike back. She had no way of knowing how many Terrans—and Protoss, for that matter—might die in the backlash. Octavia could not muster enough compassion to care whether the Zerg swarm was wiped out or not.

General Duke had treated her as if she were a hysterical child who did not know what she was dealing with. Octavia had to admit she didn't understand enough about the situation outside in the Terran Dominion, but in this case she did know more than General Duke.

Now that her efforts to persuade him to give up his ill-advised plan had failed, Octavia knew of only one place to turn. Taking a small field rover, she drove at top speed out to the ax-blade rock where she and the Dark Templar Xerana had first met. Leaving the rover behind, she scrambled up the rocky slope, calling out, "Xerana! Xerana!"

There was no answering voice, of course. The Dark Templar could not have known Octavia would come here to speak to her.

Still, when she concentrated she felt a presence at the back of her mind. Not Xerana, though. It was more like a kind of tension, a mixture of emotions she could not begin to comprehend, all rising in a wordless scream. She could tell something powerful was about to occur.

Desperate now, Octavia blocked all other thoughts from her mind and focused all her concentration on one word: *Xerana*!

She had no idea how long she stood there, the thought pulsing through her brain—*Xerana! Xerana!*—but suddenly the Dark Templar scholar was there. She looked ruffled and tired.

As soon as she saw the alien woman, Octavia blurted, "Xerana, I've failed. The military wouldn't listen. There's going to be an atomic explosion. You've got to stop it."

I too have spoken with my people. They too have chosen not to listen.

A hot ball formed at the pit of Octavia's stomach. "But they could all die. You said so yourself. We've got to stop them."

Ah. But we can only offer them our knowledge. We cannot make their choices for them. Their greed and prejudice have killed their common sense. What comes after . . . is of their own doing.

"But the Free Haven colonists shouldn't have to die because of someone else's stupidity," Octavia said.

No. The Dark Templar closed her blazing gemfire eyes, as if she were concentrating on a single deep thought.

Just then, Octavia felt that other presence again at the back of her mind, wiping out all hope of other thought or discussion. She pressed her hands to her temples as the telepathic shout grew and grew.

They were already too late.

CHAPTER 41

WHEN THE DARK TEMPLAR VANISHED BEFORE HIS eyes—escaped!—Judicator Amdor was furious. He had lost the captive he had wanted tortured, interrogated, and then executed. All of the heretics must be made into examples for the rest of the Protoss race, to keep their faith in the Khala strong.

But Xerana had used foul Void powers, tapping into forbidden dark resources that were an affront to all loyal zealots, judicators, and High Templar. Amdor could not allow it to seem that she was stronger.

After the Dark Templar scholar fled, her mind-scrambling corruption had faded. But while mentally blinded, Amdor had never seen his rigorous followers so frightened or confused. Not even the Zerg attacks had caused as much disruption and dismay as being cut off from the gentle communal flow of the Khala.

He turned to Executor Koronis, whose thoughts were carefully masked. Amdor had the strange suspicion that the calm commander was as much amused by the Judicator's discomfiture as by the Dark Templar's escape.

Amdor made up his mind. "I will not allow this traitor and heretic to sway me from going inside the Xel'Naga treasure. Enough ground troops and survey teams—I will go myself. Your dragoons never returned, nor did any of our zealot scouts. The time has come to investigate this matter personally. Will you come with me?"

To his surprise, Koronis declined. "I wish I could accompany you, Judicator, but the requirements of strategy and military duty dictate that I stay here to direct our battle."

Amdor looked at him for a moment, as if sneering, then accepted. "You are not worthy to walk in the shadow of the Xel'Naga. I will shoulder the responsibility for the enclave, and for the entire Protoss race."

The proud Judicator climbed the slope, leaving Koronis behind to reorganize his troops and shore up a line of defense where a mysterious lockdown detonation had just wiped out all of the Protoss mechanized firepower. Zerg minions were flooding into the breach, pressing their advantage. Giving mental commands, Koronis ordered more reavers to close the gap and a carrier to strike from the sky with flying interceptors. . . .

Judicator Amdor reached the opening of the artifact and sensed the pulsing presence inside growing stronger. The light increased, crackling like cold fire through the smooth translucent polymer of the labyrinthine walls. He could sense the influence of the Xel'Naga here, an intangible mark of the creator race. Amdor was certain this legacy was meant for him.

Their fruitless search, the long wanderings of the *Qel'Ha* had been a result of Executor Koronis's indecisiveness and lack of vision. When the expeditionary fleet returned to the ruins of Aiur, Amdor would bring hope and power to the Protoss race and the Conclave would reward him well.

Stepping into the tunnels, the Judicator walked quickly,

choosing curves and following a golden path in his mind. He could tell where the core of this object lay, the center of its power. It seemed to call him, drawing him deeper inside, and he rushed to answer the summons. The entity would reveal everything he had ever wanted to know about the Xel'Naga.

Oddly, despite the throbbing pulse in his mind, Amdor found the artifact to be empty and silent, as if all the other infiltrators—the Protoss zealots, Terran commandos, and Zerg invaders alike—had somehow gone away. But Amdor felt no threat in this, only a gladness that his way would not be hindered.

When at last he entered the grotto of the arctic-cold fire, it swelled and grew, drawing energy, licking the swirled sides of the cavern. Amdor stopped, and all the amazed thoughts in his mind drained away. He could no longer feel the Khala, but this *presence* was greater than even the combined mental power of the Protoss race. This was magnificent.

This was *everything*.

As he stood in front of the blazing, living heart of the artifact, Amdor could put no words to his astonishment. Then inside his head, piercing through even the awakening, utterly ancient presence of this thing, he heard the hated psi-voice of the Dark Templar, whispering to him from a distance: "Now you will believe, Judicator. This is only the beginning. This artifact is another creation of the Xel'Naga. It knows that we are all interconnected, part of the great tapestry. And the Xel'Naga plan requires all of us here, every scrap of our DNA. Their legacy needs only the energy to escape."

Amdor whirled to see if Xerana had somehow followed him inside, if she dared taint this holy place with her foul presence. But the scholar was not there, only her voice. She herself had fled to safety. "You should have listened to me, Judicator Amdor."

Then she fell silent in his head, and he looked once again

toward the shimmering core, which even now blazed brighter, focusing on him, assessing him—then lunging out for him.

Brilliant bolts shot in all directions, lacing the grotto with a fiery webwork of connections, forming the final pattern as it disintegrated the Judicator and absorbed the last scraps of information that it needed for its full awakening.

CHAPTER 42

FOLLOWING THE BRIGHT PATH PAINTED ONTO THE surface of the artifact by the Ghost's special laser, the tactical nuclear warheads plunged down through the hazy storm-breeding skies of Bhekar Ro. They were like lightning bolts hurled from the heavens by an angry god.

The Ghost, MacGregor Golding, scrambled over rock outcroppings away from the giant structure. He switched off his cloaking field and left himself exposed as all the aliens turned, some noticing him, some spotting the streaks of fire coming down from distant ships high above, some just sensing an awful doom approaching.

It was just a few tactical nukes. The GPIP (guaranteed permanent incapacitation of personnel) radius wasn't too large. A stim-charged Ghost, running all out, could get to the other side of the ridge, dive down among some thick rocks, and hope the mountainside offered enough shelter.

Before leaping down through scree and boulders, Golding raised his hands as if beckoning the awesome weapons closer.

He heard a hissing boom through the air and the scream of their passage, then all the warheads came down like sledge-hammers on top of the glowing artifact.

He found a crack in enormous talus rocks, squeezed inside to where the shadows looked dark and cool. But even there, he had to close his eyes, and through his lids the world looked bright as day. . . .

In a growing burst of light, the three tactical nukes erased the front of the mountain surrounding the artifact. A flash of spreading disintegration rippled outward.

But faster still, the awakened and hungry artifact struck, drinking deeply of the energy, absorbing it all. Within a moment—too short for any clock to measure—the outward spread of atomic annihilation halted, then was sucked inside, drawn deep into the Xel'Naga creation like a whirlpool of power. . . .

Reeling from the sonic boom, not knowing what had just happened, Executor Koronis stood by his Protoss forces, unable to believe he was still alive. He could not grasp how the artifact had responded to the nuclear attack from above, but now all the translucent biopolymer convolutions awak-ened in a burst of radiance.

The mountainside was gone, like unlocked chains that had fallen away. Recharged and fully awake, the living artifact at last cracked and broke free, its substance no longer an armor-like material. Now the whole thing was charged with pulsing electrical fire, a life force.

Alive, and searching.

The Zerg overlords, stunned by the unexpected atomic blast, reeled, losing control of their ravenous minions. The bristling, monstrous roverlisks, based on the genetics of Old Blue, bounded about, tearing into their zergling cohorts. Dragonlike mutalisks flew in circles, out of control and spit-ting a rain of Glave Wurm destruction down on all frenzied fighters.

The surviving Protoss Judicators and zealots stood in awe, looking up at the incandescent, stirring object buried by their ancient progenitors, as if a thunderous destiny were coming down upon them.

Then the web-laced blazing shell split with crackling lightning bolts as the casing spread wider, opening up like an eggshell. . . .

Or a *chrysalis*.

As Koronis stared in astonishment, feeling the thoughts of all the Protoss around him swelling with terror and anticipation, his own brain reached an overload. He thought of how wonderful it had been just to take his worn shard of old Khaydarin crystal to focus his thoughts, to calm himself and meditate. But this was too much for his brain, even in the flow of the Khala, to comprehend.

The Dark Templar Xerana had warned them. She had tried to explain that this object was not simply an artifact, but the seed of a living creature, another prototype race developed through the genetic machinations of the Xel'Naga. Now he and his armies, along with the Zerg minions and the Terran military, had not succeeded in conquering it . . . but in *reviving* it.

With a squidlike form of incandescent energy barely held within a luminous organic skin, the real creature, a glorious being, emerged from the broken shards of its cocoon. It rose like a phoenix made of giant feathery wings, grasping tentacles, and blazing suns for eyes.

Koronis stood watching the wondrous beast. It looked unlike anything he had ever seen, and yet there was nothing *wrong* about it. The creature combined elements of Terran butterfly and jellyfish and sea anemone. This being had a purity of purpose that seemed to reach a pinnacle higher than either the Protoss or the Zerg, which were the Xel'Naga's other primary creations.

The awakened entity moved quickly, rising out of the shattered chrysalis and hovering over the battlefield. Koronis felt as if he were a part of it. The creature sang a telepathic melody, a song written by the long-dead Xel'Naga, infused with a throbbing resonance that felt attuned to every strand of his DNA.

But Koronis sensed that he and his Protoss were not here just as observers. This phoenix monster needed him, and it needed the Zerg. They were resources to complete its grand metamorphosis. The buried cocoon had been placed here aeons ago, growing, incubating, waiting . . . until now.

A typhoon of wind and carefully targeted lightning bolts flew around the rising creature like a fury, and it struck out in a kaleidoscope of color across the battlefield. The Protoss and the Zerg stood helpless as the Xel'Naga–spawned being flashed them all with its high-powered scanning beams, disintegrating and absorbing them, gathering up their genetics, all the thoughts and souls of these other children of the Xel'Naga. The area for miles around glowed, not with nuclear radiation, but with a seething backwash of life force.

Now more than the sum of its parts, the magnificent phoenix creature rose through the sky, tearing apart clouds and turning them hot and orange. The adult life-form ascended into space, leaving behind the destruction and the shell of its chrysalis in the blasted mountainside.

On its way it encountered the few remaining Alpha Squadron battlecruisers in orbit.

Already on edge, knowing that the ground forces had been wiped out in the titanic three-way battle around the artifact, the captain of the wounded battlecruiser *Napoleon* opened fire with a blast of his Yamato gun. Seeing the dazzling creature hurtling toward him like a hurricane, he had no time—or desire—to wait for orders from General Duke down in his command center in Free Haven.

The captains of the other battlecruisers came to the same conclusion. Yamato guns fired at the oncoming phoenix-thing, unwittingly increasing the being's biological power reservoirs. It glowed brighter, hotter. . . .

And as it swept past, the newborn entity vaporized, absorbed, and digested the Terran battleships, drinking their power, leaving only sparkling chunks of molten debris, which flash-froze in the cold vacuum of space.

Then it engulfed and absorbed the Zerg and Protoss secondary forces that had remained in reserve above the planet.

Finally sated and eager to begin its new life, the strange blazing creature departed from its aeons-long home of Bhekar Ro and soared off through the Void into the vast and unexplored gulf between the stars.

CHAPTER 43

OCTAVIA PANTED, HER LEGS TREMBLING AS SHE forced her body to keep moving. The Dark Templar Xerana insisted that she maintain the desperate pace. They had climbed the slope together, no longer fearing any outlying Zerg infestation, because all of the aliens had drawn together into the valley war zone.

Sensing imminent danger just as they crested the ridge, though, the Dark Templar struck Octavia with the full force of her long arm, knocking her to the ground. Xerana ducked under a rock outcropping, sheltering herself and Octavia as a blaze of yellow-white fire lit up the sky and then faded . . . too quickly.

Your marines have dropped their bombs, the Dark Templar said. *But the result will not be what your commander expected.*

When the light and fire began to fade, Xerana rose to her feet with Octavia beside her, and they watched from a distance as the enormous buried chrysalis cracked open and the phoenix-being hatched out of it, rose high in the air, and min-

utes later swept over the distant battlefield, absorbing everything. Octavia hoped they were far enough away from all the
other combatants.

Welcome to the universe, Xerana said as if to the risen creature, her mental voice tinged with awe.

Octavia's mind sensed a glorious freedom and fulfillment.
She now understood the presence that had been calling her for
so long, and even though she hated what this alien thing had
done to her brother Lars, she could not resist the pull of complete wonder. She had never before seen anything so beautiful
or so utterly pure. Her eyes ached from the too-white light as
the newly born luminous beast filled the valley with its incan-
descence and then eagerly shot up to vanish into the skies.

Come, Xerana said. *There is more here we need to see.*

They scrambled down the rough, steep slope. The battlefield valley itself continued to throb and glow. A strange pulsing fog crawled over the ground, like a nebulous remnant of
life force seeping out of the stones and soil, a mist made of
diamond dust. The crown of Khaydarin crystals that had surrounded the buried artifact was now pulverized and scattered
about like myriad grains of sand . . . or seeds.

The two of them reached the valley floor and moved forward together. Only minutes ago Octavia had been exhausted,
but now she felt recharged, more rested and nourished than
she had been in years. She did not mind that the tall Dark
Templar strode along at a rapid pace. Octavia bounded beside
Xerana, practically running. She saw scars from the battle, the
twisted wreckage of destroyed machines, but no corpses—not
even any splashes of blood.

Xerana, who must have picked up her thoughts, responded.
*The Xel'Naga hatchling took all the life it could touch, and with the
energy from your military's nuclear strikes, it had more life force than
it could contain. It used that energy to combine all the genetics of the
Zerg and Protoss in order to complete its maturation. Then, on its
journey outward, the new hatchling shed some of its bioenergy, leaving it here.*

Octavia bit her lip. As she looked around and saw so many wonderful things, her anger came back. "Then why did it take Lars? What possible use could that creature have for human DNA?"

Xerana seemed saddened. *Your brother was a mistake. The hatchling had no use for your Terran energy. It was asleep and still young. It did not understand what it was doing.*

So . . . Lars had died simply because he had been in the wrong place.

Not consoled by this, Octavia walked deeper into the valley, noticing a small change that grew more pronounced as minutes passed. The soil seemed springy, and she saw tendrils of grass, tiny shoots sprouting everywhere. They grew so quickly that she could actually see the plants moving, bursting up through the ground as if anxious to return an exuberance of life to scarred Bhekar Ro. She knelt on the ground and plucked a flower, which blossomed in her hand into a brilliant crimson bloom with three pointed petals.

It is life, Xerana said simply. Octavia could feel it in her eyes, her skin, her mind.

The powerful diamond mist began to dissipate, thinning to reveal a clear blue sky that seemed to reach all the way to the stars. Then, in the distance, Octavia saw several figures, people standing dazed and confused out in the middle of the burgeoning meadow.

They were human.

Octavia started forward, hesitantly at first, afraid to hope. Many of them wore the uniforms of Terran marines, but one was dressed in settlers' clothes, serviceable coveralls . . . just like the ones her brother had worn. Octavia caught her breath, unable to believe what she was seeing. She blinked.

Xerana explained, *For the final transformation, the embryo required the genetics of the other Xel'Naga children as a biological fuel. Because these Terrans were not necessary, the creature must have rejected them from the DNA matrix.*

"Lars!" Octavia shouted, then rushed forward, breathless.

She laughed. Her resurrected brother stood in the middle of a field of flowers that looked like a fireworks show of color across the grassy valley. He turned to see her, and his face lit up. She threw herself into Lars's arms. He looked confused at first, then hugged her tightly.

"Now this *is* interesting," he said in a bemused voice.

"I can't believe you're back!" she said. Octavia grabbed his shoulders, just staring at him. Her knees felt weak. After all she had been through, this seemed the most unbelievable.

"I never thought I'd be glad to get back to this place," Lars said. Octavia hugged him again.

The Dark Templar female stood alone and apart. There was nothing more for her here. She had come to see and to learn. Her warning had not been heeded, and she'd been unable to save her Protoss brothers, but perhaps that was for the best. The newly awakened phoenix creature was also part of the Xel'Naga mystery, and Xerana was glad that she had witnessed its birth.

Without a word of farewell, the Dark Templar scholar wrapped herself in shadows again, vanished from sight, and made her way back to her own ship.

Perhaps she could follow the newborn creature, or search for other sleeping embryos that had been hidden by the Xel'Naga. She had many questions to answer and much to do . . . and all the Void in which to search.

CHAPTER 44

THE OBLITERATION OF KUKULKAN BROOD FELT like a wound ripped into Sarah Kerrigan's side. The sickly light pulsing from the living walls of the hive around her seemed oppressive.

It was not so much anger at a humiliating defeat or sadness at the deaths of so many of her minions. What she felt was the loss of an ambitious dream, a loss of resources.

Only a setback . . .

So far, she had worked without rest to guide the Zerg back into a ferocious force that was destined to conquer the galaxy. This mission to confiscate the Xel'Naga artifact had been a test for her. She had wanted to demonstrate to herself that her Zerg were undefeatable, that the destruction of the Overmind had been merely a fluke. The Queen of Blades was stronger, braver, more ambitious.

Now, though, she would have to reassess her plans, redefine her goals so that the dead planet of Char blossomed into a dark flower.

The burgeoning hives generated hordes of larvae, all of which were mutated into carefully chosen configurations, minions that would fit into an overall military strategy.

Even without Kukulkan Brood, Sarah Kerrigan still had other powerful Broods—Tiamat, Fenris, Baelrog, Surtur, Jormungand. Each one was led by a different Cerebrate. Each one had a general function in the overall Zerg social structure: to command, hunt, terrorize, attack. Each one had thousands, sometimes millions of loyal Zerg minions.

Some had been decimated in the recent war that had brought Terrans, Protoss, and Zerg to the brink of oblivion. But the Queen of Blades had brought them back together again.

She decided she would not concern herself with the setback on Bhekar Ro. It did not matter. Despair was a human condition, and Sarah Kerrigan no longer considered herself human.

This was only the beginning.

Soon she would launch her Brood War.

CHAPTER 45

ACCOMPANIED BY LIEUTENANT SCOTT AND HIS surviving commandos—all of whom had also been restored in the backwash of the Phoenix-creature's birth—Octavia and Lars made their way back to Free Haven.

Inside the settlement town, General Edmund Duke seemed completely lost and alone. They found Mayor Nikolai pounding on the door of his home. "I want my office back."

A handful of marine guards continued their duties around the town, but they seemed completely bereft of goal or direction. General Duke opened the door and, ignoring the mayor, pushed past to stand out in the middle of the street.

Nik rushed back into his dwelling and began to clear the general's paraphernalia off his desk.

Alpha Squadron had been wiped out on the battlefield. Duke's battlecruisers, Wraiths, and ground troops had been destroyed, some of them during the orbital battle, most in the abortive assault against the Zerg and the Protoss near the artifact. Now, shortly after the nuclear strike and the strange unexplained events that had occurred around the buried object, he'd lost contact with his remaining ships in space. No one answered his comm signals.

He hoped they were just scattered. Perhaps a few vessels had reported directly to Emperor Mengsk. Some might come back to search for him.

But he didn't think so.

When Octavia returned with her brother, the settlers, though beaten and in shock after the war, reacted with joy to see at least one member of their colony returned alive and well. The most joyful by far, though, was Cyn McCarthy, who ran to Lars, threw her arms around him, and burst into tears. To Octavia's surprise, Lars kissed the copper-haired young woman and proposed to her on the spot—prompting a fresh wave of happy tears.

The rest of the colonists watched in a daze. So many astonishing and terrifying things had happened to them in the last few days that they did not even question the miracles they were now seeing.

Octavia's exuberance began to awaken them. "Wait until you see the valley!" she said. "It's all fertile land now, bursting with plants. We'll be able to grow any kind of crops there. I guarantee we'll have a yield higher than anything in our colony's history. It's a new chance for us, a spot of hope. We *can* get back on our feet again."

General Duke scowled at Octavia as if she were to blame. "My military force came to rescue you and now most of them are wiped out." He shouted into the office that had, until recently, been his command center. "Mayor Nikolai, I demand that you contact the Terran Dominion and request a full extraction team, battlefield analysis, and relief for my surviving men."

The mayor poked his head out the door, looking insufferably pleased with himself. He didn't seem terribly disappointed when he said, "I'm sorry, General. All of our long-range communications systems are down. They were destroyed in the attack."

General Duke growled, as if he wanted to chew on some rocks and spit out sand. "And you don't have *any* spaceports? No star-traveling technology on this rock?"

Mayor Nikolai shook his head. "We're just a fledgling colony, General. 'Simple dirt-farmers,' I think you called us."

"Clodhoppers," Octavia added. "Don't worry, I'm sure they'll come looking for you eventually."

Duke balled his fists and planted them on his hips, glaring at all the townspeople. "Well, I'm stranded here then. Now what am I supposed to do?"

"Let's be practical." Octavia reached over to the wall of one of the dwellings and picked up a long-handled hoe that was stained with Zerg blood. She shoved the farming implement into the flustered general's hands. "You can start *weeding*. We've got a lot of new arable land to cultivate."

Duke spluttered and could think of no response. Octavia gave him a wry smile. "It's easy, General. Any child can show you how to do it."

With the help of Lars and Cyn, she gathered Jon, Wes, Gregor, Kiernan, Kirsten, and a few other settlers, to lead them out to the lush, revitalized valley and show them where they could plant fresh crops. Handsome young Lieutenant Scott, looking at Octavia with undisguised interest, volunteered to accompany them. He seemed happy and relieved, as if he was tired of warfare and might prefer to settle down here. . . .

As the colonists worked together to pick up the pieces of their scarred world, Octavia sincerely hoped they would never draw outside attention again.

SPEED OF DARKNESS

TRACY HICKMAN

ABOUT THE AUTHOR

TRACY HICKMAN is a *New York Times* bestselling author best known for his *Dragonlance* series of novels coauthored with Margaret Weis. Born in Salt Lake City, Utah, in 1955, Tracy now lives and writes with his wife, Laura, in southern Utah.

To the fine men and women of the
U.S.S. Carl Vinson (CVN-70).
May God go with you as you cross the beach
and grant you calm seas on your journey home.
Vis per mare.

CHAPTER 1

DOWNFALL

GOLDEN...

That was his word for it, that rare, perfect day that warms the soul with a golden glow of joy. There was peace in a golden day.

Some days were gray, hung with leaden clouds and rain punctuated by brilliant flashes of burning white and rolling thunder. Other days were a vibrant cold blue arching over the frost-encrusted domes and sheds of the settlement. Some days were even red—the evening sky painted by the dust in the spring winds before the crops had gotten their own hold on the soil. Some days even extended into the night with a velvety cobalt blanket across the sky.

He liked those autumn nights when he could leave his world behind by staring up into that rich darkness. God had put pinpricks in the dome of the night, he imagined, so that His light could shine through. As a child he had searched the stars, hoping to see through to the other side and catch some glimpse of this Creator. He had never stopped looking, even though he had reached his nineteenth birthday and had thought himself too mature for such things.

Each day held different colors for him. He had experienced them in all their hues. Each held a memory and a place in his heart. Yet none in his experience could compare to a golden day. It was the color of the wheat fields that rolled like waves across the low hills stretching out from his father's homestead. Golden was the warmth of the sun on his face. Golden was the glow he felt within him.

Golden was the color of her hair and the sound of her voice.

"You're dreaming again, Ardo," she whispered playfully. "Come back to me. You are much too far away!"

He opened his eyes. She was golden.

"Melani, I'm right here." Ardo smiled.

"No, you aren't." She pouted—a formidable weapon in getting her way. "You're off dreaming again and you've left me behind."

He rolled onto his side, propping his head up on one elbow so that he could get a better look at her. She was just a year younger than he. Her family had arrived back when Ardo was nine years old, another group in a long line of religious refugees that fell from the sky to join with other Saints in Helaman Township.

Refugee survivors had been gathering from nearly all the planets of the Confederacy back then—reluctant pioneers of the stars. Many devout religious groups had been among the first to be outlawed by the United Powers League on Earth back in '31. It was not a new story to Saints and Martyrs. Throughout humanity's history, those who did not understand the faithful had driven them from place to place and home to home. That they should be driven from planet to planet, then star to star, was beginning to sound painfully repetitious in their Heritage classes. Now, exiles once more, families of the faithful were scattered among the ill-fated transports of the ATLAS project, and when that mission ended in such cataclysmic failure, those families who survived searched desperately for their brothers and sisters. When communication was finally established between worlds, the Patriarchs chose an outlying region on a world they called Bountiful for their new home. Soon, orbital dropships were landing at the Zarahemla Starport daily. The newly arrived families would then make their way to the outlying settlements as best they could. Arthur and Keti Bradlaw, with their wide-eyed daughter, were one of five families that arrived that day. Ardo had joined his father as the entire township came out to welcome the new families and get them settled.

Ardo could not remember much about Melani then, although he had been vaguely aware of the stick of a girl who seemed awkward, lonely, and shy. He first took real notice of her when her fourteenth year brought some rather remarkable changes. The "stick girl" seemed to burst into his awareness like a butterfly unfolding from its chrysalis. Her features held a natural beauty—body painting and makeup were frowned upon by the Patriarchs of the township—and it had been Ardo's great good fortune to have been the first to approach her. His heart and soul fell into her large, luminescent blue eyes.

The nimbus of her long, shining hair played softly in the warm breeze drifting over the wheat fields. The wind carried the distant hum of the mill and the faint scent of the bread at the bakery.

Golden.

"I may be off dreaming, but I'll never leave you behind," he said to her, smiling. The wheat rustled about the blanket where they lay. "Tell me where you want to go. I'll take you there!"

"Right now?" Her laugh was sunshine. "In your dreams?"

"Sure!" Ardo pulled himself up to kneel on the heavy blanket he had spread out for them. "Anywhere in the stars!"

"I can't go anywhere." She smiled. "I have a test in Sister Johnson's Hydroponics class this afternoon! Besides," she said more earnestly. "Why would I want to go anywhere else at all? Everything I want is right here."

Golden. Who could ever leave on such a golden day?

"Then let's not go anywhere," he said eagerly. "Let's stay here . . . and get married."

"Married?" She looked at him, half bemused and half questioning. "I told you, I have Hydroponics class this afternoon."

"No, I mean it." Ardo had been working himself up for this for some time. "I've graduated, and things are working out really well on Dad's agraplots. He said he was thinking of giving me forty acres at the far end of the homestead. It's the sweetest place, right up near the base of the canyon. There's a spot there next to the river where . . . where . . . Melani?"

The girl with the golden hair did not hear him. She sat up, her blue eyes squinting toward the township. "The siren, Ardo!"

Then he heard it, too. The distant wail, rising and falling across the fields.

Ardo shook his head. "They always sound it at noon . . ."

"But it *isn't* noon, Ardo."

The sun was eclipsed in that instant. Ardo leaped up, wheeling around toward the darkened sky. His mouth fell open as the lengthening shadow surged across the yellowed fields of wheat. Ardo's eyes went wide with the rush of fear. Adrenaline roared into his veins.

Enormous plumes of smoke trailed behind fireballs roaring directly toward him from the western end of the broad valley. Ardo quickly reached down and pulled Melani to her feet. His mind raced. They had to run, find shelter . . . But where could they go? Melani screamed, and he realized that there was nowhere to go and no place safe to hide.

The fireballs seemed so close that both of them ducked. The flames arched over them, the thunderous sound of their fury quickly drowning the distant warning siren. The shadow of their wake covered the entire valley. Five enormous columns crossed overhead, their fingers reaching over Ardo and Melani toward the clustered buildings of Helaman Township. Then the fireballs wheeled as one, lifted over the township, and descended in roiling flames into Segard Yohansen's instantly ruined fields, about a mile past the center of Helaman.

Ardo shook—whether from fear or excitement he could not tell—but at least his stupor had ended. He clasped Melani's arm and began pulling at her. "Come on! We've got to get into the town before they shut the gates! Come on!"

She needed no further urging.

They ran.

He could not remember how they got into town.

The golden day had turned a muddy brown fading to gray from the smoke that still coated the sky overhead. It was an oppressive color, slate and cold. It seemed so out of place here.

"We've got to find my Uncle Dez," he heard himself say. "He has a shop in the compound! Come on! Come on!"

Ardo and Melani struggled to move through the center of the township, now crowded with refugees. Helaman originally had been nothing but an outpost in the far reaches of Bountiful. Its town center was the original fortress compound with the defensive wall encompassing the main buildings. Since then, the town had grown well beyond those central walls. Now more than ten thousand people called Helaman their home—and nearly all of them had poured into the safety of the old fortress compound.

He could just see the sign "Dez Hardwarez" across the packed central square.

The rattle of automatic weapons clattered suddenly from the perimeter wall. Two dull explosive thuds resounded, followed by even more chattering machine guns.

A cry arose from the crowd in the square. Ardo felt more than heard the fear in the seething mob. Shouts rang out, some strident and others calming. The smoke overhead cast an oppressive veil over the surging mob.

"Please, Ardo!" Melani said, "I . . . Where do we go? What do we do?"

Ardo glanced around. He could taste the panic in the air.

"We just need to get across the square," he choked out, then, seeing the look in her eyes. "We've done it hundreds of times."

"But, Ardo—"

"It isn't any farther than it was before. Just a little more crowded, that's all." Ardo looked at the tears welling up in those beautiful blue eyes. He squeezed her hand tightly. "Don't worry. I'll be right here with you."

Somehow, they were halfway across the square when it came.

A sheet of flame erupted beyond the fortress's outer wall. Its crimson light flashed against the blanket of smoke that hung oppressively over the town. The blood-red hue electrified the panicked crowd in the square. Screams, shouts, and cries all tumbled into a cacophony of sound, but several disembodied voices penetrated Ardo's thoughts clearly.

"Where are the Confederacy forces? Where are the marines?"

"Don't argue with me! Get the children! Stay together!"

"It can't be the Zerg! They couldn't have penetrated so far into the Confederacy . . ."

Zerg? Ardo had heard rumors about them. Nightmares, so he thought, to scare children or keep outsiders from settling in the Outer Colonies. He could not remember all the whispered tales, but the nightmare was here now, and very real.

Another voice penetrated his thoughts. He turned toward her.

"Ardo, I'm frightened!" Melani's eyes were wide and liquid. "What is it? What's going on?"

Ardo opened his mouth. He could not answer her question. No words came out. There were so many words he wanted to say to her in that moment—so many words that he would regret never having said for uncounted years to come. But no words came out.

A light flared. He felt the heat on his back. He turned, holding Melani behind him.

The eastern wall had been breached. The old rampart was being pulled down from the other side, dismantled before Ardo's eyes. It seemed as though a dark wave was breaking against the breach, an undulating silhouette. Then details lodged in his mind: a gleaming purple carapace, red-streaked ivory claws sliding from a colonist's limp body, the arching, snakelike bodies writhing across the broken stone.

It was unthinkable. . . . The nightmare had come to Bountiful.

The shoulder-to-shoulder crowd in the square roared their deep fear and turned to run from the breach. There was nowhere to go. Zerg hydralisks had already crested the opposite wall, cascading into the street like black drops from a greasy spill. Within moments, hideous cobralike hoods had unfolded above their razor-sharp talons. They arched their tails upward. Armored spikes exploded from their serrated shoulder sockets and darted with deadly effect into the western edge of the crowd.

Those facing the new threat suddenly tried to reverse direction, crushing back into the surging crowd behind them.

Ardo heard Melani gasp behind him. "I can't . . . I can't breathe . . ."

The mob was crushing them. Ardo looked desperately around him, trying to find a way out.

Movement overhead caught his eye. A bloated, bulbous form like a disembodied brain drifted over the colony wall. Tendrils hung like viscera beneath it, quivering with activity. It was reaching down for the center of the crowd. Ardo had heard tales in which the Zerg had captured colonists and taken them alive to a fate that could only be worse than death.

Tears flooded Ardo's eyes. There was nowhere to go and nothing left to do.

Suddenly the Zerg overlord drifting above the colony shuddered and slid sideways. Several explosions erupted from the side of the hideous beast. The overlord exploded in an enormous fireball. The Zerg hydralisks entering the compound suddenly hesitated.

A wing of five Confederacy Wraith fighters ripped through the smoke overhead, the scream of their engines nearly drowning out the cries of the terrified crowd below. Twenty-five-millimeter burst lasers pulsed repeatedly as the Wraiths wheeled through the air, the bolts slamming against targets on the far side of the crumbling fortress wall.

One of the Wraiths wavered suddenly, then exploded under a hail of ground fire from the outraged Zerg.

The Zerg who had entered the compound were pressing their attack, killing some and dragging others off without apparent distinction. They had corralled the humans; now all they had to do was harvest them from the edges of the crowd inward.

A second flight of Wraiths tore through the smoke-blackened sky. Then a single Confederacy dropship ripped through the air, spinning in a rapid breaking maneuver and descending toward the square. The downblast from the engines created an instant hurricane on the ground. Trees bent over nearly double. It was impossible to hear anything over the roar of the engines. People all about Ardo tumbled to the ground, shielding themselves from the gale.

Ardo blinked through the dust. The dropship continued to hover but managed somehow to lower its transport ramp into the square. He could see the silhouetted figure of a Confederacy marine beckoning to them.

Everyone else in the square saw the marine also. Mindlessly they charged the ramp. A human tide pulled Ardo along.

He lost Melani's hand.

"Melani!" he screamed. He tried to fight against the crushing press of the panicked crowd. His words were lost in the roar of the dropship's engines. "Melani!"

He saw her behind him. The Zerg were pressing their attack

with anger now. The dropship was depriving them of their prize. Ardo was appalled at how quickly the large crowd had been sundered—harvested like blood-red wheat in the field. The Zerg were already nearly at Melani's side.

Ardo clawed and fought. He screamed.

Three hydralisks grasped Melani at once, dragging her back from the edge of the crowd.

"Please, Ardo!" she wept. "Don't leave me alone!"

The mindless mob pushed him farther into the ship.

Zerg claws suddenly rang against the sides of the dropship. The pilot had played out all the time his luck would afford. The ship responded instantly to his command, lurching upward away from the Zerg and bearing Ardo away from his home, his life, and his love.

"Don't leave me alone!" Those were her last words to him, pounding through his mind and soul, louder and louder, threatening to burst his skull . . .

Ardo's world went black. It would stay black for a very long time.

CHAPTER 2

MAR SARA

"ALL RIGHT, YOU RAW MEAT! HANG ON TO YOUR asses! We're takin' the long fall!"

Private Ardo Melnikov did not bother to glance at the sergeant as he barked at them. The man was a tic—temporarily in command—for this drop. Odds were that Ardo would never see the man once they were down. It was best to just stay out of the man's way until Ardo's new platoon was sorted out for the mission. He could barely hear the tic above the screaming engines of the dropship and the thunder of their hot descent buffeting the hull. There was just something about the sergeant that seemed to require a full voice and an angry eye. In any event, it really did not matter to Ardo—the sergeant was just baby-sitting them down to the surface. Once he got there, Ardo knew there would be someone who would make his life miserable on a more permanent basis.

Ardo shrugged his shoulders, trying to lift his back away from the wall pad. The interior of the dropship was normally a hot box, but most especially during the plunge down through the atmosphere. This particular dropship was at least two cooling units shy of keeping everyone comfortable. Now a growing patch of sweat was sticking his shoulder blades to the nonporous cushion. Sweat beaded up on his face and occasionally dropped down the front of his fatigues. The restraining bar prevented him from finding any relief from the pooling discomfort gathering at various junction points of his uniform.

Worse yet, the dropship was fully loaded—packed shoulder to shoulder and bulkhead to bulkhead. The heat was not nearly so oppressive as the growing smell that was overwhelming the air scrubbers.

There was nothing for him to look at except the same slack and blank faces of the other marine recruits strapped against the bulkhead across from him. There was nothing for him to listen to except the sergeant's occasional growl and the uniform roar of the hull behind him. There was nothing for him to do but wait it out with his own thoughts . . . and that was the last thing he wanted.

They haunted him, those thoughts lurking at the back of his mind. It seemed to him sometimes that the ghosts pursued him from inside his own head. Closing his eyes never banished those specters. No sound could drown them out for long. Those ghosts were all painfully bright and beautiful, terrible and crushing. They would wait quietly, patiently at the edge of his conscious thought, kept at bay by his will alone. Sometimes he would be arrogant enough to think he had them mastered and banished once and for all. Then some smell of ripening grass or plowed earth would waft past him on a breeze, or a glint of the color of light honey, or a distant whispered laugh, or some indefinable quality of his surroundings, and the demons would rush back, overwhelming him.

He would have bled tears just at the thought of them if he could.

All he wanted was to fight. He needed to fight. It was the only thing that really kept the demons at bay. He could concentrate on the mission and its objectives . . . or at least those minor objectives that his commander deemed necessary for him to know. Grand strategy was not his purview. It was none of his business. His job was to do whatever he was told to do and with as little thought as necessary. That suited him just fine.

The howling of the dropship was tapering off. The vehicle had finally spent its energy against the atmosphere of whatever world they were plunging toward. The engines were doing their best now to make the ship imitate the grace of a bird in flight. Ardo chuckled to himself at the thought. The Quantradyne APOD-33 was the Confederacy's proof to the stars that anything with a big enough engine would fly—no matter how badly. Of course, he had made many training jumps before. Each was completely unremarkable and he really did not care to recall them in any detail.

Why reflect on something so painful as time to be still and think?

Better to concentrate on something else . . . anything else. Ardo began scanning the faces of the marines around him. It was an exercise in self-preservation. It was always a good idea to know the marines around you. You never knew when your life might depend on one of them . . . or be threatened by one.

The woman sitting across from him seemed to be a good example of one kind or the other—it was just that Ardo was not all that sure of which. She had close-cropped blond hair that stood in neat bristles from a well-shaped scalp. Her face was drawn tight, with angular cheekbones that sharply framed two shining, steel-tinged eyes. They stared unfocused at some distant point past Ardo's shoulder, unblinking yet shuttered windows into any soul she might possess. *Those eyes could freeze a river solid in midsummer,* he thought. He was left to his own imagination as to what the rest of her looked like. The powered combat suit she wore effectively hid any physical distinction she might otherwise have displayed, but it did tell him one thing: her suit markings were that of an officer.

That meant danger to a private no matter how you cut it. Avoidance of an officer is the first thing a private learns—especially in casual conversation. The last private he could remember being too familiar with his squad leader ended up with a hole where his head had been.

The female officer had not said a word since they boarded the dropship. She was perfectly welcome to let her silence continue as far as Ardo was concerned. *Speak when spoken to,* he thought. *Otherwise, do not go looking for trouble.*

At least *she* was comfortable, Ardo thought. Her suit was self-cooling, and he could see the power umbilical plugged into the dropship's power bus. Ardo suspected that her chill went well beyond the physical. Someday he, too, would learn the intricate skills necessary to wear the CMC-300—maybe even the new 400 model. That day was a long way off, of course. Still, it would be a lot better to wear in combat than a few layers of ablative cloth and one's standard-issue underwear. If he could just manage to live long enough to get a combat suit of his own, his prospects would improve considerably.

Well, hopefully they would at least give him some training in a weapon. He had not even had the chance to do that yet.

The rest of the compartment was filled with grunts just like himself. Each of them wore the standard-issue detached look of a Confederacy Security Marine. Each of them dripped Confederacy sweat through their Confederacy fatigues, as was their duty.

Ardo's eye fell for a time, however, on one particularly large private. The man was enormous—Ardo remembered the prep crew had some trouble getting his harness to lock closed—and he would not stop his incessant yammering for a moment. Ardo could not imagine where they had found a uniform that would fit him. He was dark complexioned, and Ardo vaguely recalled the ancient United Powers League back on Earth had once qualified the man as "South Seas Islander." He had broad, angular features and full lips. His hair was a long mane that flowed back from his forehead and down his neck in natural black waves. The giant was gung-ho certifiable—one of those all-for-the-wall, eat-their-hearts-for-breakfast psychotics who was the first person you would want to come and pull you out of the fire and the last person you would want to follow into one.

"Get this junkwad on the ground!" The giant laughed beneath his bright eyes. "I've got some death to deal out! Want to roast me some Zerg on a spit! Maybe eat their brains straight off!"

The islander threw his head back and laughed too loudly once more. He slapped his massive hands down on the thighs of the two marines sitting next to him. They both winced so hard from the impact that tears pooled in their eyes.

"We'll eat them for dinner, eh? Big Zerg feast! Ha! Just put this flying trashyard on the ground before I open it myself!"

The pilot in the sealed cockpit forward of the dropbay could not possibly have heard the request but seemed willing just the same to accommodate it. The ship pivoted noticeably—Ardo knew this was a standard clearing maneuver just before landing—and the engines whined a little differently. A final bump, and the engines suddenly spindled down.

The lieutenant in front of Ardo wasted no time unplugging herself from the dropship power, managing to get herself free before the restraining bar had lifted completely out of the way. A deft move with her free hand brought her duffel bag down from the overhead racks. She was already moving toward the ramp as it began lowering at the back of the ship. She even beat the islander, who seemed to be in his own hurry to get into whatever fight he could either find or manufacture.

Ardo took his time, tugging at his fatigues to pull them free of each of the places sweat had stuck them to his body. He could smell the change in the atmosphere already blowing in through the open ramp. An achingly dry breeze swept the musty dampness out of the compartment like a furnace. He pulled his own duffel bag from the racks and followed the others as they straggled out the back of the dropship.

"Get your asses out here, ladies," the sergeant snarled. "We haven't got all day!"

The air was oven-hot and dry—drier than Ardo ever remembered breathing. A stiff breeze carried the furnace heat around him. His sweat evaporated almost at once as he stepped onto the tarmac of the spaceport.

Ardo glanced grimly around.

He had stepped into hell.

The world was a rusting red, colored by the sand that seemed to add its own tint to every building and vehicle regardless of its original color. The effect was all the more enhanced by the flaming dawn just breaking over the starport . . .

Or what was left of the starport. Nearly half of the seven launch control towers originally scattered around the sprawling installation were on fire. Two of them were crested only with broken rubble. Columns of smoke from various other fires could be seen rising from buildings of the starport itself. More telling, larger columns could be seen rising from the central city district of the colony several miles beyond.

It was then that Ardo heard the sound—an all too familiar sound. Drifting toward him on the breeze, he heard the cries, the anguish, the panic.

He turned sharply. On the opposite side of the field, just short of the embarkation pads, he could see the cordon of marines surrounding the Confederacy section of the starport and the panicked mob beyond.

No!

The memories flooded over him. He stood in the colony square once more. The sounds of it filled his mind. Their cries . . . *her* cries . . .

"Don't leave me alone!" she wept.

Someone shoved Ardo hard from behind. His training took over, and he tumbled deftly before rising quickly to his feet, his hands prepared to defend and attack.

"Quit stalling, you maggot-wipe," the drop sergeant snapped. "What are you waiting for—an official welcome?

Get over to the barracks for training. You're needed on the double!"

Ardo dreaded the barracks more than any other thing in his life. There was something about them that repulsed him, that shook him to his very soul whenever he just heard the word. Ardo was slightly dazed, but he knew better even as he said, "No, Sergeant, I can't . . ."

The sergeant simply knocked him down again.

"Welcome to Mar Sara, marine! Now move!"

He moved. Gathering up his kit, Ardo joined the rest of the group from his dropship as they made their way toward the barracks at the edge of the tarmac. He had the distinct impression of swimming against the current: everyone else on the base was moving out toward the pads. "Looks like we're the cleanup crew," Ardo muttered to himself, trying not to think about the inevitability of what was coming next. He kept his eyes to the ground, refusing to look at the box-like mobile barracks unit even as he was walking up into its interior. He looked up only when he was inside, standing with the others in rough rows in the cramped deployment room at the top of the access ramp.

The tic was still there with them, mothering them with his unique touch every step of the way. "You know the drill, boys and girls. Drop your gear and strip . . . then right back here, people!"

Ardo felt a wave of nausea wash over him. There was nothing he hated more than the barracks and there was nothing in the barracks he hated more than what they were about to force on him. He told himself that it was all part of the job, but it did not make the fact of it any less revolting to him.

Ardo herded into the adjoining barracks room—like cattle into a slaughter chute, he thought, shuddering—and found an empty bunk. Whoever had called this place home ahead of him had apparently left in a hurry. Odd bits of trash remained strewn about the bedding and the floor. Ardo thought that the tic outside probably would not have approved of such sloppy behavior. With a sigh, the young marine began peeling off his sweat-stained shirt. He tried not to notice the others around him as they undressed. There were both men and women present—the Confederacy Marines were perfectly willing to allow both sexes to die for their missions—but Ardo was always deeply ashamed of being naked in front of men, let alone women. Young and inexperienced, he found it achingly upsetting every time he was so casually required to strip, and more than once he had been the source of considerable amusement to the other marines.

Ardo shivered as he stepped back into the deployment room. The dry heat was rapidly cooling the sweat still on his back. He felt physically sick. He knew what was coming next.

He tried to distract himself by glancing at the others around the room. He would barely admit to himself that his motives in doing so were more than a little tainted with puerile curiosity. The majority of those present were men, he noted—in fact, an unusually high number. He had even briefly wondered what that lieutenant would look like once taken out of her battle armor. Ardo was somewhat surprised to note that she was not among them. Was she somehow exempt from this indignity?

Two large guards with stunners were standing next to the tic. Between them, a single hatchway led into the darkened room beyond. Ardo closed his eyes, trying to calm down. The tic was reading from a hand display.

". . . Alley . . . Bounous . . ."

Ardo could not think for the pounding in his head.

". . . Mellish . . . Melnikov . . ."

Ardo took several steps forward at the sound of his name and then froze. His feet refused to move any closer to the terrifying, darkened doorway. His eyes locked on the passage beyond. Rows of man-size tubes, each filled with a blue-green liquid, lined each side of the passageway.

"Melnikov, what the hell . . . ?"

They would pack him in one of those tubes and as soon as they did the nightmare would begin.

"Melnikov!"

It was like a coffin . . . a nightmare in a coffin.

He could not move. The two guards had seen it many times before. They stepped forward casually and, as roughly as possible, helped Ardo into the darkness.

He was falling and there was no end. He did not know how he had gotten here. Was he here at all or was he somewhere else . . . someone else? He struggled to concentrate on the images and memories that were drifting past his mind, but he could not find a way to grasp them. He would reach for them, desperate to examine them, but they would fall apart like bubbles of air under water as he tried to hold them.

Bubbles of air . . .

He could breathe the water. The long clear tube was filled with the breathable water. He had tried to be brave, really he had, but in the end he had panicked and screamed and disgraced himself. They did not care, for they had seen it a thousand thousand times before. Their rough hands clamped the headpiece firmly on him and pushed him down into the tube and spun shut the seals. "We'll have to make an adjustment in this one," he heard one of them say. He held his breath as long as he could . . .

As long as he could . . . what?

What was he thinking? Why was he thinking?

Hair the color of wheat fields dancing in the summer sun. There was a golden day . . .

His hands slammed against the sides of the clear tube as his last gasp escaped his lungs. The implants charged suddenly in the headpiece and his mind exploded into a million shards.

Shards tumbled around him. Bubbles of shards.

Combat suit school. How could he have forgotten? His instructor was an old marine named Carlyle. They spent weeks there perfecting his technique—or was it months? The combat suit was like an old friend. He seemed to have lived with one all his life . . .

The combat suit. Where was that? When was that? During the seminary class? There was Brother Gabittas teaching about the fall of the ancients and the sin of pride. Peace comes from within, a joyful knowledge of the pure voice of God speaking to each man. "Thou shalt not kill," he says, but he raises an AGR-14 gauss rifle in the front of the class.

"Here, Ardo," the brother says, walking to where the boy sat near the back of the classroom. He hands the 8-millimeter automatic weapon to the young boy who has not been paying attention. "Do unto others," he says as the boy takes the weapon.

The boy drifts away in the bubble but the weapon remains, smooth and seductive. Magnetic acceleration of the projectile to supersonic speeds with enormous kinetic punch utilizing a variety of jacketless slugs from depleted uranium to steel-tipped infantry rounds. Another old friend from long ago, the rifle turns itself inside out, explodes, and then reassembles into the face of his father.

"You'll always be my son," the old man says, with a single tear coursing down his cheek. The family agrafarm stretches beyond him in the sunset. "No matter where you go or what you do . . . you'll always be my son."

Am I? Will I?

Ardo was feeling better now. He had been disoriented when he first came out of the resocialization tanks, but he was clear-headed now.

He always felt better wearing his combat suit. It was an older CMC-300 model, but he didn't mind. He had been using a 300 for years now, and it fit him just fine.

Ardo stood packed shoulder to shoulder with other marines. There were some firebats as well as regulars in the ready room. In the little space he had, he checked the power connection between his gauss rifle and the combat suit. He loved that rifle; it was his weapon of choice. He had been firing a gauss rifle for nearly as many years as he had been working with the combat suit.

Ardo looked up. The "go" lamp over the exit hatch had just turned from red to green. A roar went up from the marines as the door slid open in an instant.

He hated to leave, though.

He sure loved the barracks.

CHAPTER 3

OUT COUNTRY

ARDO WAS ONE OF A TIDE OF MARINES POURING uniformly from the barracks and into a world of chaos.

A company of marines in power armor had formed a perimeter around the Confederacy section of the starport, cordoning off the military units. Beyond them, Ardo could see as he quick-marched across the tarmac, literally thousands of colonists pressed against the marine line. Men, women, and children—a screaming mass of humanity—struggled desperately for a way off the planet.

Beyond them, the civilian side of the starport was in anarchy. All down the flight line, perhaps as many as a hundred orbital spacecraft were either clawing their way up from the surface or hovering in anticipation of launch. At least twice that number moved listlessly beyond the outer markers, the daylight glinting off their polished hulls. There was a sense of desperation in their movements. Control seemed to have been abandoned. Ships attempted to take off and land at will. Several transports hovered near the terminal building, searching for a place to put down, but the panicked mob would not, or could not, move out of the way. The still-burning wreckage of at least half a dozen ships lay strewn about the port complex. Those pilots still flying apparently paid them little heed. Like moths to a flame, they were drawn by the exorbitant ransoms they could charge anyone who managed to board. Fearful for the safety of themselves and their ships, they wanted to get in and out as quickly as possible.

If everyone is trying so hard to get out *of here, why did the Confederacy work so hard to get me* in *here?* Ardo wondered. The terribly uncomfortable, gnawing cold below his stomach reasserted itself. *I don't know these people. I don't even really know what world I'm on! What am I doing here?*

He knew his assigned transport—yet another dropship—and found himself dashing toward it with two squads of marines. Each individual knew where he or she was supposed to report. So it was that their squad formed up almost as if by some magnetic magic. Ardo found himself jogging behind that female lieutenant he had seen the day before. Next to him was the huge, dark islander in perhaps the largest powered armor suit Ardo had ever seen. He recognized it as a CMC-660 Heavy Combat Suit, complete with plasma generator tanks on the back. So the large islander was a firebat, Ardo thought: one of those plasma flame-throwing units that were occasionally as dangerous to their operators as they were to the enemy. Several others followed as well, including a single technician in a set of light fatigues. Where was *he* going, Ardo thought. On vacation?

The roar of the orbitals constantly lifting from the surrounding pads did not deter the enthusiasm of the dropship pilot, nor did it entirely drown out his shrill words.

"Step right up, boys and girls, young and old!" he screeched, punching out the words in carnival-huckster style. "Come see the greatest show in the universe! See the local colonists run for their lives! See the government collapse before your very eyes! Witness feats of panic never before attempted by civilized man! Right this way!"

Ardo made his way toward the dropship. The crackle of automatic gauss fire ripped through the air near the marine cordon. Ardo winced, trying not to think of what it meant.

"Cutter!" the lieutenant barked when they arrived at the ramp leading into the ship.

"Ma'am!" the hulking islander piped up.

"Get these drip-dry recruits loaded in five minutes." Her command voice carried even over the din of the riot that was taking place all around them. "We've got a job to do. I'll sort them out once we get on station."

"Yes, ma'am! You heard the lady! Make a line!"

The small group fell in. Cutter begin making his way down the line, making sure everyone had their gear set for transport.

The pilot leaned against the landing strut of the dropship, and grinned.

"Okay, ladies!" Cutter was enjoying himself. "Take your places inside. Let's go!"

Ardo pulled up his kit and moved forward, suspiciously eyeing the nose art painted on the side of the ship. *"Valkyrie Vixen?"*

"That's right, friend," the pilot answered smugly. "They say once you've had a Valkyrie, you'll never ride another! You've come to the right place . . . or the wrong place, if you take my drift." The slim pilot had the most outrageous hair that Ardo had ever seen. Brilliant blue spikes radiated away from his head in sharp cones, the areas between them shaved bald with precision care. His gaunt frame seemed to radiate all arms and legs, a scarecrow in a flight suit with a mischievous smile that seemed to wind halfway around his head. "Tegis Marz is the name. I'm the Angel of Death for you boys out on the periphery. Happy to serve you. You need anything—including a proper butt-saving—and I'm the man to call."

"It's a death trap, and I'm not getting on it."

Tegis turned toward the voice coming from just down the line behind Ardo. It was the technician. Ardo could not remember seeing him on the transport down to the surface; the guy must have been here longer than that.

"I can't even look at it!" said the man in fatigues. He had a slender build but was smooth-faced and sported his hair close-cropped. The guy was so clean he probably squeaked when he walked. "This piece of abandoned trash isn't even up to being *called* abandoned trash!"

Tegis stood away from the landing strut and growled menacingly. "You piece of dog puke! This ship is a thing of beauty! There's not another one like her in the entire fleet!"

"That's because the *rest* of the fleet is at least in *some* state of reasonable repair!"

"You take that back, Marcus!"

"In your dreams, Tegis!"

"You're getting on this ship right now!"

"Not if it was the last ship off this rock! I'd stand a better chance flapping my arms off a cliff than in that hurtling death trap. When you gonna grow up and get yourself a *real* ship?"

With an outraged cry, Tegis lunged at the technician. They tumbled to the ground, rolling as each pounded the other. Red dust kicked into the air around them as they fought; a blur of arms and legs. A pair of alley cats would have been hard-pressed to put up a more vicious fight.

Ardo stood there, dumbfounded. It was almost laughable.

Cutter waded into the fight and pulled the two combatants apart. "Mister Jans, I believe the lieutenant told you to get your gear on board. I think *now* would be a good time to do it."

The red-faced technician continued to claw the air in the direction of the dropship pilot. Cutter gave him a strong shake that should have loosened the man's teeth.

"Wouldn't it?" Cutter reiterated.

Marcus Jans quit struggling. "Yes. I believe it would."

Cutter turned toward Tegis Marz. The tips of the pilot's hair spikes were still quivering with rage. "And don't you have a ship to fly?"

"Yeah," Tegis replied, still seething. "And a damn fine ship, too!"

"Then, respectfully, *sir*, maybe you had better go fly it," Cutter's smile was so full of teeth that it looked like he might eat the next person who disagreed with him. "I've got a reason to be here and I don't want anyone between me and where I'm going. And right now, you are standing *in my way . . . sir*."

Tegis went slack. "I . . . I'll just get this *fine piece of machine* off the ground for you, then."

"You do that, sir. Thank you, sir," Cutter said, pushing each of them apart as he let them go. Staggering slightly, each of the former combatants found a great deal of interest in the ground at his feet as they moved off to take care of business elsewhere.

Ardo let out his breath in a sigh.

"What about you, soldier," Cutter said, turning his dark eyes toward Ardo for the first time. "You gonna get in my way?"

"No, sir," Ardo replied, regretting that he had not managed to avoid the large islander's attention longer. "I'm definitely staying out of your way, sir."

The big man grinned again. There was something both devilishly playful and at the same time dangerous in that smile. "No, friend, I'm not a 'sir.'" The gloved hand he extended was enormous. "PFC Fetu Koura-Abi, but everyone just calls me Cutter."

"PFC Ardo Melnikov," he responded, grateful that the active feedback in his glove managed to dampen what might have otherwise been a crippling handshake. "Pleased to know you."

"You're lying." Cutter grinned malevolently.

"Almost," Ardo replied.

The big man threw his head back and laughed heartily. "Fair enough! Grab your kit. I want to get out to where I can burn something! Did you enjoy the show?"

Ardo picked up his kit and began making his way up the

dropship's ramp. "What? Oh, you mean the pilot and that tech?"

"Sure!" Cutter replied, carrying his own duffel bag easily over his shoulder with one hand. "It's always fun to watch brothers go at it. The best times I had were with my own brothers . . ."

Ardo turned. "You mean . . . those two are . . ."

"It's obvious." Cutter smiled, giving Ardo a playful shove back into the jump harness that nearly knocked the wind out of him. "You can't hide the blood between brothers."

Suddenly Cutter shuddered. Ardo could see some dark thought pass over the big man's face. With a sudden cry, Cutter reached out and grabbed the sealing ring for Ardo's helmet, pulling the man's face near his own. "That's why I'm here, Melnikov. My own brothers are out there on this ball of red dust working the waterfarms in the Out Country. I will find them, Melnikov, or I will avenge them with hell's own fire! You understand me, Melnikov? You going to get in my way, Melnikov?"

Ardo calmly returned Cutter's twitching stare.

Eye for an eye, Ardo thought. Then, *Love them that hate you.*

"Ardo," he replied quietly. "You can call me Ardo, if you like."

Cutter's cheek muscles twitched. "What?"

"My name is Ardo. I hope you'll let me call you Cutter, because I don't think I caught your full name the first time."

Cutter relaxed his grip. A smile played on his lips. "Sure, Ardo. I like you. You can call me Cutter, friend. So, I guess you *are* behind me, eh?"

As far behind you as possible, Ardo thought, but aloud he said, "All the way, Cutter."

The hydraulics suddenly whined. The aft ramp was closing quickly. Cutter loosed his grip, regained his huge Cheshire Cat grin, and stepped back against the opposite wall. He was just struggling into his own drop harness when the lieutenant stepped back into their personnel bay.

"All right, listen up," she said in a solid alto voice. "I am Lieutenant L. Z. Breanne. I'm your commanding officer for this mission."

"Ooh! How about that, boys, we got a mission!"

Lieutenant Breanne continued, her voice level and authoritative: "We don't have a lot of time, people. I've given our drop coordinates to the pilot and we should be on station at the LZ in about thirty minutes.

"Fifteen days ago, outland colonist stations began going silent. Initial investigations resulted in lost recon squads. A subsequent reconnaissance-in-force ten days ago confirmed that this planet has been infested with what we now call the Zerg . . ."

"Zergs, boys!" Alley smiled.

"Pardon, ma'am, but what's a Zerg?" Mellish sniffed.

"A new species of alien life-form. We don't know too much about them at this point . . ."

"Bring on the barbecue!" Cutter chattered.

Breanne ignored them for the time being. "Given the planetwide saturation of these Zerg—whatever they are—the Confederacy has determined to withdraw its assets from Mar Sara—"

"Hey, the Confederacy is hauling its 'assets' out!" Marcus snorted.

Laughter rolled around the cabin.

"Stow it, Jans, or I'll put you in a bag myself." Lieutenant Breanne meant it, and there was not a person in the compartment who thought otherwise. "Our mission is threefold: first, hold the forward bunker position at three-nine-two-seven in support of the Confederacy evacuation; second, recon enemy activity forward of that position, and, finally, pick up a little bauble that command lost along the way. That's all."

"Uh, Lieutenant," Cutter asked. "What kind of . . . bauble?"

"You'll know when I see it, Cutter," Breanne said. "On board you'll find a scanner plug-in for your armor. It has been precalibrated to acquire the target. I don't know what the target is, and you don't really care. But if we *do* find it, it's our ticket off this rock. I'll give you more once we've got the position secure. That's all."

Lieutenant Breanne turned and took her place in her own jump harness. Once again, Ardo found himself opposite the woman, now his commander.

"Begging your pardon, Lieutenant," Ardo asked. The engines of the dropship were spinning up.

"What is it, soldier?" Breanne looked at him with those steel-cold eyes.

"You said we were here to cover the evac of the Confederacy personnel and equipment?"

"Yes, that's part of the mission," she replied over the increasing noise.

"What about the colonists?" Ardo called out over the roar. "Are we here to cover the evacuation of the colonists, too?"

If Breanne had a response, she did not bother to give it. Perhaps the engine noise was now just too great. Perhaps she simply had no answer to give him.

Ardo settled back once more into the jump harness and dreaded the next thirty minutes. He closed his eyes for a moment and could see in his mind the ruins of Mar Sara's starport receding below. Through the roar shaking the hull he could have sworn he heard the cries of the thousands below him desperate to escape.

He thought he saw Melani's face among them.

CHAPTER 4

LITTLEFIELD

ARDO FLEW OVER A WORLD OF RUST. THE SHEER faces of the distant mountains were rust. The crags that cut into the earth were rust. Even the outskirts of the settlement city were coated with a layer of rust. Only days ago, those buildings were occupied, and the fine dust that blew across the arid world was diligently kept at bay. Now the world itself was taking no time in reclaiming the surface as its own.

All of this, Ardo experienced vicariously through his combat suit. He was plugged into the dropship's main power bus, which also transmitted to him a continuous stream of data that Ardo could configure in any way that he liked. He had switched the sensor system over to external, and instantly the ship had vanished around him. He soared above the landscape alone, the internal display system automatically masking out the dropship around him and everyone inside it. He was a bird sailing the hot plasma fire that trailed behind him.

The outskirts of the central city fell quickly behind. Below was a wasteland, cratered and scarred black from the battles that had preceded him here. The scattered carnage of desperate struggles dotted the shattered land. The occasional hulks of Vulture hover-cycles and hundreds of civilian transports formed twisted, black-metal flower petals here and there.

Ardo sailed through the sky above it all and wondered at it. Where were the siege tanks, the mobile artillery, the Goliath assault walkers? Everything he could see below him was strictly light armaments and local militia trash.

More important, where were they deploying if the battle below had already been lost? Ardo looked ahead. His flight was slowing as he descended toward an outpost bunker complex and the landing zone just inside its perimeter.

"Get your head out, marine," the sharp voice of Lieutenant Breanne sounded through his com-system. "It's time to disembark."

The dropship materialized around him almost at once as his attention shifted. The lieutenant was staring coolly into his faceplate.

"Yes, ma'am," Ardo responded sharply. "Ready, ma'am!"

Lieutenant Breanne gave no more acknowledgment than a moment's look into Ardo's eyes and then turned to address the squad. Her voice cut across the whine of the engines. "We're here for a reason, boys and girls! Let's get the job done and get out. Is that clear?"

"Ma'am! Yes, ma'am!" they all barked as one.

"You have ten minutes from touchdown to find your bunk and stow your gear. You will then report to me outside the command bunker for immediate deployment." Lieutenant Breanne extended two fingers together as she indicated the marines around her. "Cutter, Wabowski, both of you will prep firebat cat-five. The rest of you prep for recon-in-force, cat-three configuration."

Ardo ran through the category-3 checklist in a moment:

power armor, Impaler gauss rifle with infantry loads, no field pack . . . fast on their feet and ready for anything. It also meant they would not be going too far from the encampment. Sounded like a pleasant afternoon after all.

Lieutenant Breanne paused a moment as she looked down the bay, filled with the members of her squad. Ardo wondered what the lieutenant was thinking.

"Be a minute late, you won't be breathing after two. Clear?"

"Ma'am! Yes, ma'am!"

The dropship lurched suddenly, landing hard. The lieutenant snatched a handhold instantly, then snapped shut her suit visor.

She had cleared the lowering exit ramp before it even touched the ground.

Ardo tried to move through the barracks hatch, but he felt so confused. He couldn't seem to concentrate very well on even simple tasks. His duffel bag got caught somewhere on the other side of the frame as he tried to enter the barracks. His face flushed red from the tittering laughter that rolled around the double rows of bunks. It spurred him to try harder, but his anger and embarrassment just managed somehow to keep him from turning the bag the right way. His mind seemed caught in some kind of a terrible loop—understanding what he was doing wrong but somehow not being able to correct it.

"Easy, soldier," said an older marine from his top bunk. "Let me give you a hand with that."

"Don't trouble yourself, mister," Ardo grumbled. Some part of him was sure the old man just meant to embarrass him further.

The older marine snorted, then rolled out of his bunk. "Look, kid, it's no trouble at all. Sometimes you just gotta let things slack off a little and they work themselves out. You're just trying too hard."

The marine gently rested his hand on Ardo's arm.

Ardo snatched back his arm angrily. The power armor protected his elbow as it slammed against the metal wall and left a rather sizable dent, but the shock of it numbed his arm. The duffel bag fell with a jumbled clank to the floor.

The older marine shook his head and smiled. Ardo could barely see the man through his own dizzying pain and embarrassment. He had iron-gray hair in long, unkempt strands, and the faint grizzle of a beard. Piercing dark eyes looked out of a scarred and twisted face. Ardo guessed that the man was in his late thirties, although the ravages of his face made that only a guess. That twisted face continued to smile at Ardo, however, putting his two hands up in front of him, palms out, in a sign of surrender. Then, slowly, the man reached through the hatchway, drew the bag into the compartment, and set it down in front of Ardo.

"Easy, brother," he said. "Looks like you're fresh out of the resoc tank. They can scramble your head up pretty good for a while."

Ardo merely nodded sullenly. The electric feeling was subsiding in his elbow.

"Jon Littlefield," the marine said as he extended his large, callused hand. "Glad to meet you, brother."

Ardo blinked. Something in the back of his mind screamed at him from a distance, but he could not understand what it was saying. The thought of being called "brother" somehow made him dizzy.

The memories bounded and rebounded within his mind in a bewildering cascade.

"Brother Melnikov!" His youth leader smiled brilliantly in the dawning light . . .

His father's voice: "All are brothers in God's eyes, son. Brothers do not kill brothers . . ."

"Brother?" Ardo blinked as he spoke, trying to steady himself.

"Sure." Jon sniffed. "We're all brothers here—brothers in arms, brothers in combat. Face it, recruit, all we've got out here is each other."

Melani's receding face, twisted in horror as the Zerg dragged her bleeding to the grass of the square.

"Yes . . . of course," Ardo said, his eyes looking down at the deck. "We're all we've got."

Jon Littlefield deftly picked up the bag and tossed it onto the bunk beneath his own. "Don't you worry, son. I've been 'on the quick' for most of my life as a marine. Stick with me, boy, and you'll do all right. We'll straighten out your head and you'll be feeling better in no time."

Ardo stared blankly at Jon Littlefield. If Littlefield was in his early thirties, then the man was old . . . older than any marine he remembered seeing. He had seen older men before, of course, back on Bountiful. The Patriarchs of the colony were all gray-haired elders. He remembered that they all seemed so wise. It had been comforting at the time to have leaders who had survived so long. They had wisdom of their own instead of borrowed from someone else. Now that he thought about it, Littlefield was about the oldest man he had seen among the marines who was anything less than a colonel.

"Old at thirty" was not on any of the recruiting posters.

What do I care? Ardo thought. *I didn't join up for the retirement plan. I owe the Zerg for what they did, and if I get my payback before they take me, all the better.*

Cutter deftly squeezed his enormous frame through the hatch. His bulk nearly filled the space between Ardo and Littlefield.

"Well, Sergeant Littlefield!" Cutter's sarcasm and disdain were evident in his tone as he looked down on the older marine. "Wasn't that *Captain* Littlefield when we last served together, *sir*?"

Ardo was shocked for a moment that a private would be so disrespectful of an officer, even a noncommissioned one.

Jon apparently chose to simply ignore the obvious insult as he smiled back his response. "It's nice to see you in my squad, Private. You'd all better get on the quick now. Lieutenant Breanne has a bee up her butt and won't stop until she's spilled a little blood on one side or the other. You've got the config, so let's get prepped and get out!"

CHAPTER 5

MISSION ELAPSED TIME

THE WIND WHIPPED ACROSS THE CRAGGY, DESO-
late landscape. Ardo could almost feel the grains of sand
digging into the joints of his Powered Combat Suit. There
was no help for it. The squad was at attention. If he even
contemplated making a move, Ardo felt sure that Lieutenant Breanne would make it his last.

Even though the combat suit carefully controlled his body
temperature to keep it at its peak performance, he felt a rivu-
let of sweat start to make its way between his shoulder blades
toward the hollow of his back. Maybe Sergeant Littlefield was
right. Maybe something was still scrambled in his head after
his resoc back at the starport. He was having a little trouble concentrating, and there was a sense of foreboding that
seemed to hover just at the edge of his conscious thoughts. His
father had often called such notions the "promptings of the
Spirit," that still, small voice that came to men to give them
divine direction. "Heed that voice," his father had said, "and it
will never lead you wrong."

Where was that warning Spirit when the Zerg had torn his parents apart limb by limb?

A sharp, blinding pain shot through the back of his right eye. Ardo winced as a wave of nausea followed. The image of spraying his breakfast hash across his battlesuit visor flitted across his mind. *Littlefield said it would pass,* Ardo thought as he struggled to regain his mental balance. *Just hang on for a moment and it will be all right.*

He tried, instead, to concentrate on Lieutenant Breanne. She stood before them, the polarized field of her bubble helmet deliberately turned down so that everyone could see her face clearly as she spoke. Everyone in the squad faced rigidly forward. No one wanted to risk catching her eye as she strode before them.

"With everyone pulling out, they're sending us in, my beauties," her voice sounded before them, only slightly distorted by the helmet she wore. Aural directional enhancers in the suits made both transmitted and external sounds seem to come from the direction of their source. "The entire Confederacy force is jumping off the surface of this rock."

But what of the colonists? Ardo thought. *Is the Confederacy leaving them as well?*

"Before we join our brothers in abandoning this dustball of a planet, we've got a job to do."

"Burning to burn 'em, ma'am!" Cutter interrupted enthusiastically in a crisp, military voice.

Breanne smiled like a wolf in response. "You'll have plenty to roast with that toy of yours before we're finished, Mister Koura-Abi. I would suggest, however, that we get the present job done first and get off this rock while we still have a way out."

"Ma'am! Yes, ma'am!" Cutter sounded a little disappointed.

"Your new home—if any of you are wondering—is Bunker Complex 3847. A week ago it was an outpost settlement. Folks used to call it Scenic, God knows why. It's all ours now.

Enjoy it while you can 'cause I don't intend to stay here one moment more than we have to for this mission.

"There's an old pumping settlement in the bottom of an impact crater just northeast of here. It's a collection of scrap called Oasis about three clicks out on a radial of thirty-five degrees from the command transmitter. Set your navigational transceivers to those coordinates. Captain Marz here"—the pilot stood squinting in the blowing dust, managing to wave his hand slightly in reluctant identification—"will be flying cover and directing us below."

"Flying cover?" It was Sejak, the young kid. "In a drop-ship?"

"The *Vixen* has been fitted with a special receiver, Mister Sejak, to help us locate this thing we are looking for. Do you have a problem with this, mister?"

The tone in her voice should have frosted over Sejak's face-plate from the inside. "No, ma'am!"

"We find this thing, we pull out and bring it with us. Clean and quick. Corporal Smith-puun will lead First Squad on Vultures with Bowers, Fu, Peaches, and Windom. Littlefield?"

"Yes, ma'am!" The old marine's voice sounded loud in Ardo's helmet. Littlefield was standing right next to him.

"You take Second Squad—that will be Alley, Bernelli, Melnikov, and Xiang. Cutter and Ekart will give you heavy support in the firebats."

Ardo took in the names of his squad as best he could. Bernelli, Xiang, and Ekart were unfamiliar to him. Cutter was still a very dangerous mystery. If they needed a squad leader, though, Littlefield gave him a little more hope than he might have had otherwise.

"Ma'am! Yes, ma'am!" Littlefield barked back enthusiastically.

Breanne barely took notice. "Jensen, you're boss of Third Squad. That's Collin, Mellish, Esson, and M'butu. Wabowski gives you firebat support."

"Yes, ma'am," Jensen replied without much enthusiasm.

Ardo hoped the man fought better than he talked. He looked as though he were about to fall asleep where he stood.

"The dropship will fly high cover and sensor support until we've got the prize. Then we dust off and get off this rock. Any questions?" When Breanne said it, it was a dare, not an invitation.

Ardo could not help himself. He stepped forward and saluted as he spoke. "Ma'am! Yes, ma'am!"

"Yes, Mister . . . Melkof, isn't it?"

"Melnikov, ma'am. Begging your pardon, ma'am!"

"What's your question, Melnikov?"

"What are we looking for, ma'am?"

Lieutenant Breanne looked away from him, her eyes focusing into the distance.

"A box, Private. Just a box."

Ardo felt wonderful. He loved running in the power armor. It seemed effortless as he bounded across the ground. The clicks rolled under him, the salmon colored dust trailing behind him and his companions.

He switched the visor of his battlesuit to navigation mode. Wherever he looked, the visor superimposed the map of their surrounding terrain and labels of the more prominent landmarks. Despite what the lieutenant had said, Scenic had been aptly named. The settlement's primary job had been to maintain the upper pumping station for the aqueduct pipes coming up out of Oasis. As such, it was situated on the sheer drop-off that marked the edge of the Basin—the remains of a major impact crater that had gouged a magnificent long bowl out of the surface. The remains of the crater rim had eroded somewhat over time. His visor labeled the razor peaks to his left as "Stonewall" and the embarrassingly appropriate peak to his left as "Molly's Nipple." The crater itself was a barren landscape, like so much of the entire world of Mar Sara, but there was a stark beauty in its ruggedness that pleased Ardo's eye.

A road snaked its way in switchbacks down the steep

incline of the crater edge. Ardo smiled again at the thought of
the local civvies slowly winding their tortured way down that
treacherous road before reaching the valley floor. The marines
were not constrained by such weakness. His entire squad had
bounded over the steep edge of the mesa and had galloped
straight down to the crater floor. The battlesuits were designed
to take a lot more punishment than a little tumble down a cliff
face. And the marines inside them were, he thought smartly,
tougher than the suits they wore.

"Hubris . . ." It was his father's voice. "Pride cometh before a
fall . . ."

Ardo frowned. His headache threatened suddenly to return.
Better not to think about it and concentrate on his job.

First Squad floated off to his squad's right on their four
hover-cycles. Normally, mobile units in siege tanks or even a
pair of Goliath Walkers would supplement the platoon. Ardo
rather thought that First Squad had arrived hoping for such
heavy equipment. They were destined for disappointment,
being issued local Vulture Hover Bikes that had recently been
"liberated" from the local militia. They were fast, light, and
highly maneuverable, and they gave their riders about as
much protection as a paper hat. The squad leader, a corporal named Smith-puun, was having some difficulty holding
back the cycles to stay even with the two other marine squads
beating feet across the floor of the crater.

Third Squad was running flank off to his left while Ardo's
own Second Squad was taking point for the group. They all
ran in a line, the slope of the crater floor gradually flattening
out. Above them all, the *Valkyrie Vixen* howled, her downward
angled jets churning a wall of dust behind the platoon's own.

Lieutenant Breanne ran slightly behind Third Squad. That
was surprising. Ardo had expected the lieutenant to stay aloft
in the dropship and run the entire show from up there. He had
served under other commanders who preferred to backseat-
drive their platoons from a pleasantly remote location. His
own estimation of Breanne went up several points.

The ground shook underfoot with each stride Ardo made. The oxygen in the suit poured into him, making him feel alive, ready and anxious to do his duty for the Confederacy.

We are tough, Ardo thought. *Everyone says so . . .* although he could not recall just who had said so or where he had heard it ever really said.

All he knew was that the outskirts of Oasis were coming up fast before him, and he would finally be able to exact justice for what the Zerg had done to him.

TRANSCRIPT / CONCOM417 / MET:00:04:23
LC: Lieutenant L.Z. Breanne, Commanding
3 Squads 1:a-e (Mech/Cycle); 2:a-g (M/Inf) / 3:a-f (M/Inf)
Support: DS (Dropship *Valkyrie Vixen* / Tegis Marz, Pilot)
BEGIN:
LC/Breanne: "Okay, grunts! Time for work! First Squad, give me a circle pass on the outpost perimeter."
1a/Smith-puun: ". . . again? Say again?"
LC/Breanne: "First Squad . . . circle Oasis and report!"
1a/Smith-puun: "Yeah, I got it. . . . Fu, break left and take it high, man, and stay tight. If you go buggin' out on me again, I'll cash you in this time, I swear!"
1b/Bowers: "Yeah, I love you, too, Corporal!"
LC/Breanne: "Second Squad, cover Third Squad at that barricade."
2a/Littlefield: "We're on it! Go!"
LC/Breanne: "Third Squad . . ."
3b/Wabowski: "Hey, we're already there, lady!"
LC/Breanne: ". . . move up and recon the . . . Cutter, you'll wait for my command or I'll be tacking your hide up on my office wall!"
3a/Jensen: "Roger, Lieutenant! We are at the breach."
Met: 00:04:24
3c/Collins: "Hey, Sarge! What is this stuff? It's all over the ground!"
3b/Wabowski: "That's Zerg shit, Ekart. They spread this crap all over the place when they come through."

2E/ALLEY: "Lordy, that's nasty! Looks like them bugs just coated the whole town with their black vomit!"

2A/LITTLEFIELD: "Shut up, Alley . . . and keep your field of fire clear! The way you're wavin' that rifle around, you'd think you were conducting a parade!"

MET: 00:04:25

2E/ALLEY: "I'm watching their back, Sarge. Don't get your panties . . ."

3A/JENSEN: "Lieutenant, this is Jensen. I'm at the breach. There's a lot of Zerg creep in here. There's got to be a colony nearby."

1A/SMITH-PUUN: "That's bullshit, Lieutenant! We've just made our circuit and there's no hive here."

1B/BOWERS: "Yeah, you tell 'em, Smith-puun!"

3A/JENSEN: ". . . all you want, Corporal, but this is hive creep and it's flowed down the length of the main street and around the buildings. I can't tell where it's coming from."

1A/SMITH-PUUN: "That's 'cause it ain't coming from anywhere, Jensen! I'm tellin' ya there . . ."

MET: 00:04:26

LC/BREANNE: "Knock it off, Smith-puun. Jensen, any contact?"

3A/JENSEN: "Just this creep, Lieutenant. Otherwise, negative."

LC/BREANNE: "Very well. Marz, how about it? Is there . . ."

1A/SMITH-PUUN: "Fu, I'm tellin' you for the last time, take that cycle higher. Windom! Tighten it up, will ya? And watch out for those aqueducts! You hit one of those and it will ruin your whole day!"

DS/VALKYRIE: "Say again, Lieutenant?"

LC/BREANNE: "Any sign of what we're looking for?"

MET: 00:04:26

DS/VALKYRIE: "Negative, Lieutenant. Sensor's still clear. No indication yet. I think you're getting too much interference from the buildings. You'll have to get . . ."

1B/BOWERS: "That close enough for you, Smith-puun, or do you want me to ride your cycle for you?"

LC/BREANNE: "Shut up, Bowers! Marz, say again?"

DS/VALKYRIE: "Your squads have to get closer. Send 'em in."

2E/ALLEY: "In there? You gotta be kiddin' me!"

LC/BREANNE: "Roger, Marz. Second Squad, move up. Third Squad . . ."

2A/LITTLEFIELD: "Roger . . . moving up."

LC/BREANNE: ". . . and recon eastern buildings up to the . . ."

3A/JENSEN: "Say again? Say again?"

LC/BREANNE: "I said spread your squad out and recon the eastern buildings up to the transmission tower. Second Squad, you . . ."

1B/BOWERS: "There's nothin' out here, Smith-puun! We're just burning circles in the air."

1A/SMITH-PUUN: "Be grateful, Bowers, 'cause if there *was* anything out here . . ."

LC/BREANNE: "Keep the chatter off the command channel! Second Squad, you take the western side. Make your way between the condensers and circle around to the administration center!"

MET: 00:04:27

2A/LITTLEFIELD: "Roger. We're on it. Sejak, you go with Mellish and check out the condensers. The rest of you come with me."

3A/JENSEN: "You all heard the lady, let's move! Cutter, you follow Alley and Xiang up the main street here. Ekart, you're with Melnikov and Bernelli. Go right down that road and then make your way north toward the . . ."

1D/PEACHES: "Hey, Smith-puun! Did you see that?"

1A/SMITH-PUUN: "You heard the lady, Windom. Cut the chatter . . ."

1D/PEACHES: "Something's moving down there!"

1A/SMITH-PUUN: "Where?"

1B/BOWERS: "There's nothin' moving, I tell ya!"

MET: 00:04:28

3D/MELLISH: "Sarge? Can we walk on this—this creepy stuff?"

3A/JENSEN: "It's called creep, Melnikov. Yeah, you can walk on it. It looks wet, but it's probably harder than your power armor."

2A/LITTLEFIELD: "Keep moving those sensors around, ladies. The sooner we find this thing, the sooner we get back for chow."

1E/WINDOM: "Peaches is right, Corp, there's something moving down there."

1B/BOWERS: "You're seeing things, Windom!"

1D/PEACHES: "No, I see it, too. Over by the com tower, in the shadows!"

LC/BREANNE: "Let's get this over with and get out. Marz, anything yet?

MET: 00:04:29

DS/VALKYRIE: "Not yet, Lieutenant . . . keep 'em moving."

2D/MELNIKOV: "Hey, I think I'm getting something here . . ."

LC/BREANNE: "Melnikov . . . what is it?"

2D/MELNIKOV: "Sarge, I think you need to take a look at this."

2A/LITTLEFIELD: "Where are you, Melnikov?"

MET: 00:04:30

2A/LITTLEFIELD: "Melnikov, say again. Where are you?"

LC/BREANNE: "Littlefield, what's going on?"

2A/LITTLEFIELD: "Ekart, where's Melnikov?"

2G/EKART: "I'm not the kid's baby-sitter, Sarge."

2A/LITTLEFIELD: "Ekart, answer me."

2G/EKART: "Look, he was behind me a minute ago!"

2A/LITTLEFIELD: "Bernelli?"

2C/BERNELLI: "He's just around the corner, Sarge."

2A/LITTLEFIELD: "Can you see him?"

2C/BERNELLI: "Well, he's just . . . Hey, where did he go?"

MET: 00:04:31

LC/BREANNE: "Melnikov, report!"

MET: 00:04:32

LC/Breanne: "Melnikov! *Report*!"

CHAPTER 6

RABBIT HOLE

ARDO FELL.

There was a timelessness about his fall, a descent into blackness that seemed never to end. His helmet slamming against the unseen sides of the dark shaft punctuated his freefall. His arms and legs wrenched and twisted with impact from time to time but were saved from serious damage by the automatic safety servos of the battle armor. Still he fell, farther and farther into the unknowable blackness beneath him.

He landed with a shock, rubble cascading around him as he slammed facedown against the hard floor of the shaft. The suit had saved his life, reacting automatically to his descent, but now the broken and collapsing edges of the shaft overhead tumbled down around him, burying him deep in the bowels of a world that was not his own.

Panic gripped him. He screamed: a scream that rattled weak and hollow in his own ears despite its rebounding within his helmet. He thrashed his arms and legs wildly against the debris, kicking at the dark objects rolling about him. He staggered to his feet, losing his balance in his haste and falling backward once more, his arms and legs flailing as he tried to find some purchase. His back slammed against the smooth wall behind him. There, his quivering legs beneath him at last, he stood leaning against the wall, gulping air and trying desperately to regain control of himself.

Darkness surrounded him, complete and utter.

Ardo shuddered, struggling against his quick and shallow breaths. *"Take a deep breath, Ardo," his mother said, concern in her eyes. "Don't say anything until you've taken a deep breath."*

He sucked in a shivering breath.

"Melnikov to . . . Melnikov to . . . Cutter!" It took him a moment to remember the name. "Cutter . . . Come in, Cutter!"

Only faint hissing sounded in his ears.

Ardo took another hesitant deep breath.

"Ekart? . . . Bernelli? Can you . . . can you read me? Come in, Ekart! Bernelli! I've fallen down a shaft at . . ."

At where? The heads-up display of his visor was blank. The navigational display was flashing LOS, which meant it was no longer in contact with the navigational beacon back at the base. How far *had* he fallen, anyway? He remembered that he had been walking along on top of the creep, sweeping down the east side toward the tower.

Ardo's breath froze. The creep!

Instinctively, he leveled the muzzle of his gauss rifle in front of him with his right hand. His left hand reached down behind him to feel along the wall at his back. The powered glove of the battlesuit slid smoothly along the ribbed, slick surface.

"Damn!" he breathed, eyes suddenly wide with fear.

Ardo gripped the gauss rifle with both hands, pushing himself away from the wall. He leaned slightly forward into the rifle as he had been trained to do. "Light! Full spectrum!"

The helmet-mounted illuminators suddenly flashed brightly to life.

The zergling was at least ten meters down the spore colony tunnel that appeared immediately to Ardo's left. The horrendous creature turned suddenly to face the light, just as Ardo got his bearings. The long, deep-ivory talons extending from each of its forearms snapped toward the terrified marine. The zergling's vomit-brown head cowl reared back as it screeched hideously.

Ardo had no time to think. Training. Instinct. He swiveled the weapon around as the display in his helmet switched automatically to attack mode.

The zergling lunged down the corridor, its massive hind legs with razor-spine edges propelling it at incredible speed directly toward the marine.

"Thou shalt not kill," the voice whispered unheeded at the back of his mind.

Ardo pulled the trigger, leaning into the rifle as he did.

Steel-tipped infantry slugs tore from the muzzle of the gauss automatic rifle at thirty rounds per second. Fifteen sonic booms rattled in the air.

Ardo released the trigger. Short bursts. Training.

Fully half the initial burst had found its mark, ripping through the flesh of the Zergling, splattering the walls with the detritus. Greenish-black ichor poured from the gaping holes punched in the creature's torso.

The zergling did not slow.

Ten meters separated them now.

Ardo pulled the trigger once more. *Longer bursts,* he thought automatically, his conscious, screaming mind pushed aside.

The gauss rifle chattered again, the tracers registering in Ardo's facial display, correcting his aim at the juggernaut of death and hatred clawing toward him. Pieces of the creature's carapace broke away, slamming against the walls and clattering to the hard floor of the spore tunnel. Black blood spurted from the exposed arteries as the creature shook with each impact.

Ardo released again.

Five meters.

The zergling, frothing from its fanged mouth, reeled with the impacts but—impossibly—found its feet and lunged forward.

Ardo, eyes wide with terror, jammed down on the trigger. The gauss rifle responded almost instantly, sending a stream of hot metal against and through his enemy. Still it pressed toward him against the steel-tipped hail slamming through it. Ardo's training evaporated in that instant. A scream, raw and unconscious in its intensity, erupted from his throat. The animal within him took hold. The Confederacy ceased to exist. The marines ceased to exist. There was just Ardo, his back against the wall, fighting for his life.

One meter.

Ardo's eyes were fixed open, unblinking, as the hideous, alien face loomed closer still.

The gauss rifle stopped chattering despite Ardo's fanatical grip on the trigger. The magazine was empty.

The smooth, mottled brown of the zergling face smashed against Ardo's faceplate. Ardo could not look away. He peered into the black, soul-less eyes just inches from his face. His hands mindlessly shook the assault rifle, hoping against reason that it would somehow, impossibly, start up again.

Ardo could not stop screaming.

Slowly, the face of the zergling slid down the faceplate, its torso bumping against Ardo's arms.

Ardo scrambled backward, the boots of his battlesuit slipping slightly as he kicked himself back away from the shattered remains of the revolting creature. Ardo shakily ejected the magazine from the assault rifle. He banged the new magazine against his head to clear any sand, more out of instinct than any real need, before he slammed it home in the rifle and primed the weapon once more.

The zergling lay at his feet. Nearly half of the carapace had been shot away. Ardo could see one of its arms had been severed and blown back to rest on the ground farther down the spore corridor. A widening pool of black was spreading across the corridor floor beneath it.

It still breathed.

"All creatures of our God and King," his mother sang. *"Lift up your voice and hear us sing . . ."*

Ardo began to shake uncontrollably.

He was twelve in Sunday school class. "But these, as natural brute beasts, made to be taken and destroyed, speak evil of the things that they understand not; and shall utterly perish in their own corruption . . ." Beasts were interesting to a twelve-year-old. . . .

The zergling twitched before him. The beast's dull, black eye stared back at him.

"And God said, Let the waters bring forth abundantly the moving creature that hath life . . ."

Ardo could not breathe.

Panicked, he suddenly dropped his rifle. His hands clawed at the faceplate release. It resisted for a moment, and then slid sideways with a definitive click. He slammed the visor open as he fell down on all fours.

His breakfast gushed in a cascade against the floor of the spore tunnel. His arms supported him but continued to shake uncontrollably. Again, he heaved; then again.

It was not until then that he noticed the stench in the shaft other than his own. He belched twice and knew he was dry. He wiped his hand on his now-soiled battle armor before he reached up and snapped the visor shut against the smell.

Finally, spent and weak, he tried to push himself back up. He found that he could not stand. So he sat with his back against the wall of the shaft and drew his armored knees up to his chest.

"Thou shalt not kill . . ."

The zergling stopped twitching. He watched it die in front of him and wondered how he could have taken a life—life that only God could grant.

Ardo had killed.

"Thou shalt not kill. . . ."

The marine began to weep quietly, rocking back and forth as he squatted at the bottom of the shaft.

He had killed. He had never killed before. He had been trained, conditioned, drilled, and simulated more ways and times than he could ever recall. But until this moment, he had never truly deprived anything of its life.

His mother had taught him it was a sin to kill. His father had taught him to respect all life, as life was a gift from God. Where were his parents now? Where was their faith now? Where was their hope? Dead with them on a distant world called Bountiful. Destroyed by these same mindless demons from hell, he told himself. Yet the words sounded hollow to him, excuses for the truth, as his father used to say to him.

"*. . . and every living creature that moveth, which the waters brought forth abundantly, after their kind, and every winged fowl after his kind: and God saw that it was good.*"

Ardo drew his knees up tighter. He could not seem to think.

The display on the inside of his visor began to flash insistently. The motion sensors had picked up activity in the blackness of the spore tunnel that stretched before him, but Ardo's mind seemed frozen, unable to grasp its importance.

"I'm sorry, Mom," Ardo mumbled through his tears. "I didn't mean to do it. I didn't mean to . . ."

The headset began to crackle in his ears.

"*An eye for an eye . . . a tooth for a tooth . . .*"

Ardo hugged his knees tighter.

". . . down . . . Sarge! . . . this hole!" The crackling began to form words. Ardo barely heard them, as if they were from a conversation a great distance away.

The faceplate display locked onto the motion. The readout began updating: sixty meters and closing.

". . . this shaft." Suddenly the sound came clear into Ardo's ears. He vaguely recognized the voice as Bernelli's. "*Shit!* Must be a hundred feet down. Hey, Melnikov! You still . . ."

Ardo blinked and took a shuddering breath.

Multiple contacts appeared on his visor display. Their number was steadily increasing.

". . . down an old well shaft, Sarge," the voice continued to crackle in his ears. "The creep must have covered it over and he fell through. I think I can see him but he ain't answerin' me."

Forty meters and closing.

Mom was gone. Dad was gone. Melani was gone. *I'm the only one left to remember them,* Ardo realized.

Thirty-five meters and closing.

He looked up. He could see the lights from Bernelli's suit flashing in the distance above.

Someone has to live.

"I'm here," he called up as he reached quickly down and retrieved his gauss rifle from the debris-covered floor. He quickly pulled the grapple from his belt and slid it down the muzzle of the rifle. "Stand back; grapple's coming up."

"Hey, man, we thought we'd lost you!"

"Not today," he called back.

Thirty meters and closing.

He fired the grapple straight up the shaft. The monofilament line whipped upward, spooling out from the automated winch in the back of his power armor.

He looked back down the shaft just as he activated the lift. A cold smile formed on his tear-streaked face as his feet quickly cleared the floor of the spore tunnel.

"Not today."

CHAPTER 7

SPIT AND POLISH

CUTTER'S ENORMOUS FISTS REACHED DOWN AND dragged Ardo up out of the hole, combat armor and all. He had barely cleared the lip of the cave-in before three of his squad began firing down into the hole he had just vacated.

"Sarge!" Alley cried out, a little more excitement in his voice than he would have liked. "They're coming up. *Shit!* There's no end to 'em!"

"Don't just stand there, *damn it!* Fire at will!" Littlefield shouted through the command channel.

"Hoggin' it all, were you, punk?" the islander growled through his faceplate pressed against Ardo's own. "Thought you might just be the hero of the hour takin' 'em on all by yourself?"

"Back off, Cutter," Littlefield said sharply. "The lieutenant wants a word with this kid right now. Alley! You keep up the suppressing fire. Ekart, Xiang, start fragging this hole right now! Bernelli, you set a charge. When you've finished with them, I don't want the Zerg even *thinking* of putting a hole here again! Soon as you can, get your butts over to the Admin Office. Keep an eye out. If there's one spore hole there's bound to be more and I don't want any of them tappin' me on the shoulder. Clear?"

The squad nodded their consent as they rained death down the hole at their feet.

"Cutter, keep an eye on these whelps and get them back to me in one piece."

"Damn it, Sarge!" Cutter protested. "I haven't killed a thing all day!"

Littlefield seemed to consider the firebat marine for a moment. There was sadness in his eyes but his voice was solid and clear. "You'll have plenty lined up for you before the day's out, Cutter. I'll need those men. Get them back to me, clear?"

"Clear, sir," Cutter sniffed. "Glass-clear."

Littlefield turned to Ardo. "On the quick, marine! Let's go!"

Sergeant Littlefield wasted no time and had bounded several steps ahead of Ardo before the younger marine caught on. Littlefield ran through the alleys of Oasis while Ardo tried desperately to keep up. The creep was still underfoot. Ardo expected at any moment to crash once more through the brittle crust and tumble into a worse situation than before. Much as he feared that, there was something deep inside him that feared disobeying the sergeant's orders even more.

The tactical channel did not give him a clear picture of what was going on, but what he understood did not sound good.

"Holy shit, man! They're not stoppin'!"

"Keep fraggin' 'em, man!"

"I am, man! I'm nearly out . . ."

"Stand back, you ladies! Time to light me some Zerg!"

Cutter, Ardo thought as he ducked down another alley, trying desperately to keep up with Littlefield.

Oasis had been a small outpost. There was little to offer here other than the work, which the wells and multiple pumping stations provided. Homes were largely of the modular variety, each showing the very temporary nature of their construction. The central district of the settlement had a small number of shops, which served the locals.

At least, they *used* to serve the locals. The creep had extended itself down the length of the central section of the town. *There must be a bloom around here somewhere,* Ardo thought, but he was having trouble keeping up with Littlefield through the maze of haphazardly placed buildings and had little time to think about it.

". . . it's shifting, Sergeant! The creep is starting to move!"

"Well, find the bloom. We find that and we can take it all out."

"I've been looking. It just ain't here."

"We'll make a high pass over the main street again. Maybe we missed it."

The four Vulture hover-cycles screamed overhead just as the central administration building came into view. It was not difficult to find. Three stories high, it towered over all the other occupied buildings in the settlement. A gaping, ragged hole had been torn in one side of the building, its external metal wall peeled back; whether by an explosion or some unthinkably powerful hands, Ardo did not care to speculate.

He was so astonished at the sight that he nearly ran directly into Sergeant Littlefield, who had stopped abruptly short of the admin building. The older man looked into the eyes of the panting Ardo, who now stood confused before him, and then keyed his transmitter to Squad Member Select. His words were for Ardo alone.

"Son, you're in a lot of trouble, but don't sweat it. Just take it like a marine and I think things are going to be okay. Understand?"

Ardo nodded even though he knew it was a lie. He was having trouble understanding much of anything at the moment. "Sir, yes, sir!"

Littlefield smiled. "Well, there isn't much they can do to

you out here that the job won't do for them. Be polite, don't talk back to Breanne, and I think you may just live to rejoin my squad. She's waiting for you up in Operations."

Littlefield gave Ardo's battle armor a quick glance, then smiled. "I wish we had time to hose you off first, son! You're gonna smell just awful for the lieutenant."

You would have thought they would have at least removed the dead, Ardo thought, as he stepped into the Operations Room.

Operations was at the top of the three-story central building in the complex. Its windows, now vacant of all but the smallest shards of glass, looked out over the settlement. The building had probably been the last stand of the colonists, and when the fight was over there was nobody left to bury the dead.

That had been several days ago. The Confederacy Marines had given the Zerg a pretty good pasting when they reached Scenic. Intel called it an "extermination" and believed that only a minimal force of Zerg remained in Oasis. Still, no one in command had thought it necessary to come back to the pumping settlement and honor the valiant fallen. After all, they *were* dead.

The Operations Room itself had seen considerable damage. Several marines from Second Squad were working to shore up the gaping holes in the outer wall. The sporadic light from their hand welders played a ghastly blue-white pall across the grisly scene. In the center of the room, the lieutenant leaned over the map table, her back toward them. Her battle armor helmet was off, sitting to one side as she tried to concentrate on the readout in front of her.

Ardo could still hear her on the tactical channel.

"Third Squad continue north toward the tower and then fall back toward Operations."

"I've got movement over here! Something's coming!"

"Shut up, man! We've all got movement . . . everywhere! They're coming out of the floor, man!"

"Keep moving! Keep moving!"

Sergeant Littlefield unlatched his helmet and quickly tucked it into the crook of his left arm. "Beggin' your pardon, ma'am? Reporting as ordered."

The lieutenant straightened and began to turn.

Ardo barely had the presence of mind to quickly remove his own helmet and salute.

The smell in the room was more familiar than what he had experienced in the spore tunnel, and therefore all the more nauseating.

Her voice was coated in frost. "Private . . . Melnikov, isn't it? How good of you to obey an order at last." Her eyes flicked over toward the sergeant. "Mr. Littlefield, do you think this fresh-out-of-the-can marine is worth my trouble?"

"Ma'am . . . by your grace, ma'am!" Ardo glanced sideways at the sergeant. There seemed to be a smile playing at the edge of his mouth.

"I doubt it," Breanne snapped. "Step forward, Private!"

Ardo panicked. He was saluting and could not move until the salute had been returned, yet he had just been ordered to move. Something in his brain seized up, and he seemed unable to do much of anything except sweat and continue to hold his salute.

Breanne seemed suddenly to understand this. She swore under her breath and offered a perfunctory salute.

Relieved, Ardo dropped the salute, and shuddered slightly as he stepped over a headless torso and arm. He could not tell if it had been a man or a woman. He did not want to know. He kept his eyes fixed on the lieutenant.

"Mister Melnikov! Did I or did I not order this team to hold weapons fire for this operation?"

It was a direct question. Ardo could not help but give an answer. "Ma'am! Yes, ma'am!"

"Did I not make it clear that this was a recon and extraction mission?"

"Ma'am! Glass-clear, ma'am!"

Breanne's face was getting uncomfortably close to Ardo's own. Her words were chilling. "Then why, soldier, did you disobey my order?"

Ardo swallowed. "Fell down a shaft, ma'am! Encountered a Zerg . . ." He stammered slightly, the memory of it flooding over him all at once. He dropped his eyes, suddenly ashamed. "I . . . I killed it!"

"Look at me when I'm talking to you, soldier!"

Ardo's eyes locked on her sharp nose.

"You think that's what we're here for, to kill Zerg?"

"Ma'am! Yes, ma'am! Send them all to hell, ma'am!"

Breanne rolled her eyes at this and stepped away, seething. "Littlefield, can you believe this? *This* is the new marine! Neural resocialization! Cookie-cutter soldiers! Press them out of the resoc tanks like so many gingerbread men, wind 'em up and send 'em off to die!"

Littlefield chuckled darkly. "Well, ma'am, it's a lot quicker than the old way, that's for sure. That's progress."

"God save us from progress!" Breanne sighed, then turned her steel eyes back on Ardo. "Mr. Melnikov, let me try to educate you the old-fashioned way. Private, we are *not* here to kill Zerg."

Ardo felt confused. "Ma'am?"

"We are here to *stop* Zerg. That's a different thing altogether. Those caseless steel-tipped infantry rounds you so dutifully loaded into your assault rifle this morning are not designed to kill. They are designed to maim."

"Ma'am, I . . . I don't understand."

"Kill a man on the field of battle and you can leave him there. The buzzards will take care of him." Breanne gestured around the Operations Room. "Look around you, Private. There was nothing we could do for the dead. You honor them when you can, but in the middle of battle there's nothing you can do for them. They are *no longer of any concern*, understand?"

"Well . . . yes, ma'am, but . . ."

"But nothing! If you *maim* an enemy on the field it takes four of his friends to haul him back from the battle and even *more* of his friends to patch him up and care for him. Kill an enemy and you decrease the force against you by one. *Maim* an enemy and you decrease the force against you by *ten*. Is any of this sinking in through that thick, resocialized brain of yours?"

Ardo thought for a moment. "Yes, ma'am."

"Then perhaps in the future you will be more careful in the field to follow my orders *to the letter*?"

"Ma'am, yes, ma'am . . . but . . ."

Breanne's eyes narrowed. "Are you trying to say something, Private?"

Ardo swallowed. "Begging your pardon, ma'am . . . but is the lieutenant suggesting that it would have been better for me to have died at the bottom of that well?"

Breanne took a breath to answer, then held it in check. A wicked smile rippled across her lips. "Well, well, well! A marine who thinks! How refreshing. There's hope for you yet, Melnikov. I—"

"Hey, Lieutentant! I think we found something!"

"Marz, here. They've got something on one of the scanners."

"Hey, I think I found it!"

Breanne spun back toward the map table. "Where? Where is it?"

"It's just a prefab house . . . I think it's in a basement."

"Lordy! The ground is breaking all around me!"

"Movement! Movement!"

"Where?"

"Everywhere!"

"Cutter!" Breanne snapped. "Get the device! Marz! They're at . . . damn it! . . . map grid thirty-six mark four-seventeen. Get them out of there!"

"They'll be vulnerable if I do, Lieutenant! Get them back to Operations and I'll pick up the lot of ya."

"Captain Marz, get that crate over there and pick up my team!"

"There's no place to set down, Lieutenant, *and if I use the extraction fields they'll be held in stasis on the ground for a few seconds. That's more than enough time for the Zerg to kill them where they stand."*

"That's just great!"

Breanne motioned for Littlefield to join her. The sergeant quickly stepped up to the map table. He began pointing to various locations as Breanne spoke.

"Second Squad, get that device. First Squad, I need high cover for Second Squad at thirty-six mark four-seventeen!"

"Hey, does she mean us, *man?"*

"You heard the lady, it's just over— Sweet shit! Where did they *come from?"*

"It's a whole goddamn wall *of 'em!"*

"More like a carpet! Where the hell *did they come from?"*

"Third Squad!" Breanne continued. "Cover fire from thirty-four mark four-sixteen to thirty-six mark four-sixteen. Hold a corridor open and then fall back."

"Say again?"

"I said, hold a corridor and then fall back with Second Squad to the operations center. We'll extract from here."

The lieutenant turned to Ardo.

"Well, you started this, Melnikov, now you can help clean it up. Join Third Squad and see if you can get your old Second Squad back here in as few pieces as possible."

The lieutenant turned back to the map.

"I think it is safe to say that they know we are here now."

CHAPTER 8

SEEING THE ELEPHANT

ARDO DASHED DOWN THE STAIRWELL, STEPPING quickly over the bodies along the way, then burst into what once was the lobby. Wabowski, the second firebat in the platoon, was already charging up his plasma flamethrower. Mellish and Esson were both fingering their gauss rifles nervously. Sejak seemed even more agitated than the others.

"Where's Jensen?" Ardo asked.

"Went to find M'butu," Sejak said, licking his lips. "He said he'd only be . . . oh, *hell*, he's overdue."

"I say we go find him," Wabowski rumbled.

"And I say we follow orders," Littlefield snapped, coming down the stairs and joining them. "The lieutenant knows what she's doing. You've got the word and you know the drill. Move it, people! On me!"

Littlefield readied his own assault rifle and moved out through the broken doors of the lobby. The broken squad glanced around at each other for a moment and then moved quickly to follow the sergeant.

The wind was blowing a steady, hot breeze from the northeast, kicking dust up over the creep that had spread across the main square. Ardo shuddered as they moved across it. They could all hear Cutter and the rest of First and Second squads on the command channel, disembodied voices struggling to survive somewhere beyond the wall of buildings surrounding the outpost's central square.

"Keep moving! Keep moving!"

"Bowers? Bowers! Where the hell . . ."

"Bowers is down!"

"Fu! Peaches! Get your asses over here, now!"

"Damn! Sarge! I'm hit! I'm hit! The cycle's dropping down! Help me! Oh, God . . . they're gonna be all over me! Don't let them . . ."

Littlefield's voice echoed in their helmets, his proximity automatically overriding the other voices, fading them below his own. "Sejak! Mellish! You two take flanking positions on the square and hold it. Wabowski, you and the rest of the squad come with me on point. I don't want anything comin' up behind me, marines!"

Ardo followed without a word, though he was shaking inside his battle armor. The private glanced to either side nervously as he moved forward purely out of training. Somewhere in the back of his mind was the instinct to run in the other direction as quickly as his battle armor would take him, but the training kept that howling animal somehow at bay.

"Alley! Get the hell out of my way! I'll burn 'em!"

"They're a frickin' wall, Cutter!"

"Keep moving! Hang onto that box, Ekart, or I swear to God I'll make you go back for it, Zerg or no! Keep moving!"

Wabowski was on Ardo's left, laden down with two fully charged plasma tanks mounted into the back of his firebat flamethrower battle armor. Esson flanked Wabowski on the far side. Though Ardo could not see him directly, his helmet display noted M'butu directly behind them. They were in the classic support position for firebats, something Ardo gave no more thought to than the others following Littlefield across the square. One might as well concentrate on thinking about how to breathe. Everything and everyone was performing by the book.

Then why, Ardo thought, *am I still shaking?*

"Hell! They're everywhere! Where are they comin' from?"

"Keep movin', grunt!"

They reached a barricade on the far side of the square that extended across the eastern road between two buildings. It had obviously been thrown together from whatever was at hand. Two heavy loaders and a mobile trencher formed the bulk of the barricade, but anything within reach appeared to have been pressed into service. Desks, beds, rocks, pieces of broken wall, even a pair of children's cycles had been tossed desperately onto the pile. From the look of the mangled dead who remained, their efforts may have bought them an extra minute and a half.

Ardo shook violently, suddenly dreadfully afraid that his teeth would chatter over the com frequency. He concentrated on what the lieutenant had said. *"There's nothing you can do for them. They are no longer of any concern, understand?"* Still, Ardo looked away, feeling vaguely ashamed.

Littlefield took no notice of Ardo's discomfort. He scanned the eastern road that wound between the buildings. Calling it a road was generous; it was more of a tortured passage that ran crookedly between modular buildings. "There they are," the sergeant said, pointing eastward.

Ardo peered between the buildings. Something was moving beyond the fine veil of blowing red dust, but he could not be sure just what. The wind was picking up with the evening, the blowing dust obscuring his vision even more. The chatter from the com channel was getting louder and more distinct. Cutter was making progress, but would it be enough?

"M'butu! Esson!" Littlefield's words were level and matter-of-fact. Just another day at the office, he seemed to be saying. "You anchor both sides of this barricade. Set up a crossfire down this passage. Melnikov!"

Ardo looked to the sergeant at the sound of his name.

"You and Wabowski come with me. Let's bring 'em in."

With that, Littlefield leveled his gauss rifle and clambered over the barricade.

Ardo could not move.

Littlefield was already getting hard to see, the blowing dust fading the sergeant's battle armor in and out.

Ardo's mind seemed to seize up. He could not move forward. He could not move back.

Suddenly, something slammed against the middle of his back, knocking him forward.

"Come on, Melnikov," Wabowski sniffed. "Move your ass! This is a rescue mission, remember?"

Wabowski's booted foot dislodged Ardo's stupor. They both scrambled over the barricade quickly, Ardo covering both the barely discernible Littlefield and Wabowski behind him.

"Left!" Wabowski yelled suddenly.

Ardo spun, crouching.

Several Zerg were clawing their way with incredible speed along the wall of a modular building. They seemed to defy gravity through raw strength. The moment Ardo recognized them, the first of them leaped from the wall, directly toward the marine.

Ardo had no time to think. He squeezed the trigger of the gauss assault rifle. The hail of slugs smashed into the monster midair. The raw strength of the creature might have impelled it forward, but the accelerated projectiles arrested the Zerg's momentum and pinned it against the wall. The remaining creatures crouched down against the wall, preparing to spring on their own.

A sudden column of plasma flame engulfed the wall, swallowing the Zerg in its fury. Ardo turned around and saw Wabowski, a huge grin on his face, hosing the wall down with the plasma stream.

He also saw the Zerg lurkers cresting the top of the building behind the smiling firebat warrior.

"On your back!" Ardo yelled, his voice sounding high-pitched in his own ears. His rifle chattered in his hands, laying down a pattern across the rooftop. Several of the lurkers dropped heavily to the ground, their claws working in the dust, struggling to bring them closer to their prey.

We are the prey, Ardo suddenly realized. He could see the smile on Wabowski's face had suddenly waxed grim. The bursts of superheated plasma were flashing toward several targets at Ardo's own back.

"Keep 'em off me, brother," Wabowski drawled. "I'm a little busy here."

The slick, dark forms suddenly seemed to be everywhere on the modules lining the street. Ardo remembered as a child once kicking an anthill on his father's farm, and the ants appeared as if by magic to be all around him at once.

I kicked this anthill, Ardo thought.

The rifle suddenly stopped chattering. Instinctively, Ardo ejected the clip, banged a new clip against his helmet, and slammed it home into the rifle. The clip had barely reached the breach when Ardo pulled the trigger again, splaying the advancing and ever increasing hordes of Zerg lurkers dropping down like rain from the southern rooftops.

"Damn! How far do we have to go?"

"We'll never make it, Cutter!"

"Shut up! Keep moving!"

"We are under heavy attack!" Wabowski's words were factual, but there was a definite edge to them. "Littlefield, if you're going to do something, now would be the time!"

"Got 'em, Wabowski. ETA your position one minute."

Ardo's second clip emptied. Sweat streaming down his face despite the climate control of the battle armor, he ejected the clip once more and pressed the third clip home even as he squeezed the trigger. The broken, mutilated bodies of the lurkers were falling on top of each other. The pile itself was drawing closer to him by the minute, scratching the ground, desperate for Ardo's blood.

Still they came over the eaves of the roof. Ardo could only imagine what Wabowski was fighting out of sight behind his own back.

Ardo's gauss rifle was warm in his hands. The suit filtered that sensation so that it would not do him any actual harm, but he knew that it meant the rifle was getting dangerously close to seizing up.

"We got contact." It was Mellish, behind them in the square. *"Fire zone here in the square. We could use some help back here!"*

One of the Zerg claws reached out from the pile, snapping blindly at Ardo's leg. He took an instinctive step back, then sent a quick burst downward that severed the limb entirely.

When he looked up, the rooftop lurkers were already in midair, leaping toward him.

They never reached the ground. A burst of flame and gauss slugs from Ardo's left obliterated them.

"Make way, kid," Cutter said, his huge firebat suit running past Ardo at full speed. There appeared to be a civilian draped over the huge man's shoulder as he plunged forward. He held the figure in place with one hand and wielded the massive plasma hose with the other. He shouted through the com channel as he ran. "Keep moving!"

Littlefield and Xiang rushed past as well, holding a metallic case by its handles between them. Bernelli continued to fire his own rifle, sometimes at real targets and sometimes at imaginary ones.

"Stay and hold 'em, Melnikov!" Littlefield shouted as he passed. The case appeared to be heavy, slowing Xiang and him down. "We're almost there! Wabowski! Buy us time! That's an order!"

Ardo turned to look east down the road.

Zerg poured down the street, their talons a wall of death and hatred. Ardo knew that they had come for him. Wildly, he thought that they knew, somehow, that he had escaped them twice before. They wanted him, his flesh, his blood.

Ardo turned and ran.

Wabowski continued to rake the walls with the plasma stream, unaware that Ardo had left him.

The lurkers on the opposite wall leaped.

Ardo turned at the scream. The Zerg lurkers had ripped the nozzle from Wabowski's hands and were savagely raking the armor, prying at it carefully. They apparently knew better than to tear haphazardly into a firebat suit. They would take it apart in moments, dragging the screaming Wabowski out and then . . .

Three hydralisks grasped Melani at once, dragging her back from the edge of the crowd.

"Please, Ardo," she wept. "Don't leave me alone!"

Ardo raised his weapon and fired a stream of armor-piercing rounds into the tanks of Wabowski's firebat suit.

Firebat suits are dangerous even under the best of conditions. The containment fields shattered, Wabowski erupted into a mammoth conflagration, a roiling ball that engulfed the buildings around it, swallowing the Zerg, who were too intent on their prey. The flames rolled between the buildings, an expanding inferno raging down the channel directly toward Ardo.

CHAPTER 9

FALL BACK

"MELNIKOV!"

Ardo turned at the sound of his name crackling in his helmet.

"Move it, marine! *Damn it,* Melnikov! Answer me!"

The fireball roiled behind him, eating the air between the buildings. He sensed its hunger and its power at his back. He began to run toward the barricade at the end of the crooked street, already brilliantly lit by the approaching flames.

Ardo's feet were like lead. His arms and legs moved in agonizing slowness. Time was working against him. He tried to cry out for help, but the words seemed malformed and incoherent in his own ears.

The brightness suddenly enveloped him. Chaos erupted in his helmet. Half a dozen different alarms rang out, but he had no time to pay attention to any of them. He was swimming through the brilliant flame and heat. The suit servos strained against the explosive force, struggling to keep Ardo's various limbs and appendages where they belonged. He tumbled through the fire, the heat overcoming the internal cooling. Ardo could feel the webflex netting of the undersuit searing his flesh. All sense of up or down, in or out, was lost as panic welled up within him.

Suddenly he fell from the sky. The ground rushed up at him, slamming his head violently against the interior of his helmet. Dazed, he felt as though he were still moving, although the rough granules of dirt and rock half burying his faceplate belied the thought. He lay still for a moment, aware of a thin stream of blood winding its way down across the clear plexithene of the faceplate and slowly starting to pool.

He jerked himself upright, the movement smearing his blood across both the inside of his helmet and his face. Littlefield was crabbing backward next to him, dragging the ungainly metal case. Xiang had been helping him with it just moments before. Ardo vaguely wondered what had happened to him. The sergeant's gauss rifle was chattering in his hands, spitting out a stream of death. Other members of the squad were backing away from the barricade as well.

"Keep moving! Keep moving!" Littlefield yelled, though they all could have heard him perfectly well through the com-system.

Ardo staggered unsteadily to his feet. Next to him, the sergeant turned suddenly on his heel, his weapon instinctively training on the movement so close to his side. Fear and desperation registered for a moment on the old veteran's features. Ardo half expected to be cut down where he so unsteadily stood, but the sergeant's trigger finger held back long enough for him to register who was suddenly in his sights.

"*Goddamn*, Melnikov! You're a hard man to kill!" Littlefield said, with a hint of hysterical laughter in his voice. Littlefield turned back to face the barricade. "Fall back! Listen to me! Fall back *now*!"

The inferno from Wabowski's explosion continued to rage enthusiastically down the length of the street beyond the barricade, preventing most of the Zerg groundlings from reaching them. Here and there, however, pockets of them somehow managed to swarm through the flames. Cutter, his huge fire-bat armor towering over the remaining members of the detail, was still pumping short bursts of plasma against the Zerg as they tried repeatedly to swarm over the barricade. Ardo gaped. Cutter was firing his plasma weapon with a single hand while still holding on with his other hand to the rag-doll survivor slung over his shoulder.

"It's working," Ardo whispered, more to himself than to the sergeant standing next to him. "We're holding them off."

"Like *hell* we are," Littlefield snapped. "They're cunning, these slime-bugs. They'll keep us occupied here with a few of their kin just long enough to circle around and take us from behind. Make yourself useful, Melnikov, and grab the other side of this case!" The sergeant turned his attention once more to the hulking firebat. "Cutter, get that civilian out of here! Sejak! Ekart! Lay down cover fire and pull back to oh-thirty-seven mark one-fifty-three. We got our little prize, now let's get the hell out of here!"

Cutter growled through the com-system, but he obeyed, falling back with the rest of the line. The shining carapaces of the zerglings leaped deftly over the barricades with a grace and speed Ardo had not thought possible. Each in turn was met by concentrated fire from the retreating marines.

"How we doin', boss?" Littlefield called out.

"Clock's running out." It was the lieutenant, still in the Operations tower that somehow in Ardo's mind was suddenly miles away. *"I can't see them on tactical, but you know they've got to be coming for us. I'm abandoning the Ops center now. Double-time to oh-thirty-seven mark one-fifty-three. We'll dust off there. You copy that, Peaches?"*

"Yes, ma'am." The voice had a strange edge to it. If Peaches was answering on the command channel, then things had not gone well for the Vulture cycle crews.

"Vixen, *you got the coordinates?"*

"*You just get your pretty ass over there, and the* Vixen *will do the rest. Pick up and delivery! ETA five minutes to dust off.*"

"Let's go, people!" Littlefield rumbled. "We don't have a lot of time!"

Cutter growled through the com-system and then turned. One glance and Ardo could see the look on the man's face. His words were for Littlefield, but his cold, black eyes were trained squarely on Ardo as he spoke. "Beg to report one fire-bat lost, sir! Wabowski, sir!"

Ardo quickly snatched at the handle on the metal box. His armor was power enhanced, but the feedback systems let him know that it was heavy.

"Let's move," Littlefield snapped.

In tandem, the two of them began running back across the square. Littlefield pointed off to the left of the Operations tower. Ardo sensed the rest of the squad falling back with them, collapsing the perimeter as they dashed toward the extraction point.

Ardo ran, but he could not clear his mind. "Sergeant . . . sir, about Wabowski, I . . ."

"That was one *hell* of a move, kid," Littlefield cut in, the box bouncing erratically between them as they ran. "Wabowski was already a dead man. You did him a favor . . . and we are wasting what little time you bought for us."

"Yeah . . . thanks." Cutter was running just behind them. The helmet obstructed Ardo's view of the huge islander, but he knew from the big man's tone that he was anything but appreciative.

"You just keep hold of that civilian, Cutter, and leave the thinking to me. As for you, Melnikov . . . if you're still alive by the end of the day"—Littlefield huffed between quick breaths—"well then, by God, son, you may be a veteran yet!"

Cutter's voice was all venom just two steps behind him. "A veteran, eh, Melnikov? Oh, then by all means, you go first. I've seen what you can do with a rifle, and I think it's better if I *follow* you."

"*ETA two minutes.* Vixen *turning downwind now. Jeez! Look at 'em down there! You really stirred up the hive, didn't you, Breanne!*"

They ran down the line of buildings, checking their flanks as they went. There was definitely something out there, but nothing Ardo could really see. Dark movement flashed in the gaps between structures. *Don't stop to look,* he told himself, the rhythm of his running steps in counterpoint. *Don't stop or they'll take you down.*

"*Hold fire! Hold fire at oh-thirty-five!*" It was Breanne's voice. Ardo glanced toward the navigation radial. Sure enough, the lieutenant was running toward them, her own rifle held at the ready. There were three soldiers running with her, two less than he had seen her with only fifteen minutes before.

"Don't stop! Keep moving!" The lieutenant did not break stride as she urged them forward. "Is that the prize, Little-field?"

"Yes, ma'am!" Littlefield picked up his pace a little to keep up with Breanne. Ardo, still clinging to the other side of the metal case, was forced to do the same.

"Nice work, Sergeant!" Lieutenant Breanne was looking toward the rapidly approaching opening at the end of the street. "So, who is the meat that Cutter is hauling out of here?"

"Don't know, ma'am. Some civvy he found still breathing when they came across the box."

"Well, Cutter, looks like you've rescued yourself a real live princess." A smile played into Breanne's voice. "Hang onto her, Private. I'll want to talk with her once we get out of this."

Ardo could hear the filtered chatter of gauss rifle fire over his intercom. Someone nearby was firing short bursts.

"Contact, Lieutenant!" It was Mellish. "On the right!"

"I see 'em, too!" Bernelli was running picket for the retreat on the left. "*Damn!* Look at 'em *move!*"

Breanne looked up as she ran. "*Vixen!* What's your status?"

"Turning base now. Keep your skirt on, Lieutenant, I'll be there in . . . oh, hell! Stand by."

The squad burst from the shelter of the surrounding buildings. The supply-landing pad for Oasis stretched out all around them. Several battered hangars and warehouses stood to either side. After the claustrophobic trails between the buildings, the area felt exposed and vulnerable. Beyond the landing pad toward the south was an open expanse of hydrofarms and the long road they had followed earlier in the day to reach Oasis. Ardo could see the vertical cliff wall of the Basin in the distant south. Molly's Nipple was hazy in the distance, and he could make out the Stonewall Peaks. Right between them, he knew, lay Scenic and their fortified base.

It seemed a million miles away.

Private William Peaches and Private Amy Windom were landing their Vulture cycles in the center of the open area. When the day began, the Vultures had numbered five. Now they were down to two.

"Littlefield! Melnikov!" The lieutenant moved toward the parked Vultures at the center of the landing pad. "Keep that box near me! Cutter! Bring that civvy, too. Everyone else, I need an extraction perimeter around me *now*!"

Ardo could see the windsock next to the landing field. He kept glancing to the south and the distant ridges where a clean bunk, a shower, and, perhaps, relative safety might be found. He had killed twice in one day. He longed for unconsciousness. If Captain Marz was following a standard approach, he should be coming from that direction.

Breanne was looking in the same direction, searching the sky for any sign of movement.

"Vixen," she called out. "Update!"

The Confederacy Marines formed a circle on the landing pad, training their weapons outward. The sands of the Basin were blowing across the flat expanse, obscuring the once carefully laid-out markings. Ardo could hear the swish of the sand blowing against the hard carapace of his own battle armor.

Nothing else.

"*Vixen.*" Breanne's voice was steady. "We are on station. What is your ETA?"

The com channel crackled with muffled background static, the gain automatically heightening as the equipment strained to hear a response.

"Lieutenant! We've got movement!"

"Where, Bernelli?"

"Just past the hangars, ma'am! They're flanking us on the east just beyond—"

"West, too, Lieutenant! Gods! Look at how *fast* they are!"

"*Vixen!* Damn it! Report!" Breanne turned back to the south. "Littlefield! Do you see him? He said he was a minute inbound. We should have seen him by now."

"He should have been here by now, Lieutenant," Littlefield replied. "There's something wrong here, ma'am."

Breanne looked south again. "*Vixen!* Come in, *Vixen!* What's your status?"

"He's not there." Littlefield's voice was heavy as he pointed to the south. "But I do see something, ma'am."

Dark figures began moving across the southern end of the landing pad.

"Zerg," Breanne breathed. "They're cutting us off."

Littlefield shook his head. "Lieutenant, I think—"

"They don't pay you to think, Sergeant!" Breanne snapped. "Peaches and Windom! Mount up! Everybody, I want new loads prepped and locked right now! When I give the order, the Vulture cycles open up with everything you have and fly straight across the Zerg line to the south. Plow me a road through those bugs. The rest of us, lead with everything you've got, charge through the hole and don't stop. Go right through and don't stop for anything, you understand?"

"Then what, Lieutenant?" Esson's voice was a little shaky.

"Then run, boy. Run for the base, and don't look back."

CHAPTER 10

THE GAUNTLET

"THEY'RE CLOSING THE GAP, MA'AM!" BERNELLI whispered hoarsely. It was as though louder noise would somehow shatter a fragile moment and bring the slowly approaching Zerg crashing down on them.

Breanne's voice was cold and level. "Hold your fire, damn it!"

"They're cutting us off, Lieutenant!"

"Shut up, Mellish," Breanne snapped. "Peaches! Can't you get that thing started?"

What remained of the detail was ever so slowly pulling in tighter and tighter around where Ardo stood. The purplish wall of Zerg, their faces locked in a hideous metallic grin, clawed at the air, anxious in anticipation of their prey. Ardo thought suddenly of the cat his mother had barely tolerated to wander about the farm. One afternoon, Ardo had watched in fascinated horror as that otherwise sweet creature had cornered a mouse in the barnyard and played with the trapped prey as though it were a toy. Eventually, that cat had clamped his jaws down on the hapless critter's skull and ended the chase in a bloody, dirty meal. Yet before that happened, Ardo seemed to recall a similar smile on the face of that cat.

And now here he was . . . the mouse.

The Vultures suddenly whined back to life. Ardo could see the sweat breaking out on Peaches as he nervously primed the forward ordnance.

Breanne's voice rose slightly in pitch. Perhaps she was looking at the same teeth as Ardo was considering. "I don't have all day, Priv—"

"I've got it, Lieutenant!" Peaches chattered back. "We're good to go!"

"Very well." Breanne turned slowly, her voice rising over the whine of the Vulture cycles. "Everyone locked and loaded? Peaches and Windom: make me a hole! *Now*!"

The Vultures screamed and lurched forward as their riders opened their accelerators clear to the stops. Bolts thundered from their forward projectors and exploded against the Zerg line even as they approached it.

The Zerg screamed, too, their own terrible voices rising in indignation that their prize would have the effrontery to challenge them.

"Now, marines!" Breanne screamed.

The encroaching outer circle of Zerg suddenly lurched inward, collapsing toward their prey. Their claws whipped through the air, intent on shredding armor, draining blood, and stripping flesh from bones.

Yet the marines were no longer there. As one they rushed toward the line of explosions before them, the billowing orange conflagration growing by the second. Their weapons trained forward in unison, a solid column of flame and death burning and blasting through the deep column of the enraged Zerg.

"Don't look back! Run, you bastards! Run!"

Ardo ran next to Littlefield, the metal case banging between them. His free hand held his gauss rifle, swinging wildly as it spewed destruction indiscriminately in his path. There was no effort to fire for effect—all he could do as he ran was random damage and add to the carnage already taking place.

They were nearly at the wall of fire they had created. Severed Zerg limbs and burning viscous fluid cascaded around them.

"Keep firing! Keep running!"

Ardo caught a glimpse of Cutter off to his left. The huge firebat thundered forward, the female civilian draped over his shoulder. She bounced with each step like a rag doll. With his free hand, Cutter poured plasma into the Zerg line.

The flames wrapped around Ardo as he crossed the line. The footing had already gotten difficult, the ground slick with charred and ruptured Zerg organs. The metal box banged against his leg, letting him know that Littlefield was still there, running and pulling him forward.

An unearthly scream tore across the com channel. It continued, an ear-piercing squeal of terror.

"Esson! *Jeez,* Lieutenant! They're all over him! We gotta—"

"Keep running, Collins! That's an order!"

"But Lieutenant, can't you *hear* him?"

"Run, damn you! Don't look back!"

The internal temperature of Ardo's battle armor was growing by the moment. He could feel his hands and feet starting to blister. Suddenly he ran directly into a standing zergling. Ardo screamed but did not stop, knocking the creature down in his rush before both vanished from each other's sight amid the conflagration.

He was shocked when, in the next instant, the flame was gone from his smoking faceplate.

Before him lay the long expanse of the southern Basin. Molly's Nipple. The Stonewall Peaks. All he had to do was reach the rim. All he had to do was . . .

The chatter of automatic fire rattled across the com channel.

"They're coming! They're nippin' at my ass! Oh gods of . . ."

A scream drove like a needle into Ardo's ear. Before it died, two more joined it, each unique in its death sound.

"Keep running, you dogs!" Breanne breathed through the com channel. Her own voice had an edge to it Ardo had never heard before. Was she winded or just afraid? "Keep running and don't look back!"

Instinctively, Ardo looked.

The Zerg were closer than he thought and more numerous than he imagined. To either side of them stretched a carpet of the aliens pouring across the landscape, streaming toward him.

Ardo stumbled at the sight. Littlefield, maintaining a death grip on the case slung between them, shot ahead. Only his companion's pull on the box kept Ardo on his feet and moving forward.

"Do that again, kid," Littlefield huffed between breaths, "and I'll leave you behind."

They were covering open ground now, their battle armor once more carrying them with incredible speed toward the steep incline of the Basin wall. Ardo briefly remembered how much fun he had had crossing this same ground and coming down that incline just a few hours ago. Or was it months ago? In the open, they were widening the distance between themselves and the Zerg behind them. Now he was faced with having to run up that sheer face. Ardo realized with a start that the vertical face would slow down his battle armor considerably, but it would not hinder the enraged Zerg pursuing him.

"Sarge," Ardo huffed. "My weapon's dry. I need to reload."

"Drop it, soldier," Littlefield chuckled with a dry throat.

"Sir?"

"Drop your weapon." Littlefield was a strong warrior, but even his training was being taxed by the full-out run. His words were gasping over his breath. "It doesn't matter anymore, son."

"But, sir!"

"Do you . . . do you know what's . . . what's on top of that cliff right there? There's a bunk and a hot meal waiting . . . for me . . . for you. It's sitting . . . sitting just inside the most beautiful Confederacy per . . . perimeter wall you've ever seen. Auto . . . auto-defense cannon turrets. Bunkers. Prettiest bunkers . . . you've ever seen full . . . full of fresh soldiers who really want to . . . play shooting gallery at a wall of angry Zergs."

Ardo looked at the top of the cliff face again. He could almost see the walls of their base at Scenic. It seemed to be a million steps from where he so desperately continued to run.

"Drop your gun, son," Littlefield croaked. "If we don't clear the rim of this basin . . . no amount of ammo . . . in that fine weapon of yours . . . will save your ass . . . or mine."

Ardo glanced at Littlefield. The old warrior smiled at him through his panting breath. Ardo noticed for the first time that Littlefield had already dropped his weapon and ammunition packs.

Ardo tossed his gun aside, put his head down, and ran.

The floor of the basin began to rise in front of them. The relatively smooth floor was giving way to the more uneven terrain leading up to the base of the rim wall. Ardo frantically scrambled across the ever steeper ground, his feet propelling loose rock behind him from time to time. The climb was getting worse with each step. The stone face of the cliff rose above them. The battle armor was powered for many things, but flight was not one of them.

He stumbled onto the access road. It crossed back and forth along the cliff face, a series of switchbacks leading up to Scenic. It was the only way up the cliff.

Ardo risked another glance back. The marines had put a hundred yards between them and the following Zerg. It would not be enough. The marines would have to navigate the switchbacks, but Ardo could already see that the Zerg were under no such restraint. The buglike creatures scrambled and leaped over the intervening rocks with barely any check. They would come straight up the cliff face.

Someone else noticed it, too.

"Marines! Prepare to hold and fire!"

Lieutenant Breanne. She was going to stop and make her stand.

"Melnikov. Littlefield. Get that case back to base! Cutter! Follow them with that civilian! That's the mission. The rest of us hold here as long as we can. Maybe it will be enough."

"Holy shit!"

"Shut up, Collins! That line of rocks at the edge of the road-way! Everybody take a position and prepare to fire." Breanne's voice was like steel. She had made up her mind, and nothing and no one could change it now.

The squad, breathless and aching, dashed to the group of protruding boulders lining the side of the road like broken teeth. The Zerg swarm swept toward them.

"Littlefield! Get out of here now or I'll—"

A bright tone sounded suddenly in Ardo's helmet. By the sudden reaction from the remaining platoon members, they all heard it, too.

Ardo, looking at Breanne's face at the time, saw her eyes go wide. She looked up. Ardo followed her gaze and caught a glimpse of a brilliant arching contrail etching itself across the bright sky.

"Turtle down, marines! Now!" the Lieutenant barked.

Ardo, out of trained reflex more than thought, tossed himself to the ground behind the nearest boulder. He closed his eyes, but to little effect.

The world suddenly went painfully white.

He could feel the concussion through the ground a moment afterward. He had experienced this many times before, but there was still something about being under such primal, unquestioning power that shook him to his soul. It was coming, the great beast, and the shaking ground only heralded its approach.

The shock wave from the tactical nuclear blast had compressed the air in front of it into a wall of force. Distance had dissipated its effect, but it was nevertheless deadly. It passed over Ardo and his battlesuit, shaking him through the armor until he thought his teeth would be dislodged.

It would only be a moment, he knew. Either way, it would only be a moment.

Then the moment passed . . . and he was still there.

Ardo staggered to his feet.

The outpost that had been Oasis was hidden beneath the roiling red cloud—probably *was* the roiling red cloud, Ardo realized. The line of Zerg had not had any warning. Most were dead from the shock wave. Those few who remained seemed either confused or blind from the flash.

This certainly was no time to question which.

"Move it, marines!" Breanne whooped. "Let's get home before these Zerg pigs figure out what happened!"

Ardo grabbed the handle on the battered metal case and turned, grinning, toward Sergeant Littlefield. "That was one amazing rescue, eh, Sarge?"

"Is that what that was?" To Ardo's astonishment, Littlefield's face was grim. "Let's get this box home. I need a shower and my bunk."

CHAPTER 11

HOMECOMING

THEY DRAGGED THEMSELVES OVER THE CREST OF
the Basin wall. It was a site Ardo had wondered if he would
see again. The walls of Scenic Outpost, dark in the failing
light, thrust up out of the sandstone. Beyond its walls lay
bunks, showers, meals, and, most of all, some measure of
security. The Command Center towered over it all, beckoning Ardo like a siren. Its flashing beacons were so beautiful
that it almost moved the marine to tears.

Breanne straightened them all up on the ridge. It would
not do to have them straggle in like a bunch of whipped dogs,
she said. She formed them up, admonished them in no uncertain terms to keep themselves tall and proud or she would
personally insert something unnatural into their anatomy
that would force them to stand up straight. Then, with snap
and precision, she marched them toward the garrison's deployment gate. Their fear of her overwhelmed their tiredness.
What remained of the detail approached the compound like
some sort of dust-caked military parade. If Breanne had had a

flag, Ardo was certain she would have been waving it by now.

Ardo afforded himself a single backward glance. The great atomic cloud was dissipating over the Basin, its angry glow spreading eastward over the red mountains beyond. It had been an airburst: a detonation at a designated altitude that slammed down like a fist on anything beneath. The result was heavier physical damage but also a much lower radioactive fallout rate than from a ground detonation. Still, Ardo wondered if anyone had mentioned these facts to any settlers who might be remaining downwind of the deadly cloud's fallout. Most likely not, he decided. The Zerg are probably all that remain east of here anyway.

Their formation was much smaller than it had been earlier in the day. Ardo counted heads as they marched. The platoon of marines was down by about half. Ekart, the second firebat from his own squad, was missing and presumably either shredded or smashed flat on the floor of the Basin somewhere around Oasis. The same fate apparently had been visited upon Collins and Esson.

At least he hoped they were dead. It was entirely possible, he realized, that for some of them the nuke had blown the Zergs off them and welded the seals in the battle armor, but not completely crushed them in the blast wave. Sealed inside your own battle armor, unable to move on an abandoned, radioactive plain . . . The aching in his head was returning. Probably best not to think about it.

So it was another glorious day for the Confederacy Marines. Half their number had been left behind, but Ardo knew the mission would be chalked up as victorious. No, he realized, it was more than half. The Vulture cycles had not waited for them to return, but he recalled they had lost all but two before they had fled Oasis, and he did not actually know if either of them had survived to reach the garrison.

Glorious. All for a little metal box banging incessantly against his thigh and a single civilian draped over Cutter like a broken doll.

Breanne and the remains of her squad marched up to the east gate with all the dignity they could muster. A vibrant rust-colored sunset silhouetted the dark metallic walls of the garrison compound. There was something unnatural as they approached, something Ardo could not put a name to in his mind. As they approached the main lock, however, Breanne must have sensed something, too. She suddenly held up her left fist. The marines all stopped at once, wary.

Breanne stood there for a moment. Ardo could not tell if the lieutenant was concerned or simply undecided.

"Breanne to Scenic Ops," she called over the com channel.

Silence. That was it, Ardo realized. He had not heard anything over the com channel but their own chatter as they approached the wall.

"Breanne to Scenic Ops. Respond, please."

The wind was picking up in the evening, the sound of the blowing sand hissing around their helmets. Ardo looked at the low bunkers set on either side of the lock. The dark slits had been comforting a few moments before. He had imagined each filled with sentry troops prepared to defend them against any assault. Now they seemed ominously empty and dark. He tried to see if there was any movement beyond the black slits, but it was impossible to tell.

The marines glanced uneasily at each other.

The com channel crackled slightly.

Breanne signaled the platoon to ready weapons. It was not until that moment that Ardo realized he was without his gauss rifle. He felt suddenly quite vulnerable. He glanced accusingly at Littlefield, still holding the other handle on the metal box between them. Littlefield took no notice, his eyes shifting over the darkening walls of the garrison.

"Why don't they answer?"

"Could be a com problem."

"*Could* be? What if it ain't?"

Breanne stepped up to the keypad entry panel next to the

massive, sealed gate. It took her several attempts before she managed a proper sequence the gate would accept.

Ardo felt it more than heard it. The massive gate through the garrison main lock groaned slowly upward. Breanne raised her weapon but held her ground. The others in the platoon followed her lead.

"Mellish, Bernelli, on point! Move!"

The two marines hesitated only a moment, then moved quickly forward, gauss assault rifles held high. Each took up a position on either side of the darkened lock, peering in over their gun sights.

"Clear, Lieutenant!" Mellish called with a decided lack of conviction.

The inner door of the lock began to grind open as well. Its mass rose slowly, revealing the center of the garrison compound beyond bathed in the deepening rust of the sunset.

"Lieutenant?" Bernelli asked with a nervous edge to his voice.

"Hold your ground, Private!" Breanne stepped forward, her eyes trying to see beyond the narrow lock opening. "Cover us. Xiang, you're with me."

Breanne stepped into the lock, followed by the private. Both were swallowed at once by the dark corridor, their outlines etched against the deepening red of the compound clearing beyond. Just as quickly both figures stepped back into the light as they left the confines of the lock.

"Everyone, move up," Breanne called. "Quickly, people!"

Ardo glanced once more at Littlefield. The old veteran nodded, and they quickly moved forward with the rest of the platoon.

The clearing beyond the lock was not much more than a rally point set amid the too closely spaced buildings of the garrison. The Confederacy liked to keep their military bases tight and efficient: the smaller the area, the easier it is to apply resources and the less terrain you have to guard. At least, that was the doctrine engrained in all their commanders. The result was often a crowded hodgepodge of structures built far enough apart so that ground vehicles could maneuver between them. When fully staffed, this made any Confederacy garrison like an anthill, its narrow passages teeming with marines, support personnel, and command staff all in a hurry to get somewhere.

Stepping hesitantly out of the lock space, Ardo noted once more that Scenic Garrison had been deployed like every other base he had ever served in, with one very notable exception.

No one was home.

The lock entered the clearing through the east side perimeter wall. The clearing itself had served as the landing area for the dropships. Several buildings crowded in on the marginal open space. A ragged line of supply depots had been constructed in a tightly fitted puzzle on both the north and south sides of the clearing. A matching pair of missile turrets rose above them on either side. Their deployment heads still rotated as their homing systems searched automatically. To the west of the clearing, directly across from the lock, stood the three barracks units they had so casually left that same morning. A wide passage just to the south led back to the massive Command Center, the top of which could be seen towering above the barracks. The upper parts of the factory center and machine shop could just be made out farther beyond. A pair of SCVs stood next to a stack of supply containers on the north side of the clearing. Everything was exactly where it should have been.

"Mellish, cycle the lock." The lieutenant's voice was calm and quiet. Ardo used to talk the same way to the horses on his father's farm to calm them down when they were skittish. "Let's get that door closed. No sense being surprised from behind."

"Yeah," someone muttered over the com channel. "Especially since we got plenty to surprise us in front."

"That's enough, Bernelli." Breanne's voice remained ice calm. "You get that door closed yet, Mellish?"

"Yes, sir. Lock's secure."

"It's like they all just got up and left," Xiang muttered.

"Yeah," Littlefield agreed, "but look: I can see them leaving the supply huts and turrets—those are all built here—but the barracks are mobile. Hell, even the Command Center flies itself on those repulsor pads. They're all mobile units, and still in good repair by the looks of 'em. If they were evacuating, why not take the hardware, too?"

"All good questions, but what we need are answers." Breanne had made her decision. "Let's sweep the area. There may be people trapped or hurt or otherwise unable to communicate. Something's happened here, and whoever you run into is probably going to be a little nervous."

"You got *that* right!"

"Just take it easy and relax your trigger a little, got that? I don't want anybody blowing holes through our own just because we don't know what's going on. Littlefield and Melnikov, stay with me. Cutter, how's that civvy doing?"

"She's starting to come around, Lieutenant." Cutter held the woman cradled in both arms now. Against the massive islander, the woman looked tiny and frail, but Ardo could see she was stirring. "You want me to put her down?"

"No, there's an aid station in the Command Center." Breanne was frustrated. There was not much left for her to command. "Let's do this together. We'll start with the north barracks and then—"

"Lieutenant, I've got movement!"

"Where, Bernelli?"

"Looks like about fifty meters at about two-seven-eight degrees."

"That's the Command Center! Track it, Bernelli. Stay sharp, people!"

Bernelli's voice was rising ever so slightly in pitch as he spoke. "Tracking . . . moving south."

"We're in the open here, Lieutenant," Littlefield breathed.

Breanne understood at once. "Deploy forward! Take positions under the northern barracks. Use the landing struts for cover. Move!"

The platoon dashed quickly across the clearing. Ardo ran awkwardly next to Littlefield, the two of them still struggling with the metal box between them. Ardo fleetingly thought about the supply huts just a few meters away from him. Within one of them would be a brand-new rifle for him and a fresh supply of ammo. Instead, here he crouched, cowering in the landing well of a mobile barracks with nothing to defend himself except harsh language, spit, and this stupid metal box which, as far as he was concerned, could have stayed in Oasis and become part of the great radiant cloud drifting off to the east.

"Bernelli?" Breanne spoke quietly, despite the fact that the battle armor kept her words restricted to the com channel.

"Still tracking, Lieutenant. Moving fast. Fifteen meters on the two hundred radial. Maintaining an eastern line."

"It's coming down the road," Littlefield rumbled.

"Fifteen meters still. Should be able to see it . . ."

Ardo crouched lower behind the strut.

A single figure, bathed in the dying light of the day, staggered out into the clearing.

"Oh, *shit!*" Breanne spat. She stood up, snapping back the faceplate of her battle armor and yelling across the clearing. "Marcus, what in the name of *hell* are you doing?"

The figure turned. His fatigues were no longer crisp or clean. He had lost his snappy hat, revealing a head of straw hair that seemed to stick out in directions of its own free will. Nevertheless, Ardo recognized him as the technician who had joined them on the flight out to Scenic just yesterday.

"Ma'am, oh!" Sergeant Marcus Jans snapped to a rigid salute. "Welcome home, ma'am!"

Lieutenant Breanne returned the salute casually, then asked, "Permission to enter the garrison?"

"Uh, ma'am?"

"I assume you are in charge of this post, Sergeant, or someone else would have greeted us by now."

"Oh." Jans seemed confused. "Yes, ma'am, I guess I am . . .
except for you . . . now, I mean."

Ardo was suddenly reminded of his cat and the mouse
once more.

"Then I'm reporting my platoon as having returned from
a glorious mission on behalf of the Confederacy." Breanne's
voice was tired and her temper was starting to give it an
edge.

Jans looked past Breanne to where Ardo and his companions had taken cover. "You mean, the marines hiding under
the barracks?"

"So much for our glorious return," Cutter rumbled.

"Yes." Breanne spoke the words through her teeth. "The
marines hiding under the barracks are asking permission to
enter your garrison, Sergeant, and then I want to know where
the *hell* the *garrison has gone!*"

Jans blinked as Breanne's final words seemed to rock him
back on his heels.

"But . . . but, Lieutenant . . . I thought *you* could tell *me!*"

CHAPTER 12

GHOST TOWN

"WHAT THE HELL ARE YOU TALKING ABOUT, TINKER?" Breanne was in no mood to guess. The wrath in her voice might just melt the technical sergeant right down into his scuffed boots.

"Well, ma'am, they just all pulled out," Marcus stammered. The dirt on the sergeant's face was marred by the streaks of sweat starting to run down from his hairline. "I thought, you being in the command loop and all, you'd know about it, that's all."

Littlefield stepped toward Breanne and the tech sergeant, dragging Ardo closer by virtue of the metal box still hanging between them. He spoke in a low voice, confidentially, but Ardo was too close to avoid hearing. "Lieutenant, it's getting dark, and we've got no place else to hide."

Breanne's gaze had been locked with building fury on Jans but Littlefield's words somehow penetrated her rage. Her head snapped up, and she seemed to be seeing the fading sky for the first time above the dim walls of the garrison.

"We probably don't have a lot of time," Littlefield whispered toward the ground, but the words were meant for the lieutenant.

"The post has been abandoned," Breanne announced suddenly. "Some sort of SNAFU is my guess. I'll get it straightened out. Meanwhile, Cutter . . ."

"Yes, ma'am."

"There's an aid station in the Command Center. Take that woman there, strap her to a bunk, and then report back to me. Littlefield, take Melnikov and go with Cutter. Have Melnikov keep an eye on that treasure chest of yours and the woman—if he can handle it."

"He'll do fine, Lieutenant. I'll see to it."

"Well, would you also 'see to it' that he gets a new rifle, and pick one up for yourself while you're at it." Breanne's lips very nearly smiled. "Then get back here to me. We've got to set up a perimeter."

Cutter grunted once and shifted the position of the moaning woman still in his arms. There was disappointment in his voice as he spoke. "Not much fun tonight, Lieutenant. We just nuked the Zerg into bloody little bits. All that's left now is to call for the bus to take us out. War's all finished here." The big man shook his head sadly. "No, ma'am, not much fun tonight at all."

Littlefield glanced at Breanne, but if he was looking for any reaction, he did not get the satisfaction.

"You have your orders." The lieutenant spoke with an even chill. Then she turned back to the tech sergeant. "As for you, Sergeant Jans, you stay with me. I have a lot of questions for you, and I don't want you getting lost before I can ask them."

Night was falling quickly as they made their way to the infirmary. The wind had picked up considerably from the west, its sounds moaning and wailing among the buildings of the Confederacy garrison compound. Ardo shuddered at the sound. The deserted buildings seemed to stare back at him as he moved between them. The place was altogether too still for the massive amount of equipment remaining here. Everywhere he looked he was greeted by visions of things that were entirely in place and yet somehow wrong. The ground beneath his feet was packed hard under the treads and repulsors of various vehicles that had trod over it. The bright lights still burned in each of the modules as they passed. One supply depot access door was open, its interior work lights spilling into the street. An SCV loader stood within, its vaguely humanoid metal-and-plastic shape poised to pick up a shipping module. Its operator, however, was long gone, like a spirit who had abandoned its physical body in death. Everywhere he looked, there were the bootprints of marines and technicians who should have been walking over that same ground still, but were somehow missing. Now they only existed here as ghosts. Ardo was not sure whether he would be more surprised by actually seeing someone else or by the constant strain of *not* seeing anyone at all.

The main access roadway wound around the back of the southern barracks module, curving across the flattened ground toward the hulking Command Center. The building was massive, as wide as it was tall, the suggestion of a flattened metallic spheroid in its general shape. It had obviously been built for function rather than aesthetics. Some Confederacy technical draftsman back at R&D Division probably had an impassioned affair with this design at one point, but he was alone in his appreciation. The Command Center was all business. Massive repulsor landing claws supported the main bulk of the structure, their thick struts disappearing into wide housing cowls. External ablative plates reinforced the armored hull. Above that, at a level three stories higher than the ground, a variety of observation towers, antennae, sensor domes and other technical gadgetry were arranged in what appeared to the casual observer to be utter chaos. Above it all sat the Operations Center, an armored block with windows on all sides that lorded over the entire complex. The lights were shining brightly from those windows, but there was no movement behind them as far as Ardo could see.

The main access ramp to the Command Center had been lowered, the hydraulic arms fully extended to either side. The main command bay was well lit, but Ardo could not help but feel that they were all walking into the mouth of some great, dark beast.

The brightness of the bay helped, however, once they were inside its glow. The fewer shadows the better. The main bay towered over them through two decks. To his left and right, Ardo knew that the Command Center held the mineral and gas processors, which were the heart that sustained any mobile command base. Their bulk took up most of the Command Center's internal space.

Overhead, squeezed into a space between the massive processors, was the SCV maintenance bay. "Maintenance" was something of a misnomer: the fabricators on that level could create an SCV from scratch just using the mineral processor output alone. Several T-280 Space Construction Vehicles hung suspended from their construction racks overhead. They swayed slightly. Ardo had to remind himself that it was probably the ventilation system moving the suits.

He noticed his annoying headache had returned. Littlefield continued forward toward the lift at the end of the bay. Ardo kept up with him as he held the metal case. They both turned as they stepped onto the lift platform. Cutter, still cradling the woman in his arms, joined them, and then Littlefield activated the lift.

As they rose, Ardo tried to get a better look at the woman. The massive tangle of her long, filthy hair was his first and strongest impression. Her face was turned away from him, toward Cutter's chest. She wore the ubiquitous jumpsuit of a colonist worker, probably a worker in the engineering or waterfarm projects out in Oasis. The sole of one of her boots was partially torn away from the top leather. It struck him as an odd thing, considering everything else that must have happened to her companions down in that outpost town.

At least, now that the town was drifting in a glowing cloud to the east, they would not need to go in and clean up the dead.

Clean up the dead?

The phrase caught in his mind, but he could not attach any significance to it. Besides, his head hurt too much to think about it much more. Better to just get on with the current task and forget about it.

The lift quickly rose into the overhead shaft, then stopped at Level 3. Cutter turned with the woman and carried her down the narrow hall. It was a difficult feat, especially in the huge firebat armor, but Cutter managed it without much trouble. He seemed to wear the armor like a second skin.

"Let's go," Littlefield urged with a nudge against the box that carried into Ardo's thigh. Ardo shook himself from his own thoughts and began moving down the corridor.

The infirmary was well encased by the rest of the Command Center. It was situated nearly in the exact middle of the structure. There were no regen tanks here or really much of anything that citizens of the Confederacy might consider standard equipment for a medical facility. The infirmary was more of a first-aid station, a stopping place on the journey of an injured marine to keep him just alive enough so that he could reach better care and facilities.

There were several bunks mounted against one wall. Most of these were neatly and crisply made up in the traditional marine style. One, however, was in disarray, its sheets dropping casually toward the floor.

Cutter entered the room, his bulk seeming to take up most of it. He found a middle bunk that seemed to suit his requirements and lay the groaning woman down. The big man finally was able to flip open his helmet faceplate just as Ardo and Littlefield entered the room. Ardo could see the sweat streaming down the islander's brown face.

"That wasn't good," he huffed. He quickly released the locking rings on his gloves and pulled his hands free. In moments he was strapping the bed restraints around the listless woman's hands, chest, and feet. "Need more exercise. Gotta work out more."

Ardo smiled and shook his head. Cutter had just run several kilometers with that woman either on his back or in his arms. Even with the help of the suit, that was a remarkable performance. Ardo smiled to think that Cutter would consider it a sign of weakness.

Littlefield motioned Ardo over to the right. Against the opposite wall from the bunks, a desk stood away from the wall with a chair on its far side.

Littlefield stopped. "Will you look at that!"

Ardo and Littlefield both stopped.

The desk was clean and uncluttered except for a partially downed cup of coffee and a half-eaten sandwich.

Cutter gazed at it as well for a moment, then he reached forward with his massive right hand and picked up the cup.

"Still warm," he said, then downed the coffee in a single gulp.

Ardo and Littlefield stared at him, amazed.

"Needed sugar," Cutter reflected as he gathered up the remains of the sandwich and began stuffing it into his mouth. The rest of his words were barely discernible through the bread. "I'm heading out. You two need anything, just shout. I'm sure *someone* will come."

Cutter grabbed his battle gloves and stepped out of the room, the infirmary door sliding closed behind him.

Littlefield returned Ardo's astonished look, then both men broke into a hearty laugh.

"Unbelievable," Ardo gasped between laughs.

"No, not really," Littlefield responded with good nature. "He's really not that bad once you get to know him."

Ardo sat down in the desk chair, not an easy thing to do in his battle suit. "You know him?"

"Sure," Littlefield said as he sat on the edge of the desk. "He served under me for a while. Our styles didn't mesh very well. I guess my style didn't mesh very well with a lot of people."

Ardo could not think of anything to say in the silence that followed.

"Well," Littlefield went on, looking away, "it's a nice infirmary but you *are* on duty. Guard duty now that I think of it. Here's the box—whatever the hell it's supposed to be—and I don't think that woman will give you any trouble. Still, keep on the com channel, and whatever you do, stay awake! I'll go find us a couple of nice new rifles and fresh ammo. Breanne wants to set the watches, then we'll see about some chow. I'll be back before you know it."

"Sure, Sarge." Ardo nodded. He had not realized how tired he was until he sat down. "I hear you."

Littlefield smiled. "Head still bothering you?"

Ardo nodded slightly. "A little."

"I guess the resoc is taking after all. And hey, you're a veteran now! You've made your first kill and survived to tell about it."

The zergling twitched before him. The beast's dull, black eye stared back at him.

"And God said, Let the waters bring forth abundantly the moving creature that hath life . . ."

Ardo could not breathe.

Ardo frowned suddenly and looked away. "Yes, sir."

Littlefield frowned slightly. "You're going to be all right, kid. I won't be long."

The sergeant stood up and walked purposefully toward the door. The door obliged him, slipping out of his way and then closing once he had passed.

Ardo took a deep breath.

There was nothing for him to do but wait. He could imagine nothing worse than to be left with his own thoughts.

"I'll never leave you behind," he said to her. The wheat rustled about the blanket where they lay.

He was falling into her luminescent blue eyes.

Golden . . .

Ardo stood up. There had to be something he could do. His head was throbbing once again.

The woman on the bunk was apparently not faring much better. She was starting to struggle dazedly against the restraints, her moans increasing.

Ardo quickly started searching through the wall cabinets of the infirmary. He wet down a towel in the wall basin and moved over toward the woman.

"Easy, lady," Ardo spoke in soothing tones. "Nobody is going to hurt you."

The woman's head flailed from side to side beneath her nimbus of matted, tangled hair. Her struggles were getting more pronounced by the moment.

"Hey . . . look, lady, you've got to relax! We're here to help you." It was not working. Ardo grabbed the woman by the shoulders and shook her. "Stop it! Listen to me!"

The woman suddenly stopped struggling.

"You're safe now," Ardo sighed as he released her shoulders. He took up the wetted towel again and moved to brush aside the hair covering the woman's face. "You're in the Confederacy Garrison at Scenic. No one is going to . . ."

His voice trailed off.

Golden.

He blinked, then shook.

The woman stared at him from the bunk.

The nimbus of her long shining hair played softly in the warm, gentle breeze drifting over the wheat field.

Tears welled up unbidden in Ardo's eyes. "Melani? Melani! It's you! My God, it's a miracle! A miracle!"

Overwhelmed, Ardo clasped the woman's head lovingly in his hands.

He drew his lips close to hers.

The woman screamed.

CHAPTER 13

MERDITH

ARDO JUMPED BACKWARD AS THOUGH HIT BY AN electric shock. IIis head was pounding. "Melani! Please, stop! It's me!"

The woman screamed again, her eyes wide with fright.

Ardo held his hands up, trying to will her to calm down. His eyes stung, filling with tears. His head throbbed, almost blinding him as well. "Please! I won't hurt you. You're confused . . . and . . . and hurt. It's been so long, I . . ."

"Get away from me, you bastard!" The woman's teeth chattered as she struggled to control her fear. "Where the hell am I?"

"You're in the infirmary at . . . uh . . . at . . ." Ardo winced against the pain exploding in his skull. He was finding it hard to think. "At the Scenic Garrison . . . on Mar Sara. It's a Confederacy outpost base . . ."

She struggled against the restraining straps once more, rattling the framework of the wall-mounted cot. Cutter had done his job well. In a few moments, exhausted, she lay back panting.

"Please, Melani." Ardo blinked back tears. He struggled

with the lock rings on his gloves, desperate to remove them, as he spoke. "If only you knew how much I've dreamed of this . . . how much I longed for you. I've seen your face a thousand times in the crowd . . ."

She turned her face toward him, still blinking, struggling to remain conscious. "This is a Confederacy base?"

"Yes!" Anguish in his face, Ardo stepped toward her. "Oh, Melani, if you only knew how sorry I am . . ."

The woman yelled at him with all her strength. *"Take one more step you sonofabitch and I'll kill you!"*

Ardo stopped, frozen, unable to move forward or retreat. The thundering pain in his head overwhelmed him. He gave a single, choked cry and collapsed to the floor, sobbing uncontrollably. Memories washed and flooded across his mind. Golden fields. Golden hair. Screams and crimson blood.

It was some time before he heard her voice, quietly talking to him.

"Hey, soldier-boy, it's all right. Relax, it's gonna be fine."

Ardo looked up through the blur of his tears.

"Just take it easy, okay? We'll talk . . . just talk . . . all right? I'll help you make it better. Deal?"

Ardo nodded slowly. He was spent, sitting ignominiously in his battlesuit on the floor of the infirmary, his back propped against the desk.

"That's fine." The woman's voice was calm and deliberate, as though she were talking a suicide away from the edge of a cliff. "You just sit there and we'll talk for a minute and get all this sorted out, okay?"

Ardo nodded vaguely again.

"My name is Merdith. What's yours?"

Ardo sucked in a ragged breath.

"Look at me."

Ardo did not know if he had the strength. "Oh, Melani . . ."

"Look at me," Merdith said a little more forcefully.

Ardo raised his eyes.

"Look at me closely." Merdith lay still, concentrating her

dark eyes on Ardo's face. "Look at my hair . . . look at it. Is that, uh, Melani's hair?"

Ardo struggled to concentrate.

"Look at it . . . see it. Is that Melani's hair?"

The hair was different. It was obviously much darker, even without the dirt. Melani's hair was so beautifully fine and . . .

"My eyes," Merdith ordered once more. "Are these Melani's eyes?"

Ardo shifted and gazed into the woman's dark, almost black eyes. They were like deep pools in a cavern. Melani's own eyes were such a brilliant blue . . .

Ardo looked away. "No . . . those are not Melani's eyes."

"Hello. My name is Merdith," the woman tried quietly once more. "What's yours?"

"Ardo . . . Ardo Meln . . . Private Ardo Melnikov, ma'am." Ardo still could not look at the woman on the bunk. "I'm . . . so very sorry, ma'am. I don't know what happened to me. Please . . . accept my apologies."

"It's all right, soldier, no harm done." Merdith looked up at the ceiling, considering before she spoke. "You're a resoc, aren't you?"

"Ma'am?" The throbbing in Ardo's head had left for a moment but was making a definite comeback.

"A resoc—neural resocialization—training through memory overlay, right?"

"Yes . . . I guess that makes me a 're-sock' or whatever you call it." Ardo was suddenly very tired again. "Look, ma'am, I said I was sorry for what I did and I meant it. Now . . . well, maybe it's just better we didn't talk anymore."

He gathered up his battle gloves and pushed himself up from the floor. He still could not bring himself to look at her again. He moved back around to the other side of the desk, trying hard to be alone.

But he was never alone, especially now. The ghosts in his mind continued to torment him. The thought of sitting down and waiting for Littlefield to come back was torment.

He needed something else to think about, something else to occupy his mind than the black idle thoughts that were always a moment away from overwhelming him.

The metal case sat before him.

The treasure that had nearly gotten him killed—had killed others already.

There was a puzzle to occupy his mind. The case had two handles on either side. What appeared to be the top was held down by six separate latching mechanisms. They were not locked—which seemed to Ardo to be reasonable enough invitation to open them.

He reached forward and snapped open the first latch.

"I, uh, I wouldn't do that if I were you."

Ardo looked up. Merdith was still strapped to the bunk. She was speaking to Ardo, but her eyes were on the box.

"Why not?" Ardo asked in a flat tone.

"Well . . . you might not want to know what's inside."

Ardo snorted, then snapped open a second latch.

Merdith started visibly.

"I'm serious, soldier-boy."

"I'm sure you are," Ardo sighed, idly snapping open the third latch.

Merdith's voice rose slightly in pitch and urgency. "There's an ancient earth legend about this woman named Pandora. You ever hear about that, soldier-boy?"

"Yes," Ardo answered irritably. He was having trouble with the fourth latch. It seemed to be stuck. "We're not all bumpkins in the colonies, you know. I studied mythology in school."

Ardo grunted, and the fourth latch swung open.

"Is that where you met her?" Merdith asked quickly. "Is that where you met Melani?"

Ardo stopped. "What the *hell* are you talking about, lady?"

"Melani, I'm asking about Melani." Merdith licked her lips nervously. "I just . . . I just wanted to know where you met her, that's all."

"Look, uh . . . ."

"Merdith. I'm Merdith."

"Yeah. Look, Merdith, that was a long time ago on a planet you probably never heard of and probably couldn't care less about even if you *had* heard of it." Ardo shook his head, looking for the next latch. "It just doesn't matter anymore."

"What happened there?" Merdith pressed on. "What happened to Melani?"

Sharp pain flashed behind Ardo's right eye. He winced.

"Tell me . . . tell me what happened to her."

He saw her behind him. The Zerg were pressing their attack with anger now. The dropship was depriving them of their prize. Ardo was appalled at how quickly the large crowd had been sundered—harvested like blood-red wheat in the field. The Zerg were already nearly at Melani's side.

Ardo shuddered. "It doesn't matter . . . You shouldn't ask . . ."

"I want to know," she pressed him. "What do you remember, soldier-boy? What do you see in your mind?"

They were already nearly at Melani's side.

Ardo clawed and fought. He screamed.

Three hydralisks grasped Melani at once, dragging her back from the edge of the crowd.

"What do you *see*?"

"Leave me alone!"

"Please, Ardo!" she wept. "Don't leave me alone!"

The mindless mob pushed him farther into the ship.

Merdith urged again. "Tell me!"

"*She's dead, all right?*" Ardo raged. "She's dead! The Zerg attacked our settlement. The Confederacy came to evac us and I tried to save her and I failed, okay? I tried . . . I tried to get her into the dropship but the crowd was between us . . . and I . . . and I couldn't . . . I just couldn't . . ."

Ardo's voice trailed off. To his surprise, he saw his own sadness mirrored in Merdith's eyes.

"Oh, soldier-boy," she spoke quietly. "Is that what they told you? Is that what you believe?"

The com channel chimed in his headpiece, the sound carrying into the room. Somewhere in Ardo's mind he recognized it but could not bring himself to answer its call.

"I'm so sorry for you, soldier-boy."

The com channel chimed once more. What was this woman trying to tell him?

The com channel chimed a third time.

"You gonna answer that?" Merdith asked.

Ardo shook himself from his confused thoughts and toggled the com to Open Vox. "Melnikov here."

"Littlefield here. You all right up there, son?"

Merdith continued to keep her eyes on Ardo. The marine had become more than a little suspicious of the woman. He stepped back around the desk, and hopefully out of range for the woman to overhear the com channel.

"Yes, sergeant, we're just fine here."

"Are we, indeed? Well, I've found us a pair of very clean and very new Impaler C-14's fresh out of storage for us both. I'll be with you directly. What's the condition of your prisoner?"

"She's talkative," Ardo replied, drawing a wry smile from the woman.

"Well, let's hope she remains that way. The lieutenant wants both her and that box brought up to Operations as soon as I join you. I'm at the Command Center entrance now. Littlefield out."

Ardo toggled the com channel to Standby once more and quickly began closing the latches on the box.

"I hope we'll get a chance to talk again, soldier-boy." Merdith's words were silken. "I know something about Melani's fate that you really should be told."

"You couldn't possibly know anything about it."

"But I do."

"Like what?"

"That it's all a lie, soldier-boy. It's all a lie."

CHAPTER 14

DIMINISHING RETURNS

"HEY, MELNIKOV! THE LIEUTENANT WANTS US UP AT Operations on the—Melnikov, you all right?"

Ardo had barely noticed Littlefield moving through the door. He was still staring at Merdith, his eyes narrowing. "What did you just say?"

Littlefield mistook Ardo's words as being meant for him. "I said the lieutenant wants us up at Operations. Lose something?"

The sergeant tossed a new C-14 gauss rifle to Ardo. Feeling its weight in his hand was reassuring. Without thinking, Ardo checked the breach, noted the load count on the clip, and armed the weapon. It felt good to be doing something mindless.

"How's the woman?" The sergeant carefully set his own new weapon on top of the metal case, then walked quickly over to the bunk where Merdith remained bound. "Oh, I see you're awake, ma'am. How are you feeling?"

"Restrained," Merdith answered flatly.

Littlefield laughed to himself as he checked the dilation of her eyes. "Well, I see you haven't lost any humor. Anything broken? Anything sprained?"

"I'm portable," Merdith responded.

"Yeah, but I'll bet you're hard to move," Littlefield chuckled as he leaned back. "All right, miss, I'm going to let you loose now. The lieutenant wants to have a few words with you. There's nothing to worry about—we just pulled you out of a bad spot and this is just routine, you understand?"

Merdith nodded.

"So you aren't going to give me any trouble, are you?"

"And if I did?" Merdith sniffed.

"Well, we both have very big guns, ma'am."

"That's what they all say," Merdith laughed in turn. "I won't be any trouble, Sergeant, and I very much want to talk to your lieutenant. I'll be polite."

"Now that's what I like to hear," Littlefield said pleasantly as he began undoing the restraining straps from the bunk. "I'm sure we'll all be really good friends as soon as we get a few things cleared up. Isn't that right, Melnikov?"

"Sir, yes, sir," Ardo responded automatically. Somewhere inside the depths of his brain he was not all that certain.

Littlefield undid the nearest ankle strap last and then took a large step back.

"Frightened?" Merdith said as she sat up.

"Cautious, ma'am," Littlefield replied as he reached back behind him and took his weapon. "Just cautious."

"How about your treasure chest over there?" Merdith's voice seemed casual to Ardo in a very studied, dangerous sort of way. "Does it get to come with us?"

"Why is that any concern of yours?" Littlefield's eyes narrowed.

"I've been baby-sitting that little crate for quite a while now. Let's just say we've gotten to be quite attached to each other." Merdith slid off the side of the bunk, carefully trying to stand. Her left foot bent over wrong, however, and she had to catch herself before she fell.

"Hurt, ma'am?" Littlefield asked.

"Just the pride." Merdith lifted her foot to examine the ruined boot. She shook her head. "And these were my favorite pair, too. Well, as my mother used to say, 'Make do or do without.' You think you can find me some duct tape around here somewhere, Sarge?"

"Duct tape?" Littlefield laughed. "Isn't that a bit old-fashioned?"

"Ask an engineer," Merdith said as she limped toward the infirmary door. "You can fix anything with duct tape."

The Operations Room was situated at the very top of the Command Center. The Great Designer—whoever he was—had decided to make it into a large box with sloped armor and a ring of transsteel windows running around the entire room. An officer could see in all directions through those windows by walking along a raised platform that ringed the room on all four sides.

The centerpiece of the Operations Room, however, was the command island, a raised circular platform situated in the center of the room. From here the central command staff could monitor activities not only through the windows beyond but at the various stations around the Operations Room.

Command consoles were situated on the underside of the walkway platform as well as on the command island. These could monitor nearly every aspect of operations that a remote base of the Confederacy might be called upon to perform. They were rarely ever used all at once. They only had their transport covers removed when the demands of the base's mission required them. It was said that one could get a good feel for what a base was tasked to accomplish just by knowing which consoles had been uncovered for use.

As the lift platform brought Ardo, Merdith, and Littlefield up into the Operations Room, Ardo was struck by the number of consoles still secured under their transport covers. He had not been in Scenic long enough to get more than a limited look at the base—just the barracks, actually, before they set out on the morning mission. As he stepped off the lift with Littlefield, a quick glance around told him that there really wasn't much more to the base than just the barracks. There was a factory console open with its machine shop console next to it as well. They could make basic things here, apparently, but not much more. A single supply station was uncovered, too. He was more interested in what was missing: those consoles that were still covered and never pressed into service. Armory, Engineering, and Starport support were all still sealed. More important, the refinery controls remained locked up, meaning that they had no means of producing their own gas to power any larger pieces of equipment. All they could rely on would be whatever remained in the depot stores. At least there was one console he was just as glad was still secure: there apparently was no Academy here, either.

Not much to work with, Ardo reflected. *Why is this base even here?* he wondered.

Lieutenant Breanne stood hunched over the command table on the island. Cutter stood nearby, intent on Breanne's instructions as she pointed at the surface display on the table.

"The perimeter fencing extends only about three-quarters of the way around the base. It ends here . . . and here . . ." —Breanne pointed again at the display—"at the top of this cliff face. There's about a thirty-foot drop straight down and then another twenty feet of loose dirt and rock to the base of the ravine. The face is sandstone—pretty slick stuff even for the Zerg. The ravine empties down into the Basin, most of which is a nuclear slag pile now. I don't expect 'em from this direction, but I don't exactly want to be surprised by them either."

"Lieutenant?" Littlefield spoke up.

Breanne did not look up from the display as she spoke. "Yes, thank you, Sergeant. Cutter, get out to the perimeter. Have Xiang and Mellish give the defense towers a quick look to make sure they're all operating, then set the watch as we discussed."

"At your will, Lieutenant," Cutter replied with a stiff salute.

He jumped down off the island, his heavy firebat suit causing the floor plates to ring with the impact. His broad face flashed into a massive smile as he saw Merdith. "Well, Princess! Nice to see you with your eyes open!"

"Flattered, I'm sure," Merdith yawned.

"Hey, you should be. Not every woman gets to be rescued by Fetu Koura-Abi!" The huge islander thumped the chest-plate of his firebat suit, then rumbled as suavely as he could muster. "No need to thank me now. I'm sure you can think of better ways to thank me later!"

Merdith batted her eyes at him with exaggerated motion. "Gee, thanks for bringing me here, you big, strong marine you!"

The sarcasm was completely lost on Cutter. "Hee-hee. You find me later and I'll take care of you better than ever."

Cutter strutted to the lift, missing completely Merdith's rolled eyes and soured face.

It was not, however, lost on Lieutenant Breanne, who now stood facing them from the island with her arms folded across her chest. Her short-cropped hair seemed to bristle on its own. "My name is Lieutenant L. Z. Breanne of the Confederate Marines. And you are?"

Merdith eyed the lieutenant carefully, sizing her up. "I'm Merdith Jernic. I am . . . well, was . . . an engineer down at Oasis Station."

"An engineer?"

"Yes, that's what I said."

"And what did you engineer?"

"Thermal wells and condenser systems for the water supply."

"I see." Lieutenant Breanne stepped down from the island, her hands still folded across her chest. "And you were found in possession of that case."

"Well, I . . . don't know," Merdith replied levelly. "I believe I was unconscious at the time."

Breanne chuckled darkly. "How convenient for you."

"Well, ma'am, if you're about to be eaten by the Zerg, I certainly recommend being unconscious first."

Breanne's eyes leveled with Merdith's. "Do you know what is in that case?"

Merdith hesitated for a moment, then responded, "Do you?"

Breanne smiled thinly, then strode directly over to where Littlefield and Ardo still held the metallic box between them. "Let's find out."

"Wait," Merdith said quietly.

Breanne snapped open two of the latches in a swift move.

"Wait," Merdith spoke more insistently.

The lieutenant turned her icy eyes toward Merdith. "You have something to say."

Merdith licked her lips.

Breanne took two quick steps, her sharply angled face suddenly within inches of the civilian's. "What is so important in this case?"

Merdith looked away.

Breanne's voice was low and dangerous. "I've had a very long day, lady, and I don't have any intention of making it any longer. The Confederacy Marine Command sent me and my people here to retrieve this damn box . . . and I don't ask any questions. They drop me in the middle of some godforsaken planet in the outer colonies . . . and I don't ask any questions. Now that I've got the damn thing, I've been left here high and dry, my evac has deserted me, a tactical nuclear device drops behind me unannounced . . ."

Unannounced? Ardo thought. *The lieutenant had not even been warned of the incoming?*

". . . half my platoon is wasted dragging their asses out of this mess only to find my sortie base is suddenly a ghost town . . . and *now, now at last,* I have some questions. And you are going to answer them."

Merdith's eyes flashed with anger.

"What is in this case?"

"It's proof."

"Proof of what?"

"Proof that the Confederacy brought the Zerg to Mar Sara," Merdith snapped. "Proof that the Confederacy is developing a terrible weapon capable of destroying the civilian population on entire worlds."

Breanne let out a grunt of disbelief and walked back to the case. She once more began flipping open the latches. "So now you show up with a box full of papers and documents and other such 'proof' and expect me to believe—"

"Please, stop!" Merdith shouted.

Breanne pulled out her side arm in a single swift motion, leveling the muzzle between Merdith's eyebrows. "Why should I?"

"Because," Merdith spoke quietly, her voice as level as her eyes fixed on the lieutenant's gun, "that box contains the device that called the Zerg here. If you open it, you'll activate it, and every zergling, hydralisk, or mutalisk within ten thousand clicks of this building will move heaven and earth to get into this very room."

"You're insane," Breanne murmured.

"No, ma'am," Merdith countered, her voice subdued. "With all due respect, I think you are describing the people who would build such a thing."

Ardo held his breath. He felt almost detached as he watched the exchange taking place not more than a meter in front of him.

Breanne's gun remained steady. "You stole this . . . this device?"

"No, ma'am, like I told you: I'm an engineer. Some members of the Sons of Korhal brought it to me for examination."

"'Sons of Korhal'?" Littlefield tilted his head skeptically. "Who the hell are the 'Sons of Korhal'?"

"Damned if I know," Breanne sniffed. "Some local troublemakers, probably. Korhal is a planet in the core Confederacy worlds that rebelled some time ago. I think it was under quarantine blockade last time I heard anything about it. We've seen a lot of these lately—small, isolated rebel groups trying to undermine the integrity of the Confederacy."

"We're growing," Merdith sniffed proudly. "We may be small now, but soul by soul, house by house, planet by planet we threaten this so-called Confederacy."

"Terrorists," Breanne snapped.

"Revolutionaries," Merdith returned.

"Gnats with delusions of grandeur," Breanne snorted. "So these terrorists brought the box to you . . ."

Breanne's voice lowered to a whisper.

"And you opened it . . . didn't you?"

Merdith continued to gaze at the gun muzzle, but remained silent.

Breanne lowered her weapon and holstered it.

"Merdith Jernic, I'm placing you under custody pending an investigation into the theft of Confederacy property."

Merdith smiled to herself as she shook her head. It struck Ardo as ludicrous to arrest the woman, but Breanne always seemed to do things by the book, regardless of how little sense it might make.

"I will investigate your statements and, if they are found to be substantially truthful, you will be released. Do you understand?"

Merdith nodded with a chuckle. "More than you may know."

"Littlefield, leave that 'evidence' here with me and escort this woman down to the barracks for some chow. Have her back here in an hour."

"Begging your pardon, ma'am," Ardo spoke up.

"You have something to contribute, Private?"

The iced steel eyes swung on Ardo, making him most uncomfortable. "Yes, ma'am. I'll take the duty, ma'am. I could use some chow myself and it might relieve the sergeant for more pressing duties."

"You're volunteering, Private?"

"Yes, ma'am . . . if it's quite all right."

Breanne shrugged. "Be my guest. Littlefield, find that Tech Sergeant Jans and get him up here. We'll see if we can get this puzzle put together. And, Melnikov . . ."

"Yes, ma'am?"

"Have her back here in one hour," the lieutenant emphasized. "I want her none the worse for wear, but don't lose her."

"Yes, ma'am."

Ardo took Merdith by the arm and guided her toward the lift. The lieutenant may have no more questions, but Ardo had plenty of his own, and he had no intention of losing Merdith now.

CHAPTER 15

MIND'S EYE

ARDO PROPELLED THEM BOTH DOWN THE MAIN ramp of the Command Center and toward the nearest barracks entrance just to their left. The wind was howling out of the west, whipping the dry dirt in the compound. The whirls of sand whispered and moaned between the buildings. Ardo, still in his combat suit, was relatively unaffected by the gale. The woman next to him, however, was exposed to the elements. Her right arm held the lapel of her worker's coveralls across her face, her left arm still held firmly by the marine.

Ardo was in a hurry to get her inside, and not because of her exposure to the weather.

They passed between the massive landing struts and repulsor pads of the southern barracks. A column of golden light poured from the access ramp, making it easy to find.

He loved the barracks, he thought suddenly, but wondered why they always made him feel queasy in the stomach. He did not take time to think about it, however: there was too much to think about as it was. Still holding Merdith's arm in a firm grip, he marched them both up the ramp and into the deployment room.

Deployment was one of the larger spaces in a very cramped arrangement. It sat at the top of the ramp and was used by marines for staging. All around him there were weapons and equipment racks. Most were ordered and locked, although a few of the cabinets hung open. A maintenance kit sat on the floor in front of one of them. Someone apparently working on a battlesuit had just left it there.

The entire site had been abandoned, apparently without much notice. More questions. They made his head hurt, but he thought he might have some of the answers quite literally at hand.

"You all right, ma'am?" Ardo asked casually. "That wind is pretty awful tonight."

Merdith coughed a couple of times as she patted the dust off herself with her free hand. "That wind is pretty awful *every* night, soldier-boy. We're raised on sand here. It doesn't bother us." She sighed and then winced, looking up at Ardo through his faceplate. "Say, if I promise not to run away, do you think you could let go of my arm?"

Ardo blinked, letting go. "Oh, uh, yes, ma'am. You wouldn't do anything stupid, would you?"

"I promise I won't dance with anyone else all night." She smiled, then looked around for a moment. There were numerous exits from the Ready Room that led deeper into the barracks. "So, where do you go around here to buy a girl a cup of coffee?"

"That hatchway on the right," Ardo gestured with the muzzle of his C-14. "You first. . . . I insist."

Merdith arched her eyebrows and smiled casually. Ardo smiled back, pressing open the visor on his combat suit with his free hand. Merdith nodded and moved ahead. The massive pressure door swung open easily.

Dim light illuminated the corridor beyond. The passage was

lined with large transparent tubes. Each appeared to be filled with a blue-green liquid that circulated constantly. Monitors above each showed them to be in ready mode. Each had its own separate panel of controls, while at the end of the corridor to the left of another pressure door stood a raised control booth.

"By the gods," Merdith spoke almost reverently. "These are neural resocialization chambers, aren't they? These are the things they put you people through."

"Keep moving," Ardo said. "Just through to the other side."

"What's wrong? Are you all right?"

"Just keep moving," Ardo snapped.

"You don't like this place, do you? You're frightened of it. I can feel it."

"Lady, I said *move!*"

Merdith winced at the shout and quickly walked to the opposite door.

"Go right," Ardo ordered. He felt slightly dizzy. He loved resoc . . . he hated resoc . . . he looked forward to resoc . . . he would rather shoot himself than do resoc again.

Merdith quickly opened the door and stepped off into the brightly lit corridor beyond, with Ardo too closely on her heels. They moved past the barracks cells proper, including the one where Ardo had stowed his gear earlier, and passed through the final doorway to the galley.

It was a cramped but efficient room. Whatever had happened to take the personnel of the base away had apparently not been during anyone's regular dining shift. The compartment was pristine. Ardo was just as glad that no one had left anything behind. He was weary of the constant reminders that the place had been so fully occupied hours ago and was now so completely desolate.

"Nice place you have here," Merdith observed casually. "Sterile, but nice."

"The food dispensers are back along that wall," Ardo said,

motioning with the rifle again. "They're not hard to operate. Just—"

"I know my way around a kitchen, soldier-boy." Merdith stepped toward the bank of meal and drink dispensers. "You want anything? Cup of coffee?"

"No, ma'am. Don't drink coffee."

Merdith pulled a cup from the dispenser and began filling it. "Really? That's interesting. Did you know that coffee was one of the things most people begged to have sent with them when the original colonies were exiled from Earth?"

"Yes, ma'am, I'd heard that."

Merdith turned around with her steaming cup and leaned back against the wall. Silence fell between them. There was so much that Ardo wanted to ask, but the questions tumbled through his mind, running into each other. What was she saying before Littlefield came in? Something about it all being a lie? But now that he thought about it, he couldn't recall what they had been talking about exactly.

"So, we gonna be disturbed anytime soon?"

Ardo came back from his thoughts, realizing angrily that letting himself drift away like that while guarding this woman might well get him killed. "Sorry? What, ma'am?"

"Are we alone? Anyone gonna be bothering us for a while?"

Ardo flushed. "Please, ma'am, I really don't think you ought to be talking that way. It isn't . . . isn't right."

Merdith started to answer but stopped. Her slack mouth quickly became a delighted smile. "You thought I wanted to—"

"Now, ma'am, it doesn't matter what I thought." Ardo could feel his face going beet red and knew there was not a thing he could do to stop it. "I'm . . . I'm guarding you and it wouldn't be proper."

"Proper?" Merdith was having entirely too much fun and Ardo knew it was at his expense.

"Yes, ma'am! Proper!"

"I don't believe it." Merdith took a long sip of her coffee and then tipped it in salute toward Ardo. "You're a virgin."

Ardo knew his voice was too loud when he opened his mouth. "I don't see that it's any of your business, ma'am!"

"Now I *know* I've seen everything!" Merdith was delighted. "A virgin Confederacy Marine!"

"It wouldn't be honorable, ma'am . . . not to either one of us. Now, why don't you just sip your coffee and relax . . . I mean . . . we've got an hour before you're due back . . ." The more he talked, the worse it seemed to get. Finally Ardo just let his words trail off into a frustrated silence.

Merdith looked away, amusement still in her eyes. "Don't worry, soldier-boy, your secret is safe with me." She sat down smoothly at one of the tables. "Besides, that really isn't what I meant. You're a nice guy and all, soldier-boy, but all I honestly want to do is talk. That is what you had in mind, isn't it?"

"Yes, ma'am. I—"

"Call me Merdith."

"Oh, I don't know if I—"

"Sure, it's just us. Let's be friends."

"Okay . . . Merdith. I'm . . . I'm PFC Ardo Melnikov."

The woman tipped her cup again in thanks. "Okay, Ardo. It's nice to meet you. So . . . tell me. How is it that you fine marines came to rescue my sorry soul?"

Ardo thought for a moment. "I'm sorry, ma'am, I can't discuss mission details with—"

"With a civilian, I know," Merdith finished the sentence for him. "I'm just curious about how you got me out of there. The last few days are a bit hazy for me. Where did you find me?"

"Oh, I didn't find you, ma'am. That was Cutter—PFC Koura-Abi. That big guy you met earlier in Ops."

"Of course. So where did *he* find me?"

"Don't really know, ma'am. First thing I saw he had you over his shoulder and was running back to join the rest of us at the barricade."

Merdith's eyes smiled warmly at him. "I see. So how did

we get out of there? The lieutenant mentioned something about her 'evac' deserting her?"

"Oh." Ardo shrugged. "There was a dropship with us that was supposed to extract us when we had that box. We fought our way to the extraction landing zone, but . . . it never showed up."

"I thought you said it was with you?"

"Yeah. Strange, that. I heard it talking about its final approach to the landing zone—it's all on the com channel—but we never saw it. It just—I don't know—wasn't there. The Zerg had cut off our retreat and it looked like it was time for us all to cash our last paycheck. The lieutenant, though, she had us fight our way out of there. We lost a few along the way, but what's left of us are still here. If the dropship had come, we'd have been okay. Some sort of SNAFU, I guess."

"A SNAFU?" Merdith nodded absently with a slight smile playing on the edge of her lips. "Yeah, I guess it could be that, although your lieutenant seems to have more than her share of them. What was all that about a nuke?"

"Oh, that." Ardo shrugged again, but his face settled into an uncertain frown. "Well, after we hightailed it across the Basin, the Confederacy nuked Oasis. Just a little tactical. Good thing, too, or those Zerg would have followed us and taken us all out at the wall."

"Well, we wouldn't have wanted that," Merdith sighed, but her brows were knit together in deep and troubled thought. She came to a conclusion, her brow smoothing as she looked up again with a quickly flashed smile at Ardo. "Well, we made it thanks to you—me to my life of thermal wells and you to thoughts of that girl of yours. What was her name? Oh, yeah, Melani."

Ardo swallowed. "What do you know about Melani? You said she was a lie, or something was a lie. What were you talking about?"

Merdith gazed down into her coffee. She looked for all the world to Ardo as though she were reading the swirls like some kind of gypsy divination rite.

"The truth is dangerous, Ardo. You're a nice little soldier-boy. Maybe it's better not to discuss these things."

Ardo put his boot on the bench opposite where Merdith was sitting and leaned forward. "Ma'am—Merdith—a wise man once told me that truth is the only thing that is real. Truth is what's left when all the shadows and darkness are torn away. I believe that and I think you do, too."

"What I believe isn't the point here," Merdith replied, looking at Ardo as if for the first time. "The point is what you believe."

Ardo did not understand what she was saying. All he knew is that he wanted to know the truth, that he was tired of the shadows haunting his mind and driving him slowly mad. "What happened to Melani? What happened to my parents? What happened to my world?"

Merdith sighed. "Ardo . . . You remember we were talking about Pandora's box?"

"What?" Was she changing the subject on him? "Yeah, we were talking about the metal case we found with you . . ."

"Yes, that's true, but I'm asking if you remember the story?"

"Sure I do. What's the point?"

"You've got a Pandora's box inside you. Do you really want me to open it? Once it's open, you can never, ever close it up again."

Ardo winced. His head was beginning to pound once more. "You're saying the answer is inside of me?"

Merdith seemed to come to a decision. "Tell me about that last day. Tell me everything about that last day with Melani on your old home world."

The pounding in his skull increased. "What does that have to do with—"

"Just tell me," Merdith insisted. "Start at the beginning of where things went wrong—you know there was a moment when things just started to go wrong—what were you doing just before that?"

Ardo winced against the pain. Why was she making him do this? Why was he allowing himself to do this? He didn't know this woman. She was probably a spy or anarchist or God knew what.

He had to know. He had to know the truth.

"We . . . we were in a field . . ."

Golden . . . a perfect day that comes along all too rarely . . .

". . . having a picnic. It was the most beautiful day. Warm in the spring. Oh, God . . . do I have to . . ."

"It's all right," Merdith assured him. "I'm here with you. We'll walk through the day together and I'll be there with you. What changed that perfect day?"

"The siren in the township went off. The alarm siren. I thought it was the usual noonday test, but Melani said it wasn't noon and then . . . they came."

"Who came?"

The sun was dowsed in that instant. Enormous plumes of smoke trailed behind fireballs roaring directly toward him from the western end of the broad valley.

"The Zerg came."

"Can you see them? What do they look like?"

"I can't see them . . . just balls of fire coming down through the atmosphere."

"What kind of entry would cause that, Ardo?"

Ardo blinked. "What do you mean?"

"What would cause the Zerg to make big fireballs and smoke contrails in the sky like that?" Merdith pressed. Her eyes were locked on his as she spoke.

"High speed, I guess. A lot of heat builds up on atmospheric entry, I suppose," Ardo replied.

"But have you *ever* heard of the Zerg entering a planetary atmosphere that way?" Merdith asked softly. "They swarm across space. Their arrival is soft and silent."

Ardo closed his eyes. The light in the room seemed to be hurting them. "What . . . what are you saying?"

"*I'm* not saying anything. I'm *listening*," Merdith said. "Just try to relax and remember. Talk to me. Please . . . what did you and Melani do next?"

"Well . . . we ran! We ran toward the township. The old colony had a defensive wall and we thought we might be safer inside. I don't know how we got there, but the next thing I remember was that we were inside along with everyone else."

The rattle of automatic weapons clattered suddenly from the perimeter wall. Two dull explosive thuds resounded, followed by even more chattering machine guns.

"What was it like?" Merdith urged quietly, her eyes fixed on Ardo as she sipped her coffee.

"Well . . . chaos! The Zerg were attacking and—"

"No, I mean, tell me what you *saw*. Tell me what you *did*." Ardo closed his eyes.

"Please, Ardo!" Melani said. "I . . . Where do we go? What do we do?"

Ardo glanced around. He could taste the panic in the air.

"We were in the square. It's a large open area in the middle of the town. We used to have concerts there or plays in the summer evenings. I'd never seen it so crowded. We were shoulder to shoulder. Melani . . . I held her hand and we tried to cross the square."

"Yes, that's right." Merdith put the cup down. Her unblinking eyes remained fixed on Ardo. "What did you see next?"

Ardo felt suddenly cold. His eyes shut against the images that came unbidden from the depths of his mind.

A sheet of flame erupted beyond the fortress's outer wall. Its crimson light flashed against the blanket of smoke that hung oppressively over the town. The blood-red hue fell across the panicked crowd in the square. Screams, shouts, and cries all tumbled into a cacophony of sound, but several disembodied voices penetrated Ardo's thoughts clearly.

"It's the Confederacy forces! It's the marines!"

"No!" Ardo reeled backward from the table, his combat suit slamming into the wall behind him. The plastic wall cracked under the sudden impact. "That's not what he said!"

"What *did* he say, Ardo?" Merdith was standing now, leaning forward, both her hands on the table. "What did you *hear*?"

"He said . . . he must have said . . . '*Where* . . . *where* are the Confederacy—'"

"That's a lie, Ardo!" Merdith shot back. "Remember! Think! Neural resocialization can't replace memories; it can only cover them over with new ones! What did you *hear*?"

"Ardo, I'm frightened!" Melani's eyes were wide and liquid. "What is it? What's going on?"

There were so many words he wanted to say to her in that moment—so many words that he would regret never having said for uncounted years to come.

"Tell me what you *see*!" Merdith demanded.

The eastern wall had been breached. The old rampart was being pulled down from the other side, dismantled before Ardo's eyes. It seemed as though a dark wave was breaking against the breach.

"Stop it!" Ardo screamed. "What are you doing to me?"

"You wanted the truth. You've opened the truth, in yourself," Merdith said. "The ugly, horrible truth and it won't go back in the box, Ardo. Not again. What did you *see*, Ardo? What happened next, Ardo?"

Ardo slid along the wall toward the door of the mess room, reeling backward away from Merdith. He wanted to run, wanted to get as far from this woman as possible, but somewhere in his mind he knew that he was not trying to run from her but from the beast lurking in his own mind.

Ardo heard Melani gasp behind him. "I can't . . . I can't breathe . . ."

The mob was crushing them. Ardo looked desperately around him, trying to find a way out.

Movement overhead caught his eye. The angular, bloated form of a Confederacy dropship, still glowing from the fast atmospheric interface of landing, was dropping down overhead.

Tears flooded Ardo's eyes.

Tears flooded Ardo's eyes.

The downblast from the engines created an instant hurricane in the panicked crowd. Ardo blinked through the dust as the dropship lowered its transport ramp into the square. He could see the silhouetted figures of Confederacy Marines . . .

They grabbed him.

They tore him from Melani's hand.

"Melani!" he screamed.

"Melani!" Ardo screamed in the mess hall.

"Please, Ardo! Don't leave me alone!" she cried as the marines dragged him into their ship.

Ardo struggled to escape them as the ramp closed. Something hit him from behind and his world went black . . .

Slowly, the world grew brighter. Ardo was sitting on the floor. His eyes focused slowly on Merdith. She knelt beside him, her hand on his tear-streaked cheek.

Her voice was heavy with emotion. "Poor soldier-boy. It's been that way all over the colony worlds, from what we hear. The Confederacy needs to build an army as fast as they can. They've been press-ganging boys for over a year now and then using their neural resocialization to layer as many false memories on top of their existing ones as necessary—until their manufactured soldier-boys believe whatever the Confederacy *needs* them to believe. They go where they are told to go. They die when they are told to die."

"Then Melani . . . my folks . . ." Ardo struggled for breath.

"I don't know, Ardo, but they almost certainly didn't die the way you remember it happening, and most likely didn't die at all."

"Then everything I know is a lie," Ardo said weakly.

"Perhaps," Merdith said. "But if you're willing to help me, I think we both may be able to get off this cursed world. I can help you if—"

Ardo pressed the muzzle of his rifle firmly under Merdith's chin.

CHAPTER 16

BARRICADES

"WHAT HAVE YOU DONE TO ME?" ARDO SHUDDERED, his hand quivering on the trigger of the C-14 assault rifle.

Merdith held very still. Her voice was quiet and terribly deliberate as she spoke. "Not a thing, Ardo. Not one blessed thing."

"Get back!" Ardo could hardly see beyond the pain banging against the back of his forehead. He was having trouble focusing. "Just back off slowly."

"I'm so sorry, soldier-boy."

"Don't touch me!" Ardo squealed, his voice shaking with terror and outrage. The gun muzzle shivered under Merdith's chin.

Merdith slowly raised both her hands, palms open toward the marine. "Okay Ardo. I'm going to back away now. Just relax."

Merdith rose up with aching slowness, smoothly backing against the mess hall table. Her eyes were locked with Ardo's, unblinking and holding his attention.

Ardo steadied his rifle but found its aim wandering dangerously. He could not seem to keep it steady. He wanted to stand, to get some distance between himself and the woman sliding slowly back to sit on the table.

She had done something to him, something to his mind. It was a trick, some sort of drug or attack that he had not seen. He tried to remember the way it had been—that perfect, golden day turning blood red. He could see the Zerg pouring through the breach in the town wall, and he could see the Confederacy Marines doing the same thing. The Zerg were tearing at Melani and the marines were dragging her away all at the same time and in the same place. He had two truths in his head at the same time. He knew that they could not both be true, but that knowledge did not help him choose between them. He longed for sleep, some blessed place of unconsciousness where he could awake from this nightmare and his thoughts would have all been sorted out for him.

Both memories could not be real, but inside himself he realized that somehow they both *were* real and that the full truth lay beyond both memories. He dreaded the answer, either way, but he also knew that he had to have it, whatever the cost. Something within him demanded the truth.

Ardo staggered to his feet, regaining his composure as best he could. He breathed deeply to calm himself. His rifle aim steadied.

Merdith made no move, no sound.

"What did you do to me?" Ardo asked levelly.

"*I* didn't do anything to you," she replied calmly. "You might ask that same question of the Confederacy—"

"Cut the crap, lady," Ardo snapped. "I may not be playing the same game you are, but that doesn't mean I can't read the score. You did something to my head"—Ardo jammed the rifle muzzle toward her head for emphasis—"so what did you do to me?"

"I didn't plant anything in your mind, if that's what you mean."

Ardo raised the rifle to his shoulder, squaring his aim between her eyes.

"Easy!" Merdith leaned back slightly, her arms still raised. "I swear. All I did is . . . unkink what was already there. Look, I'm a psych, okay? I'm an unregistered psych. I fell through the screening process—it happens sometimes in the outer colonies. They never suspected. I wasn't interested in the Confederacy psych program, so I just kept quiet about it. I'm not trained or anything—I just have a gift for helping people get their minds straightened out sometimes, that's all. I swear, that's all."

Ardo lowered the weapon slightly. He considered her words for a moment before he spoke again. "Tell me: what *really* happened to my family? What happened to Melani?"

"I don't know."

Ardo brought the weapon up quickly again.

"I don't know!" Panic, anger and frustration tumbled through Merdith's voice, her words rushing in staccato sounds as she spoke. "I don't know! Maybe they're alive! Maybe not! How should I know? They're your memories, not mine!"

"Aahh!" Ardo grunted as he lowered his weapon in disgust. "Worthless! You're absolutely worthless!"

"Look, soldier-boy, I didn't do this to you," she answered. "Neural resocialization just layers new memories on top of old ones—it doesn't replace them. All I did was help you straighten out your head a little."

Ardo shook his head. "But you still can't tell me which memory is the real one and which is the false one, can you?"

"You were the one who wanted to know the truth," she said sullenly.

"Yeah? What truth?" Ardo growled. "*Which* truth?"

"I don't *know* which truth. But you *do* want to know what the truth really is, don't you?"

Ardo look at her and considered. She had opened his mind. There was no closing Pandora's box now. "Yes . . . I have to know!"

She sighed through a slight smile. "Then help me and I'll help you find that truth. I know some people who can get us off this world. Help me get in touch with them . . . reach them . . . and they'll help us, too. We'll go back to your planet . . . uh . . ."

"Bountiful," he finished for her quietly. The word was almost too painfully beautiful to say.

"Yes, back to Bountiful. And we'll find the truth together."

Ardo was about to answer her when the com channel chimed in his ear. He responded automatically. "Melnikov here."

"Escort the prisoner to Operations on the double, Private." Littlefield's voice sounded somehow different to Ardo, but the private had enough worries of his own to think about it much.

"By your word, sir," Ardo responded, then turned to Merdith. "That's enough coffee and conversation. Let's go."

The lift had not even cleared the Level 3 landing before Ardo could hear the voices yelling overhead.

". . . supposed to do once we storm the transport? You've heard the tactical channel traffic. Do *you* have a better option?"

"I don't know! I don't have all the answers! All I know is that I'm not giving up on these grunts, Breanne! They deserve better than this!"

"Yes, they do, and that's exactly my point. If we'd been good little soldiers we would have sat under that *nuke* and caught the damn thing with our teeth. That's what they wanted, isn't it? But we're here and still breathing."

"So just what the hell are you telling me, ma'am?"

"I'm saying I don't like this any more than you do, Littlefield, but we are running out of options! You have a better idea, then fine! Let's hear it right now!"

The lift seemed agonizingly slow. Ardo glanced at Merdith.

Her face was a blank, but Ardo could see that her eyes were focused and intent. She was soaking in every word drifting down from above.

"I don't *have* an answer!" Littlefield rumbled. "Someone must have screwed up! If we just get on the tactical channel, we can get this thing straightened out with CHQ!"

The lift cleared the floor plates of the Operations Room. Breanne was standing on the island, her arms folded defiantly across her chest as she leaned back against one of the consoles, staring down at the map table. Littlefield's face was ruddy as he faced her, his large fists gripping the edge of the map table. His knuckles were nearly white with fury. Between them stood Tinker Jans at the far side of the island. He looked to Ardo as though he were caught in a crossfire and trying to make himself as small and as still as possible.

"Look for yourself! That's satellite data, Sergeant. Clean band and updated in real time." Breanne's finger stabbed out suddenly, indicating each location as she spoke. "Zcrg infestations moving in from the northeast in a ragged line here, here, and here. Advanced recon groups will be reaching those outer settlements in the next few minutes. The rest of the northeast settlements will be hit within an hour after that. Where are our marines on this map, Sergeant?"

Littlefield stared at the map and said nothing.

"They're all at Mar Sara Starport," Breanne answered for him. "Confederacy dropships have been evac'ing every position for the last three hours. All of the heavy equipment is gone. There are still ground forces being brought to the central transports at Mar Sara Starport, but those will be loaded within the hour. Dropships are returning from the outposts now with the last remaining marines. Tinker's brother, the esteemed Tegis Marz, is returning from his last run now."

"The same guy that left us high and dry last time?" Littlefield was incredulous. "What makes you think that he'll go out of his way to come back for us now?"

"Because we aren't the ones who are going to do the asking," Breanne replied, her eyes flashing. "Tegis has been choking the com channels for the last half hour trying to find out who brought his brother out of our little garrison here. Apparently he doesn't know his brother got left behind."

"Hey, it wasn't my fault!" Tinker said. "I went out to repair the downlink. Who knew the SCV was balky. It quit on me out there and I had to hoof it back. I ran like hell when I saw the dropships hovering over the base, but by the time I got back they were gone."

"I'm glad you did." The lieutenant's smile was wicked. "You're my new best friend, Tinker. You'll call your brother once he's on the ground over the com channel and convince him to come and get you." She looked up at Littlefield. "When Tegis comes to get his brother, we rush the ship and take it back to the Starport. Then we'll straighten out this SNAFU and get the hell off this planet."

"You can't do that!" Merdith interrupted.

"Ah, Ms. Jernic." Breanne noticed Ardo and his prisoner for the first time since they arrived. "It seems you'll be joining us on a little trip."

Merdith ignored the remark. "Without the Confederacy outposts, there will be nothing left to stop the Zerg!"

Breanne shrugged. "Well, there's always the vaunted local militia . . ."

"They don't have either the equipment or the numbers to stop a planetary infestation!" Merdith started to walk toward the command island, but Ardo grabbed her arm, firmly restraining her. "What about the civilians? What about *their* evacuation?"

"The Confederacy," Breanne grumbled, "has apparently written off the planet . . . including its civilians."

Merdith struggled against Ardo's grip, but the marine held her back. "Written us off to the Zerg? It was that Confederacy device that *brought* the Zerg here! With all their weapons and all their starships and all their soldier-boy marines, they wanted more power. So they built that box, not even comprehending the death it would bring with it. They thought they could control them or capture them. They had no idea what they had unleashed. And now they're just 'writing us off' as though we were some cipher on a balance sheet!"

No one in the room had an answer for her.

Merdith stopped struggling, anger still in her face.

"A planet full of monsters. I just thought I'd never see them among my own kind."

Breanne looked up, her wicked smile returning under the bristle of her hair. "You never know, do you?"

"Lieutenant," Littlefield interrupted. "Tac-com one-twenty-nine."

"On speakers," Breanne commanded.

"*This is the* Vixen *on radial three-four-zero, forty-five clicks to MS Station . . . stand by to refuel for immediate dustoff.*"

"*Negative,* Vixen. *Report to the OOD for evac on landing.*"

"Hey, he'll be on the ground there inside of ten minutes," Tinker said nervously. "Maybe . . . maybe they won't let him leave again once he's on the ground."

"*Any word on my request regarding Scenic Station?*"

Ardo looked up at the speakers.

"*Negative. No contact.*"

"*What about that personnel request? I gotta find that tech!*"

"*CHQ has no information for you at this time.*"

"All right, you know the drill," Breanne said. "Jans, get on the horn and call—"

"*Lieutenant, this is Xiang! We have multiple contacts bearing oh-five-five degrees!*"

Breanne glanced down at the map table, her eyes suddenly wide. "Where? How many?"

"*There's a . . . Stand by . . . There's about twenty . . . maybe twenty-five passing to the south. Hydralisks, I think, ma'am. And . . . oh, hell! There's a flight of eight mutalisks above them.*"

"They're not on the map," Breanne seethed. "Why aren't they on the map?"

"*The mutalisks are turning. They are vectoring toward the base. Permission to fire, ma'am?*"

Breanne continued to stare angrily at the map table.

"Permission to fire, ma'am?"

All of the color drained from Tinker's face.

Littlefield looked up. "Breanne?"

The lieutenant shook herself from her frozen state. "Negative! Hold your fire!"

"What . . . what do you mean, hold your fire?" The technician's eyes darted around in fear.

"Listen to me! We don't want this fight right now." Breanne motioned everyone else up to the command island. "Everyone take cover! If anyone is spotted, open fire, but until then stay out of sight. Don't transmit, just monitor. There have been reports that the Zerg can follow transmissions to their source. Just wait for my command, and hope like hell they pass us by!"

"What is the universe coming to," Littlefield muttered, "when marines start hiding under desks!"

Ardo propelled Merdith up the short ladder to the command island. As he did, light blossomed to the west. Through the windows he saw in the east the glowing trail of the first Confederacy evac ship arching into the sky.

CHAPTER 17

WEAK LINKS

ARDO VAULTED UP THE LADDER TO THE COMMAND
island. The space was crowded enough with the large equipment banks nearly completely surrounding the map table
in the center. The combat suit only made things worse in
the cramped space. Still, the consoles were built to marine
specs and designed for durability as much as for functional-
ity. They had a clear path to the lift. Ardo wondered why
they did not all just disappear into the bowels of the Command Center rather than try to duck for cover behind the
consoles of a fish bowl like Operations.

Breanne crouched behind the map table. It was not the
first time Ardo was struck with her catlike movement. She
switched off the display on the map table, then smoothly
pulled a large set of field binoculars up to her eyes. "Six of
them . . . no, make that seven. Mutalisks flying cover for a
ground force of . . . let's see . . . maybe fifteen or twenty
hydralisks about a half mile to the south." Breanne slid back
down next to the table, out of sight of the windows. "There

may be more beyond that, maybe a mile or two. It's difficult to say. The main force seems to be passing us by. Everyone stay put. Let the flyers have their fun ogling the 'old abandoned human base.' Once they're a few clicks safely away from here we'll make the call and catch our ride home."

Ardo sat with his back against a console directly opposite to Jans. The engineer was intent on every word Breanne was saying. He was pale even in the dim light of the Operations Room and nodded rather more vehemently than he probably should have. Jans swallowed hard, then his head slowly turned toward the ladder exit from the island just to his left. Ardo followed the man's gaze. He was staring toward the tactical communication panel just below the catwalk to the west. It was still lit, the muted words of the chatter of the starport still pouring out of it through the speakers mounted above the island.

"Transit alpha four-oh-niner, cleared for immediate departure pad seven. Transit alpha oh-six-five hold short at pad fourteen. Transit gamma eight-zero-zero cleared to pad twelve. Transit delta two-two-zero, hold at Lima for cross traffic . . ."

Jans's eyes grew large as a second flare of light erupted through the western windows above the tac-com console. "There goes another one," he breathed.

"They aren't wasting any time getting out," Littlefield muttered. The sergeant seemed distracted and detached, his mind working on a different problem.

Ardo knew it was his imagination, but the knowledge did not help him. The chatter from the speakers seemed unbearably loud. "Shouldn't we shut that off?"

Breanne shook her head, looking up as she listened. "Too late. They're here."

Ardo realized he could hear it, too: the fingernails-on-slate sound of the mutalisks screaming at each other as they neared the human base. The sound cut through the windows to reach their ears, mixing with the constant chatter from the tac-com open channel.

"Transit alpha oh-six-five cleared for immediate departure pad fourteen . . ."

"Control. Vixen *inbound requesting vector . . ."*

Jans caught his breath.

"Vixen, hold at nav marker Ta-shua and stand by; the pattern is full."

"Roger, control, holding at Ta-shua."

Another column of flame and smoke tore upward through the darkening atmosphere.

Merdith crouched next to Ardo, hugging her knees to her chest. "Looks like you soldier-boys are going to miss your boat."

Breanne's eyes reflected a practiced indifference. "We're not finished yet, Ms. Jernic."

"No, of course not," Merdith responded evenly. "All I'm saying is that if you *did* happen to miss your boat, you might want to consider other means of departure."

"Ah," Breanne smiled back at her, baring her teeth, "you mean throw our lot in with a spy and a traitor, perhaps?"

"Sorry to disappoint you, Lieutenant." Merdith shrugged. "But I'm no spy."

"No, of course not." Breanne casually looked away toward the windows. "Not a spy, not a collaborator, not an expert doing weapons research for the Sons of Korhal. You are just an innocent civilian engineer who was found in accidental possession of a highly classified piece of Confederacy equipment." Breanne stopped, turned to Merdith, and smiled frostily. "Look, Ms. Jernic, I choose to believe you. I choose to believe you because if I choose otherwise I'll have Mister Melnikov here take you out of this Command Center and shoot you as many times as necessary to insure that you are very permanently dead. Now, you don't want me to choose *not* to believe that, do you?"

Merdith considered the angular face in front of her carefully. "No, Lieutenant, I most certainly do not."

"Then, Ms. Jernic"—Breanne sniffed derisively—"for the time being, you keep your company and I'll keep mine."

"Whatever you say, Lieutenant," Merdith spoke casually. "However, may I point out that *your* friends are apparently leaving the planet in droves while *my* friends may soon be the only ones with a ticket off this planet. Even if you *do* manage to get back to the starport somehow, just how pleased will your superiors be to see you? Nobody likes to see a dead man walking in the door . . . especially when it's in everyone's best interest that the body *stay* dead."

A horrible scraping sound rang through the tritanium roof of the Operations Room. Ardo winced against the sound, pulling his rifle up closer to his chest in his sudden tension.

"Hold still." Breanne breathed out her words as quietly as she could manage. "They're here."

Everyone looked up. The sound of scraping scales on serrated tails dragged casually across the armor shivered through the plates overhead. The sound occasionally obliterated the surreal voices so casually communicating from the still operating tac-com transceiver.

"*Transit gamma eight-zero-zero, cleared to depart pad twelve immediately. Transit epsilon four-three-three, hold short at rho-beta intersection.*"

There were two additional scraping impacts on the roof plates. Ardo could clearly hear the dreadful, screeching voices of the mutalisks as they slithered about the rooftop. He glanced at Jans across from him. The man was sweating profusely, his eyes fixed on the transceiver as though somehow he could crawl through the device and somehow join the distant voice on the other side.

"*Transit epsilon four-three-three clear to proceed to pad ten . . .*"

"*Control, this is* Vixen *holding at Ta-shua. What's the delay? I've got to see the base commander and . . .*"

"Vixen, *you are cleared to land. Report at outer marker. Over.*"

"*What about my brother? I don't know . . .*"

Jans gritted his teeth. Another voice came across the com channel, not nearly so detached.

"*Marz, for the last time, he's probably already off-planet in an* unreported transport. *Get your ass down out of the sky right now.*"

"Copy that, sir! Vixen *on final appr . . . repor . . . outer mark . . .*"

Ardo glanced at Littlefield, whispering. "The transmission's breaking up?"

"The mutalisks," Littlefield sighed. "They're playing with the antenna dishes."

"*. . . final appr . . . tand by.*"

"*. . . oger . . . ansit epsilon four-three . . . eared for . . . mediate departure pad seven-left. Vixen, taxi left to platform seven-three for shutdown.*"

"Roger, control. Vixen *taxiing to platform seven-three.*"

Breanne pointed to her ear and then toward the ceiling. Ardo strained to hear.

The scraping sound had stopped.

Littlefield put his thumbs together and moved his hands like flapping wings. Breanne shrugged and shook her head, her eyebrows knitted together in doubt.

Ardo unconsciously held his breath. He was concentrating so hard on the sounds overhead that he did not notice Merdith's nudge until her second try.

She was pointing toward Tinker Jans.

Ardo could see at once that the man was in bad shape. His pale skin glistened with sweat. He was physically shaking, his lips moving as he spoke to himself. His eyes were fixed on the transmission console just a few steps from the base of the command island.

"*Transit kappa oh-seven-five cleared for immediate departure. Vixen, what is your status?*"

"Are they gone?" Littlefield hissed.

Breanne shook her head. She did not know.

"*My load has disembarked, control. I'm clean.*"

"Roger, Vixen. *Shut down and proceed to platform five-right. Report to the section chief there for embarkation and departure.*"

"No!" Jans whimpered. "Don't leave me here!"

"*Don't leave me alone!*" Melani wept. Ardo froze.

"Vixen, *roger that. Shutting down . . .*"

"No!"

Jans hauled himself up in a single movement. Ardo lunged for him, but he was too late. The engineer propelled himself through the gap between the consoles of the command island, running across the floor plates.

"Quick! Stop him!" Breanne snapped.

Ardo sprang to his feet, clearing the access ladder in a jump, but he could not reach the engineer.

Tinker Jans swept up the dangling communications microphone and keyed the transmit button.

"Tegis! It's Jans! I'm here! Don't leave me! I'm back at the base at Scenic! They left me behind, they—"

Ardo had no time to think as he ran across the floor. When he reached Jans, he simply drew back his combat suit fist and launched it at the engineer's head.

The power-enhanced, armored glove did its job well. Jans fell unconscious to the floor.

"Jans! Jans! I'm coming to get you! Just hold on and . . . hey! Let go of me! That's my brother out there! You can't—"

Shattering windows drowned the words out. The transparent panes exploded into the room. Instinctively, Ardo ducked away from the cascading crystal. He heard the sudden chattering of automatic fire in the room.

Above the screeching, Ardo heard Breanne's unmistakable voice filling the com channel. "Open fire! Open fire and kill them all!"

CHAPTER 18

JAWS OF VICTORY

ARDO DOVE BACK TOWARD THE COMMAND ISLAND, instinctively arming his rifle. He was still rolling upright when he began discharging his weapon.

Three mutalisks launched themselves through the framework of the shattered windows. Their purplish wings were shredded on the remaining shards, but the creatures were oblivious to the damage they were inflicting on themselves. There was madness in their flat, blood-brown eyes: mindless, relentless, and deadly. Ear-piercing screams erupted from their wide, gaping mouths as they charged.

"Keep firing! Keep firing!" Breanne shouted through the com channel. Ardo was happy to oblige. His gauss rifle joined the hail of death erupting from the guns on the command island just behind him.

Wing membrane, cartilage, skin, muscle, all exploded in shreds from the ugly beasts as they fanatically moved forward. The wet pieces slammed against the panels, ceiling, and floor, exploding into acrid smoke. Within seconds the entire command chamber was filled with the swirling, thick stench that even the outside wind, now howling through the shattered windows, could not dissipate.

Ardo continued to press his fire. He could see the nearest mutalisk open its mouth, its jaw muscles working. He had a glimpse of fanglike projections on either side of its massive jaw.

It's attacking, Ardo suddenly realized. He dove to his left.

A gush of bat-winged abominations disgorged from the creature's maw toward the base of the command island where Ardo had just squatted. The sightless creatures splayed against the metal, erupting on impact. The floor plates melted away in a terrible, high-pitched squeal. The mutalisk shifted the fowl stream, attempting to follow Ardo, but the marine was too quick for the creature. His feet under him, he sprang forward toward the alcove of the elevator door.

The deadly eruption continued to follow him, the mutalisk now fixed on Ardo as its only thought. The vomited creatures slammed in a line across the floor, the plates dissolving like water under their impact. Acrid smoke filled the room, making it difficult for Ardo to breathe with his faceplate still up. He scrambled toward the elevator alcove. The curved door was closed. To the left and right of the elevator were the raised platforms above the control stations. There was no other cover. He was running out of places to hide.

He reached the elevator bay and slammed his hand against the call button. He turned quickly, his open palm repeatedly smashing down on the button. He glimpsed the hellish rush of winged abominations issue from the mutalisk's maw, evaporating metal in a straight line toward him.

Suddenly the mutalisk's horrible attack stopped. Ardo looked up. The head of the mutalisk exploded under a stream of tracer fire from the command island. Bits of the creature rained down around the room. Several greasy pieces impacted on Ardo's battle armor, the creature's latent acid clawing at the metal fabric of the suit. Ardo yelled incoherently as he brushed the pieces away quickly with his gloved hands. His suit was badly pocked, but he did not think anything had burned all the way through.

His pursuer fell heavily to the floor, the impact almost immediately dissolving the plates beneath him. A gaping, smoking hole was all that was left of the place where the creature fell as it burned down through the deck. By the sounds coming from the fissure, it was still burning its way down through several decks of the Command Center.

Ardo, his back to the elevator door, raised his weapon again. He searched desperately through the smoke swirling madly about the room, but he had lost sight of his companions. For that matter, he suddenly realized, the weapons from the command island had gone silent.

"Lieutenant?" Ardo asked tentatively.

Overhead, Ardo could still hear the tac-com channel. "*. . . Repeat,* Vixen, *return to base at once. That is a direct order!*"

"*Jans! Hold on! Tegis is on the way! I'm comin' for ya, kid!*"

Marz! Ardo realized. He must have gotten the message! He was inbound right now. All they had to do was . . .

Ardo swallowed. All they had to do was be here.

The rotating emergency lights flashed through the swirling, acrid smoke. Jans might just be his ticket out of here, he suddenly realized. If everyone on the command island were dead, then he could pull Jans out to the dropship. He could tell Tegis that he had been left behind, too. What the hell did he care about the mission or that damn box! If he could get off-world then maybe he could find a way out of the resoc tanks and make his way back to Bountiful. Maybe he could get his life back all over again and to hell with the marines and their Confederacy! Then, maybe he could find out if his life had been a lie. Maybe, just maybe, Melani was still there somewhere, looking for him, waiting for him. Maybe, just maybe . . .

Ardo shouldered his weapon. The smoke was still thick in the room, but Ardo remembered where Jans had fallen. He quickly began picking his way across the gaping rifts in the floor. Jans had fallen somewhere near the transmitter console to the left of the command island. If he could just get there before anyone noticed him, he could slip out AWOL in the confusion and then use Jans to get off this rock. He could quit this damn Confederacy and its marines and get back his life.

The marine moved with a wary anticipation. There were still at least two more mutalisks out there somewhere. Maybe they were dead but more likely they were lurking nearby.

"Scenic Base, this is the Vixen *five miles out from the marker! Jans, please respond! Jans! Please respond . . ."*

Ardo reached Jans. The tech was still out cold where Ardo had decked him.

Something struck the side of his combat helmet. Ardo did not notice it at first, but it was followed by a second light impact.

Ardo quickly grabbed his weapon and swiveled toward the command island. Heart suddenly racing, he saw Lieutenant Breanne through the swirling smoke, crouching next to the map table. Merdith was just behind her. Littlefield crouched on the other side of the map table.

Breanne signaled for Ardo to hold his position. She then pointed her first two fingers toward her own eyes and then pointed at Ardo.

Ardo understood the standard signal and looked once more around the compartment. The smoke was quickly clearing from the room. Acid had clearly damaged many of the consoles, and there were several melted troughs in the room. Smoke still poured from the hole burned by the fallen mutalisk, but otherwise the room appeared clear. Ardo looked back at Breanne and shook his head.

Breanne nodded a curt acknowledgment and then pointed down at the technician.

Ardo looked down quickly. There was a nasty bruise coloring a rather large knob rising on the side of his head. He certainly didn't envy the man the headache he'd have later . . . if he woke up. Ardo realized with a start that he did not actually care if the man ever woke up, as long as he could use him to get on that dropship.

Ardo looked back at Breanne and held out his hand palm down and level. Stable, he signaled.

Again, Breanne nodded. She pointed at Jans, then at Ardo, and then signaled the marine toward the elevator.

He had forgotten about the elevator! Ardo glanced behind him. The curved door had rolled back and the elevator itself now stood open and ready for them. He nodded again toward Breanne. He reached down and grabbed the unconscious technician by the collar of his fatigue jacket and began to drag him slowly across the floor toward the waiting elevator. His eyes were fixed on the little compartment, brightly lit and welcoming.

"Jans! It's Marz! I'm a mile out . . ."

Ardo glanced through the broken panes of the command deck. In the distance, to the west, he could just make out the dropship: a dot silhouetted against the multiple con-trails of Confederacy transport ships reaching into the sunset beyond.

"Don't you . . . orry broth . . . be . . . ith you . . . ust a few . . ."

Something bright fell between him and the elevator, splashing against the floor plate.

It was smoking where it landed.

Ardo quickly looked up.

A ribbon of molten silver ran in a ragged arc across the ceiling. Its curve continued toward itself, circumscribing a circle in the ceiling directly above the command island.

"Lieutenant! Move! Now!" Ardo screamed into the com channel.

Breanne and Littlefield looked up at the same time. The structural cross supports were melting under the rain of acid. Already they could hear the low groan of the metal giving way under its own weight.

They needed no further urging. Breanne leaped over the

console bordering one side of the island. Littlefield grabbed Merdith's arm and ran for the stairs. He propelled her ahead of him, launching Merdith toward the catwalk around the room's perimeter before jumping clear himself.

With a wrenching groan, the ceiling of the Operations Room gave way, crashing downward toward the command island. The weight of the ceiling hull plates and cut structural supports crushed the island consoles with a thunderous sound. The entire communications antenna farm came crashing down with it, twisting into a barely recognizable tangle as the heavy hull plating slid down off the wrecked island and against the acid-weakened floor plates.

Ardo pulled furiously on Jans, trying to stay out of the way of the massive avalanche of writhing metal. The technician, however, was beginning to struggle against him as he regained consciousness. *His timing is lousy,* Ardo thought, but he needed this man to make his escape from this hell.

"Get ready!" Breanne shouted. "They're here!"

Breanne had already rolled painfully to her feet. A deep gash on her shoulder was bleeding freely through a tear in her combat suit. Littlefield was on the other side of the ruined island with Merdith. Ardo could see the two of them moving, trying to get around the wreckage to the elevator.

It was then that he spotted them: winged shapes rushing down through the ragged opening in the ceiling. The mutalisks had carved a new way into the Command Center, scattering the humans from their protective cover. The prey were in the open now and vulnerable.

Ardo released Jans quickly beside him. They were at the open elevator. The now listless body lay across the threshold so as to keep the elevator door from closing again. It was all that the marine had time to do before raising his weapon.

Merdith struggled to her feet, glanced up, and screamed— more out of honest surprise than fear, Ardo supposed. It was hard to think of that woman being truly afraid of much of anything. Whatever the reason, Ardo noted it got their attention. The remaining mutalisks dove down through the opening, sailing into the room en masse.

Breanne did not wait. Her assault rifle began chattering away at once, slamming the winged nightmares into the wreckage. Two of them had impaled their wings on the twisted spikes of the broken antennae and support frames. They writhed and screamed in outrage against the indignity of being knocked out of the air, tearing themselves against the sharp edges of the torn metal.

Ardo had no time to concern himself with Breanne's fight, however. A leathery darkness of his own rushed toward him with impossible speed. He opened up with his own weapon, knocking it, too, out of the air. The creature refused to stop, however, and began writhing its way across the ruined floor. Ardo shredded its wings, blasting away at the membrane with deliberate effort. Some cool part of his mind took over, a part that he thought he would like to forget but that stepped forward now to save him when he needed it. Ardo ran as he fired, out of the alcove and toward his target. It continued to press toward him, relentless and heedless of the damage it was taking. Ardo continued to eat away at the creature's wings. *A few more feet should do it,* he thought. Ardo stepped slightly to his left.

The mutalisk suddenly coiled, then sprang.

Ardo was waiting. He shifted his fire the moment the mutalisk attacked. The stream of slugs from his rifle slammed against the chest bone of the mutalisk, pushing it backward in midair and over the gaping chasm its brother had burned through the floor before him.

The mutalisk flapped its wings but there was little left of them to catch the wind. It screamed in outrage as it tumbled down through the hole. Ardo stepped forward, shifting the stream of his fire now to the head as well as the chest and felt strangely satisfied.

"Thou shalt not kill . . ."

"An eye for an eye . . ."

"Love those that hate you . . ."

A wave of nausea passed over him, but he could not stop—would not stop. He shifted fire once more toward the mutalisks still struggling to reach Breanne. Their combined fire was quickly shredding the beasts. Caught in the metal framework of the antennae, their own acid blood was working against them. Every wound ate into the metal around them, melting it and causing the antennae to collapse down on them even further, pinning them in place.

"Run! Merdith, run now!"

Ardo turned quickly toward the sound. It was Littlefield.

The sergeant was blasting away at a mutalisk of his own, but it was dangerously close. Ardo could see from where he stood that the shower of acid from the approaching creature was eating into Littlefield's armor. Merdith was behind him. They were both on the opposite side of the Command Center.

Littlefield's own stream of fire was ripping through the beast, showering the debris between them with smoking bits of ichor.

Merdith started to run, but the mutalisk shifted toward her. Littlefield quickly darted between them, continuing his fire. The beast slithered toward them.

Ardo shifted fire from his own dying targets, but hesitated in frustration. The mutalisk was between him and Littlefield. If he began firing on it, he would risk not only hitting both Merdith and Littlefield but spraying them with acid from the disintegrating creature. He yelled, "Littlefield! Get out of the way!"

Ardo could see the sweat beading on Littlefield's forehead.

The sergeant glanced at him, grinned, and then leaped directly toward the mutalisk. Burying his weapon in the gut of the creature, Littlefield reached out with his free hand and gripped the monster by the throat. Enraged, the mutalisk coiled its razor-edged tail around Littlefield.

"No!" Breanne roared.

"Run!" Littlefield shouted, his voice rising in agony. "Run, Merdith!"

The mutalisk was coming apart under Littlefield's fire. The acid pouring from its body was melting the sergeant's combat suit, merging the two bodies hideously.

Merdith, the color drained from her face, ran around the wreckage in the center of the room. She joined Ardo on the far side but could not bring herself to look.

Breanne moved up, shouting, screaming. "Get away, Littlefield! Let go and get away!"

Littlefield's weapon continued to fire. Ardo thought surely the flesh from his hand had been eaten away by now. Perhaps only the melting armor of the suit kept the gun firing. The mutalisk stopped struggling as the pool of acid formed beneath them.

The floor plates groaned once more, and Sergeant Littlefield with his defeated foe vanished from view.

Ardo was shaking so hard that he found it difficult to hold on to his weapon. Outside they could hear a different scream, more familiar and higher pitched.

Merdith looked up toward the sound and then shouted, "Look!"

The dropship. The *Valkyrie Vixen* hovered thirty feet away, its engines shrill and beautiful to their ears.

Ardo sucked in a ragged breath and turned around. Jans was leaning up against the side of the elevator, dazed but with his eyes open. Ardo stepped gingerly over to him across the buckled floor plates and pulled him to his feet. "Mister, it's time you got us the hell out of here."

They moved quickly toward the remains of the window. Ardo could see Marz through the cockpit canopy.

Breanne breathed out and then spoke. "We're leaving."

Merdith, standing beside her, seemed troubled. "Lieutenant, how many of those winged horrors did your sentries report inbound when all of this started?"

"Eight. Why?"

"Well, did any of your sentries report any kills? I mean, I don't think I . . ."

Breanne's eyes went wide. She turned to the dropship and began waving at him. She was shouting. "Get out! Go around!"

He was smiling and waving back.

"No! Damn it! Get out!" Breanne shouted, waving more emphatically. "What the hell is the tactical channel? I can't seem to raise him on the—"

"Oh, no!" Merdith breathed.

The remaining three mutalisks soared up over the command center. Marz was too intent on finding his brother to notice. By the time he realized they were on him, the mutalisks were already disgorging their spawn into the engine intakes and against the canopy.

Breanne raised her weapon and began firing. Ardo joined her, but it was too little and too late. Desperately, Marz throttled open the engines and the unsuspecting mutalisks were sucked into the intakes. The acid flowed into the engines, separating turbine blades from high-speed shafts. In moments the dropship began tearing itself apart.

Marz managed to get his *Vixen* only a hundred yards to the west before it exploded, sending shards raining down throughout Scenic Outpost. It crashed into the ravine just west of the base, burning furiously as the hypergolic tanks collapsed.

Beyond the thick column of smoke, Ardo saw more Confederacy transports arch gracefully into the sky, their contrails glowing salmon-orange against the crimson horizon of the setting sun.

There were not nearly as many as he had seen before.

CHAPTER 19

DEBTS

ARDO STOOD IN SHOCK. HIS MIND DID NOT WANT TO register what he had just seen. Suddenly, it seemed hard to breathe. He began gulping down long, shuddering breaths. What was there left to do?

He turned to face Lieutenant Breanne. Her eyes were staring unfocused at the burning hulk beyond the perimeter as though she were seeing completely through it.

"Lieutenant?" Ardo spoke quietly, somehow afraid to disturb her. "What do we do now?"

Breanne blinked. She did not—could not—look in his direction. "We . . . I . . . I don't . . . know. I . . ."

"What do I do, Lieutenant?" Ardo repeated, his voice shaking with an anger that was welling up from deep within him. "Give me an *order*, Lieutenant! Tell me what to *do*, Lieutenant! How do I *fix this for you, Lieutenant*!"

Breanne turned toward Ardo. Her eyes were watery and unfocused. "I think . . . maybe Littlefield would . . ."

"Littlefield is *dead*, Lieutenant!" Ardo's voice was loud and shaking. The beast that always seemed caged somewhere in the back of his mind broke free, yelling into the face of his superior officer. "He's *gone!* He can't help you out of this one, Lieutenant! He's not going to save you. He's not going to make you look good. And he most definitely isn't going to keep you alive this time! It's *you,* Lieutenant, here and now! You give the orders! You show us the way out of—"

"*Bernelli to command.*"

The tactical channel was still functioning. Bernelli's voice cut through some intermittent static.

Ardo stared at Lieutenant Breanne, waiting.

Breanne swallowed, beads of sweat forming on her forehead and among the bristle of her short-cropped hair.

"*Bernelli to command; Come in, command.*"

Ardo grimaced and keyed the channel open on his own suit. "Bernelli," he replied curtly. "The lieutenant specifically ordered everyone to stay off this channel."

"*Not much need, now, Ardo. They're leaving.*"

"What?"

"*The Zerg. They're moving on past us to the west. The whole line of them just passed us right up.*"

"That doesn't make sense," Ardo mused over the channel.

"*Sense or not, that's what they're doing.*"

"*He's right, Melnikov.*" It was Mellish's voice this time. "*I'm watchin' 'em through the bunker. They went by us like a line of locusts and left us behind. I've got a good eye on 'em through these field glasses and they're all slitherin' off to the west. I guess they're all lookin' forward to a night on the town.*"

Ardo blew softly through his lips. Mar Sara City was to the west, now abandoned by the marines and essentially defenseless.

"Cutter, this is Melnikov. I'm with the lieutenant in Operations—or what's left of it. Where are you?"

"*I'm in Bunker Four on the southwest perimeter. What the hell happened up there? Where's Littlefield and the lieutenant?*"

"Get up here on the quick," Ardo snapped without explanation. "The, uh, lieutenant needs you."

"Yeah, well, if the lieutenant needs me, she *can ask for me, and
not some snotty-nosed, trigger-happy preemie of a—"*

"Cut the crap, Cutter," Ardo barked. "Lieutenant wants
you here, so *move*!"

"On my way," Cutter responded in a cold tone. *"If nothing
else, I'd be interested in seeing you. I hope you've kept that woman
warm for me, preemie. I'm sure she'll be glad to see a* man *after having to put up with you."*

Ardo angrily keyed his tactical communications to Off,
then turned toward the elevator bay. "I'm sorry, Merdith. I'll
see to it that Cutter doesn't bother—"

The elevator door was closed. The indicator lights on the
panel in the alcove showed the lift descending. A feeling of
dread rushed over Ardo.

Merdith was gone.

Ardo cast his eyes quickly around the room. The fallen section of the overhead hull now sat at an awkward angle to the
floor. The consoles on the left side of the command island were
crushed nearly to the floor plates by its weight, but the right
side remained elevated. Ardo quickly made his way across the
buckled and acid-torn floor plates.

"Melnikov?" Breanne spoke as though she were just waking up. "Damn it! What the hell are you doing?"

"It was sitting on the floor just a few feet from me," Ardo
muttered as he leaned forward peering between the consoles
on the right side.

The box was gone, too.

Ardo roared, his voice a wordless expression of animal outrage. He glanced at the elevator. Too long, he realized. He'd
never catch her that way. He turned and pulled himself up
the short ladder to the catwalk that now was a ripple of bent
metal around the room. Grasping the open pane of one of the
shattered windows, he pulled himself forward into the howling wind and looked down.

The dark, curving hull dropped away below him in the fading twilight. Pools of light emanated dimly from the windows of the Command Center and from the anticollision markers that blinked mournfully from the various equipment pods jutting from the main hull. Just beyond the curve of the hull, a large bright patch of yellow light extended from the main doors of the Command Center across the small patch of compressed dirt between the dark patchwork of the base buildings.

There, a long shadow emerged. It was cast by a single, small female figure struggling to run with a heavy case.

Ardo glanced at the power indicators just below the lip of his helmet. He had not yet dipped into the power reserve. It would be plenty to catch up with her.

In a single movement, Ardo pulled himself through the window opening and began running down the slope of the Command Center. His booted footfalls rang against the hull as he made his way down the various sensor armatures around the hull. Such a suicidal dash would have been impossible without the combat suit, but despite the whine of the servos in complaint of the abuse, he quickly made his way down the ever-increasing slope of the outer hull. Merdith was running west toward the factory unit. Ardo checked her position as he ran. Within moments the slope became too steep to support him, but he was already within twenty feet of the ground. He held on to a protruding thruster pod for a moment, then jumped into the air.

He landed hard, rolling on the ground as his training had taught him. The suit absorbed most of the impact, the servos whining as he rolled to his feet and set off in pursuit at a dead run.

Turning the corner, Ardo saw an array of vehicles in front of him. Each had been parked outside of the automated factory that had churned them out on demand, only to be abandoned. The evening wind was whipping blinding dust between the various SCVs, ground support trucks, and a line of enclosed Vulture cycles.

Ardo stopped. She was in there somewhere, he knew. All he had to do was find her.

The wind was howling around his head, but he turned up the external audio sensors anyway. He switched the tactical channel to standby. He knew Breanne would start asking after him soon enough, and he did not want the distraction.

Ardo moved slowly forward through the machines, stepping carefully and quietly. He thought absently how amazing it was that as complicated a piece of military hardware as a battlesuit was, it could still move with deadly quiet when required. He raised and readied his weapon. He knew that he was perfectly willing and able to shoot Merdith through the head if necessary—and quite possibly even if it was *not* necessary.

The sand-obscured SCVs stood as still as sentinels. The armored titans were just over ten feet tall. Ardo wove his way between them smoothly, his rifle at the ready.

Something creaked in the wind to his right. He spun around, his rifle quickly leveled in the direction of the sound. The vision augmentation in his closed faceplate illuminated the culprit at once: an open maintenance hatch on an SCV leg flapped in the wind. He turned back again on his ragged course, picking his way forward.

An engine turned over with agonizing slowness somewhere just ahead of him. Ardo smiled thinly to himself and stepped smoothly around another SCV that was blocking his line of sight.

It was a hauler, a truck nearly as tall as an SCV. The chassis was suspended between six massive balloon tires, three on a side. The control cab jutted out from the front. Ardo could just make out the glow from the cab's windows through the wind-whipped sand.

Getting into the cab was something of a problem. One had to climb up a vertical ladder to get to one of the side hatches. He could do it in the combat suit, of course, but he suspected the lieutenant would prefer Merdith alive. A direct assault was not the best way to achieve this objective. He suddenly had a better idea. Smiling to himself, he made his way around to the back of the vehicle, being careful to stay out of the sight lines from the extended mirrors on either side of the control cab. Then he ducked down and began crawling down the length of the truck chassis. Halfway down, he heard the low agony of the starter motor once again. He began to hurry. The engine sputtered twice, then died.

Under the cab, Ardo slowly brought himself into a crouch just below the driver's-side door. He could see shadows moving in the cab, heard various switches being toggled and Merdith's low mutters.

Ardo quickly stood up and wrenched open the driver's-side door. With his free hand he grabbed the astonished Merdith by the arm, intent on pulling her out of the cab and throwing her to the ground.

Ardo jerked Merdith from the driver's seat in a single motion, his combat suit bringing him incredible strength. The woman tumbled out of the cab, her hands desperately fastening on Ardo's grip. Her flailing legs kicked against the truck cab, pushing Ardo unexpectedly backward with additional momentum. Ardo fell away from the cab, dragging the panicked Merdith with him.

Both of them tumbled to the ground. Ardo quickly rolled to his feet, his weapon already in hand by the time he was standing. Merdith lay painfully on the ground, groaning in the wind at his feet.

"Get up," he said. "You're going back."

Merdith looked up, gasping for air.

"You're my prisoner," he said flatly, raising his weapon.

"Prisoner?" she coughed, her words derisive. "Prisoner of *what*?"

"Prisoner of the Confederacy," Ardo explained dutifully.

Merdith snorted derisively. "That makes two of us."

"Shut up!" Ardo growled.

"Listen, I've been monitoring the com traffic from here."

Merdith pointed up to the cab of the truck. "The Confederacy forces are done with their evac, soldier-boy. Hell, they're probably already out of the system by now."

"So we'll find another uplink!" Ardo was beginning to sweat. "We'll call for an evac. They'll come back and—"

Merdith snapped. "Wake up, Ardo! We're *supposed* to be *dead!* You think that nuke just dropped out of the sky on its own? We were all supposed to *eat* that nuke, soldier-boy! CHQ sent you and your pals out there to find me and my box—that goddamn poison box—and the moment they knew you had it they *called off* your evac and lobbed a big one with you and me and that box as ground zero. They knew your situation top to bottom. They set you up. The only reason they sent you out there was to find me and that lousy box and *die with it*!"

"We're soldiers, lady." Ardo's face flushed red. "Soldiers die! It's our *job* to die!"

"No." Merdith's voice lowered but remained intense. "It is your job to *fight*. You fought today and we lived. CHQ cut you off without a prayer and you *still* fought and you *still* lived. Make no mistake about it, Ardo. As far as they are concerned we are all dead and they prefer it that way. Jeez, they *planned it* that way! No one is supposed to know about this box. If you show up with it at CHQ, they'll make sure that you're all a whole lot deader than they *think* you are now."

"Shut up! Why the hell can't you just *shut up*?"

She pleaded with him over the screaming wind. "Don't throw away your life on phantoms, soldier-boy! The Confederacy lied to you, robbed you of your love, your family, and your entire past. They sent you here to do a dirty job for them, and once you did it they casually tried to murder you. Underneath all that programming and brainwashing and 'social reconditioning' there is still a man—Ardo Melnikov—who deserves to have a life and to live it." Merdith sighed into the wind. "There must be something left deep inside of that noble boy who was raised by loving parents."

Ardo blinked. He was sweating, and the combat suit cooling systems did not seem to be helping. "What . . . what are you suggesting? What are you saying?"

Merdith nodded, their eyes locked. "I'm saying we get out. They think we're dead—let's just leave it that way. We get off-planet and find a new life somewhere else and let someone else do the dying for us."

Ardo smiled sadly. "And just how are we supposed to leave? Walk? The Confederacy left. They took the last of the commercial transports with them. Even if I said yes, even if I trusted you, there's no way off this rock."

Merdith stepped forward, smiling. "Oh, yes, I think there is one way off this rock."

Ardo raised his gun slightly. Merdith took the hint and stepped back.

"The Sons of Korhal," she said levelly.

"The Sons of Korhal?" Ardo snorted. "A handful of delusional fanatics?"

"Yes." Merdith nodded, smiling. "Because a fleet of transport ships of those 'delusional fanatics' is five hours out and inbound to this same rock right now. They'll be landing here to evac anyone they can—anyone who's left—and, my good soldier-boy, I suspect they will be especially anxious and grateful to accept our ticket."

Ardo shook his head but didn't say anything.

"Ardo, we give them that box and we're off on the first flight out!" Merdith pressed her point fervently. "All we have to do is get out of here with that box and stay alive for the next six hours. I know where there is an enclave, the last place the Zerg are going to move against. The Zerg will almost certainly move against the cities first."

"What?" Ardo suddenly realized what she was saying.

"The enclave should be able to hold out until the fleet arrives. The cities will slow the Zerg advance so we'll have enough time to—"

"The cities?" Ardo was suddenly galvanized by his own thoughts. "Civilians being slaughtered by those nightmares—

thousands of them—and all you can do is count them by the number of minutes that they buy for *your* escape?"

Merdith swallowed hard. "We all have to make sacrifices, Ardo. Sometimes they're hard, but . . ."

Patriarch Gabittas was speaking to him in the seminary class. "What profit is a man if he gain the whole world and lose his soul . . ."

Melani smiled at him under a golden sun.

"And so their sacrifice—thousands of lives—has meaning because you and your precious rebellion can live?" Ardo shook with his anger. "Littlefield gave his life for you! He stepped up and threw his life down so that you could live. Isn't that enough? How many people is your life worth, Merdith? Hundreds? Thousands?"

Merdith's eyes flashed. Ardo turned angrily and raised his rifle overhead. With an outraged cry, he smashed the butt of the rifle through the lower window in the cab door. It didn't seem to help. He threw the weapon through the vacant pane into the cab with another howl. He turned back to Merdith, gripping her shoulders roughly with both hands.

"What about my life, Merdith? How many people is my life worth? How many should die for me?"

Ardo's grip tightened. Merdith winced in pain.

"What about my soul, Merdith? My soul is mine. No one can have it. Not the Confederacy. Not your precious rebellion. You can't buy my redemption. What is my life worth, Merdith? How many . . . how many people can I buy with my life?"

His father was reading to the family. "And fear not them which kill the body, but are not able to kill the soul: but rather fear him which is able to destroy both soul and body in hell."

Ardo stood frozen, transfixed.

Merdith looked up, still in his painful grip. "What is it?"

Melani stood in the field of golden wheat. She was handing him the box and reciting something from Scripture.

"Please." Merdith grimaced. "You're hurting me!"

"It is better that one man should perish than that a nation should dwindle and perish in unbelief . . ."

Ardo suddenly let Merdith go. "How many ships are coming?"

"What? Maybe a hundred—whatever they could scrape together, I guess—but they'll never reach the cities in time."

"No, but what if the Zerg didn't make it to the cities?" Ardo turned back to the truck as he spoke, pulling open the door and climbing up into the cab. "Thousands could be saved, couldn't they?"

"You can't stop the Zerg, soldier-boy!"

Ardo jumped back down from the cab.

In his hands he held the metal case.

"No, we can't," Ardo said. "But we might—just might—be able to slow them down."

CHAPTER 20

SIRENS

"YOU ARE COMPLETELY OUT OF YOUR FRAGGED mind, you know that?"

Ardo looked around the Operations Room. The faces he saw looking back at him for the most part seemed to be in agreement with Cutter's statement.

A cascade of sparks rained down from the ceiling of the Operations Room. Tinker was outside in an SCV. The technician had managed to clear most of the broken antennae and sensor probes away and lifted the fallen section of the hull back up to where it belonged. Now he was welding additional plating over the acid cuts in the metal overhead to hold it all in place and reinforce the structure.

The rest of the surviving detail had been called back into the Operations Room. Ardo was facing all that remained of the platoon that had left that same morning—a morning that seemed to Ardo to be years in the past. Private Mellish sat wearily on the catwalk, his legs dangling down over one of the console covers. He was all that was left of Jensen's original squad and now apparently wanted to look anywhere but at Ardo. Privates Bernelli and Xiang stood leaning back against the floor consoles opposite Mellish. Xiang's eyes seemed unfocused and distant while Bernelli's appeared to bore right through Ardo with laser intensity. Lieutenant Breanne stood with her back turned to the room on the catwalk behind Xiang and Bernelli, her arms folded across her chest. One might have thought that she was gazing out the still broken window into the darkness beyond, but Ardo knew that she saw nothing out there and that her mind was very much in the room.

As was Cutter, the mammoth islander in the plasma firebat suit, who was having no trouble expressing his views. He stomped back and forth across the newly welded floor plates in front of the elevator bay. "You are absolutely meltdown fragged in the head!"

"Maybe I am," Ardo said, fingering the metallic case resting awkwardly on the bent floor of the command island next to him. Merdith was leaning against the back of one of the crushed panels of the island, her hands in the pockets of her jumpsuit, her eyes cast down toward the floor in thought. "Maybe I am, but I don't see that it makes much difference to us, and it *might* make a lot of difference to someone else."

"Not much difference to us?" Cutter gaped. "You want to turn that Zerg homing beacon on—draw every mutalisk, hydralisk, and I-don't-know-what-lisk within a thousand clicks right down on top of us—and you figure we won't *care*?"

"That's not what I said." Ardo shook his head.

"By the gods, I hope *not*!"

"What I said was, it won't *make* much difference to us." Ardo set his combat helmet down on top of the case and removed his combat gloves. "Look, the Confederacy left us for dead—hell, they flat-out *wanted* us dead! They're not coming back for us even if they knew we were here. They've written off this entire world—and every colonist on it. Just think, Cutter! The Confederacy's little secret device here *called* the

Zerg down on this world. We've got the proof right here in this box. You think they want anybody to know that they're responsible for the flat-out cue-balling of this entire planet?"

Bernelli spoke up. "But . . . but what about these Sons of Kohole or Korhal or whoever. They got evac ships coming. Can't we hook up with them?"

Ardo nodded. "We could barter with the Sons of Korhal. We could trade them this box and probably find a way off this planet, if anyone can. We'd have to break through the Zerg front, find them, and make the deal. But these Sons of Korhal have their own plan. The rescue ships they have coming certainly aren't enough to evac the entire planet. It's just public relations—show some pictures of them rescuing a few left behind. What they do *not* want everyone to know, however, is that they are also responsible for the Zerg coming here."

Xiang turned to Ardo suddenly. "The Korhal bunch? I thought that was a Confederacy gadget."

Ardo turned to Merdith. "Tell them."

Merdith squirmed uncomfortably. "It's true that you could make a deal with the Sons of Korhal—"

"No," Ardo said, and Merdith winced at his tone. "Tell them who activated the device!"

Merdith continued to look at the floor. "Some sacrifices have to be made for the continuation of the Cause. The . . . atrocities of the Confederacy leave the rebellion no choice . . . ah . . . but to use the device against further Confederacy aggression. By using their own weapon against them—"

"By the gods, Melnikov!" Xiang was shocked. "It's mass murder! Planetary genocide!"

Merdith looked up, her eyes flashing. "The Sons of Korhal have a legitimate claim to—"

Mellish spat on the floor in disgust. "Oh, shut up, lady! The Sons of Korhal don't give a shit about the civilians any more than the damn Confederacy does. Near as I can tell, they're just the flip side of the same coin—and just as tarnished."

Ardo shook his head sadly. "And when this is all over, this

Korhal bunch certainly won't want us breathing any more than the Confederacy will. The Confederacy may have made the box, but it was the Sons of Korhal who opened it. We know what happened here and how many died . . . because of *both* sides." He sighed. "No, boys, we're all dead. About the only thing left for us to decide is *how* we die and what we die *for*."

"Well, isn't that a pretty speech," Cutter sniffed, his large nostrils flaring. "So you're all hero and sacrifice, are you, Melnikov? I've seen just how much of a hero you are, boy! You were perfectly willing to sacrifice Wabowski back there at Oasis—plenty willing, by my reckoning! Now you're all the big man wanting to sacrifice the rest of us!"

"There's families out there, Cutter." Bernelli sounded tired. "Women and children . . ."

"Yeah, and some of them are mine!" Cutter's deep black eyes were wide and watery. "But I didn't sign up for this!"

"Seems to me you wanted a fight when you landed on this rock," Mellish added, his words rising in tone. The private did not care for Cutter in the least. "Now you're looking for the back door?"

"Cutter never took a back door in his life, sister! Give me a stand-up fight! Bring 'em on and I'll eat their hearts for breakfast. But *this*,"—Cutter pointed angrily at Ardo—"*this* latrine cleaner tells me to sit still and *die* for a bunch of civvies I have never met, who will never know what I did for them and probably wouldn't give a shit even if they did! *That's* insane!"

"So that's why you're here, Cutter?" Ardo's frustration seeped into his voice. "You want someone to give you the credit? Throw you a parade or shed some tears? Is that what's important here, that you're remembered as the hero? Innocent people are gonna *die* out there, Cutter, and we're the only ones who can help them, whether they know it or not!"

"I'm here to find my brothers. They're out there and I've got to find them!"

Ardo was about to say something but stopped. Cutter's

brothers. He had not thought about it much before now, but if his own memories had been so blatantly tampered with and altered by the resoc tanks, what had they done to the huge islander? Were his brothers even on this rock? Did Cutter, for that matter, in reality even *have* any brothers? How could Ardo possibly ever explain that to the volatile marine?

Bernelli sighed. "Well, if we're gonna die, I'd like to at least know it was for something more than my pension."

"Well, if *I'm* going to die," Cutter seethed, "it won't be because of this butt wipe . . . and it won't be *alone*!"

Cutter moved so fast that Ardo had no time to react. In two quick steps the huge man crossed the floor and wrapped his right hand around Ardo's throat.

Ardo tried to speak, but he was not able. The firebat suit reinforced Cutter's intense grip. Ardo struggled uselessly. In moments bright stars began to burst in his vision and the world began to blur. Everyone was shouting at once. Shadows moved around the periphery of his vision, but all he could see was the outraged face of the islander with murder in his eyes.

A voice. "Drop him! Drop him, now, Cutter!"

Suddenly, Cutter released him. Ardo tumbled like a cloth doll to the floor, gasping for breath. He looked up.

Lieutenant Breanne was holding her gauss rifle against Cutter's temple. "Cutter, you want to save your brothers? You ever think that they might be part of those civilians waiting for a way out of this? You ever think that the only way you're gonna have a chance of saving any of your brothers is by making sure those Zerg don't reach the city before the transports?"

Cutter blinked furiously. His voice was low and quiet when he replied. "No, ma'am. I . . . I hadn't thought of that."

"Then stop trying to think," Breanne screamed. Her voice was shrill and unnerving. "I'll think for you. You're not *paid* to think!"

Breanne pulled the weapon back from Cutter's head and motioned him back with its muzzle. "I've spent a lifetime fighting everyone else's wars, for other people's ideals and other people's causes! Melnikov is right! Each of our lives could buy hundreds of others, maybe thousands. They'll never know it, never appreciate it, but if I have to die, let me die for something worthwhile!"

Breanne turned to the box and with quick, firm motions, released the latches. The metallic box was open.

The lieutenant turned to the astonished faces in the room. "We have, by my rough estimate, approximately an hour and a half before the first Zerg arrive. I suggest that we make use of the time."

Ardo was on his fourth trip to the various bunkers. He was tired, but he knew that he would not have to be tired much longer. There was a peace waiting for him that was long and permanent. He found that he was rather looking forward to it. The teachings of his youth kept bubbling back to the surface of his memory: tales of faith and hope and peace in an afterlife. Strange, he thought, to consider such things here in the center of hell.

Tinker had been using the SCVs to construct several new bunkers around the Command Center. This would be the defensive core inside the outer perimeter. They would start their defense on the outer ring, taking ranged shots on the approaches to the base. When the Zerg threatened to overrun the outer position, then the plan was to fall back to the inner ring of linked bunkers for the final defense. After that, they would hold on as long as they could . . . and hope that it was long enough.

Meanwhile, Mellish had taken a couple of the others out in an APC with every mine they could salvage from the compound. Ardo had grinned when Mellish had come to him with the idea. Now the private was out happily sowing mines in a specific pattern around the compound as though he were a farmer working the back forty. Ardo hoped Mellish would enjoy a bumper crop from the seeds he was sowing.

Ardo busied himself in the factory manufacturing new ammunition for the rifles. Breanne had even taken Ardo's point about the Zerg never stopping for their wounded. It was a fairly easy calibration. Rather than the standard infantry rounds, he reprogrammed the replicator to produce hollow-point spread rounds. Unlike their standard issue, these rounds would flatten and expand on impact with the target. These were not designed to wound, but to kill and inflict as much damage as possible. Ardo was looking forward to seeing if they worked.

Tinker was still working on the south perimeter bunker as Ardo approached. Tinker had not said more than ten words to anyone since his brother's dropship went down. Ardo was more than a little concerned about the man, but there was no time to deal with his problems at the moment—perhaps no time to deal with them ever. Ardo walked up to the low domed building and entered the open access hatch.

Bunkers were standard equipment for SCV manufacture, and it could truly be said that once you had seen one bunker, you had seen them all. Their thick metal shell held sufficient quarters for four, with weapons ports on all sides. They were not the most comfortable of quarters, but they had the benefit of being as safe a place as you could find on any Confederacy base. Once assembled, they were incredibly difficult to take apart. Just how difficult he was sure they were about to learn.

He stepped into the central compartment, loaded down with his ammo cases, and was surprised to see Merdith staring out of one of the weapons ports.

"Oh, excuse me," Merdith said. "I'll get out of your way."

"No, it's all right." Ardo set the boxes down and began stowing them under each of the weapons ports. "You're no trouble. If you're here for the view, you're looking in the wrong direction."

"Yeah. I never was one for being a tourist." Merdith laughed tiredly. Then she turned back to the port. "Which way do you think they'll come first?"

"I don't know," Ardo said, moving to stand next to her and gazing out across the red plain. "The last units we saw were passing to the west. My guess is that they will be the first to arrive. I'd look for unwanted company coming from there first."

Merdith nodded. A short silence passed between them.

"Hey, soldier-boy?"

"Yes, ma'am?"

"If I don't get a chance to tell you . . . I think what you've done here is . . ." Her voice trailed off.

Ardo glanced at her. "Is what?"

"I . . . I don't know. I was going to say 'good' or 'right' but the words didn't seem quite big enough." She rested her folded arms on the sill of the weapons port, laying her head down on them as she spoke. "Maybe even . . . epic."

Ardo laughed. "Epic?"

Merdith laughed, too. "Okay. Maybe not epic, either. Whatever it is, I'd like to tell you thanks."

"I wouldn't thank me, ma'am. I just got us all killed."

"But how many more are going to live because of what we do here? I'd never really thought of it before." Merdith looked at him. "They may not say thank you. They may never know what happened here or even who we were, but I'll say thanks for them."

Ardo nodded, then thought for a moment. "You know . . . I'm not even sure of who I am anymore. I've been programmed and reprogrammed so many times that I've forgotten who I was and why I was and where I was even going. Yet there was always *me* here somewhere—that part of my soul that they could never program over or take away. I used to fear that, but now it's all I have to hang on to. You helped me find my soul, ma'am, and for that, *I* want to say thanks to you."

Ardo reached down picked up a new gauss rifle, and tossed it over to Merdith. He said, "You know how to use it, don't you?"

Merdith caught the rifle, then primed it expertly with a single motion. "You trust me with this?"

"Hey, if you kill one of *us*, it just means there's one less person to watch *your* back!" Ardo smiled.

Merdith smiled back. "I'll have to be careful about that, won't I?"

"I wish you had met Melani. I doubt you'd have had much in common, but she—"

"Mellish reporting. I've got a visual from the west. We've got company."

Ardo grimaced. "They're early."

CHAPTER 21

SIEGE

"STAND BY, PEOPLE!" IT WAS BREANNE'S VOICE over the tactical net. *"Outer perimeter first, then fall back on my command to the inner perimeter. Flash status!"*

Ardo keyed his tac-com transmit key twice. "Melnikov, Outer Five, southwest."

"Mellish, Outer Four, northwest! They're comin' hard and—"

"Cut the chatter, Mellish! Flash status!"

"Xiang. I'm here. Outer Three, northeast."

"Bernelli at Outer Two. I'm . . . uh . . . I'm southeast."

"Cutter, Outer One, south, Lieutenant."

"Status complete! Hold fire until they breach the outer mines. Report the breach, then open fire, understood?"

Ardo smiled. Even in the middle of a hopeless cause, Breanne was going to do this by the numbers. If there was a way to *die* by the numbers, he knew that she would do it, too.

"What is it?" Merdith asked, seeing the look on Ardo's face.

He leaned forward, his eyes narrowing as he peered out the firing slits in the bunker.

"By the gods! What *is* that?" Merdith breathed in disbelief.

The horizon to the southwest was blurred, its crisp line smudged. It might have been a sandstorm rolling toward them, but Ardo knew it was something far more deadly.

Ardo opened the tac-com channel. "Lieutenant; Melnikov. I've got a line of Zerg approaching rapidly from the west . . . about three clicks out. I can't make out the ends of the line."

"Mellish here. I think I have the end of the line of advance here on about a two-ninety radial. Hell, I didn't think there were that many Zerg in the whole—"

"This is Cutter. I can't seem to make out the end of the line on my end."

"Ardo! What's going on?"

The marine looked over at Merdith. "What? Oh, *damn!* You don't have a tactical com set. That's them coming now—a line of Zerg that just about covers the horizon and God only knows how deep they are behind that line. That little box of yours apparently works a lot better than I thought."

"So." Merdith swallowed hard, her mouth suddenly dry. Her fingers gripped her rifle so hard they were white. "What happens now?"

"We wait for them."

"Wait?" Merdith blinked. "Wait for what?"

"Wait until they hit the mine perimeters." Ardo shook his shoulders and rolled his head. He was tense, and that was a bad way to go into battle. "Mellish and Bernelli sowed two perimeters of minefield around the base. There's one at a thousand meters and a second at five hundred meters. They're a combination of hopper and shape-charge mines with heuristic sensor links—"

"Whoa, slower! They've got heuristic what?"

"Sensor links. The mines talk to each other on a dedicated, low-power network and learn from each other what to look for in an enemy passing over them. The more they detonate, the smarter they get about killing whatever crosses them. Then they can modify their own blast patterns to maim more effectively. We've had to change their programming a little . . ."

"Because you don't want them just to maim," Merdith finished for him. She turned to gaze out the gun port of the bunker. The hazy line was getting much closer. "You want them to kill as many and as quickly as possible."

"That's right," Ardo replied, then leaned even closer to the gun port. "Incredible! Just listen to that."

The low rumble was felt before it could be heard—a pounding of the ground that nervously shook everything resting on top of it. In moments it grew to audibility—thousands of Zerg rushing heedlessly toward them in an enraged fury. The ear-piercing screech of their voices punctuated the roar, chilling Ardo to his bones.

"By the gods! What have we done?" Bernelli yelled across the com channel.

"Hold your fire!" Breanne's voice crackled over the channel in response. *"I've got to know where they hit the perimeter first!"*

A single dull thud shook the bunker. Dust from the upper ammunition racks sifted loose toward the floor. Ardo saw Merdith's eyes go wide. Then a quick succession of thuds rolled through the open ports.

"Bernelli here! Perimeter contact at radial two-twenty!"

The mine explosions rattled in quick succession now, one nearly on top of the other. They were sounding closer to Ardo.

"They're shifting!" Bernelli shouted. *"They're coming left, Melnikov!"*

Ardo quickly picked up his field glasses. He pushed Merdith back and pressed the glasses through the rightmost gun port.

He could see them clearly now: a solid wall of Zerg writhing and squealing nearly a thousand meters away. Every kind of hideous nightmare of their kind seemed to be present, charging in his direction, and then, as though heeding some unheard dance music, they all began shifting to the right.

The thudding explosions followed them. A wall of dirt, flame, and torn flesh surged into the air like a continuous curtain of death. Each Zerg in its turn charged forward, probing for the weak spot in the perimeter, searching for the opening that humans always left in the field through which they could pass and attack. Ardo smiled. He was looking into the mind of his enemy and knew something it did not know: that there was no opening through which they could pass because they knew they would never be leaving.

"Melnikov here!" Ardo shouted into the com channel over the thunderous barrage. "They're throwing their lead elements against the perimeter. Moving eastward around the outer minefield. Cutter? You got 'em?"

"Yeah, I see. Sweet Sister Sin! Look at 'em! They're moving to surround the base! I've never seen so many ugly bastards in my life! Come to me, you sweet meat! I'm digging a pit just for you! I'll roast you for dinner, you ugly—Heads up! Incoming!"

The curtain of destruction continued to explode before him, cutting off all sight of the Zerg beyond it. Ardo frantically searched with his field glasses for some sign of a breakthrough.

"The towers have a lock! Weapons release!"

He heard it before he saw it. The rockets leaped from the defensive towers. Merdith's scream was obliterated by the wail of the high-speed thrusters clawing their way toward the Zerg. Ardo followed their trails to their targets: mutalisks in droves were soaring over the mine perimeter, their numbers nearly blanking out the bright sky beyond. The rockets slammed into them, their bright blossoms burning into the creatures with deadly accuracy. The beasts began falling like a grotesque rain on the perimeter area. A few of them triggered mines of their own when they slammed into the ground, but Ardo noted with grim satisfaction that the mines were already recognizing these new targets as being dead when they landed and were saving themselves for better and more threatening targets.

Suddenly, an almost deafening silence descended. The

smoke and dirt around the perimeter began to settle, its curtain falling slowly back to earth.

Merdith and Ardo glanced at each other. The quiet after the initial barrage was unnerving.

"It stopped them." Merdith smiled, almost giddy at the thought. "Ardo! It's incredible! You stopped them!"

Ardo lifted his glasses once more and tried to peer beyond the settling dust, smoke, and debris. He could see them moving, shifting positions.

"Oh, damn." Ardo's voice shuddered as he spoke. "They've figured it out."

Merdith looked desperately out of the gun port, trying to see what Ardo was seeing. "Figured it out?"

Ardo keyed open his com. "Melnikov here! They're spacing out! Get ready for it!" Then he turned to Merdith. "Arm your weapon! This is it! The Zerg are spacing themselves out so that the mines will only take out one of them at a time. Then they'll charge the minefield all the way around."

Merdith's jaw dropped. "You mean . . . That's suicide!"

"No," Ardo said, quickly priming his own gauss rifle and laying its muzzle through the gun port. "That's just the Zerg. They don't value individual lives. That's why they don't bother with the wounded. They're cold and they're cunning, and they'll do whatever it takes to get to us and that box. They'll throw thousands of their warriors at us and won't think a second thought. They know that they won't run out of Zerg before we run out of mines."

"They're bringing up the zerglings!" It was Cutter's voice. *"Guess they're wanting to keep the big boys for after they've cleared the minefield."*

"Setting the mines to discriminate. We'll let the smaller ones through both perimeters for now and concentrate the mines on the larger targets."

"Roger, Lieutenant. Here, kitty, kitty, kitty . . ."

Even with his unaided eyes, Ardo could see the changes in the Zergs a thousand meters out. The larval zerglings were the smallest creatures known among the Zerg, the closest thing the monsters had to children. Ardo thought bleakly that it was another clear difference between their races, but then wondered if it was such a difference after all. Humans seemed equally willing to throw their own youth away on war, and Ardo knew that he was ample evidence of that.

"Here they come!" Bernelli announced, his voice rising. *"Make 'em count!"*

The multilegged zerglings began skittering across the blackened and pocked ground of the outer perimeter. Ardo snapped shut his combat helmet, saw the targeting display come up at once, and began aiming his gauss rifle at the nearest of the creatures.

The targeting was eerily effective. The laser designator pinpointed the location of Ardo's shots. The gun jerked repeatedly with each shot as he shifted targets quickly from one zergling to the next. The new ammunition was doing its job well. The explosive-tipped bullets smashed open the carapace of each approaching zergling, blowing open the exit wound in a horrific, deadly display.

"Whoo-ho! It's a shootin' gallery out here!"

"I'm goin' for the high score today, marines!"

How does this game end? Ardo thought. He continued to shift targets, but he was firing faster and faster trying to keep up with the onslaught. It was like trying to push back the tide. The zerglings continued to come in wave after wave . . . and they were nearing the inner minefield.

Ardo glanced at Merdith. Her weapon had a built-in target designator. Her grip on the weapon had not eased as she fired faster and faster.

Suddenly, a deafening, high-pitched shriek from a thousand Zerg tore across the sand.

Shaken, Ardo's eyes went wide. "They're charging!"

The second line of hydralisks thundered toward the outer minefield. Instantly the entire perimeter exploded in a deafening cacophony of fury and death. The defensive towers erupted again as well, the mutalisks driving forward at the same time. Again the mutalisk dead rained down, but their bodies were falling closer and closer to the outer walls of the base. Ardo could not be distracted, however. The crawling carpet of zerglings was crossing the inner minefield and was now only five hundred meters away and closing quickly on the outer wall.

Ardo's gun suddenly went dry. He ejected the clip and slammed home another from the racks above him. When he raised his weapon again, the zerglings were within four hundred meters.

"Lieutenant! The zerglings are about to pass the inner mines!" Ardo called out over his quick succession of shots. "We're not holding 'em!"

"You've got to hold! We need the mines for the bigger Zerg!"

The zerglings were within a hundred meters. Closing in on the base, they were forced by their numbers to come closer together, a nearly solid carpet of scarablike locusts looking, in Ardo's mind, to devour Ardo personally. Ardo switched his rifle to automatic and began spraying the approaching horde indiscriminately.

He was so preoccupied that he failed to register the thunderous sound of the mine detonations suddenly dropping off in the distance beyond. It shocked him when in a flash they resumed, this time only five hundred meters out. Towering columns of smoke, dirt, and rock shredded the charging Zerg. Their deafening roar surrounded the entire base as they charged from all sides simultaneously. The sun was blotted out by the waves of destruction. The detonations, no longer distinguishable one from another, now merged into one seemingly continuous demonic roar.

Stones and charred Zerg flesh began raining down on the bunker and the space beyond. Ardo continued playing his deadly stream of explosive shells against the zerglings, who were now within a few meters of the bunker. Beyond them, the demon wall of death continued to march toward him, its sound shaking the plates of the bunker and threatening to knock him off his feet. The wall of mine explosions was now within a hundred meters of his position.

Ardo knew that the minefield ended within eighty meters of where he stood.

"Lieutenant! They're breaking through!"

"Fall back! Fall back now!*"*

Ardo did not have to hear the order twice. He grabbed Merdith's arm, quickly pulling her away from the gun port. He shouted. "We gotta go *now*!"

Merdith stepped quickly back from the port. As she did, the armor plates above the port began to peel upward.

A zergling scrambled through the opening, hit the floor, and instantly leaped toward her.

Ardo fired his weapon, slamming the creature away from her in midair, exploding it across the front wall of the bunker.

"Fall back!" Ardo yelled at her. "Run!"

The last thing Ardo saw as he slammed the hatch closed behind him was a wall of zergling underbellies covering the gunports as they climbed up toward the torn opening.

CHAPTER 22

FAREWELL

THE SOUND WAS OVERWHELMING. THE DEFENSIVE towers were firing into the sky, disgorging their contents in a frenzy of flame and destruction. The missiles must have been arming just as they left their protective tubes, since their targets were close and pressing closer still.

Merdith ran in front of Ardo. The dusty stretch of ground between the outer wall and the inner bunkers was a veil of ash, smoke, and burning Zerg falling like a black snow from the sky. Acid splashes smoked against the ground here and there. Ardo followed the woman quickly. The intervening street between them and the inner bunker complex had never looked so far before.

Ardo sprang into the street at once. He looked up as he ran, desperate to protect himself. The defensive towers above him were scarred with repeated acid splashes, two of them already twisting under their own weight on their weakened frames. The sky beyond them was a roiling wall of flame and smoke with occasional patches of sky flashing through by some whim of chaos.

The bunker was ahead of him. Its main hatch stood open. Framed in it, he could see someone waving him onward.

Then he heard it—a sound he had heard before. It was a thunderous roar that overwhelmed even the sound of their own desperate battle. He looked up.

The rescue transports! They were coming in hot, bleeding off their speed in enormous heat through the atmosphere. The Sons of Korhal ships arched through the sky, their flaming contrails falling toward Mar Sara Starport to the west. They would be on the ground soon—their most vulnerable time as the ships tried to evacuate anyone who could reach them.

Time. They needed more time . . .

Gauss rifles suddenly chattered to life through the gun ports on either side of the bunker hatch, shocking Ardo into action. He leaped for the hatchway. Hands grabbed him and pulled him inside. His feet barely cleared the hatch seals before it slammed closed.

Ardo scrambled to his feet. Merdith was firing a stream through one of the gun ports. Bernelli had pulled him in, yelled something unintelligible at him, and then jammed his own rifle through the second set of gun ports.

Ardo quickly took his place beside Bernelli, positioned his gun, and then looked down his sights into hell.

Hydralisks were pouring over the base outer wall. They had thrown enough of their own against the minefield until there was nothing left to explode. There must have been thousands dead surrounding the complex but still they kept coming. Now they slid like a terrible wave over the wall, approaching the bunker en masse.

The tactical channel continued to chatter.

"Xiang! Report!"

"Xiang's down, Lieutenant! We've gotta get outta here! I can't hold 'em back!"

Bernelli continued to yell as he fired. Ardo joined him, the exhilaration of the sound in his own ears driving him as he poured death from the muzzle of his rifle.

Still the tide of dark horror tried to advance over the bodies of their own dead, but now the constricted field of fire was working against them, The dead were piling up before them, but they were not getting any closer to the bunker.

"Melnikov! You copy?"

Ardo ejected a cartridge, holding the fire trigger down even as he was slamming the new cartridge home. "A little busy here, Lieutenant!"

"We're coming in!"

"What?!"

"We're falling back to your position!"

"Affirmative," Ardo grimly replied. "Bernelli, keep 'em off! I'll get the back door!"

Ardo moved to the back section of the bunker. Through the ports he could barely see the vehicle pad off to his left. Behind that, he could make out the other two bunkers on either side of the Command Center. The left bunker had been Xiang's but was swarming with hydralisks. Ardo could see them tearing at the plating, pulling apart the seams even as the bunker burned furiously. *Good-bye, Xiang,* Ardo thought.

Hydralisks were also tearing at the bunker on the right, but there a bright light suddenly flared to life. *Cutter,* Ardo realized. The rolling flames from the firebat's plasma weapon were getting closer and closer. Ardo pressed his weapon through the port and blasted away at the hydralisks trying to flank his own bunker and get to easier targets. At the last moment, Ardo smashed his hand against the release and opened the rear hatch.

Breanne stumbled through first, dragging the cursed box and Tinker Jans with it. They all fell heavily to the plated flooring. Cutter stood in the open hatchway, his plasma fire scorching several enraged hydralisks in the process. With a final burst, Cutter took a step back through the hatchway. Ardo instantly slammed the hatch shut.

They were firing from all points around the bunker now. The dead Zerg were piling up in shining heaps.

Suddenly, the Zerg stopped advancing. The hydralisks drew back into the shadows of the inner base complex. Within moments, there were no targets left to them, and their firing stopped.

"Hey, what's going on?" Cutter demanded. "They givin' up?"

Lieutenant Breanne was breathing heavily, whether from adrenaline or exertion, Ardo could not tell. "No. They *never* give up. They're just drawing up their forces . . . gathering strength. As soon as they're ready, they'll walk in here and take us."

Bernelli laughed nervously. "Oh, well, as long as we're not losing . . ."

"We *are* losing," Breanne said, flipping open her helmet and pushing her fingers back through her short-cropped hair. "We won't last ten minutes in here once they decide to make their move. You saw those ships coming down on Mar Sara! They're on the ground right now—fat civilian transports shoveling passengers in with a loader if they can. They're sitting ducks on the ground, and I can tell you that the best of them won't be able to get turned around inside forty minutes. Some longer."

"So?" Bernelli shrugged. "These Zerg slugs couldn't cross that distance in half a day, let alone an hour."

"The problem isn't the crawlers." Merdith shook her head. "It's the flyers—the mutalisks. The only thing holding them here is that box. As soon as it's destroyed, the flyers will head straight for the starport, and all this would have been for nothing."

"All we need is to hold out for thirty minutes," Ardo said. "Just a lousy thirty minutes."

"Yeah," Breanne sneered. "And who's gonna buy you those thirty minutes?"

"I will."

They all turned.

It was Tinker Jans.

"I'll do it. I'll buy you your thirty minutes," the engineer said coolly. "But I'll need help."

Bernelli glanced out the port. "Hey, I think they're moving up!"

"You've got to get me into an SCV!" Jans said. "You've got to do it now!"

Breanne thought for a moment, then decided. "Cutter! Melnikov! You heard the man! Get him to an SCV!"

"There's definite movement out there!" Bernelli yelled.

Ardo punched the rear hatch release. Grim-faced, Cutter jumped out through the opening. Jans followed him, looking shaky and vulnerable in his soiled fatigues. Ardo ducked out after them, snapping closed his combat helmet—not that he thought it would help him much.

The ground was carpeted with the mutilated bodies of Zerg attackers. There was no time to think. They ran toward the vehicle pad, stumbling across the slick, greasy ground.

The nearest SCV stood silhouetted against the burning factory unit. Jans released the front access hatch, which popped open with a satisfying hydraulic whoosh.

"Come on! Come on!" Cutter encouraged nervously.

Jans clambered up the footholds in the face of the suit and settled backward into the control cabin. The access hatch started to lower smoothly.

"Here they come!" Breanne called out.

Ardo could see them. They were charging around the factory, over the compound wall, around the Command Center. They were everywhere.

"*Now* what do we do?" Cutter demanded of the engineer.

"Get back inside! Quickly!" Jans replied.

"And leave you here?" Ardo was shaken.

"Do it now, and just keep 'em off me as long as you can!"

Ardo had no time to argue. He and Cutter ran back toward the bunker. He could already see the tracer fire ripping through the gun ports in all directions. The hydralisks were pouring across the ground, surging toward the bunker itself. Their carapace shells were distended, their armor-piercing spine quills at the ready for the attack.

Ardo fell back through the hatchway just as the hydralisks attacked. The spines shot through the open hatch, slicing through the outer layers of his combat suit as though it were cotton cloth. Searing pain erupted in his leg, a quill having passed completely through and lodging in a neosteel beam.

Cutter helped him off the floor. "You dead yet?"

Ardo winced, unwilling to look at his leg. "Not yet."

They both took up their own port firing positions, dreading what was coming next.

The hull of the bunker suddenly rang with the sound of a thousand armor-piercing darts. It was a deadly hail, hammering repeatedly on the metal exterior, the acid-coated quills shearing away pieces of the metal shell with each impact.

"Kill them! Kill them all before they can get to us!" Breanne raged. The hull overhead was already buckling downward, large indentations pressing down into their space.

Firing desperately through the port, Ardo saw the SCV start to move.

The motion barely attracted the attention of the Zerg around them. The creatures appeared so intent on reaching the bunker that they barely took notice of the single craft.

If I could just get to one of those Vulture cycles, Ardo thought to himself wildly. *I could slip away . . . I could . . .*

He shook his head. Who would die because he lived? How *many* would die because he ran when his own life could buy so many others? No one would ever know who he was or why he was here. Anyone who ever cared for him would never know his fate. Maybe God would know. No matter what the Confederacy told him he was, Ardo knew who he was at last, and that he had something of his own that he could give.

The SCV lumbered up to the bunker complex. Tinker had left a stack of armor plating next to the bunker. Ardo wondered suddenly if the engineer had planned this all along. Jans picked up the plating with the massive arms of the SCV, looked at the bunker, found the weakest point, and slammed the plate across it. Holding it in place with one mechanical arm, Jans activated the plasma welder on the other and began reinforcing the hull.

The Zerg must have realized what Jans was doing. Several of the hydralisks wheeled suddenly on the SCV.

Cutter and Ardo both saw it. In a moment, they shifted their fire. "Keep 'em off him, he said!" Cutter sneered through his sweat. "And just how are we supposed to do *that*?"

Jans continued to work frantically around the bunker, welding, reinforcing, replacing plates as quickly as possible. The marines kept up their stream of death against the invaders, knocking down the hydralisks in row after row as they advanced and fired.

The battle raged in an agonizing stalemate. Ardo's gun was hot in his armored hands. Somehow, Jans was keeping up with the repairs as quickly as the hydralisks were damaging the bunker.

"Hey, I think it's working!" Bernelli laughed. "I think—"

The hydralisks surged forward.

"No!" Ardo raged.

Jans could not see them coming in the SCV. Several of the hydralisks had gotten shots at the work vehicle, and it was badly damaged but still operating. Suddenly, the fiendish wave had reached him. They were swarming about the SCV. Jans tried to beat them off the shell of the machine. In moments, however, they had dragged him and the entire SCV up and out of sight of the gun ports.

"They've got Jans!" Cutter yelled.

"We lose him and we're done for!" Breanne yelled back.

With a terrible cry, Cutter hit the hatch switch and dove outside.

Great sheets of plasma flame erupted outside the ports. Ardo could barely make out what was happening outside.

Then he caught a glimpse of Cutter, his huge form standing outside the hatchway pouring out his superheated carnage.

Ardo's gun suddenly silenced. He ejected his cartridge instantly and then reached for the next in the overhead rack.

There was none.

"I'm out!" Ardo shouted.

Breanne tossed him another clip. "Make it count, kid. We're all low!"

He slammed home the clip and turned back toward the port.

Cutter was gone.

Ardo looked desperately through the ports but could not see the huge man anywhere. "Tinker!" he called through the tac-com channel. "Where's Cutter?"

"They . . . gone . . . they're all over me! Can't last . . ."

Breanne pitched back from the gun port. A single spine from a hydralisk had found its way through the port opening, slamming through the faceplate of the lieutenant's combat suit. Hideously, it passed through her head and pinned her combat helmet to a neosteel support. Lieutenant L. Z. Breanne hung there, still standing.

Ardo glanced at Bernelli and then at Merdith. "I'm going out to save Jans. He can buy you some time. Bernelli, you got a clip left?"

"Yeah," he sighed.

Ardo looked at Merdith. "He'll take care of you."

Merdith nodded and looked away.

"See you on the other side," Ardo said to them both, then turned to the rear hatch.

"Hey, soldier-boy?"

He turned back to Merdith.

"Please, Ardo!" She wept. *"Don't leave me alone!"*

"Thanks, soldier-boy."

Ardo nodded, then hit the switch.

The gauss rifle responded instantly to his trained hand. The Confederacy had taught him well. His swiftly shifting aim kept the hydralisks at bay and blew them clear of the SCV as well. As he stood there in the doomed yard, his sensations seemed heightened. The world around him was clearer than he had remembered it in years, perhaps clearer than he had ever experienced it. He took it all in: the horror around him that he was keeping at bay, the smoke over the compound that had turned to wisps in the lowering twilight. The sounds. The smells. All were alive for him.

Ardo was himself at last. He knew there was something that could never be taken from him: a victory more glorious and satisfying than anything experienced on any real field of battle.

As the last of his ammunition ran out, Ardo looked up. The transports, heavy with their precious human cargo, were arching into the sunset of his most glorious day. A hundred— maybe a thousand—cascades of thunderous exhaust climbed skyward. They would never know who had fought so hard for their lives. They would never hear his name nor sing songs to praise him. He alone would know of his triumph.

As the darkness closed over him, Ardo smiled at his last thought.

The contrails of the escaping ships . . . were all golden.

UPRISING
MICKY NEILSON

ABOUT THE AUTHOR

MICKY NEILSON is a writer and voice director at Blizzard Entertainment, where he worked on *World of Warcraft*, the most popular massively multiplayer online role-playing game of all time. He was also a writer and the voice director for *WoW*'s expansion: *World of Warcraft: The Burning Crusade*. Micky's other game writing credits include *StarCraft, Warcraft III*, and *Lost Vikings II*. Micky is a television and movie fanatic, and with his writing partner Sam Didier, has completed three feature-length screenplays: *The Hunt, Vamptown,* and *Ushers,* all currently in various stages of development.

I would like to give my sincerest thanks and gratitude to the people who have been and continue to be instrumental in shaping my life: to my brothers, Sammy, Rider, Eric, and Tony. Thank you always.

To my love, Tiffany, thank you for being a pillar of strength.

A special thank you also goes out to: Chris Metzen, for his continued faith in my talent; to Allen Adham, Paul Sams, and Mike Morhaime for their endless support; to Marco Palmieri at Pocket; and to all my co-workers, my friends, you know who you are. Thank you.

Finally, I would like to thank my father, Shihan Calvin Neilson, for always allowing me to exercise my imagination.

CHAPTER 1

THE SEEDS OF REBELLION

THROUGHOUT THE COURSE OF EVERY PERSON'S life, a large-scale catastrophe is certain to occur. At some point, fate will hand everyone the ultimate test: a tragedy so profound and so inescapable that it will forever alter the remaining course of the life affected. This event will have one of two outcomes. The people confronted with the catastrophe may be defeated in the test, and live the remainder of their lives as shadows of the people they once were. Or they might transform and become strengthened by their experience, transcending all self-imposed limitations and flourishing in a way they had never deemed possible.

Arcturus Mengsk was one of the latter. He had overcome a tragic event in his life, and now it had changed him, forever molded him into a being of single-minded purpose and unshakable determination. Lesser men would have been broken by the tragedy. Lesser men would have just given up. But *lesser* men did not take their place in the proud annals of Terran history.

During his formative years, young Arcturus would often awake from dreams in which he had seen himself as a figure of importance, a preeminent leader of men. Mostly, Arcturus would dismiss the dreams as whims of an overactive imagination. In the waking world, Arcturus did not see himself as the leader-type at all. He didn't care about the affairs of others; he didn't care about the Confederacy. All he cared about was serving his time in the Confederate military and how much money he might be able to earn as a fringe-world prospector when that time was done. He had certainly done his duty, and, lack of desire to lead notwithstanding, had ascended to the rank of colonel before the climate changed; before he realized he was not fighting for what he believed in, and of course, before the tragedy.

Now, in the wake of the tragedy, things had changed. The man he once saw himself as seemed no more than a distant relative.

For the most part, up until now, it had all been about preparation: keeping in constant communication with his colleagues in the underground network on Korhal (although they had become so vocal of late that the term "underground" no longer applied); recruiting like-minded, eager civilians for training; and observing the actions of the Confederacy here among the relative safety of the Umojan Protectorate.

Preparation was well and good, and Arcturus prided himself on planning ahead. But he believed that the time had now come for action. Blowing up supply route bridges on key planets, hacking into Confederate mainframes, and staging mine-worker revolts were all well and good, but the time had come to strengthen his numbers and to set out on his quest in earnest. The time had come to raise hell.

And so General Mengsk now stood looking into the determined eyes of the roughly twenty or so Umojan men before him. They were an able-bodied lot, though not as many as he had hoped for, and he was fairly certain that none of the men had ever seen combat. Still, they were capable, and they were willing to fight for what they believed in, and that was where the seeds of rebellion truly began to germinate.

The general greeted each man's eyes in turn. Once he was confident that he held their attention, he spoke. "You men are gathered here today because you share common beliefs and a common desire. Among the beliefs you share is the tenet that no man or body of government should have authority to treat you unjustly; the desire you share is the pursuit of independence. Make no mistake, men—these are the ideals that wars are made of. The least of the troubles that lie ahead for all of you is a life of forced seclusion, of being branded as seditionist by the very government that would impose her unfair laws upon you. The worst of what you may face—of what we all face—is death. Pollock and I and the rest of our fighters are, as you know, already considered turncoats by the Confederacy. . . ."

Arcturus motioned to a man standing at parade-rest to his left. Pollock Rimes was a man who looked the part of a battle veteran—his bald head and face were covered with scars, and the upper left hemisphere of his skull bore a slight indentation the size of a fist. His left ear was mostly missing and the bridge of his nose formed a backward S. Pollock's eyes stared ahead blankly as Arcturus continued. "It is important that all of you go into this knowing that there exists a very real possibility that you may not live to see it through."

As Arcturus allowed his words to sink in, his eyes fell on a man outside the room, visible through one of the large windows. The man, of Asian descent, wearing the clothes of a low-level prospector, seemed to be intrigued by what was going on inside. When the man looked up and saw Arcturus staring at him, he held the gaze for a second before looking away. He seemed to be wrestling with some kind of decision. Just then Arcturus heard the sound of one of the men clearing his throat. He turned to see a somewhat crazed-looking older man standing near the front of the group whose face bore a web of wrinkles and whose white tonsured hair circled his bald dome like wispy clouds hovering around a particularly worn mountain peak. "My mother, may she rest easy, used to say that there wan't nothin' worth living fer that wan't worth dyin' fer."

Arcturus allowed himself a half-smile. "What's your name?"

"I'm Forest Keel, and I seen my share o' friction in the seven cycles I served in the Guild Wars."

"I'm sure you did. And I'm sure you made your superiors proud." Old Forest beamed a gap-toothed smile as Arcturus's eyes once again scanned the nearby window, where the prospector was still standing, nervously undetermined. Arcturus turned his attention back to the group. "Well, men, the time has—"

Just then Arcturus was interrupted by the sound of an entryway opening. Looking to the far side of the room, the general saw Ailin Pasteur—one of the Protectorate's ambassadors—stick his head in. The usually unflappable man looked pale and distressed.

"I'm sorry to interrupt, General, but there is a situation that requires your immediate attention."

The Spy Deck was an area where mining foremen watched image-enhanced holograms of planets within the system that might be fertile grounds for prospecting. For the enlistment of its current purpose, the Spy Deck could not have been more aptly named. Not long ago, Ailin Pasteur had served under the command of Arcturus's father, Angus. Angus had saved the man's life on one occasion and Ailin had repaid the favor by being one of the voting members of the Ruling Council that appointed Arcturus to the rank of general, and leader of the revolution. The Council also allowed Arcturus to use the Protectorate as a base of operations, and to use the Spy Deck as a somewhat archaic means of surveillance. The imaging program contained detailed charts of all the planets within the known systems. It was also capable of charting the progress of freight ships carrying their valuable cargo through the trade routes in real-time—a primitive kind of "radar" system to be sure, but more than adequate for Arcturus's needs. It was here on the Spy Deck that the Ruling Council of the Umojan Protectorate stood, their haggard faces revealing collective concern.

Ailin turned to Arcturus and spoke in a halting voice: "We received an anonymous transmission suggesting that we keep an eye on this sector."

Arcturus looked at the sector currently being displayed. He recognized the planet at the display's center immediately. "Korhal," he said, to no one in particular.

The superintendent nodded slightly. Arcturus noticed that the man was sweating heavily. "Yes."

Several smaller objects that looked like orbiting satellites of some kind surrounded the image of the planet. Arcturus had an idea, even before the superintendent spoke, of what the objects really were.

"Battlecruisers," Ailin confirmed. "We make out twenty of them. We've been monitoring the military channels and have overheard nothing that might explain this."

"Nothing they're willing to admit, anyway," offered Mengsk. "But you can bet your last credit that the Confederates are the source of your anonymous tip. And if those ships are orbiting Korhal on Confederate orders, they mean to start trouble. Send an intelligence report to Achton immediately."

In Korhal's capital city of Styrling, Colonel Achton Feld—the elected leader of the rebel forces in the absence of General Mengsk—was busy shouting orders, standing atop a guard-walk at the city's perimeter, the myriad antiair missile turrets that served as outer defenses forming a jagged outline on the horizon behind him. At one time, this fortress in the center of the city had been a Confederate post. That was before the revolution. Now it served as the rebel headquarters on Korhal.

The rebels had of course known about the presence of Confederate ships in their orbit, but their limited surveillance systems had been unable to uncover what the recent intelligence transmission confirmed: that the orbiting ships numbered twenty—quite a number, especially with the capacity of each ship to hold hundreds of marines, dropships, siege tanks, even armored Goliaths. And those were just the ground forces. They were sure to be bombarded from the air first. But none of that mattered now. The rebels had spent almost a full cycle beefing up their antiair defenses and had recruited enough of the planet's population to form a sizable army.

The confrontation with the Confederate forces was inevitable. And even now, in the midst of all the fear and the panic and the anticipation, Achton was glad. He was glad that the waiting was over and that the battle was about to begin. The Korhalians were about to send a message to the Confederates: that they were the citizens of a free planet, and that they would fight to ensure that freedom. *Let them come*, thought the Colonel, *let them bring their armored walkers and their cloaked fighters, but just let them come.*

Colonel Achton smiled and waited for the first dropships to appear.

The holo-image now showed several tiny objects, no more than minuscule dots. They came from the ships in swarms, like locusts, leaving the battlecruisers and snaking their way toward Korhal's atmosphere.

"Dropships?" Ailin responded to the unasked question on everyone's mind.

Mengsk shook his head. "No. Too small. They look more like . . . no, no that couldn't be, just could not—" Mengsk continued shaking his head, refusing to believe, because he knew that if he believed, that just might make it all the more real.

He watched with the others as the scores of tiny, luminescent dots began descending into Korhal's dense atmosphere.

Achton waited, looking out at the array of defenses beyond Styrling's walls. A lieutenant raced up onto the guardwalk, out of breath. He had the harried look of a man who suddenly wished he were somewhere else.

"Sir, we're tracking hundreds of incoming objects that have locked onto several positions across this side of the planet. I'm not sure, but I think we got a report from the Underside that they're tracking objects as well."

"Hundreds, you say?" The colonel's calm veneer was slipping, and the naked fear began to become apparent on his face.

"Yes, sir. Too small for us to identify just yet, but they're coming fast."

Just then the colonel heard a low hum, barely detectable, like the whine of a small insect. Then he looked to the horizon and saw a swarm of small objects descending, trailing tails of smoke from behind, and he knew. "No . . ." he whispered.

But the lieutenant did not hear him. The hum had become almost deafening now. As the lieutenant looked up and saw more of the objects descending on them from directly above, he began to scream.

On the Spy Deck, silence pervaded as pools of brilliant light began spreading across the surface of the already luminescent image of Korhal. They continued from multiple locations until the majority of the planet was engulfed in that brilliance and no one in the room could question what they had just seen.

"By the fathers, it's gone . . . Korhal's gone. Everybody. Billions of people . . . " Ailin seemed on the verge of fainting.

Arcturus felt his stomach tighten and was aware of nothing but that image in front of him, the image of Korhal burning. After a short time, the pools of light began to fade, and the holo-image of Korhal became a darker, featureless facsimile of its former self.

In the midst of his shock and denial, Arcturus managed to speak three words: "Gather the men."

★　　★　　★

The case of Korhal was, like many others throughout history, an example of a government attempting to suppress
upheaval among its populace through tyrannical means and
thereby only strengthening the determination of its dissent-
ers. Inside the ready room where twenty men had stood just
moments before, a throng of over fifty now crowded, exchanging angry and violent discourse over the loss of Korhal and
the impudence of the Confederacy.

A hatchway slid open at the head of the room and Arcturus entered, looking like a lion that had stalked its prey into
a corner and is savoring the moment just before the kill.

"You all know what has just transpired. For those of
you who want the specifics—and I think you all deserve to
know—twenty battlecruisers just launched about a thousand
Apocalypse-class missiles from Korhal IV's orbit. The missiles
impacted on the planet's surface and 35 million people were
murdered. You need no stirring speeches; you need no coer-
cion or coaxing. You all know the difference between right
and wrong. Now the time has come to fight for the values you
hold dear and to challenge those who would strip you of your
individual freedoms. Are you with me?"

Fifty fists raised into the air simultaneously as the mob
responded with a deafening roar. Mengsk waited for the din
to subside before continuing. "As of this day, I declare that
you are all no longer civilians. You are now soldiers. And we
are now at war." Mengsk prepared to go on, then stopped as
a hatchway at the side of the room opened, and the Asian
prospector he had spotted outside earlier now stepped in. The
crowd was silent. Mengsk's eyes traveled to the newcomer.

"I want to join," he said.

Mengsk approached the smaller man and stood before him,
an intimidating presence.

"I saw you before. You seemed hesitant."

The Asian man nodded. "I wasn't sure yet. But I am
now."

Somewhere among the crowd a mocking comment was

made. A man near the general muttered "Fringe-squib" under his breath. The general silenced the man with a glance, then turned back to the Asian. "Indecision on the battlefield costs lives, boy."

The smaller man held the general's gaze. "Sir, all I'm asking is that you give me a chance."

"Will you follow orders without question?"

"I will."

Mengsk searched the other man's eyes for a moment, then finally nodded. "What's your name?"

"Somo. Somo Hung."

"Welcome aboard," said the general before he walked back to his spot next to Pollock and surveyed the men. "As I said, from now on . . . you are soldiers. And you will bear that mantle proudly. And as for the name of our little army, the name that shall be the bane of the Confederacy's existence, I think it only appropriate that we call ourselves the Sons of Korhal!"

Once more the room erupted, this time with spirited cries of "Mengsk! Mengsk! Mengsk!"

Ailin stood next to the general, looking out into the docking bay where a battered, barely recognizable craft hung suspended. Workers pored over the behemoth busily, their torches spraying out sparks of light as final fittings and adjustments were made.

"She's not exactly pristine, but she'll serve her purpose," Ailin offered, nodding his head toward the craft outside.

"That she will, my friend." Arcturus was visibly pleased with the progress.

The battlecruiser was the casualty of a navigational systems error, much like the snafu that landed four supercarriers, carrying convicted criminals onto a few inhabitable worlds (including Umoja) into the deepest reaches of space just a few millennia ago. Those criminals were the forefathers of the Terrans, a blanket term that applied to all the generations of humans who followed and spread, inhabiting world after world and marching ever onward.

The battlecruiser now in the docking bay had crashed onto a fiery planet not far from the Protectorate, but well out of range of the Confederacy's hailing frequencies. Ailin and Mengsk went to the crash site immediately and stripped the craft of its tracking beacon. In the cargo bay they found several SCVs as well as a fully operational siege tank, and in the launching bay they found two CF/A-17G Wraith fighters, as well as four dropships.

The Protectorate shepherded the cruiser into one of its many docking bays. The Confederacy was obviously angered by the loss of one of their ships, but without proof of the Protectorate's subversion, was unwilling to start another war. The crew was pronounced dead, and offered better pay and shorter hours to remain among the Protectorate and remain silent (a proposition no one balked at), and not too long after that the displaced ship's captain became Arcturus's most trusted soldier, Pollock Rimes.

It seemed like so much time had passed since then, though it was only a cycle. The craft had remained, being upgraded and modified slowly and methodically, until it became what Arcturus now saw before him, a battlecruiser he could call his own.

Ailin interrupted the general's thoughts briefly. "What would you like to call her?" he asked.

Mengsk thought for a long moment.

"Hyperion," he said at last. "I'll call her the *Hyperion*."

Just then Pollock approached the two men. "The soldiers request an update of status, General."

Arcturus turned his bright eyes to Pollock. "Tell them we set out at next interval."

Pollock's lip lifted slightly, the closest thing to a smile Arcturus had ever seen cross the man's face.

"Yes, sir."

CHAPTER 2

THE CALM BEFORE
THE STORM

SARAH KERRIGAN WAS HAVING A NIGHTMARE. IN THIS nightmare, she spent seemingly endless intervals trapped in dark rooms, bound, with the feeling of unseen eyes watching her. From the darkness she would hear a noise, a moist smacking sound accompanied by slithering, the sound of a giant slug methodically traversing the tile floor. The sound seemed to come from all around her. Then she would feel something wet, something alive, crawling up her leg and then . . . the nightmare would start all over again.

Sarah awoke to find that she was living the nightmare.

She was in a small, dimly lit room with no visible doors, her hands and feet bound with metal shackles, in a seated position. At the far end of the room she could barely make out a closed container with a hazard label affixed to it and beyond that, a large, dark pane of glass reflected her image back to her. Sarah knew that she was being watched from behind that glass. She was also vaguely aware of a sound from somewhere outside the room, the constant sound of rushing wind.

Her mind felt almost disconnected, her body sluggish and numb. She knew that she had been drugged, although she could not remember how she came to be in this place, or even what her name was. She began to fight the drug's effects. As she did so, she heard the sound of a door opening. As she watched, a small arm extended from an aperture above and behind the container. The arm slid into a ring on the container's top and lifted. There was a slight gushing sound of trapped air escaping. The arm then retracted back into the aperture and disappeared. A small door slid shut and the room was sealed once again.

There was a noise from the container then, like a pocket of air escaping a vat of molasses.

As Sarah watched, a purplish, viscous blob rose to the top of the container and began spilling over its sides. It moved down the outside of the container seemingly of its own volition, crawling onto the floor and spreading outward. Sarah watched it creep up the wall behind the container and across the floor. On the wall, as the substance reached and finally touched the glass, there was a quick hissing sound, like a drop of liquid touching an extremely hot surface. The substance began moving around the glass, framing it as it continued to cover the surrounding surface.

The creeping mass made its way inexorably across the floor. Sarah wanted to scream, but resisted. She kept telling herself that this was just all part of the nightmare and soon she would wake up at her . . . home? Sarah couldn't remember having a home, or even a life prior to being in this room, and that made the nightmare more real than ever.

As the material made its way to the lights on the ceiling, it moved across, and the already dim room grew even darker. The glob was translucent. The diffused, softened light silhouetted a host of veins and arteries inside the mass, pulsing with some form of life.

Sarah had begun to shiver as the substance made its way to within inches of her feet. She shook her head, willing with all her might for the substance to halt its progress, and much to her amazement and relief, it *did*. The material continued to slide across the walls and ceiling, now closing in the wall behind her, but it had stopped at her feet and simply sat there now, as if waiting.

Straining to turn her head, Sarah could see that the wall behind her was now fully covered. The creeping fungus was crawling up the sides of the metal chair she was bound to, and once again Sarah willed for the movement to cease, and once more, the effort was greeted with success.

Virtually the entire room was now covered, save for Sarah herself and the window across from her. A voice came from the room then, a masculine voice, muffled, being transmitted through some speakers somewhere that were, like everything else in the room, smothered in the mass.

"I want you to call the substance onto your arm, without speaking. Do it now."

Sarah certainly did not want to do any such thing, but that was simply not an option. Her inability to refuse the order was more than just a conditioned response; it was somehow hard-wired into her mind that she could never, under any circumstances, refuse a direct order . . . *unless that order is issued by an enemy of the Confederacy*, her brain reminded her. She didn't know where that information had come from, or what exactly the Confederacy was. Neither did she know that the voice she heard was not that of an enemy of the Confederacy. But her drugged brain was in no condition to work out such reasoning, and so, Sarah complied and willed for the substance to touch her arm.

It moved fast. Faster than its previous behavior indicated it was capable of moving. It wrapped around Sarah's arm and she could feel it, probing at her skin hungrily . . . .

She screamed then, and willed it to back away. It complied, and Sarah could see that she had willed it with such force that it pulled back as one, all around her.

Sarah felt a pricking in the back of her neck, and her vision began to fade as more drugs were administered to her system.

Before long, Sarah Kerrigan drifted back to sleep and returned to her troubled dreams.

Inside the observation room, Doctor Flanx was busily noting the results of the experiment.

"I've never seen it move like that before," said his assistant. "The way it reacted to her was amazing. Nothing like the interaction with the other telepaths." He was still looking out through the window at the slumped figure of Sarah in the chair. The alien substance had begun to close in on her once again.

The doctor did not look up from the screen as he typed: *Patient appears to have innate ability to interact with subject matter.* "Yep. Looks like the brass was right for once. Let's start the evacuation process."

The assistant nodded and pressed a button on the console before him. In the other room, beneath the mass, several red lights along the floor and walls suddenly illuminated. There was an audible hissing sound, and the substance began to retreat from the heat sources, being ushered back toward the safety of the container. No matter how many times the process was repeated, the assistant still marveled at the fact that the substance could spread from just a few tiny spores. The doctor pressed a button. A moment later a disc ejected from the console. He handed the disc to the assistant. "I want this sent underground for Lockston immediately, to be transmitted to Tarsonis."

The assistant nodded, then motioned toward the other room. "What's next for her?"

The doctor sighed. "We'll move her up to the next stage, see how she interacts with the larvae. Until then keep her drugged."

The assistant nodded, watching as the final remains of the creep, as the scientists had come to call it, disappeared back into the container.

The *Hyperion* was moving steadily through Protected Space, on the Umojan side.

Inside the cargo bay, Forest Keel was learning how to operate a siege tank. The old man sat inside the metal behemoth, the control panel lights bathing his smiling face in an array of primary colors. One of Mengsk's officers, Sela Brock, sat in the vehicle's rear, educating Forest on the tank's finer points in her sultry, almost hypnotic voice.

"The Arclite Siege Tank is a dual purpose vehicle," she explained. "Once a forward unit has reached an optimal position for insertion—" Forest chuckled somewhat at this comment; Sela either did not notice or chose to ignore the infraction and continued "—the tank can be transformed into siege mode, where it will provide cover artillery fire with the 120mm shock cannon."

Forest rubbed the palms of his hands together in eager anticipation. "You just show me which button to push, little lady."

Sela sighed and moved forward to show Forest how to transform the tank.

In the mess hall, Somo Hung sat alone. He had become used to isolation, having grown up in the outer limits of what was called the Fringe Worlds, a belt at the farthest reaches of the galaxy's inhabitable planets.

Fringe Worlders for the most part were considered to be ignorant, expendable sources of cheap labor. The Fringes offered the hardest work for the cheapest pay, though the work was steady. Those who settled the outer ring kept mostly to themselves. Some of the Fringe workers had begun reviving forgotten religions, and some had created new religions that enjoyed a following that sometimes bordered on the fanatical.

Somo's parents had never been caught up in the new religions or the old, and though they had sacrificed education for stability, they had never wished the same fate on their only son. And so they saved their credits, and when Somo reached his eighteenth cycle, they paid for him to be transported to Umoja, a bustling mecca of opportunity.

And there he stayed. He taught himself to read, and began collecting Digi-tomes on everything from philosophy and poetry to the recorded histories of several of the key planets. Two cycles later an outbreak of cholera ended a score of lives on his home planet, including that of his mother and father. But still Somo pressed on, in their memory, bearing the burden of their loss in silence and striving to become the man they would have wished him to be.

Just now Somo was reading his favorite Digi-tome, the *History of the Guild Wars*. He was aware of the whisperings from the nearby tables. At one table in particular, a group of warp-rats sat staring. Warp-rats were the engineers who maintained the warp drives that were standard on all space-faring craft.

Somo tried to ignore the large, bald engineers whose intent gazes were growing more and more persistent by the moment. It wasn't long before the largest of the men shouted: "Who you tryin' to impress, Fringe-squib? We all know you can't read." The other men at the table snickered. Somo looked up and offered a brief smile before returning to his book.

The leader of the men, bolstered by the others' reactions, stood up and approached Somo's table. "Hey there squib, I'm just tryin' to make friendly conversation, and you're ignoring me. That's not polite."

Somo turned in his seat, facing his back to the man, and continued reading. The larger man then snatched the tome out of Somo's hands and flung it at the nearest wall. Somo stood, his face red, his lips pressed together.

"Whatcha gonna do, squib?" the other man said through clenched teeth as he stepped closer.

The moment was then interrupted by a low, somewhat hoarse voice that said, "Any man who causes trouble will forfeit half of his period stipend." The men turned to see Pollock Rimes. He approached slowly, his hands clasped behind his back. "What's the cause of this disturbance?" Pollock stopped, his patchwork face very close, eyeing each man in turn.

"This squib's the one causing the trouble, sir." The large

man looked back at his cronies, who began nodding ada-
mantly. "Yep, Fringe-World trash is all he is," voiced one of
the men.

Pollock leaned close to Somo, studying his eyes. "If I catch
you being insubordinate, Private, I'll see to your discipline
personally."

Somo stared back. "I didn't make trouble. They wanted to
make trouble, not me."

"You'll find no sympathy here, squib," Pollock replied. He
smiled, revealing a field of crooked teeth. "Now double-time
it to the cargo bay. It's time to begin your instruction on the
proper use and maintenance of your CMC 400 powered combat suit."

Somo nodded, looked back at the remains of the Digi-
tome, and left.

"Thank you, sir," offered the engineer. Pollock turned to
the large man, facing him at eye level. "Return to your seat,
warp-rat." The man emitted a small laugh to indicate that he
knew the lieutenant was joking. The lieutenant's steady gaze
indicated that he was not. The warp-rat returned to his seat.

The next few intervals passed without incident. The forty-
six new recruits in General Mengsk's army were all trained in
the use of marine-issue combat suits, gauss rifles, and basic
military protocol. The men, who had clearly signed on for
action, soon began to grow restless and wondered when they
would strike a blow to the Confederacy.

The mess hall became more of a gambling hall, where credits were won and lost and then won again (Somo was never
invited to these games, nor did he wish to attend). Mengsk,
during this period, was nowhere to be seen, and as a result, his
legend grew. Whisperings and rumors abounded that Mengsk
was a recluse, that he spent his time in meditation, or that
he simply didn't care (at one point Somo heard a rumor that
the general had been stricken with a debilitating disease and
didn't have much time left among the living).

Finally, mercifully, much to the delight of the new recruits (and the relief of the alarmists), the general called for a briefing.

The briefing was held in the main cargo bay, where an expansive area had been cleared, and a holo-projection system had been set up. The forty-six new recruits as well as roughly thirty of Mengsk's original troops waited nervously for the arrival of their fearless leader. Sela Brock stood impassively near the projection system. Before long, a metallic droning sound was heard as the cargo bay lift arrived. Sela called attention. The lift doors opened, and Pollock Rimes stepped out, followed by Arcturus Mengsk.

The general walked to a spot near the projector and nodded to Sela as Pollock stepped up and assumed a position to Mengsk's right. The lights in the bay were dimmed, and the holo-projector came to life, emitting a glowing image of a small rotating planet.

"Stand easy," Pollock ordered. The men went from attention to a resting position and waited in silence for Arcturus to begin speaking.

"Men," he began, "Umojan intelligence sources have recently provided us with the necessary information to deal our first substantial blow to a key target in the Confederacy." There was a murmur of excitement. "At ease," Pollock barked. The murmuring ceased and Mengsk continued: "Our target is on the planet Vyctor 5 in the Koprulu system." Mengsk motioned toward the image. "As some of you may know, Vyctor 5 is renowned for a particular feature on its desert surface: a weather anomaly unlike any other previously recorded in the known systems." Mengsk turned to the glowing planet, and nodded once again to Sela. "Bring us closer."

The edges of the planet began to fade out as the program zoomed in on the desert surface and now the assembly was treated to a first-person view, skimming along the planet's relatively flat surface until a massively tall, rotating windstorm appeared on the horizon.

"It is known as the Fujita Pinnacle—a complex mass of conflicting pressure systems and staggering updrafts that have created what is, in simple terms, a stationary, volatile vortex of immense size and unlimited life. It is four leagues wide and over twenty high. To give you a rough idea, its diameter is that of two battlecruisers placed end-to-end, and its height is twice that of the tallest superstructure on Tarsonis."

There was silence among the men as Mengsk stood in front of the swirling column of light. "Long ago, before the Guild Wars, a research center was built in the eye of the tempest, to study it." The perspective of the holo-image changed once more, moving through the cyclone winds of the anomaly, into its center, where a sprawling complex of structures were seen to rest on the sandy floor.

"That facility has since been taken over by the Confederacy and, we have just learned, is being used by them for some highly secretive experiments. We have arranged for a falsified message to be sent to a detachment of marines at the Fujita facility, informing them of a change in their rotation. They are expecting to be replaced at the end of this cycle, so they have already alerted sector patrol to be on the lookout for a carrier—our carrier. I believe the marines will be excited enough about the transfer that they will not question its authenticity and we should have little trouble getting to the planet. That, however, is only the first step. The marines will be expecting their replacements to come to them via underground transit. . . ."

One of the men near the front, a Private Saunders from Umoja, blurted out: "I've been to Vyctor 5. The transit's terminal has more guards than the Council headquarters on Tarsonis!" Some of the more experienced members of Mengsk's militia, who had already learned not to interrupt the general during his briefings, threw the man derisive stares but remained silent.

Mengsk acknowledged the man briefly with a flat gaze, and then returned to the image. "The facility is supplied via underground transit systems that run from the closest city, Lockston, fifty leagues away. To attack the city, as our friend so aptly pointed out, would be too risky. To try and break into the underground tunnels from the desert would be too difficult and time consuming. So . . . we will breach the facility's defenses from above, with a squadron of four dropships led by a Wraith fighter. Two of the dropships will carry armed forces, while the other two will bring back any civilians we run across, or any Confederates who wish to surrender."

New recruits, Somo thought.

"One aspect of the anomaly that works in our favor is that it blocks virtually all ground-based surveillance, scanning and transmissions. They won't even know we're there until we're on top of them."

The image moved outside the column once more, then up. Once at the top the angle tilted down and the view was from above the windstorm, looking down its winding tunnel at the structures below. "The facility's defenses, due to its already formidable location, are minimal. There are four missile turrets around the facility's perimeter to discourage an attack from above." The perspective moved forward, down the wind tunnel, leveling out at the bottom and circling to provide a view of the four turrets.

"The turrets must be taken out before the airdrop can take place. Like I said, although they are expecting our carrier, they are expecting it at Lockston, not the facility. Those turrets will be live, and will fire on anything that comes down the funnel. The only way to get past them is to sabotage them from the ground."

Another private, a dark-skinned man named Tibbs asked, "How do we get to the turrets without going through that storm?"

Mengsk waited patiently for a moment before answering. "We don't. That's where Sergeant Keel comes in. He's going to take four soldiers with him, and he's going to drive a siege tank right through the Pinnacle's outer barrier and into the belly of the beast."

There was a stunned silence among the assembly, and many eyes turned to Forest. He simply beamed a smile back, although Somo doubted he had any idea how he was going to get through the tempest, and until now, hadn't even known Keel was a sergeant.

Another private managed to stammer out, "But with the force of those winds . . . that's impossible."

Mengsk sighed angrily. He told Sela to bring the lights back up and proceeded to explain exactly how Forest Keel and four of his companions were going to achieve the impossible.

CHAPTER 3

INTO THE EYE
OF THE STORM

ARCTURUS HAD TO EXPLAIN THE CONCEPT TO Forest three times, and Forest still didn't really understand it, but it went something like this: the problem was that once the tank reached the hurricane winds of the Pinnacle, it would be swept up into the air and hurled across the wastes like some child's toy if it was not somehow "rooted" to the ground. The solution lay in the fact that, long ago, even before the landing of the forefathers on the inhabitable planets, mankind's technology had advanced to a point where it could simulate and control gravity. The same technology that was used on battlecruisers to create artificial gravity was used to a smaller degree in combat suits and in siege tanks, to allow for their use on orbiting platforms—although most platforms had their own version of the gravity technology, to have a platform's power supplies fail and subsequently allow a tank to float out into space simply would not do. Therefore, tanks, marine combat suits, Goliath walkers, and Vulture cycles all had accelerator technology in place.

So the siege tank that Forest Keel now piloted across the arid wastes of Vyctor 5 carried modified accelerators that would, with the press of a button, increase the downward G-forces of the tank to six times normal; the inside of the tank, much like a pressurized cabin, would remain unaffected.

This particular technique had never been tested in field conditions before to anyone's knowledge, and the soldiers were not exactly thrilled to be the pioneers of its inception, but, as Mengsk had explained, their options were limited and time was a factor.

Intercepted Confederate transmissions indicated that in just under an interval a Mammoth-class carrier—a real Confederate carrier—was due to arrive on the planet. It would proceed to Lockston, but to get to Lockston it would pass through the outer orbit where the *Hyperion* now waited. The Confederate carrier was certain to be escorted by several fighters, and perhaps even a battlecruiser, and so it was imperative that Mengsk's operatives slip in and out as quickly as possible.

Entering Confederate space had been fairly easy. Umojan operatives were masters at pilfering both military and commercial passage codes. The Sector Patrol for Vyctor 5 was expecting the *Hyperion*, and remarked that they must be the cause of the cancellation of the massive tour ship that had been scheduled to visit the Pinnacle until just a few intervals ago. Mengsk, of course, had known of the cancellation and its purpose: the canceled tour coincided with the legitimate carrier's arrival. The Confederacy didn't like civilians snooping around when they were going about their shady business.

The tank had been dropped several leagues away from the Pinnacle, just beyond the restricted area warning markers, and just inside the elevated Lookout Plateau where the people of Lockston and other visitors could rent telescopic sights to view the anomaly. On ground level the Pinnacle was not yet visible past the rolling dunes. Old Forest wondered if civilians at the lookout had noticed the dropship, or if they noticed the tank as it now rolled toward its destination, then figured that most people who paid to view the Pinnacle would not bother with inspecting the trackless desert surrounding it, and even if they did see the tank they probably wouldn't care; or if they did care, by the time they finally got around to reporting it and the squadrons at Lockston acted, it would be too late. Forest then decided that he was thinking too much and decided to concentrate on the situation at hand.

On the interior vidscreen, Somo watched the horizon through his combat suit face shield. Just now the tank had begun to encounter several small cresting hills, and the journey soon began to simulate the effects of being on a vessel at sea. As the small dunes grew larger, Somo suddenly felt that he might be sick. He closed his eyes and concentrated, then glanced around at the others. They didn't seem to be faring much better, except for Pollock of course, who simply returned Somo's glance with a cold stare. Somo's condition was not helped by the fact that the tank was incredibly hot, despite the cooling unit inside the suit. And to add to the discomfort, the space inside the tank was cramped and claustrophobic. Somo wasn't sure exactly how many personnel the tank was made to accommodate, but he was fairly sure it wasn't five. At least not five fully suited.

The dunes continued to grow in size, and at each crest and downward descent, Somo felt more sure that he would vomit, until, mercifully, the tank would level out. Then before long, it would begin another upward climb. After several of these, Forest finally stopped on the crest of a particularly large dune.

"I'll be a swampbat's uncle," the old man said. There was a touch of awe in his voice that made Somo and the others crowd forward to share a look at the forward vid-screen. Only Pollock remained seated.

What they saw looked like a solid towering pillar of sand

rising up and up and finally disappearing into the open sky. It was possible to note a certain amount of movement in the funnel, but from here it looked as if the winds were moving in slow motion, like a video recording being played at half speed. There was an immense cloud of dust at the Pinnacle's base that roiled and shifted like a nest of angry hornets.

"Enough gawking. Let's move," Pollock ordered.

Somo and the others sat back down. There was a tickling sensation in Somo's stomach that he was not used to. He took several deep breaths and told himself to remain calm. *Everything's going to be just fine*, he thought. *No problem.* There was a lurch as Forest engaged the forward drive and the tank began descending the large dune.

Sela stood on the bridge of the *Hyperion* looking over General Mengsk's shoulder at a spy screen that displayed a large red dot, and not too far below it, a small green dot. She was wearing her flight suit and had her piloting helmet tucked under one arm. The green dot on the screen stopped briefly, and then began to move again, toward the red.

Mengsk sat with his chin resting on his closed fists, watching intently.

"All right, Lieutenant," he said finally. "Prepare to drop."

Sarah Kerrigan was reliving the nightmare. This time it was just a little different: a glowing red line cleanly bisected the dark room, keeping the purplish substance at bay on the other side. Wherever the shifting mass would touch the heat source, it would retract instantly. As before, Sarah was bound, facing a dark window. She was still groggy from the latest dose of drugs, and had grown emaciated and sickly.

Below the window across from her and to one side, Kerrigan saw an opening. She had not noticed it upon waking, and now that she looked closer she could see that the mass extended into the depths of the aperture. She heard a sound coming from the hole then, a sticky, wet, sucking noise, like someone trying to free a foot that has been stuck in mud.

The sound was becoming louder, more insistent, and it became obvious that whatever was making the noise would soon be in the room with her.

Sarah still believed that there was a chance she was dreaming, and that before the thing in the hole entered the room, she would wake up.

Then the creature emerged.

They were past the rippling dunes now. The area just outside the tempest was in fact so perfectly level that it almost seemed unnatural. All of the loose sand in the area had long since been swept into the storm and what remained was hard-packed ground, layered with spider-web cracks. The wind was intense, and Somo could hear it buffeting against the tank's armor even through his combat suit helmet.

"We're within two leagues," Forest informed the others.

The tickling sensation in Somo's stomach was gone. Mostly what Somo felt now was a kind of detached disbelief; disbelief that he was playing at being a soldier, disbelief that he had come so far on his own, and disbelief that he was about to enter a raging tempest in the name of the rebellion.

As these thoughts traveled through his mind, he felt the tank begin to slow, heard the sound of the engine ramping up, working harder to push through the wind, and wondered if the vehicle was powerful enough to even get them to the storm's outer barrier.

"We're under one league," Forest croaked. The wind was making it increasingly difficult to hear, and when Pollock spoke, he had raised his voice to be heard over it.

Pollock looked to Forest, who was waiting for the order, and nodded. "All right, time to get heavy."

Forest activated the gravity accelerator and the tank began to crawl, moving at an agonizingly slow pace.

Seemingly an eternity later, tiny flecks of sand could be heard pelting the tank's outer armor, and Somo realized as he looked over at the monitor that they had reached the sand-storm at the tempest's base.

For a long time, no one spoke. They sat there listening; to the wind punishing the tank's outer shell; to the impact sounds of the gritty sand like a constant rainfall; and to the now high-pitched, persistent drone of the overworked engine.

After another infinite stretch of time, Forest's voice was heard once again. "We're just now at the outer perimeter. Engine's in the red. I don't know how much more it's gonna take."

Pollock shot Forest a withering glance. "I didn't know you were an authority on siege tank engines. Continue ahead full." Pollock's voice was breaking up, even in the interior suit mikes. Somo knew that pretty soon, when they were inside the funnel, their transmitters would not work at all.

"Aaallrighty," muttered Forest as he turned back to panel. "Here goes the farm." The tank then lumbered through the outer barrier and into the Fujita Pinnacle.

Arcturus Mengsk sat watching a timer on his console. He then thumbed a button on his lapel and spoke into a collar mike. "They should be in now, Lieutenant. Proceed with insertion."

"Roger that, sir," returned Sela's sultry voice.

Arcturus leaned back and closed his eyes. *This is where it truly begins*, he thought. They would soon learn whatever secret the Confederacy was hiding, and, most importantly, they would embark upon the road to revenge. And then, maybe at long last, there would be atonement for his life's catastrophe.

The creature appeared to be some kind of insect. It had a segmented, multilegged body that trailed a mucous-like sub-stance behind it. It crawled forward on its tiny legs, shimmy-ing like a snake, its tail section creating the sucking noises that Sarah had previously heard. It moved to the edge of the purple mass, and then stopped as two small antennae on its head probed the empty air. The creature wriggled to a position just in front of Sarah, maneuvering to face her. It rose up onto its hind section until it had reached a height that was on Kerrigan's eye level. Its tiny legs moved back and forth as the creature inclined its head slightly.

Sarah stared into the creature's multifaceted eyes. There was a mutual, unspoken recognition that Kerrigan did not understand. She wasn't sure but it seemed as if the creature was waiting . . . the way a foot soldier would wait to be given an order.

Inside the observation room, Doctor Flanx was stunned. He began typing feverishly. The assistant was watching the scene in the opposite room with an open mouth.

"Well, I'd say it's clear that there is some kind of communication taking place," he offered. The doctor nodded, then looked back into the room. The larva was waiting there, sitting in front of the patient like a pet begging for food. It was truly amazing.

"Now what?" asked the assistant.

The doctor shrugged. "I don't really know . . . ." It was clear that telepaths, and especially this patient in particular, had an effect on the alien species. But could she control it? "We'll see if she can give it orders," the doctor finally replied.

Forest, Somo, and the others were inside the vortex making their way slowly toward the inner wall. The vehicle had tilted slightly as the side facing the wind was lifted, and at some point something (hopefully nonessential) had been ripped from the tank's top and was carried away into the maelstrom. The sound in the funnel was a constant, almost deafening roar. Somo was quite sure that had he not been wearing the helmet he would be forced to plug his ears.

The progress seemed almost nonexistent to those inside, but they were, at least, moving forward. The engine had now developed a disconcerting rattling noise from somewhere deep inside, but Pollock and the others knew that they were close to making it into the storm's eye.

Somo had glanced at the monitor in front of Forest on several occasions, but the view never really changed. All the monitor showed was a blur of sand. But now, as Somo watched, he actually believed he could make out the first structures of the Fujita facility.

It was like coming upon a landmass in the midst of a dense fog. The facility and its outlying constructions were just dark shapes glimpsed through the sandy wall, but, as Somo watched, they became clearer and clearer until finally, he could make out more details such as antennae and dishes. The roar of the funnel *moved* then, working its way back as the tank emerged into the storm's center. Then, the noise was simply gone, replaced by what sounded like nothing more than a strong wind.

As the tank rolled to a stop Pollock gave the hand signal to move out.

Somo was the first one out of the tank. He vaulted to the ground, stumbled a few feet, and hit the visor button for his helmet. (They had been informed during the briefing that Vyctor 5's air was breathable. The suits were to protect against human enemies, not the atmosphere.) He felt heat in his throat, and then his stomach tightened and he doubled over, vomiting his last two meals. He wiped at his mouth, then looked up, and froze.

Behind the facility the Pinnacle was a counterclockwise rotating wall of sand. Somo could hear the furious winds now, but it was muted somehow, not nearly the same as on the outside. Somo turned slightly, following the blur of the inner wall until he saw where the tank had come through. Then he looked up, and became instantly dizzy, and thought he might puke again. It was like being inside a living, raging tower.

Pollock grabbed Somo by the arm and spun him around.

"You'd better wake your dimwitted ass up!" he yelled. "Pick up your weapon and start firing at that turret!"

The plan was to take out all of the four antiair missile turrets. The closest one was just a few strides in front of the tank. The foot soldiers would take care of that one, but it would take some time. The other three, however, could be taken out in one shot each with the shock cannon. Luckily, the siege tank's targeting computer keyed in on heat sources, and therefore was not affected by the Pinnacle's dampening effects. Forest's fingers danced across the control panel nimbly. He felt a shifting underneath him as the tank's support legs extended. The entire vehicle then rose up slightly, and a moment later a light flashed indicating that the tank was now in siege mode. *Well, color me giddy!* Forest thought as he put on his ear protection and targeted the first turret.

A voice, the same voice that had told Sarah to invite the mess onto her arm in a previous nightmare now told her to order the maggot-thing to move back across the room. This order Sarah had no problem complying with, since the proximity of the creature repulsed her. She was in the midst of sending the thought when her concentration was interrupted by what sounded like . . . gunfire. The gunfire was followed by a blast that caused the ground to shake. Somewhere an alarm was sounding. Sarah wondered what was happening, then realized as she looked to the far side of the room that the creature had complied. Somehow, the thing understood her. Even in the midst of her delirium Sarah knew that this was significant, that she had established some kind of connection.

There was more gunfire, and an explosion. Sarah felt a stabbing at the base of her neck, and heat, and then nothing as the world faded away.

Doctor Flanx had just told Sarah to command the insect away when the gunfire began outside. Shortly following the gunfire, a perimeter alarm sounded. The assistant had turned white as snow.

"I think we're being attacked," he stammered. The doctor looked back into the room where the subject was being held. He saw that the creature had obeyed the subject's command. *Not now*, he thought. *We can't be under attack now.* There was a ground-shaking explosion then. The doctor pressed a console button and the patient in the other room was knocked out. The assistant was standing frozen, staring dumbly at the wall where the sounds were coming from.

"What do we do? What the hell do we do?" he cried, and then looked to the doctor.

"Stay calm. We're just going to wait here. Remember, we have an entire marine detachment to protect us."

"Yeah . . . yeah. That's right." The assistant smiled and wiped sweat from his forehead. "We're gonna be just fine."

The support legs were designed to absorb the recoil of the cannon, but the force of it was intense nonetheless. The entire tank had jarred dramatically when the shock cannon fired, and Forest, who had not strapped in to his seat, was in the process of picking himself up from the floor. He returned to his seat somewhat dazed, harnessed himself in, and prepared to continue firing.

The Wraith CF/A-17G fighter had led its entourage of four dropships through Vyctor 5's atmosphere and was now hovering far above the Fujita Pinnacle. Sela sat in the pilot's seat, and canted the craft so that she could look down at the spectacle through her canopy window. It was breathtaking, and even this high up she could feel the turbulence it created. She looked down at her computer readout, which was set to key in on heat signatures. There were four red dots representing the missile turrets, and one of them now blinked out. Sela smiled. Then, another of the dots faded. *Two to go*, Sela thought, and then returned her eyes to the beauty of the Pinnacle as she waited for the last two turrets to be destroyed.

Gunnery Sergeant Mitch Tanner had almost cried when he received the Vyctor 5 duty assignment. The last thing he wanted to do was baby-sit the science geeks while they did whatever top-secret crap they were supposed to do. He knew the experiments involved some kind of newly discovered, buglike aliens, but beyond that, he really didn't care. The aliens didn't carry guns, and hadn't seemed to want to put up a fight yet, so they were about as exciting as pulling fire-watch duty in the frozen wastes of Saluset. And the geeks weren't much better; they didn't drink, and they didn't gamble, so what good were they? The Pinnacle was neat to look at . . . for a while. The novelty wore off after the first planetary month. Mitch had cleaned his weapon and combat suit so many times he could do it in his sleep. He knew that the men were just as bored as he was, but they had made the best of it, and now they had finally gotten the good news that replacements were coming, and Mitch and his Gamma Squadron could go back to forcibly settling claim disputes and ridding the miners' daughters of their pesky virginity.

Mitch was in the middle of cleaning his suit . . . again, and working on a decent buzz with the aid of a bottle of Scotty Bolger's Old No. 8 Whiskey—Tarsonis' finest—when he heard what sounded strangely like . . . gunfire. Mitch bolted up in his seat, and listened harder. It *was* gunfire. A dispute among the men, maybe? A drunken argument carried to the extreme? Too many mother jokes? *Could be* . . . Mitch thought, and then he heard the perimeter alarm. *By the fathers, we're being attacked!* Mitch thought now as he started suiting up. He wondered just how in the known systems anyone could have made it through the Pinnacle. They couldn't have come in from above, or he would have heard the turrets firing. There was a massive blast then, what sounded incredibly like a siege tank firing. *They're taking out the turrets*, he thought. That meant that this was the real thing; they were in it, deep. If they were blasting the turrets, they meant to bring in air support. Just then there was an explosion, different from the first blast, and the gunfire stopped momentarily. *They took out one of the turrets with small arms*, Mitch thought. *That means there's two left.*

And I thought this would be a boring assignment, Mitch thought as he finished suiting up and reached for his gauss rifle.

Outside, Pollock and the others had finally destroyed the closest turret. Forest targeted the third, and fired. The tank rocked. On the targeting computer, the dot representing the third turret disappeared. *I hope the fat lady's warmed up and ready to crow*, Forest thought as he targeted the last turret on the facility's far side. There was a buzzing sound. Forest frowned, looking at the bottom of the screen where a red warning had appeared. *Target out of range*, it read. Well, that was no problem. Forest would just take the tank out of siege mode and drive it around the perimeter until it was in range.

The tank lowered slightly, and Forest could hear the support legs retracting. He put the tank in forward, and accelerated . . . and nothing happened. The rattling noise in the engine had now returned, and was significantly louder. Then whatever was making the noise came loose with a loud pop, ricocheted off of something else, and the engine died completely.

Forest removed his hearing protection and popped the top hatch on the tank. Pollock, standing near the remains of the turret they had sabotaged with rifle fire, looked over questioningly. Forest pointed down at the tank and made a swiping motion across his neck with his right hand. Pollock nodded, and called Somo and the others to his position.

Something is wrong, Sela thought as she waited for the last dot on her screen to fade out. They should have destroyed the last turret by now. The dot representing the tank had not moved. It was possible that it had become incapacitated. Sela decided to contact Mengsk.

"Sir, the last turret is still in place. Please advise."

Mengsk's voice came through the mike. "We're running out of time, Lieutenant. That carrier is on its way, and it has a battlecruiser escort. If the last turret isn't down in five ticks, I want you to proceed and destroy the target with your burst lasers. Your shield should hold up. No matter what, those dropships must land, and soon. We still have a marine detachment to worry about."

"Roger that, sir." Sela waited, wishing for the dot to disappear. She really didn't relish the thought of heading into the Pinnacle with one turret still active.

"All dropships, be advised, we move in five." *One way or the other*, Sela thought as she looked back down at her screen.

The dot was still there.

Pollock had called the men to his position, raised his visor and told them that the tank was out of range to hit the last turret, and that it was immobilized by some kind of engine failure. So the men would have to make their way to the opposite side of the facility and use their gauss rifles to destroy the remaining turret.

"Be aware that we should be seeing enemy resistance shortly," Pollock yelled as he and the others trotted around the facility's northeast side. Somo knew what "enemy resistance" meant; it meant an entire detachment of Confederate marines, at least twenty-five of them. Math had never been Somo's strongest point, but he knew without a doubt that twenty-five against four were not good odds.

Gunnery Sergeant Tanner and his men had exited the barracks and seen the remains of the turret on the facility's southern side. It was completely destroyed. He could not see the other turrets from his current position, but he remembered the explosions he had heard from his quarters; the only direction he had *not* yet heard an explosion from was the northeast side, and so he led his men around the facility's power generators and was rewarded with the sight of an undamaged, fully operational missile turret.

He and his men took a position in front of the turret, and a few seconds later they saw a combat-helmeted head peer out from behind the South Lab.

Pollock and the others were pinned down, the tank was useless, and the enemy had taken a position around the last turret. A barrage of suppressing fire was now pelting the structure Somo and the others were taking cover behind. Somo wondered just how they might get out of this predicament when suddenly the whole environment darkened.

There wasn't much light inside the funnel anyway, but when the Wraith fighter and four dropships appeared at the funnel's top, it had the effect of eclipsing what little light there was. Somo peered up and watched the craft descend. Once they reached the funnel's halfway point, the turret came to life. The Wraith positioned itself to take the entirety of the barrage of automatic missile fire. Bright coronas erupted around the fighter as several missiles struck the outer shields. There were smaller impacts as well, and Somo realized that the marines must have begun firing at the fighter . . . but at least that meant the marines were distracted.

"Let's lay it down! Now!" Pollock yelled as he took a kneeling position and began firing. The dropships had almost reached the ground behind Somo's position and out of the line of the marines' fire. Somo knew the Wraith would not take much more punishment, and the turret needed to be destroyed before they could leave. He leaned out, watching as clouds of whitish back-blast smoke from the rapid-fire missiles engulfed the marines.

Somo lifted his weapon to fire, and stopped. He had never shot at another human being before, and he hesitated. The others had begun firing now, and Somo watched as some of the marines fell, and others began returning fire. Somo ducked back behind the structure. Pollock stood and smacked the side of Somo's helmet.

"You'd better lay down some fire before I toss your worthless ass into this storm!" he yelled. Somo nodded then, and made the decision that his desire to live outweighed his reluctance to kill.

Pollock went back to his kneeling position and continued firing. Somo leaned out and pressed the trigger, aiming his sights at the first marine he saw. A second later twenty of Mengsk's men rushed up to support Pollock's position and sealed the fate of the Confederate marines.

Sela was taking heavy fire. The shields were almost gone, but at least the turret didn't have much left. A steady stream of fire from her burst lasers was wearing the weapon down, but not fast enough. The marines were all but gone now; just a few left who were exchanging fire with the ground troops, but the missiles were still doing enough damage.

Gunnery Sergeant Tanner knew that this was it. Most of his men were lying at his feet now, and the dropships had landed. This position could not be held much longer, and the turret was just about finished. The Wraith had taken a barrage of fire, and couldn't have many shields left. The attackers were too well covered for him to get a very good shot, so Sergeant Tanner turned his weapon on the last target he could attack with any degree of effectiveness: the Wraith.

Sela realized then that she was taking additional fire from one of the marines. Her shields finally gave, and the first rocket to penetrate impacted with her right-side wing, sending the fighter up and sideways, into the massive wall of sand that rotated around it. In a blinding instant her control over the craft was gone and the fighter was swept into the maelstrom. The cockpit was spinning then, and the only thing her eyes could focus on were the tiny lights on the control panel.

She felt an impact soon after, and wondered if she was still alive. Then her world turned dark.

Somo watched as the Wraith was sucked into the pinnacle. It was gone in the blink of an eye, spewed out now into the desert somewhere. Somo wondered if Sela could have survived the crash. He became aware that Pollock had charged out from their position, and stepped out to provide cover fire. Pollock didn't need it; all of the marines had now been dispatched, save one, who stood looking skyward with an air of satisfaction.

Pollock charged forward, firing as he did so. The steady stream of fire knocked the survivor back, until he too came into contact with the wall of the Pinnacle and was swept away. To Somo he looked like a child's toy, some kind of action figure as he pinwheeled through the tempest's wall, up and around, and then was gone.

Doctor Flanx and his assistant were sitting on the floor in the observation room, waiting for the conflict to end.

"Listen," said the doctor. "The firing's stopped." He smiled. "I told you it was going to be okay." The assistant nodded feverishly, laughing and returning the doctor's smile. They heard steps then, pounding metallic steps as booted feet traveled down the hall outside. The hatchway to the observation room opened, and a man in marine combat suit armor strode in. The armor he wore did not bear the markings of the Confederacy. Doctor Flanx stood, his smile fading.

Pollock raised his weapon and pointed it at Doctor Flanx's face. "You are now a prisoner of the rebellion," he said. Three more suited men entered the observation room. One of them leveled his weapon at the doctor's assistant.

Somo entered the room, noted the men at gunpoint, and noticed a window that looked out into another room. Somo approached the window and stopped, not really believing what he was seeing.

Half of the room was covered in a purplish goop. Seated in a chair in the room's opposite side was a woman with her head slumped to her chest, wearing a plain green robe. Her hair was a deep, striking red. In front of the woman was a creature that resembled an oversized beetle. It had curled up into a ball, as if waiting for the woman to awake.

"What in the known systems . . ." Somo began. Pollock stepped up to Somo's side and looked into the room.

"We take everything back with us that we can. We've got ten minutes. What we can't take, we burn. Let's move."

Several minutes later, the four rebel dropships lifted off and away from the burning remains of the Fujita facility. Miraculously, after several tries, the tank's engine came to life long enough for Forest to board it onto one of the craft. The last turret had finally been destroyed, and the ships met no resistance as they rose out of the Pinnacle and traveled to a spot where one of the pilots had detected a faint heat signature in the desert. Sela Brock was taken from her half-buried craft, unconscious but alive, carried into the ship, and was soon on her way with the others back to the *Hyperion*.

CHAPTER 4

GHOSTS OF THE PAST

THE UNIVERSE NEWS NETWORK COVERAGE OF THE rebel attack on Vyctor 5 was saturated with omissions, embellishments, and all-out lies, as the government-controlled media coverage always was. Nothing aired on UNN that was not edited for content by the Confederacy, and so the attack on Vyctor 5 was presented as a vicious, terrorist rebel strike on an environmental research facility in which several civilians were killed and valuable scientific data concerning the Fujita Pinnacle was lost.

Arcturus wondered how long the people would allow themselves to be misled. As long as the media cowered to the Confederacy they could paint whatever pictures they chose, and the Sons of Korhal were making nothing more than the tiniest of dents in the Confederacy's armor. Something would have to be done, something on such a grand scale that not even the media could cover it up.

But, all things in their time, the general reminded himself. The scientists were now in the process of studying the dead alien creature (Pollock had decided it was easier and safer to transport it that way) and the substance. Arcturus had never seen anything like it. There had actually been contact made with an alien presence, and the Confederacy had concealed the information from its people. Based on what he had seen so far, Arcturus's best guess was that they intended to develop some kind of biological weapon. It was obvious, according to what Pollock and Somo had told him, and on the confiscated report that was taken from the lab, that the Confederacy was conducting experiments to study the interaction between the aliens and humans. And this woman, who now lay before him, was the only human test subject left. What had happened to the others? What else had the Confederacy already learned about the aliens? But most of all, Arcturus wanted to know, why *her*? And how important was she to the Confederacy? Mengsk was beginning to think that she might turn out to be a valuable ally. But . . .

Somo entered the sick ward where Arcturus was seated, looking thoughtfully at Sarah as she lay unconscious in the bed before him. The general did not look up when Somo entered.

"Sir?" Somo said. Arcturus looked up at him then.

"Sir, will she be all right?" Somo motioned toward Sarah.

Arcturus looked back at her, contemplating the very same question. "We'll see. We'll know when she comes out of surgery."

"I didn't know it was that bad."

The distant look in Arcturus's eyes returned. He didn't process Somo's statement for a long moment. "Hm? Oh. It's not her injuries from the facility that necessitate her operation. All the medics at that lab did—physically, anyway—was drug her."

Arcturus stood, and walked to the bed. He lifted Sarah's fiery hair and pulled back the upper part of her left ear. There was scar tissue on her neck.

"You see this scar?"

Somo nodded, and the general continued. "It means that our 'patient' here is a Ghost—one of the Confederacy's most highly trained and dangerous operatives. It also means that she's a telepath."

"You mean she can read minds?" Somo had the awe-filled look of someone who was suddenly thrust into the presence of a superior being.

"Yes, and perhaps more. Telepaths have powers that not even the Confederacy fully understands yet. That's why they ensure the compliance of their Ghost soldiers by putting 'neural inhibitors' inside their brain." Mengsk pointed to the scar. "It makes them highly responsive to orders, and in most cases, inhibits their memories."

"Why do they want to repress their memory?" Somo asked.

Arcturus waited for a moment, choosing his words carefully. "Because Ghosts are only sent on the blackest of operations. They are assassins, infiltrators, and murderous automatons under Confederate control. The inhibitors are implanted so the Ghosts cannot remember the things they have done, and therefore if captured cannot give up any Confederate secrets to the enemy." Arcturus stood over Kerrigan, looking down at her. Unreadable emotions passed over his face. "We're going to have her inhibitor removed."

Pollock Rimes stepped into the room. He glared savagely at Somo for a moment before turning to General Mengsk. "Our new doctor has finished his examination of Lieutenant Brock. She appears to be just fine. Doctor Flanx seems more than eager to prove himself in his new capacity."

Mengsk nodded. "Good. We'll allow our friendly doctor to prove beyond a doubt that his loyalty has been subverted." The general looked down at Sarah. "Tell him to report to me immediately."

"Yes, sir." Pollock turned his eyes to Somo. "After I speak with the doctor, I want to have a talk with you."

"Something's the matter, Lieutenant?" asked Mengsk.

"Nothing a little discipline can't handle, sir." Pollock nodded at Mengsk; Mengsk nodded back and Pollock left the room. Somo looked after him questioningly, wondering what the lieutenant wanted to yell at him about now.

Arcturus turned back and continued staring at Sarah Kerrigan. Somo found himself looking at her also, hoping that she would come through this okay, desperately wanting just to speak with her, to see what kind of individual she was. If Mengsk was right, she had spent her life as an unwilling participant in horrible acts that she could not remember. She had probably lived her life as a recluse and an outcast. Somo knew what it was like to be shunned, and he felt a sudden bond with the prone woman.

I wish I could read her mind, Somo thought.

Sarah knew that she had been having nightmares, but she couldn't remember what they had been about. Every time she tried to remember, horrible images flickered through her mind's eye, too brief to fully grasp: dark rooms, a strange, creeping substance, a maggot-like creature . . . but what before that? Where was she now? *You're still dreaming*, she told herself. *It's not time to wake up yet, Sarah. Soon.* That voice was not hers; she couldn't place it, but she thought it must be her mother's. She struggled to remember things about her mother, what she had looked like, sounded like, been like . . . but nothing came. Then she tried to remember her father, and again nothing came. It was as if all the doors inside her mind were locked, and she no longer held the key. She knew that she had possessed the key at one time, but had no idea how or where she had lost it.

She seemed to hear voices then, distant murmurings that would fade in and out, sometimes becoming distinct enough that she thought she might be able to understand what was being said, but then the voices would slip away again to a faint mumble and would be gone.

Underneath those voices was something barely discernible,

hidden deep within the insular regions of her mind: a calling; a beckoning invitation that was not expressed in words but only in thought, foreign and distant and not capable of being translated into language. Sarah was aware of this only briefly before the recognition of it was lost and her mind returned to trying to unlock the sealed doors of her memory.

"If you freeze up again during a mission, you won't be coming back. You got that?" Pollock's eyes were wide, looking back and forth between Somo's, searching for the slightest hint of protest or defiance, any excuse for Pollock to make an example out of the young recruit. Somo did not give it to him.

"I won't freeze up again. That was the first time I—" Somo started.

"Don't give me excuses, Private; I've heard plenty, and from better men than you. In case you haven't figured it out yet, you're not my favorite person. I don't think you belong here. But even though you're more trouble than you're worth, I've put up with more than I usually would because we need every man we've got. But don't think for a minute that our lack of personnel gives you any wiggle room to be a screw-up."

"Like I said, it won't happen again." Somo held Pollock's eyes, making every effort not to glance at the concave indentation in the lieutenant's head (he doubted that would help his situation any).

"If it does, the next time will be the last." Pollock spun and exited the room.

Somo proceeded directly from the break room where Pollock had pulled him aside back to the sick ward to check on Sela, and of course, the other female patient, the Ghost. He hoped that she had made it through the surgery okay.

For the longest time there was only blackness. Then there was a sensation of slowly returning to reality, like coming to the surface of dark waters. Her mouth was dry, and her head ached dully. There was a brightness perceived through her closed eyelids. There were noises: the hum of equipment, the low deep rumble of massive engines. There was also a thought pattern, difficult to discern, multilaycred and complex, like no other pattern she had read before. The basic gist of the thought stream was that the person considered her to be important, and that was why she was still alive.

Sarah Kerrigan opened her eyes. She was in a bright room. There was a man seated next to her bed, watching her intently. He was a stern older man with long hair tied back in a tail, whitening in places. A large mustache graced his lip and a protruding brow sheltered piercing gray eyes. He wore a uniform that resembled that of the Confederacy only slightly.

"Hello," the man said.

Sarah stared back at him for a moment, then replied. "Where am I?"

"You are on board the *Hyperion,* a battlecruiser under my command. You are here as a guest of the Sons of Korhal. My name is Arcturus Mengsk."

"Sons of Korhal? Who—" Sarah began as the hatchway to the room slid open. Somo poked his head in, and saw that the general was there.

"Sorry. I just wanted to see if she was okay." Somo looked at Sarah and offered a smile. He was a young man, not unattractive. Kerrigan stared back at him, showing indifference. She still did not know where she was, and who these people were, so she reminded herself to stay on the defensive. "I'll just, uh . . . go." Somo stepped back out and the hatchway slid shut.

Arcturus returned his attention to Sarah. "We liberated you from a Confederate test facility on the planet Vyctor 5. You were being subjected to some kind of experiments involving an alien species. Do you remember any of that?"

Sarah thought for a moment. There was a montage of images parading through her mind: the inside of living quarters aboard a carrier. She was being transferred, although she couldn't remember from where; then, a massive funnel cloud, and the carrier descending to a complex at the vortex's base. She was taken to a lab and given drugs. Then things became more indistinct. Dark rooms, strange substances covering the walls and floors, reaching out for her . . .

"I remember some things. I don't know why I was there, or everything that happened."

The general nodded. "Do you remember—"

"What I did before I came to the facility . . ." Arcturus had almost forgotten that telepaths had a disconcerting habit of completing other people's sentences. He simply nodded and waited patiently.

Sarah concentrated. There were brief flashes: visits to distant worlds, stalking through hallways, traversing open battlefields, raising a weapon to fire . . . then a glimpse of something far more dark and sinister, a blade across a throat, and gushing blood.

"I don't know."

Arcturus knew that she was lying. And Sarah, being a telepath, knew that Arcturus knew. However, she did not read any animosity in his thoughts—at least, not on the surface. There was animosity there, but it was buried deeper than Sarah was able to penetrate.

"You were a Ghost, a Confederate soldier. Before you became a soldier, a chip—called a 'neural inhibitor'—was implanted in your brain. Part of the function of the inhibitor is to repress memory. The rest of your memory loss is due to the drugs administered during the experiments. We have removed the chip, and the drugs' effects are not permanent. I believe that with time, and patience, and the proper guidance, you may regain your memories. All of them."

"And what do you want in return?"

"For now I just want you to rest. We can discuss the subject in greater detail at a later date. I don't want you to feel, at any time, that you are a prisoner here. You will have access to any part of this ship you like, and my door will always be open to you. I think that once you have regained your memory, without the interference of the chip, you will come to the conclusion that you were fighting for the wrong side. But it's important that you reach this conclusion on your own."

Sarah was unsure how to respond. She could not remember ever having been treated this way. Arcturus offered a brief smile and rose.

"If you have any questions, do not hesitate to ask me." The general walked to the hatchway, then stopped and turned back. "By the way, do you remember your name?"

A name rose to the surface of her consciousness then, without any prompting on her part; she blurted it out uncertainly, aware of how strange it sounded to her, as if she had not spoken it in years.

"Sarah . . ."

But Sarah what? For now, she could not remember the rest. At the hatchway, Arcturus smiled once again. "Well, Sarah, rest easy." The general then turned and was gone.

The containment cell was meant for patients who suffered contagious viral infections. It was a climate controlled, airtight chamber that could be supplied with oxygen when necessary. At this time the chamber was not oxygenated, which made the state of its contents (that was the only word that really fit; "inhabitant" just didn't seem right) all the more puzzling.

A container marked as hazardous had been taken from the Fujita facility. Scanning equipment determined that a living organism resided within the container, and the decision was made to open the container inside the cell. Within a few short minutes the organism within the container had propagated to an alarming degree, covering every surface in the room, and it had done so without the benefit of oxygen.

The cell walls were transparent. Arcturus Mengsk stood now beside Helek Branamoor—a Umojan scientist who had spent his pre-rebellion life as a geologist—staring at the substance on the other side. It was almost jellylike, laced with veins and arteries, and pulsating with life.

"The self-replicating cell structure is unlike anything I've ever seen. It's incredibly resilient. The only adverse reaction I've noted so far is to extreme heat. It doesn't like fire very much." The professor smiled, obviously very excited about his work.

Arcturus reached up and laid his hand on the glass. The substance churned and contracted. Professor Branamoor smiled and motioned for the general to follow him down the hall. "If you like that, you're going to love this. . . ."

Inside Research Lab One, Professor Branamoor led the general to an incubator-like device near the center of the room that was currently housing the dead alien larva. The creature had been dissected, its belly opened up, the skin removed to expose a complex network of inner organs.

"I think it's basically just a larva, a precursor, if you will, to something bigger. Within this creature's DNA are countless sequences, carrying billions of patterns and nearly infinite possible combinations. I think what we're seeing now is just the first stage of its life cycle." The professor was still grinning eagerly.

"If I'm following you," said Arcturus, motioning to the larva, "you're saying that once this creature enters the metamorphosis stage, it could become almost anything."

"That's just a theory, mind you, but I believe it's very possible."

"So how does it determine what it will become?" Arcturus asked.

"I don't know. Perhaps a catalyst within the environment, or some kind of predetermining factor in the creature's life cycle."

Arcturus nodded gravely. "Is it dangerous?"

"At this stage in its development I really don't think so. But post-metamorphosis . . . who knows?"

Arcturus was quiet for a moment. The professor wondered

what thoughts were taking place inside his mind but decided not to ask. Finally Mengsk spoke. "Thank you, Professor. Let me know anything else you find immediately."

"Of course," the professor replied. The general took one last look at the creature and left the room.

For the briefest moment, Sarah thought she could remember her mother's face. It was there and gone again, more like a hallucination than a memory, but it had been pleasant and strong and beautiful, and Sarah clung to it. Over the course of the past few intervals, Sarah had begun to remember more and more, but the memories were always snippets; pieces of the greater whole. She remembered more of the Fujita facility, of the experiments, and those memories she chose not to focus on as much.

She tried to remember her last name, her last birthday, her father's face . . . all these things still eluded her. Most of her life still eluded her, now that she thought about it. She could not remember her training at the Ghost Academy, or how she even came to join the Confederacy. She could not remember her childhood years, or her teenage years. She could not remember most of the missions she had performed as a Ghost. What little she could remember seemed surreal and fantastic, more of a dream than reality, for in these memories she was an invisible warrior, unseen and unheard, and she was an assassin. These half-memories frightened her most of all; she would watch herself through her own eyes as she committed ruthless and horrific acts of violence (she could never see the faces of those she killed, though, and she was thankful for that). In those moments she told herself that she had been in some kind of altered state, that she was not herself, that the real Sarah would not do those things. But even then, a part of her knew the truth.

The hatchway in the room slid open and Sarah opened her eyes. The Asian man who had looked in on her before stood in the entryway somewhat awkwardly.

"You might want to step into the room before the hatchway slides shut," Sarah said, nodding at the entryway. The other man laughed and took a step into the room. The hatchway slid shut behind him.

"Hi, my name's Somo. I'm the one who . . . uh, brought you from the . . . from Vyctor 5 here on board. I just wanted to see how you're coming along."

The man was obviously very nervous, and obviously very taken with her. She didn't need to be a telepath to realize that. When she did read his thought patterns, she found him to be sincerely concerned for her. His mental signature was unlike that of a lot of the men she encountered. She detected a strength that came from deep within him, as well as an amazing willpower and a genuine appreciation of life.

"So . . . how do you like the *Hyperion* so far?" Somo asked. Sarah picked up an immediate self-chastisement in him then for blurting out what he perceived to be a stupid remark. It went something like: *"How do you like the* Hyperion*?" You idiot! She's going to think you're a moron*. Somo offered a nervous smile and Sarah began to laugh. It was the first time she could remember laughing in a very long time. As a matter of fact, she couldn't remember the last time she *did* laugh. It felt good and for a while she could not stop.

"I don't think you're a moron," she finally offered.

Somo started to smile, and then his features froze as he realized he had only been *thinking* what she had just responded to; then his smile returned as he remembered she was a telepath.

Sarah simply smiled back at Somo knowingly.

"You know, I get the feeling that we just had a conversation on two different levels," Somo said. "That's pretty weird."

"I think it can be quite efficient," Sarah responded. "It's a great way of cutting out all the crap."

Somo nodded. "Since I'm trying to think of the best way to ask you if you'd like to have coffee sometime, and you know that's what I'm thinking, then I suppose I don't really have to ask, unless thinking of it doesn't really count as asking, which brings me right back to—"

"Let me help you out. I would like to sometime, but right now I'm still tired and I want to get some rest."

"Okay . . . sure, great. I'll let you get back to, uh, resting, then." Somo walked back to the hatchway and waved at Sarah before stepping through.

"I'll see you later," she said. Somo nodded happily and the hatchway slid shut.

As Sarah lay in her bed, gazing up at the ceiling, she began to wonder when Arcturus would call on her to discuss what he wanted in return for rescuing her from the Fujita facility. Eventually she decided that the general would approach her in his own time, and she drifted into sleep.

Doctor Flanx had already decided that he would do whatever it took to get out of this situation alive. If that meant telling the revolutionaries what they wanted to know, so be it. The doctor was convinced, however, that the Confederacy would soon overcome their little rebellion, and when that time came, he meant to cast himself in the best possible light. Perhaps he could even have a hand in vanquishing the Sons of Korhal, if he could gain enough of their trust. And then, when the time came and the Confederacy squashed their little uprising, Doctor Flanx would be a hero. Perhaps he could even become a special adviser to one of the ruling fathers. Maybe have his own penthouse suite in one of Tarsonis' superstructures. Hell, maybe he could own the whole building. And his name would be forever recorded in the Digi-tomes of history.

With these thoughts in mind, Doctor Flanx proceeded down one of the *Hyperion*'s labyrinthine hallways, escorted by two combat-suited marines. He was led to a hatchway and told to enter.

Inside the room Pollock Rimes stood near an empty chair, facing a bare table. Across from the empty chair sat Arcturus Mengsk. There was another fully suited marine in the far corner, and as the doctor stepped in he thought he detected yet another seated in the nearest corner on Pollock's side. The two marine escorts waited in the hall as the hatchway slid shut.

So, this is it, the doctor thought. He knew it was just a matter of time before the rebels got around to their interrogation of him. He was surprised it had taken this long. Then, he thought, maybe they wanted him to settle into a false sense of security.

The doctor nodded at Pollock, who simply barked out, "Sit."

Doctor Flanx settled into the chair and looked across at the grave face of General Mengsk. Pollock remained nearby, close enough, it seemed, to cuff the doctor on the head if he stepped out of line during the questioning.

"I want to know when and how the Confederacy became aware of the alien presence."

"Um . . ." The doctor threw a sheepish glance at Pollock, who glared back, then turned back to Mengsk. "As far as I know, the species was detected nearly five cycles ago, on a fringe planet in the Koprulu sector. It was reported to a local marshal, and several scientists were sent to investigate. It, hm-mm," (the doctor cleared his throat and swallowed; his voice had begun to go hoarse), "it was determined that the species was not indigenous, but beyond that, little to nothing was known about the organisms, aside from their staggering proliferation abilities. Um . . . then more reports came in, from neighboring planets. It seemed that the infestation was extensive, and it was determined that the aliens should be studied."

The silence in the room was painful. The doctor looked hopefully at Mengsk, who only glared back. He looked at the marine in Mengsk's corner, who seemed ready and more than willing to use his gauss rifle at the first signal from the general. The doctor tried to glance behind him, at the marine seated in the corner, but Pollock stepped forward and blocked his vision.

"Why experiment on humans?" The general's eyes were twin drills now, boring through the doctor's skull and peering right into his mind. The doctor could almost actually feel the general mentally probing him.

"Wh—uh, I was of course acting under orders to experiment with human subjects, but only to determine how the creature and the uh, Creep, as we call it, would interact with people."

"Why was the Ghost the only subject left?" Arcturus leaned forward, resting his elbows on the table.

"Well, it's interesting, actually. We found that both the alien substance and the larva had a specific reaction to telepaths; or at least that's what we thought. We couldn't really prove it until we performed the tests in an isolated environment and it turned out to be true. The female subject, though, the Ghost . . . she seemed to provoke the strongest reaction in both the creep and the larva. So, we decided to continue with her and discontinue the experiments with the others."

"What did you do with the other subjects once they were no longer needed?" There was an edge to the general's voice that made the doctor even more uncomfortable.

"I don't really know—"

"I'm warning you not to lie to me," the general said flatly. The doctor decided that the best course of action would indeed be to tell the truth, because he could pass the buck onto someone else. "I believe that the marines were ordered to . . . uh, eliminate them and dispose of their remains, due to the top secret nature of the experiments."

"So they were killed. And what happened to the inhabitants of the Fringe planets, where the species was originally discovered? Surely the Confederacy didn't have all of them eliminated." The calmer Arcturus remained, the more uncomfortable the doctor became. He could feel his hands trembling against his knees under the desk.

"Well, as far as I heard, uh . . . a genetically engineered disease was released on those planets. I believe they said it was cholera."

Arcturus nodded at the doctor. He turned and glanced at the marine in the corner behind him, and the doctor was just barely able to prevent himself from urinating in his pants. "Escort the doctor out," the general said. The marine nodded and approached the table.

Doctor Flanx stood shakily. Pollock once again blocked the doctor from seeing the marine in the corner near the doorway, and the doctor began to wonder if the lieutenant was doing it on purpose. *Hey, at least you're alive,* he thought.

"One more thing," said the general. "Why the Fujita facility?"

The doctor turned. "Well, in order to prove conclusively that the aliens were reacting to the telepaths, we needed to ensure that there was absolutely no outside interference. The Pinnacle provided that naturally, and already had facilities in place."

The general nodded again, then looked to the marine. "Introduce our new friend to Professor Branamoor," he said. The marine nodded inside his helmet.

Once the doctor was escorted out of the room, Pollock turned to the combat-suited marine seated in the corner. Sarah removed the helmet of the suit, stood, brushed past the lieutenant, and sat at the table where the doctor had sat sweating just a moment before. She returned Arcturus's cool gaze with equal confidence.

"Was he lying?" the general asked.

Sarah shook her head. "No. He was scared to the point of passing out, but he was telling the truth."

"Good," the general replied. "I hope that some of what he said was helpful to you, as well."

Sarah looked down at her lap, conceding in her own mind that she had indeed been fighting for the wrong side. "It was helpful. And now that I don't have the chip to interfere, I know that what the Confederacy is doing is wrong. I want to help you."

"I think that you could be a powerful asset to our cause.

I welcome you." The general offered a smile, the first that Sarah had seen cross his face. She was tired from the constant probing of the doctor's mind, and she now had a great deal more to think about, so she nodded back to the general and said: "Thank you. Right now I'd like to get some more rest."

The general stood. "Of course. When you feel up to it, I'd like to speak with you some more."

Sarah stood and nodded her acknowledgment. Pollock led her to the door. "I can find my way, thanks," she said to the lieutenant. Pollock looked at Mengsk, who shook his head slightly. Pollock clenched his jaw, staring at Sarah. She did not like what was going through the lieutenant's mind.

"Hey," she said to Rimes on her way out, "I heard that." Sarah walked through the hatchway and out into the hall. *I'll have to take care to remember her little ability,* Pollock thought as the hatchway door slid shut.

CHAPTER 5

AN UNINVITED GUEST

OVER THE NEXT SEVERAL INTERVALS, MANY OF THE facts (as well as an abundance of speculation) regarding the alien race were spread among the various soldiers, technicians, engineers, and other remaining rank-and-file personnel aboard the *Hyperion*.

General Mengsk in fact carefully monitored the dissemination of these rumors, even from within the inner sanctum of his personal quarters and from his post on the bridge. Certain key people (including Sarah, a fact not lost on Lieutenant Rimes) were entrusted with the information and allowed to propagate it. Mengsk knew that from there the rumors would snowball into an entirely different beast, that conjecture would lend its hand and transform the facts and that the end result, whatever it may be, would only fuel the fire against the Confederacy.

The *Hyperion* returned to Umoja for five planetary days. Mengsk sat in on several meetings with the Umojan ambassadors, and important decisions were made. A course of action was decided upon, and wheels were set in motion. During the leave, Sarah kept mostly to herself, remaining in the quarters provided and refusing Somo's invitations to "hang out" on several occasions. She had begun to remember more, and the more she remembered, the more disturbed she became. Forest Keel and several others engaged in liberal alcohol consumption, and the on-site medical staff had its hands full for quite a while, especially with Forest, who reportedly drank a bottle and a half of Scotty Bolger's Old No.8 by himself. Lieutenant Brock rejected several propositions but finally relented to Private Tibbs during a night of drunken carousing and a lapse in her normally resolute judgment. Pollock Rimes, for his part, took his alcohol to his quarters and drank alone. On the morning of the sixth day, the *Hyperion* was restocked and the rebels were transported back to dry dock where they boarded the now familiar ship and settled in for another long voyage.

There was no indication of what their next mission might be, or when it would take place. In the meantime, the soldiers were occupied with training exercises and drills until they could don their combat suits in less than sixty ticks and could disassemble, clean, and reassemble their weapons with blindfolds on.

The *Hyperion* was at the border of Protected Space and was about to cross over into the Confederate dominion. Once again the rebels had become anxious and ready to see more action.

They would not have to wait for very long.

Even though she could see, Sarah knew that the hallway was in fact pitch black. Her vision was tainted by a reddish hue and objects in the distance were blurry and indistinct, but a mapping display in the left-hand corner of her field of vision told her exactly where to go.

She ascended a set of steps and made her way through the halls of the manor's upper story. She arrived at the open door of the master bedroom. Inside, she approached two sleeping figures. There was more light here, moonlight streaming in from an open window somewhere nearby. Sarah approached the large canopy bed. She withdrew a blade from somewhere on her person, and she grabbed the figure in the bed, pulling him up against the corner post of the canopy and in one smooth motion swiping the blade across his throat. The blood began to gush then, as the figure stumbled back into the moonlight, revealing—

Here was where the memory ended. This particular recollection was the most vivid and complete to date—as well as the most disturbing. Sarah sat up in the bunk, burying her face in her hands. Regaining her memory was all well and good, but sitting in this tiny room and reliving the same troubling events over and over was taking its toll on her. She needed to get out, to talk with other people, to try to remind herself that she was normal and human and capable of putting her past deeds behind her forever.

Sarah walked through the claustrophobic ship's hallway, toward compartment 17. Navigating the halls reminded her somewhat of the memory she just had, and she tried with all her power to force it out of her mind. She stood before the hatchway of number 17 and pressed the call button.

The hatchway slid open and Somo, reclining in his bunk reading a Digi-tome, sat up. His eyes widened to the size of credit chips.

"Hello!" he managed. Then, with concern, "Is everything okay?"

"Yeah . . . I just thought I might take you up on that coffee." Somo's mouth opened in a wide smile, revealing a set of near-perfect teeth. Sarah felt a wave of pure joy wash over her from the younger man, and it felt good.

The mess hall was unusually crowded and Somo and Sarah had to hunt for a place to sit. Although Somo had avoided more encounters like the one involving the warp-rats, the derisive stares continued, and Sarah sensed these and felt the negative thoughts of the men as they made their way through the mess hall and took their seats. She was equally aware of the appreciative and, in some cases, lascivious glances and thoughts that followed her across the room. Somo sat in an empty spot next to Forest, and Sarah sat across from him.

Forest, for his part, had been among the few who did not treat Somo with the same cold indifference as the others. Somo nodded to the old man now, who was in the process of masticating a particularly large cut of Umojan skalet meat.

"I'll tell ya what," exclaimed Forest, turning his wild eyes to Sarah briefly, "they sure know how to grow 'em on Umoja! Milk-fed, that's the way to go every time. Straight from the teat."

Sarah smirked at the old man amusedly, sifting through his thought patterns. It was, to her, like a garden that had been overrun and neglected.

The old man sat, still chewing, looking back and forth between the two of them and holding one utensil in each hand, his fists resting on the tabletop. "My mother, may she be granted eternal solace, used to cook up skalet that would make your toes curl. I bet your mom could make some mean skalet herself," he said to Somo.

Sarah felt Somo's mood change. "She used to," was all he said.

"Ah, she don't cook no more, huh? Poor lad." Forest was still chewing, and shaking his head.

Sarah read the thoughts going through Somo's mind then, searching for the most polite way to say that his mother was gone.

"I'm sorry," Sarah offered. Somo looked up, and in spite of himself, he smiled just a little. "You're amazing."

"Wait a minute, sorry for wha— Oh, she's not— Well, kick me in the nuggets, boy. I'm sorry. I didn't even think—how did it happen?"

Somo was now thinking that tact was not among Forest's finer points, even as he answered. "Cholera. My mother and father both."

"I heard something about that. Affected a few of the Fringe worlds, if I remember right. Wiped out entire populations." Forest was shaking his head. "I'm sorry to hear that, boy. Well, suppose I better get some beauty sleep before the next drill." Forest stood up and grabbed his tray (with the utensils still in his hands), offered a brief "see ya," and was on his way.

Somo looked at Sarah then. Her head was tilted, her mouth slightly open. She was staring deeply and pensively into Somo's eyes.

"What is it?" he asked.

"Maybe I shouldn't tell you this, but I think you have a right to know." Sarah leaned forward. "Your parents were victims of an epidemic that was engineered by the Confederacy to silence any possible witnesses of this new alien species."

Sarah could feel Somo's thoughts swirling, his mind going over the statement she had just made again and again. His first reaction was disbelief.

"How do you know?" he asked, looking suddenly very lost.

"The doctor from the facility, the one who was doing the tests on me, he told Mengsk. I was there. I know he wasn't lying."

"But they didn't even know . . ." Somo was looking down at the table, his eyes distant. Sarah felt pity for the man.

Just then Sarah detected Pollock behind her. "It's time for your weapons drill, Private," the lieutenant said to Somo.

"Not now," replied Sarah without looking up. "He's just received some distressing news." Somo was just about to say, "It's okay," when Pollock spoke up. "Our schedule does not revolve around your friend's emotions."

"Your schedule can wait," Sarah replied hotly.

"Don't you dictate to me—" Pollock began as he laid his hand on Sarah's shoulder to turn her to face him.

Somo did not see Sarah move. Nor did he see her stand. It just seemed that in one instant she was sitting there, and the next she was up, holding Pollock's hand in a painful looking, twisted position, her hand on Pollock's face and her thumb hovering over the lieutenant's eye. Her eyes were blank, emotionless adornments on her face. "Don't ever lay a hand on me, Lieutenant," she said through half-clenched teeth.

Somo stood and ran around the table. By the time he got to the other side, Pollock had jerked back and withdrawn a knife. Somo stepped in between the two of them, holding his arms out.

"Listen! Both of you! I just found out that the reason I'll never see my parents again is because the Confederacy arranged for them to be eliminated. I'm not about to let the two of you stand here and kill each other when the enemy is out there! If we fight each other then it's all over! Don't you understand?"

Pollock sheathed his blade, looking around at the gathered spectators. "She was the cause of this altercation. Assaulting a superior officer is an offense punishable by court martial. You all saw what she did," Pollock said, waiting for affirmation. When none came he looked to the nearest table, where the group of warp-rats who had cornered Somo were seated. "You are all witnesses. Right?" Pollock was looking directly at the warp-rats' leader now.

The warp-rat shrugged his shoulders slightly. "I wasn't really looking when it happened." He turned his back and continued eating. The others either looked away or remembered urgent business elsewhere. As Pollock looked around the mess hall, he could not find one pair of eyes that would hold his. Sarah had not moved. She still stared at Pollock with that blank look, a look that accompanied the blank state her mind was in, where thoughts of right and wrong held no place, where there was only action and instinct. It was, Sarah realized, a part of her Confederate conditioning. She forced herself to relax a little.

"I expect you at the weapons drill in five ticks," said Pollock. He glanced once more at Sarah, and she could tell he was making every effort to keep his thoughts hidden from her. She knew if she concentrated hard enough, she could expose those intentions. She decided to wait.

A moment later the lieutenant turned and stormed out of the mess hall. The remaining personnel soon returned to their meals.

General Mengsk stood on the deck of the bridge, looking out at the vista of needlepoint stars that twinkled against the black vastness of space—Confederate space. The *Hyperion* was a minnow swimming through shark-infested waters. They would have to be very careful. Somewhere behind the general a hatchway slid open and Sarah stepped onto the lower deck. She looked around. The bridge seemed more like the general's living quarters than his official post. There were several Digi-tomes, a full-service bar, and even a smattering of archaic strategy games, including one Sarah recognized as chess. On the lower level, directly in front of Sarah, were several banks of monitors showing myriad systems. Some of the dots on those screens, shown in red, represented Confederate vessels. Sarah immediately felt that even in the vast expanses of space, those dots were too close.

"You called for me?" she asked, directing her attention to the imposing figure before the lookout.

Mengsk spoke without turning around. "Yes. I felt it was time that we had a more in-depth conversation, you and I. By the way, I heard of the incident in the mess hall." Sarah did not detect accusation, in his tone or in his thoughts.

"Lieutenant Pollock laid his hand on me. If he does it again I'll put a matching dent in that head of his." Although the general was not facing her, Sarah could tell that he was smiling.

"I think you put a scare into Rimes. That's not a minor feat. Rimes is the kind of person who simply does not scare." The general turned now, facing Sarah. He stood with his hands behind his back, a silhouette against the stars. "We had information that the Confederacy was conducting studies on Vyctor 5," he began. "But that's not entirely the reason I chose the planet as the Sons of Korhal's first operation. The reason . . . was you."

The general paused. Sarah could detect something beneath Mengsk's thoughts, something that he wished to keep hidden, and he was doing an amazingly fine job of it. His was proving to be the most formidable mind Sarah had ever encountered. And she respected him all the more for it.

"The Umojans knew of your transfer to the Fujita facility. They made that information available to me, and I made the decision to release you. I had my reasons, of course."

"And those were?"

The general paused again. Sarah knew that what the general was about to say was not the whole truth. "Because I believed you could be . . . rehabilitated, for lack of a better word. Also, within your memory rests valuable information, such as the details of the security measures at the Ghost Training Academy on Tarsonis."

Sarah could not hide her amazement. "You mean to attack the Ghost Academy? On the capital planet of the Confederacy?"

"That's exactly what I mean to do. Until now the efforts of the rebels have been largely ignored in the Confederate-controlled media. I doubt even *they* could ignore an event of such magnitude."

The general stepped forward now, and Sarah could see his features. His eyes were wildly intent, focused, piercing. "I have a policy of not informing my soldiers of our missions until the last minute, but I'm telling you now. Not only because I trust you . . . but also because I want you to lead the assault. We have reason to believe that there are more alien specimens at the Academy. And they're using the recruits for tests, just like they did with you. You know the Academy. You trained there. Even if you don't remember it all right now, you will in time."

Sarah began to understand, although she still had the nagging feeling that the truth, in its entirety, was not being presented to her. What was Arcturus concealing, and why? No matter what the general was hiding, inexplicably, Sarah felt that she could trust him. Perhaps it was the gesture of trust that he was offering to her.

"You needed me. So you rescued me from the facility and helped me regain my memory to convert me to your side so I would lead your assault. You've had this planned for quite a while."

As Sarah waited for Mengsk to answer, there came a hailing from the nearby comm. Sela Brock's wavering voice broke the silence in the room. "Sir . . . this is Lieutenant Brock. I was attacked outside my quarters. I just woke up. Didn't see who . . . took my uplink code key."

Uplink code keys were used to send out transmissions, either from one of several comm stations in the limited access areas, or via remote terminals located throughout the ship. "Report to the sick ward immediately," the general answered to the lieutenant, then pressed another button on the comm. "Communications officer, I want you to monitor any outgoing transmissions starting now. Notify me of any unauthorized activity."

The general walked around to the bank of vidscreens. He focused on the monitor showing their current location, and then looked to nearby corresponding monitors, which showed the activity in the next closest sectors.

A voice from the comm announced: "Sir, I'm showing an unauthorized transmission was made just moments ago from a remote terminal on the cargo level."

"Nav!" the general blurted.

A voice answered: "Yes, sir."

"Prepare to go to subwarp."

"Preparing for subwarp."

On a monitor near the one in front of the general, one of the red dots disappeared from the screen.

"Too late," the general whispered to himself.

As Sarah glanced upward at the lookout there came a bending, a rippling in the field of stars outside. Sarah's eyes grew wide as the broadside of a massive metallic craft seemingly appeared out of nowhere, directly in the *Hyperion*'s path. An alert was sounded.

Arcturus turned and moved to the comm. "Sir, a craft has just warped into our—"

The general pressed a button on the comm and responded. "Yes, I can see that, Nav. Full stop."

"Full stop, yes, sir," the navigator responded.

Just then a large vid monitor to the general's left illuminated, displaying the face of a gray-haired colonel wearing a Confederate uniform. He began to speak with a heavily accented drawl. "Attention derelict vessel. This is Colonel Edmund Duke of the Confederacy Flagship *Norad II*. Identify yourself immediately."

General Mengsk pressed a button on the comm. "Notify *Norad II* that we are a Confederate vessel on a training exercise, and send them our pass code."

On the vidscreen, Colonel Duke looked away for a moment, then looked back.

"There are no exercises authorized in this area. Do not attempt to engage your engines, and prepare to be boarded. If you attempt to interfere with our boarding party in any way, you will be fired upon."

The *Hyperion* was just now coming to a complete stop. The *Norad II* loomed before them, a hulking technological giant. The general knew that the ship itself could not fire at them sideways from its current position, but the squadrons of Wraith fighters that were now leaving the docking bay could. The *Norad II* had positioned itself the way it did simply to prevent the *Hyperion* from going to subwarp and leaving the *Norad II* to eat its wake. A textbook maneuver. The general's mind began working out the situation. The range of the remote terminals was severely limited; the *Norad II* had been the closest and probably the only ship to receive the transmission. And if the general knew Colonel Duke, the stubborn old codger did not report his situation before knowing all the facts. Which meant that for right now, all they had to deal with was the *Norad II*.

The general pressed a button on the comm panel and spoke: "Nav, notify *Norad II* that their boarding party is cleared to land in docking bay one." Mengsk pressed another button. "Private Hung, this is General Mengsk. I want you to grab seven of your comrades, get suited up and armed, then report back to me. As fast as you can possibly move."

"Yes, sir," came the reply.

"Would you like me to suit up as well?" Sarah asked.

"No," the general answered. Sarah surprised herself by being disappointed. She found that she desperately *wanted* to engage the enemy. Her bloodlust, it seemed, had not been dulled by the removal of the inhibitor. But beyond the disappointment, she wondered if maybe the general did not trust her. She could detect no suspicion in him, but still . . .

"No, I would rather have you here to protect me, if it becomes necessary." The general turned to Sarah then, and a moment passed between the two of them.

The general returned to the lookout, briefly glimpsing at the chronometer on the nearest console. His mind was working out the situation, weighing their chances, and thinking of a way out. Sarah watched and waited in respectful silence.

Colonel Edmund Duke couldn't believe his luck. Every Confederate officer in the known systems was on the lookout for the whereabouts of their lost Ghost, and mere moments ago they received a communication from an anonymous party giving them exact coordinates! *If I don't make general for this I'll eat my own pressure suit*, the colonel thought as he sat at his command station.

"Sir, the boarding party is ready to depart," stated a voice from the comm.

"Excellent. Send 'em away," replied the colonel.

The colonel looked at a vidscreen that showed a view from portside of the older model cruiser and wondered if the captain of the vessel could possibly be the renowned leader of the rebels . . . wouldn't that be a hoot? To bring in this upstart Mengsk . . . the Confederacy would make Edmund Duke a general for sure. The colonel had known of Mengsk, back when he was fighting for their side. He had never really liked the man then, and now he liked him even less. Bringing him in would be a pleasure.

Duke relaxed in his chair and waited to see what would unfold.

On the lookout deck, General Mengsk had not moved. Sarah had waited patiently, scanning his thoughts but trying not to be invasive. This much she knew: the general had a plan. *Somehow,* she thought, *this is one person who always had a plan.*

Arcturus turned and stepped onto the lower level. He stood near the comm, watching the chronometer above it. He pressed a button.

"Sergeant Keel, this is Mengsk. Listen carefully . . ."

The doorway of docking bay one had opened to receive the Confederate dropship. It closed now, as the dropship landed. A moment later the walkway lowered and ten fully armored Confederate marines jogged down onto the docking bay deck. They proceeded to the nearest open hatchway, where Pollock Rimes waited.

"I'm Sergeant Roosevelt Brannigan of the Confederate marines. This vessel is hereby commandeered under orders of the Confederacy. Take us to your captain immediately." Pollock nodded at the sergeant, turned, and began leading them to the nearest lift.

The charting screens cast Arcturus Mengsk's features in a medley of primary colors as he watched and waited. He pressed a button on the comm.

"Sergeant Keel. Are you ready to proceed?"

Sarah heard the old man's voice answer. "I still don't get what I'm doin', but yeah, I'm ready." Suddenly there was a nagging, underlying disturbance in the back of Sarah's mind. She could not pinpoint the source of it, but believed it had something to do with the Confederate boarding party. Certainly it couldn't be any of their thoughts . . . not at this range.

"Good. Stand fast." The general glanced at the chronometer and pressed another button. "Nav, give me forward, fifteen degrees port at half speed, on my mark."

"Yes, sir," came the reply.

The general was unwaveringly focused on the chronometer now. If they were to survive this, the general knew, the timing would have to be perfect. Sarah, in the meantime, pushed any and all disturbing mental commotion to the back of her mind so that she could concentrate on the trouble at hand.

The lift in front of Pollock opened and Doctor Flanx rushed out, waving his hands and smiling.

"Thank the fathers! I'm one of you! This is a rebel ship, and I've been taken prisoner here. This man is a rebel as well! Don't trust anything he says! I'll take you to the captain myself!"

The sergeant spoke into his helmet mike: "Colonel, are you receiving this?"

The colonel's voice responded. "Yeah, I'm readin' ya! Follow him."

"Yes, sir," the sergeant responded. He nodded to the doctor, who turned and led the marines (two of whom now had their weapons trained on Rimes) into the lift.

On the bank of monitors, the general was taking particular interest in the displays of the *Hyperion*'s interior corridors and lift systems. He watched as a display showed the lift from docking bay two ascending to the Meridian level. Another monitor showed a camera view of the marines as they exited the lift and proceeded down the corridor. The general seemed relieved, even though Doctor Flanx was now leading the Confederate troops. Sarah waited anxiously. The general spoke into the comm.

"Computer: close off section A-6 on Meridian. Sergeant Keel, proceed now."

The siege tank had been repaired when the *Hyperion* docked at Umoja, and Forest had not trained in it since. But he had no trouble now as he guided the vehicle through the towering crates of the cargo bay and through the adjoining doorway to docking bay two. The general's directions had been bizarre to say the least, but Forest trusted the man and was willing to do what he was told without question. So now he sat at the tank's controls, fully suited, steering the tank into the empty bay. He then parked it in front of the outer seal door, as he was told, and engaged it in siege mode. The legs extended, the vessel lifted several feet, and Forest sat, staring at the forward monitor, which showed nothing but a massive, sealed door. He engaged the gravity accelerator to five G's, as he had been told. He put on his hearing protection, strapped into the driver's seat, and waited.

General Mengsk watched on the vid monitor as the Confederate troops made their way single-file through the narrow corridor. He spoke once more into the comm.

"Nav. Give me forward, half speed, fifteen degrees port . . . now."

"Forward, half speed, fifteen degrees port. Yes, sir."

The mammoth ship began moving forward toward the *Norad II*. Sarah was unwilling to believe that the general was actually doing what he seemed to be doing. She grabbed onto a nearby railing anyway.

On board *Norad II*, the word arrived to Colonel Duke's command post that the *Hyperion* was on the move. The colonel assumed that the vessel was retreating, perhaps trying to reposition to make the subwarp jump. He asked for clarification, and was told that the vessel was moving *forward*.

Those sons of Fringe-Worlders actually mean to ram us, the colonel thought. "Shields to full! Shields to full! And take crash positions!" the colonel yelled. "Sergeant Brannigan, report!"

The sergeant's voice returned to him immediately. "En route to bridge, sir."

"That ship is moving on our position. You get to the captain and stop that cruiser now! Double time!"

"Yes, sir."

In all his years of captaining a ship, Colonel Duke had never once strapped himself into his command seat.

He did so now.

Somo waited, sweating inside the combat suit. He knew vaguely what the plan was, but that didn't change the fact that it was dangerous. And he knew, like the others around him, that he was facing sentencing in Confederate courts and eventual death if he was captured. That was assuming, of course, that he lived to stand trial.

Doctor Flanx led the soldiers to an L turn in the corridor. The hallway stretched on, past personal quarters, to another turn, and then they would be at the hatchway to the main deck. They were halfway down the passageway now, and the doctor was smiling; he was picturing himself accepting a medal of valor from one of the ruling fathers. *Then the promotion, of course,* he thought, *and a life of affluence on Tarsonis. Maybe even—*

Just then a hatchway to the doctor's right opened. Pollock stepped into the room immediately, where four fully suited soldiers stood. One of the men passed Pollock a gauss rifle. The doctor then heard shouting. He looked down the corridor and saw that another hatchway had opened, just before the next turn. Two rebels stepped out; one kneeled. Both trained their weapons down the hall at the Confederates. They had their visors up and they yelled for everyone to drop their weapons.

In the hallway behind them, the hatchway they had just passed opened and two more rebels stepped out. Doctor Flanx saw his world unraveling around him; saw his fantasies of the easy life on Tarsonis shattered. His eyes grew impossibly wide and his brow knotted as he screamed: "You ignorant grunts! Get me outta here!" Something in the doctor snapped. He snatched a gauss rifle from the nearest Confederate, pointed it into the compartment to his right, and began firing.

They were almost on top of the *Norad* now. Sarah could hear minor impact noises from the strafing Wraiths outside. It would take a long time for the fighters to break through the *Hyperion*'s shields. But the behemoth cruiser before them was another matter altogether.

"Bring shields to full."

"Shields to full, yes, sir."

"And brace for impact."

The general looked at Sarah then and motioned to his chair, indicating that she could strap herself in there if she liked. She glanced at the chair briefly, then shook her head, unable to keep her eyes from the lookout for very long. She could see small details on the looming, larger ship now, hatches, panels, and outer compartments—the kinds of things a person saw on another vessel just before a collision.

The *Norad II* was not moving. Sarah took a deep breath. *We're really doing this,* she thought as the hatches and panels grew closer; she fancied that soon she would be able to read the serial number on the other ship's cooling compartment.

There was a brilliant flash just outside as the shields collided. The clash was accompanied by a horrific screeching noise and a massive, gut-wrenching jolt. Sarah clasped her hands to her ears, shutting her eyes tight, fighting to maintain her balance, but to no avail.

She fell to the deck in a fetal position, her hands against

her ears. On the upper level, Arcturus had been forced to his knees, and was likewise clutching his ears, but managed to keep his eyes on the lookout screen. Outside, brilliant flashes and ear-piercing shrieking accompanied the abrasion of the two shield systems. But slowly, incredibly, they were still moving forward, pushing the other ship away and aside in a rotating circle so that the bridge of the *Hyperion* would soon be flanking the bridge of the *Norad II*. Soon, the two ships would be side-by-side.

General Mengsk managed to stand. He stumbled to the comm, shouting to be heard: "Seal off docking bay two and open the outer doors, now!"

Long ago, General Mengsk had read of ancient battles, back on Earth, from a time when men crossed oceans in bulky, cumbersome wooden craft. At that time, when these ships fought, they would position themselves alongside each other and blast away with cannon. That had always fascinated the general. Now, millennia later, in the boundless ocean of space, Arcturus Mengsk decided to try his hand at naval warfare.

The rebel next to Somo, Saunders, he thought his name was, was down and, judging by the amount of armor-piercing spikes Doctor Flanx had pumped into him, dead. The marines in the hall began firing, into the room and in opposite directions down the hall outside. Pollock, who was being targeted by one of the marines outside, had taken cover against the wall next to the hatchway. Doctor Flanx now swung his weapon toward Somo. There was a piercing, high-pitched noise, accompanied by a monumental jarring that knocked Hung onto his back. The doctor fell against the marines in the hall, who some-how managed to remain standing, and with eyes completely devoid of the last vestiges of sanity, now pointed the barrel of his confiscated rifle back down at Somo. Somo let loose with a short burst of fire, aiming at the doctor's chest. The weapon ran away from him slightly, and when Somo looked at Flanx, he saw a trail of gaping holes starting from the man's sternum and ending in his forehead. Somo watched the doctor's wide, lifeless eyes as the man fell back against the huddled marines and then slumped to the floor like a discarded puppet. On either side of Somo, three rebels had recovered from the jolt and began directing fire back into the hallway. A few marines had managed to take flanking positions on either side of the hatchway and were still firing bursts into the room.

The door was opening. Minute debris swept out into the vacuum of space as the outer seal was broken. The tank, moored by augmented G-forces, held steady. Beyond the door was a massive beast of metal, the *Norad II*. Forest Keel now understood the general's plan. A smile spread across his face as the old man became giddy with anticipation. Then the general's voice came through Forest's helmet mike. The shields outside had now been worn to almost nothing, and a great deal of the noise had died down. Still, Forest had to strain to hear. "Sergeant Keel, you may fire when ready."

"That's all you had to say, skipper! Yeee-haaa!!" Forest engaged the shock cannon. There was massive recoil, and when Keel looked back at the targeting monitor, he saw a satisfying impact wave spreading across the neighboring vessel's shield. The blast was enough to force the defensive barrier to collapse. A bright ripple ran through the shield and then it was gone. Forest fired again. This time, the impact tore through the *Norad*'s outer hull.

"What in the name of all the charted planets was that?" It seemed every warning Klaxon in the ship was sounding at once. A voice from the comm announced to the colonel that there was a breach in the outer hull, and that sections G–L of the Median deck had been compromised.

"I want to know just what in the name of the fathers is firing at us!" the colonel yelled. "Start scanning! Hell, they're right next to us for Krydon's sake. Go to a lookout and give me a visual!"

A moment later a voice returned. "Sir, our scanners indicate the source of the incoming fire to be a . . . siege tank. Firing from one of their docking bays."

For the first time in many cycles, the colonel was actually speechless. Another explosion came then, followed by news of another breach. "Send the Wraith fighters to knock out that tank," he finally managed.

"Sir, the shields are spent," the Nav informed Mengsk. "The Wraith burst lasers are beginning to damage the outer hull."

They're not doing nearly as much damage to us as we're doing to them with that siege tank, the general mused. Another roaring *boom* was heard then, punctuating the general's line of thought. With both shields gone, the jarring had ceased, as well as the deafening noise. Sarah was standing, watching as the last of the *Norad II*'s bridge disappeared on the starboard side of the lookout and out of sight.

"Nav, are we clear for subwarp?" the general asked anxiously. There was a moment of silence, then: "That's affirmative, sir." Another *boom* from the docking bay resounded.

"Comm, lower transmission screen and contact *Norad II*."

Somo rolled to his left, narrowly avoiding a barrage of deadly fire from the hallway. The marines flanking the hatchway had resorted to thrusting their gauss rifles into the room and shooting blindly. Pollock, who had taken a position against the wall and near the hatchway, grabbed the gauss rifle with his bare hands the next time the barrel was poked into the room, and yanked. Somo, on the opposite side of the compartment, caught a glimpse of the dumbfounded marine in the hallway as his weapon was ripped from his hands. In a different situation, the look on that marine's face would have been comical. But here it simply conveyed shock and defeat. The marine stood with his hands waving in the air; he hit a button to raise his helmet visor and began shouting: "I'm unarmed! I'm unarm—" the marine then stepped just enough in front of the doorway so that Pollock could get a clean shot. The lieutenant unloaded a full burst into the man, then proceeded into the hall, where he fired a second burst, point-blank, into the remaining marine crouched near the hatchway.

Colonel Duke was staring at an update screen, showing a top-down, wire-frame view of the *Norad II*, with damaged or compromised areas shown in red. There were four large red areas on the *Norad*'s port side, four breaches that would take months to repair.

Through the lookout, the colonel could now see the bridge of the *Hyperion*, inching forward on their port side. To the left of the colonel's command seat, a vidscreen crackled to life and on it, the composed figure of a man in rebel outfitting began to speak.

"Colonel Duke, this is General Arcturus Mengsk, leader of the Sons of Korhal. When you run back to your masters, tell them that free men still live in Confederate space. Tell them that we are learning their secrets, and that their avarice will be their undoing. Tell them that twilight has settled upon their regime and the changing of the guard is close at hand; and tell them Arcturus Mengsk sends his regards."

With that, the transmission ended. There was a rippling wave that surrounded the *Hyperion*'s bridge for the briefest moment before the vessel disappeared completely.

"Sir, the enemy craft has engaged subwarp," the Nav offered.

"Thank you for keeping me apprised of the situation, Nav," the colonel responded hotly. *It's okay, let them subwarp,* the colonel thought. Once they'd received the anonymous transmission, they had followed the Confederate protocol that had been dictated to them just an interval earlier—and it was a good thing they did. The colonel thought he might still make general out of this whole mess yet.

The battle in the hallway was over. Doctor Flanx, as well as the ten marines who had boarded the *Hyperion*, lay dead on the floor. Pollock, who had seemed enraged, shouted at Somo and the two remaining rebels in the compartment to clean the mess up, then stormed off down the hallway. Inside the compartment, two rebels lay still. In the hallway, two more rebels, one on each side, had fallen. The remaining soldiers approached the compartment, stepping over the marines and looking down at the bodies in a dazed, almost somnambulant manner. Somebody asked for Section G-6 to be opened and called for a medic.

Somo looked at the carnage around him, shaking his head, trying to convince himself that these were the men who were responsible for the death of his family. But as he stared down into the lifeless faces he saw only people; people who had simply been caught up in fervor and circumstance. He stood there for a long time, even after the medics arrived and carried away one of the wounded from the hallway. He stood and wondered how long this would go on, and whether or not he would live to see the end of it.

One of the other privates had gripped a fallen marine under the arms and was attempting to drag him away. He looked up at Somo in irritation.

"Are you gonna help clean up this mess or—" The rebel's sentence was cut off by a *cha-chink* sound, a noise any experienced soldier would immediately recognize as a C-10 canister rifle being cocked. There was a *boom* then, thunderous and deafening in the confined space. The private arched forward, rocking onto the toes of his boots. His mouth hung open as he dropped the marine and fell forward. Somo stared in shock: even from his vantage point farther down the hallway, he could see the gaping hole in the private's back. There was another cocking sound. Somo, ignoring the ringing in his ears, strained to see, because he could swear that the sound he just heard came from the empty space at the end of the hall, but there was no one there. Another private, standing between Somo and the hallway's opposite end, was rushing toward his fallen comrade.

There was a second booming sound, almost like that of a miniature shock cannon. The private was lifted off of the deck by the blast. When he fell onto his back a microtick later, there was a steaming concavity where his chest had once been.

Somo could not see where the blast had come from; the end of the hall was still empty, but he had an undeniable feeling that whoever or whatever the unseen foe may be, *he* was going to be the next to die. He stepped backward and into the compartment where the trap had been set for the marines, sealing the hatchway door even as he heard another *cha-chink* sound. He waited there, inside the compartment, and he believed he could actually feel a physical presence on the other side of the door. The feeling was brief, but it was strong. A moment later the feeling was gone.

The mental disturbance Sarah had felt when the dropship landed had increased now to the point where she could no longer push it to the back of her mind. She struggled to figure out just what the disturbance was, knowing that she should know, but she just couldn't remember. It was like forgetting a word she had just spoken.

The *Hyperion* had broken out of subwarp now and was cruising near the outer Fringe. General Mengsk, satisfied that they were safe for the time being, turned to Sarah. An immediate concern showed on his face.

"What's wrong? You're white as a—"

"Ghost," Sarah blurted. *That's it,* she thought. *Of course that's it . . .*

"I was going to say a sheet, but—" The general was interrupted by Somo's frantic voice from the comm.

"Sir, it's Somo. I don't know if I'm going crazy, but I think there's an enemy still alive on board. He just killed two of our guys and I think he's on his way to you. I know this sounds nuts, but . . . I couldn't see him. I think he must have some kind of cloaking, I don't know. I locked myself in one of the compartments."

"There's a Ghost on board, general." Sarah advanced to the monitors showing the ship's interior. She moved to a diagram of the upper deck, scanning the maze of halls and corridors.

"Stay there and await my orders, Private," Mengsk spoke into the comm.

Sarah held out her hand, palm up. "Give me your weapon."

"Pardon?"

"Your sidearm, General. Give it to me now. I just watched you pull us away from the brink of destruction; well, now it's my turn to save the day. None of your soldiers have dealt with a Ghost before. He'll kill everyone on this ship if you don't do as I say."

The general considered this for a moment, then nodded. There was, as always, something in his thoughts that she just could not read. He handed his weapon to her. "I want you to activate the fire suppression systems in all corridors on the upper deck." Sarah pointed to several hallways just outside. "Shut down all lifts to the lower levels. We need to keep him isolated. There isn't much time. I assume you have a filtration mask somewhere on the bridge?"

"Of course." General Mengsk proceeded to a small hatch in a nearby wall. He opened the compartment, withdrew a filtration mask, and handed it to Kerrigan. She began to strap it on. When she spoke, her voice was muffled.

"Lock yourself in here and don't open the door until you hear from me." The general looked up at Sarah with equanimity. "Okay," he said. "Good luck."

Sarah nodded at him and exited quickly through the hatchway. Mengsk sealed the door behind her and activated the fire suppression systems.

Sarah stood in the hallway as the fire suppressant showered over her in a fine mist. A red warning light began flashing; a computerized voice warned all personnel to evacuate the corridors.

Sarah knew that the Ghost could breathe, even in the fog

created by the fire suppressant. The headpiece the Ghosts wore acted as chemical agent masks. She remembered wearing one herself. The real purpose of activating the suppressant was to render the Ghost visible. The substance was wet and sticky, and would adhere to the Ghost, rendering the cloaking system in his hostile environment suit useless.

Both ends of the corridor Sarah now stood in were lost in a misty fog. She had a choice of two directions: left or right. She knew the logical direction would be left, since that led to where Somo and the others had been attacked, but she had to be sure. Having been temporarily overcome by the adrenaline surge that accompanied her decision to take action, Sarah had effectively muted the interference from the Ghost's alpha waves. Now she stood perfectly still, eyes closed, allowing her mind to open itself completely and receive the mental bombardment that the neural inhibitor had once suppressed. She could sense the pattern, but it was difficult to tell which direction it originated from. She concentrated harder, forcing all other thoughts from her mind. Finally she came to a decision and turned left, proceeding down the hallway.

The atmosphere inside the foggy, deserted corridors was eerie and surreal. To Sarah it felt as though she were walking through a cloudbank, the only reminder of her physical surroundings being the corridor walls that emerged from the mist as she progressed. The pattern was stronger now, and she knew that she was on the right track. As she stepped forward her foot caught on something. Sarah lowered her firearm toward her feet and kicked outward. Her foot met metal. She kneeled and felt around the dense mist. It was a fallen soldier in a combat suit. She grabbed the upper portion of the chest piece and pulled upward. She recognized the face of the private, one of the men she had glimpsed in the mess hall. He was dead now, his eyebrows gathering tiny crystals from the fire suppressant being let in through his open visor.

She was at the spot in the corridor where the trap had been set for the marines, and where Somo had been attacked. The

Ghost was nearby, but not too close. She could tell now. His alpha pattern was like a beacon. Sarah glanced at the hatchway door to her left. Probably where Somo had taken refuge. She made her way slowly through this part of the corridor, her foot occasionally coming into contact with one of the dead. Once at the end of the hall, she made a right, then an immediate left.

The pattern was stronger now, emanating from the end of the corridor. Sarah held Mengsk's weapon out in front of her as she came to an open hatchway.

Inside the compartment were several sinks, ranges, and ovens. She was in the upper level kitchen. The fire suppressant had not been activated in here and what little had drifted in from the corridor had thinned out enough to allow her to see: several upright shelving units held trays, containers, pots and pans, forming rows down the center of the room. A plethora of steel utensils hung from the bulkheads. The compartment was large, almost the size of the bridge, lined with cabinets and sinks. There were a host of hiding places within the cluttered space.

The Ghost is in here, she thought. The magnitude of the alpha patterns was almost overpowering now, like being locked in a small room with speakers blaring deafening music from all four walls. It was impossible to tell just where in the room the Ghost was. She had to concentrate.

She made her way down a row formed by two of the storage units, heading toward the wall at the kitchen's far end, glancing in between the shelves on either side for any hint of movement. Once at the end of the rows, she looked to her right and saw an open door. She walked toward it, trying with all her might to pinpoint the source of the alpha patterns. Was it beyond the door? She approached the doorway that opened into a cold storage vault. Inside, shelving units containing frozen foods formed several more aisles within the room—more places for the Ghost to hide.

Sarah tried with every fragment of mental acuity she could

muster to lock in on the source of the Ghost's patterns. She had to know if it came from within the room before she entered and risked having the Ghost close the door behind her, locking her in. Once again she forced all excess thought from her mind, focusing intently on the patterns.

Behind me, she thought as she dropped to one knee, spinning to face her opponent, raising her right arm. The barrel of the invisible canister rifle was knocked upward and away. There was a *boom!* that left Sarah temporarily in a world with no sound. She fired her weapon, knocking the Ghost back into one of the shelving units. Even with the thin coating of fire suppressant material, her foe was still incredibly difficult to see. A crystalline veneer hinted at a human form beneath but beyond that, the Ghost was still invisible. Moving with lightning speed, the figure lunged forward, attempting to wrest the weapon from Sarah's grip. She spun with her opponent's charge, circling around and redirecting the assailant into a nearby bulkhead. An arm reached up, snatching a large knife from one of the hooks. The figure made another lunge. Sarah jumped backward. The Ghost slashed across, from left to right, missing by inches, then raised the weapon for a downward slice.

Sarah gripped her opponent's wrist with her right arm, threading her left arm around the Ghost's, grabbing her own wrist and yanking downward with all the weight of her body. She felt her opponent's wrist break as the figure hit the floor. In a blur of action she removed the knife and plunged it into the Ghost's chest. She withdrew the knife, preparing to plunge it downward again. Her eyes were wide, her teeth clenched; she was aware of an almost primordial growl emanating from her throat. She stumbled backward, dropping the knife, forcing herself to regain control. A moment later she contacted Mengsk, telling him that the Ghost was dead.

CHAPTER 6

A BRIEF RESPITE

THERE WAS AN EXPANSIVE FIELD, WITH TALL GRASS
that reached her chest. She held out her hands as she ran,
allowing the blades to pass between her spread fingers. She
was laughing, happy to be out of the house, in a playful
mood. The sun was directly overhead, and the day would
have been hot if not for the cool breeze that lifted her hair
away from the back of her neck and caused her eyes to
water just a little.

Sarah was five years old.

She heard a voice then, the voice of her father. As she
turned she saw him in the distance, hands placed firmly and
disapprovingly on his hips. He called out her name: "Sarah
Louise Kerrigan, you get back in the house this instant! You
still have chores to do!"

She began walking toward him then, and when she was
close enough to see his features, she saw Arcturus Mengsk
standing in his place. She suddenly became aware that she
was no longer in the field. She was in a long, metallic corridor.

Ahead of her on either side were large windows that looked into sealed rooms. Sarah continued walking, approaching the first window. She stared in and saw herself, at the age of eight, sitting in a metal chair, restrained. A man in a Confederate uniform paced back and forth in front of the chair, his mouth moving in speech. Sarah could not tell what he was saying. The man turned to her, staring at her through the window. He stopped pacing, his eyes drilling into her. He began to yell, but she could not hear him. She continued walking.

The next window she came to offered a view of her father, clamped into a chair similar to the one from the first room. He was not the young version of her father she saw in the field. He was older now, gaunt and sickly; his wide eyes looked out with a blank gaze. Sarah beat against the window, yelling: "Daddy! Daddy, it's me! Daddy!" but the eyes did not register any recognition of her; they instead continued to stare forward without blinking, conveying only apathy. Dejected, Sarah turned and looked toward the end of the hall. There was a staircase there now that had not been there before. She turned and walked toward it.

As her foot touched the first step the scene became instantly familiar. She had walked this staircase before, in her memory; it was a recollection that her mind would not fully divulge, yet could not let go of. *It* was the haunting; she was the Ghost. She ascended the stairs and made her way down a long hall toward an open doorway. Inside two figures lay sleeping. She grabbed the figure nearest to her, pulling him to his feet; she withdrew a blade, slashing the figure's throat. The person stumbled back toward the moonlight coming in through the open window. Just as the light was about to hit the person's face . . .

Sarah awoke.

The dream left her with a strange, uneasy feeling. It was more than the act of the killing itself; there was a deeper meaning that she was thus far unable to decipher. Sitting up in the bed, she ran her fingers through her hair, wiped the bleariness from her eyes and began to get dressed.

General Mengsk stood looking at the prone body of the deceased man. He still wore the Ghost uniform, but he was visible now, laying on the gurney here in the sick ward; he looked very real, very pale, and very dead. The cloaking system shut off automatically once the suit's sensors detected that their host was no longer registering a pulse. The cloaking would have worn off before too much longer anyway; the length of time these soldiers were able to remain invisible was finite.

Mengsk stared down at the identification number on the right breast of the suit, just above the puncture hole where Sarah had driven the knife into the man's heart. It read: No. 24506. All members of the Ghost program were nothing more than numbers—but this man meant far more, especially to Arcturus Mengsk, because he was one of the three.

"The three what, General?" a voice behind him asked. The general turned, and Sarah felt his mind close off immediately. It simply became a blank void where she could find no trace of thought or intention. Mengsk was incredibly good at it. "Hello Sarah," he offered.

"Sarah Kerrigan. I finally remembered my last name, just a short time ago."

"Well in that case, congratulations, *Lieutenant* Kerrigan."

Sarah smiled. The general turned back toward the body on the gurney. "It's not exactly your size," Mengsk said, motioning toward the suit, "and it will need some repair work, but with the proper alterations I think it may prove useful to you."

Sarah approached and looked down at the suit. Seeing it now under the harsh lights prompted a feeling of disgust inside her; she connected the hostile environment suit with the person she had once been, and never wanted to be again . . . but if wearing the suit meant accomplishing the mission, she would don it.

"Do you think he came here to kill you?" Sarah asked after a long moment.

"No. I don't think the Confederacy considers me that much of a threat yet. I think he came to retrieve *you*. Those in power are unsure why the alien race has reacted to you the way it did, and they want to know more."

"I think you're right," Sarah offered.

"Even if you didn't technically save my life, I still want to say thank you for killing him."

Sarah simply shrugged. "I did what I had to."

Precisely one interval after the Ghost incident aboard the *Hyperion*, the Sons of Korhal arrived at the Kal-Bryant Mining Conglomerate, docking in orbit around the planet Pridewater. Pridewater was on the Fringe system (located several planets away from the deserted, cholera-ridden planets where Somo's parents died), and was a rich source of several rare minerals. The docking station housed the *Hyperion* inside one of its empty bays, where it would remain hidden until the mission was complete. Surprise inspections by the Confederacy were not uncommon, but since one had been conducted several intervals ago, it was a safe bet that another would not occur for some time. The foremen at Pridewater had secretly sided with Umoja during the Guild Wars, and now further displayed their loyalty by providing information and support to the Umojans when circumstances permitted.

The liaison with Pridewater was set up during the *Hyperion*'s docking at Umoja, based upon a suggestion by Mengsk. Pridewater provided a staging area from which the Sons of Korhal would be able to launch their most audacious attack yet—the raid on the Ghost Academy on Tarsonis.

Once every cycle a cargo ship from the Conglomerate, loaded with minerals, would dock at the receiving terminal—an orbiting platform in Tarsonis' upper atmosphere. From there, the miners would take a transport to the capital planet itself where they would spend several intervals drinking away their concerns and cavorting with Tarsonian females. This time, however, the cycle would be different; the passengers aboard the cargo ship would not be miners from the Kal-Bryant Conglomerate, and the trip to Tarsonis would not be one of revelry.

The plan had been explained to the rebels during a briefing at the Conglomerate docking bay and now the soldiers were informed that they had a single interval before they would once again be called into action.

Sarah Kerrigan (who had repeated her full name to herself several times since remembering it—it was like trying on an old set of clothes and finding out that they still fit) sat inside a cantina at the edge of one of Pridewater's two major oceans. She could not remember ever having seen an ocean. She sat now, looking out the bay window from her table at the rolling waves. It was beautiful, and had a calming effect on her that she embraced.

She had found this quiet place by accident, wandering the streets alone, trying desperately to escape the cacophony of thoughts, the duplicity, the posturing, the impudence of those around her. It had been quite a long time since she had sat down and enjoyed a good drink. The last time was—well, she couldn't remember when the last time was, but she knew it had been too long.

She sensed an awkward yet sincere, nervous individual in her midst then and knew that Somo had entered the cantina. She smiled to herself as the Fringe-Worlder approached her table. "Hi, Somo," she said without turning.

"Hey . . . I saw you leave and come this way. I thought maybe you could use some company. If you wanted to be alone I could just—"

"Sit," Sarah interjected.

"Sure . . . thanks. So are you nervous about tomorrow?"

Sarah was still staring out at the waves, mesmerized by them. The sun was hovering just above the horizon. She did not turn to Somo as she spoke. "No. It's nothing I haven't done before."

Somo found himself taken by Sarah's beauty, every nuance of her features enhanced by the soft light of the setting sun. Sarah smiled, and then began to laugh. "Thank you," she said at last.

A deep crimson hue crept into Somo's face. He stopped staring and raised his hand for a drink. Sarah spoke: "Sometimes I wish the chip hadn't been removed, that I had just continued without any knowledge of what I was doing. I know it's wrong, but I think it just the same. I sometimes wish I couldn't see what goes on inside people's heads; but then, sometimes someone comes along who makes me glad to have the abilities that I do."

A waiter brought Somo's drink. Sarah turned to Somo finally, gazing *into* him. "You're one of those people. You make me glad I'm telepathic, because you're genuine, and you're good. I should know; I've read every kind of human being you could imagine. You're like a breath of fresh air. You represent to me what people can become; you represent hope, and that's something worth fighting for."

Somo searched his mind for a response, but none seemed appropriate. "I—" he began, but Sarah cut him off as she leaned in and kissed him firmly on the lips. Sarah felt a wave of adoration wash over her and she did her best to reciprocate as the sun cast its final light of the day over the waves outside.

Once again Arcturus Mengsk stood before a gathering of soldiers, although this particular gathering was smaller than usual; it consisted of twenty rebels, the exact number of miners who were scheduled to dock at the receiving terminal above Tarsonis. The rebels carried the proper pass cards, and wore the proper clothes, and the cargo ship that would transport them to the terminal—the Giant-class *Homage*—carried the proper load of minerals for appraisal and processing.

Having briefed them on the finer points of the mission, General Mengsk stood now, looking at each one individually. Among them was Somo, smiling and looking to be in an especially good mood, which was encouraging; Forest Keel was there, though he was obviously hung over from excessive carousing during his one-night stay on Pridewater; Sela Brock was present and accounted for, exchanging amorous glances every once in a while with the dark-skinned Private Tibbs; Pollock was at the far right of the formation, apparently unbothered by the fact that he would be taking orders instead of giving them this time around; and finally, Sarah was present, standing to the right of Mengsk, looking every bit as determined and redoubtable as ever she had before.

"I know this won't be the last opportunity to say it before we part company, but I'm going to say it right now, anyway: I know that each of you has his or her own reasons for joining in the fight, and I won't pretend to know what all of you have been through, but suffice it to say that you are all fighting for what is right, for what you believe in . . . and for that I want to wish all of you the best of luck. Dismissed."

Sarah turned and began walking away. General Mengsk called out, "Lieutenant, a moment please."

Sarah returned. The general looked at her confidingly. "I want you to seek out a specific soldier at the Academy, and bring him to me. His number is 24718. He is one of their trainers, and our intelligence suggests that he resides within the Academy barracks. I know it poses a bit of extra risk, but I would not ask if it wasn't important."

"How do I find him?" Sarah asked.

"The Academy's commanding officer will carry a locater, designed to home in on each Ghost's neural inhibitor. Simply enter his number."

Sarah thought for a moment. "If he's there, I'll bring him back. Forcibly, I presume."

The general nodded. As always, his thoughts were his own. Sarah continued. "How will I know this commander?"

"He is the Post Commander. His name is Major Rumm. He oversees the experiments."

The name sparked an immediate response within Sarah's mind: A memory flashed across her inner vision, of being confined in a room with a man dressed in a Confederate lieutenant's uniform pacing back and forth before her. Rumm was his name, she remembered now. Lieutenant Rumm.

The flash of memory was gone then, and Sarah noted a speculative look in the general's eyes. Sarah met his eyes, but gave away nothing.

"I'll take care of it," she said, and then turned to catch up to the others.

CHAPTER 7

THE TARSONIS GHOST ACADEMY

THE JOURNEY TO TARSONIS TOOK ALMOST A FULL interval, and gave Sarah plenty of time to think about the man she had known as Lieutenant Rumm.

The very mention of his name had opened up a host of doors within her mind, and memories filed through those doors at a slow, steady pace until she was able to piece together the series of events that led to the implanting of the neural inhibitor inside her brain.

She was eight years old. Her mother had died, she couldn't quite remember how, and she had been taken from her father, whose mental health had declined severely. She became a ward of the Confederate court system and was remanded to a fledgling science program that was being overseen by Lieutenant Rumm; a program whose sole purpose was to research and develop psychic potential within young telepaths.

She had undergone several tests, to induce her to display her mental powers, but she steadfastly refused (she thought the reason she refused had something to do with her mother, though she was unsure what the connection was). She had been allowed to play with a kitten for a long period of time. Apparently, the scientists had believed that Sarah possessed the ability to cause hemorrhaging within a person's brain simply through force of will. To test this theory, a tumor was implanted in the kitten and Sarah was ordered to mentally ablate the tumor, or to put the kitten out of its misery. Still, she had refused to cooperate.

Lieutenant Rumm then did the unthinkable. He confined Sarah to a metal chair. She was allowed to see her mentally vapid father, who was likewise confined in an adjacent room. Rumm then threatened to have an orderly inject Sarah's father with the same serum that created the tumor in the kitten, unless she was willing to display her powers. Even in the face of this ultimatum, she refused, threatening to kill herself and her father if Rumm continued.

It was shortly after that incident that Lieutenant Rumm gave the okay for the scientists to implant the neural inhibitor inside her head. She had been a puppet of the Confederacy ever since, and for that, she held Rumm personally responsible.

Sarah's thoughts were interrupted as the navigational computer announced that they were preparing to dock at the receiving terminal.

Once at the terminal Sarah and the other "miners" were cleared through security, and herded into a small bay where they awaited a transport to take them down to Tarsonis. From this point on, they were truly on their own. General Mengsk had remained behind at the Conglomerate, and was probably watching his screens even now from the bridge of the *Hyperion*.

As the transport dropped into Tarsonis' lower atmosphere, Sarah went through the plan in her head: She would use the Ghost suit (being worn even now under her mining overalls) to cloak and infiltrate the Academy. She would seek out the section of the institution where the experiments were taking place. Further, she would attempt to track down Major Rumm, and retrieve the tracking device he carried (what she chose to do to Major Rumm at that juncture, she would not dwell on just yet). She would sabotage the base's security and allow the others access, whereupon the rebels would destroy the facility, Sarah would extract Ghost No. 24718, and any alien specimens would be destroyed. They would then rendezvous with Sela.

It was risky, and incredibly dangerous, but Sarah truly believed that if all went according to plan, it could actually work.

Sarah glanced across the transport at Somo, who glanced back, winked, and offered her a smile. She returned the smile, then turned to look out the window next to her. The transport had just descended through the massive cloud base and the capital city of Tarsonis was spread out below, a tightly packed metropolis of towering superstructures and bustling commerce. It was nighttime on Tarsonis, approaching early morning, but the city was very much alive. Lights twinkled from seemingly every window and people still occupied the streets, commuting in their vehicles or perambulating along the myriad walks.

Mixed emotions flooded over Sarah as she was bombarded with the immediate reactions of those around her: anxiousness, dread, nervousness, doubt, and hope were all among them.

They angled toward a circle of lights that indicated the landing pad of the Tarsonis Starport. The transport leveled out and touched down. Sarah watched Lieutenant Brock make her way to the cockpit. She had struck up a conversation with the pilot before lift-off from the terminal, and was now in the process of coaxing the man into joining her for a drink. When she emerged from the cockpit she would give a signal. If the ploy was a failure they would be forced to restrain the pilot, and if he resisted, resort to more drastic measures. Sarah, for one, wanted to keep the body count to a minimum.

Sarah stood as her comrades near the front of the cabin headed for the gangplank. A moment later Sela emerged from the cockpit, smiling, running her right hand through her hair. Sarah relaxed. The pilot followed Lieutenant Brock out, helping her along with a playful slap on the backside. Sela giggled. Nearby, Tibbs made a guttural noise of disapproval. "Let's go," Sarah said.

A short trip aboard a transit shuttle delivered the group to the Starlite-Starbrite, a pub in the city square that was located three leagues away from the Ghost Academy's main gate.

The interior of the Starlite was a chaotic frenzy of light and noise, with a grinding bass-driven techno beat that seemed to be on a perpetual loop. There were tables available near the back, and that is where most of the group ended up; a few stayed outside and a few others actually took to the dance floor. It was part of their responsibility to represent themselves as off-world miners who had not been in a social setting for some time, and were in serious need of recreation. Sela ordered drinks for herself and the pilot, whose name was Castomar, and retreated to a corner table. Tibbs kept a watchful eye on the two as they toasted and the pilot began to drink.

Sarah decided that the time had come for her to depart. She approached Somo and told him that she was leaving. He was about to tell her to be careful, she could tell. She simply put the palm of her hand to his face and said, "I know," and then she was gone.

Inside the stall of the female lavatory, Sarah slipped out of her overalls, exposing the hostile-environment suit beneath. She had a shoulder bag, which she now opened, that contained her headpiece and gloves. The cloaking equipment was integrated into virtually every fiber of the suit, including the gloves, which rendered anything the Ghost held during cloaking invisible. Sarah waited until the occupant of an adjoining stall left, then donned the headpiece and activated the cloaking mechanism. It was disturbing how familiar it all seemed, how she moved automatically now, instinctively. Her vision through the goggles was tinted a reddish hue. She raised her hand before her eyes and flexed her fingers. The goggles allowed her to see her hand perfectly. She stepped out of the stall, staring at her reflection in the mirror, which the goggles also allowed her to see.

The headpiece was a strange-looking contraption, and not all that flattering. Seeing herself there in the mirror, she was forced to repress a wave of memories, of prior missions spent in these very same trappings. The door to the lavatory opened then, and a rather large woman with green hair entered and stopped. There was a brief, horrifying moment where Sarah thought, *she can see me,* before the woman clutched at her mouth, turned, and began vomiting in the sink. Sarah realized then that the woman had only stopped to maintain her balance. Sarah retreated silently to the back of the room. The woman stayed for a while, moaning, until another female who bore similar features (probably a sister) entered and hauled the first woman back through the door. Sarah then opened a window that led to a small side street at the building's rear. She crawled through and made her way into the night unseen.

Somo was seated at a nearby table with Tibbs, watching Sela and Castomar. She had been sipping her drink for some time now, while Castomar had downed two and ordered a third. It looked as if that part of the plan was going very well, at least.

Tibbs was watching, flexing his right hand nervously. Castomar put a hand on Sela's leg.

"That motherless—" Tibbs began.

"Hey, calm down. She's just doing her part."

Tibbs did not answer, but watched intently. Somo surveyed the rest of the room. The last time he had seen Forest, the old man had been on the floor, engaged in a dance that looked something like a cross between a bird imitation and a cardiac arrest. Forest was actually at the bar now, conversing with

a much younger, and fairly attractive local. Somo shook his
head and glanced down at the communicator on his hip. He
knew the device would vibrate when Sarah sent the signal,
but he looked anyway, if for no other reason but to ensure
that the communicator was still there. He then scanned the
room once again, and came to a sudden realization: he had
not seen much of Pollock Rimes the entire night. He scruti-
nized the crowd more closely, and then began looking behind
him to the tables in the dark corners at the very back. Seated
at one of these was the lieutenant, reclining comfortably with
a drink in front of him. He returned Somo's gaze. After a
moment Somo turned away and rejoined Tibbs in his scrutiny
of Sela and Castomar.

The main gate of the Academy would not have been difficult to find, even for someone who had never been there
before. One had only to look for the monolithic statue of
Major General Brantigan Fole, a popular and integral figure
during the Guild Wars, which stood in the midst of well-kept
grounds facing the city square. At the statue's base, near the
edge of the grounds, was a square, concrete tunnel that cut
into the earth, leading down at a shallow angle and ending
at a set of clear, code-locked doors that Sarah estimated to be
somewhere below the major general's feet.

Sarah made her way down the impressively lit tunnel until
she reached the set of doors. Just beyond the doors a sentry
was posted at a small desk, reading a Digi-tome, his weapon
lying on the ground at his feet. Sarah remembered serving
duty at that same post on more than one occasion. It was so
strange to be back here, in this place once again, to be here
with all her faculties about her, not as some mindless drone.
She leaned against the concrete wall and waited, remembering
the nights she had spent here, most of it spent in an ambigu-
ous haze, not differentiating one day from the next, only living for the training. Others went out into the city and drank;
most people drank to forget, but Sarah thought that many of

the recruits who had been "resocialized" with the implanting of the neural inhibitors drank to try to remember; remember who they had been before they came here, what their lives had once been like.

It wasn't long before two drunken recruits stumbled up to the clear doors, one of the men obviously worse off than the other, his arm draped limply over his companion's shoulder, as the first man attempted at length to retrieve his code-card. Down the hallway inside, the sentry continued reading.

The first recruit finally found his card, attempted to wave it before the card scanner, missed, tried again, and was finally successful. The doors opened, the men entered, and Sarah slipped in behind them.

The sentry forced the two men to stop and asked for their ID numbers and cards. The first man stammered out his number and produced his card. The second man, when prompted, muttered something unintelligible. The first man began digging into the second man's pockets.

Sarah walked past the sentry and the drunken men, making her way to the tunnel's end, which split into two hallways on either side. Directly in front of her were two lifts. Taking a glance backward, Sarah noticed that the more inebriated of the two men was now lying on the floor, singing at the top of his voice as the sentry and the second man attempted to lift him to his feet. She used the opportunity to press the nearest lift's call button.

Castomar, now well into his fifth drink, had begun to stoop in his seat. His eyes had become bloodshot, and he had begun speaking louder, even though Sela was sitting right next to him. Lieutenant Brock ordered the pilot another drink. As she did so, Castomar began massaging her shoulder.

At Somo's table, Tibbs had begun grinding his teeth. Somo, for his part, was busy trying to work out a conundrum that had been vexing him since their departure from Pridewater.

During this entire mission, Pollock Rimes, the man who

had done nothing but bark orders incessantly and charge into the thick of battle at every given opportunity, had not made his presence known once since the incident in the mess hall. Somo figured that it was possible that Sarah had scared him that much, that he had simply given in and resigned himself to following along with the other soldiers, but Somo didn't really believe that. Somo didn't believe that Pollock was capable of stepping down without a fight. As a matter of fact, it almost seemed to Somo that Pollock had gone out of his way to blend in with the rest, to fade into the background to such a point that he had unintentionally drawn attention to himself by doing so—at least in Somo's mind. *Perhaps I'm wrong,* Somo thought; *perhaps I'm just being paranoid.*

He decided he would keep a close eye on the lieutenant just the same.

The lift descended to the second level. The doors opened and Sarah exited. It had been a long time, but she was struck immediately by how little the Academy had changed. The walls, although they had been repainted, were still the same vaguely disturbing green color they had been when she was last here. She proceeded past several closed doors, some quiet, some with pounding music coming from inside the rooms, and occasionally she would hear voices. The mental presence of other telepaths was strong here—she was on the barracks level, where the recruits shared tiny rooms, sometimes two to three per domicile. The mental bombardment was disorienting for a moment, as Sarah felt herself right in the middle of it, being jostled from all sides, like floating in the midst of a raging ocean. She set up a barrier inside her mind, using her willpower to mute out the swarming alpha waves. Once this was done, she continued to Area C.

All of the personnel who worked in the limited-access fields roomed in Area C. These were the men and women in charge of security (and some of the heaviest drinkers in the bunch). Once she entered this hallway, she heard a great deal more noise, and immediately spotted two open doors. The first door she came to revealed a seemingly deserted room. She heard voices emanating from the second, farther down the hall. Sarah figured the man who occupied the deserted room had just come off his rotation and was socializing with someone across the hall. Sarah entered the room.

The inside was not completely deserted, as she heard the faint, deep breathing sounds of someone fast asleep. In one corner of the room, a man slept on the top of two bunk beds. On the lower bed was one of the jackets that the security personnel wore while on duty. Inside the jacket was a code card.

I hope the rest of the mission goes this smoothly, Sarah thought as she exited the room and made her way back to the lift.

Inside the Starlite-Starbrite, Castomar was now unable to maintain focus, even on Sela, who had stopped drinking a long time ago and was now in the process of coaxing the pilot to continue (she had ordered him a double). Tibbs had calmed down, much to the relief of Somo, who had begun to grow slightly concerned about Sarah. He wished he had some way of knowing if she was all right.

A man, who had obviously been doing his own share of drinking, approached the table, leaning against it for support and directing his bloodshot eyes to Somo.

"You guys are miners, huh? Where from?" he asked.

"Pridewater," Somo answered.

"Pridewater . . . wow, that's great. I grew up there."

Somo and Tibbs exchanged glances. The man continued: "Hey, who's marshal now that Skoldmeier resigned?"

Somo looked to Tibbs for help. Tibbs shrugged slightly as if to say, *your guess is as good as mine.* The intoxicated man looked back and forth between the two, waiting for a response. Somo suddenly felt as if everyone in the pub was listening, waiting for him to give the wrong response. Of course it was silly, but the idea was not helped by the fact that a couple of other men with similar haircuts were now looking at their table.

"Brodie," Somo answered finally.

The man stared at him blankly for a moment. "You mean Brady? Stylus Brady?"

"Yep, that's him." Somo nodded. The man looked at Tibbs, who said, "Stylus, that's right."

The man looked absolutely dumbfounded. "Stylus Brady's dead. He died three cycles ago."

Somo began trying to think of a way out of their situation. Tibbs sighed heavily and shifted in his seat.

The man frowned. "At least I thought he did."

Somo threw Tibbs a questioning glance. Tibbs shrugged once again. "I just started here at the Academy. I've been going through some conditioning. . . . To tell you the truth, I don't remember things so good, like I used to, anymore."

Somo felt pity then, for this younger man who had already started losing his memories to the neural inhibitor inside his head. *Just a lost boy, really, that's all he is,* Somo thought. *But, when the time comes, he could prove useful.* The other men who had been looking toward Somo's table returned to their conversation.

Once inside the lift, Sarah punched the button for the bottom floor, the security level. In a few ticks she was there, on her way to the security control booth.

She had only actually seen the control booth on one occasion, and that was during her orientation. She did not remember exactly where it was, and walked down several corridors, eventually becoming disoriented. Every hallway looked the same, the only differentiating feature being a section number at each terminus. At one point two men approached from the other end of the hall Sarah was navigating. There were no doorways to slip into, and if Sarah tried to rush back the way she came, she would certainly make noise; so, she pressed herself as tightly as possible against the corridor wall. The conversation of the men became clearer as they drew near.

"All I'm sayin' is *somethin's* going on. Training exercises, my ass. I don't believe in aliens any more than the next guy. But there's definitely somethin' they're not telling us. . . ."

The man who was speaking came closer. Sarah drew in a deep breath and held it. The material on the man's shoulder brushed against Sarah's chest. The man wiped absently at his shoulder as he spoke, continuing on down the hall.

"Besides, if all they're doing's renovating, why all the secrecy? That's all I'm saying. . . ."

The men reached the end of the hall and turned the corner. Sarah exhaled and moved once again in the opposite direction. She looked at a monitor on her wrist, which displayed how much "cloaking" time she had left. The bar was almost at zero. After wandering a few moments more, she finally came upon a circular room with a sealed, windowless three-man enclosure in the middle. It was the security control booth.

Sarah wasted no time. She waved her card before the scanner. The door to the control booth slid open and Sarah rushed inside.

The man nearest the door turned his head just in time to receive a palm strike to the point of the chin, knocking him immediately unconscious. The next man stared, open-mouthed, as he looked down at his fallen friend. Maneuvering inside the cramped space, Sarah worked her way to the man's rear, delivering a double-fisted blow to the base of his neck. He fell, but was not out. The third man had risen from his seat, stumbling backward, his eyes wide, looking around the room as if expecting the walls to suddenly come alive. Sarah wrapped both hands around the back of the man's head, yanking downward with all her strength as she shot the point of her knee up into the man's forehead. The man crumpled. Sarah turned her attention back to the second man, delivering a full-force blow to the back of his neck. The man fell onto his chest and moved no more.

Sarah closed the door and uncloaked, allowing the device time to recharge. Next, Sarah surveyed the booth and the banks of monitors and keyboards that filled nearly every inch of space. She picked out the monitors that displayed views of the main gate, the armory, and the officers' quarters. Next, Sarah began searching for any monitor that might provide a clue as to the whereabouts of the alien specimens.

Near the doorway, behind where the first man had been seated, were two monitors that displayed the recreational facilities, according to the tags above each screen. The screens themselves, however, were blank. The words "Under Renovation" were written across each screen. Sarah thought back to the conversation between the two men in the hall; she believed she now knew where the experiment with the aliens was taking place . . . but it would be up to Somo and the others to find out for sure.

Somo almost jumped out of his seat when the hip communicator went off.

He and Tibbs had kept a conversation going with the young recruit. Castomar was now passed out, his head laying flat on the table. Somo stood and looked to Sela, indicating the communicator, which had a small light that was flashing green. Sela nodded. Tibbs excused himself from his conversation with the recruit, went to Sela and exchanged a few words, then kissed her and returned. Somo looked back at the table where Pollock had been seated. The lieutenant was no longer there. Looking past the dance floor toward the front of the pub, Somo saw Pollock making his way to the entrance. The others were aware that the time had come, glancing over at Somo (all except for Forest, who was still talking to the attractive young Tarsonian). They began making their way out to the street.

"You know what," Somo confided to the recruit, "I've been on this planet several times and I've never even seen the Academy."

The recruit's eyes drifted for a moment, then found Somo's. "What? Are you serious? The main gate's like, just a few leagues away. I can't get you in but I can show you. There's a big statue and everything. Follow me."

The man led the way out of the bar, colliding with a few dancing patrons on the way out, mumbling apologies. Somo grabbed Forest—who seemed perturbed at the intrusion but acquiesced after repeated farewells to the lady—and made his exit to the front of the pub, where the others waited. The recruit looked at the eighteen gathered men somewhat apprehensively.

"You're all comin'?"

Somo intervened. "None of us have seen it. At least not when we were sober enough to remember it the next day."

The recruit smacked Somo on the shoulder, cackling. "Heh heh, yeah, sober. That's a good one. All right, assault troops, follow your leader!" With that the recruit shot out his right arm, index finger pointing forward, and stumbled in the general direction of the Academy.

Sarah's next order of business was to uncover the whereabouts of Major Rumm. She sat before the monitor displaying the hallway outside the officers' quarters, a segregated, obviously more deluxe spread of accommodations where each domicile was the size of a luxury apartment in one of Tarsonis' top hotels. This was where all officers stayed during their two-cycle assignment as Academy instructors, forgoing the off-post housing accommodations granted to instructors at other Confederate institutions. But after all, they lived rent-free. Most officers she had known when she served here didn't seem unhappy about it.

Sarah navigated a computer screen to find a listing of room assignments. Major Rumm resided in the largest dwelling, in Section G-7. Sarah scanned the O.Q. monitors for the one displaying G-7. She soon found it. With the press of a button, she was able to review all footage that had been taken of the hall outside Rumm's quarters for the past ten intervals. It did not take long for her to come to a point in the video where Rumm could be seen entering the domicile. She paused the video there, staring at the tiny monitor that showed a shadowed face beneath a Confederate officer's hat. She felt her stomach tighten. She pushed out the memories that immediately began to surface; memories of the dying kitten with the bulging tumor, of her father, staring mindlessly from the adjacent room while Rumm, then a lieutenant, paced back and forth before her. She forced all of these memories away as she took the code cards from the unconscious security guards on the floor and began dragging them, one by one, to the latrine outside the booth and down the hall.

Outside the Academy's main gate, Somo and his group stood staring at the statue of Major General Brantigan Fole.

The recruit looked up, swaying, and would have fallen if Somo had not offered a steadying hand. The man then started walking down the tunnel. "Come on, I'll show you the gate." Somo and Tibbs followed. The rest stayed near the mouth of the tunnel. The recruit approached the set of clear doors, waving at the sentry, who eyed Somo and Tibbs wearily. The sentry reached for his gun and began approaching the doors as the recruit dug inside his pockets for his code card.

The sentry arrived at the doors, holding the weapon ready. The recruit waved his card before the scanner, and waved a hand at the sentry, motioning toward Tibbs and Somo. "It's okay. They're off-world miners. Just looking." Somo and Tibbs nodded, offering the most genuine smiles they could muster. The recruit turned and shook Somo's hand. "Well, it's been great hanging with you guys. . . ." The sentry appeared to relax slightly.

Tibbs's foot launched out through the open doorway, catching the sentry square in the midsection. The man folded over, dropping his weapon. Tibbs rained a heavy fist down onto the back of the man's head and the sentry collapsed. Somo looked at the recruit, who stared back in bafflement. "Sorry," he said as he grabbed the recruit's hair and rammed his head forward into the clear section of barrier just above the scanner.

The rest of the group ran down the hallway and through the gate. Somo and Tibbs grabbed the sentry. Forest and Pollock took the recruit. Another soldier grabbed the sentry's gun and a portable wordlink from the sentry's post. Together, they dashed toward the lifts at the end of the hall.

Sarah watched the main gate events transpire from inside the booth. The three security personnel were now locked inside the latrine (short-circuiting the automatic doors was actually very simple, once you knew how) and Somo and the others had finally made it inside the gate. Sarah tracked their progress as they entered the two lifts. She began typing a message on a nearby keypad to the sentry's wordlink. Once she finished, she disabled all of the monitors and used the emergency override to render the security doors outside the armory, recreation areas, and officers' quarters sector inoperative. She then left the booth to begin searching for Major Rumm.

Inside the lift, the soldier who had grabbed the wordlink flipped up the top, which doubled as an LCD screen. A message began appearing.

"Got it," he said to the others. Tibbs was in the process of removing the sentry's clothes. The rest were stepping out of their overalls, under which they had worn the same kind of "off duty" clothes that recruits would wear on a night out. Somo grabbed the sentry's shirt and began putting it on. A hand shot out and grabbed his arm. The hand belonged to Pollock.

"Hold fast, soldier. I'll take over the sentry's position."

Somo looked at Pollock quizzically. "That wasn't the plan—"

"I've decided it will be easier this way. In the absence of Lieutenant Kerrigan, I'm still the senior ranking officer. Now hand me that jacket."

Somo pulled his arm out of the jacket sleeve and offered

it to Pollock, who began putting it on as the lift reached level H, the trash collection and cleaning supply storage level. "The rest of you continue as planned. You know where I'll be. Come get me when the time comes." Pollock slipped on the sentry's pants, then boots. He took the sentry's gun and hat as the rest stepped out onto the third level, hauling the unconscious Confederates with them. Pollock hit the button for the top level. Somo watched as the lift's doors slid closed.

Tibbs and three of the others dragged the bodies toward a large swing-open door in the wall, a rubbish chute. "This is gonna stink, but you'll thank us later," Tibbs offered as he dropped the recruit in. One of the soldiers stepped up on another's knee and removed one of the overhead ceiling tiles. The others handed their overalls to the man, who stashed them in the ceiling. All the while, Somo kept looking back at the lift where Pollock had gone back up to the top level.

None of Pollock's behavior made sense, and it unnerved Somo to a large degree. He had done absolutely nothing all night, displayed no desire to assume leadership, until it came time to replace the sentry. All of a sudden he steps up out of nowhere and changes the plan. Somo didn't like it. Something about Pollock's behavior just didn't feel right, and Somo intended to do something about it.

Having disposed of the two bodies, the soldiers reentered the lift. Tibbs was busy looking at the message Sarah had typed into the wordlink. He turned to Somo. "She gave us the section numbers to both the armory and some recreation area. She must think that's where the specimens are." Somo nodded. The lift descended to L level. The doors opened. The others stepped out as the rest of the group stepped out onto the level from the adjacent lift. Somo grabbed Tibbs's arm before he could leave.

"I'm going back up," he said.

"What?"

"Something's not right about the way Pollock's acting. If I'm wrong, I'll catch up with you guys. If I'm right . . . well, if I'm right we could be in trouble if someone doesn't do something."

Tibbs looked deep into Somo's eyes, saw he was serious, and nodded. "Okay. The armory's in section L-14. We'll meet you there."

Sarah's plan was simple: to enter the first lift she came to and ascend to G level. The problem was, she was lost. On an ordinary mission when she had been an assassin for the Confederacy, a map readout in her field of vision, displayed against the left lens of her goggles, would have provided any necessary topical information. In this case, however, the intelligence was not available to create a map, and she was on her own.

After reaching the end of a seemingly endless hallway, Sarah arrived at a computer room. She turned around, making her way back to the intersection where she had entered. She went the opposite way this time, and was eventually rewarded with the sight of a lift. Unfortunately, one man was standing inside the lift, holding the door, while the other was standing outside, talking. Sarah was cloaked, but she could not get past the man inside the lift; there simply wasn't enough room. So, once that person finished his conversation, Sarah had to wait as the first man ascended and the second man left before she could call the lift back down again.

When Somo returned to the top level and stepped out of the lift, his worst fears were realized: Pollock was nowhere in sight. The sentry post was vacated, which was bad enough in itself, but what was worse was that Pollock was roaming free inside the facility, with a security code card and a weapon. Somo turned and looked at the readout above the second lift. It was currently stopped at the security level. Somo could suddenly feel his heart pounding inside his chest. Somo felt certain that the lieutenant meant to sabotage the mission, and unless someone stopped him, Pollock would succeed.

If only that boot-licking doctor hadn't screwed it all up the first time, Pollock thought, *things never would have gotten this far.* After he had sent the message to the *Norad II*, it had been Pollock's plan to take a separate lift, leading the Confederate soldiers around the port side of the ship and circumventing the trap. Then the soldiers could have arrested Mengsk and hopefully killed that intransigent cur of a woman whom the general had become taken with. That's the way it *should* have happened. But the good doctor had met them in the bay, and inadvertently took them up to the starboard side and led them directly into the trap. Moron. Now Pollock had to do his best to clean things up if he still expected to come out of this a Confederate hero. It would be difficult, and required perfect timing and more than just a little luck. But Pollock certainly figured his odds to be better than that of the others.

He had taken a different route than that which Sarah had taken not long before him, and after only a few wrong turns, he made it to the security control booth. *Things are looking up already*, Pollock thought. Using the sentry's code card, Pollock accessed the booth. All of the surveillance systems had been sabotaged, but that mattered little. Pollock immediately tripped the silent alarm system located near the door, sat down at the central computer, and began typing.

Tibbs, Forest, and the others reached the Armory without a hitch. Inside they found several gauss rifles, a host of fragmentation grenades, as well as harnesses, holsters, and of course, canister rifles. Most of them had never seen canister rifles, and didn't know how to use them, so they grabbed the gauss rifles. Forest donned a harness and packed in as many fragmentation grenades as he could carry. Tibbs decided one gauss rifle wasn't enough and opted to carry two.

Tibbs looked down the corridor for any sign of Somo. There

was none. He hoped the private was okay, but knew that they could not afford to wait. Somo knew the plan. He could catch up to them in the recreation area.

Within moments the rebels were outside the Armory on their way back to the lift. So far, they had not been spotted. Tibbs only hoped that their luck would continue to hold.

The officers' quarters were laid out inside a sector that almost resembled a miniature city in itself. Walkways led between the detached buildings, which even had small "backyards" with chairs and tables. Sarah had never been to this sector, and had taken some time to get here, since G sector was located well away from anything having to do with the enlisted men. *The officers of the Ghost Academy may be forced to live on base, but they certainly aren't being slighted,* Sarah thought as she made her way past several of these buildings, some with lights still on, others with snoring sounds emanating from open windows. She made her way to the far side of the sector and found the major's residence there, nestled in the corner. A flagpole stood in front of the house waving the Confederate flag. Sarah approached cautiously, alert for any signs of movement. The lights within the domicile were off.

Sarah approached one of the front windows and peeked in through the drapes. A small amount of light was cast on the living room area from a wordlink on a nearby table. The back of the device was facing her so she could not read the words on the screen. She flipped a switch on her belt and her goggles immediately shifted to infrared vision. There were no heat sources emanating from within the building. Sarah switched back to normal vision and crossed to the home's front door.

Incredibly, there next to the door, on a digitized message pad, was a note. It read: *Out to training area, section P-4 at 03:00.* Sarah checked her timepiece. It read *02:55.* It seemed strange to Sarah that the major would be doing anything in the training area at this particular time, but nothing the military did ever really surprised her. Could it be some kind of trap? How could the major possibly know? Sarah found herself suddenly wishing she had a way of contacting the others. The fact that Tarsonis held some of the most sophisticated de-scrambling communications surveillance technology in the world did not help their situation any. It had left them cut off from Mengsk, and effectively cut off from each other.

Despite all of this, Sarah made her way to the nearest lift and punched the button for section P, hoping that she was not walking into an ambush.

Somo, once he made it to the security level, ended up retracing nearly the exact same route Sarah had navigated before him. The security level was a labyrinth of hallways. At one point Somo rounded a corner and stopped in his tracks as he saw a security officer approaching from the other end. The officer was intent on the digital clipboard he held before him, and had taken no notice of Somo. Somo slipped back the way he had come and darted down a side alley just as the man reached the intersection and went in the opposite direction.

Somo decided to continue down the corridor in which he presently found himself. At the end of it was a sealed doorway. Somo had no idea how he would get through any secured doors; he hoped that Sarah had disabled all of them, but he knew she probably hadn't. For now, all he could do was hope that he found Pollock before the lieutenant did anything to jeopardize the mission.

Once at the end of the hall, Somo waved his hand in front of the scanner beside the door. There was no response. The door was locked. Just as Somo was about to turn around to try to find another way, however, the door slid open.

Standing on the other side, wearing a look of surprise on his face, was Pollock Rimes.

Tibbs, Forest, and the rest of the rebels were heading toward the recreation area. As they rounded the corner just before the entrance, they noticed two sentries flanking the doorway. One of the men frowned, making no attempt to raise his weapon. The second man was quicker to react; he immediately shouted for the soldiers to identify themselves, even as he began raising his gauss rifle.

Tibbs did not wait for the second man to take aim. He began firing immediately, knowing that the noise may draw attention (the gauss rifles were nowhere near as loud as the canister rifles, but the spikes they fired tended to create quite a racket when they ricocheted), but also knowing that they had little choice. The man who had raised his weapon was pinned to the wall by the gunfire, hanging there for a moment, his arms outstretched, before sliding to the floor. The first man simply looked at his comrade in shock and disbelief.

Tibbs and the others knew that they had come to a point where lives could no longer be spared if they were to make it out in one piece. Tibbs turned his weapon on the first sentry and fired a final burst.

Once at the doorway Tibbs waved his hand before the scanner. The doors opened. Sarah had done her job. Forest stopped for a moment, looking down at the dead sentries before he joined the others filing through the doorway into the recreation area.

Major Rumm sat at a wordlink inside one of the training center's control booths, wondering if he would turn out to be the victim of some cruel practical joke. He kept repeating, over and over in his head, the emergency message that accompanied the alarm that had woken him from a fairly pleasant sleep. It had read: *The Academy is being attacked. There are several rebels en route to recreation area and a Ghost on her way to you. Get out now and take action before it is too late.*

The first thing the major did was to check the source of the message. It was sent from the security control booth. Likewise, the silent alarm had been triggered at the booth. Even then, the major was not convinced that the Academy had been infiltrated. What he found more likely was that some drunken security officer thought it would be fun to get cute with his superiors—until, of course, Major Rumm typed a message to the sentry at the main gate and received no reply.

At that point it would have been easy to deliver an emergency message to the Battalion Command Center requesting a dispatch of soldiers. But, if the whole thing turned out to be a hoax, the major would be the one who would look like the idiot. Besides, the purpose of the Academy was to train the deadliest soldiers in all the known systems. They could handle their own problems.

That was why Major Rumm dispatched a message to several Ghost officers (who had already been awakened by the alarm) to suit up, retrieve their weapons from the Armory, and proceed to the recreation area.

The tricky part was the infiltrating Ghost. Was he one of theirs? He would have to be. The Academy was the only place that trained Ghosts, although the major had checked and no rogue operatives appeared on his tracker, meaning the Ghost no longer possessed its neural inhibitor. These thoughts had passed through the major's head as he left the note on the message board outside his door (an admittedly amateur ploy, but the only thing the major could think of at the time) and proceeded to the training area. Here was the only place he knew of where he could possibly set a trap.

Now as he waited, he continued to ponder the identity of the invisible spy. Perhaps one of the recruits had a breakdown as a result of the resocialization. But the message had mentioned *rebels*. The major knew that a Ghost had been deployed by the *Norad II* to retrieve . . . Kerrigan. It couldn't be. It wasn't possible—or was it? *What an interesting possibility*, he thought as he waited. He did not want to call for backup, not until he knew exactly who or what he was dealing with.

The training section took up two levels, P being the uppermost. It was here that Sarah stepped out of the lift and proceeded into an expansive, open space. Set into the wall on the far side of the room were clear doors that led to a small chamber, followed by another set of clear doors, and beyond that . . . Major Rumm.

He sat at a terminal near what looked like a control booth, ostensibly absorbed in his work. To Sarah's right was a railing where the floor dropped off into a massive intake shaft that spanned the width of the room. She could not remember participating in any training exercises on this level, so the surroundings were foreign to her. Still, there seemed to be no concealment from which to stage an ambush, being that the area was open and devoid of cover. Sarah switched to infrared. The only heat sources she detected were from machinery in the walls. She furtively made her way toward the first set of doors.

As she drew nearer, she recognized more of the major's features. He was far older, but his eyes had remained the same. There was no doubt in Sarah's mind that he was the one; the one who had threatened her invalid father and subjected her to a full cycle of mind games and psychological terror. She felt her adrenaline surge, her view narrowing to tunnel vision, locked on his face. She continued forward, past the first set of doors into what appeared to be some kind of small chamber, focusing all of her intent on the man in the uniform.

She read something disturbing in his thoughts then: suspicion, awareness of danger, and she realized that he knew.

But it was already too late.

She felt a crunching under her foot and heard the sound of fragmenting glass. She looked down, seeing the tiny shards, littered over the floor just inside the first set of doors. Major Rumm's head shot up. He hit a button at the terminal and the doors nearest him slid shut. Sarah turned, just as the doors behind her came to a close. She was trapped. The major looked into the room as he stood and made his way to the control booth. Inside the booth was a small, circular window where Major Rumm continued to look out into the chamber as he worked the booth's controls.

Sarah had just enough time to wonder what was happening when the floor opened up beneath her.

Pollock Rimes recovered from his surprise at seeing Somo with remarkable speed, raising his weapon and taking aim at Somo's chest. Somo grasped the barrel of the rifle and pushed it aside as Pollock fired. Turning, Somo shot an open hand full-force into the lieutenant's face. Pollock fell back, and Somo, not wanting to release his grip on the weapon and unable to wrench it from the other man's grasp, fell with him.

Somo reared backward and cocked his fist for a downward strike. Pollock kicked inward with his left leg, bringing his right knee up and across Somo's stomach, knocking the rebel off balance. Somo rolled, still gripping the weapon tightly, now with both hands. Pollock yanked backward on the rifle so hard it flew from his grasp, colliding with the now-closed doorway behind them and clattering to the floor.

Pollock stood. As he did so, Somo grabbed both of the man's ankles, pressing his knees inward and thrusting his hips up as he pulled. Pollock hit the floor tailbone-first, grimacing in pain. Somo reared a leg back and stomped at Pollock's face. Pollock spun in time to avoid the blow, crawling on his stomach toward the weapon as Somo desperately clutched at Pollock's ankles.

Pollock's fingers reached the barrel just as Somo bolted to a crouching stand. Pollock swung the weapon around, smashing it into the side of Somo's knee. Somo groaned through clenched teeth and collapsed as Pollock shifted the gauss rifle into a firing position.

Tibbs and the others walked into a renovated area that now housed several small chambers, all sealed, with a purplish, pulsating substance in each that covered the walls. Something on the windows prevented the material from covering the glass, allowing the rebels to look inside each chamber.

Forest approached one of the chambers at the far end of

the section. Looking inside he saw what appeared to be a large insect, almost some kind of maggot. Forest reached his hand out to the glass, and then drew it back as his fingertips touched the scalding-hot pane. "Youch!" he yelped. "Whatever you do, don't put your hands on the glass."

So that's what keeps this mess off of the windows, Tibbs thought. Through the glass before him, he watched as a multilegged bug crawled from an aperture in the wall, into the chamber, approaching the glass.

This is what everyone's so worried about? he thought. *They don't look like much to me.*

"All right," Tibbs said, "let's do what we came to do."

Tibbs raised his weapon to fire into the chamber. Just then a chorus of noises rang out, echoing inside the cavernous room. *Cha-chink! Cha-chink! Cha-chink*—the sound of numerous canister rifles being cocked at once. The rebels began glancing around in every direction, but there was no one in sight. The voice of a Ghost came to them from somewhere in the room.

"Drop your weapons and kick them toward the door," the voice advised.

Everyone in the room stood still, waving their weapons back and forth, looking to each other for guidance.

"We will fire upon you. Drop your weapons now."

Tibbs knew that if they surrendered here, they would be tried and put to death for sedition, so he took his best guess as to where the Ghost voice was coming from and began firing.

Sarah fell into a wide, cylindrical cell. She saw the floor beneath her and had no idea of how she might break her fall, when suddenly, her body stopped plummeting, like a weight at the end of a string. Glancing around her, she saw twinkling flashes—the falling glass, also suspended. It was like being surrounded by thousands of tiny stars. She continued to fall, but agonizingly slowly; she was floating, and she instantly knew where she was: she was inside the zero-gravity training cell, one of the harsh environment simulators that all Ghosts qualified in; except when she had gone through the exercise as a cadet, she had entered from the bottom, not the top where the control booth was.

She glided effortlessly down; unsure of why the major had decided to use this place to ensnare her, or what exactly his intentions were. As her toes finally brushed the cell's floor, she found out.

She felt an unstoppable force drawing her downward, and realized that the gravity inside the cell could be controlled. Right now, the gravity was being increased. Sarah fell to her knees, and then was forced to lie on her stomach as the downward G-forces became stronger. If the pull continued, she would soon be unable to move, and soon after, her bones would be crushed.

On top of all that, Sarah knew that it wouldn't be very long before she uncloaked.

Somo angled to the side even as Pollock began firing. He brought his weight forward, stretching his right hand up to the lieutenant's face. He felt sure that he was going to die at this point, and he vowed to do everything within his power to take Pollock Rimes with him.

With Somo on top of him, Pollock didn't have much room to maneuver, but he still had enough to do damage. Somo felt the spikes of the gauss rifle tearing chunks from his ribs on the right side and chipping away pieces of bone; but even though Pollock had the rifle, Somo still had weapons of his own. He brought his forefinger and thumb up to Pollock's eyes and thrust down.

Pollock screamed as Somo felt the skin at the inner corners of the lieutenant's eyes give way. In his pain and shock, Pollock finally released the rifle, scrambling on all fours, scurrying away, desperately pressing against his unseeing eyes with the palms of his hands.

Somo rolled to his left and turned the rifle around. As Pollock turned and stood, hands still pressed to his face, Somo engaged the trigger. Pollock danced backward as the spikes ripped through his chest and spewed gore out his back. The lieutenant finally struck the door, then turned and fell to his side, emitting gurgling noises from his throat, the bloody remains of his eyes staring wide. He shook for a brief moment and then lay still.

Tibbs thought that he had gotten at least one of them. There was gunfire in all directions, spikes ricocheting off of walls, and sometimes, Tibbs thought he could see intermittent muzzle flashes from the canister rifles. He aimed for one of these, and saw his spikes simply disappear. *Good,* he thought. *I know I got one.* He heard a cocking noise so close to him that it was audible even above the cacophony of gunfire that filled the massive room, and he knew it was over.

Forest fell back to the rear wall, firing on either side. He saw Tibbs's back rupture outward. The dark-skinned man fell to his knees, then onto his side. Four other rebels were down. Forest began shouting for them to fall back. On Forest's right was a door. He began making his way toward it, still firing on either side, shouting for the others to join him.

The group closest to Forest glanced over their shoulders and retreated toward the wall. The Ghosts weren't firing as much now; they were picking their shots carefully, which scared Forest even more. He and eight others made it finally to the door. Forest reached out and waved his hand before the scanner—but nothing happened.

The door was locked.

Sarah could feel her body being flattened, pressed against the floor as if by a giant unseen hand. Then there was a voice. It was the voice of Major Rumm, of course, confident and pleased, self-assured and inquisitive.

"Show yourself, and tell me who you are," the voice demanded.

Sarah tried desperately to get a sense of her surroundings.

The door was to her left, within sight, but still at the edge of the room. Five or six paces at most that might just as well have been fifty or sixty leagues.

"I am quite sure that you are aware of the hopelessness of your situation. Your friends are likewise endangered. I would say that by now they are most likely dead."

Sarah tried to tell herself that he was lying, that the others were safe; but if *she* had walked in to a trap . . .

"I am growing weary of these games. Why don't you just reveal yourself? There is still a chance for the courts to decide your fate."

Sarah felt an increase in the G-forces. It was now becoming incredibly difficult to breathe.

"This is the last time I will make the request. De-cloak and show me your face."

A warning flashed in Sarah's upper left field of vision then. She was about to uncloak whether she liked it or not. The warning flashed critical and then disappeared. She was visible.

There was a moment of silence, and then the sound of a very satisfied voice, like honey: "Well, well . . . I do believe we've met."

Somo had taken Pollock's code card and limped to the security booth. Inside, he was able to discover where Sarah had cut off the main feed to the monitors. He restored it. He felt himself becoming light-headed, and knew that he was losing blood; but he also knew that as long as there was a chance the others were still alive, he must do everything within his power to help.

A look at the recreation area monitor confirmed his worst fears. There was a firefight raging. Somo felt his heart sink as he watched Tibbs collapse to the ground in a pool of blood. As much as he hated to, he tore his eyes away from the scene to look for any signs of Sarah. There was some scattered activity in a few of the hallways, some aimless scurrying, but nothing that gave any indication where—

Then he saw a video monitor displaying a view of one of the control booths in the training area. He saw a man in a Confederate uniform at a computer terminal. The man was looking down at a monitor and talking. Somo punched a series of keys on the pad below the monitor until another screen next to it began changing views: one of a weight-lifting room, another of an indoor track, and then . . . an empty, cylindrical room, and to Somo's amazement, he saw Sarah appear right before his eyes. She seemed to be pinned to the floor. He saw her hand move ever so slightly, and he knew that she was alive.

So now, Somo was faced with an impossible decision: help Sarah, or try to save the others. A tag above the monitor he was now looking at told him Sarah was in section G-7. He took a last desperate look at the monitor showing the recreation area. A computer screen below showed an overhead map of the room. On the monitor, the rebels had fallen back to a door that they could not seem to get through. Somo looked at the computer screen, hit arrow keys until the door at the back of the room was highlighted, and simply continued punching keys until the door changed from a grayed-out white to green. He then watched as the doors opened and the rebels ran through. Satisfied that he had done what he could, he fought off the urge to simply lie down and go to sleep and set out to find Sarah.

Miraculously, the door behind Forest and the remaining rebels opened on its own. Without bothering to wonder how, the old man yelled to the others and fell back into the hallway.

At least in here they can only come at us two at a time, he thought, *and only from one direction.*

Two of the rebels near the door fell. The men directly in front of Forest began retreating. The group came to an elbow in the hall that led to another long corridor. Two more men fell before they made the turn.

Aside from Forest, there were now two soldiers left. The

corridor dead-ended at a closed door, a door marked with a hazard symbol, but at least it appeared that it did not require a code card to open. Forest and the two rebels reached the door, which slid open automatically. There was a blast, and one of the men fell.

Forest backed up to a large tank, and he realized that he was in a room housing one of the Academy's power reactors. The last man crumpled from a shot to the back just as he entered the doorway. Forest pressed against the tank, knowing that the Ghosts could not fire at him without blowing them all to bits.

The old man held his ground as one by one, the Ghosts around him began to de-cloak.

Inside the cell, Sarah found that the G-forces had abated somewhat, at least allowing her to breathe.

The maddening, rambling voice of the major continued. "I only know of one female Ghost who is unaccounted for; who may have been exposed to someone with the resources and audacity to try and pull of a stunt like this. I know it's you, Sarah. I've eased the pressure a little. Why don't you turn and look upward so I can see you?"

Sarah knew that she was in a desperate situation; but she also knew that the last thing she wanted to do was give this human pile of waste the pleasure of seeing her face.

"I remember when you were just a little girl. I remember the hard time you gave me then. That was a time when neural resocialization wasn't proven yet, and I wanted to avoid it if possible; but in the end you left me little choice. I also remember your father . . ."

Sarah found herself desperately wishing that the major was in the same room with her. Even if she couldn't physically harm him, she knew that if he was in the room she could reach out with her mind and—

"That one wasn't my call either. Your father died on his own, of course. Didn't need the Confederacy's help to do that.

I did what I could on your behalf, you know, I really did, but in the end I think you got what you deserved. Now why don't you show me your face before one of my recruits arrives and takes you into custody?"

Sarah desperately tried to crawl, but it was no use. She was immobilized. All she could do now was wait.

Somo moved with the kind of single-minded determination that only a dying man can muster. Even with a nearly useless right leg, he managed to hobble to the nearest lift, and make his way to G level.

As he entered G-7 he saw two sets of clear doors and beyond that, a control booth with a small round window. The head of a Confederate officer inside the booth bolted up at Somo's entrance. Somo raised his weapon. The man inside the booth hurriedly punched buttons, then took cover as Somo fired.

The glass around the doors shattered. Somo moved forward. He entered some kind of chamber with what looked like a trapdoor under his feet. He moved through the second shattered wall of the chamber, pointed his weapon into the control booth, and fired off a full burst.

Looking to the other side of the room, Somo saw handrails leading down into some kind of open chasm. He went to the edge, where he found an enclosed ladder, and began descending to the next level.

Forest watched the five remaining Ghosts de-cloak. They stood surrounding him in a semicircle, canister rifles pointed at his chest. They began to close in.

The old man pulled two fragmentation grenades from the harness he wore. The Ghosts paused, and then began to step backward.

Forest offered an imperfect smile, looking to each soldier and nodding. He saw recognition of what he was about to do from some of them; recognition and fear, and that was reward enough.

"My mother, may she welcome me with open arms, used to say, 'There ain't nothin' worth livin fer that ain't worth dyin' fer.'"

With that Forest pulled the pins on each grenade, and before the Ghosts could rush in to stop him, released both clips.

Sarah felt the weight on her body simply dissipate. She heard muffled rifle fire. Weakly rising up on her hands and knees, she looked upward. The doors at the top of the cell were closed. She shook her head, desperately trying to regain her strength. She was finding it difficult to stand.

A moment passed as Sarah waited. There was a tremendous *boom!* that shook the entire structure. She thought it must have come from above. Then, the door at the edge of the cell slid open. Sarah looked up to see Somo standing in the doorway. He was badly wounded, and favoring his left leg, but he was smiling, glad to see her alive. "We'd better get out of here," he said.

"The door—" Sarah croaked. Even speaking was still difficult. She tried with all her might to stand, and finally rose up on shaky legs. "Get away from the—"

Sarah heard the report of small-arms fire from the room outside. Somo's smile faded as he looked down at his chest, where blood began to spread across the fabric of his shirt. Somo fell forward.

Stumbling to where he lay, Sarah retrieved his weapon. Major Rumm appeared in the doorway just long enough to see that Sarah possessed superior firepower, and then disappeared. Sarah fired a burst anyway, and then returned her attention to Somo, gently turning him onto his back, laying his head on her arm.

Somo tried to smile. "I screwed up. Sorry. It was a tough decision, but in the end there really was no choice. . . ." Sarah was unsure what Somo meant, not knowing of his decision to come to Sarah's aid at the expense of the others.

"You know I'm in lo—" Somo exhaled and Sarah felt his body go slack. Sarah did not need to be a telepath to understand what he had wanted to say. She knew; of course she knew that Somo had been in love with her, and she so desperately wanted to tell him that she knew, and that she had held for him the deepest feelings possible; that what she felt for him was even greater than love, but it was too late; the essence of what had made the man in her arms Somo Hung was gone.

All her pity, all her sorrow, all her despondency was replaced then by rage, and by pure, unfettered primordial hate. In that moment, Sarah forsook all within her that was human and became a predatory beast. The only thing that mattered now was the kill.

Suddenly galvanized, Lieutenant Kerrigan snatched up the weapon at Somo's side and raced from the cell.

The bottom of the cell connected to a guardwalk that led out to the far wall, then across to an "open" lift that, unlike the others, attached to a track in the wall of the chasm. This lift was now moving upward. Sarah knew that Major Rumm was inside. She also knew that a Ghost was approaching her on the guardwalk. Her concentration was so acutely focused in this state that she could pinpoint him exactly.

As the Ghost cocked his canister rifle Sarah took a step forward and shot out her hand, wedging it in the man's throat. She placed a hand at the back of his head and pulled, smashing her elbow into the man's face. She felt his nose crack like an eggshell. Gripping the weapon with one hand she pulled the man by his hair, over the railing, dropping him into the seemingly bottomless steel pit.

All canister rifles fired not only high explosive projectiles, but were also capable of firing "lockdown" rounds, concentrated EMPs that shorted out any electrical device or vehicle they struck. Sarah raised the rifle, took a bead on the lift, and fired. The round hit its mark; the lift froze halfway up the wall, enclosed in a field of crackling energy.

Inside the lift, Rumm suddenly felt that matters had taken a major turn for the worse. He waited, listening intently, repeatedly hitting the top-level button on the lift, to no avail. Suddenly the repair hatch at the top of the structure flipped open. Rumm fired several shots into the lift's ceiling, then waited.

He barely heard Sarah's feet hit the floor when his gun flew from his grasp. She had recharged enough to cloak once again, even if only temporarily. The major tried to put his back to the wall but he was on the floor of the lift before he could move. He felt an immense pain in his head then, a swelling. It felt as if his brain was expanding, pressing against the insides of his skull. He felt fire racing through a vein in his forehead and along his brow. The major began to scream.

Sarah did not stop her mental assault, even after Major Rumm's eyes exploded from their sockets.

After her business in the lift was done, Sarah used the major's tracker to find Ghost No. 24718. She found him, uncloaked, in what was left of the recreation area, unconscious from a spike wound to the head. She also found the remains of her fellow soldiers. An entire section of the far wall was gone, and the alien creatures there had been destroyed. There were a few left in the cells against the remaining wall. Sarah went to one of these and looked inside. She felt the calling, the beckoning she had vaguely felt from the creature once before; it seemed stronger now in her current, feral state. As she watched, the maggot-like creature rolled into a ball. It began to pulsate, forming into an egg-like sac. It was becoming something else, mutating into its next stage. And it was calling to her.

Sarah had seen enough. She fired through the glass, rupturing the egg inside, killing it once and for all. She then fired explosive rounds from the canister rifle into each remaining cell, setting the substance inside on fire.

She cloaked, took the Ghost, activated his cloaking device, hauled him over her shoulder, and took a lift to the top level, making her way out through the main gate and to the rendezvous point with Sela's transport.

The news of the deaths of the others—especially Tibbs—struck Sela hard. She did not speak as she guided the transport up and out of Tarsonis' atmosphere. The small craft was hailed several times, first by Flight Control and then by Sector Patrol as they made their way from the planet. The Confederacy would of course send Wraiths to intercept the vehicle, but it made no difference, since the *Hyperion* warped in long enough for the transport to board (and for Mengsk to send a brief message), then warped out again.

Sarah brought Ghost No. 24718 to the bridge. He went willingly enough, still dazed from his head wound.

When Arcturus Mengsk saw the younger man, he temporarily seemed to forget everything else: the deaths of the other rebels, the destruction of the Academy, and the eradication of the aliens. The Ghost stared back at Mengsk, waiting. The general turned to Sarah. "I'm sorry about your comrades. They were all noble, courageous warriors who died for—"

"I don't really want to hear it right now," Sarah blurted.

Mengsk nodded, then motioned for the Ghost to sit in his command chair. The man obeyed. The general turned to the lookout and began to speak once again: "Not long after I ended my service in the Confederacy, something happened to me; my life's great catastrophe, as I often describe it to myself. You see my father, Angus, was a revolutionary. Back then I didn't share his views, but he caused quite a stir among the people around him. The Confederacy considered him a threat . . . and they had him assassinated."

Mengsk turned, staring at the man in the chair. "Three Ghosts were tasked to complete the job. Sarah killed one of them on this very vessel not long ago. You, No. 24718, were one of the three. You probably don't even remember doing it. That's why I wanted to tell you before you died."

The general drew his side arm and fired a single shot into the man's chest. The soldier put his hand to the wound, his eyes drifting. He slumped forward and onto the floor.

Sarah felt the rage within her surfacing once again. "All of this, since the beginning, has been some kind of personal vendetta? You used me . . . you used all of us!"

"The targets I chose were military targets, and their destruction will aid the revolution greatly. But, I admit that certain of those choices were made for personal reasons."

Sarah clenched her fists. "I'm tired of being used. I've been putting up with it my whole life and I'm done. Whoever the third Ghost is, you can find him on your own."

Sarah turned to leave. "I already found the third Ghost. Quite a while ago, on a dust-bowl planet called Vyctor 5. That Ghost, the most important of the three, the one who killed my father, is you, Sarah."

Sarah froze. Memories rushed unbidden into her mind: the ascent up the staircase, the stalking into the bedroom, the form lying on the bed. She saw herself yanking the figure to his feet, slicing the blade across his throat, saw him stumbling back into the moonlight revealing . . . revealing features remarkably similar to the man standing behind her, the features only a relative could share. He was older, gray-haired, but he had Arcturus's same eyes, the same hawkish nose.

"It's true. I originally traced you to Vyctor 5 to have you brought aboard and killed. But then I decided that you might serve better as an ally. Yes, I decided to use you to get to the others, to infiltrate the Academy, but somewhere in the course of it all I came to see you as the singular, incredible person that you are. You gave me hope, Sarah."

Sarah's eyes had begun to well with tears. "And that's something worth fighting for."

"Yes, and worth dying for, Sergeant Keel might have said."

Sarah turned to face Mengsk then. She felt no animosity toward the other man, no enmity.

"I forgive you, Sarah. I forgive you for killing my father. But that won't make any difference until you're able to forgive yourself."

Sarah's face tightened; she began to cry, letting out emotions that she had kept bottled within her for so long, emotions that she was unsure how to deal with. For now, she just needed to get away.

"Thank you, sir," she said. Unable or unwilling to say more, at least for now, she turned and left the bridge.

Mengsk returned to his chair, pushing aside the body of the young Ghost. He pressed a button and a vidmonitor lowered. A UNN report came to life on the screen as a reporter began to speak.

"Breaking news: the Confederate regime here on Tarsonis has been rocked by an assault on one of its core facilities, an academy for the training of elite soldiers. Just moments after the strike we received a transmission from a rebel leader taking credit for the action." Mengsk's face filled the screen then. "Let it be known that freedom will not perish; that we will fight until the very last man to topple the Confederacy and that we are responsible for the destruction at the Tarsonis Ghost Academy." There was a pause then, a jump where Mengsk had mentioned something about a secret being kept from Tarsonis' citizens. The message concluded: "We are The Sons of Korhal."

Mengsk smiled. *Finally,* he thought. *Finally a message that got through.* The road ahead would be hard. The Confederacy would fight back, but Mengsk would not stop until they fell. The general believed they had not seen the last of the aliens. But for now, all was well. Arcturus leaned back in his seat. The reporter then came back on. "There you have it, a communication delivered to us through Confederate channels, obviously edited for content at some point, but the unshakable truth is that today a deadly blow has been dealt to the once untouchable empire that was the Confederacy."

Behind the reporter was a wall where a symbol had been spray-painted: a black arm holding a whip in its fist, the whip forming a circle around the arm. "Student uprisings have begun taking place in several universities all across Tarsonis. In this reporter's humble opinion, perhaps it is a portent of things to come. Reporting for Universe News Network, this is Michael Daniel Liberty, signing off. . . ."